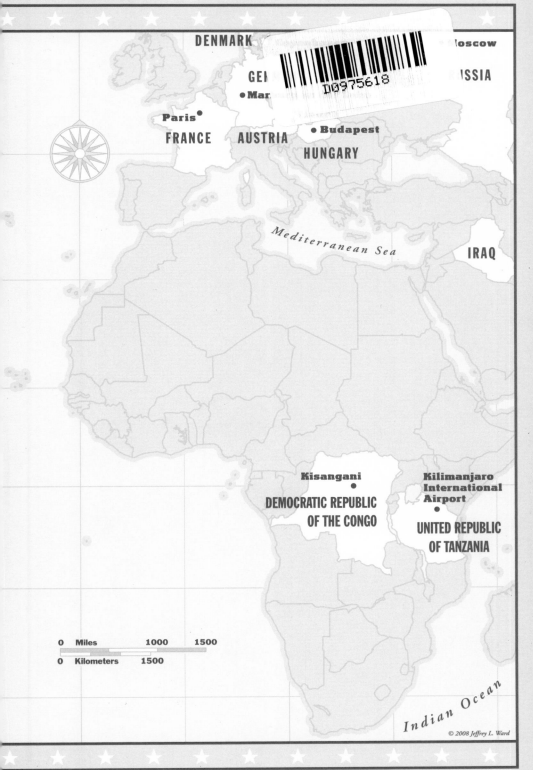

DENMARK

GER

Moscow

●Mar

SSIA

Paris●

FRANCE   AUSTRIA   ●Budapest

HUNGARY

IRAQ

Mediterranean Sea

Kisangani
●

Kilimanjaro
International
Airport
●

DEMOCRATIC REPUBLIC
OF THE CONGO

UNITED REPUBLIC
OF TANZANIA

| 0 | Miles | 1000 | 1500 |

| 0 | Kilometers | 1500 |

Indian Ocean

© 2008 Jeffrey L. Ward

BLACK
OPS

BLACK OPS

W.E.B. GRIFFIN

G. P. PUTNAM'S SONS

NEW YORK

S

PUTNAM

G. P. PUTNAM'S SONS
Publishers Since 1838
Published by the Penguin Group
Penguin Group (USA) Inc., 375 Hudson Street, New York, New York 10014, USA • Penguin Group
(Canada), 90 Eglinton Avenue East, Suite 700, Toronto, Ontario M4P 2Y3, Canada (a division of Pearson
Canada Inc.) • Penguin Books Ltd, 80 Strand, London WC2R 0RL, England • Penguin Ireland,
25 St Stephen's Green, Dublin 2, Ireland (a division of Penguin Books Ltd) • Penguin Group (Australia),
250 Camberwell Road, Camberwell, Victoria 3124, Australia (a division of Pearson Australia Group Pty Ltd) •
Penguin Books India Pvt Ltd, 11 Community Centre, Panchsheel Park, New Delhi–110 017, India •
Penguin Group (NZ), 67 Apollo Drive, Rosedale, North Shore 0632, New Zealand (a division of
Pearson New Zealand Ltd) • Penguin Books (South Africa) (Pty) Ltd, 24 Sturdee Avenue,
Rosebank, Johannesburg 2196, South Africa

Penguin Books Ltd, Registered Offices: 80 Strand, London WC2R 0RL, England

Library of Congress Cataloging-in-Publication Data

Griffin, W.E. B.
Black ops / W. E. B. Griffin.
p.   cm. — (The presidential agent bk. 5)
ISBN 978-0-399-15517-8
1. United States. Army. Delta Force—Fiction.   2. Undercover operations—Fiction.
3. International relations—Fiction.   I. Title.
PS3557.R489137B55   2009   2008042220
813'.54—dc22

Printed in the United States of America
1   3   5   7   9   10   8   6   4   2

This is a work of fiction. Names, characters, places, and incidents either are the product of the author's imagination
or are used fictitiously, and any resemblance to actual persons, living or dead, businesses, companies, events, or locales
is entirely coincidental.

While the author has made every effort to provide accurate telephone numbers and Internet addresses at the time of
publication, neither the publisher nor the author assumes any responsibility for errors, or for changes that occur after
publication. Further, the publisher does not have any control over and does not assume any responsibility for author
or third-party websites or their content.

26 July 1777

The necessity of procuring good intelligence is apparent and need not be further urged.

George Washington
General and Commander in Chief
The Continental Army

FOR THE LATE

WILLIAM E. COLBY
An OSS Jedburgh First Lieutenant
who became director of the Central Intelligence Agency.

AARON BANK
An OSS Jedburgh First Lieutenant
who became a colonel and the father of Special Forces.

WILLIAM R. CORSON
A legendary Marine intelligence officer
whom the KGB hated more than any other U.S. intelligence officer—
and not only because he wrote the definitive work on them.

FOR THE LIVING

BILLY WAUGH
A legendary Special Forces Command Sergeant Major
who retired and then went on to hunt down the infamous Carlos the Jackal.
Billy could have terminated Osama bin Laden in the early 1990s
but could not get permission to do so. After fifty years in
the business, Billy is still going after the bad guys.

RENÉ J. DÉFOURNEAUX
A U.S. Army OSS Second Lieutenant attached to the British SOE
who jumped into Occupied France alone and later
became a legendary U.S. Army counterintelligence officer.

JOHNNY REITZEL
An Army Special Operations officer
who could have terminated the head terrorist of the seized cruise ship
Achille Lauro but could not get permission to do so.

RALPH PETERS
An Army intelligence officer
who has written the best analysis of our war against terrorists
and of our enemy that I have ever seen.

AND FOR THE NEW BREED

MARC L
A senior intelligence officer, despite his youth,
who reminds me of Bill Colby more and more each day.

FRANK L
A legendary Defense Intelligence Agency officer
who retired and now follows in Billy Waugh's footsteps.

**OUR NATION OWES ALL OF THESE PATRIOTS
A DEBT BEYOND REPAYMENT.**

I

It was a picture-postcard Christmas Eve.

Snow covered the ground. It had been snowing on and off all day, and it was gently falling now.

The stained-glass windows of the ancient Church of St. Elisabeth glowed faintly from the forest of candles burning inside, and the church itself seemed to glow from the light of the candles in the hands of the faithful who had arrived to worship too late to find room inside and now stood outside.

A black Mercedes-Benz 600SL was stopped in traffic by the crowds on Elisabethstrasse, its wipers throwing snow off its windshield.

The front passenger door opened and a tall, heavyset, ruddy-faced man in his sixties got out. He looked at the crowds of the faithful, then up at the twin steeples of the church, then shook his head in disgust and impatience, and got back in the car.

"Seven hundred and sixty-nine fucking years, and they're still waiting for a fucking virgin," Otto Görner said, as much in disgust as awe.

"Excuse me, Herr Görner?" the driver asked, more than a little nervously.

Johan Schmidt, the large forty-year-old behind the wheel, was wearing a police-type uniform; he was a supervisor in the security firm that protected the personnel and property of Gossinger Beteiligungsgesellschaft, G.m.b.H. Otto Görner was managing director of the holding company, among whose many corporate assets was the security firm.

Schmidt's supervisor was in charge of security for what in America would be called the corporate headquarters of Gossinger Beteiligungsgesellschaft, G.m.b.H., in Fulda, another small Hessian city about one hundred kilometers from Marburg an der Lahn. The supervisor had arrived at Schmidt's home an hour and a half before, and had come right to the point.

"Herr Görner wants to go to Marburg," he'd announced at Schmidt's door. "And you're going to drive him."

He had then made two gestures, one toward the street, where a security car was parked behind the SL600, and one by putting his thumb to his lips.

Schmidt immediately understood both gestures. He was to drive Herr Görner to Marburg in the SL600, and the reason he was going to do so was that Herr Görner—who usually drove himself in a 6.0-liter V12-engined Jaguar XJ Vanden Plas—had been imbibing spirits. Görner was fond of saying he never got behind the wheel of a car if at any time in the preceding eight hours he had so much as sniffed a cork. The Mercedes was Frau Görner's car; no one drove Otto Görner's Jag but Otto Görner.

Görner's physical appearance was that of a stereotypical Bavarian; he visually seemed to radiate *gemütlichkeit.* He was in fact a Hessian, and what he really radiated—even when he had not been drinking—was the antithesis of *gemütlichkeit.* It was said behind his back that only three people in the world were not afraid of him. One was his wife, Helena, who was paradoxically a Bavarian but looked and dressed like a Berlinerin or maybe a New Yorker. It was hard to imagine Helena Görner in a dirndl, her hair in pigtails, munching on a *würstchen.*

Frau Gertrud Schröeder, Görner's secretary, had been known to tell him no and to shout back at him when that was necessary in the performance of her duties.

The third person who didn't hold Görner in fearful awe didn't have to. Herr Karl Wilhelm von und zu Gossinger was by far the principal stockholder of Gossinger Beteiligungsgesellschaft, G.m.b.H. Görner worked for him, at least theoretically. Gossinger lived in the United States under the polite fiction that he was the Washington, D.C., correspondent of the *Tages Zeitung* newspaper chain—there were seven scattered over Germany, Austria, Czechoslovakia, and Hungary—which constituted another holding of Gossinger Beteiligungsgesellschaft, G.m.b.H.

It was commonly believed that the heir to the Gossinger fortune seldom wrote anything but his signature on a corporate check drawn to his credit and instead spent most of his time chasing movie stars, models, and other female prey in the beachside bars of Florida and California and in the après-ski lounges of Colorado and elsewhere.

"I said it's been seven hundred and sixty-nine fucking years, and they're still waiting for a fucking virgin," Görner repeated.

"Yes, sir," Schmidt said, now sorry he had asked.

"You do know the legend?" Görner challenged.

Schmidt resisted the temptation to say "of course" in the hope that would end the conversation. Instead, afraid that Görner would demand to hear what the legend was, he said, "I'm not sure, Herr Görner."

"Not sure?" Görner replied scornfully. "You either do or you don't."

"The crooked steeples?" Schmidt asked, taking a chance.

"Steeple, singular," Görner corrected him, and then went on: "The church was built to honor Elisabeth of Hungary, twelve hundred seven to twelve hundred thirty-one. She was a daughter of King Andrew II of Hungary. He married her off at age fourteen to Ludwig IV, one of whose descendants was Mad King Ludwig of Bavaria, who lost his throne because he became involved with an American actress whose name I can't at the moment recall, possibly because, before this came up, I got into the wassail cup.

"Anyway, Ludwig IV, the presumably sane one, went off somewhere for God and Emperor Frederick II of the Holy Roman Empire. While so nobly employed, he caught a bug of some sort and died.

"Elisabeth, now a widow, interpreted this as a sign from God and thereafter devoted her life and fortune to good works and Holy Mother Church. For reasons I have never had satisfactorily explained, she came here and founded a hospital for the poor, right here behind the church—our destination, you understand?"

"I know where we're going, Herr Görner."

To see a dead man, he thought. *A murdered man.*

So why am I getting this Gottverdammt *history lesson—because he's feeling no pain?*

Or because he doesn't want to think about the real reason we're here?

"That was before the church was built, you understand," Görner had gone on. "The church came after she died in 1231. By then she had become a Franciscan nun and given all her money and property to the church.

"So, they decided to canonize her. Pope Gregory IX did so in 1235, and in the fall of that year, they laid the cornerstone of the church. It took them a couple of years to finish it, and nobody was so impolite as to mention that one of the steeples was crooked.

"But everybody saw it, of course, and a legend sprang up—possibly with a little help from the Vatican—that the steeple would be straightened by God himself just as soon as Saint Elisabeth's bones were reburied under the altar. That happened in 1249. The steeple didn't move.

"The legend changed to be that the steeple would be fixed when the first virgin was married in the church." He paused, then drily added, "Your choice, Schmidt—either there was a shortage of virgins getting married, or the legend was baloney."

Schmidt raised an eyebrow but said nothing.

"The steeple was still crooked three hundred years later," Görner continued, "when Landgrave Phillip of Hesse threw the Romans out of the church and turned it over to the Protestants. That was in 1527, if memory serves, and it usually does.

"He threw the Dominicans out of their monastery on the top of the hill"— Görner turned and pointed over his shoulder—"at about the same time and turned it into a university, which he modestly named after himself. That's where I went to school."

"So I have heard, Herr Görner."

"Enough is enough," Görner said.

"Sir?"

"It could be argued that inasmuch as poor Günther is dead, there is no reason for us to hurry," Görner said. "But an equally heavy argument is there is no reason we should wait while they stand there with their fucking candles waiting for a fucking virgin. Sound the horn, Schmidt, and drive through them."

"Herr Görner, are you sure you—"

Görner reached for the steering wheel and pressed hard on the horn for what seemed to Schmidt an interminable time.

This earned them looks of shock and indignation from the candle-bearing worshippers, but after a moment the crowd began to make room and the big Mercedes moved through the gap.

In the block behind the church, at Görner's direction, Schmidt illegally parked the car before a PARKEN VERBOTEN! sign at the main entrance to the hospital, between a somewhat battered silver-and-white Opel Astra police car and an apparently brand-new, unmarked Astra that bore a magnet-based police blue light on its roof.

[TWO]

There were two men sitting on a bench in the corridor of the hospital. One was a stout, totally bald, decently dressed man in his fifties, the other a weasel-faced thirty-something-year-old in a well-worn blue suit that had not received the attention of a dry cleaner in a very long time.

When they saw Görner, they both rose, the older one first.

"Herr Görner?" he said.

Görner nodded and perfunctorily shook their hands.

"Where is he?" Görner said.

"You wish to see the victim, Herr Görner?"

Görner shut off the reply that sprang to his lips, and instead said, "If I may."

"The 'mortuary,' using the term loosely, is down that way," the older man said. "But I was ordered to have the body moved here from the coroner's morgue."

Görner nodded. He had been responsible for the order.

When the security duty officer at the office had called Herr Otto Görner to tell him he had just been informed that Herr Günther Friedler had been found dead "under disturbing circumstances" in his room in the Europäischer Hof in Marburg, the first thing Görner had done was to order that his wife's car be brought to the house with a driver to take him to Marburg. Next, he had called an acquaintance—not a friend—in the Ministry of the Interior. The Interior Ministry controlled both the Federal Police and the Bundeskriminalamt, the Federal Investigation Bureau, known by its acronym, BKA. The acquaintance owed Otto Görner several large favors.

Görner had given him—"And yes, Stutmann, I know it's Christmas Eve"—two "requests":

One, that Görner wanted a senior officer of the BKA immediately dispatched to Marburg an der Lahn to "assist" the Hessian police in their investigation of the death of Günther Friedler, and, two, that while that official was on his way, Görner wanted the Hessian police to be told to move the body out of the coroner's morgue; Saint Elisabeth's Hospital would be a good place.

"What's this all about, Otto?"

"I don't want to talk about it on the phone. Your line is probably tapped."

There was no blood on either the sheet that the weasel-faced plainclothes policeman pulled from the naked corpse of the late Günther Friedler or on the body itself. There were, however, too many stab wounds to the body to be easily counted, and there was an obscene wound on the face where the left eye had been cut from the skull.

Someone has worked very hard to clean you up, Günther.

"Merry Christmas," Otto Görner said, and motioned for the plainclothes policeman to pull the sheet back over the body.

The completely bald police official signaled for the plainclothes policeman to leave the room.

"So what is the official theory?" Görner asked as soon as the door closed.

"Actually, Herr Görner, we see a case like this every once in a while."

Görner waited for him to continue.

"When homosexual lovers quarrel, there is often a good deal of passion. And when knives are involved . . ." He shook his bald head and grimaced, then went on: "We're looking for a 'good friend' rather than a male prostitute."

Görner just looked at him.

"But we are, of course, talking to the male prostitutes," the police official added.

"You are?" Görner asked.

"Yes, of course we are. This is murder, Herr Görner—"

"I was asking who you are," Görner interrupted.

"Polizeirat Lumm, Herr Görner, of the Hessian Landespolizie."

"Captain, whoever did this to Herr Friedler might well be a deviate, but he was neither a 'good friend' of Friedler nor a male whore."

"How can you know—"

"A senior BKA investigator," Görner said quickly, shutting him off, "is on his way here to assist you in your investigation. Until he gets here, I strongly suggest that you do whatever you have to do to protect the corpse and the scene of the crime."

"Polizeidirektor Achter told me about the BKA getting involved when he told me you would be coming, Herr Görner."

"Good."

"Can you tell me what this is all about?"

"Friedler worked for me. He was in Marburg working on a story. There is no question in my mind that he was killed because he had—or was about to have—come upon something that would likely send someone to prison and/or embarrass someone very prominent."

"Have you a name? Names?"

"As far as I know, Polizeirat Lumm, you are a paradigm of an honest police officer, but on the other hand, I don't *know* that, and I never laid eyes on you until tonight, so I'm not going to give you any names."

"With all respect, Herr Görner, that could be interpreted as refusing to co-operate with a police investigation."

"Yes, I suppose it could. Are you thinking of arresting me?"

"I didn't say that, sir."

"I almost wish you would. If you did, I wouldn't have to do what I must do next: go to Günther Friedler's home on Christmas Eve and tell his widow that her thoroughly decent husband—they have four children, Lumm, two at school here at Phillips, two a little older with families of their own—will not be coming home late on Christmas Eve because he has been murdered by these bastards."

[THREE]
3690 Churchill Lane
Philadelphia, Pennsylvania
1610 24 December 2005

After carefully checking his rearview mirror, John M. "Jack" Britton, a some-what soberly dressed thirty-two-year-old black man, turned his silver Mazda MX-5 Miata right off Morrell Avenue onto West Crown Avenue, then almost immediately made another right onto Churchill Lane.

Churchill Lane—lined with clusters of two-story row houses, five to eight houses per cluster—made an almost ninety-degree turn to the left after the second cluster of homes. Britton followed the turn, then pulled the two-door convertible (he had the optional hardtop on it for the winter) to the curb in front of the center cluster. He was now nearly right in front of his home.

Britton got out of the car, looked down the street, and then, seeing nothing, walked around the nose of the Miata, pulled open the passenger door, and accepted an armload of packages from his wife, Sandra, a slim, tall, sharp-featured woman who was six days his senior in age.

They had come from a Bring One Present Christmas party held in a nearby restaurant by and for co-workers. Jack Britton had changed jobs, but he and his wife had been invited anyway. They came home with the two presents they had received in exchange for each of theirs, plus the door prize, an electric mixer for the kitchen that seemed to be made of lead and for which they had no use. On the way home, they had discussed giving it to Sandra's brother, El-wood, who was getting married.

Knowing that her husband couldn't unlock the front door with his arms full, Sandra preceded him past the three-foot-high brick wall that was topped with a four-foot-high aluminum rail fence—one that Britton bitterly complained had cost a bundle yet had done absolutely nothing to keep the local dogs from doing their business on his small but meticulously kept lawn.

Sandra was just inside the fence when Jack looked down the street again.

This time he saw what he was afraid he was going to see: a pale green Chrysler Town & Country minivan. It was slowly turning the ninety-degree bend in Churchill Lane. Then it rapidly accelerated.

"Sandy, get down behind the wall!" Britton ordered.

"What?"

He rushed to his wife, pushed her off the walkway and down onto the ground behind the wall, then covered her body with his.

"What the hell are you doing?" she demanded, half angrily, half fearfully.

There came the sound of squealing tires.

Britton reached inside his jacket and pulled a Smith & Wesson Model 29 .357 Magnum revolver from his shoulder holster. He rolled off of his wife and onto his back, bringing up the pistol with both hands and aiming at the top of the wall in case someone came over it.

There then came the sound of automatic-weapons fire—*Kalashnikovs*, he thought, *two of them*—and of a few ricochets and glass shattering, and the tinkle of ejected cartridge cases bouncing on the macadam pavement of Churchill Lane.

And then squealing tires and a revved-up engine.

Britton crawled to where he could look out the gate to the street. He saw the Town & Country turn onto Wessex Lane but knew there wasn't time for a shot at the minivan. And he realized he couldn't have fired if there had been time; another cluster of houses was in the line of fire.

He stood up, put the pistol back in the shoulder holster, then went to Sandra and pulled her to her feet.

"What the hell was that, Jack?" she asked, her voice faint.

"Let's get you in the house," he said, avoiding the question. "Into the cellar."

He took her arm and led her up the walk to the door.

"I dropped the goddamn keys," Sandra said.

He ran back to the fence, drawing the pistol again as he ran, found the keys, and then ran back to his front door.

There were half a dozen neat little holes in the door, and one of the small panes of glass in the door had been shattered.

He got the door unlocked and propelled Sandra through the living room to the door of the cellar, which he had finished out with a big-screen TV, a sectional couch, and a wet bar.

"Honey," he said, his tone forceful, "stay down there until I tell you. If you want to be useful, make us a drink while I call the cavalry."

"I don't think this is funny, Jack, goddamn you!"

"I'll be right outside. And when the cops get here, I'm going to need a drink."

He closed the cellar door after she started down the stairs. Then he went quickly to the front door, took up a position where he could safely see out onto the street, and looked. He saw nothing alarming.

He took his cellular telephone from its belt clip and punched 9-1-1.

He didn't even hear the phone ring a single time before a voice said: "Nine-one-one Emergency. Operator four-seven-one. What's your emergency?"

"Assist officer! Shots fired! Thirty-six ninety Churchill Lane. Thirty-six ninety Churchill Lane." He'd repeated the address, making sure the police dispatcher got it correct. "Two or more shooters in a pale green Chrysler Town & Country minivan. They went westbound on Wessex from Churchill. They used automatic weapons, possibly Kalashnikov rifles."

He broke the connection, then looked out the window again, this time seeing something he hadn't noticed before.

The MX-5 had bullet holes in the passenger door. The metal was torn outward, meaning that the bullets had passed through the driver's door first.

If we had been in the car, they would've gotten us.

Goddamn! The car's not two months old.

When he heard the howl of sirens, he went outside. He looked up and down the street, and then, taking the revolver out of its holster again, walked down to the sidewalk to see what else had happened to the Miata.

The first unit to respond to the call was DJ 811, a rather rough-looking Ford Crown Victoria Police Interceptor patrol car assigned to the Eighth District. The howl of its siren died as it turned onto Churchill Lane, and when Britton saw it coming around the curve, he noticed that the overhead lights were not flashing.

Britton turned his attention back to the Miata. The driver's-side window was shattered and several bullets had penetrated the windshield. The windshield had not shattered, but Britton couldn't help but think how the holes in it looked amazingly like someone had stuck all over it those cheap bullet-hole decals that could be bought at most auto-supply shops.

He walked around the front of the car and saw that it had taken hits in the right fender, the right front tire, and the hood.

He smelled gasoline.

Oh, shit! They got the gas tank!

Then he heard a voice bark: "Drop the gun! Drop the gun! Put your hands on the top of your head! Put your hands on the top of your head!"

Britton saw that two cops in a patrol car had arrived.

They were both out of their car and had their service Glock semiautomatics aimed at him from behind the passenger door and across the hood.

Both looked as if they had graduated from the academy last week.

The order reminded Britton that he was still holding the Smith & Wesson. At his side, to be sure, pointing at the ground. But holding it.

Not smart, Jack. Not smart!

"Three-six-nine! Three-six-nine!" Britton shouted, using the old Philadelphia police radio code for police officer.

The two very young cops, their Glocks still leveled on him, suddenly looked much older and in charge.

The one behind the driver door repeated the order: "Drop the gun! Drop the gun! Put your hands on the top of your head! Put your hands on the top of your head!"

Britton's problem was that he did not think he could safely do as ordered—"Drop the gun!"

The Smith & Wesson Model 29 is a double-action model, meaning he could squeeze the trigger to fire a round with the hammer forward or cocked back. The latter required less pressure from the trigger finger.

It was Britton's belief that one well-aimed shot was more effective than a barrage of shots aimed in the general direction of a miscreant. He also knew that a shot fired in the single-action mode—with the hammer drawn back—was far more likely to strike its intended target than one fired by pulling hard on the trigger with the hammer in the forward—or uncocked—position. The extra effort required to fire from the uncocked position tended to disturb one's aim.

He had, therefore, formed the habit, whenever drawing his weapon with any chance whatever that he might have to pull the trigger, of cocking the hammer. And he had done so just now when he walked out of his front door.

If I drop this sonofabitch, the impact's liable to release the hammer, which will fire off a round, whereupon these two kids are going to empty their Glocks at me.

"Three-six-nine!" Britton said again. "I'm Jack Britton. I'm a detective. This is my house. My wife and I are the ones who were—"

"I'm not going to tell you again, you sonofabitch! Drop the gun! Drop the gun!"

"May I lay it on the ground, please? The hammer—"

"Drop the fucking gun!"

"Take it easy, fellows," a new voice said with authority.

Britton saw two more Philly policemen, a captain and a sergeant. He had not seen another car drive up, but now noticed there were four police cars on

Churchill Lane. The wail of sirens in the distance announced the imminent arrival of others.

"Hello, Jack," the captain said.

Britton now recognized him. He had been his sergeant, years ago, when Officer Britton was walking a beat in the Thirty-fifth District.

"If I drop this gun, the hammer's back, and—"

"Holster your weapons," the captain ordered firmly. "I know him. He's one
of us."

When the police officers had complied with the order—and not a second
before—the captain walked to Britton and squeezed his shoulder in an affectionate gesture that clearly said, *Good to see you, pal.*

"Jesus, Jack, they shot the car up, didn't they?"

"It's not even two months old," Britton said.

"What the hell happened here, Jack?"

"Sandra and I were at the Rosewood Caterer's, on Frankford Avenue, at the
Northeast Detectives Christmas party. I thought I was being followed—2002,
2003 Chrysler Town and Country, pale green in color. I didn't get the tag."

"Tommy," the captain ordered, "put out a flash on the car. . . ."

"Black males, maybe in Muslim clothing," Britton furnished, "armed with
automatic AKs, last seen heading west on Wessex Lane."

"Yes, sir," the sergeant said. He grabbed the lapel mike attached to his shirt
epaulet, squeezed the PUSH TO TALK button, and began to relay the flash information to Police Radio.

"Kalashnikovs?" the captain asked, shaking his head. "Fully auto ones?"

Britton nodded. "And they got the gas tank." He pointed.

The captain muttered an obscenity and then turned to the young policemen.

"Put in a call to the fire department—gasoline spill," he ordered, and then
looked at Britton.

"Well, although I thought for a minute they weren't following me, they
were," Britton said. "They came around the bend"—he pointed—"just as Sandra and I got inside the fence. I tackled her behind the wall and then all hell
broke loose. . . ."

"She all right?"

"She's in the basement. Shook up, sure, but all right."

"Why don't you put that horse pistol away, and we'll go talk to her?"

"Jesus," Britton said, embarrassed that he hadn't already lowered the hammer and put the Smith & Wesson in its holster.

The captain issued orders to first check to see if anyone might have been injured in the area, and then to protect the scene, and finally gestured to Britton to precede him into his house.

Sandra had left the cellar and now was in the living room, sprawled on the couch. There was a squat glass dark with whiskey on the coffee table, and she had one just like it in her hand.

"You remember Captain Donnelly, honey?"

"Yeah, sure. Long time. Merry Christmas."

"You all right, Sandra?" Donnelly said, the genuine concern of an old friend clear in his tone.

"As well—after being tackled by my husband, then having those AALs shoot up our house and our new car—as can be expected under the circumstances."

"AAL is politically incorrect, Sandra," Captain Donnelly said, smiling.

"I can say it," she said, pointing to her skin. "I can say African-American Lunatics. I could even say worse, but I'm a lady and I won't."

"Take it easy, honey," Britton said.

"I thought Jack was finished with them," Sandra said. "Naïve little ol' me."

Britton leaned over and picked up the whiskey glass.

"Can I offer you one of these?" he said to Donnelly.

"Of course not. I'm a captain, a district commander, and I'm on duty. But on the other hand, it's Christmas Eve, isn't it?"

"I'll get it," Sandra said, rising gracefully from the couch. "I moved the bottle to the kitchen knowing I would probably have more than one."

Donnelly looked at Britton.

"Tough little lady," he said admiringly.

"Yeah. Those bastards! I understand them wanting to whack me, but . . ."

"Jack, let's get a few things out of the way."

"Like what?"

"I heard you left the department, but that's about all I know. You're still in law enforcement?"

"I guess you could say that," Britton said, and took a small leather wallet from his suit jacket and handed it to Donnelly, who opened it, examined it, and handed it back.

"Secret Service, eh?"

"Now, if anyone asks, you can say, 'The victim identified himself to me by producing the credentials of a Secret Service special agent . . .'"

"'. . . and authorized to carry firearms,' " Donnelly finished the quote. "You guys carry Smith & Wesson .357s?"

"I do."

"What have they got you doing, Jack?"

"I'm assigned to Homeland Security."

"That's what Sandra meant when she said she thought you were through with the AALs?"

Britton nodded, then suddenly realized: "And speaking of Homeland Security, I'm going to have to tell them about this before they see it on Fox News. Excuse me."

He took his cellular telephone from its holster and punched an autodial number.

[FOUR]
The Consulate of the United States of America
Parkring 12a
Vienna, Austria
2105 24 December 2005

The counselor for consular affairs of the United States embassy in Vienna, Miss Eleanor Dillworth, was aware that many people—including many, perhaps most, American citizens—were less than thrilled with the services the consular section offered, and with the very consular officials who offered them.

An American citizen who required consular service—for example, having pages added to a passport; registering the birth of a child; needing what amounted to notary public services—could acquire such services only from eight to eleven-thirty each morning, Monday through Friday—*provided,* of course, that that day was neither an American nor an Austrian holiday and, of course, with the understanding that the said American citizen could not get the passport pages added *and* make any inquiry of any consular official regarding visas.

Consular officials could not be troubled by being asked about the status of a visa application by anyone—including, for example, but not limited to, an American citizen wondering when his foreign wife was going to get the visa that she not only had applied for but was entitled to under the law.

Miss Dillworth understood that such dissatisfaction spread around the world.

A colleague—one Alexander B. Darby, who was the commercial attaché of the United States embassy in Buenos Aires, Argentina—had told her that a well-known American artist living in Buenos Aires was going about loudly saying to anyone who would listen that whenever he went to the embassy there, he was made to feel by the consular officials as welcome as a registered sex offender seeking overnight lodging at a Girl Scout camp.

Eleanor and Alex had exchanged horror stories for at least a half hour when they had run into each other in Washington. They had even come up with an explanation why the Foreign Service got away with its arrogance and, indeed, incompetence.

It was, they concluded, a question of congressional oversight . . . or wanton lack thereof.

A farmer, for example, who felt that he had been mistreated by a farm agent would immediately get on the phone to his congressman or senator and complain, whereupon the congressman or senator would call the secretary of Agriculture, expressing his displeasure and reminding the secretary that the function of his agency was to serve the public, not antagonize it.

Doctors—and maybe especially lawyers—thought nothing, when they felt they were being improperly serviced, of going directly to the surgeon general, or the attorney general, with their complaints. Similarly, bankers would raise hell with the secretary of the Treasury, businessmen with the secretary of Commerce, *und so weiter*.

And they got results.

The only people who took a close look at the Foreign Service were members of Congress. They performed this duty by visiting embassies around the world—usually in places like Paris, London, and Tokyo—traveling in either USAF VIP jets or in the first-class compartment of a commercial airliner, and accompanied by their wives. On their arrival, they were housed in the best hotels and lavishly entertained, the costs thereof coming from the ambassadors' "representational allowance" provided by the U.S. taxpayer. Then they got back on the airplanes and went home, having become "Experts in International Affairs" and bubbling all over with praise for the charming people of the State Department, those nobly serving their country on foreign shores.

There were exceptions, of course. Alex Darby couldn't say enough nice things about the ambassador in Buenos Aires, even though he didn't seem able to do much about his consular staff enraging American citizens—not to mention the natives—living in Argentina.

But Alex and Eleanor were agreed that the Foreign Service could be greatly improved if every other diplomat arriving for work in his chauffeur-driven embassy car—with consular diplomatic tags, which permitted him to ignore speed limits and park wherever he wished—were canned, and those dips remaining were seriously counseled to get their act in gear or be canned themselves.

At first glance—or even second—it might appear that Counselor for Consular Affairs Eleanor Dillworth and Commercial Attaché Alexander B. Darby were disgruntled employees and probably should never have been employed by the Foreign Service in the first place.

The truth here was that neither was a member of the Foreign Service, despite the good deal of effort expended to make that seem to be the case. In fact, Dillworth and Darby were the Central Intelligence Agency station chiefs in, respectively, Vienna and Buenos Aires, and the salary checks deposited once a month to their personal banking accounts came from the funds of the Clandestine Services Division of the Central Intelligence Agency, Langley, Virginia.

It was in this latter—which was to say real—role that Eleanor Dillworth sat in her consul general's office on Parkring, waiting to have a word with a bona fide diplomat, Ronald J. Spearson, who was, as no one at the moment served as ambassador to Austria, the Chargé d'Affaires, a.i. of the American embassy.

"In case this somehow slipped by you, Eleanor, it's Christmas Eve," Spearson said when he walked into the office. He was a tall, trim man in his early forties.

"Well, in that case, Merry Christmas, Ronnie."

Spearson believed that embassy staff should address him as "Mister," and he did not like to be called "Ronnie," not even by his wife.

He gave her a dirty look.

"I'm in no mood for your sarcasm," she said. "I know what day this is, and I wouldn't have asked you to come here unless it was important."

"I meant no offense, Eleanor," he said after a moment. "If an apology is in order, consider that it has been offered."

She did consider that a moment, then nodded.

"Kurt Kuhl and his wife have been murdered," she said.

"Kurt Kuhl of Kuhlhaus? That Kuhl?"

She nodded.

"About half past six tonight," she said. "The bodies were found behind the Johann Strauss statue in the Stadtpark."

She gestured in the direction of a window that overlooked Parkring and the Stadtpark.

"Well, I'm . . ."

"They were garroted," she went on evenly, "with a metal garrote of the type the Hungarian secret police—the Államvédelmi Hatóság—used in the bad old days."

"Eleanor, what has this to do with me? With the embassy?"

"As a result of which," she went on, ignoring the questions, "there will be a new star on that wall in Langley. Two, if I have anything to say. Gertrud Kuhl is entitled to one, too."

Spearson looked at her for a long moment.

"You're not suggesting, Eleanor, are you, that Kurt Kuhl was one of your—"

"I'm telling you that Kurt Kuhl has been in the clandestine service of the company longer than you're old."

"I find that very hard to believe," Spearson said.

"I thought you might. Nevertheless, you have now been told."

"My God, he's an old man!"

"Seventy-five," she said. "About as old as Billy Waugh."

"Billy Waugh?"

"The fellow who bagged Carlos the Jackal. The last time I heard, Billy was running around Afghanistan looking for Osama bin Laden."

Again he looked at her a long moment before replying.

"If what you say is true . . ."

"I just made this up to give you a little Christmas Eve excitement," she said sarcastically.

"Then why wasn't I told of this before?"

"You didn't have the Need to Know. Now, in my judgment, you do."

"And the ambassador? Did he know?"

"No. He didn't have the Need to Know, either."

"You made that decision, is that what you're saying?"

"I was given the authority to tell him if I thought it was necessary. Or not to tell him."

"That violates the Country Team principle."

"The secretary of State signed on to what the DCI told me."

"What was Kuhl doing for the CIA?"

"You want a thumbnail or the whole scenario?"

"I think I had better hear everything."

"Okay. Kuhl was a Hungarian Jew. His family had been in the pastry shop business for a long time, way back before World War One. They saw what was happening and got out of Hungary to the States in 1939. Kurt was then ten years old, the youngest of their children.

"There was already a Kuhlhaus store in New York City and another in Chicago. The family went back to work in that business. When war came, his older brother, Gustav, went into the Army, was promptly recruited by the OSS, and was one of the original Jedburghs."

"The original what?"

"Agents for the Office of Strategic Services trained at Jedburgh, Scotland, to jump into German-occupied Europe. Bill Colby, who, I'm sure you remember, went on to become DCI in '73, was one of them. Gustav was captured in France, sent to Sachsenhausen, and executed there just before the Russians arrived.

"In 1946, just as soon as he turned seventeen, Kurt, by then an American citizen, enlisted in the Army. Getting to Europe to see what family assets he could salvage was one reason. Avenging his brother was another.

"He spoke German and Hungarian and Slovak, etcetera. He was assigned here as an interpreter at the Kommandatura—the Allied Control Commission. 'Four men in a jeep.' Remember that?"

Spearson shook his head.

"Toward the end of his tour, they found out that Corporal Kuhl had been sneaking in and out of what was then Czechoslovakia and Hungary and East Germany. That was in 1949. He should have been court-martialed, but somebody in the CIA was smart enough to offer him a deal.

"If he was willing to be of service, unspecified, if called upon, he not only would not be court-martialed but would be allowed to remain in Vienna to salvage what he could of the family business, and he would be helped to do that.

"He took the deal. I don't know what he did between '49 and '56, but he was so helpful during the Hungarian uprising that the agency put him on the payroll, as field officer, clandestine service. He's been on it ever since."

"He's been a spy all this time?"

"Not in the James Bond sense. What he has been doing—and if you think about it a moment, you'll see how valuable this has been—is identify people the company could turn. He didn't turn them. He just identified those people he thought could be turned. He became their friend, learned their strengths and weaknesses, and passed it to the company.

"The diplomatic and intelligence services of the old Soviet Union, and its satellites, as well as the Western countries, do—as we do—tend to move their people between assignments in an area. In this case, Eastern Europe. Their dips would be in Warsaw on one assignment, Vienna the next, maybe Rome, and later Budapest, then back to Vienna . . ."

"And we wouldn't recruit them here, but when they were somewhere else?"

"Precisely. An Austrian passport was arranged for him. That happened to many ex-Hungarians who couldn't get a Hungarian passport. He became a Viennese, the heir to the Kuhlhaus pastry shops. It was a perfect cover. When the wall came down, no one raised an eyebrow when Kuhlhauses were opened or reopened—in Prague, Budapest, all over—and no one thought it was in any way suspicious that Kurt Kuhl moved around Eastern Europe supervising his business."

"Well, apparently someone did," Spearson said. "If he was murdered."

"Nobody ever accused the SVR of stupidity. I suppose we should have expected he would get burned. . . . My God, he was doing his job for fifty years. He didn't think so. I tried to warn him it was just about inevitable."

"You've been in touch with him?"

She nodded.

"About once a week. At the Kuhlhaus store on the Graben. He often took me in the back room for a little *café mit schlagobers*. And I will go to his funeral. I think it will probably be held in Saint Stephen's. Over the years, he made a lot of important friends. I will go as an old customer, not as the counselor for consular affairs."

"What am I supposed to do?"

"I hope nothing. But I thought you should know who he really was, and what he was doing, rather than be surprised when you read it on the front page of the *Wiener Tages Zeitung*."

[FIVE]
Restaurant Oca
Pilar, Buenos Aires Province, Argentina
1855 24 December 2005

In the opinion of Liam Duffy—a short, muscular, blond thirty-nine-year-old—there was a good deal to recommend the Restaurant Oca on a blistering hot Christmas Eve, starting with the fact that it would stay open until seven. Most other restaurants in this country of devout Catholics closed just after lunch to celebrate the night before Christ's sacred birth.

The food was good, but the basic reason he had suggested to Mónica, his wife, that they take a ride out to Oca in Pilar from their apartment in Barrio Norte was the geese.

Oca was adjacent to a residential country club called The Farm. Just inside the gate to the guarded community of larger-than-ordinary houses, and immediately behind the restaurant, was a small lake that supported a large gaggle of geese.

The geese had learned to paddle up to the rear of the restaurant and beg for bread scraps. The Duffy kids—there were four, two girls and two boys, ranging in age from two to seven years—never tired of feeding them.

This meant that Liam and Mónica could linger over their dessert and coffee without having to separate the children from sibling disputes. These occurred often, of course, but far more frequently when the kids were excited, as they were by Christmas Eve and when the temperature and humidity were as oppressive as they were now.

Duffy ignored the waiter standing nearby with their check in hand as long as he could, but finally waved him over. Mónica collected the kids as her husband waited for his change.

From here, they would go to Mónica's parents' home in Belgrano for the ritual Christmas Eve "tea." They would have Christmas dinner tomorrow with his parents and four other Duffy males and their families at their apartment in Palermo.

Mónica appeared with the children, holding the hand of the youngest boy and the ear of the elder. The other two children seemed delighted with the arrangement.

Duffy shook hands with the proprietor, whose smile seemed a little strained, then left the restaurant and got in the car. He handed the car-parker a five-peso note instead of the usual two. It was, after all, Christmas Eve.

And he was driving a year-old Mercedes-Benz 320 SUV, which suggested that he was affluent and could afford a five-peso tip. He wasn't; the car belonged to the government. But the valet, of course, had no way of knowing this.

To get in the southbound lane of the Panamericana Expressway, it was necessary to pass through a tunnel under the toll road itself. As Duffy came out the far side of the tunnel and prepared to turn left onto the access ramp, an old battered white Ford F-150 pickup truck pulled in front of him, causing Liam Duffy to say certain words, ones Mónica quickly pointed out to him should not be used in the presence of children.

Duffy followed the Ford up the access ramp, where the sonofabitch driving the pickup suddenly slammed on its brakes.

Duffy stopped just before ramming him.

And then, as the hair on his neck curled, he looked over his left shoulder.

Holy Mary, Mother of God, not on fucking Christmas Eve!

He jammed the gearshift into low, spun the steering wheel to the right, and floored the accelerator. He rammed the right rear of the Ford. The pickup's tires screamed as Duffy pushed it out of the way. The SUV—which was why Duffy had chosen it—had full-time four-wheel drive.

Mónica screamed.

Duffy then heard bullets impacting the Mercedes. By the time he reached the top of the access road, he had both offered a prayer for the safety of his family and drawn from under his shirt his semiautomatic pistol, an Argentine-manufactured version of the Model 1911A1 .45 ACP Colt.

He held down the horn with the hand holding the pistol as he drove through the traffic on the toll road.

Mónica was screaming again.

"The kids?" he shouted.

She stopped screaming and tried and failed to get into the backseat.

"Mónica, for Christ's sake!"

"They're all right," she reported a moment later. "For God's sake, slow down!"

Yeah, and let the bastards catch up with us!

He didn't slow down, but did stop weaving through traffic.

Five kilometers down the toll road, he saw a Policía Federal police car parked in a Shell gasoline station.

He pulled off the highway and skidded to a stop by the car. The policemen inside looked at him more in annoyance than curiosity.

Duffy pushed the button on his door panel that rolled down his window.

"Comandante Duffy, Gendarmería Nacional!" he shouted at the Policía Federal policemen. "We have just been ambushed. Shot at. Look for a battered white Ford 150."

They took him at his word.

The driver, a young officer, jumped out of the car, drew his pistol, and looked up the highway. The passenger, a sergeant, walked to the SUV.

By then Duffy had the microphone of his radio in his hand.

"All gendarmería hearing this. Comandante Duffy has just been ambushed at kilometer forty-six on the Panamericana. I want the nearest cars at the Shell station, kilometer thirty-eight, southbound. En route, stop all old white Ford 150 pickups and inspect right rear of vehicle for collision damage."

It will do absolutely no fucking good, Duffy thought. *The bastards are long gone.*

But nobody's hurt, and cars are on the way.

Holy Mary, Mother of God, thank you for answering my prayer.

Duffy got out of the car, put the pistol back in the holster in the small of his back under his shirt, then opened the rear door of the Mercedes.

He picked up the seven-year-old José and said, "Why don't we go in there and get a Coke, and then we'll go see Abuela?"

His wife, holding the baby, looked at him.

"Well, we'll have something to talk about when we get to your mother's, won't we?" Liam asked.

"Goddamn you, Liam!" Mónica said.

[ONE]
7200 West Boulevard Drive
Alexandria, Virginia
1145 25 December 2005

A yellow Chrysler minivan with the legend *Captain Al's Taxi Service To All D.C. Airports* painted on its back windows drove through the snow of the long, curving driveway up to the big house and stopped before the closed four doors of the basement garage.

The sole passenger—a trim woman who appeared to be in her sixties but was in fact a decade older, her jet-black hair, drawn tight in a bun, showing traces of gray—slid the door open before the driver could get out of the van to do it for her.

There was a path up a slope from the driveway to the front of the house, but there were no footprints in the snow to suggest that anyone had used it recently.

The driver took a small leather suitcase from the rear of the van, thought about it a moment—*What the hell, it's Christmas Day*—and then said, "I'll walk you to the door, ma'am."

"That's very kind of you."

She followed him up the path. When he had put the suitcase at the foot of the door, she handed him a folded bill.

"Thank you," she said. "And Merry Christmas."

He looked at the money. It was a hundred-dollar note.

The fare was thirty-three fifty.

"Ma'am, I can't change this."

"Merry Christmas," she said again, and pushed the doorbell button.

"Thank you very much, and a Merry Christmas to you, too."

He got back in the van, waited to make sure that someone would answer her ring, and then drove away.

The door was opened by a large, muscular young man in a single-breasted suit.

"Yes, ma'am?"

"Merry Christmas. Colonel Castillo, please."

"There's no one here by that name, ma'am."

"Yes, there is," she said politely but firmly. "Tell him his grandmother is here."

The muscular young man considered that for a moment, then appeared to be talking to his suit lapel. It wasn't the first time she had seen someone do that.

"Roger that," he said again. "She says she's Don Juan's grandmother."

Not ninety seconds later, a large, fair-skinned, blue-eyed man of thirty-six suddenly appeared at the front door. Lieutenant Colonel Carlos G. Castillo, Special Forces, U.S. Army, was wearing brown corduroy slacks and a battered sweatshirt with USMA printed on it. He held what could have been a glass of tomato juice in one hand, and a large, nearly black, eight-inch-long cigar in the other.

At his side was a very large silver-and-black shaggy dog about one and a half times the size of a very large boxer. At first sight, the dog—a one-hundred-forty-pound Bouvier des Flandres named Max—often frightened people, even dog lovers such as the muscular young man in the business suit who had answered the door, and who took some pride in thinking he was unflappable.

He flapped now in shock as the old lady, who, instead of recoiling in horror as Max rushed at her, dropped to her knees, cooed, "Hello, baby! Are you happy to see your old Abuela?" and wrapped her arms around Max's massive neck.

Max whined happily as his shaggy stub of a tail spun like a helicopter rotor.

The old lady looked up at the man in the West Point sweatshirt.

"And what about you, Carlos? Are you happy to see your old Abuela?"

"Happy yes," he said. "Shock will come later. What the he— What are you doing here?"

"Well, Fernando, Maria, and the children spent Christmas Eve with me at the house. Today I was faced with the choice of spending Christmas with Maria's family or getting on the plane and spending it with you."

"How'd you find the house, Abuela?"

"I told Fernando I was going to send you a turkey, and he gave me the address."

"In other words, he doesn't know you're here?"

"Probably not," Doña Alicia Castillo confessed as she stood up. "But the way that works, darling, is that I'm the Abuela and you and Fernando are the grandchildren. I don't need anybody's permission."

"Welcome, welcome, Abuela," Castillo said, smiling, and wrapped his arms around her, lifting her off the floor.

"I echo the sentiment," a deep voice with a slight Eastern European accent said. "Until you arrived, Doña Alicia, I was sick with the thought of having to spend the day alone with these barbarians."

Eric Kocian, a tall, erect man with a full head of silver hair, who also appeared to be in his sixties but was in fact eighty-two years of age, was in a starched white dress shirt, pressed woolen trousers, and a blue-striped chef's apron. He walked to her and with great formality kissed her hand.

"Count your fingers, Abuela," Castillo said. "And make sure you still have on your wedding ring."

"Merry Christmas, Billy," Doña Alicia said, using his nickname, and rising on her toes to kiss his cheek. "I don't think I've ever seen you in an apron."

"When one is being fed by vulgarians, one is wise to keep one's eye on the cooks."

"Well, I'm glad to see you. I somehow had the idea you'd gone back to Budapest."

Kocian sighed dramatically. "I pray daily that I will soon be released from durance vile. So far the Good Lord has ignored my devout pleas."

"I had no idea you were living here with Carlos."

"I'm not," he said a little too quickly. "Mädchen and I—with those few pups Karlchen has not torn cruelly from their mother—are staying in the Mayflower."

"Four of those adorable pups, as I suspect you well know, Billy, are making this Christmas even more joyous for some very nice people."

Kocian ignored that. He said, "May I offer you a glass of champagne, Doña Alicia? I took the precaution of bringing some, knowing that if the inhabitants of this monastery had any at all, it would be vinegar."

" 'Monastery'?"

"That's what they call it," Kocian said with a nod at Castillo. "Their sense of humor is as perverse as their taste in food and wine."

"I would love a glass of champagne," Doña Alicia said, smiling.

"If you would be so kind as to follow me?"

Doña Alicia saw that the kitchen was large—even huge—and that the sliding doors open to the adjacent living room showed that it was sizable, too, causing her to idly wonder what exact purpose this great big house—and all these people—served for her grandson. There were seven people in the kitchen, six men and a woman, not counting Eric Kocian or Charley Castillo. Most were sprawled in chairs holding what could have been glasses of iced tomato juice, but what Doña Alicia knew had to be Bloody Marys. The woman and two of the men were standing at the stove, which was in an island in the center of the room.

There was also another Bouvier des Flandres, this one a third smaller than Max and lying on the floor beside an infant's crib that held four sleeping puppies. She clearly was the mother—Mädchen—and sat up attentively when the others came into the room.

Castillo gestured toward the woman and one of the men at the stove. Dressed casually in nice blue jeans and sweaters, both were in their forties, a pleasant-looking pair yet average to the point that they would not stand out in a crowd on Main Street, U.S.A.

"Abuela," Castillo said, "this is Dianne and Harold Sanders. They take care of us. This is my grandmother, Mrs. Alicia Castillo. Have we got enough to feed her?"

"No problem, Colonel," Harold Sanders said as he stirred some dark sauce in a large pot. He looked at Abuela and nodded once. "It's our honor to meet you, ma'am."

"You know everybody else, right, Abuela?" Castillo went on.

"Enough," she said, and went to Dianne Sanders. "My grandson should have given you Christmas off."

"Unless we cooked dinner, ma'am," Harold Sanders put in, "they'd poison themselves and we'd be out of a job."

"If you say so," she said with a smile.

She went in turn to the others, kissing the cheeks of the men she knew, shaking the hands of those she didn't and saying she was happy to get to know them.

These included a young Chinese American whose name was David Yung; a nondescript man in his late fifties, wearing somewhat rumpled trousers and an unbuttoned vest, who introduced himself as Edgar Delchamps; a well-set-up man about Castillo's age by the name of John Davidson; a ruddy-cheeked, middle-aged man who said he was Tom McGuire; and another middle-aged man whose name was Sándor Tor. Most were wearing suits, but not the jackets thereto.

And there were two others in the house: the muscular young man in the suit who had opened the front door to Doña Alicia, and another muscular young man in a suit who could have been his brother were he not a very dark-skinned African-American.

These two muscular young men were special agents of the United States Secret Service. Their mission was to provide security to the personnel of the Office of Organizational Analysis. While both the Secret Service and the OOA were in the Department of Homeland Security, almost no one knew of the OOA's existence and even fewer were in fact members, including these special agents.

Of course, there were very good reasons for this—indeed, top secret ones—chief among them that the OOA had come into being only five months earlier at the direction—if not the fury—of the President of the United States:

```
TOP SECRET—PRESIDENTIAL


THE WHITE HOUSE, WASHINGTON, D.C.


DUPLICATION FORBIDDEN


COPY 2 OF 3 (SECRETARY COHEN)


JULY 25, 2005.


PRESIDENTIAL FINDING.


IT HAS BEEN FOUND THAT THE ASSASSINATION OF J. WINSLOW
MASTERSON, CHIEF OF MISSION OF THE UNITED STATES
EMBASSY IN BUENOS AIRES, ARGENTINA; THE ABDUCTION OF
MR. MASTERSON'S WIFE, MRS. ELIZABETH LORIMER MASTERSON;
THE ASSASSINATION OF SERGEANT ROGER MARKHAM, USMC; AND
THE ATTEMPTED ASSASSINATION OF SECRET SERVICE SPECIAL
```

AGENT ELIZABETH T. SCHNEIDER INDICATES BEYOND ANY
REASONABLE DOUBT THE EXISTENCE OF A CONTINUING PLOT OR
PLOTS BY TERRORISTS, OR TERRORIST ORGANIZATIONS, TO
CAUSE SERIOUS DAMAGE TO THE INTERESTS OF THE UNITED
STATES, ITS DIPLOMATIC OFFICERS, AND ITS CITIZENS, AND
THAT THIS SITUATION CANNOT BE TOLERATED.

IT IS FURTHER FOUND THAT THE EFFORTS AND ACTIONS TAKEN
AND TO BE TAKEN BY THE SEVERAL BRANCHES OF THE UNITED
STATES GOVERNMENT TO DETECT AND APPREHEND THOSE
INDIVIDUALS WHO COMMITTED THE TERRORIST ACTS PREVIOUSLY
DESCRIBED, AND TO PREVENT SIMILAR SUCH ACTS IN THE
FUTURE ARE BEING AND WILL BE HAMPERED AND RENDERED LESS
EFFECTIVE BY STRICT ADHERENCE TO APPLICABLE LAWS AND
REGULATIONS.

IT IS THEREFORE FOUND THAT CLANDESTINE AND COVERT
ACTION UNDER THE SOLE SUPERVISION OF THE PRESIDENT IS
NECESSARY.

IT IS DIRECTED AND ORDERED THAT THERE IMMEDIATELY BE
ESTABLISHED A CLANDESTINE AND COVERT ORGANIZATION WITH
THE MISSION OF DETERMINING THE IDENTITY OF THE
TERRORISTS INVOLVED IN THE ASSASSINATIONS, ABDUCTION,
AND ATTEMPTED ASSASSINATION PREVIOUSLY DESCRIBED AND TO
RENDER THEM HARMLESS. AND TO PERFORM SUCH OTHER COVERT
AND CLANDESTINE ACTIVITIES AS THE PRESIDENT MAY ELECT
TO ASSIGN.

FOR PURPOSES OF CONCEALMENT, THE AFOREMENTIONED
CLANDESTINE AND COVERT ORGANIZATION WILL BE KNOWN AS
THE OFFICE OF ORGANIZATIONAL ANALYSIS, WITHIN THE
DEPARTMENT OF HOMELAND SECURITY. FUNDING WILL INITIALLY
BE FROM DISCRETIONAL FUNDS OF THE OFFICE OF THE
PRESIDENT. THE MANNING OF THE ORGANIZATION WILL BE
DECIDED BY THE PRESIDENT ACTING ON THE ADVICE OF THE
CHIEF, OFFICE OF ORGANIZATIONAL ANALYSIS.

MAJOR CARLOS G. CASTILLO, SPECIAL FORCES, U.S. ARMY, IS
HEREWITH APPOINTED CHIEF, OFFICE OF ORGANIZATIONAL
ANALYSIS, WITH IMMEDIATE EFFECT.

SIGNED:

[signature]

PRESIDENT OF THE UNITED STATES OF AMERICA

WITNESS:

Natalie G. Cohen

SECRETARY OF STATE

TOP SECRET—PRESIDENTIAL

There at first had been only one member of the Office of Organizational
Analysis—Castillo, who had recently returned from Afghanistan and was then
assigned as an aide to Department of Homeland Security Secretary Matthew
Hall—but the staff had quickly grown.

To guide the young Army major through the swamp of Washington bureaucracy and to protect him as much as this could be done from the alligators
dwelling therein, Secretary Hall had given up two members of his personal
staff, Mrs. Agnes Forbison and Thomas McGuire.

Mrs. Forbison, who was forty-nine, gray-haired, and getting just a little
chubby, was a GS-15, the most senior grade in the Federal Civil Service. She
had been one of Hall's executive assistants before being named deputy chief for
administration of the Office of Organizational Analysis.

Tom McGuire, a supervisory special agent of the Secret Service, had been
transferred to OOA because he knew the law-enforcement community and because—although he was not told this—Hall knew that whatever Castillo was
going to do, it would take him far from Washington, and the secretary thought
that getting away from Washington would take McGuire's mind off the recent
loss of his wife to cancer. He had been devastated.

The search for the assassins of J. Winslow Masterson had taken Castillo from Buenos Aires to the U.S. embassy in Montevideo, Uruguay. There he had met David W. Yung, Jr., ostensibly one of more than a dozen embassy "legal attachés"—actually, FBI agents—investigating the money laundering that was taking place in that small republic and its surrounding countries in what the U.S. State Department types called the Southern Cone.

About the time Yung had pointed Castillo toward a Uruguayan antiquities dealer—who was really one Dr. Jean-Paul Lorimer, an American employee of the United Nations *and* Elizabeth Masterson's brother *and* deeply involved in the Iraqi–UN oil-for-food scandal—Castillo had learned that Yung—who spoke five languages, none of them Oriental—had been assigned duties in Uruguay that neither the ambassador nor the other "legal attachés" knew about.

The secretary of State and the U.S. attorney general had him investigating money laundering by prominent Americans of profits from the oil-for-food cesspool.

After Yung's investigation helped unmask Lorimer, Castillo decided the best way to deal with the situation was to repatriate Lorimer to the United States—willingly or otherwise—where he could be interrogated by people like Tom McGuire.

Castillo then launched an *ad hoc* helicopter assault on Lorimer's estancia, Shangri-La, to accomplish this. He used a helicopter borrowed from Aleksandr Pevsner, a Russian arms dealer living in secret in Argentina, and the few personnel immediately available to him, including Yung and a young—very young—U.S. Marine Corps corporal, Lester Bradley.

Castillo had sent Bradley—the clerk-typist of the Marine Guard at the American embassy in Buenos Aires, and thus best tasked to drive a truck on some unexplained mission—to Uruguay, at the wheel of a GMC Yukon XL, smuggling in two forty-two-gallon barrels for the refueling of the helicopter.

The raid, even though conducted by what Castillo painfully acknowledged were mostly amateurs, initially went well. But just as Castillo was about to tell Lorimer that he was being returned to the States—and right after he'd had Lorimer open his safe—a burst of small-arms fire announced that others were interested in Dr. Jean-Paul Lorimer. He was killed instantly.

In the next five minutes, the estancia became littered with bodies, including one of the two Special Forces soldiers on Castillo's team. Sergeant Seymour Krantz had been garroted to death. The other six dead were all of the unknown men who had begun the attack. One had been shot by David W. Yung, Jr., who for the first time in his law-enforcement career had drawn his pistol, and two others by Corporal Lester Bradley, who took them out with head shots from a sniper's rifle at more than one hundred yards away.

Bradley later modestly confessed he had been a "designated marksman" when the Marines had marched on Baghdad, and there had been no question at all in his mind that he could make the shots at the estancia when he laid the crosshairs of the telescopic sight on the heads of the bad guys about to fire on Yung and Castillo.

The assault team immediately departed Estancia Shangri-La by helicopter, leaving behind Dr. Lorimer's body but taking with them the body of Sergeant Krantz, the garroted Delta Force soldier; David W. Yung, Jr.; Corporal Lester W. Bradley, USMC—and some sixteen million dollars' worth of what amounted to bearer bonds that Yung had found in Lorimer's safe.

Castillo had ordered Yung aboard the helicopter for two reasons:

One, that Yung—even if he didn't know it—had more information about the oil-for-food business behind the Masterson assassination than Castillo had been able to draw from him, and, Two, that Castillo didn't think Yung would be able to keep his mouth shut during the interrogations that would begin the moment the black-clad bodies of whoever had attacked them were discovered at the estancia.

And so far as Corporal Bradley was concerned, this was an even worse situation. If Bradley went back to his duties at the embassy without the GMC truck, his gunnery sergeant in Buenos Aires was naturally going to ask, "So where's the Yukon?"

Bradley obviously could not be allowed to reply that a Special Forces major had torched the vehicle with a thermite grenade during a clandestine helicopter assault on an estate in Uruguay—which was precisely what Bradley would understand that he would have to reply when so asked.

Marines learn at Parris Island that when a gunny asks them a question, they *will* respond with the truth, the whole truth, and nothing but the truth.

By the time they got to Washington, Yung had figured out a likely scenario to explain the money, and why they had been attacked at the estancia: Dr. Lorimer—by now identified as the bagman for oil-for-food bribes and payoffs—had stolen the sixteen million bucks from his as-yet-unidentified employers.

These people had kidnapped Lorimer's sister—Mrs. J. Winslow Masterson—then murdered her husband before her eyes to impress upon her that they were quite serious about being willing to kill her and her children unless she told them where in hell they could find Lorimer and their sixteen million. But she hadn't told them because she didn't know.

The bad guys had found Estancia Shangri-La by themselves.

That they arrived there to reclaim their money and eliminate Lorimer ten minutes after Castillo's covert team had arrived to repatriate Lorimer was pure coincidence. Not to mention damn bad luck.

"They didn't expect to find anything at the estancia, Mr. President, but Dr. Lorimer and the sixteen million dollars in bearer bonds," Castillo had explained the next day in the presidential apartment in the White House.

"Surprise, surprise, huh?" the President replied. "You have no idea who these people were, Charley?"

"I don't think they were South American bandits, Mr. President. But aside from that—"

"Find out who they are, Major," the President interrupted, "and render them harmless."

Castillo noted that he'd been formally addressed. And, as such, so ordered.

"Yes, sir."

"Anything else, Charley?"

"Mr. President, what do we do with the money?"

"Sixteen million, right? Where is it? Are you sure you can cash those bearer bonds?"

"Sir, to make sure we could retain control of money, we already have. It's now in the Riggs Bank."

"I'm not going to get involved with dirty money," the President said. "You understand that, of course?"

"Yes, of course, Mr. President."

"But on the subject of money, and apropos of nothing else, Charley . . ."

"Yes, sir?"

"I funded OOA with two million from my discretionary funds. That's really not very much money, and I have a good idea of how expensive your operations are. Sooner or later, you're going to have to come to me for more money, and right now I just don't see how it will be available. It's something to keep in mind."

"Sir, are you suggesting—?"

"Major, I have no idea what you're talking about. What sixteen million?"

Thus was established the Lorimer Charitable & Benevolent Fund, with an initial donation the next day of nearly sixteen million dollars from an anonymous well-wisher.

On the same day, David W. Yung, Jr., and Corporal Lester Bradley were placed on indefinite temporary duty with the OOA.

At the time, there was only one true volunteer in the ranks of the OOA, essentially because very few people had even heard of it. Sergeant Major John K. "Jack" Davidson had learned of OOA from Corporal Bradley, whom Castillo, perhaps unwisely, had sent to Camp Mackall—the Special Forces/Delta Force training base near Fort Bragg, North Carolina—"for training" but actually to get him out of sight—and out of truthfully answering questions from his gunny and any other superior—short-term until Castillo could figure out what to do with him long-term.

Davidson's function at Mackall was to evaluate students to see if they were psychologically and physically made up to justify their expensive training to become special operators. He had taken one look at nineteen-year-old Corporal Bradley—who stood five-four and weighed one thirty-two—then decided that someone with a sick sense of humor had sent the boy to Mackall as a joke.

Davidson put Bradley to work pushing the keys on a computer.

The next day, Lieutenant General Bruce J. McNab, commanding general of the John F. Kennedy Center for Special Warfare, disabused Davidson of this notion that whatever the kid was, he was no warrior.

The general had choppered out to Mackall to take Corporal Bradley to Sergeant Krantz's burial at Arlington National Cemetery. Davidson had no Need to Know, of course, but he and General McNab had been around several blocks together, and so the general told him what had happened to Krantz on Charley Castillo's *ad hoc* assault, and how, had it not been for Corporal Bradley's offhand hundred-yard head shots, Charley would be awaiting his own interment services at Arlington alongside Krantz.

Davidson, as he reminded General McNab, also had been around the block several times with Charley Castillo. He further reminded General McNab that the general knew as well as he did that while Charley was a splendid officer, he tended sometimes to do things that he would not do if he had a sober, experienced advisor, such as Davidson, at his side to counsel him.

General McNab, who first met Castillo when Castillo had been a second lieutenant, and who thus had been around the block with him on many occasions, considered this and agreed.

Sergeant Major Davidson was sent to OOA.

It was Davidson who had recruited Dianne and Harold Sanders to run the

OOA safe house on West Boulevard Drive. Master Sergeant Harold Sanders, who had been around the block several times with both Jack Davidson and Charley Castillo, had been unhappy with his role after he had been medically retired. Sanders said that he had become a camp follower, because CWO3 Dianne Sanders had remained on active service. But recognizing the situation, she then had retired, too.

Living the retired life in Fayetteville, North Carolina, however, then caused the both of them to be bored—almost literally—out of their minds.

They had jumped at the chance to work again with Charley and Jack, even if it only would be guarding the mouth of the cave. Still, both suspected that Charley would sooner or later require the services of a cryptographic analyst—and Dianne, recognized as one of the best code-breakers around, would be there.

Edgar Delchamps had been the CIA station chief in Paris, France, when Castillo, running down Dr. Lorimer's various connections, first met him. Men with thirty years in the Clandestine Services of the agency tended to regard thirty-six-year-old Army officers with something less than awe, and such had been the case when Delchamps laid eyes on then-Major C. G. Castillo.

He had told Castillo that he was the station chief in Paris as the result of an accommodation with his superiors in Langley. They didn't want him to retire because his doing so would leave him free to more or less run at the mouth concerning a number of failed operations that the agency devoutly wished would never again be mentioned. Langley reasoned that if Delchamps was stationed in Paris—the only assignment he was willing to accept—he couldn't do much harm. Paris wasn't really important in the world of intelligence.

"Despite my name, I'm a Francophobe, Ace," Delchamps had told Castillo. "My files say all sorts of unkind things about the Frogs. They are sent to Langley, where, of course, they are promptly shredded—unread—by a platoon of Francophiles humming 'The Last Time I Saw Paris.' "

Delchamps made it perfectly clear that he had no desire whatever to become in any way associated with OOA. When, a month or so later, Castillo decided he had to have him whether or not he liked it, and Delchamps received orders to immediately report for indefinite temporary duty with OOA, he first had stopped by Langley to fill out his request for retirement, effective immediately.

He was dissuaded from going through with his retirement when Castillo told him he was going after the oil-for-food people with a presidential carte blanche to do what he thought had to be done, and that the carte blanche specifically ordered the Director of Central Intelligence to grant access to OOA to whatever intelligence—raw, in analysis, or confirmed—the CIA had in its possession. Castillo said he thought Edgar Delchamps was just the man to root around in Langley's basement. It was an offer Delchamps could not refuse.

And there was one man in the kitchen who was neither an American nor a member of OOA. Sándor Tor was the chief of security for the *Budapester Tages Zeitung,* of which Eric Kocian was the managing director and editor in chief. Tor didn't feel uncomfortable among the special operators and senior law-enforcement officers, as might be expected. Before he had gone to work for the newspaper, he had been an inspector on the Budapest police force and, before that, in his youth, a sergeant in the French Foreign Legion.

There were other people assigned to OOA, but all of those who had families—Corporal Lester Bradley, for example, and Major H. Richard Miller, Jr., USA (Retired), a West Point classmate of Colonel Castillo and OOA's chief of staff—had been turned loose by Castillo to be with them at Christmas.

[TWO]

One of the pair of wall-mounted telephones in the kitchen rang a little after two o'clock.

The young, muscular black Secret Service agent answered it.

Castillo wondered idly who was calling. Neither of the telephone numbers was listed in the phone book. Both rarely were used; everyone had their own cellular telephone or two. There were two secure telephones, one in what was Castillo's bedroom and the other in what he called his office, an anteroom off the great big living room.

Castillo was surprised when the Secret Service agent held out the phone receiver to him, indicating the call was for him. He crossed the room, took the phone, and, after putting his hand over the mouthpiece, asked with his eyebrows who was calling.

"Mr. Görner, Colonel. He's on the list."

Castillo nodded his thanks, and in German cheerfully said into the phone, "Merry Christmas, Otto!"

Nice that Abuela is here, Castillo thought, glancing across the room and making eye contact with her. *She and Otto can talk.*

"I hope you know where Billy Kocian is," Görner said by way of greeting, his voice completely devoid of Christmas bonhomie.

Castillo turned his gaze just slightly. "As a matter of fact, I'm looking at him."

"Thank God!" Görner exclaimed, his genuine relief evident in his tone. "There was no answer at the Mayflower."

"Why do I think you're not calling to wish him a Merry Christmas?" Castillo said.

"I'm calling first to tell you to make sure he's safe."

"He is. He frequently complains that he can't go anywhere without being followed by two or more men who wear hearing aids and keep talking to themselves."

Castillo expected to get a chuckle, if only a reluctant one. He didn't.

"Günther Friedler has been murdered," Görner went on, "his corpse mutilated."

Who? Castillo thought.

Shit! Someone close to Billy obviously . . .

"Where are you?" Castillo asked quickly, his tone now one of growing concern.

The others in the kitchen picked up on that and Castillo's body language, and had expressions that asked, *What?*

"In the office," Görner said.

"I'll call you right back," Castillo said. "I can't talk from this phone."

He put the handset in its cradle before Görner could reply. He saw that Edgar Delchamps was looking at him. He nodded just enough to signal Delchamps to follow him, then left the kitchen to go to his office.

The anteroom was barely large enough to hold a small desk and a skeletal office chair, but the door to it could be closed and was thick enough to be mostly soundproof. Castillo picked up the telephone. It could be made secure when necessary, and came with earphone sets on long cords so that others could listen to the conversation. It also had a built-in digital recorder so that conversations could be replayed for any number of reasons.

He pushed the RECORD button, then dialed a long number from memory.

"Görner."

"Karl. Who is Günther Fiedler?"

"Friedler," Görner corrected him. "He *was* a staff reporter."

Castillo knew enough of the operations of the *Tages Zeitung* newspapers to know that a staff reporter was analogous to a reporter for the Associated Press or other wire service in that the reporter's stories were fed to all of the *Tages Zeitung* newspapers, rather than to any individual paper.

"I don't think I knew him," Castillo said.

"Probably not," Görner said on the edge of sarcasm. "Billy did. Billy gave him his first job on the *Weiner Tages Zeitung* years ago. Billy was godfather to Peter, Günther's oldest son."

"Great news on Christmas Day. Who killed him and why?"

"He was working on a story about German involvement in that oil-for-food obscenity. Does that give a hint, Mr. Intelligence Officer?"

Castillo's face tightened.

"Otto, I'm about to tell you to call back when you have your emotions under control."

"I want to tell Billy before somebody else does."

"But you can't do that, can you, unless I put him on the phone?"

There was a ten-second silence—which seemed much longer—before Görner replied, "I suppose I am a little upset. Günther was my friend, too. I put him on that story, and I just now came from his house. On Christmas Day, as you say."

Castillo realized it was as much of an apology as he was going to get.

"Okay. Do they have any idea who killed him?"

"The police tried to tell me it was a fairy lovers' quarrel. My God!"

"What was that about his body being mutilated?"

"I couldn't count the stab wounds in his body."

Delchamps, holding one can of an earphone set to his ear, touched Castillo's shoulder, and when Castillo looked at him, handed him a slip of paper on which he had quickly written, *That's all?*

Castillo nodded and said into the phone, "You said 'mutilated'?"

"They cut out his eye. That's what I mean by mutilated."

Delchamps nodded as if he expected that answer.

"I don't think you should tell Billy that," Castillo said. "And in your frame of mind, I really don't think you should talk to him at all."

He let that sink in a moment, then went on: "If I put Billy on the phone, can you leave out the mutilation?"

"That wouldn't work, Karl, and you know it. No matter what I tell him, he's going to look into it himself. And just as soon as he gets off the phone with me, he'll be on the phone himself. And he has a lot of contacts."

Shit, Castillo thought, *he's right!*

When Castillo didn't reply, Görner added, "And it's already all over the front pages of the Frankfurt newspapers, the *Allgemeine Zeitung* and the *Rundschau*. And Berlin and Munich won't be far behind. And as soon as Billy gets to reading his newspapers online, he's going to find out. You can bet your ass on that."

He paused again, then gave what he thought would be the headline: " '*Tages Zeitung* Reporter Murdered. Police Suspect Gay Lovers Spat.' Merry Christmas, Frau Friedler and family."

Castillo was ashamed of the irreverent thought that popped into his mind—*Is there no honor among journalists?*—which immediately was replaced by another disturbing thought, which he said aloud: "Billy will want to go to the funeral."

"Oh, God! I didn't even think about that!"

"Right now, he's surrounded by Secret Service agents. How am I going to protect him in Fulda?"

"Wetzlar," Görner corrected automatically. "He lived in Wetzlar. He's from Wetzlar." Another brief pause. "You can't keep him there?"

Castillo didn't reply.

In as many seconds as it takes Otto to hear what he just said, he will realize that the only way to keep Billy Kocian from doing whatever he wants to do is convince him he really doesn't want to do it, and that's not going to happen.

A moment later, Görner thought aloud: "Let me know what flight he'll be on and I'll have some of our security people waiting at the gate. Better yet—I have some friends—send me the flight number and I will get agents of the Bundeskriminalamt to take him off the airplane before it gets to the gate."

"I'll bring him in the Gulfstream," Castillo said. "For one thing, he won't leave the dogs, and I don't want—"

"I thought you went out of your way not to attract attention," Görner interrupted.

"Here's a headline for you, Otto: '*Tages Zeitung* Publisher Returns from America for Friedler Last Rites.' "

"Okay," Görner said after a moment. "But don't bring anybody from the CIA to mourn with you."

Castillo looked at Delchamps and smiled.

He would no more have gone to Germany without Delchamps than he would have gone without shoes, but this was not the time to argue with Görner about that, or even tell him.

As a practical matter, before this came up, they had been planning to go to Europe, taking Billy Kocian with them, and not only because they knew Kocian was out of patience with living in the Mayflower Hotel and spending his days searching his copious memory to fill in the blanks of the investigation.

Delchamps and FBI Inspector John J. Doherty—another at-first-very-reluctant recruit to OOA—were agreed that the time had come to move the investigation out of the bubble at Langley and onto the ground.

They would start in Budapest, Doherty had suggested—and Delchamps had agreed—then move almost certainly to Vienna, then to Berlin and Paris and wherever else the trail led, preceded by a message from either—or both—Secretary of State Natalie Cohen and Director of National Intelligence Charles M. Montvale ordering the ambassadors and CIA station chiefs to provide the people from OOA whatever support they requested, specifically including access to all their intelligence.

All that this latest development had changed was that they first would go to Hesse in Germany—seeing Otto Görner in Fulda had been on the original agenda—rather than to Budapest, and that they would go as soon as possible, rather than "right after the first of the year."

"If you think you have your emotions under control, Otto," Castillo said, "I'll go get Billy."

Görner got his emotions under control to the point where he was able to say, in a reasonably civil voice, "Thank you."

Delchamps followed Castillo through the office door, touched his arm, and softly said, "I presume you know, Ace, that cutting out someone's eye is Middle East speak—and, come to think of it, Sicilian—for *This is what happens to people who get caught looking at things they shouldn't.*"

Castillo nodded, then said, "But setting up something like this to look as if it's a homosexual love affair gone wrong isn't Middle East speak, is it?"

"That may have been a message to your Onkel Otto," Delchamps said. "You keep sending people to look at things they shouldn't be looking at, and the way we take them out will humiliate their families *and* the *Tages Zeitung.*"

Castillo considered that a moment, then nodded.

"Billy, can I see you a moment?" he said, and mimed holding a telephone to his ear.

Kocian came back into the kitchen ten minutes later, which told Castillo that he had subjected Otto Görner to a thorough interrogation, which in turn meant Kocian knew all the sordid details of his friend's death. But there was nothing on his face to suggest anything unpleasant.

He's one tough old bastard, Castillo thought admiringly.

Doña Alicia was more perceptive.

"Not bad news, I hope, Billy?" she asked.

"I'm afraid so. A dear friend has passed on unexpectedly."

"Oh, I'm so sorry," Doña Alicia said. "And at Christmastime!"

"I'll have to go to the funeral, of course," Kocian said, and looked at Castillo. "How much of an inconvenience for you would it be, Karlchen, if we went to Germany very soon—say, tomorrow—rather than after New Year's?"

"That can be arranged, I'm sure," Castillo said, adding mentally, *because I know, and you know I know, just how quickly the Hungarian charm would vanish if I even looked like I was going to suggest it would be "inconvenient."*

"You're very kind, Karlchen. You get that from your mother." Kocian paused. "I refuse to let my personal loss cast a pall on everybody else's Christmas. So while you're making the necessary arrangements, I will open an absolutely superb bottle of wine from a vineyard that was once the property of the Esterhazys."

[THREE]

Colonel Jacob D. Torine, United States Air Force, answered his cellular telephone on the third buzz.

"Torine."

"Merry Christmas, Jake. How would you like to go to Germany?"

"That would depend on when," Torine replied, and belatedly added, "And Merry Christmas to you, too, Charley."

"Early tomorrow morning. Something's come up."

"You want me to get on a secure line?"

"I'll explain when I see you."

"This is going to cost me two hundred dollars," Torine said.

"Excuse me?"

"At dinner, I said something to the effect that it was nice, for a change, to be home for the holidays, to which my bride replied, 'I've got a hundred dollars that says you won't be here through New Year's Day,' to which I replied, 'Oh, I think I will be,' to which she replied, 'Double down if the phone rings before we're finished with dinner.' "

"I'm sorry, Jake. If it's a real problem, I can get Miller to come down from Philly."

"Thank you just the same, but I don't want to have to explain to *your* boss why I wasn't driving—and you and Gimpy were—when you got lost, ran out of gas, and put the bird down in the North Atlantic, never to be seen again. I'll be at Signature at half past seven. That will mean I will have to tear Sparkman, weeping piteously, from the bosom of his beloved, but that can't be helped."

"I thought you said he wasn't married?"

"He's not. What's that got to do with anything, Don Juan?"

Castillo caught the crack, smiled, but ignored it. He instead replied, "Do it, Jake. It's important we get to Rhine-Main."

"I have told you and told you, Colonel, that Rhine-Main is only a memory of our youth. I'll have Sparkman file a flight plan to Flughafen Frankfurt am Main."

"I'm really sorry to have to do this to you, Jake."

"Yeah," Torine said, and broke the connection.

Captain Richard M. Sparkman, USAF, was the most recent addition to OOA. After five years flying an AC-130H Spectre gunship in the Air Force Special Operations Command, he had been reassigned to the Presidential Airlift Group, 89th Airlift Wing, based at Andrews Air Force Base, Maryland.

His superiors—the ones in the Pentagon, not those at Hurlburt Field, home of the AF Special Operations Command—had decided that it was time to rescue him from those regulation-busting special operations savages and bring him back to the *real* Air Force. He was, after all, an Air Force Academy graduate, and stars were in his future.

It was solemnly decided that flying very important people—very senior military officers and high-ranking government officials—around in a C-20, the Air Force's designation for the Gulfstream III, would broaden his experience and hopefully cause him to forget the outrageously unconventional things he had learned and practiced in special operations.

When he had politely asked if he had any choice in the matter, he was politely told he did not and advised that down the line he would appreciate what was being done for him.

Shortly after he'd begun seriously contemplating resigning his commission—sitting in the right seat of a G-III and flying a Deputy Assistant Secretary of Whatever around was not what he'd had in mind when he applied for the academy—he'd run into Colonel Jacob Torine again.

Torine was sort of a legend in the Air Force Special Operations community. Sparkman had flown his Spectre in a black mission that Torine had run in Central America, and had come to greatly admire him. So when he'd come across Torine again, he'd told him of his frustrations—and of his thoughts of getting out to go fly commercial passenger airliners. "If I'm flying taxis, I might as well make some money at it."

Torine, as one ring-knocker to another, had counseled him against that.

And Sparkman had taken the advice, and some time later wound up then and again in the right seat of a Gulfstream V that ostensibly "belonged" to Director of National Intelligence Charles W. Montvale, though he'd yet to meet the man or have him on board.

Sparkman had heard that when Torine later had been given command of a wing of Lockheed Martin C-5B Galaxy aircraft, he had been as enthusiastic about it as Sparkman had been when ordered to park his AC-130H and get in the right seat of a Gulfstream, even though a colonel's eagle had come with Torine's reassignment.

And small wonder, Sparkman had thought, considering what Torine had to leave behind.

It wasn't much of a secret that Torine had been in charge of the Air Force's contribution to the Army's Delta Force and the even more clandestine Gray Fox unit. Nor was it super secret that a certain C-22, the Air Force designation for the Boeing 727, sat in a heavily guarded hangar at Pope Air Force Base, which adjoins Fort Bragg, North Carolina. This aircraft had been extensively modified; it was whispered to have almost twice the range of the standard 727, was capable of being refueled in the air—and had a passenger compartment that could be depressurized at 35,000 feet so that Delta Force and Gray Fox special operators could make undetected high-altitude, low-opening (HALO) parachute jumps.

It also was rumored that in two hours, the so-called Delta Force 727 could be painted in the color scheme of any airline in the world.

Sparkman thought that that seemed a bit over the top—*a two-hour paint job?*—but he had never seen the aircraft, so he didn't *know* for sure anything about it, save that a Delta Force 727 existed.

But he believed another story going around: that Torine had used the aircraft in a black op in which another 727, a stolen one, had been recovered from a fanatic Islamic group that planned to demonstrate its disapproval of everything American by crashing the fuel-bladder-packed aircraft into the Liberty Bell in Philadelphia.

Sparkman *did* know a little about that. He had been the co-pilot on a Gulfstream flight that had flown a hurry-up mission to take the Vice Chief of Staff of the Air Force to MacDill Air Force Base in Tampa.

As they taxied to MacDill Base Operations, Sparkman had seen a great deal of unusual activity on the field. Yellow fire trucks had lined the main runway, and that implied an aircraft in trouble. But alongside the fire trucks were a half-dozen HUMVs manned by airfield Security Forces. Not only were there .50-caliber machine guns in the ready position on the HUMVs, but belts of ammunition gleamed in the sun. That rarely happened.

Even more interesting were two vans conspicuously labeled EXPLOSIVE ORD-NANCE DISPOSAL.

Minutes later, two F-15s made a low-speed pass over the field, giving Spark-man time to remember that that was the type of aircraft he had expected to fly after joining the Air Force. Not some itsy-bitsy VIP aerial taxi.

And then something else very interesting appeared: a Costa Rican Air Trans-port Boeing 727 on final, about to touch down.

Costa Rican Air Transport? he'd thought.

MacDill was closed to civilian traffic.

The 727 had made a perfectly ordinary landing but was not allowed to leave the runway. The fleet of emergency vehicles—now joined by a half-dozen staff cars, most of these bearing general officer's starred license plates—rushed out to meet the plane.

Then a U.S. Army Blackhawk helicopter of the 160th Special Operations Aviation Regiment fluttered to the ground as a pickup truck with mounted stairs backed up to the forward door in the civilian transport's fuselage.

The plane's door opened and two men got off. They were wearing jungle camouflage uniforms and their hands and faces were streaked with the grease-paint normally worn by special operators deployed in the boonies.

The taller one, seeing all the brass, saluted, and it was then that Sparkman recognized Colonel Jacob D. Torine, USAF.

There was no way—not with all the brass around—that Sparkman could make his manners to Colonel Torine and politely inquire what the hell was going on.

But when he heard the rumors that Torine and a Special Forces major had stolen a 727 back from Muslim fanatics who had taken it with the idea of each of them collecting a harem of heavenly virgins just as soon as they crashed it into the Liberty Bell, he thought there might be something to it.

Especially after he heard two weeks later that Torine had been awarded an-other Distinguished Flying Cross, for unspecified actions of a classified nature.

The next time Captain Sparkman had seen Colonel Torine was at Andrews, as Sparkman was taxiing a Citation III to the runway for takeoff, this time haul-ing a senator to Kansas to give a speech.

Torine was in civilian clothing and doing a preflight inspection walkaround of a Gulfstream. A *civilian* G-III, which was interesting because Andrews also was closed to civilian aircraft.

Sparkman again had no idea what was going on, but he was determined to find out. If the Air Force insisted that he fly itsy-bitsy aircraft, he would see if he could fly Torine's.

It took some doing, but Sparkman was an enterprising young officer, and within a few days, he learned that Colonel Torine had been assigned to some outfit called the Office of Organizational Analysis, which was under the Department of Homeland Security, which had its offices in the Nebraska Avenue Complex in Washington.

When Sparkman went there, though, the security guard denied any knowledge of any Colonel Torine or of any Office of Organizational Analysis.

Which of course really got Sparkman's attention. And so he took a chance: "You get on that phone and tell Colonel Torine that Captain Richard Sparkman has to see him now on a matter of great importance."

The security guard considered that for a long moment, then picked up his telephone. Sparkman couldn't hear what he said, but a minute later, an elevator door opened, and a muscular man, who might as well have had *Federal Special Agent* tattooed on his forehead, got off.

"Captain Sparkman?"

Sparkman nodded.

"ID, please, sir."

Sparkman gave it to him. He studied it carefully, then waved Sparkman onto the elevator.

Colonel Torine, in civilian clothing, was waiting for the elevator when it stopped on the top floor.

"Okay," Torine said to the agent. "Thanks." He offered his hand to Sparkman. "Long time no see, Lieutenant. Come on in."

"Actually, sir, it's captain."

"Well, sooner or later they finally get to the bottom of the barrel, don't they?"

Torine had an impressive office. Behind a massive wooden desk were three flags: the national colors, the Air Force flag, and one that Sparkman had never seen before but correctly guessed was that of the Department of Homeland Security.

Torine sat in a red leather judge's chair. He waved Sparkman into one of two leather-upholstered chairs before his desk.

"Okay . . . Dick, right?"

"Yes, sir."

"What's the matter of great importance?"

"Sir, I thought maybe you could use a co-pilot for your Gulfstream."

Torine's eyebrows rose, but he didn't speak for a long moment.

"How do you know about the Gulfstream?" he asked finally.

"I saw you doing a walkaround at Andrews, sir."

Torine shook his head.

"Make a note, Captain. You never saw me with a Gulfstream at Andrews or anywhere else."

"Yes, sir."

"Still driving a gunship, are you, Sparkman?"

"No, sir. I'm flying the right seat of mostly C-20s for the Presidential Air-lift Group."

"How did you get a soft billet like that?"

"Over my strongest objections, sir."

"How much Gulfstream time do you have?"

"Pushing six hundred hours, sir."

Torine tapped the balls of his fingers together for perhaps fifteen seconds, then shrugged and punched buttons on a telephone.

"Got a minute, boss?"

"Sure," a voice came from a speaker Sparkman could not see.

"Put your shoes on and restrain the beast. I'm on my way."

Torine led Sparkman through an inner corridor to a closed door. He knocked, but went through it without waiting for a reply.

Sparkman found himself in an even more impressive office. It was occupied by a very large—six-foot-two, two-twenty—very black man, a slightly smaller white man, and a very large dog that held a soccer ball in his mouth with no more difficulty than a lesser dog would have with a tennis ball.

When the dog saw Sparkman, he dropped the soccer ball, walked to Spark-man, and showed him what looked like five pounds of sharp white teeth.

The white man said something to the dog in a foreign language Sparkman could not identify, whereupon the dog sat on his haunches, closed his mouth, and offered Sparkman his paw.

"Shake Max's hand, Sparkman," Torine ordered.

Sparkman did so.

Pointing first at the black man, then at the white man, Torine said, "Major Miller, Colonel Castillo, this is Captain Dick Sparkman, whom, I believe, the good Lord has just dropped in our lap."

Sparkman saw the nameplate on the desk: LT. COL. C. G. CASTILLO.

A light bird, he thought, *and Torine, a full bull colonel, calls him "boss"?*
And his office is fancier than Torine's. . . .

"I have this unfortunate tendency to look your gift horses in the mouth, Jake," Castillo had said as he took a long, thin black cigar from a humidor and started to clip the end.

"Do you remember Captain Sparkman?"

"I just did. You were driving a Gulfstream that gave me a ride to Fort Rucker, right?"

"Yes, sir."

"Captain Sparkman has nearly six hundred hours in the right seat of a G-III," Torine explained.

"Ah!" Lieutenant Colonel Castillo said.

"Before that, he was flying an AC-130H gunship out of Hurlburt," Torine went on. "We once very quietly toured Central America together."

"Ah ha!" Lieutenant Colonel Castillo said.

"And he saw me doing a walkaround of our bird at Andrews."

"And, Captain, who did you tell about that?" Major Miller asked.

"No one, sir," Sparkman said.

"And how did you find Colonel Torine, Captain?" Lieutenant Colonel Castillo asked.

"I asked around, sir."

"And how did you get past the receptionist downstairs?" Major Miller asked. "He's supposed to tell people he has never heard of Colonel Jake Torine."

"The receptionist did," Torine said. "The captain here then told him, forcefully, to get on the phone and tell me that he had to see me on a matter of great importance."

"Ah ha!" Lieutenant Colonel Castillo said.

"Which was?" Major Miller inquired.

"That if I had to fly the right seat of a Gulfstream," Sparkman offered, "I'd rather fly Colonel Torine's."

"Ah ha!" Lieutenant Colonel Castillo said for the third time, then looked at Major Miller, who paused a moment for thought and then shrugged.

"Tell me, Captain," Castillo said. "Is there any pressing business, personal or official, which would keep you from going to Buenos Aires first thing in the morning?"

"I'm on the board for a flight to Saint Louis at 0830, sir."

"Jake, call out there and tell them the captain will be otherwise occupied," Castillo said, and then turned to Sparkman. "Prefacing this with the caveat that anything you hear, see, or intuit from this moment on is classified Top Secret

Presidential, the disclosure of which will see you punished by your castration with a very dull knife, plus imprisonment for the rest of your natural life, let me welcome you to the Office of Organizational Analysis, where you will serve as our most experienced Gulfstream jockey and perform such other duties as may be required."

"Just like that?" Sparkman blurted.

"Just like that, Dick," Torine said, chuckling.

"Go pack a bag with enough civvies—you won't need your uniform—for a week, and then come back here," Castillo ordered. "Major Miller here will run you through our in-processing procedures."

At the safe house in Alexandria, Castillo cut his end of the cellular telephone connection with Torine, put the telephone in his trousers pocket, then picked up the handset of another secure telephone on his office desk. He pushed one key on the base and said, "C. G. Castillo."

It took a second or two—no more—for the voice-recognition circuitry to function, flashing the caller's name before the White House operator.

"White House," the pleasant young female operator's voice said. "Merry Christmas, Colonel Castillo."

"Merry Christmas to you, too. Can you get me Ambassador Montvale on a secure line, please?"

The rule was that those people given access to the special White House switch-board circuit were expected to answer their telephones within sixty seconds. Charles W. Montvale, former deputy secretary of State, former secretary of the Treasury, former ambassador to the European Union, and currently United States director of National Intelligence, took twenty-seven seconds to come on the line.

"Charles Montvale," he said. His voice was deep, cultured, and charming.

"Merry Christmas, Mr. Ambassador. Colonel Castillo for you," the White House operator told him. "The line is secure."

Castillo picked up on the ambassador's failure to return the operator's Christmas greetings.

"Merry Christmas and a *very* happy New Year, Mr. Ambassador," Castillo said cheerfully.

The ambassador did not respond in kind, but instead said, "Actually, I was about to call you, Charley."

"Mental telepathy, sir?"

"Does the name Kurt Kuhl mean anything to you, Colonel?"

Montvale's tone, and the use of Castillo's rank, suggested that Montvale was displeased with him. Again. As usual.

There is an exception, so they say, to every absolute statement. The exception to the absolute statement that the director of National Intelligence exercised authority over everyone and everything in the intelligence community was the Office of Organizational Analysis, which answered only to the commander in chief.

Ambassador Montvale found this both absurd and unacceptable, but had been unable to take OOA under his wing beyond an agreement with Castillo that he would be informed in a timely fashion of what Castillo was up to.

On Castillo's part this meant it was frequently necessary to remind the director of National Intelligence of the great difference between Castillo *telling* Montvale about taking some action and Castillo *asking* Montvale's permission—or even Montvale's advice—about taking some action.

"No, sir. It doesn't ring a bell. Who is he?"

There was a perceptible pause before Montvale replied: "Kuhl *was* a deep-cover CIA asset in Vienna and elsewhere in that part of the world."

"Past tense?"

"I was informed an hour or so ago that he and his wife were found garroted to death behind the Johann Strauss statue in the Stadtpark in Vienna yesterday."

"They know who did it?"

"I was hoping you might be able to offer a suggestion. I seem to recall that you have some experience with people who are garroted to death."

"Sorry. I never heard of him."

There was a moment's silence while Montvale considered that, then he abruptly changed the subject: "What's on your mind, Castillo?"

"I'm going to Germany in the morning."

"Is that so? And are you going to share with me why?"

"Otto Görner called a few minutes ago to tell me that a *Tages Zeitung* reporter was found murdered in interesting circumstances."

"How interesting?"

"The body was mutilated. First, Otto thinks, to make it look as if it was a homosexual lovers' quarrel—multiple stab wounds."

"And second?"

"One of the victim's eyes was cut out."

"Suggesting the message 'This is what happens when you look at something you shouldn't'?"

"That's what Mr. Delchamps suggests. It follows, as Otto says this reporter was working on the oil-for-food scheme."

"And your—our—interest in this tragic event, Colonel?"

"Eric Kocian insists on going to the funeral. The man was an old friend of his."

"He can't be dissuaded?"

"Not a chance."

"How hard did you try?"

"Not at all. It would have been a waste of time."

"The President happened to mention at dinner that he hadn't seen you since he visited you at Walter Reed, and perhaps there would be a chance to do so over the next few days. What am I supposed to tell him?"

"That in keeping with the accord between us, I told you where I was going and why."

"How much is this going to delay the investigation?"

"It might speed it up."

"You need anything, Charley?"

"Can't think of a thing."

"Keep in touch," Montvale said, and broke the connection.

"Anything else, Colonel?" the pleasant young female White House operator's voice asked.

"That'll do it. Thanks very much. And Merry Christmas."

"You, too, Colonel."

Castillo put the handset back in its cradle and thought hard about what else he had to do.

After a long moment he decided that he had done everything necessary, and that it was highly unlikely that anything else was going to come up and interfere with their Christmas dinner.

That carefully considered prediction proved false about seventeen minutes later, when the cellular in his trousers pocket vibrated against his leg while his grandmother was invoking the Lord's blessing on all those gathered at the table.

He of course could not answer it while his grandmother was praying.

Sixty seconds later, the White House phone buzzed imperiously. One of the Secret Service agents quickly rose from the table to answer it.

Thirty seconds after that, surprising Castillo not at all, the agent reappeared and mimed that the call was for Castillo.

Doña Alicia looked at him as he rose from the table. He wasn't sure if she was annoyed or felt sorry for him.

The legend on the small LCD screen next to the telephone read: SECURE JOEL ISAACSON SECURE.

Castillo picked up the handset, said "C. G. Castillo," waited for the voice recognition circuitry to kick in, then said, "What's up, Joel?"

Joel Isaacson was the Secret Service supervisory special agent in charge of the protection detail for Homeland Security Secretary Matt Hall. But the tall, slim, forty-year-old Isaacson, who had once been number two on the presidential detail, was *de facto* more than that.

In the reorganization after 9/11, the Secret Service, which had been under the Treasury Department, was transferred to the newly formed Department of Homeland Security.

The chief of the Secret Service had assigned two old and trusted pals, Supervisory Special Agents Joel Isaacson and Tom McGuire, to the secretary's protection detail. It was understood between them that their mission was as much to protect the Secret Service from its new boss—new brooms have been known to sweep out the good and keep the garbage—as it was to protect him from Islamic lunatics.

It had worked out well from the beginning. The secretary quickly learned that if he wanted something from the Secret Service—about whose operations he knew virtually nothing—Isaacson or McGuire could get it for him. Similarly, the chief of the Secret Service quickly learned that if he wanted something from the secretary, it was better and quicker to make the request of McGuire or Isaacson than directly of the secretary, who made no decisions involving the Secret Service without getting the opinion of one or the other.

And then when the President issued the Finding setting up the Office of Organizational Analysis—which in the chief of the Secret Service's very private opinion was not one of his wiser decisions—Tom McGuire was one of the first people assigned to it. The chief did not entirely trust Isaacson's and McGuire's opinion that despite his youth, junior rank, and reputation, Major C. G. Castillo was just the guy to run what the chief very privately thought of as the President's Own CIA/FBI/Delta Force.

The assignment of McGuire to OOA left Isaacson as the chief's conduit to the secretary, and that was just fine. But he worried about Tom McGuire getting burned when someone burned the OOA, which seemed to the chief to be inevitable.

My God, that crazy Green Beret launched an invasion of Paraguay to rescue a DEA agent the druggies had kidnapped.

That the mission had succeeded did not, in the chief's opinion, mean the operation was not as lunatic an operation as he had ever heard of, and he'd been around the Secret Service for a long time.

"Jack Britton and his wife are on their way out there, Charley," Joel Isaacson announced without any preliminaries. "I need you to talk to him. Okay? As a favor to me?"

"Talk to him about what?" Castillo replied, and then: *"And his wife?"*

"They had to take him off the Vice President's protection detail. And he's pretty annoyed."

"What did he do to get canned?"

"Somebody, most likely those AALs in Philadelphia, tried to take out him, and his wife, yesterday afternoon."

"Is he all right?"

"They weren't hit, but the supervisor in Philadelphia told me he counted sixteen bullet holes in Britton's new car. Plus about that many in his front door, picture window, etcetera. They used automatic Kalashnikovs."

"What's this got to do with him getting taken off the Vice President's protection detail?"

There was a just-perceptible pause before Isaacson said, "Think about it, Charley. These people try to take him out again when he's on duty, then the Vice President becomes collateral damage."

"Stupid question. Sorry. Britton didn't understand?"

"What he didn't understand was being brought here. Standard procedure when something like this happens. Gets them out of the line of fire."

"That made him mad?"

"What made him mad was being told that he was going to be placed on administrative duties in—I forget where; probably Saint Louis—until the matter is resolved. When he heard that, the kindest thing he had to say to the supervisor on duty downtown was that the supervisor could insert the whole Secret Service into his anal orifice. That's when they brought him to me."

"What's Jack want to do?"

"He wants to go back to Philly and play Bat Masterson with the people who shot at his wife," Isaacson said.

"This is probably the wrong thing to say, but I can understand that."

"You're right. It is the wrong thing to say. Charley, I assumed responsibility for them. The big brass are determined he will not go back to Philadelphia; they wanted to hold him—them—as material witnesses to an assault on a federal officer."

"Can they do that?"

"They could her. What I told the supervisor was that they were going to have a hard time convincing a judge that a member of the Vice President's protection detail—and a highly decorated former Philly cop—was going to vanish so that he wouldn't have to testify against the bad guys who had tried to whack him and his wife. That's when they turned them over to me. They'd rather that I be responsible for putting this little escapade on the front page of *The Washington Post*."

When Castillo didn't immediately reply, Isaacson went on: "Or for a headline in *The Philadelphia Inquirer*: 'Secret Service Agent Guns Down Area Muslims; Alleges They Tried to Kill Him and His Wife.' "

"So that's the priority? Keeping egg off the face of the Secret Service?"

"That, and keeping Jack out of jail."

"What am I supposed to do with them?"

"Convince him that going back to Philly would be stupid, then put them on ice someplace until this can be worked out."

"Personally, I'll do anything I can for Jack. But why me?"

"Because the chief of the Secret Service has been told that any inquiries he wishes to make about OOA will have to go through me."

"Jesus Christ!"

"Indeed. Merry Christmas, Charley. Please don't tell me what you decide to do with them; that way I'll truthfully be able to say I don't know where they are when I'm asked. And I will be asked."

"Jesus Christ!" Castillo said again.

But no one heard him.

The legend on the screen now read: CALL TERMINATED.

III

"Not more bad news, I hope, Carlos?" Doña Alicia asked as Castillo took what Davidson referred to as the "paterfamilias seat" at the head of the table.

Castillo looked at her and had the first not-unpleasant thought he'd had in the last five minutes: *This is not classified. I won't have to take Delchamps and McGuire into the office or, even worse, ask Abuela to leave the room so we can discuss it.*

"There's some good news," he said. "And . . ."

"Let's have that first," Doña Alicia said. "The good news."

"Okay. Jack Britton and his wife will appear here shortly."

"Oh, good!" Tom McGuire said. "You'll like them, Doña Alicia. Particularly her. Great sense of humor. As my sainted mother used to say, she's the kind of girl who can make a corpse sit up in his casket at the funeral and start whistling."

"Tom, that's terrible," Doña Alicia said, but she was smiling.

"And the bad news, Ace?" Delchamps asked.

"They have been wrapped in the protective arms of the Secret Service."

McGuire's smile vanished. He liked Britton. He had recruited him for the Secret Service.

"Why?" he asked softly.

"Isaacson told me that that's standard procedure when a special agent is attacked. As is taking a member of the Protection Service off the detail and assigning him administrative duties."

"Somebody attacked Jack?" Davidson asked.

"And Sandra," Castillo confirmed. "Sixteen bullet holes in his new Mazda convertible. And that many more in the picture window of his house."

"Oh, my God! How terrible!" Doña Alicia said.

"The African-American Lunatics?" David W. Yung asked.

Doña Alicia looked at him in confusion.

"Who else?" Castillo said.

"Where are they sending him?" McGuire said. Before Castillo could reply, he added, surprised, "They want to keep him here?"

"They wanted to send them to Saint Louis, or someplace like that."

"And?" McGuire pursued.

"When they told him that, Jack said something very, very rude to the supervisor who told him, and then said he was going back to Philadelphia. That's when he was turned over to Joel." He paused. "And then Joel turned him over to me."

McGuire grunted. "Philadelphia's not an option," he said. "And I don't know about here. There's a train from Union Station to Philadelphia about every hour."

"Nuestra Pequeña Casa," Delchamps suggested. "Better yet, Shangri-La."

McGuire considered that a moment, then nodded. "That'd do it."

Doña Alicia's face showed that she didn't understand any of what had been said.

"Ace, you think your lady friend would go along with one more legal attaché in Buenos Aires or Montevideo?" Delchamps asked.

"Probably. But asking her on Christmas Day?"

"Good point," Delchamps said.

"Let's get them down there and worry about that later," McGuire said. "Worst case, they make us bring them back."

"Why don't we wait and see what kind of a frame of mind Jack's in before we do anything?" Davidson asked.

"If I could repeat in mixed company what he told the Secret Service supervisor, Jack, that would give you a good idea," Castillo said. "But for the moment, would someone please pass me the cranberry sauce?"

Special Agent and Mrs. Britton arrived fifteen minutes later. They were accompanied by four Secret Service agents. All of the men at the table stood when they came into the dining room.

"If you have any clout with the guards, Tom," Sandra Britton said, "I'd really like to have a little something to eat before I'm strip-searched and put in my cell."

"Sandra!" McGuire said uncomfortably.

She went on, unrepentant: "The only thing the prisoners have had to eat today is an Egg McMuffin as we began our journey and, for Christmas dinner, a hamburger in a Wendy's outside Baltimore."

She directed her attention to Castillo.

"You're the warden, right, Colonel? When do I get my one telephone call? I just can't wait to talk to the ACLU."

"Just as soon as I introduce you to my grandmother," Castillo said, laughing. "Abuela, this is Sandra Britton. Sandra, Doña Alicia Castillo."

"I'm very happy to meet you," Sandra said. "But what in the world is a nice grandmother doing sitting down with this company?"

"I told you you'd like her, Doña Alicia," McGuire said.

"Or are you also under-arrest-by-another-name?" Sandra pursued.

"Sit down, my dear," Doña Alicia said. "We'll get you some dinner."

"I understand why you're a little upset, Sandra," McGuire said.

" 'A *little*'?"

"My dear young woman," Billy Kocian said. "I recognize in you not only a kindred soul, but someone else suffering velvet-cell incarceration at the hands of these thugs. May I offer you a glass of champagne? Or perhaps something stronger?"

"Both," she said. "Who the hell are you?"

Kocian walked quickly to her and kissed her hand.

"Eric Kocian, madam. I am enchanted."

"As well you should be, Billy," Doña Alicia said.

"Pray take my seat, and I'll get the champagne," Kocian said.

"Hey, Jack!" Davidson said. "How goes it?"

Britton shook his head.

"Ginger-peachy," he said. "How could it be otherwise?"

Kocian took a bottle of champagne from a cooler, poured some in a glass, and handed it to Sandra.

"Please excuse the stem. It originally came, I believe, filled with yogurt and decorated with a picture of Mickey Mouse."

"Thank you," Sandra said. A smile flickered across her lips.

"As a prisoner, of course, I am told nothing," Kocian said. "So I am therefore quite curious about your obvious distress. What have these terrible people done to you?"

"You sound like a Viennese," Sandra said.

"How perceptive of you, dear lady. I was born and spent many years in that city."

"I'm a semanticist—I teach at the University of Pennsylvania. Or I *was* teaching at the university before I was hustled into the backseat of a Secret Service SUV and hauled off before my neighbors." She paused. "You're familiar with Franz Kafka?"

"Indeed."

"He would have had a ball with this," she said.

"You are implying bureaucracy run amok?"

"Am I ever."

"Tell me all, my dear."

Sandra sipped appreciatively at her champagne, pursed her lips, and then drained the glass.

"Was the offer of something stronger bona fide?"

Kocian nodded.

"In that case, Colonel, I will have one of your famous McNab martinis, thank you ever so much."

"My pleasure," Castillo said, and went to a sideboard loaded with spirits and drinking paraphernalia.

"So, what happened, Sandra?" David W. Yung asked.

"Cutting to the chase, Two-Gun," Sandra said, "ten minutes after my better half here assured me that all was well as the Secret Service was on its way to our bullet-shattered cottage by the side of the road—before which sat our bullet-shattered new car—they did in fact arrive, sirens screaming, lights flashing. I expected Bruce Willis to leap out and wrap me in his masterly arms. By then, of course, the AALs who had turned tranquil Churchill Lane into the OK Corral were in Atlantic City. But what the hell, I thought, naïve little ol' me, I shouldn't fault them for trying."

"Then what happened?" Davidson asked.

"The first thing they did was tell the Philly cops to get lost," Sandra said. "My living room was now a federal crime scene. And they hustled Jack and me into the back of one of their SUVs and drove off with sirens screaming. I thought they had word the AALs were coming back."

"The what, my dear?" Doña Alicia asked.

"African-American Lunatics, make-believe Muslims who don't like Jack very much."

"Why not?" Doña Alicia asked.

"I kept an eye on them for the police department," Britton said.

"What he did, Abuela," Castillo said, "was live with them for long years. He wore sandals, a dark blue robe, had his hair braided with beads. They thought his name was Ali Abid ar-Raziq."

"And for that they tried to kill him?"

"Actually, they came pretty close to killing both of us," Britton said.

"Sandra," Yung said reasonably, "an attack on Jack, a federal officer, made it a federal case."

"Is that why they took Jack downtown and took his gun and badge away? The way that looked to me was that Jack was the villain for getting shot at."

"They took your credentials and weapon, Jack?" McGuire asked.

"And it was my pistol, not the Secret Service's."

"Had you fired it at the bad guys?"

Britton shook his head.

McGuire looked at the four Secret Service agents who had brought the Brittons to the house.

"Who's in charge?"

"I am, sir," the shortest one, who held a briefcase, said.

"Where's his credentials and weapon?"

"I have them, sir," the agent said, holding up the briefcase. "Mr. Isaacson said I was to turn them over to you."

"Give Special Agent Britton his credentials and his pistol."

"Sir, I don't—"

"That was an order, not a suggestion," McGuire said. "And then you guys can wait in the kitchen."

They did.

"Just to keep all the ducks in a row, Tom," Britton said as he carefully examined the revolver, reloaded it, and put it in his lap, "Joel didn't take them. The clown in Philadelphia did."

" '*The clown*'?" McGuire asked. "Supervisory Special Agent in Charge Morrell? *That* clown, Special Agent Britton?"

"Right. Just before he told me I was being transferred to Kansas or someplace just as soon as the, quote, interview, close quote, was over."

"And was that the clown you told what he could do with the Secret Service, Jack?" Delchamps asked.

"You're not being helpful, Edgar," McGuire said.

"No. I told that to the clown here in D.C.," Britton said thoughtfully. "But I think he was a supervisory special agent in charge, too."

Castillo, Delchamps, and Davidson laughed.

Britton picked up his Secret Service credentials, examined them, and held them up. "Does this mean, as they say in the movies, that I'm 'free to go'?"

"Not back to Philly to shoot up a mosque, Jack," McGuire said. "Think that through."

"Where the hell did you get that? From the clown in Philly?"

"I got that from Joel," Castillo said. "I think he got it from the clown in Philly. You apparently said something about knowing, quote, how to get the bastards, unquote."

"By which I meant I was going to go to Counterterrorism—I used to work there, remember?—and see if we couldn't send several of the bastards away on a federal firearms rap. In the commission of a felony—and shooting up Sandra and my house and car is a felony—everybody participating is chargeable. Use of a weapon in the commission of a felony is another five years, mandatory. Not to mention just having a fully auto AK is worth ten years in the slam and a ten-thousand-dollar fine." He paused and exhaled audibly. "Did that ass . . . Sorry. Did that *supervisory special agent in charge* really think I was going to walk into the mosque and open fire? For Christ's sake, I'm a cop."

"I don't think you left him with that good-cop impression, Jack," Davidson said, chuckling. "I think he saw you as Rambo in a rage."

"The Philly cops could have gotten a judge to give us a probable-cause warrant to search both the mosque and the place in Philadelphia because of the attack on Sandra, and the Secret Service wouldn't have been involved," Britton went on.

"Sandra, do you happen to speak Spanish?" Castillo asked.

"Why? Is that also some sort of Secret Service no-no?"

"Yes or no?"

"Now, why in the world would you suspect that a semanticist might speak Spanish?"

Castillo switched to Spanish: "Fiery Spanish temper, maybe?"

She flashed her eyes at him, then laughed.

"Yeah," she replied in Spanish. "Classical, Mexican, and Puerto Rican Harlem. What's that you're speaking?"

"I was hoping it would sound Porteño."

It took her a moment to make the connection.

"Yeah," she said. "You could pass."

"So how do you think you're going to like Buenos Aires?"

"I don't know. I seem to recall another ex–Philly cop got herself shot there."

"I would say it's Jack's call, but that wouldn't be true, would it? Your call, Sandra: You two go to Buenos Aires, or stay here and Jack continues his war with the Secret Service. And he's going to lose that war. They are not going to put him back on the Protection Detail. . . ."

"It's not fair, Sandra," McGuire said. "But that's the way it is. They just don't take chances with the President and the Vice President. As a matter of fact, there's an old pal of mine . . . " He stopped.

"Go on, Tom," Castillo said. "They'll find out anyhow."

" . . . There's an old pal of mine who fell off the side step of the Vice President's limo. It didn't matter that it was covered with ice. He fell off. And he was off the detail."

"And what happened to him?"

"He's in Buenos Aires."

"So . . . is this what you're saying?" Britton asked a bit bitterly. "That Buenos Aires is sort of a Secret Service gulag? The dumping ground for Protection Service rejects?"

"Enough is enough, Jack," Castillo said, his tone now cold. "What's it going to be?"

"If we go down there, what happens to my job?" Sandra asked.

Castillo didn't reply.

Sandra then answered the question herself: "The same that would happen if we went to Saint Louis, Kansas City, or wherever that guy said. How long would we have to stay?"

"As long as Tom and I think is necessary," Castillo said.

"And the AALs walk on this," Britton said more than a little bitterly.

"Not necessarily," Castillo said. "But you're never going back on the Protection Detail."

"So then what finally happens to me?"

"Tom and I will, sooner or later but probably sooner, find something for you to do."

"You mean go to work for you?"

Castillo nodded.

"You didn't mention that," Britton said.

"You didn't give him much of a chance, Rambo," Davidson said.

"I'd like that," Britton said simply. "Thank you."

"When do we go?" Sandra asked.

"As soon as we can get you on a plane," Castillo said. "Maybe even tonight."

"All we have is an overnight bag," Sandra said.

"They have wonderful shops in Buenos Aires," Doña Alicia said.

"Let's give Tony a heads-up," McGuire said, and added to the Brittons: "Tony Santini's the old pal who fell off the limo."

"We have a state-of-the-art communications system down there," Castillo said, "but in his wisdom the kindly chief of OOA figured the odds of anything happening today were slim to none, and so told the guys sitting on the radio to take Christmas day off. So we'll have to use this primitive device."

Castillo put his cellular telephone on the table, pushed a speed-dial button, then the speakerphone button.

Proof that the system worked came twenty seconds later when a male voice answered, "Boy, it didn't take long for Munz to call you to tell you, did it, Charley?"

"And a merry, merry Christmas to you, too, Tony. It didn't take Munz long to call me to tell me what?"

"You haven't heard about your Irish pal Duffy?"

"What about him?"

"They tried to take him out about seven o'clock last night. He had his wife and kids with him. Out in Pilar. He's one pissed-off Irishman."

"Anybody hurt?"

"No. Thank God."

"They get the people that did it?"

"No. But this is not the time to be on the roads in a Ford F-150 pickup with a dented rear end. Duffy rammed his way through what was supposed to be a stop-and-shoot ambush. Every gendarme in Argentina is working Christmas looking for it."

"Is Alfredo looking into who did it?"

"I thought it was probably him on the phone just now."

"Have him send what he finds out to Miller."

"Done."

"What I called about, Tony: You remember Jack Britton?"

"Sure."

"Party or parties unknown—probably those Muslims he was undercover with—tried to take him and his wife out yesterday afternoon."

"Well, so long Protection Detail. Is he all right? His wife? Where are they going to send him? I could sure use him down here when they're through with him."

"How about as soon as I can get them on a plane?"

"That's a little unusual, isn't it?"

"He said unkind things to the supervisory special agent in charge when he told him he was off the detail. Isaacson turned him over to me just before they were going to handcuff him. I need to put him on ice."

"He told off the SAC? Good for him! I wish I had."

Delchamps laughed.

"Who was that?" Santini said.

"Edgar Delchamps," Delchamps said. "Ace has you on speakerphone, Tony. We've got a whole host of folks at the Christmas dinner table working on this."

"Glad to hear it," Santini said.

"Why do you need Britton, Tony?" Castillo said.

"I keep hearing things like there's a raghead connection with our friends in Asunción that we didn't pick up on. He can pass himself off as a raghead, I seem to recall."

"I don't want him going undercover."

"Why not?"

"Say, 'Yes, sir, Charley. I understand he's not to go undercover.' "

"Yes, sir, Charley."

Castillo thought he heard a mix of annoyance and sarcasm in the reply. He knew he saw gratitude in Sandra Britton's eyes.

"Okay," he went on, "as soon as we have the schedule, we'll give you a heads-up. Put them in Nuestra Pequeña Casa. If Munz wants to tell Duffy, fine. Otherwise, not. I have a gut feeling."

"Yes, sir, Charley, sir."

Castillo ignored that. He said, "Alex Darby presumably knows about Duffy?"

"Yeah, sure. And anticipating your next question, Alex called Bob Howell in Montevideo so that he could give a heads-up to the China Post people sitting on the ambassador at Shangri-La. He told me that Munz had already called Ordóñez to give him a heads-up. I'd say all the bases are pretty well covered. But what the hell's going on, Charley?"

"I wish I knew. You'll be among the first to know if I ever find out. I'll be in touch, Tony. Take good care of the Brittons."

"Anybody who says rude things to a SAC is my kind of guy, Charley. Try to stay out of trouble."

Castillo broke the connection.

He looked at Britton.

"Masterson's mother and father—ambassador, retired—lost their home in New Orleans to Hurricane Katrina. They're now living on the estancia in Uruguay—Shangri-La—which he inherited from his late son, who was the bagman for the oil-for-food cesspool. I couldn't talk the ambassador out of it. And I really had a hard time getting him to agree to having four guys from China Post—even on our payroll, not that he couldn't have easily afforded paying them himself—to go down there to sit on him."

" 'China Post'?" Mr. and Mrs. Britton asked in unison.

"Some people think that Shanghai Post Number One (In Exile) of the American Legion," Davidson explained, "is sort of an employment agency for retired special operators seeking more or less honest employment."

"What Santini just told me," Castillo said, "was that Alex Darby, the CIA station chief in Buenos Aires, has given Bob Howell, the station chief in Montevideo, a heads-up, and that Alfredo Munz, who works for us . . ."

"Sort of the OOA station chief," Davidson injected drily.

". . . down there has given a heads-up to Chief Inspector José Ordóñez of the Interior Police Division of the Policía Nacional del Uruguay," Castillo went on. "A really smart cop, even if he doesn't like me very much. One of the first things I want you to do down there is get with him. Bottom line, I think, as Santini said, we have all the bases covered down there."

"Carlos," Doña Alicia said. "Did I understand correctly that another friend of yours has been attacked? He and his family?"

He looked at her for a long moment before replying.

"It looks that way, Abuela. But Liam Duffy is more a friend of Alfredo Munz than mine."

"Just a coincidence, would you say, Karlchen?" Kocian asked. "Two such incidents on the same day?"

Plus your friend, Billy. That makes three.

And the deep-cover asset in Vienna makes four.

Shit . . . five if you count his wife.

Castillo said: "What Montvale described as a deep-cover asset in Vienna, a man named Kuhl and his wife—"

"Kurt Kuhl?" Delchamps interrupted, and when Castillo nodded, he asked, "What the hell happened to him?"

"Merry Christmas," Castillo said. "The Kuhls were found garroted to death behind the statue of Johann Strauss on the Ring in Vienna yesterday. You knew him?"

"Yeah, I knew both of them well," Delchamps said.

"You're talking about Kurt Kuhl who ran the chain of pastry shops?" Kocian asked, and looked at Delchamps.

"I think it has to be him," Delchamps said. *"Them."*

"Then so did I know them," Kocian said. "They were friends for many years." He paused, then asked incredulously, "'Deep-cover asset'? You're not suggesting he had a connection with the CIA?"

"For longer than our leader here is old," Delchamps said. "If there's going to be a star on the wall—and there should be two stars; Gertrud was as good as Kurt was—it should be studded with diamonds."

"I don't understand," Doña Alicia said.

"There's a wall in Langley, Doña Alicia, at the CIA headquarters, with stars to memorialize spooks who got unlucky."

"I didn't know," she said softly.

"Am I permitted to ask what Kurt and Gertrud did for the CIA?" Kocian asked.

After a moment, Delchamps said, somewhat sadly: "Well, why not? They turned people, Billy. Or they set them up to be turned. . . ."

"Turned?" Doña Alicia asked softly, as if she hated to interrupt but really wanted to know.

"They made good guys out of bad guys, Abuela," Castillo said. "They got Russian intelligence people to come to our side."

"And East Germans and Poles and Czechs and Hungarians," Delchamps said. "What I can't understand is why they were just killed. Excuse me, *garroted.*"

"Instead of 'interviewing them' at length?" Davidson asked. "Getting a list of names? Some of them, I'll bet, are still being worked."

"A lot of them are still being worked," Delchamps said matter-of-factly. "I had three in Paris. One in the Bulgarian embassy and two in the Russian."

"At the risk of sounding paranoid, I think there's a pattern to this," Castillo said.

"Just because you're paranoid, Ace, doesn't mean that ugly little men from Mars—or from Pushkinskaya Square—aren't chasing you with evil intentions."

That got some chuckles.

"Pushkinskaya Square?" Doña Alicia asked.

My God, Castillo thought. *She's not just being polite; she's fascinated with this business.*

What kind of a man discusses multiple murders—or attempted murders—with his grandmother at the Christmas dinner table?

"It's in Moscow, Doña Alicia," Delchamps explained. "It's famous for two things: a statue of Pushkin, the Russian poet, and an ugly building that's the headquarters of the SVR, which used to be the KGB."

"Oh, yes," Doña Alicia said politely, then asked, "Does 'garroted' mean what I think it does?"

"Why don't we change the subject?" Castillo said. "It's Christmas!"

"Yes, dear," Doña Alicia said. "I agree. But I'm interested."

"They put a thing around your neck, Doña Alicia," Delchamps said. "Sometimes plastic, sometimes metal. It causes strangulation. It was sort of the signature of the ÁVH, the Államvédelmi Hatóság, Hungary's secret police. When they wanted it known they had taken somebody out, they used a metal garrote."

"The sort of thing the Indian assassins, the thugs, used?"

"So far as I know, they used a rope, a cord, with a ball on each end so that they could get a good grip. What the Hungarians used was sort of a metal version of the plastic handcuffs you see the cops use. Once it's in place, it's hard, impossible, to remove."

Davidson saw Castillo glaring at Delchamps.

"What kind of a garrote was used in Vienna, Charley?" Davidson asked innocently.

Castillo moved his glare to Davidson.

"How long does it take for someone to die when this happens to them?" Doña Alicia asked.

McGuire saw the look on Castillo's face and took pity on him.

"You think there's a pattern, Charley?" McGuire asked, moving the subject from people being garroted. "What kind?"

Castillo shrugged. "All these hits were on the same day."

"First," Delchamps went on, "the victim loses consciousness as oxygen to the brain is shut off. After that, it doesn't take long."

"Is it very painful?" Doña Alicia said.

"I would suppose it's damned uncomfortable," Delchamps answered. "But I would say it's more terrifying; you can't breathe."

"How awful!" Doña Alicia said.

Castillo's cellular rattled on the table as the vibration function announced an incoming call. He looked at the caller identity illuminated on its screen.

"Quiet, please," he ordered, and pushed the SPEAKERPHONE button. "Homicide. Strangulation Division."

"I don't suppose you know, Gringo, you wiseass, where Abuela might be?"

"Abuela," Castillo said. "It's your other grandson. The fat one."

"That's not kind, Carlos. Shame on you!" Doña Alicia said. "And Fernando, you know how I feel about you calling Carlos 'Gringo.'"

"Abuela, you could have told me you were going there."

"I didn't want to bother you, my darling. Merry Christmas!"

"I was worried sick. There was no answer at the house. I was just about to get in the car and go over there."

"Nobody answered the phone because I gave everybody the day off. Did you have a nice Christmas dinner?"

"Very nice, thank you."

"We had a wonderful dinner," she went on as others around the table exchanged grins. "Billy Kocian is here and he made some sort of Hungarian dessert with cherries, brandy, and brown sugar with whipped cream. It was marvelous! And now we're sitting around chatting. And having a little champagne, if it is the truth you really want. There's no cause for concern."

"When do you want to come home?"

"If it wasn't for Carlos going out of town tomorrow, I'd stay awhile. But sometime tomorrow, probably."

"I'll come pick you up."

"You're not thinking of coming here in the plane, Fernando?"

"The plane" was the Bombardier/Learjet 45XR owned by the family company and piloted more often than not by one Fernando Lopez, the company's president and Castillo's cousin and Abuela's grandson.

"Yes, I am, Abuela."

"That's very kind, darling, but I know what it costs by the hour to fly the plane; and that there's no way that we can claim it as a business deduction and get away with it. I'm perfectly capable of getting on an airliner by myself. Now, get off the phone and enjoy your family at Christmas!"

"Fernando?" Castillo called.

"What?"

"A penny saved is a penny earned. Try to keep that in mind while you're running our family business."

"Gringo! You son—"

" 'Bye, now, Fernando!" Castillo called cheerfully, and quickly broke the connection.

"You were saying, Edgar," Doña Alicia said, "that being garroted is more frightening than painful?"

[TWO]
Signature Flight Support, Inc.
Baltimore-Washington International Airport
Baltimore, Maryland
0725 26 December 2005

Major (Retired) H. Richard Miller, Jr., chief of staff of the Office of Organizational Analysis, and Mrs. Agnes Forbison, the OOA's deputy chief for administration, were in the hangar when the convoy of four identical black GMC Yukon XLs drove in through a rear door and began to unload passengers and cargo.

The first passenger to leap nimbly from a Yukon was Doña Alicia Castillo, who had been riding in the front passenger seat of what the Secret Service had been describing on their radio network as "Don Juan Two Four." That translated to mean the second of four vehicles in the Don Juan convoy. Don Juan was the code name of the senior person in the convoy.

When the director of the Washington-area Secret Service communications network had been directed to add then-Major Castillo to his net, a code name had been required. For example, the secretary of Homeland Security, who was well over six feet and two hundred pounds, was code-named Big Boy, and the director of National Intelligence was Double Oh Seven. Having seen the dashing young Army officer around town—and taking note of the string of attractive females on his arm—the communications director had to think neither long nor hard before coming up with Don Juan.

Doña Alicia walked quickly to Miller and kissed his cheek. She had known him since he and Castillo had been plebes at West Point.

The second exitee—from Don Juan Four Four—was Max, closely followed by the Secret Service agent attached to him by a strong leash. Max towed the agent to the nose gear of a glistening white Gulfstream III, where he raised his right rear leg and left a large, liquid message for any other canines in the area that the Gulfstream was his.

Gulfstream Three Seven Nine actually belonged to Gossinger Consultants, a wholly owned subsidiary of Gossinger Beteiligungsgesellschaft, G.m.b.H., of Fulda, Germany, which had bought the aircraft from Lopez Fruit and Vegetables Mexico, a wholly owned subsidiary of Castillo Agriculture, Inc., of San Antonio, Texas, whose honorary chairman of the board was Doña Alicia Castillo, whose president and chief executive officer was Fernando Lopez, and whose officers included Carlos Castillo.

The Office of Organizational Analysis "dry leased" on an "as needed" basis the Gulfstream from Gossinger Consultants on an agreed price of so much per day, plus an additional amount per flight hour.

OOA provided the crew and paid fuel, maintenance, insurance, and other costs, such as the hangar rent at Signature Flight Support. The Lorimer Charitable & Benevolent Fund reimbursed the OOA on a monthly basis for all of its aviation expenses involved with providing members of the LC&BF staff with the necessary transportation to carry out their charitable and benevolent duties.

It was the perhaps immodest opinion of David W. Yung, Jr.—BA, Stanford University, and MBA, Harvard Business School, who enjoyed a splendid reputation within the FBI and the IRS of being an extraordinarily talented rooter-out of money laundering and other chicanery—that if anyone could work their way through this obfuscatory arrangement he had set up, they would have to be a hell of a lot smarter than he was.

And there was little question in the minds of the cognoscenti that Two-Gun Yung was one smart character. It was he who had first found and then invisibly moved into the LC&BF account in the Riggs Bank in Washington a shade under forty-six million dollars of illicit oil-for-food profits that Philip J. Kenyon III—chairman of the board, Kenyon Oil Refining and Brokerage Company, Midland, Texas—thought he secretly had squirreled away in the Caledonian Bank & Trust Limited in the Cayman Islands.

That transaction was described, perhaps irreverently, by Edgar Delchamps as selling a slimeball a $46,000,000 Stay Out of Jail Card.

Castillo, who had been riding in the front passenger seat of Don Juan Four Four, walked to Max at the nose of the Gulfstream.

"Sit," he ordered sternly in Hungarian. "Stay!"

Max complied.

"Okay, Billy!" Castillo called, motioning with a wave of his arm.

Eric Kocian got out of Don Juan Three Four. He removed Mädchen—on a leash—and walked her to the rear of the Yukon. Edgar Delchamps and Sándor Tor next got out somewhat awkwardly, because they each held two of Mädchen's pups, and also walked to the rear of the truck. By then the Secret Service driver had gotten out from behind the wheel, gone to the rear, and opened the door.

He took out a folded travel kennel. He expanded it, but not without some difficulty that bordered on being comical to those who tried not to watch. The pups were placed in the travel kennel, and then, as Billy Kocian and Mädchen watched warily, Sándor Tor and the Secret Service agent picked up the kennel and followed Delchamps to the stair door of the Gulfstream.

Delchamps went up the stairs and into the plane, then turned so he could pull the kennel through the door.

He swore in German.

"I could have told you it wasn't going to fit through the door, sweetie," Jack Davidson called in a somewhat effeminate voice from near Don Juan One Four. "If you'd only *asked*! You *never* ask. You think you know *everything*!"

Delchamps made an obscene gesture to Davidson, which Doña Alicia and Agnes Forbison, who by then had walked over to Castillo, pretended not to see.

"What this reminds me of is sending Carlos and Fernando off to Boy Scout camp," Doña Alicia said.

"Yeah," Agnes agreed.

"You didn't have to come out here, Agnes," Castillo said.

"No, I didn't," she said. "But I thought you might need a little walking-around money."

She handed him a zippered cloth envelope marked RIGGS NATIONAL BANK. It appeared to be full.

"Thank you," Castillo said.

When he had put it in his briefcase, she handed him a receipt to sign. He used the briefcase as a desk to sign it, and gave it back.

"How long are you going to be?" Agnes asked.

"I don't know," Castillo said. He paused. "Abuela, don't let him know I told you, but Billy's friend didn't die of natural causes."

"I'm not surprised. It was in his eyes."

"What I'm saying is that Billy is now pretty angry, and that may help us with Otto."

"I don't think I understand," Doña Alicia said.

"He doesn't like us using the *Tages Zeitung* as a source of information."

"But you're the boss," Agnes said.

"I don't want to have to confront him more than I already have," Castillo said. "I don't want him to quit."

"He wouldn't do that," Doña Alicia said. "Not only is the *Tages Zeitung* his life, but he loves you."

"He also has the journalistic ethical standards he got from my grandfather, and he doesn't think my grandfather would give the CIA the time of day."

"But you're not CIA," Agnes said.

"I don't think Otto believes that," Castillo said. "Anyway, Billy was closer to my grandfather than Otto was—closer than anyone else ever was—and what I'm hoping is that he will go through the *Tages Zeitung* database like a vacuum cleaner on overdrive and Otto will get the message. We'll see."

The rear door of the hangar rose with a metallic screech.

"For what we're paying for this place, you'd think they could afford a little grease," Castillo said.

Three cars drove into the hangar. A total of five uniformed officers got out.

"Here comes the bureaucracy," Castillo said. "I guess we can leave now."

"Not until you arrange the dogs," Agnes said. "How long is that going to go on?"

"Otto's kids get one of the puppies, whether or not Otto likes it—"

"Carlos!"

"One pup I'm keeping for a friend of mine in Argentina," Castillo went on. "That leaves two. One of which Delchamps says he wants."

"Of course he does! Didn't you see him on his knees with the puppies yesterday?"

"And Billy says he wants one to keep Mädchen company. So that's it. Once we get Billy back to Budapest, no more airborne Noah's ark."

"And you keep Max?" Doña Alicia asked.

"It will be Max and me alone against the cold cruel world."

"Billy doesn't want him? Or he's just saying that to be nice to you?"

"I don't know, Abuela," Castillo said. "I asked him. He said he doesn't think Mädchen will betray him the way Max has."

"He doesn't mean that," Doña Alicia said.

"Yeah, I know. But he's already named the pup Max, making that his Max the Tenth or Twelfth." Castillo looked at Agnes and changed the subject. "Are you going to put my grandma on her plane?"

"After we have a nice lunch in the Old Ebbitt Grill, I will," Agnes said.

"What do I do about the apartment in the Mayflower?"

"When does the lease run out?"

"The end of next month; you have to give them ten days' notice."

"Well, let's see what happens toward the end of next month," Castillo said. Then he saw Jake Torine and Dick Sparkman walking across the hangar floor toward them. "Well, here come the airplane drivers. I guess it's time to go."

[THREE]
Above Antwerp, Belgium
2045 26 December 2005

Jake Torine said, "You've got it, Dick," then removed his headset, unstrapped himself, and went into the passenger compartment.

It was crowded. The travel kennel was in the aisle at the rear. Mädchen was lying in the aisle in front of it, keeping an eye on Max, who was lying in the aisle just inside the passenger compartment—and attached to Jack Davidson by a strong leash. Max was having trouble understanding not only that the honeymoon was over, but that the mother of their offspring had decided that he was a bad influence on their progeny and didn't want him anywhere near them.

There were two couches, one on each side of the aisle. Billy Kocian—in a red silk dressing gown—was sprawled regally on one of them, reading, and Jack Doherty was on the other, snoring softly with his mouth open. David W. Yung was in the right forward-facing seat and typing on the computer in his lap. Edgar Delchamps was sitting, asleep, in the forward-facing seat nearest the stair door. Sándor Tor, also asleep, sat in the rear-facing chair across from Delchamps.

Across the aisle, Davidson, with Max attached to him, was sitting in the rear-facing seat across from Castillo, who was on the telephone. When Castillo saw Torine, he held up a finger to signal Jake to wait.

"I don't think there'll be a problem with our ambassador," Castillo said. "But this will make sure there's no problem with the other one." He paused to listen, then said, "Thank you very much, ma'am."

This strongly suggested to Torine that Castillo was talking to Secretary of State Natalie Cohen.

"Yes, ma'am, I will," Castillo said. "Thank you again, Madam Secretary." And then he said: "Break it down, please, White House," and put the handset in its cradle on the bulkhead.

"What was that all about?"

"The secretary of State is about to telephone our evil leprechaun in Montevideo—"

"I thought Duffy was our evil leprechaun."

"Comandante Liam Duffy is our evil leprechaun *in Argentina*. I was referring to our evil leprechaun *in Uruguay*, one Ambassador Michael A. McGrory."

"Oh. Thank you for the clarification. And what is the secretary going to say to the ambassador?"

"That she is dispatching a Secret Service agent by the name of Britton—recently a member of the Vice President's Protection Detail—to ensure the safety of Ambassador Lorimer, and that he is to be given what support he asks for and not to be assigned other duties."

"Did you happen to mention the circumstances under which Britton left the protection detail?"

"Yeah. I don't try to con her. She's (a) too nice and (b) too smart. I told her just about everything except his rudeness to the SACs. And then I asked her what she thought about sending him to check on the ambassador's security arrangements, and she thought that was a splendid idea."

"You knew she would. She really likes the old guy. You don't consider that conning her?"

"No, I don't."

Torine shook his head.

"You noticed that thanks to a lovely tailwind we didn't have to land for fuel?" Torine asked.

Castillo nodded.

"We're about two hundred miles—half an hour—from Flughafen Frankfurt am Main," Torine went on. "There was an in-flight advisory just now; we are to be met by unidentified government authorities."

Castillo raised his eyebrows, then looked at Davidson. "Jack, make sure to remind me to remind everybody my name is Gossinger."

"Jawohl, Herr Oberst."

"Just 'herr,' Jack. My grandfather was the oberst. I'm the ne'er-do-well heir to the fruit of his hard labor."

"I knew that," Davidson said.

Ground Control directed the Gulfstream to a tarmac and collection of buildings away from the main terminal. Castillo thought—but wasn't sure—that it was probably what was left of what had been Rhine-Main USAF Base.

A number of vehicles—Castillo recognized both Otto Görner's company Mercedes-Benz S600 and his personal Jaguar XJ—were waiting for them. Görner was out of his Jaguar and headed for the airplane before the stair door swung open.

When Görner came up the stairs, Max growled.

"Get your goddamned animal under control, Billy!" Görner almost shouted.

"That's Karlchen's goddamned animal, Otto," Kocian replied. "Talk to him."

Görner looked around the cabin, then at Castillo.

"I thought you were coming alone," he said unpleasantly, the translation of which was *I told you not to bring anybody from the CIA with you.*

"Obviously, you were wrong," Kocian said, then nodded in the direction of the crowd outside his window. "Who are all these people, Otto?"

"Some are from the Bundeskriminalamt, some are our security people, and some are the press."

"The *press?*" Castillo asked incredulously.

"The *Tages Zeitung* is going to offer a reward—fifty thousand euros—for information leading to the arrest of the people who killed Günther Friedler," Görner said evenly. "And that announcement will be made by you, Herr von und zu Gossinger, as chairman of the executive committee, just as soon as you get off this airplane."

He handed Castillo a sheet of paper.

"I took the liberty of preparing a few words for you to say when you make the announcement," Görner said.

Jack Davidson saw the look in Castillo's eyes.

"Easy, Charley," Davidson said softly in Pashtu, one of the two major languages of Afghanistan, the other being Afghan Persian. "Be cool. Count to two thousand five hundred eleven. By threes. In Russian. Slowly."

Görner looked at Davidson, clearly annoyed that he didn't understand what had been said.

Castillo met Davidson's eyes. He nodded and smiled just perceptibly. He was aware that he was furious, and had already ordered himself to put his mouth on total shutdown.

He glanced at Görner and thought: *Since I don't think you want me set up to be killed, Otto, what the fuck were you thinking?*

Is this punishment for bringing what you think is the CIA with me?

No. You wrote my speech before you knew I had.

What this is, is Teutonic stupidity!

He looked back at Davidson and said in Russian, "Two thousand five hundred eight. Two thousand five hundred eleven."

Now both Kocian and Görner looked at him in confusion.

"Daddy's proud of you," Davidson said in Pashtu, and meant it. He had been witness to Castillo losing his temper. "You get a gold star to take home to Mommy."

"That's a very good idea, Otto," Castillo said in English. "And thank you for this." He held up the sheet of paper. "After I announce the reward, what happens?"

"We go to Wetzlar so that you and Billy can pay your respects to Frau Friedler."

"I see a couple of problems with that, Otto. One is that I didn't know Herr Friedler or his wife and feel that I would be intruding on Frau Friedler's time with Billy."

Kocian grunted his agreement.

"Another is the dogs," Castillo went on. "I don't think Billy wants to take Mädchen and the pups, and I know I don't want—"

"Pups?" Görner asked. "You mean baby dogs?"

"Four of them," Castillo said, pointing down the aisle at the travel kennel. "One of them is a gift from Billy and myself to your kids, our godchildren."

"We can talk about that later," Görner said.

"And I want to get Inspector Doherty and Special Agent Yung—"

"Who?"

"They're FBI, Otto. I want to get them together with the German police as quickly as possible—"

"Karl, I don't know about that," Görner protested.

"We're going to need all the help we can get to find these murderers, Otto," Billy Kocian said. "And Doherty and Yung are recognized experts in their fields."

He didn't say which fields, Castillo thought admiringly.

I don't think either one of them knows much about investigating a murder. But Billy knows Otto can be a self-righteous pain in the ass unless you control him.

And already Billy is acting in charge, letting Otto know, as I'd hoped.

"I'll get on the phone," Görner said.

"So what I'm thinking, Otto, is that it would be best if you took Billy to Wetzlar and I took Doherty and Yung to Marburg—put them up in the Europäischer Hof, where they could get together with the authorities first thing in the morning. Then I'll take everybody else—including the dogs—with me in either the Jag or the Mercedes and the van to the Haus im Wald. That make sense?"

"It does to me," Billy Kocian said, his tone suggesting his opinion settled the matter once and for all.

Görner looked at him for a long moment, made a face of resignation, and nodded.

"Take my Jaguar," he said. "I suspect I will need a drink—several drinks— in Wetzlar, and I don't want to drink and drive."

[FOUR]
Route A5
Near Bad Homburg
2210 26 December 2005

"Please do so," Castillo said in response to an announcement from the information operator that, having found the number he asked for, they would for a small fee be happy to connect him directly.

Castillo was driving the Jaguar. Edgar Delchamps was in the front passenger seat. David Yung and Jack Davidson were squeezed in the backseat with Max between them. Max looked out the rear window at the Mercedes-Benz van that was following them and carrying Jack Doherty, Jake Torine, Dick Sparkman, Mädchen, the puppies, two members of the Gossinger Beteiligungsgesellschaft, G.m.b.H., security staff, and their luggage.

"Europäischer Hof," came over the speaker system of the Jaguar. *"Guten Abend."*

"Here is Karl von und zu Gossinger, of Gossinger Beteiligungsgesellschaft," Castillo replied more than a little imperiously in German.

"And how may we be of service, Herr von und zu Gossinger?"

"I will require accommodations for the next few days for two business associates. A suite with separate bedrooms would be preferable, but failing that, two of your better singles."

"We will be honored to be of service, Herr von und zu Gossinger. When may we expect your associates?"

"In about an hour. I presume there will be no difficulty in billing this directly to the firm?"

"None whatever."

"We will wish to eat. Will that pose a problem?"

"We will keep the restaurant open for your guests, Herr Gossinger."

Castillo's face wrinkled as he continued looking forward and mentally counted heads.

"There will be nine of us."

"We look forward to serving you, Herr von und zu Gossinger."

"Thank you very much," Castillo said, and reached for the telephone's OFF button on the spoke of the steering wheel.

Edgar Delchamps applauded.

"Very good, Herr von und zu Gossinger," he said. "Just the right touch of polite arrogance. I could hear him clicking his heels."

"Well, you know what they say, Edgar. 'When in Rome,' or for that matter, in *Das Vaterland . . .*"

"That said, don't you think it's about time to bring your business associates up to speed about where everybody, including you, fits into the landscape?"

Castillo was silent a long time as he considered that. Then he made a small frown that suggested, *Why not?*

"Okay," he said. "Take notes. There will be a quiz. Think Stalingrad. The Red Army is firing harassing and intermittent artillery at the Germans. They get lucky and make a hit on a Kublewagon—"

"A what?" Yung asked.

"The military version of the Volkswagen Bug," Davidson furnished. "They were selling them in the States a while back."

"Oh, yeah. I remember," Yung said. "Cute little car!"

"If I may be permitted to continue with the history lesson?" In the rearview mirror, he saw Yung mouth, *Sorry.* "Thank you. Said Kublewagon was carrying a light bird, general staff corps, on Von Paulus's staff—"

"I remember Von Paulus," Delchamps said. "He got on the phone to Hitler, told him they were surrounded, out of ammo, down to eating their horses, and could he please surrender? To which Der Führer replied, 'Congratulations, General, you are now a field marshal. German field marshals do not surrender. You do have, of course, the option of suicide. . . .'"

"Really?" Yung asked.

"And the next day, Field Marshal von Paulus surrendered," Delchamps finished, "in effect telling Hitler, 'Screw you, my Führer.'"

Castillo said: "If I may continue: The light bird in the Kublewagon suffered life-threatening wounds and would have been KIA had not an eighteen-year-old *Gefreite*—a corporal—from Vienna dragged him into the basement of a building and applied lifesaving measures. No good deed goes unpunished, as you know. The next couple of H-and-I rounds hit the building, causing the corporal to also suffer grievous wounds.

"The next day, the medics found both of them and loaded them—my grandfather the light bird and Billy Kocian the corporal—on one of the last medical evacuation flights back to the Fatherland . . ."

"No shit!" Yung said wonderingly.

". . . where both were put into an army hospital in Giessen, which is not far from where we're going. Billy got out first. To keep him from being sent back to the Eastern Front, good ol' Grandpa got him assigned as his orderly. When Grandpa got out of the hospital, they put him in charge of an officer's POW camp in Poland. He took Gefreite Kocian with him.

"This place was the nearest officers' POW camp to the Katyn Forest, near Smolensk, in Russia. A couple of hundred miles—"

"You're losing me, Charley," Jack Davidson said.

"When the Germans and Russians were pals, and they invaded Poland in 1940, the Russians took almost five thousand Polish officers who had surrendered out to the Katyn Forest. First they made them dig holes . . ."

"Okay," Davidson said. "I'm now with you."

"I'm *so* glad, Jack," Castillo said. "After the officers had dug the holes, the Russians wired their hands behind them, shot them in the back of the head with small-caliber pistols, and dumped them in the holes, which were then covered up."

"Nice people, the Russians," Delchamps said. "Anybody who knows me knows I've always said that."

Castillo went on: "When the Germans and the Russians were no longer pals, and the Germans invaded Russia, and they got to Smolensk, they found the graves. The Russians denied any knowledge, said if anybody shot Polish POWs, it had to be those terrible Germans.

"*How to get the truth out?* wondered those terrible Germans.

"One of the prisoners in my grandfather's POW camp was Patton's son-in-law. My grandfather was ordered to take him and a bunch of other American field-grade officers, including some doctors, to the site, and proved to them that their Russian buddies were the bad guys.

"The story didn't come out for years, but the Americans who had been taken to Katyn knew about it, and remembered the German officer who had taken them to see the graves.

"Okay. So now the war is over. My grandfather and Billy are released from our POW camps and go home. Grandpa goes home and finds that all of his newspapers have been bombed and that most of his farmland is on the wrong side of the fence between the American and Russian zones. Meanwhile, Billy goes home to Vienna and finds that all of his family was killed the day we bombed Saint Stephen's Cathedral and the Opera House.

"Billy then makes his way to Fulda. My grandfather had become a father figure to him. And vice versa. The two of them dig into the rubble that had been the printing plant of the Fulda *Tages Zeitung* and put together one Mergenthaler Linotype machine from what was left of two dozen of them.

"That machine is now on display in the lobby of Gossinger Beteiligungsgesellschaft, G.m.b.H. It was used to set the type for the first postwar edition of the *Tages Zeitung*.

"When my grandfather had applied to the American Military Government for permission to publish, he thought he had one thing going for him. A classmate at Philipps University—an American brigadier general—was military governor of Hesse and knew my grandfather was not a Nazi.

"Actually, Grandpa had three things going for him. Second was that counterintelligence had found his name on a Gestapo hit list; he was involved in the 1944 bomb plot. The only reason he hadn't been shot—or hung on a butcher's hook—was that the Gestapo thought he was already dead. And, third, the officers he'd taken to Katyn remembered him as a good guy.

"The first post-war *Tages Zeitung* was in Fulda. Then Kassel. Then Munich. Billy Kocian was sent to Vienna to get the presses up and running and then to look around for a staff, including editors, for my grandfather to vet. He was then twenty-one or twenty-two. The next time my grandfather heard from Billy was when Billy sent him the first edition of the *Wien Tages Zeitung*. The masthead read: *Eric Kocian, Associate Publisher and Editor in Chief.*

"My grandfather in effect said, 'What the hell, why not? Give him a chance. See if he sinks or swims.' Billy swam."

"Herr Oberst," Yung said. "Billy Kocian's history is fascinating, but is there a bigger point to all this?"

"Bear with me," Castillo said. "So things were looking up. My grandfather had two children, my Uncle Willi and my mother. Uncle Willi went to Philipps, took a degree in political science, and went to work for Gossinger Beteiligungsgesellschaft, bringing with him his buddy Otto Görner.

"My mother was the princess in the castle. Everybody thought that as soon as she was old enough to make it socially acceptable, she would marry Otto, who was being groomed to handle the business side—as opposed to just the newspaper side—of the business.

"And then into the princess's life appeared the evil American—in the right seat of a D-model Huey—playing war with the Fourteenth Armored Cavalry, which in those days patrolled our fence line with East Germany. And three or four days later, said evil American disappeared, never again to be seen by the princess.

"The kindest thing my grandfather had to say when he was told he was going to be a grandfather was that he thanked God my grandmother wasn't alive to be shamed by my mother's blatant immorality.

"When I asked why I didn't have a daddy like the other kids, Grandpa would walk out of the room and my Uncle Willi would tell me—little Karlchen— that that was not to be discussed. All my mother would say was that my father was an American army officer who had had to go away and would not be coming back, and that I was not to talk about him to Grandpa, Uncle Willi, or 'Uncle' Otto.

"Then, when I was about eleven, Uncle Willi, with my grandfather next to him on their way home from Kassel, drove his Gullwing Mercedes off a bridge on the A7 Autobahn at an estimated one hundred thirty miles an hour.

"That left my mother and me alone in the Haus im Wald, the family castle, which actually looks more like a factory. Mother again declined Otto's offer of marriage. She inherited her one-quarter of Gossinger Beteiligungsgesellschaft, the other three-fourths going to Uncle Willi and Uncle Billy and yours truly in equal parts. Uncle Willi had left everything he owned—his quarter—to my mother in the belief that she would eventually come to her senses and marry Otto. So she got that share, too.

"But it wasn't in the cards for my mother to live happily ever after with Little Karlchen in the castle. Six months after Uncle Willi and Grandpa went off the A7 bridge, she was diagnosed with pancreatic cancer. Terminal. Two months to live."

"Jesus!" David Yung exclaimed.

"At which point, Mother, apparently deciding that the orphan-to-be needed to establish contact with his father, whether or not the father was going to be pleased to learn that he had left a love child behind in Germany, turned to the 14th Armored Cavalry for help, giving them the father's name—Castillo—that she had steadfastly refused to give her father.

"The Fourteenth's regimental commander turned over the task of locating the father to one of his majors, one Allan B. Naylor—"

"Who now has four stars—that Naylor?" Davidson asked.

"That's the guy," Castillo confirmed. "He had a little trouble locating a Huey jockey named Castillo who had once maneuvered with the Fourteenth. Reason being: He was in San Antonio, in the National Cemetery there, with a representation of the Medal of Honor chiseled into his headstone."

"Your father won the Congressional Medal of Honor?" Yung asked softly.

"It's properly just the 'Medal of Honor,' David. And you don't win it. You receive it."

"No offense, Charley."

"None taken. Well, this changed things a good deal. The illegitimate offspring of a Medal of Honor *recipient* can't be treated like just one more bastard among the maybe a hundred thousand bastards spawned by the U.S. Army of Occupation. And Naylor, being Naylor, had also found out that I would own, when my mother died, all of Gossinger Beteiligungsgesellschaft with the exception of Billy Kocian's quarter-share.

"That raised the very real possibility that a wetback Texican family living in squalor on the riverbank in San Antonio was suddenly going to get their hands on the considerable fortune of the grandchild, nephew, cousin, whatever, they didn't even know existed.

"Naylor was dispatched to reconnoiter the terrain in San Antone while the brightest Army lawyers gathered in emergency session to come up with some way to protect the kid's assets from said wetbacks.

"What Naylor found, instead, was that my so-called wetback grandfather was just about convinced that some greedy fräulein of loose morals was trying to get her hands into the Castillo cash box and he was going to do whatever had to be done to keep that from happening.

"My grandmother had no such concerns. She took one look at the photo of Karl Wilhelm von und zu Gossinger that Naylor had shown her and said she could tell from the eyes—which were the same as his father's—her son's—that this was her grandson. Two hours after she met Allan Naylor for the first time, she went wheels-up with Naylor in my grandfather's Lear for New York, where they caught the five-fifteen PanAm flight to Frankfurt that afternoon.

"My grandfather caught up with her the next day. A week after that, clutching his brand-new American passport, Carlos Guillermo Castillo got on another PanAm 747 at Rhine-Main with his grandmother. My grandfather stayed in Germany a little longer. He buried my mother—she didn't want me to see her in her last days of that horrible disease—and he left Otto Görner in charge—temporarily—of my assets. He's still in charge.

"As far as the German government is concerned, I am Karl Wilhelm von und zu Gossinger, which means I have a German passport. That's proven useful more than once in our line of work, and when, for example, I need a couple of hotel rooms in a hurry."

"Ace, if you think I'm going to be nicer to you," Delchamps said, "now that I know how rich you are—well, then, yes, sir, your excellency, mine Führer, you handsome, wise, charming sonofabitch, I certainly will be."

"Screw you, Edgar," Castillo said. Then he exhaled audibly and added: "Okay, that's the story. Aside from bringing Jack Doherty and Sparkman up to speed—Jake has already heard all this—I'd really appreciate your keeping it— especially the soap opera details—to yourselves."

IV

[ONE]
Das Haus im Wald
Near Bad Hersfeld
Kreis Hersfeld-Rotenburg
Hesse, Germany
2315 26 December 2005

"We're almost there," Castillo said as the Jaguar swiftly moved down a macadam road winding through a thick pine forest.

A moment later, he braked very sharply and with a squeal of tires made a right turn onto an almost identical road. The driver of the van behind them decided it best not to try to turn so fast and went past the turn, then stopped and backed up, then followed.

The headlights of the Jaguar lit up reflective signs on each side of the road. Each two-foot-square sign showed a skull and bones and the legend, ZUGANG VERBOTEN!!!

"Looks like they expect you, Ace," Edgar Delchamps said. "Welcome home!"

Then the headlights picked up the form of a heavyset man standing in the middle of the road. He was swinging a heavy-duty flashlight back and forth as a signal to stop. The man was wearing a heavy Loden cloth cape, the drape of which was distorted by what Castillo professionally guessed to be a submachine gun, probably a Heckler & Koch MP7A1.

He approached the car. Castillo put the window down.

"*Wie gehts,* Karlchen?" the man said, offering Castillo his hand.

From the backseat, Max moved so that his front paws were on the console between the front seats. He showed his teeth and growled deep in his chest.

"Oh, shut up, Max," the man said. "You know me."

Max sat down.

"*Guten Abend,* Siggie," Castillo said, chuckling.

"It is good to see you again, Karlchen."

"It's good to see you."

"You have Max. Are Herr Görner and Herr Kocian close behind you?"

"I have Max and family. His wife, so to speak, and four of their pups are in a van coming right behind me. Otto and Uncle Billy went to Wetzlar; they should be along shortly."

"Frau Görner will be overjoyed. You know how she loves dogs."

Castillo grinned broadly. "Wait until she learns one of the pups is for Willi and Hermann."

The man returned the grin. "It will make her Christmas complete, Karlchen."

The man noticed movement coming up behind the Jaguar. It was the van. He then stepped back and waved both vehicles down the road.

The House in the Woods appeared in the headlights five minutes later. It sat against a hill, near the top, and did in fact look more like a collection of factory buildings than a residence.

As the Jaguar and the van stopped on a cobblestoned area, floodlights came on. Castillo got out, motioned for the people in the van to follow him, then walked across a shallow flagstone verandah to a large double door, opened the right side without knocking, and stepped inside.

Frau Helena Görner was standing just inside the vestibule. With her were two young boys, the housekeeper, and a maid. No one seemed surprised at his presence.

As Castillo approached, he decided that Siggie—"Siggie the Game Warden," he'd explained to all in the car, "stops everyone who gets past the skull-and-bones signs and announces that he's making sure they're not poachers before turning them away"—had either a cellular telephone or a radio, and then changed his mind: *Siggie has a cellular* and *a radio, and called ahead with one or both.*

"It's always good to see you, Karl," Helena said, offering him both her hand and her cheek, both of which were nearly as cold as her smile.

"You're looking as lovely as always, Helena." He turned to those following him. "Gentlemen, may I present our hostess, Frau Helena Görner? And my godsons, Willi and Hermann?"

Max towed Jack Davidson to the boys, who were obviously as glad to see the dog as Max was to see them.

Helena was not touched by the sight. She offered a strained smile, extended her hand to Edgar Delchamps, and said, "Welcome to our home. We have dinner waiting for you. I'm sure you must be . . ." She looked past the visitors toward the van. "What the hell is that they're carrying in?"

It was hard to know what tested Frau Helena Görner's good manners more in the next couple of minutes: her learning that she had gone to the trouble of having dinner prepared for her guests only to be told they had already eaten in Marburg; her learning that not only was Max going to spend the night—or the next few days—in her home but that he had his family with him; or her learning that one of the pups—which would certainly grow as enormous as his parents—was going to stay forever.

But Helena prided herself on being a lady, and the only expletive she uttered was the mild one that she had used when inquiring about the travel kennel being carried to the house, and five minutes after the visitors had walked into the vestibule, they now were all in the big room of the House in the Woods and having a little something liquid to cut the chill.

The big room was on the top—third—floor of the house, and was reached by both an enormous wide set of stairs and an elevator. It served as a combined reception and dining room for guests. The Görner family had their own dining and living rooms on the floors below.

One entire wall of the big room was curtained; the heavy curtains were now drawn. When uncovered, plateglass windows offered a view of the fields in the valley below. The housekeeper and a maid began to reset the dining table for breakfast.

The pups had been freed from the kennel and were playing with the boys in front of the fireplace. Max, lying next to Castillo, was whining because the moment he moved, Mädchen's teeth told him that he was not welcome to join in the fun.

There was the clunking sound of the elevator car rising, then its doors opening.

"Are they likely to soil the carpet?" Helena inquired of Castillo.

"Unless you get some newspapers on it, they certainly will," Eric Kocian announced as he walked from the elevator toward the dogs.

Otto Görner and Sándor Tor followed him off the elevator.

"Otto, darling," Helena greeted him, her tone somewhat less than warm. "I was thinking I'd make a place for the dogs in the stable."

"That won't work, Helena," Kocian said. "It'd be too cold for the pups in the stable. Mädchen and the pups will be in my room. For the time being, I suggest newspaper—appropriately, considering Karlchen's recent plagiaristic writings therein."

He squatted beside Mädchen and scratched her ears.

"Sándor," Kocian called. "Be a good fellow and get me a little Slivovitz from the bar, will you, please?"

He held his hand over his head, his thumb and index fingers at least three inches apart to indicate his idea of a little sip of the 120-proof Hungarian plum brandy.

Then he stood and turned to Castillo. "I am after the numbing effect, not the taste."

"It was bad in Wetzlar?" Castillo asked.

"That qualifies as an understatement, Karlchen," Kocian said. He exhaled audibly, then went on, measuring his words, "As does this: I want to get the *Gottverdammt* sonsofbitches—"

"Eric, the children!" Helena protested.

Kocian flashed her an icy look, then went on: ". . . who did this to Günther Friedler and his family. And the *Tages Zeitung* newspapers will do whatever we can toward that objective. Starting with doubling that reward to a hundred thousand euros." He took a sip of Slivovitz, then added, "And—if I have to say this—by providing our Karlchen-the-intelligence-officer and his friends with whatever we have in the files that might help them to find these bastards."

"Eric, the children shouldn't hear this!" Helena said, moving toward the boys, presumably to usher them out of earshot.

"They can read; they've seen the newspapers," Kocian said. "And so far as Helena's concern with my language, I remember you, Otto, and Willi teaching Karlchen all the dirty words when he was a lot younger than your two boys."

Sándor Tor handed Kocian a water glass three-quarters full with a clear liquid. He raised it to his lips and drank half.

He looked at Helena.

"I was led to believe there would be something to eat when we got here."

She flushed and then walked quickly out of the room.

Otto looked uncomfortable.

And so did everybody else in the room. Including Willi and Hermann.

Castillo thought: *You can't honestly say there's no excuse for Billy's behavior. There is. He obviously regards Friedler's murder as far more than the loss of a faithful employee under sordid circumstances. There was an emotional relationship between the two—maybe even father and son–like—but whatever it was, it was apparently a lot closer than anyone, maybe even Otto, suspected.*

Maybe Billy started out blaming Otto for putting Friedler on the story, knowing it was dangerous. But Billy has had plenty of time to think that through, time to conclude that maybe Otto didn't know that Friedler was in the line of fire.

And if Otto didn't, the blame for that was not Otto's; it was his.

And now Billy knows it, and that hurts.

Otto has known the pecking order around Gossinger Beteiligungsgesellschaft, G.m.b.H., from the time he came here. He wasn't in on Gossinger Beteiligungsgesellschaft, G.m.b.H., from the beginning; Billy was.

Even as a kid I knew that order: Grandpa—the Herr Oberst—was Lord and Master of all he surveyed. Then came Onkel Billy, Tier Two. Then Onkel Willi, Tier Three. And finally Otto, Tier Four.

Otto might've jumped to the top after Onkel Willi went off the bridge with Grandpa. But Grandpa's will hadn't left him much money—and not a single share of Gossinger Beteiligungsgesellschaft, G.m.b.H. And my mother didn't marry him.

And since she didn't have a clue on how to run the business, she turned to Uncle Billy, who not only knew how to run it but owned a quarter-share of it.

And the wisdom of that was confirmed when my other grandpa got in the act when my mother died. Otto moved into the Herr Oberst's office, took on the titles and ran things—and was paid damned well for it. But Don Fernando's bimonthly trips to Vienna and Billy's bimonthly trips to San Antonio or Midland had nothing to do with Grandpa having discovered Wiener schnitzel or Billy having a newfound interest in the Wild West.

Grandpa controlled my three-quarter interest in the firm, and he and Billy decided between them that Otto, with the proper guidance, was well qualified to run the firm. And that they—with every right to do so—would provide that guidance to Otto.

It worked out well, and certainly a lot of the credit for its success goes to Otto. He's paid an enormous salary and has a lot of perks. But the bottom line is that he doesn't own any of Gossinger.

Billy and I own all of it.

Including this house.

*I guess I should have gone into that when I was delivering the soap opera sce-
nario in the car on the way here. The explanation would have helped to avoid the
unease the others are feeling.*

But I didn't, and it's too late now with Otto here.

*There is, of course, a silver lining for me in the black cloud of Billy's embar-
rassingly bad manners. He gave me what I so far hadn't worked up the courage
to ask him for:* "The Tages Zeitung *newspapers will do whatever we can toward
that objective. Starting with doubling that reward to a hundred thousand euros.
And—if I have to say this—by providing our Karlchen-the-intelligence-officer
and his friends with whatever we have in the files that might help them to find
these bastards."*

Kocian drained his glass of Slivovitz and looked around for Sándor Tor, who
was nowhere in sight—*probably taking Billy's luggage to his room,* Castillo decided—and then, muttering, headed for the bar, which was actually an enormous antique sideboard, obviously intending to get a refill.

Castillo got up and followed him.

"Easy on the sauce, Billy," Castillo said softly.

Kocian raised one bushy, snow-white eyebrow.

"What did you say?"

"I said go easy on the Slivovitz."

"You don't dare tell me what to do, Karlchen!"

"I don't like her any more than you do, Billy, but we don't need to humiliate her, or Otto, and make everybody else uncomfortable. Including Hermann
and Willi."

"Go fuck yourself, Karlchen!"

Castillo shrugged.

"Suit yourself," he said. "I know better than to argue with an old drunk wallowing in self-pity."

"*Self-pity?* You arrogant little . . ."

By then Castillo was halfway back to his chair.

That was not one of my smartest moves, Charley thought as he went.

Why the hell did I do that?

Not as a considered move.

I guess the Boy Scout in me suddenly bubbled up and escaped.

Well, I certainly managed to make things worse than they were.

Helena reappeared several minutes later.

"It'll be just a few more minutes, Billy," she said.

Castillo looked at Kocian, who he found was already glaring at him.

Kocian drained his second glass of Slivovitz.

"Helena," Kocian said, "it has been pointed out to me that my behavior toward you and your family tonight has been shameful."

"I don't know what you mean, Billy," she said.

"Pray let me finish." He waited until she nodded, then went on: "I can only hope you can find it in your heart to forgive an old drunk wallowing in self-pity over the loss of a man who was like a son to him."

"Billy, you've not said nor done anything to apologize to me for."

"Otto," Kocian announced, "your wife is a lousy liar. One with a kind and gracious heart. She's much too good for you."

Helena went to Kocian and kissed him.

Kocian looked at Castillo.

"In case you're curious, Karlchen, that was my heart speaking, not the Slivovitz."

Castillo felt his throat tighten and his eyes start to water. He quickly got out of his chair.

"Did you drink all the Slivovitz, Onkel Billy? Or can I have one?"

"I think," Otto Görner said, "that we should get into the arrangements for tomorrow."

[TWO]
Das Haus im Wald
Near Bad Hersfeld
Kreis Hersfeld-Rotenburg
Hesse, Germany
0830 27 December 2005

The drapes over the plateglass windows had been opened, and everyone at the breakfast table could see what Castillo was describing in what he called Lesson Seven, Modern European History 202.

"You see that thing that looks sort of like a control tower? In the middle of the field?"

"There was an airstrip, Charley?" Jack Davidson asked.

"No. And don't interrupt teacher again unless you raise your hand and ask permission first."

Hermann and Willi, sitting on the floor playing with the puppies, giggled. Castillo turned to them. "And laughing at your godfather also is verboten!" They giggled again.

"As I was saying before I was so rudely interrupted," Castillo went on, "was that that thing that *looks sort of like a control tower* was sort of the command post for half a dozen other, simpler control towers, three on each side. There were telephones in the smaller ones, and the larger one had telephones and radios connected to the next level of command—"

Davidson raised his hand.

"Yes, Jackie, you may go tend to your personal problem," Castillo said. "But don't forget—as you usually do—to wash your hands when you're finished."

Hermann and Willi giggled again.

"Why is it still there?" Davidson asked. "Too expensive to knock down?"

"Otto and I decided to leave it up, 'Lest we forget,'" Kocian said. "It did cost a small fortune to take down the other towers and, of course, the fence itself."

"Thank you, Professor Doktor Kocian," Castillo said. "Turning to the fence. You see, about three hundred meters this side of the tower, a road—or what's left of one?"

Everybody looked.

"The road is a few meters from what was the actual border. The fence was a hundred meters inside East Germany. They reserved the right—and used it— to shoot onto their land this side of the fence. They also tried to mine it, but were frustrated in that endeavor by good old American ingenuity."

"You want to—" Captain Sparkman began, then abruptly stopped, raised his hand, and said, "Sorry."

"You're going to have to learn like Jackie here to take care of that sort of thing before coming to class, Sparky."

That got the expected reaction from Hermann and Willi. Even Otto smiled.

"American ingenuity?" Sparkman pursued.

"As my heroes, the stalwart troops of the Fourteenth Armored Cavalry, made their rounds down the road, they could of course see their East German counterparts laying the mines. And they of course could not protest. But once the field was in, and grass sown over the mines so that those terrible West Germans fleeing the horrors of capitalism for the Communist heaven would not see the mines and blow themselves—"

"Onkel Karl is being sarcastic, boys," Otto said. "The fence was built to keep East Germans from escaping to the West."

"Onkel Karl, you said, 'my heroes'?" Willi asked, his right arm raised.

"When I was your age, Willi, what I wanted to be when I grew up was a member of the Black Horse regiment, riding up and down the border in a jeep or an armored car or even better"—he met Otto's eyes, then Billy Kocian's—"in a helicopter, protecting the West Germans from their evil cousins on the other side of the fence. I could not tell my grandfather or my mother or anybody this, however, because, for reasons I didn't understand, they didn't like Americans very much."

"Why?" Willi asked.

Otto and Kocian both shook their heads.

"Getting back to the minefields," Castillo said. "Once the minefields were in—Bouncing Betties; really nasty mines—"

"Bouncing Betties?" Hermann asked.

"You didn't raise your hand, but I will forgive you this once. When someone steps on a Bouncing Betty, it goes off, then jumps out of the ground about a meter, then explodes again. This sends the shrapnel into people's bodies from their knees up. Very nasty."

The boys' faces showed they understood.

"Trying this one more time," Castillo went on, "after the minefields were in and the Volkspolizei and the border guards and the Army of the German Democratic Republic were congratulating themselves, a trooper of the Fourteenth reintroduced one of the oldest artillery weapons known, the catapult."

Willi's hand shot back up.

"The what?"

"I will demonstrate." Castillo reached for the sugar bowl, took out an oblong lump of sugar, and put it on the handle of a spoon. "What do you think would happen if I banged my fist against the other end of the spoon?"

"They get the idea, Karl," Otto said. "You don't have to—"

BAM!

The lump of sugar flew in a high arc across the table and crashed against the plateglass window.

Hermann's and Willi's eyes widened.

"That is a catapult," Castillo said. "So what the troopers of the Black Horse did was build a great big one, big enough to throw four cobblestones wired together. They mounted it on a jeep and practiced with it until they got pretty good. And then they waited for a really dark night and sneaked the catapult close to the minefield—and started firing cobblestones. Eventually, one landed on a Bouncing Betty. It went off. There is a phenomenon known as sympathetic explosion, which means that one explosion sets off another. Bouncing Betties went off all over the minefield.

"The troopers got back in their jeep and took off. The Communists decided that they'd caught a whole bunch of dirty capitalists trying to sneak into their Communist paradise. Floodlights came on. Sirens screamed. Soldiers rushed to the area. All they found was a bunch of exploded Betties and some cobblestones."

Hermann and Willi were obviously enthralled with the story.

Castillo was pleased.

"After that happened a couple of times," he went on, "they started placing their mines on the other side of the fence. That was out of range of the catapult—"

"Excuse me, Herr Gossinger," a maid said as she entered the room and extended a portable telephone to Castillo. "It's the American embassy in Berlin. They say it's important."

"Thank you," Castillo said, and reached for the telephone.

"Hello?"

"Have I Karl Wilhelm von und zu Gossinger?" a male voice asked in German.

Sounds like a Berliner, Castillo thought. *Some local hire who will connect me with some Foggy Bottom bureaucrat too important to make his own calls.*

"*Ja.*"

"My name is Tom Barlow, Colonel Castillo," the caller said, now in faultless American English. "Sorry to bother you so early in the day, but the circumstances make it necessary."

Okay, the American guy speaks perfect German. So what? So do I. So do Edgar and Jack.

But he called me "Colonel Castillo"?

"What circumstances are those, Mr. Barlow?" Castillo asked, switching to English.

"I thought that you would be interested to know that an attempt will be made on your life today during the services for Herr Friedler. Actually, on yours and those of Herr Görner and Herr Kocian."

"You're right. I find that fascinating. Are you going to tell me how this came to the attention of the embassy?"

"Oh, the embassy doesn't know anything about it."

"Okay, then how did it come to your attention?"

"I ordered it. I'll explain when we meet. But watch your back today, Colonel. The workers are ex-Stasi and are very good at what they do."

There was a click and the line went dead.

Castillo looked at his godchildren. They were looking impatiently at him to continue the stories of fun and games with Communists in the good old days.

[THREE]

When Castillo had been growing up in das Haus im Wald, he lived in a small apartment—a bedroom, a bath, and a small living room—on the left of the Big Room on the third floor. It had been his Onkel Willi's as a boy. To the right had been "The Herr Oberst's Apartment," twice the size and with one more bedroom that had been converted into sort of a library with conference table.

Everyone still referred to it as The Herr Oberst's Apartment, but it was now where Castillo was housed. Enough of the Herr Oberst's furniture had been moved out to accommodate Karlchen's bed and childhood possessions. The furniture removed had gone into the smaller apartment, which was now referred to as "Onkel Billy's Apartment."

Castillo had wondered idly who had made the decision for the change, but had never been curious enough to ask.

He remembered that now—*probably because of the soap opera and history lectures,* he thought—as he led everyone into The Herr Oberst's Apartment.

The room assignment was to mark the pecking order.

Although occupied as a perk by our managing director and his family, the house in fact belongs to Gossinger Beteiligungsgesellschaft, G.m.b.H.

I am the majority stockholder thereof, and so have been given the larger apartment. And Billy, because he owns what stock I don't, has the smaller apartment.

But who made the assignment—Billy or Otto?

"I hated to run the boys off that way," Castillo said as he waved everybody into chairs around the conference table. "But I didn't think they should hear this."

"Who was on the phone, Ace?" Delchamps asked as he sat down and pushed toward Castillo an ashtray that had been made from a large boar's foot.

"The name Tom Barlow mean anything to anybody?" Castillo asked as he found, bit the end off, and then carefully lit a cigar.

When everyone had shrugged or shaken his head or said no—or various combinations thereof—Castillo continued: "This guy told the maid—probably in German—that he was from our embassy in Berlin and wanted to speak to Gossinger. When I got on the line, he asked me—in German, Berliner's accent—if I was Gossinger, and then, when I said I was, he switched to English—American, perfect, sounded midwestern—called me Colonel Castillo, said his name was Tom Barlow, and that he hated to call but thought I would be interested to learn that an attempt will be made on my life—and on Otto's and Billy's—during the Friedler funeral."

"My God!" Görner said.

"I asked him how the embassy came into this information, and he said that the embassy didn't know. Then I asked him how he knew. And he said because he had ordered the hits, and that he would explain that when we met, and that I should be careful as the hitters are ex-Stasi and good at what they do."

"Why do I think we've just heard from the SVR?" Edgar Delchamps said. "I wonder what they're up to."

"You think this threat is credible?" Görner asked. "That the SVR is involved?"

"I think it's credible enough for us to stay away from the funeral," Castillo said.

"Prefacing this by saying I'm going to Günther Friedler's services," Billy Kocian said, "what I think they're up to, Edgar, is trying to frighten us, and I have no intention of giving them that satisfaction." He paused and looked at Castillo. "There will be police all over, Karl. The SVR is not stupid. They are not going to spray the mourners with submachine gun fire or detonate a bomb in Saint Elisabeth's."

"Uncle Billy has a point, Ace," Delchamps said.

"Karl, what I think we should do is contact the police," Görner said, "the Bundeskriminalamt. . . ."

"Otto," Castillo said, "we're pressed for time. We don't have time to convince the local cops or the Bundeskriminalamt that there even is a threat. All we have is the telephone call to me. And I'm not about to tell the local cops, much less the Bundeskriminalamt, that this guy called Gossinger is really 'Colonel Castillo.' And unless I did, they would decide that all we have is a crank call from some lunatic."

"So what do you suggest?" Görner replied.

"The first thing we do is circle the wagons."

"What?" Görner asked.

"Set up our own defense perimeter," Castillo said. "Protect ourselves. Everybody's here but the FBI. Now, we don't know if these people know about Yung and Doherty, but we have to presume they do. So the first thing we do is get them out of the Europäischer Hof."

"Get them out to where?" Kocian asked.

"Someplace in the open," Castillo said. "Where we can meet them and where we can see people approaching." He paused and then went on: "I think Billy's right. We should not let these bastards think they've scared us. Which means we will go to Saint Elisabeth's. You game for that, Otto?"

"Of course," Görner said firmly after hesitating just long enough to make Castillo suspect he really didn't think that was such a good idea.

"The boys and Helena?" Kocian asked.

"Surrounded by our security people," Castillo said. "Not sitting with us. We have reserved seats?"

"Of course," Görner said. "But I can change the arrangements for them."

"Okay. Now, what we need is a place in the open not too far from Saint Elisabeth's where we can meet. Suggestions?"

No one had any suggestions.

Finally, Castillo had one: "Otto, you know the place, the walk, just below the castle? That's open, not far from the church. . . ."

Görner nodded.

"That'd do it," he said.

"How quick can we get our security people over to the Europäischer Hof to take Yung and Doherty there?" Castillo asked. "They're armed, right?"

"Yes, of course they're armed," Görner said. "And I can call the supervisor."

He reached for the telephone on the table and began to punch numbers from memory.

"That raises the question of weapons for us," Castillo said. He looked around the table and asked, "Weapons?"

Everybody shook his head.

"This is Otto Görner," Görner said into the telephone. "Who's in charge?"

"It would take a couple of hours to get the weapons from the Gulfstream," Jake Torine said. "Presuming we could smuggle them off the airfield."

"So that's out," Castillo said. "Damn!"

"Hunting weapons here, Charley?" Davidson asked. "Rifles, shotguns, anything?"

"There's a cut-down single-shot Winchester .22 rifle in the wardrobe. Or there was the last time I looked. I didn't see any cartridges." Castillo paused in deep thought, listened as Görner finished his call, then said: "We have to get weapons from someplace. Otto, does the security service or whatever you call it have some sort of arsenal we can get into?"

Görner didn't answer directly. Instead, he reported, "The supervisor will move four men from the church to the Europäischer Hof, and take your men to the Philipps Castle. Which means there will be that many fewer to protect the Friedlers."

"The bad guys are not after the Friedler family," Castillo said. "They're after you and Billy. And me. Now, get back on the phone and call whoever you have in the Bundeskriminalamt and tell them you have learned of a credible threat to you and Billy and the Friedlers—no details—and to act accordingly. Let them deal with the local cops."

Görner reached for the telephone.

"Before you do that, Otto," Castillo said, "tell me about weapons. Is there anything here? Hunting rifles, shotguns, anything? Or can we get some from the security people?"

"I very strongly suggest we go to the police," Görner said. "They know how to deal with situations like this."

"Otto, right now I'm not asking for suggestions. I asked where we can get our hands on some goddamn weapons! Answer the question!"

"Cool, Charley, cool," Davidson said in Pashtu.

"Otto," Kocian said. "He may not look like it, but Little Karlchen is actually very good at what he does. If there are any guns, tell him."

Görner's face, which had been flushed, now turned pale.

"The Herr Oberst's drilling is over the mantel in my living room. There are several shotguns. And the game wardens, of course, are armed."

"Bingo!" Castillo said. "We have just found a Heckler & Koch submachine gun. Otto, get Siggie Müller on the line for me, please."

"The guy on the road?" Delchamps asked.

"That was an MP7 under his coat," Castillo said. "Maybe he'll know where we can find something else we can use. I don't want to walk into church trying to hide a drilling under my coat."

"Siggie'll know," Kocian said as he reached impatiently for the telephone Görner had just finished dialing.

Castillo looked at Kocian with curiosity but didn't say anything.

"What's a drilling?" Sparkman asked.

"A side-by-side shotgun," Castillo said. "Usually sixteen-gauge. With a rifle barrel, usually seven-millimeter, underneath."

"I never heard of anything like that."

"That's because you went to the Air Force Academy, Captain Sparkman," Castillo said. "At West Point, we learn all about guns."

"Screw you, Charley," Torine said loyally.

"Siggie, here is Eric Kocian," Billy said into the telephone. "I need to see you just as soon as you can get here. We're in the big room. Bring your weapon, preferably weapons."

[FOUR]

Müller appeared five minutes later. By then Görner had spoken to the Bundeskriminalamt, and was just hanging up the phone after speaking with his security supervisor.

"You been in the attic lately, Siggie?" Kocian asked.

Müller looked uncomfortable. He nodded but didn't reply.

"What's in the attic?" Görner asked.

"Something the Herr Oberst and I put there and didn't want you and Helena to worry about. Siggie did not like keeping it from you. I insisted."

"What the hell are you talking about?"

"When the Herr Oberst and I escaped from the Russians—"

"Escaped from the Russians?" Castillo asked. "I thought you were captured by the English?"

"That's the story the Herr Oberst told. He did not wish to further alarm his wife unnecessarily. We were captured by, and escaped from, the Red Army. We walked from near Stettin—now Szczecin, just inside Poland—to here. We saw the rape of Berlin. We saw the rape of every other place the Red Army went. It very much bothered the Herr Oberst."

"I don't think I understand," Castillo said.

"I know I don't," Görner said.

"Let's show them what we have in the attic, Siggie," Kocian said.

"*Jawohl,* Herr Kocian."

Müller led them to a closet off the sitting room. He took a chair into the closet, stood on it, put his hands flat against a low ceiling, and pushed hard upward. There was a screeching sound and one side of the ceiling folded upward.

"Over the years, there have been improvements to what was originally here," Kocian said. "The ceiling—the door—is now hinged, for example. We used to have to prop it open. And there were no electric lights here in the old days."

As if it had been rehearsed, Siggie stretched an arm into the hole. There was a click and electric lights came on. Then he heaved and grunted, and let down from the attic a simple, sturdy ladder.

He looked to Kocian for direction.

"I'm really too old to be climbing ladders," Kocian said, then climbed nimbly up it.

Müller gestured for Castillo to go up the ladder. He did so and found himself in something he realized with chagrin he had never even suspected existed. The area was as large as the apartment beneath. The roof was so steeply pitched, however, that there was room for only three men standing abreast in the center.

Against each side of the room were six olive-drab oblong metal boxes on wooden horses, just far enough toward the center so that their lids could be raised.

On each box—on the top, the sides, and the front—was a stenciled legend, the paint a faded yellow. Castillo squatted to get a look.

```
STIELHANDGRANATE 24
20 STUCK
BOHMISCHE WAFFENFABRIK A. G. PRAG
```

It was a moment before he remembered that under the Nazis, Czechoslovakia had been the "Protectorate of Bohemia and Moravia" and that the "Bohemian Weapons Factory" in Prague was the Czech factory that the Germans had taken over.

Kocian saw him looking.

"Hand grenades aren't the first thing that comes to mind when you hear 'Bohemia,' are they, Karlchen?"

"No," Castillo replied simply.

Delchamps came off the ladder, saw the boxes, read the labeling, and said, "I was really hoping for something a little less noisy than potato mashers."

Castillo and Kocian both chuckled.

Kocian went to one of the boxes and opened it with an ease that suggested this wasn't the first time he'd opened a crate of hand grenades.

What the hell. Why not? He was a corporal in Stalingrad when he was eighteen. He's probably opened several hundred ammo boxes like these.

Otto Görner, wheezing a little, came off the ladder.

"Ach, mein Gott," he said softly when he saw the ammunition boxes.

Kocian took something wrapped in a cloth from the box and extended it to Castillo.

"I considered giving you this when you finished West Point. But I thought you would either lose it or shoot yourself in the foot with it."

Castillo unwrapped the small package. It held a well-worn Luger pistol, two magazines, and what looked like twenty-odd loose cartridges.

"You know what it is, presumably?" Kocian asked.

West Point—or maybe Camp Mackall—came on automatically. Castillo picked up the pistol with his thumb and index finger on the grip, worked the action to ensure it was unloaded, then examined it carefully before reciting in English: "Pistol 08, Parabellum. Often referred to as the Luger. This one—made by Deutsche Waffen und Munitionsfabriken, Berlin, in 1913—is 9 by 19 millimeters. Also called 9mm-NATO."

Castillo looked at Kocian.

"It was the Herr Oberst's," Kocian said. "He had that with him at Stalingrad. And before that, the Herr Oberst's father, your great-grandfather, carried it in France."

"Jesus!" Castillo said.

"It is now yours, *Oberstleutnant* Castillo," Kocian said with emotion in his voice, and not a hint of his usual sarcasm.

"How the hell did it survive the war?" Castillo asked.

By then, without thinking about it, he had stuck his finger in the action and was moving it so that light would be reflected off his fingernail and into the barrel for his inspection.

"It's been used, but there's no pitting."

"I have taken care of it, Karlchen," Müller said. "Herr Kocian told me it would one day come to you."

"I envisioned somewhat different circumstances from these today," Kocian said, and Castillo heard the sarcasm now was back in his voice.

Castillo looked at Müller and again asked, "How the hell did it survive the war?"

"When the Herr Oberst—after he was freed from the hospital—was given command of the Offizier POW Lager, he left it here. He told me the war was lost, and he didn't want his father's pistol to wind up in the hands of some Russian commissar."

"Here in the attic?"

"No. Actually, he had me bury it in a machine-gun ammo box under the manure pile behind the stable. It was after the war that it—that all this material—was moved and placed up here."

"Tell me about that," Castillo said.

"Karl, we're pressed for time," Görner said.

"Not that pressed," Castillo said.

"I don't know, Otto, if you've ever heard this story," Kocian said.

"I have no idea what story you're going to tell," Görner replied.

"Well, by the time the Herr Oberst and I got here," Kocian went on, "this house was occupied by a company of American engineers. So we went to a farmer's house—Müller's father's house—on the farm. The Herr Oberst then became ex-Gefreite Gossinger, as he didn't want to be rearrested by the Americans as he would have been as an oberstleutnant. When I came back here from Vienna, he and Siggie's father were plowing the field with the one horse that had miraculously escaped both the German Army and hungry people.

"Two weeks after that, the Russians arrived. The border between the Russian and American Zones was then marked off, our horse stolen, and we were evicted on thirty minutes' notice from Müller's father's house.

"We came to the big house. The Herr Oberst planned to beg the American officer, a captain, for permission to live in the stable, and perhaps to work for food.

"As we walked across the field, a small convoy of Americans arrived at the big house. Two jeeps, an armored car, and a large, open Mercedes. On seeing this, we turned and tried to hide. No luck. We were spotted. A jeep with three MPs and a machine gun caught us before we'd made a hundred meters.

"We were then marched in front of the jeep up to the big house. As we got close to the Mercedes, we saw there was a senior officer in it. The Herr Oberst said, 'One star, Billy, a brigadier.'

"Then this brigadier general stood up and motioned for our captors to bring us close.

" 'I am General Withers, the Military Governor of Hesse-Kassel,' he said in perfect German. 'I came here today in what my staff told me was going to be a vain search for an old and dear friend. Hermann, the same bastards told me they had proof you had been murdered by the Gestapo!'

"The Herr Oberst . . ." Kocian went on, but then his voice broke. "The Herr Oberst . . . The Herr Oberst came to attention and saluted. General Withers got out of the car and they embraced, both of them crying."

"I had not heard that story," Görner said. "I knew that he knew the military governor, but . . ."

"The Herr Oberst was a proud man. He was ashamed that that friendship got him, got us, special treatment."

"You mean," Delchamps asked, "permission to start up the newspapers again? Charley told us about that."

"That came later," Kocian said. "That day, that very day, we were fed American rations—unbelievable fare; we had considered one boiled potato a hearty meal—and the engineer captain was told that his unit would be moved, and until it was, Herr Gossinger would look after the property. Staying in the apartment on the third floor.

"The Americans were gone a week later. A sign was erected stating the property had been requisitioned for use by the military governor. American rations mysteriously appeared on the verandah. American gasoline mysteriously appeared in the stable, in which captured German vehicles suitable for adaptation to agricultural purposes had also mysteriously appeared. Getting the picture?"

"What about the weapons?" Castillo asked.

"There had been several ack-ack—antiaircraft—batteries on the property," Kocian explained. "We found some of the weapons, and all of the hand grenades in the magazine of one of them. And others turned up. The Herr Oberst believed—as did your General George S. Patton, by the way—that it would be only a matter of time before the Red Army came through the Fulda Gap. We had seen the raping of Berlin and elsewhere. The Herr Oberst decided many would prefer to die fighting than fall into the hands of the Reds. So we moved the weapons here. Fortunately, they weren't needed. Until now."

"What else is in the boxes, Billy?" Jack Davidson asked from behind Castillo.

Castillo looked at him in surprise; he hadn't seen or heard him coming up the ladder. And then he saw something else that surprised him. Without making a conscious decision to do so, Castillo had been feeding the loose cartridges into his pistol's magazine. One was already full, the other nearly so.

"A little bit of everything," Kocian replied. "One of the boxes is full of hand grenades. Several kinds of *maschinenpistols*—MP-40s, MP-43s—plus a number of pistols, mostly Walther P-38s, but some Lugers. There's even American .45s."

"You just said the magic words, Billy," Davidson said. "MP-43 and .45."

"Jack, you can't go anywhere near the church—you can't go anywhere—with a Schmeisser," Castillo said.

"I can, Karlchen," Müller said. "I am licensed to have a machine pistol."

"Which means," Davidson said, "we can have a couple of spares for Herr Müller on the floorboard of the car he's in."

"That's if Siggie is willing to involve himself in this," Castillo said.

"*Ach,* Karlchen!" Müller snorted, suggesting the question was stupid.

"See if you can find a P-38 for me in there, Billy," Delchamps said.

"And a couple of .45s for me and Sparkman," Torine said. "And for Charley, too. Charley is a real .45 fan."

"Not today, Jake," Castillo said, in the process of slipping the Luger into the small of his back as he approached the ladder.

[FIVE]
"The Castle Walk"
Philipps University
Marburg an der Lahn
Hesse, Germany
1040 27 December 2005

The castle of the Landgraves of Hesse-Kassel—now the signature building of Philipps Universität—had been built at the peak of a steep hill. What had probably been a path hacked out of the granite had been broadened over the years—most likely centuries—into a two-lane cobblestone road against the castle wall. Sometime later, an area perhaps two hundred meters long and thirty-five meters wide had been somehow added to the steep sides of the hill. A neat little wall kept people and cars from going over the edge into the city below.

Castillo, the collar of his trench coat up and buttoned around his neck against the cold, sat with his feet dangling over the wall, clenching an unlit cigar between his teeth. Max, his natural coat clearly making him immune to the cold, lay contentedly by the wall. Siggie Müller, the drape of his Loden cloth cape revealing the outline of what had indeed turned out to be a Heckler & Koch MP7A1 submachine gun, leaned against the hood of Otto Görner's Jaguar.

Castillo was trying to follow his own advice—and for once being successful—which was that as soon as you have decided what to do, and put the decision into action, stop thinking about it and think of something else. That way, your mind will be clearer if you have to revisit your decisions when something goes wrong.

What he had decided to do was send Jack Davidson to have a look at the church. Davidson was a recognized expert in being able to spot places where a sniper—or something else dangerous, such as an improvised explosive device, or IED—might be concealed.

That decision had been implemented without even discussion. Edgar Delchamps suggested that it might be a good idea if he, too, went to the church and looked around. So both Jack and Edgar were at the church.

It had been Castillo's intention to send Inspector Doherty and Two-Gun Yung to das Haus im Wald. Both had made it clear that anyone refusing the services of two FBI agents—one of them very senior and the other a distinguished veteran of the Battle of Shangri-La—in these circumstances was not playing with a full deck.

Doherty and Yung, now equipped with P-38s from the grenade cases in the attic, were melding themselves into the crowds of mourners and curious—mostly the latter, according to a telephoned report from Inspector Doherty—at Saint Elisabeth's.

So were Colonel Jacob Torine and Captain Richard Sparkman of the United States Air Force, both of whom had shot down Castillo's theory that it might be a good idea if they went to Flughafen Frankfurt am Main and readied the Gulfstream for flight, in case they had to go somewhere in a hurry.

"We'll be ready to go wheels-up thirty minutes after we get to the airport," Colonel Torine had said. "That's presuming you can tell us where we're going. And while you're making up your mind about that, Captain Sparkman and I will pass the time in church."

Eric Kocian and Otto Görner and his wife and children, surrounded by twice their number of security guards, had gone to Wetzlar so they could be part of the funeral procession. Castillo was more than a little uncomfortable that Willi and Hermann were involved, but that decision, too, had been taken from him. Otto had decided there was no way the boys could be left at home without telling Helena why, and he wasn't up to facing that.

Otto said Helena would decide that if there was a threat to her and the boys, then there also was a threat to her husband, and he would just have to miss the Friedler funeral, something he had no intention of doing.

What Castillo was thinking of, to divert his attention from those things now out of his control, was "the castle walk" itself.

He had been here more times than he could count, from the time he was a small boy. He thought it was about the nicest place in Marburg. But when he had "suggested" to Otto that he have the security people bring Yung and Doherty here from the Europäischer Hof, he couldn't think of its name. It hadn't been a problem. Otto, an *alt Marburger*, had of course known where and what Castillo meant by "the castle walk." But Castillo hadn't heard him when Otto talked to the security people, so he hadn't heard what name Otto had told them.

It had to have a name—Universitätstrasse, or Philippsweg, or even Universitätplatz—and not remembering—maybe not knowing—what it was annoyed Castillo. So as he drove Otto's Jaguar up the hill, and then onto it, he started looking for signs. He had found none by the time he'd brought the car to a stop and he and Siggie had gotten out.

The castle walk was as he had remembered it, and he thought it had probably looked just about the same when his grandfather had begun his first year at the university. Or his great-grandfather.

Castillo remembered sitting here with his mother, eating a *würstchen,* and then, when his mother wasn't watching, throwing the sandwich over the edge and watching it fall. It was a long way down. Twice, he had managed to hit a streetcar. He had never been caught.

"Karlchen," Müller called softly, looking across the car and down the road.

Castillo looked over his shoulder.

A black Volkswagen Golf was coming up the road. The windows were darkened, and on its roof were multiple antennae neither available from nor installed by the manufacturer. It wasn't the car that had taken Davidson and Delchamps to the church, but Müller obviously recognized it as a security car—he hadn't bothered to move off the Jaguar, even when the Golf pulled in the parking space beside it—and Castillo was not surprised when Davidson and Delchamps got out.

Delchamps held a large, somewhat battered briefcase in his hand, and Castillo decided that was where he was carrying the P-38 he'd taken from the hand grenade box in the attic.

Castillo swung his legs off the wall and stood up. Max sat up, too.

"A very interesting development, Ace," Delchamps said.

Castillo raised his eyebrow but didn't say anything. Then he noticed that Delchamps was wearing gloves, some sort of surgeon's gloves but thicker.

Delchamps went into the briefcase and came out with what at first looked to Castillo like a small unmarked package of Kleenex, the sort found on hotel bathroom shelves and which some petty thieves, including one C. G. Castillo, often took with them when checking out.

Delchamps went into the package and pulled from it another pair of the gloves. He handed them to Castillo.

"Rubber gloves, Ace. Never leave home without them."

Castillo pulled them on.

Delchamps went back into his briefcase and took out a business-size envelope.

"Eagle Eye here spotted this in your prayer book," he said.

"What?"

Davidson said, "Your seats—yours, Billy's, and Otto's—were in the second row, right side. There were prayer books, hymnals, whatever, in a rack on the back of the front row of seats—"

"Pew," Castillo corrected him without thinking.

"Okay. *Pew.* A printed program was stuck in each prayer book. I saw this peeking out of the program in the center prayer book."

"And you opened it?" Castillo asked. "You ever hear of ricin?"

"Edgar opened it," Davidson said. "And yeah, Charley, I've heard of ricin."

"I stole those gloves from the lab at Langley," Delchamps said. "They're supposed to be ricin-proof. And a lot of other things proof. When the lab guy showed them to me, he said they cost thirty bucks a pair."

"Well, if we start soiling our shorts then dropping like flies, we'll know he wasn't telling the truth, won't we?" Castillo said and reached for the envelope.

"I don't think they want you dead, Ace. If they did, they would have just put whatever on the prayer books." Delchamps pulled, then released the wrist of his left glove; it made a *snap*. "But 'Caution' is my middle name."

He went into the briefcase again and came out with three red-bound books.

"Billy and Otto don't get no prayer books," he said. "They'll just have to wing it."

Castillo examined the envelope. It was addressed—by a computer printer, he saw; no way to identify which one—to "Herr Karl v. und z. Gossinger."

The envelope had been slit open at the top with a knife.

Castillo reached inside and saw what looked like calling cards. He took them out. There were four, held together with a paper clip. They were printed, again by a computer printer. One read "Budapest"; the second, "Vienna"; and the third, "Berlin."

An "X" had been drawn across "Berlin" by what looked like a felt-tip permanent marker. The fourth card had "Tom Barlow" printed on it.

Castillo looked at Delchamps and Davidson. Both shrugged.

Castillo handed the cards to Davidson, then took from the envelope a sheet of paper that had been neatly folded in thirds. He unfolded it.

It was a photocopy of two pages of the data section of a passport. Castillo saw first that it was a Russian passport, and a split second later saw that it was a Russian diplomatic passport.

Across the bottom of the first page was the legend SECOND SECRETARY OF THE EMBASSY OF THE RUSSIAN FEDERATION IN THE FEDERAL REPUBLIC OF GERMANY.

The second page had a photograph of a man of about Castillo's age. His neatly trimmed, light-brown hair was nearly blond. He wore a crisp white shirt with a neatly tied, red-striped necktie.

He looks, Castillo thought, *more Teutonic than Slavic.*

It gave his name as Dmitri Berezovsky. It said he was born in the USSR on 22 June 1969.

Which makes him four days younger than I am.

What the hell does that mean—if anything?

Castillo looked at Delchamps, who met his eyes and then said, "I think the passport is real, Ace."

Castillo waited for him to go on, and when he didn't, said, "And? Come on, Ed!"

"None of that could be traced back to your friend Dmitri. All you've got is four blank calling cards on which the names of three towns and Tom Barlow have been printed by a cheap computer printer. Berlin is X-ed out. So far as the photocopy of the passport is concerned, that could come from the Germans or whoever else's border Dmitri has crossed and had it stamped. Just about everybody routinely photocopies the passports of interesting people."

"All of which means?"

"First wild-hair scenario," Delchamps said. "What we could have here is a spy who wants to come in from the cold and has decided you have the best key to the door of freedom. And, of course, the CIA's cash box.

"He's proved that he knows who you are, knows where to find you, and suggests either Budapest or Vienna, but not Berlin, is where he would like to meet."

Castillo grunted, and looked at Jack Davidson.

"This guy is good, Charley. If he wanted to take you out, I think he could have," Davidson said.

"And Edgar's scenario?"

"I think he's on the money, Charley."

"No second scenario?"

Davidson shook his head.

"I don't know if this is a second scenario or not," Delchamps said, "but I wouldn't be surprised if this guy knows who whacked the Kuhls. And I'd sure as hell like that information."

"So what do we do now? Go to Vienna or Budapest and wait?"

"Yeah," Delchamps said. "But right now we have to go to the church. It's supposed to start in ten minutes."

"And you don't think anything'll happen at the church?"

"Dmitri told you he ordered the hit. And you responded the way he thought you would. The place is now crawling with cops and private security. I don't think any Stasi guys are going to commit suicide to get you or Billy or Otto. Not when they can do it quietly elsewhere. So you stay alive, which is what Dmitri wants."

Castillo looked at Davidson, who nodded his agreement.

"Okay," Castillo said. "Let's go to church."

Delchamps held out his hand for the envelope, and when Castillo gave it to him, dropped it in his briefcase.

V

[ONE]
The Big Room
Das Haus im Wald
Near Bad Hersfeld
Kreis Hersfeld-Rotenburg
Hesse, Germany
1630 27 December 2005

Hermann and Willi Görner went straight from the elevator to Onkel Billy's apartment, where Mädchen and the puppies had been left. Onkel Billy and everybody else went straight to the bar.

The service in Saint Elisabeth's had lasted almost an hour. Otto Görner had delivered the eulogy. Castillo had heard only a little of it. He hadn't known—as Otto conveniently had not mentioned his role in the services—that Otto was going to make himself a perfect target in the pulpit for almost ten minutes.

Castillo thought it quite possible—if unlikely—that Otto would be shot in front of his boys.

That didn't happen. Nothing untoward happened in the church, or in the cemetery later, if you didn't count the behavior of the goddamn press. When that had happened—both at the church and in the cemetery—Castillo suddenly had been conscious that press passes can readily be forged, and that the still and video cameras shoved in the mourners' faces could easily have concealed a weapon, if not a modified firearm then a compressed air system to launch darts tipped with ricin or some other lethal substance.

That didn't happen either.

The only thing out of the ordinary at the cemetery was that Eric Kocian told Otto Görner he was getting a little short of breath and felt dizzy and thought it would be best if he went back to das Haus im Wald rather than to the Friedler home.

Görner wanted to call for an ambulance, but Kocian insisted that he would be all right once he had lain down for a few minutes, and that he would ask Karlchen to drive him to Bad Hersfeld.

The minute Charley had driven the Jag carrying Billy, Max, and Jack David-son out of the cemetery, Castillo had asked Kocian if he was sure he didn't want to go to a hospital, or at least see a doctor.

"My medicine is in the house in the woods. Now just drive me there, Karlchen, at a reasonable speed, and spare me your concern. I know what I need."

Castillo thought he heard a snicker from the backseat, but when he glanced in the rearview mirror all he saw was Max putting his head on Davidson's lap and Jack ostensibly taking in the view of the glorious German countryside.

At the house, Delchamps, Torine, Yung, and Doherty were in the Big Room when Max led in Castillo, Kocian, and Davidson.

They all had watched as Kocian made a beeline for the liquor bottles and poured four inches of Slivovitz into a water glass, drank half, then smacked his lips and set the glass down.

"You want me to get you your medicine before you drink the rest of that?" Castillo said.

Kocian shook his head in disbelief, raised the glass, and finished off the Slivovitz.

"I just took my medicine, Karlchen, thank you very much."

Castillo laughed. "You old fraud! You weren't dizzy or short of breath!"

"Karlchen, which would have been kinder: To tell Gertrud Friedler that I thought I had expressed my sympathy enough and what I was going to do now was find the sonsofbitches who did this to him? Or to announce I wasn't feel-ing well?"

"*Touché.*"

"Pressing my advantage, Karlchen, I suggest that in the morning you and I—and the dogs, of course—catch the nine-oh-five fast train from Kassel to Vienna."

"You do?"

"That will put us—after a nice luncheon on the train—into the West-bahnhof a little after five."

"You don't want to fly down?"

"I don't like to fly, period. And the dogs have suffered enough from the mir-acle of travel by air."

"And have you a suggestion about what I should do with the airplane?"

"Aside from the scatological one that leaps to mind, you mean?" Kocian asked innocently, looked smugly around the room, then went on: "Jacob and Richard can fly the others to Schwechat, go to their hotel, the Bristol, and wait for us. Unless, of course, we get there before they do, which is a possibility. As soon as I have another little taste of the Slivovitz, I shall get on the telephone and ask Frau Schröeder to get us on the train." He looked at Davidson. "And, Jack, I will call the manager of the Bristol, a friend of mine, to beg him not to put you and your friends in those terrible rooms he reserves for you Americans."

Davidson laughed appreciatively, but said, "I'll be going with you on the train, Billy. I'll need a room where Charley's staying."

Kocian made a face no one would confuse with being friendly. "At the risk of sounding rude, Jack, I don't recall inviting you to go along."

"You didn't have to. McNab did."

Castillo chuckled.

"Who is McMad?" Kocian demanded.

"Mc*Nab*. And if I told you, I'd have to kill you," Davidson said.

Torine and Delchamps chuckled. Kocian glared at them.

"Think of him as Charley's fairy godfather, Billy," Delchamps offered.

"That," Davidson put in, "is a *very* dangerous choice of words."

"Yes, it was," Delchamps agreed. "I hastily withdraw that description and replace it with 'Charley's guardian angel.' "

"I thought that the Boy Marine was his guardian angel," David Yung said.

"Corporal Bradley is Charley's guardian *cherub*, Two-Gun," Torine went on. "General McNab is Charley's guardian *angel*."

Everybody laughed.

"Another very dangerous choice of words, Colonel," Davidson said.

"But, oh, how appropriate!" Delchamps said. "Charley's Cherub!"

"You do have a death wish, Edgar," Davidson said. "If Bradley hears that you called him that, you'll have one—probably two or more—Aleksandr Pevsner Indian beauty spots on your forehead."

"I have no idea what any of you lunatics are talking about," Kocian said.

Davidson took pity on him.

"Billy, General Bruce J. *McNab*," he explained, "is who I work for. When he sent me to work with Charley, his orders were to keep Charley out of trouble and never let him out of my sight. I hear and I obey. It's not open for discussion."

Kocian looked at Castillo, who nodded.

"Jack goes," Castillo said. "Jake, any problem about taking the Gulfstream to Vienna?"

"Not today. I've been—I am—tippling. But if I get to the airport by noon,

I can probably be in Vienna about the time you get there. Unless the weather really gets bad, of course."

Castillo turned to Inspector John "Jack" Doherty.

"Jack, any reason for the FBI—you and/or Two-Gun—to stick around here?"

"The guy from the Bundeskriminalamt showed us what they had, and what the local cops had. Conclusion—mine and Two-Gun's—is that it was a professional hit by people—probably ex-Stasi—who knew what they were doing and who now are probably in Russia. He said if anything turned up he'd let Otto know."

"So you guys can go to Vienna with Jake?" Castillo asked.

Doherty nodded.

"Okay, Billy," Castillo said. "Call Frau Schröeder. Set it up."

"Thank you," Kocian said. "And there"—he pointed to a small table near the elevator—"is a second line you can use for your call, or calls."

"And you have, I'm sure, a suggestion—or suggestions—of who I should call?" Castillo asked sarcastically.

"Well, Karlchen, I thought you might possibly be interested in learning what you can about Dmitri Berezovsky. Or is your relationship with the CIA one in which you feed them information, and they tell you only what they think you should hear?"

They locked eyes for a long moment, during which no one else even coughed.

Finally, Castillo said, "I would say 'touché' again, Billy, but that wasn't a gentle tap with a fencing saber. You just nailed me to the wall with a battle-ax, and that's my blood you see all over the carpet." He paused. "I guess I forgot for a moment what a tough old codger you are."

"Sonofabitch would be more accurate, Karlchen. I tend to be a real sonofabitch when someone doesn't seem to be as anxious as I am to find the bastards who murdered someone very dear to me."

Kocian walked to a coffee table, picked up the telephone there, then sat down on a small couch. Holding the telephone base on his lap, he began to punch a number.

Castillo pushed himself out of his chair, walked to the telephone by the door, and entered a long telephone number from memory.

"Lester," Castillo said thirty seconds later, "this is Colonel Castillo. Is either Major Miller or Mrs. Forbison there?"

"I think the cherub answered the phone," Delchamps said.

No one laughed.

[TWO]
Aboard EuroCity Train "Bartok Bela"
Near Braunau am Inn, Austria
1325 28 December 2005

They had two first-class sleeping compartments. Castillo, Jack Davidson, and Max were in one, and Kocian, Sándor Tor, and Mädchen and her puppies in the other.

Mädchen was missing one of her puppies, the male that Hermann and Willi had selected. She had decided that Max was somehow responsible and, when they were in sight of one another, either snarled or showed her teeth at him, making it plain she would like to remove at least one of his ears and very likely other body parts as well.

Max had assumed an attitude of both righteous indignation and self-defense. He obviously had done nothing wrong to the mother of their offspring and naturally felt obliged to show his teeth to let her know that he wasn't too fond of her, either.

Under these conditions, having the "nice lunch" on the train between Munich and Vienna that Kocian had promised posed a problem. Because they could not leave the dogs alone, it was finally decided that Davidson and Castillo would eat first. Sándor Tor would move into their apartment to restrain Max. Then, after Castillo and Davidson had eaten, Castillo would ride with Mädchen and the puppies, and Davidson with Max.

The dining car was two cars ahead of theirs on the train. At the rear, where Castillo and Davidson entered, it was sort of a diner, with plastic-topped tables. Farther forward, separated from the diner by a bar and serving counter, was a more elegant eatery. There were tablecloths and wine bottles and hovering waiters.

Castillo and Davidson headed for the forward end of the car.

Castillo saw something that made him suddenly stop. At the split second that Davidson walked into Castillo, Jack saw what had stopped Charley, and, as a reflex action, nudged him.

At the last table on the right were four people, a man and three women. Or—more accurately, after they had a good look—a man, two women, and an adolescent girl.

The man, who had made eye contact with Castillo, held his fork halfway between his plate and mouth. Then, as Castillo resumed walking, he put the food in his mouth.

He looks older than his passport photo, Castillo thought.

But that's not unusual.

It's him.

Castillo walked to the table and said loudly in English, "Well, I will be damned if it isn't ol' Tom Barlow! How the hell are you, Tom?"

Castillo thrust out his hand.

"Carlos Castillo, right?" Dmitri Berezovsky said. He stood, took the extended hand, and pumped it enthusiastically.

"Actually, it's 'Charley,' Tom, but what the hell! Jack, this is Tom Barlow. You've heard me talk about him."

"I sure have," Davidson answered, then shook Berezovsky's hand. "Jack Davidson, Tom. Going to Vienna, are you?"

"A business conference," Berezovsky said, and looked at Castillo. "*Charley,* I don't think you've met the better half, have you?"

"No, I haven't," Castillo said.

"Honey, this is Charley Castillo," Berezovsky said. "Charley, this is my wife, Laura, and our daughter, Sophie, and my sister, Susan Alexander."

The girl's about the age of Aleksandr Pevsner's daughter, Elena, Castillo thought.

And my Randy.

Except that but for blood my Randy's not my Randy.

The wife and daughter smiled a little uneasily, offered their hands, but said nothing.

The sister said, "How are you? Nice to meet you," as she offered her hand.

Nice English, Castillo thought. *But the Russian comes through.*

And then he noticed that she was beautiful.

I missed that until now?

What is that, tunnel vision?

"Charley, you know what?" Berezovsky said. "I was going to see if I could find you in Vienna. A little business opportunity I'd like to discuss with you."

"Oh, really? I'm always open for a good business opportunity."

"Well, we're still a couple of hours from Vienna. What I was thinking was if we could find someplace to talk. . . . I don't like to talk business in front of my family."

"I understand," Castillo said. "Well, how about my compartment? That is, unless you don't like dogs."

"Excuse me?"

"I have my dog with me. Some people are afraid of dogs."

"I love dogs," Berezovsky said.

"We're two cars back," Castillo said.

Davidson took tickets from his pocket, looked at them, and announced, "Compartment four, wagon three."

"Compartment four, wagon three," Berezovsky repeated. "Say, in thirty minutes?"

"Fine," Castillo said. He offered his hand again to Berezovsky's wife and then to his sister. "It was nice to meet you. Perhaps we'll meet again."

He smiled at the girl, who smiled shyly back. Berezovsky's wife again said nothing. The sister said, "That would be nice."

"There's a very nice Wiener schnitzel," Berezovsky said. "And the beer's Czech, from Pilsen."

Castillo smiled at him, then turned and motioned for Davidson to go to a table across the aisle.

The waiter appeared almost immediately. They both ordered the Wiener schnitzel and, at the waiter's recommendation, two bottles of Gambrinus, which he said came from eastern Bohemia and he personally preferred over the better-known Pilsner Urquell.

The beer was served immediately.

Three minutes later, as the waiter approached their table with the food, Berezovsky and party rose from their table and walked down the aisle.

Castillo waited until they were almost out of the dining car before asking, "Well, Jack, what do you think?"

"Nice ass on the sister."

"Nice boobs, too, but that wasn't exactly what I had in mind."

Davidson sipped thoughtfully from his beer, then said, "We'll just have to see what happens. I have the feeling that guy's a heavy hitter."

"Yeah. I think he is. And I think I'm in over my head with this. I wish Delchamps was here."

[THREE]

Castillo and Davidson had been in their compartment no more than five minutes when there was a knock at the door.

Davidson opened it a crack, then slid it fully open.

The sister moved gracefully through the door. She held four beer glasses by their stems in one hand.

Max stood up and looked at her, wagging his stump of a tail.

"Hello," the sister said.

"Hello," Davidson said.

Berezovsky stepped into the compartment. He held two foil-cap-topped bottles of Gambrinus in each hand. Max stiffened, showed his teeth, growled deep in his throat, and looked poised to jump at Berezovsky.

"Sit, Max," Castillo ordered sternly in Hungarian.

Max sat down but continued to show his teeth.

Berezovsky, who had frozen two steps into the compartment, smiled uneasily.

"Well, you know what they say, Tom," Castillo said in English, "about dogs being good judges of character."

"But I come bearing gifts," Berezovsky said, raising—slowly—the beer bottles.

"And you know what else they say, 'Beware of Russians bearing gifts'—or is that 'the Greeks'?"

"It's the Greeks and you know it," the sister said in English.

Nice voice. Nice teeth.

She sat down and crossed her legs.

Nice legs.

"Let the nice man in, Max," Castillo said in Hungarian. "I'll let you bite him later."

"Your Hungarian is very fluent," Berezovsky said in Hungarian. "You could be from Budapest."

"Yes," Castillo agreed.

The sister smiled.

Castillo smiled back.

"May I sit down?" Berezovsky asked.

"Make yourself comfortable," Castillo said.

Berezovsky sat down. Davidson slid the door closed.

The sister leaned forward and put the glasses on the small window-side table. Berezovsky almost ceremoniously opened a beer bottle and half-filled two of the glasses. Then he opened a second bottle and poured from it into the other two glasses. Then he passed the glasses around.

I would have opened all the bottles, Castillo thought, *and handed everybody a bottle and a glass. Why did I notice the difference?*

"What is it they say in New York?" Berezovsky asked in Russian. " 'Mud in your eye'?"

"Some places in New York," Castillo replied in Russian, "they say, 'Let us drink to the success of our project.'"

"Not only is your Russian as fluent as your Hungarian, but you know our drinking toasts."

"Yes," Castillo agreed.

And again the sister smiled.

And again Castillo smiled back.

"Not that you're not welcome here," Castillo said to her in Russian, "but I seem to recall my ol' buddy Tom saying that he didn't like to discuss business with the family around."

"Well," Berezovsky answered for her, "there's family, Charley, and then there's *family*. Permit me to introduce myself and my sister—that is, unless you already know who I am?"

"I know who you want me to think you are," Castillo said. "And when we get to Vienna, I expect to learn not only if that passport is the real thing, but a whole lot more about you."

"I'm sure there's quite a bit of information about me—and my sister—in Langley."

"In where?"

"In the CIA's Order of Battle in Langley."

"Well, there may well be, but—I don't want to mislead you, Tom—I'm not CIA. If that's what you thought."

Castillo saw surprise in Berezovsky's eyes.

"DIA?"

"And I'm not associated with the Defense Intelligence Agency, either."

Castillo saw more surprise.

Hell, he thinks I'm lying to him, and that surprises him.

Or worries him?

Castillo held up his right hand, the center three fingers extended.

"What's that?" Berezovsky asked suspiciously.

"Boy Scout's Honor. I am not an officer of the CIA, the DIA, or, to put a point on it, any of the other alphabet agencies, such as the FBI, the ONI, or even the notorious IRS."

Davidson chuckled, which earned him a dirty look from Berezovsky.

"You're playing with me, Castillo," Berezovsky said coldly. "And this is serious business."

"What I'm doing is telling you the truth," Castillo said.

"Then who do you work for?"

"That I can't tell you."

"If he did, Tom," Davidson said conversationally, "I'd have to kill you."

Berezovsky glared at him in disbelief, then stood.

"Let's go, Svetlana. We're wasting our time with these fools."

Max got up and growled softly.

"I don't think Max likes you, Tom," Castillo said.

The sister, still seated, smiled at Castillo, then looked at her brother.

"Sit down, Dmitri."

"I thought your name was 'Susan,'" Davidson said innocently.

She smiled at him and shook her head.

"Permit me to introduce myself," she said. "I am Lieutenant Colonel Svetlana Alekseeva of the Sluzhba Vnezhney Razvedki. Presumably, you know what that is?"

"The Russian Foreign Intelligence Service," Castillo replied. "Sluzhba Vnezhney Razvedki—SVR—is the new name for the same branch of the Service for the Protection of the Constitutional System. If I didn't know better, I'd think someone was trying to fool somebody."

Her expression showed Lieutenant Colonel Alekseeva did not share Castillo's sense of humor.

"Specifically, I am presently the *resident* in Copenhagen. My brother, Colonel Dmitri Berezovsky, is the SVR resident in Berlin. If I have to say so, he is also a member of the Service for the Protection of the Constitutional System. We are willing, if our conditions are met, to defect."

"Wow!" Castillo said, then parroted: " 'If our conditions are met'!"

"Come, Svetlana," Berezovsky said. "We don't have to put up with this."

"It is said that Dmitri would already be a general if his brilliance were not tempered with his impatience," Svetlana said, then added to her brother, "Sit down!"

She turned to Castillo and locked her eyes on his.

"Are you interested?" she asked evenly. "More importantly, if you are, are you in a position to deal?"

She does that look-you-in-the-eye thing like Aleksandr Pevsner does.

Does it come naturally? Or did somebody teach them how to do it?

She has eyes like Alek's, too. Light, sky blue. Very attractive.

"Am I permitted to ask why you would like to defect?" Castillo asked, his tone now serious.

"If I told you the truth, you wouldn't believe me," she said. "So I will say financial considerations."

"What figure did you have in mind?"

"Two million dollars," she said simply.

"And what would we get for our two million dollars?"

"That implies you have access to that kind of money," she said.

"And if I did, what would it buy me?"

"Our complete cooperation."

"I don't know what that means."

"The name, for example, of the officer who is replacing Lieutenant Colonel Viktor Zhdankov," she said. "Other names . . ."

"Viktor who?"

"The man . . ." she began, then stopped. "You know very well who I'm talking about, Colonel."

"The two million is the only consideration you're talking about?" Castillo asked.

She looked at her brother. He shook his head.

Castillo said, "While you two are mulling over answering that question, Colonel, why don't you tell me the reasons that I won't believe why you'd like to defect?"

She met his eyes again.

"I'll tell you that when I think you will believe me," she said. "After we go forward with this situation. *If* we go forward with this situation."

"That would depend in large measure on your other conditions," Castillo said.

"You're on the train," Berezovsky challenged. "Where is your airplane?"

"Assuming Schwechat is open, it should be there by now," Castillo said.

"And is it in condition to make a long flight on short notice?"

Which obviously translates to mean that you not only want to defect, you want to defect now.

Which means that you think somebody suspects that you want to defect.

And that would further translate to "I've got you now, Tom, ol' pal."

If the Service for the Protection of the Constitutional System and the Fight Against Terrorism is onto you, I don't need two million dollars to get you to change sides.

All I have to do is provide a way for you to keep running.

Where's the elation that's supposed to come with learning something like this?

Did I just fall into Svetlana's sky-blue eyes?

Well, what the hell. James Bond is always having some damsel in distress throw herself into his arms. Why not me?

"How close behind you are they?" Castillo asked, this time turning the tables on Lieutenant Colonel Alekseeva of the SVR and looking deeply and intently into her eyes.

"Are you going to answer the question?" Berezovsky asked angrily.

"We don't know that they are," Svetlana said.

"But the death of the Kuhls makes you think there's that possibility?"

He saw in her eyes that the question had touched a chord.

"Who?" Berezovsky said without much conviction.

"Come on, Colonel," Castillo said. "You know damned well what I mean."

"You just admitted you're CIA, you realize," Berezovsky said. "How else would you know about him, about them?"

"If you want to think I'm with the agency, suit yourself. But I just saw in Svetlana's eyes that I hit home when I asked about the Kuhls. . . ."

Berezovsky's eyes flashed to his sister.

And so did that look, Tom, ol' buddy.

"So, answer my question: How close behind you are they?"

Berezovsky gave him an icy look.

"We don't know that they are," Svetlana repeated evenly.

Castillo met her eyes.

"But the termination of the Kuhls makes it a possibility?"

"It is likely what happened to the Kuhls was intended as a message to somebody. It could be a message to us."

"Are you a believer in the worst-case scenario, Colonel?" Castillo asked, and then made a clarification: "Colonel Alekseeva?"

"Sometimes that's useful," she said.

"Do they know you're going to Vienna?"

She nodded. "The Hermitage is loaning to the Kunsthistorisches Museum Bartolomeo Rastrelli's wax statue of Peter the First. Do you know it, by chance?"

Castillo nodded. He had seen the early-eighteenth-century Madam Tussaud–like wax statue in the museum in Saint Petersburg.

"I'm surprised that the Hermitage would let it out the door," Castillo said.

"As a gesture of friendship and a hope for peace between old enemies," she said evenly. "Mr. Putin is now a friend of the West, in case you hadn't heard."

"I have heard that, now that you mention it."

She smiled at him again.

"It is very well-packed and traveling under heavy guard by road. From Vienna it will go to Berlin, then Copenhagen . . . and some other cities. This gives us a chance to see people we sometimes don't often get to see."

"The worst-case scenario being they will grab you at the Westbahnhof?"

"Or wait for confirmation of our treason when we meet our contact, or our contact tries to contact us. Both scenarios, of course, presume they know our intentions."

So this Let's Defect business didn't start last week, huh?

I should've known it didn't. . . .

"Who's your contact in Vienna?" Castillo asked.

"I've answered all of your questions," Svetlana said. "Now answer my brother's question about your airplane."

"Okay. What was it you wanted to know, Tom?"

"First, is it under your control?"

Castillo nodded.

"Is it available on short notice for a long flight?"

"Define 'long flight.' "

"Twelve thousand kilometers."

"Not without a fuel stop. The range is about thirty-seven hundred nautical miles. Where do you want to go?"

"Twelve thousand kilometers from Vienna," Berezovsky said.

"Buenos Aires," Svetlana added.

That shouldn't have surprised me—she mentioned Zhdankov—but it did.

"Why there?"

"That's none of your business," Berezovsky said.

"It is if I'm going to take you there. . . ."

"We have family there," Svetlana offered, "who can help us vanish."

"I'll need the details of that," Castillo said.

"When we're under way," she said. "At the fuel stop, I'll tell you."

Am I supposed to believe that?

"You are going to take us there, aren't you?" Svetlana asked.

She said, staring soulfully into my eyes.

Nice try, sweetheart.

Somebody must have told you of my reputation for being a sucker when beautiful women in distress stare soulfully into my eyes.

Who was it who said that the most important sex organ is between the ears?

But I'm not a sucker right now, thank you very much.

What I have to do right now is scare them a little.

"What I have to do right now is confer with Mr. Davidson to decide if what I might get out of helping you outweighs what you're trying to get out of me," Castillo said.

He saw disappointment in Svetlana's eyes.

And that makes me feel lousy, sweetheart.

But right now I'm doing what I know I have to.

Castillo went on: "So, what I think you should do now is go back to your compartment. On the way, see if anybody's tailing you. In twenty minutes, one of you—not both—come back, having decided between you what else you're going to tell me besides the name of a dead SVR officer's replacement to entice me to stick my neck out by not only trusting a couple of SVR agents I have never seen before and know nothing about in the first place, and then flying them halfway around the world with their former comrades in hot pursuit."

He stood, said in Hungarian, "Stay, Max," then stepped to the door, unlatched it, slid it open, and almost mockingly waved Berezovsky and Svetlana to pass through it.

"Twenty minutes should give you enough time to talk things over," he said.

Berezovsky gave him a dirty look as he left. Svetlana avoided looking at him.

Castillo slid the door closed after them, then looked at Jack Davidson.

"Give them ninety seconds to get off the car, then we'll see if Sándor can come up with some way to get them safely off the train."

"You got thirty seconds to listen to me, Charley?"

"Sure."

"Prefacing this by saying you did a good job with those two—which, considering the make the lady colonel was putting on you, couldn't have been easy. . . ."

"If you have something to say, Jack, say it."

"The only way I could get McNab to send me to work for you, Charley, was to promise on the heads of my children—"

"You don't *have* any children."

"Well, if I *did* . . . you get the point. I had to promise McNab—and mean it—that I would sit on you when it looked to me like your enthusiasm was about to overwhelm your common sense, as it has been known to do. I think that time has come."

Castillo looked at him for a moment.

"As a point of order, Jack, when the hell was the last time my enthusiasm overwhelmed my common sense?"

"Oh, come on, Charley! I don't know when the last time was, but I was there when you stole the helicopter."

"I didn't steal it. I borrowed it. And if memory serves, you were enthusiastically manning the Gatling in the door of that helicopter when we went after Dick Miller."

"I knew I couldn't stop you, Charley."

"And you can't stop me now, Jack. I think those two are just what we're looking for."

Davidson met his eyes for a moment, then shrugged.

"Okay. I tried. I'll go see if Sándor knows how we can get Mata Hari and her brother off the train."

[FOUR]

Castillo was surprised fifteen minutes later when he slid the compartment door open a crack and saw that both Berezovsky and Svetlana were standing in the corridor.

He expected to see Berezovsky alone—Berezovsky was, after all, the full colonel and she the lieutenant colonel and kid sister—or Svetlana alone, playing the damsel in distress.

He glanced over his shoulder at Jack Davidson, made an angry face that said, *What the hell?*, then motioned them inside and closed and latched the door.

"If this is going to go any further," Castillo said sharply, "you're going to have to learn to take orders. I said I wanted one of you back, not both. Now one of you leave."

"I don't want my brother making decisions with my life," Svetlana said evenly. "Either we both stay or we both go."

He met her eyes, hoping she would think he was doing so coldly.

After a moment, he nodded.

"Okay. What are you offering besides blue sky?" Castillo said.

" 'Blue sky'?" Svetlana repeated.

"All I have to do to find out who's replaced Colonel Zhdankov is get on the telephone. I don't have to risk anything."

Brother and sister looked at each other for a moment, and then Berezovsky asked, "What do you want, Colonel?"

"The names of the people who eliminated Friedler; ditto for the Kuhls."

"As you may have guessed, Friedler was dealt with by ex-Stasi," Berezovsky said. "I can give you the names they used, but they won't do you any good. Their papers were phony. I borrowed them from the Special Center. There was no reason for me to know their names, and they weren't given to me."

"You borrowed them for that one job?"

Berezovsky nodded. "I didn't want to run the risk of exposing my own people for that job. General Sirinov agreed and sent me men from the Special Center pool."

"Why did you eliminate Friedler?"

"If your question, Colonel, is why was he eliminated, I think you know. He was asking the wrong questions of the wrong people—the Marburg Group—about their past activities in the international oil trade and the medical-supply business. If you meant to ask why did I execute the operation, General Sirinov delegated that action to me."

"I'll want the names of your men."

"I understood that. But they won't be of much use to you. Once I turn up missing, they will be transferred. The unlucky ones will be shot for failing to learn what I was planning."

"And the Kuhls?"

"I can't help you with the Kuhls, except to say that that action was most probably carried out by the rezident in Vienna on orders from Sirinov. He probably used Hungarians—ex–Államvédelmi Hatóság—because I read in the paper that a metal garrote was used."

"You knew nothing about that action?"

Berezovsky shook his head. *"Nyet."*

"But you think it may have been a warning to you?"

Now Berezovsky nodded, and exchanged a long glance with his sister. "Svetlana thinks that may be. And it may have been. On the other hand, it may have been decided it was finally time to reward the Kuhls for their long service to the CIA."

You really are a cold-blooded bastard, aren't you?

Castillo looked at Svetlana.

And what about you?

A cold-blooded bitch, a chippie off the same block?

"So, what else have you got to offer me?" Castillo asked.

"I will answer—Svetlana *and* I will answer—any questions put to us to the best of our ability."

"And, of course, volunteer nothing," Castillo said. "I have heard nothing that sounds like it's worth two million dollars and putting my South America operation at risk."

"What I have to tell you is worth the two million dollars," Berezovsky said. "And more."

"Unfortunately, Tom, ol' buddy, you're operating in a buyer's market," Castillo said unpleasantly, "and this buyer doesn't think so."

"Tell him," Svetlana said.

Berezovsky didn't respond.

"Tell me what, Svetlana?" Castillo asked.

"There is a chemical factory in the former Belgian Congo," she said.

"There're also several in Hoboken, New Jersey. So what?"

"Weapons-of-mass-destruction chemical factory," she said.

Castillo felt the muscles at the nape of his neck contract involuntarily.

"That sounds like more blue sky," he said.

"If you've made up your minds not to help us," Svetlana said, "please be kind enough to tell us."

"Tell me more about the Congo."

"We know which German companies sold chemicals to it before Iraq fell," Berezovsky offered reluctantly, clearly unhappy, if not uncomfortable, that that chess piece had been put into play. "We know which German companies are selling chemicals to it now. And running it, of course."

"Running it for whom?"

"Who would you think, Colonel?" Berezovsky asked sarcastically.

"Answer that question, Colonel, and any others I might pose, or get the hell out of here."

Berezovsky glared at him for five full seconds.

"Iran, of course," he said.

"Why isn't whatever is being made for the Iranians in this factory in the Congolese jungle—"

"I didn't say it was in the jungle," Berezovsky interrupted.

"—not being made in Iran?" Castillo finished.

"How modest of you," Berezovsky said. "Because if it were, that information would have been in Langley years ago. The CIA is not nearly as inept as they would have us believe."

Castillo had a quick moment to look at Davidson. It was enough to see in his eyes that he, too, believed what they were being told.

"You know where this factory is?" Castillo said.

Berezovsky nodded. "Somewhere between Kisangani and Lake Albert."

"That's a large, empty area."

"That's why it was chosen in the first place."

"Chosen by whom?"

"Some chemical manufacturers in what was then known as East Germany. They said they wanted the land to grow various products for medicinal use."

Castillo looked at Davidson and mimed flipping a coin in the air and then looking to see how it came up.

"You just won, Colonel," he said. "That's the good news. The bad news is that if I find out you've been less than truthful with me, I guarantee that I personally will hand you over to the Federal'naya Sluzhba Bezopasnosti."

Berezovsky nodded calmly.

"Like yourself, Colonel," he said, "I am an officer. You have my word."

Jesus Christ, does he believe that? Does he think I will?

"You ever hear that Roman Catholic priests assigned to the Congo—at least in the old days—were excused from their vows of celibacy?" Castillo asked.

Berezovsky looked at his sister and chuckled.

"Is true, Svetlana."

"Well, much the same thing happens to West Pointers such as myself. When they give us jobs like mine, we are perfectly free to lie, cheat, steal, and get to be pals with other people who do."

Berezovsky thought that was amusing. Castillo saw in Svetlana's eyes that she did not.

"Okay, what happens now is that when the train pulls into the Westbahnhof, there will be *Wiener Tages Zeitung* trucks on each platform."

" 'Each platform'?" Svetlana parroted.

"You're familiar with the station?" Castillo asked.

Both nodded. Vienna's Westbahnhof—Western Station—was a major Austrian railway terminal.

"There're two tracks between the platforms. There will be a truck on each one. Nothing suspicious about them; they're there every day to load newspapers on the trains for the boonies—the countryside.

"When the train pulls in, you will already be at the end of the car with your luggage. If everything looks kosher—looks all right—two men will come to the car from the truck on the platform you'd normally use. They will load you into the truck.

"However, if it appears that people are looking for you on the platform, the men in the truck will create a diversion, and you will leave the train by the other door, which means you'll have to jump onto the tracks, get onto the other platform, and then get into the truck on the other side."

"And what if there is a train on the other track?" Svetlana asked.

"Then a man will help you pass through it," Castillo said.

"Where will they take us?" Berezovsky asked.

"I honestly don't know," Castillo said. "Somewhere safe. A man named Sándor Tor will be with you. I don't think we should risk being seen together."

"Is this man good at what he does?" Berezovsky asked.

"He was a Budapest police inspector and, before that, he did a hitch in the French Foreign Legion."

"I wish you were coming with us," Svetlana said.

So do I, sweetheart!

But are you saying that just to save your ass?

Or did those sky-blue eyes just tell me you meant it, that you're back to putting the make on me?

Careful, Don Juan!

"I think you should leave one at a time," Castillo said. "You first, Svetlana."

[FIVE]

The corridor side—as opposed to the compartment side—of the sleeping car was next to the platform as the "Bartok Bela" backed into the Westbahnhof.

Castillo waited until he saw that both trucks with *Tages Zeitung* logotypes on their sides were on the platforms and then stepped into the corridor. The trucks were much smaller than he expected; it was going to be a tight fit with four people and their luggage.

As Davidson waited in the compartment, Castillo looked up and down the platform but couldn't see anyone he wanted to see.

It would have been helpful, 007, if you had asked the nice people which car they were in!

Then he saw something he didn't want to see.

A departing passenger, a well-dressed stout gentleman of about forty, was suddenly hit in the stomach by an eight-inch-thick bound stack of the newest edition of the *Tages Zeitung*. The mass of newsprint knocked him onto his rather ample gluteus maximus and caused him to say very unkind things in a very loud voice to and about the cretins in the newspaper truck.

Castillo moved quickly back into the compartment. Davidson pointed.

Berezovsky was hoisting his wife onto the adjacent platform by her hips as Sándor Tor did the same for the girl. Svetlana was throwing their luggage onto the platform. A man in a gray smock took the luggage and threw it into the *Tages Zeitung* truck there.

Almost simultaneously, Berezovsky and Tor hoisted themselves onto the platform. Tor directed Berezovsky to the truck, then extended his hand to assist Svetlana onto the platform.

She was well ahead of him. She had hoisted her skirt to her waist, which revealed that she was wearing both red lacey underpants and, on her inner thigh, some sort of small semiautomatic pistol in a holster.

She then leapt to the platform with the agility of a gazelle, and, adjusting her skirt in the process, ran quickly to the truck and got in.

"I have always been partial to women in red panties," Davidson said.

"Being a professional, I was of course more interested in the pistol."

"You didn't notice the red panties, right?"

"In passing, of course."

"I noticed the pistol in passing. I have no trouble walking and chewing gum at the same time. It was more than likely a Model 1908 Colt Vest Pocket, in more than likely .25 ACP, although they made some in .32 ACP."

"It was my in-passing snap judgment that the garment in question was Victoria's Secret Model 17B, which comes with a label warning that there is not enough material in the garment for it to be used to safely blow one's nose."

"You don't think she gets cold, do you?"

"Russian women have a reputation for being warm-blooded."

"You better keep that in mind, Charley. I think that dame is trouble."

Castillo grunted. "That would appear to be the understatement of the day."

He picked up his briefcase and waved Davidson ahead of him out of the compartment.

There were three burly men in the corridor. Two of them were carrying the travel kennel. It now had Mädchen inside with her pups.

That was a good idea, Charley thought. *If Mädchen and Max had gotten into a fight, that would've been a real diversion.*

The third burly man blocked their way until Billy Kocian came out of the compartment and vouched for them.

As they walked down the platform and then down the stairs to cars waiting for them on the street, Castillo saw four different groups of men—two pairs, one trio, and one quartet—who could have been waiting for Berezovsky and the others. Or who could be waiting for anyone else.

The trio seemed unusually interested in Billy Kocian and the procession following him. Which of course could be attributed to Max and Mädchen, who were growling at each other.

A silver Mercedes S600 with Budapest tags was waiting at the curb. Kocian opened the kennel, motioned Mädchen inside the automobile's backseat, took a pup in each hand, and followed. A burly man closed the door, and the car immediately drove off.

A much smaller and older Mercedes pulled up. The burly man opened the front and rear right-side doors and motioned for Davidson and Castillo to get in. Max did so first, taking his place in back.

"Where are we going?" Davidson asked as the vehicle lurched forward.

"The Sacher," Castillo said.

"As in Sachertorte? The cake of many layers?"

Castillo nodded. "It was invented there. Billy has an apartment there."

"Room enough for us?"

"Room enough for us and half a dozen other people."

[SIX]
The Bar
The Hotel Sacher
Philharmonikerstrasse 4
Vienna, Austria
1925 28 December 2005

Colonel Jacob Torine was surprised to find Castillo feeding Max potato chips in the bar when he walked in, so surprised that he opened the conversation with the question: "They let dogs in here?"

"Only if they like you," Castillo said.

Sparkman and Delchamps chuckled; Torine shook his head.

"Let's get a table," Castillo said, nodding to a table in the corner of the red-velvet-walled and -draped room.

"When did you get here?" Castillo asked. "More important: Have you got something for me?"

Delchamps handed him a padded envelope sized to ship compact discs.

Castillo took his laptop computer from his briefcase, laid it on the table, and booted it up. He then pulled an unmarked recordable CD from the envelope and fed it to the computer.

"We were here—over in the Bristol—at eleven," Torine said. "Did you have a nice train ride down here?"

"A very interesting one," Castillo said.

Delchamps moved so he could see the laptop screen.

"I was about to mention that that disc is classified," Delchamps said. "But I see I won't have to. It's not working. What the hell happened?"

" 'United States Central Intelligence Agency,' " Castillo read off the screen. " 'Foreign Intelligence Evaluation Division. Top Secret. This material may not be removed from the FIED file-review room or copied by any means without the specific written permission of the Chief, FIED.' "

"How come I can't see that?"

"You're getting a little long in the tooth, Edgar. When was the last time you had your eyes checked?"

"Come on, Charley!"

"It's got a filter over the screen," Castillo said. "Unless you hold your head in exactly the right position—dead straight on—you can't read the screen. More important, other people can't read your screen."

"Where'd you get it?"

"Radio Shack," Castillo said. Then: "Really. I think it cost four ninety-five." Then he said, "Oh, good, this has got Lieutenant Colonel Alekseeva's dossier on it."

"You know about her?" Delchamps asked, surprised.

"Charley and I can even tell you the color of her underwear," Davidson said. "Professionally, of course."

Delchamps looked at him, shook his head, but didn't respond exactly.

"We had some trouble getting that disc, Charley," he said.

"Tell me," Castillo said, not taking his eyes from the laptop screen.

"Well, we got on the horn the minute we took off from Frankfurt. I told Miller what you wanted, and he said, 'No problem. I'll put Lester in a Yukon and send him over there. He's feeling underutilized anyway.' "

"And then?" Castillo asked.

"Dick called me back as we were about to land here, and said Langley was giving Lester trouble and the best way he could think to handle it was to go over there himself. That raised the question of how we were going to get the data without taking one of the AFC portables to the hotel and going through all the trouble of setting it up.

"Then Sparkman volunteered . . ."

Sparkman snorted.

". . . to stay at Schwechat and get the plane fueled, etcetera, and listen to the radio."

"That came in about an hour ago, Colonel," Sparkman said. "Major Miller said he had to call Ambassador Montvale to have him personally call the DCI."

"Montvale was supposed to have told Langley to give us whatever we ask for," Castillo said.

"That was my impression, too, Ace, but that's what Miller told Sparkman," Delchamps said.

Sparkman nodded and went on: "Major Miller said that some guy he didn't know said something about not wanting to interfere in any way with an on-going operation of the highest importance. He wouldn't say what that operation was. Miller said the guy shit a brick when the DCI said, 'Give him the dossiers.'

"And Miller said that's when, reluctantly, they gave him the female's dossier. What he said was that, when the DCI was in the file room, he said you wanted everything, and the DCI said, 'Give them everything.' That's one good-looking woman; who is she, Colonel?"

"Berezovsky's sister," Castillo said, then asked, "Edgar, how'd things go with the local spook?"

"Bad karma, Ace. Your reputation has preceded you."

"Explain that," Castillo ordered.

"Well, the spook is a her. Miss Eleanor Dillworth, ostensibly the counselor for consular affairs. She's a friend of Alex Darby's—or so she said; I'd like to check that with Alex—and I've never heard anything bad about her. But she was not what you could call the spirit of enthusiastic cooperation when I asked her what she could tell me about the Kuhls. And that was *before* your name came up."

"How did my name come up?"

"She asked what I was doing in Washington, and I told her I worked for you." He paused. "Ace, to respond to that pissed off look on your face, OOA is no longer a secret within the intelligence community."

"Shit. I guess I've got to get used to that. Okay, so how did she respond when my name came up?"

"She said, and this is almost verbatim, 'I know all about that sonofabitch and I want nothing to do with him.' I naturally inquired of the lady what she meant, and she said that, first, you ruined the soaring career of a Langley pal of hers and, second, you actually got said pal fired."

"Is that so?" Castillo said, his tone somewhat sarcastic. He looked at Delchamps. "She give you a name?"

"No. Is this none of my business?"

"The lady in question is Mrs. Patricia Davies Wilson. She was some kind of an analyst at Langley, and when she fucked up doing what she should have done with that stolen airliner, she tried to put the blame on the local spook. She said that not only was the local spook incompetent but a drunk, the proof of that being that while in his cups, he made improper advances to her, knowing full well she was a married woman. She probably would have gotten away with it had she not been, at the time Dick Miller was supposedly trying to rape her—"

"*Our* Dick Miller?" Delchamps interrupted.

Castillo nodded. "—Had she not been fucking me at the time. She lied that Miller was working his wicked way on her. That got her transferred. Then she went to C. Harry Whelan, Jr., the infamous journalist, and tried to blow the whistle on me. Whelan then went to Montvale with the dirt that he had on me, which was what Mrs. Wilson had leaked to him.

"Montvale—and I owe him big-time for this, as I frequently have to remind myself—not only turned Whelan off but taped their conversation, in which Whelan referred, several times, to Mrs. Wilson as 'his own private mole in Langley.'"

"Jesus Christ," Delchamps said disgustedly.

"Then Montvale played the tape for the DCI. And *that's* what got her fired."

"Women in this business are dangerous," Delchamps said.

"I was saying exactly the same thing to Charley earlier today," Davidson said innocently.

Castillo slid the laptop to him.

"Take a quick look at this, Jack, and tell me what you think."

Delchamps said: "I don't think the truth would impress Miss Dillworth very much, Charley. You're an unmitigated sonofabitch. What I think I should do is get on the horn to Alex Darby and get his take on the lady. Then I think I can deal with her. I'll start out by telling her what a sonofabitch I know you to be."

Castillo held his hand up as a signal for Delchamps to wait. He was looking at Davidson.

Finally, Davidson raised his eyes from the computer screen.

"It looks like the Big Bad Wolf and Little Red Under Britches are who they say they are, doesn't it?"

"Yeah, it sure does," Castillo said. "Jake, how soon can we go wheels-up?"

"I told you before: thirty minutes after we get to the airport. Where are we going?"

"Edgar, you can discuss Miss Moneypenny with Alex personally," Castillo said.

"Why are we going to Buenos Aires, Charley?" Delchamps asked warily.

"Because when Colonel Berezovsky and Lieutenant Colonel Alekseeva, the spies who want to come in from the cold, do come in from the cold, that's where they want to go."

"He's already been in touch? Christ, you just got here."

"I work fast," Castillo said. "Can we get out of here tonight, Jake?"

Torine nodded, and repeated, "Thirty minutes after we get to the airport."

Castillo looked at his watch. "It's seven-forty. Let's shoot for a ten o'clock takeoff. Sparkman, get out there and file a flight plan to Prestwick, Scotland. Then we file a new en-route flight plan to Morocco or someplace else that's our best and safest route to Buenos Aires. That'll work, Jake, right?"

Torine nodded. "Let me get this straight. We're taking this Berezovsky character with us?"

"And his wife and daughter. And, of course, Little Red Under Britches."

"What the hell does that mean?" Delchamps asked. "Why are you calling the sister that?"

Castillo exchanged glances with Davidson and grinned. "That's undercover spy talk, Edgar. You wouldn't understand."

"And if we told you, we'd have to kill you," Davidson added.

"Until this moment, Jake, I thought we were having our chain pulled," Delchamps said. "Now I don't know." He looked at Castillo. "You've actually got the SVR's Berlin rezident in the bag?"

"Plus the Copenhagen SVR rezident."

"I'll believe this when I see it," Delchamps said.

"Oh, ye of little faith!" Castillo said.

"If you think they hate you at Langley now, Ace," Delchamps said, "wait until they hear about this."

VI

[ONE]
General Aviation Apron West
Schwechat Airport
Vienna, Austria
2145 28 December 2005

"Work the radios, First Officer," Colonel Jake Torine said.

Castillo checked the commo panel, saw that the radio was set to the correct frequency, and pressed the TRANSMIT button on the yoke.

"Vienna Delivery, Gulfstream 379," Castillo announced.

"Gulfstream 379," the traffic controller replied in English, "this is Vienna Delivery. Go ahead."

"Gulfstream 379 at Block Alfa Six-Zero. We are a Gulfstream Three with ATIS information Bravo. Request clearance to Prestwick, Scotland, please."

"Gulfstream 379, Vienna Delivery. Your clearance is ready. Advise when ready to copy."

"Gulfstream 379 ready to copy."

"Roger, Gulfstream 379. You are cleared to Prestwick, Scotland, via the Lanux One Alpha Departure, then flight-planned route. Expect flight level three-four-zero ten minutes after departure. Squawk code 3476."

"Roger, Vienna Delivery. Understand we are cleared to Prestwick via the Lanux One Alfa Departure, flight-planned route, expect flight level three-four-zero, one-zero minutes after departure. Squawk three-four-seven-six."

The routing they had been given would take them briefly across the airspace of Czechoslovakia, Germany, and Belgium. Then, after crossing the English Channel, they would fly over the British Isles. Finally, they would be "handed off" to Scottish control for their final routing into Prestwick.

"Gulfstream 379, read-back is correct. Advise when fully ready."

"Vienna Delivery, Gulfstream 379 fully ready."

"Gulfstream 379, contact Vienna Ground on one-two-one-decimal-six for engine start and taxi."

"Gulfstream 379. Roger. Good day."

Castillo punched in 121.6 on the radio control panel, then keyed the yoke's TRANSMIT button.

"Vienna Ground, Gulfstream 379 at Block Alfa Six-Zero. Request engine start."

"Roger, Gulfstream 379. Engine start-up approved. Advise when ready to taxi."

"Gulfstream 379. Roger."

Castillo looked at Torine, raised an eyebrow, and drew circles with his index finger.

Torine shrugged, said, "Why not?" and reached for the Number One Engine start button.

"Vienna Ground, Gulfstream 379 ready to taxi. Block Alfa Six-Zero with information Bravo."

"Gulfstream 379, Vienna Ground. Taxi to Runway One-One via Alfa One-Two. At runway holding point, contact tower on frequency one-one-nine-decimal-four when ready for departure."

"Roger. Gulfstream 379 taxi to Runway One-One via Alfa One-Two."

"Gulfstream 379, Vienna Ground. That is correct. Have a nice flight."

"Gulfstream 379. Roger. Good day."

Castillo reached to dial in the new radio frequency of 119.4 as Torine rolled the aircraft to the threshold of Runway 11.

"Vienna Tower, Gulfstream 379 ready for takeoff Runway One-One at Alfa One-Two."

"Gulfstream 379, Vienna Tower. You are cleared for takeoff Runway One-One."

"Gulfstream 379 cleared for takeoff Runway One-One. Roger. Three-Seven-Nine rolling."

The Gulfstream began to move.

"Take it, Charley," Torine said. "You need the practice."

Castillo put his right hand on the yoke and his left on the throttle quadrant.

"I have it," he said.

Torine held up both hands in the air to show that he had relinquished control.

Billy Kocian had suggested, at just about the moment the same thought had occurred to Castillo, that Inspector Doherty and Two-Gun Yung would be more useful in Europe tracing the money trail than they would be in South America, so they had stayed in Vienna.

The only problem Castillo had with that was that he worried Two-Gun might not be as capable as Two-Gun thought he was in setting up the AFC satellite communications device. Two-Gun assured Castillo that Corporal Lester Bradley had taught him everything he needed to know about the radio, which forced Castillo to consider again that, as Two-Gun was not the typical FBI agent whose primary expertise was in tracing dirty money, Lester had skills far beyond those expected of a Marine Corps corporal two years short of being legally able to purchase intoxicants in the country for which he served.

For example: Having been tutored in the use and maintenance of the AFC satellite communications device by its inventor, Aloysius Francis Casey, Ph.D., MIT.

Casey—once a Special Forces A-Team commo sergeant in Vietnam and now chairman of the board of the AFC Corporation—maintained his association with the Green Berets by providing Delta Force—free of charge—with the absolute latest developments in communication.

The proof of that came thirty minutes after they had taken off. Two-Gun had called on the device to report, somewhat smugly, that he and the device had arrived in his room at the Bristol forty-one minutes before, and here he was already bouncing the deeply encrypted signal off a satellite twenty-seven thousand miles away.

Once contact with Vienna was in place, Castillo used the device to call Sergeant Bob Kensington, the Delta Force communicator who had been left behind in Argentina to man the device in Nuestra Pequeña Casa—OOA's safe house in the Mayerling Country Club in Pilar.

He told Kensington to give Alex Darby, Alfredo Munz, and Tony Santini— and absolutely no one else—a heads-up that they were coming, his best guess of their ETA, and to lay on wheels at the Jorge Newbery airport to transport eight people, plus Max, to the safe house.

He asked Kensington the whereabouts of the Sienos and was disappointed to learn that they were in Asunción, Paraguay. Susanna and Paul Sieno didn't have an AFC radio. Castillo told Kensington to get word to them as quickly as he could that he wanted the husband and wife at the safe house as soon as possible—preferably both together, but the wife absolutely soonest.

Susanna—a trim, pale, freckled-skin redhead—and Paul—with olive skin and dark hair—were CIA agents in their thirties. They had worked before for Castillo—for the OOA—but after the last operation Castillo had returned them to the CIA. Now he needed them back, especially Susanna.

Naturally, Kensington had asked what the hell was going on.

"I'll tell you when I see you, Bob. Right now, the fewer people who know we're coming the better."

Then Castillo made a final secure call on the AFC device, one to the safe house in Alexandria, Virginia. Corporal Lester Bradley answered the radio.

Castillo asked him to tell Major Dick Miller where he was headed, but again not why, and when Lester said, "Yes, sir," Castillo gave in to an impulse.

"And tell him to get you on the next flight to Buenos Aires, Lester. Go directly from the airport to the safe house there."

"Yes, sir," Bradley replied with considerably more enthusiasm than he had with his previous use of the words.

Castillo took off the headset and unstrapped himself. He looked at Jake Torine, who was in the pilot's seat.

"And was the cherub happy?" Torine asked.

Castillo gave him the finger. He pushed himself out of the co-pilot seat and went into the cabin. Sparkman then got out of his seat and went into the cockpit.

Castillo looked around the cabin.

Lora Berezovsky was sleeping on the left couch, daughter Sof'ya on the right. Both puppies were cuddled asleep with the girl. Max had begun the flight on the corridor floor next to them, but then apparently had—without disturbing either the girl or the pups—moved onto the foot of the couch, where he was curled up and asleep.

Colonel Dmitri Berezovsky was dozing in the forward-facing seat in the rear of the cabin. Lieutenant Colonel Alekseeva was in the rear-facing seat by the forward bulkhead, with Edgar Delchamps in the seat facing opposite to hers. Lieutenant Colonel Alekseeva was reading *People* magazine, shaking her head in disbelief from time to time.

As Castillo moved into the seat Sparkman had been using—the forward-facing seat across the aisle from her—this caused him to wonder, *Where the hell did that magazine come from? I hope she doesn't think it's mine.*

Jack Davidson walked up the aisle from the galley and went into the cockpit. He liked to watch the pilots—their piloting. Jack had a lot of time in the co-pilot seats of various aircraft that Castillo had flown, and he was actively working on somehow getting into flight school and staying in Special Operations at the same time. Everybody said that was just about impossible, but everybody didn't know Davidson as well as Castillo did.

Thirty-five minutes later, the public-address system speaker beeped three times, signaling that something was to be fed to the passengers.

"Rhine Control, Gulfstream 379," Torine's voice came over the speaker.

"Gulfstream 379, Rhine Control. Go ahead."

"Gulfstream 379. We need to amend our flight plan with a destination change. Our new destination is Dakar, Senegal, Identifier Golf-Oscar-Oscar-Yankee. Request present position direct Geneva. Over."

"Ahhh, roger, Gulfstream 379. I can clear you with routing direct Geneva, but I do not have the authority to clear you beyond Rhine airspace. You must coordinate further routing with Euro-control for clearance beyond Geneva. I suggest you contact Euro-control on frequency one-three-two-decimal-eight-five-zero for further clearance. Once I have received further clearance, I will contact you on this frequency. For now you are cleared present position direct Geneva. Maintain flight level three-four-zero."

The tone of the controller's voice suggested he had neither the time nor the inclination to deal with such a significant change to a cleared routing.

Torine didn't mind. What he wanted to do was at least get the Gulfstream pointed in the right direction—toward Senegal. He knew that Geneva was on the edge of Rhine Control's airspace boundary and probably would not be cleared beyond that. Also, he knew that making such a major change in their flight plan would take some time to coordinate with air traffic control. While en route to Geneva he would have Sparkman coordinate a new routing that would take them, after Geneva, over Toulouse, France; Malaga, Spain; Casablanca, Morocco; Tenerife, in the Canary Islands; then down the Atlantic Ocean just off the west coast of Africa; and finally into Dakar, Senegal.

"Roger, Rhine," Torine replied cheerfully. "Gulfstream 379 cleared direct Geneva. Maintain flight level three-four-zero. We will coordinate our request with Euro-control and will remain on this frequency. Thank you ever so much."

Castillo looked back into the cabin. Berezovsky's eyes were wide open.

What the hell, I'm a very light sleeper myself when my ass is in a crack.

Berezovsky was still awake and alert when the loudspeakers beeped three times again.

"Gulfstream 379, Rhine Control. I have your revised clearance. Advise when ready to copy."

"Gulfstream 379 ready to copy."

"Gulfstream 379, you are now cleared to Golf-Oscar-Oscar-Yankee. After Geneva direct Toulouse, direct Malaga."

This time, when Castillo glanced down the aisle to see if Berezovsky was showing any reaction to hearing the air traffic control conversation, the Russian was coming down the aisle. He reached Castillo and squatted beside him.

"I presume this aircraft has GPS capability?"

He has to ask?

Are the Russians really that backward?

Hell, he's my age; GPS has been around our generation practically forever.

Castillo nodded.

"May I see it?"

Castillo considered yelling for Davidson to open the cockpit door, then looked around the aircraft. Most everyone, including the women and child, were sleeping. He reached behind him and picked up the aircraft intercom phone.

"Jack!"

Davidson appeared in the cockpit door a moment later. He held a phone handset to his ear.

"Show the colonel where we are on the GPS," Castillo ordered into the phone.

Davidson waved Berezovsky into the cockpit.

The Russian went up the aisle and into the cockpit.

A minute or so later, Berezovsky reappeared and approached Castillo.

"Tom, you're just going to have to learn to trust me, ol' buddy."

Berezovsky didn't reply. He simply walked back to his seat.

Castillo sensed Svetlana's eyes on him.

Guess she wasn't exactly sound asleep.

"We have a training tape, a simulator, that shows that we're approaching Sheremetyevo," Castillo said to her, referring to the Moscow airport. "I should have had that running."

Svetlana shook her head. But he thought he noticed a smile.

"You're going to have to remember that he's a senior SVR colonel," she said.

"*Was* a senior colonel. Now he's what's called a defector."

"And that makes me?" she asked.

"*Former* Lieutenant Colonel Alekseeva, a much prettier defector," he said. "Who should also learn to trust me."

"Trust has to be earned, Colonel." She held up the *People* magazine. "You read this all the time?"

"From cover to cover," he said.

She smiled.

"Are you about to tell me the real reason—that I won't believe—why you're defecting?" Castillo asked.

"I told you that I'd tell you why we are—why we have—defected when the time was right. That's not yet."

"You promised to tell the details of the family you have in Argentina."

"I told you that I would tell you that at the fuel stop. We're not at the fuel stop, are we?"

"No, we're not."

"Where is the fuel stop?"

"Dakar, Senegal. From there we'll go to São Paulo, Brazil, then down to Buenos Aires. If we're lucky we should be in B.A. about five in the afternoon, which is noon in B.A. And since December is the middle of winter in Vienna, it will be the middle of summer in B.A. In other words, hot, very hot, and humid."

There's always a silver cloud. I'll very probably get to see Little Red Under Britches in a swimsuit at the safe house pool.

"We'll be flying through most of the night and most of what would be the day in Vienna. You might consider getting some sleep. That seat goes down almost flat."

"I think I will," she said with a smile.

"It might be easier to sleep if you took off your pistol."

She looked at him with what could have been surprise or indignation—or both.

"That holster must be uncomfortable," Castillo went on. "And you're really not going to have to shoot anybody anytime soon."

I'll be damned; she's actually blushing!

"Or would you rather I took the holster off?" Castillo added.

Svetlana's eyes turned to ice.

She unfastened her seat belt, stood, then marched down the aisle to the lavatory. Ninety seconds later, she was back. Without looking at him, she dropped the holstered pistol in his lap, got back in her seat, adjusted it almost flat, then turned on her side, facing away from him, and closed her eyes.

When Castillo took the pistol from the holster he saw that Davidson had been right: It was a 1908 Colt Vest Pocket. But chambered for .32 ACP, not .25 as Jack had guessed. He carefully ejected the magazine and worked the action. A cartridge flew out. He tried but failed to catch the live round, so he went looking for it. He found it under the seat, put it into the magazine, then put the magazine back in the pistol and the pistol back in its holster.

The elastic straps were still warm from her body, and he had a quick mental image of her leaping onto the platform at the Westbahnhof.

Careful, Charley.

Little Red Under Britches is a professional. One proof of that being she carries her pistol with a round in the chamber, just like big boys do.

He put the pistol into his briefcase, lowered his seat, and promptly fell asleep.

When they landed at Yoff-Léopold Sédar Senghor International Airport in Senegal, and Max made his routine visit to the nose gear, both pups and the girl followed him. Delchamps followed the pups. Castillo had thought that the only words to really describe the pups bouncing happily after Poppa, and then trying—and failing—to emulate his raised high leg, were *cute as hell.*

Castillo had glanced at Svetlana. She was smiling at the scene warmly, maternally, causing Castillo to think, *She sure don't look like no SVR rezident who goes around with a pistol next to her crotch.*

Svetlana didn't volunteer any information about her family when they had a mostly unsatisfactory French breakfast—bitter coffee and stale, too sweet croissants—making Castillo wonder if that was something she had invented to explain why they wanted to go to Argentina, and that there was, in fact, no family to help them disappear.

He didn't press her.

[TWO]
Aeropuerto Internacional Jorge Newbery
Buenos Aires, Argentina
1240 29 December 2005

Castillo had taken his turn at the controls on the Vienna–Dakar leg and again on the last, short leg from São Paulo, Brazil, to Buenos Aires. On the latter—having relieved Jake Torine, which put him in the left seat—he had, without thinking about it, made the approach and landing.

At the end of the landing roll, he glanced at Dick Sparkman in the right seat and saw the look on his face.

"I hope you were paying attention, Captain," Castillo said straight-faced. "If after much practice and study you can make a landing like that, then there may be hope that one day you can sit in the captain's seat yourself."

Sparkman shook his head, started to say something, and stopped.

"You may speak, Captain Sparkman."

"I don't know how to say this. . . ."

"Give it a shot."

"Colonel Torine told me . . ." He paused again, then said, "How many landings have you made in a Gulfstream?"

"Not many. Torine usually takes it away from me whenever we get within fifty miles of our destination."

"How many?"

"You could count them on my fingers. With a thumb, maybe both thumbs, left over."

"Colonel, you had a gusting crosswind, thermals, everything that usually adds up to a bumpy landing—and you greased it in. Colonel Torine said you were a natural pilot. I didn't know what he meant. Now I do."

"Flattery will get you everywhere, Sparkman."

"That was more surprise, maybe even awe, than flattery, Colonel."

As Castillo taxied to the private aircraft tarmac, his pleasure at the compliment was more than a little tempered by some reflection. If all the threats to a smooth landing that Sparkman mentioned had indeed existed—and Castillo had no doubts about Sparkman's judgment as an aviator—he hadn't seen them.

Which means I hadn't been paying attention as I damned well should've been.

That sobering thought left his mind as he approached the general aviation complex. He could see their welcoming party. In addition to immigration and customs officials, and their vehicles, he saw Alfredo Munz, Alex Darby, and Tony Santini standing in front of the wheels he had asked them to bring.

All I have to do now is get everybody through customs and immigration, off the airport, and to the house in Pilar without calling to us the attention of anybody really important—say, the Buenos Aires SVR rezident or Comandante Duffy of the Gendarméria Nacional.

How he was going to deal with Duffy—when he inevitably had to—was one of the things he had been thinking about when he had not been thinking about gusting crosswinds and thermals rising from the runway baking in the noonday sun.

"Shut it down, Sparkman. And keep everybody on the plane until I see what the hell's going on outside."

When Castillo opened the stair door, and the decreasing whine of the engines filled the cabin, he called out, "Everybody stay on the plane until I give the okay."

He went down the stair door and then across the tarmac. He saw Alex Darby, Tony Santini, and Alfredo Munz start walking on the heels of the Argentine officials who were already headed for him and the Gulfstream.

At the top of the stairs, Max shouldered Sparkman out of the way. He made his way down the stairs for his ritual visit to the nose wheel. One of his pups followed him, and then the other. Sof'ya Berezovsky went after the pups. Former Lieutenant Colonel Svetlana Alekseeva of the SVR, in her role as aunt, went after Sof'ya. Edgar Delchamps went after Colonel Alekseeva.

One of the Argentine officials, not smiling, put out his hand. "Documents, please."

"I'll have to get them," Castillo said in Spanish with a smile. He hoped that if he sounded like a Porteño he might get a smile in return.

He turned and saw for the first time that Delchamps, Svetlana, Sof'ya, and the dogs were off the airplane.

He walked back to Svetlana, who was standing at the foot of the step door.

"Get back on the airplane," he ordered. "Get everybody's passports." He looked up and into the airplane and saw Davidson. "Jack, get the airplane's papers and the Americans' passports."

Svetlana went up the stairs.

A moment later, Davidson and Sparkman came down the stairs with all the passports and the aircraft's documents.

They formed a fire-bucket line, and their luggage began to come off the plane. Castillo saw that Svetlana had taken her place in the line.

And then he saw that Svetlana's skirt was either Loden cloth or something heavy like it.

Jesus, that's about the worst thing she could be wearing here.

This is the hottest part of the summer.

The customs officer began a perfunctory inspection of the luggage. A man from Jet Aviation Service began to deal with Torine about landing fees, parking fees, and fuel.

"Very nice, Charley," Santini said to Castillo, vis-à-vis Lieutenant Colonel Alekseeva. "I have always been partial to redheads."

Redhead?

Castillo looked. What had looked like dark brown hair now indeed, in the bright sunlight, looked red. Dark red, but red.

"My relationship with the lady is purely professional, Tony," Castillo said.

"Sure it is."

"She is—they are—people I want to get to our house in Pilar safely and without attracting attention. When that's done, I'll tell you all about them."

"Who are they?"

"Later, Tony."

Santini heard the tone in his voice and didn't push.

"Wheels?" Castillo asked.

"I have my car and an embassy Suburban," Darby said, offering his hand. "Welcome back, Charley."

"And I've got my car," Tony Santini said. "And Munz has his."

Munz saw there was some problem with the customs or immigration officers and went to deal with it.

"The Sienos?" Castillo asked.

"He's not coming," Darby said, "and she couldn't get on the morning plane. She may not be able to get a seat on the afternoon plane, either."

"Shit!"

"Kensington said that Miller called and said Bradley would be on the Aerolíneas Argentinas flight out of Miami tonight."

"What's going on, Charley?" Darby asked.

"It'll have to wait until we're in Nuestra Pequeña Casa," Castillo said, nodding toward Munz, who was walking back to them, his left fist balled with the thumb extended, signaling that all was okay.

[THREE]
Nuestra Pequeña Casa
Mayerling Country Club
Pilar, Buenos Aires Province, Argentina
1545 29 December 2005

"Our Little House" in the exclusive Mayerling Country Club in the Buenos Aires suburb of Pilar had been rented on a two-year lease for four thousand U.S. dollars a month by Señor Paul Sieno and his wife, Susanna. The owner believed them to be fellow Argentines, an affluent young couple from Mendoza.

That the attractive pair was affluent seemed to the owner to be proven when they didn't try to bargain about the monthly rent or his demand that he be paid the first and last months' rent plus a security deposit equal to another two months' rent *before* they moved in. He had the money in hand—sixteen thousand dollars, in U.S. currency—the day after he had asked for it.

Nuestra Pequeña Casa—the owner had named it—could fairly be described as a mansion in a neighborhood of mansions. Mayerling was several kilometers off the Panamericana, a toll superhighway, and fifty-odd kilometers from Plaza del Congreso, the monolith in front of the Congress in central Buenos Aires, from which all distances in Argentina are measured.

Argentine law defined "country club" as a gated community in which at least thirty percent of the land was given over to such things as polo fields, golf courses, and other green areas. Further, a "gated community" in Argentina meant a private neighborhood enclosed by ten-foot-tall fences topped with razor wire, equipped with motion-sensing devices, and patrolled by private security guards armed with pistols, shotguns, and in some cases Uzis.

Mayerling far exceeded the minimum green-space requirements of the law. There were five polo fields and two Jack Nicklaus–designed golf courses. The smallest lot within its ten-foot walls was one hectare, or 2.45 acres.

"Mayerling," Castillo had noted when the Sienos first rented the property, was also the name of the Royal and Imperial hunting lodge outside Vienna where—depending on which version one chose to believe—Crown Prince Rudolph had shot his sixteen-year-old mistress and then himself, or Crown Prince Rudolph had been shot at the orders of his father, Emperor Franz Josef, who believed young Rudy was planning to split the Austro-Hungarian Empire by becoming King of Hungary.

Many of the homes in Mayerling were built on two or more lots. Nuestra Pequeña Casa was built on two, and had six bedrooms, all with bath and dressing room, three other toilets with bidets, a library, a sitting room, a dining room, a kitchen, servants' quarters (for four), a swimming pool, and, in the backyard near the pool, a *quincho.*

A quincho was something like an American pool house, except that it was primarily intended as a place to eat, more or less outdoors, and had a wood-fired grill for this purpose.

Our Little House's quincho was solidly built of masonry and had a rugged roof of mottled red Spanish tiles. It had a deep verandah, which also was covered by the tile roof, and a wall of sliding glass doors that overlooked the pool.

Like most of the houses in Mayerling, Nuestra Pequeña Casa was individually fenced on three sides, the fences concealed in closely packed pine trees. They, too, had motion-sensing devices. Motion-sensing devices also protected the unfenced front of the house.

The house—indeed all of Mayerling—had been constructed on a cost-be-damned basis to provide its residents with luxury, privacy, and, above all, security, as kidnapping of the rich was one of the more profitable cottage industries in Argentina.

And all of this, of course, made Nuestra Pequeña Casa ideal for the Office of Organizational Analysis, which needed a safe house. Within the intelligence community, a safe house was defined as a place the bad guys didn't know about, a place where one may hide things and people.

Jack and Sandra Britton and Bob Kensington, all in bathing suits, were standing on the verandah of Nuestra Pequeña Casa when the little convoy rolled up. The housekeeper and a maid stood behind them.

The moment Castillo opened the door of the embassy Suburban, the heat and humidity of an Argentine summer afternoon hit him. He stood there and again thought of the Russian women in clothing intended for winter in Northern Europe.

Castillo slammed the door shut and walked up to the house.

"Well, we didn't expect to see you so soon," Britton greeted him, putting out his hand.

"Unexpected things happen," Castillo said lightly, then changed his tone. "From this moment, we're going to run this place tight. First thing: We get everybody out of the vehicles and into the foyer. Kensington, get a weapon."

Sergeant Kensington took one step backward into the house, reached down, and came up holding an Uzi at his side.

"I should have known better, Bob. Sorry."

Castillo saw Sandra Britton looked like she was about to say something. "Sandra, please go inside and save your lip for later."

She gave him a dirty look, glanced at her husband, but went into the house.

The expression on Jack Britton's face showed he didn't like Castillo's curtness to his wife, though he didn't say anything.

"Bob," Castillo went on, "stay where you are. Jack, go to the Suburban and open the rear door. Tell the people in there to get out and into the house."

"Who are they?" Britton asked.

"Indulge me, Jack. Just do it."

Max erupted from the Suburban the moment the rear door was opened and ran into the house. Then Sof'ya, holding one of the pups, slid off the seat and to the ground.

"Bring him into the house, sweetheart, please," Castillo called to her in Russian.

The smile on Sof'ya's face vanished when she saw Kensington and the submachine gun. She looked back at the Suburban, then at Castillo.

"It's okay, sweetheart," Castillo called as Sof'ya's mother, holding the other puppy, slid awkwardly off the Suburban's high seat and onto the ground.

"Right this way, please, Mrs. Berezovsky," Castillo said, and then, switching to English, called, "Now the Mercedes, Jack. Watch this one!"

Kensington went to the second vehicle, Alfredo Munz's Mercedes 230 SUV. He opened the front passenger door, then, seeing no one in the front passenger seat, closed it and opened the rear door.

Lieutenant Colonel Alekseeva got out, with a show of leg, and looked around.

"Over here, please, Colonel," Castillo ordered in Russian, gesturing toward the open door.

She walked quickly to the house and went inside without looking directly at Castillo.

"And now Santini's car," Castillo called in English. "And really watch this one."

Britton opened the passenger door of Santini's Peugeot sedan. Colonel Berezovsky got out and looked around. Santini came quickly around the front of the car as Edgar Delchamps got out of the backseat.

Delchamps gestured for Berezovsky to go into the house. After a moment— long enough to demonstrate that he wasn't going to jump at anybody's command—Berezovsky walked to the house and went inside.

Castillo followed Berezovsky into the foyer.

"We're now going to move to the quincho," Castillo announced in Russian. "Before we go out there, I want to tell you the area is fenced. You are forbidden to get closer than two meters to the fence. If you do, you will be shot."

He turned to Jack Davidson. "Get a weapon . . ."

"Behind you in the closet," Kensington offered.

". . . and take them out there. I'll have something cold sent out for them to drink. And while you're doing that, and the luggage is being brought in from the cars, I'll bring everybody up to speed."

[FOUR]

"Okay," Castillo said, winding up his briefing of Alex Darby, Tony Santini, and the Brittons in the main house. "That's about it."

"It's hard to believe that woman is a Russian spy," Sandra said.

Castillo flashed her a cold look, and then, seeing her face, immediately recognized he was wrong. Sandra wasn't being clever; she was stating the obvious.

"Well, she is, Sandra," he said. "And what is it they say about 'the female being the deadlier of any species'?"

Sandra almost sadly nodded her understanding.

"Oops," Castillo said. "Code names. I don't want anybody using their real names or the phrase 'the Russians' or anything like that. So, from this moment, when you're talking about them, Berezovsky is Big Bad Wolf. His wife is Mrs. Wolf. Sof'ya is the Cub. Colonel Alekseeva is Little Red Under Britches."

Sandra's eyebrow rose at that, but she didn't say anything.

"Dealing with Little Red Under Britches is going to be a problem until Susanna Sieno can get here from Asunción, probably before noon tomorrow. Until then, we're fucked." He heard what he had said. "Sorry, Sandra. It's been a long couple of days, and I'm a little . . ."

" 'Fucked up'?" Sandra replied. "I've heard the word, Charley. Not only am I a semanticist, for many long and painful years I have been married to a Philadelphia cop. They tend to use the 'For Unlawful Carnal Knowledge' acronym at least once every sixty seconds."

He smiled at her. "Is that what it means?"

"According to Sherlock Holmes, that's what the London bobbies wrote on their blotter when they locked up a hooker for practicing her profession."

Castillo glanced at Jack Britton, then said, "According to *your* Sherlock Holmes, you mean?"

"I think the other one's dead," Sandra replied, straight-faced, and then went on: "Charley, I don't want to put my nose in where it doesn't belong, but this schoolteacher volunteers for anything you think I can do."

Jack Britton said: "Little Red Riding Hood—"

"'Under Britches,'" Castillo automatically corrected him. "Little Red Under Britches."

"I'd *love* to know the etymological root of *that*," Sandra Britton said.

"—doesn't know that Sandra's a professor," Jack Britton finished.

Sandra added: "And while I don't think I could render the lady colonel *hors de combat* with a karate chop, I am famous for my icy stare's ability to silence a roomful of obstreperous students."

"Jack, did the State Department issue you a diplomatic passport?"

"The embassy gave us both one the minute we walked in the door. I don't even know what it's good for."

"It identifies you as a diplomat," Castillo explained. "Which means you can't be searched and then arrested for carrying a concealed weapon."

"Really?" Sandra said. "When do I get my gun?"

"Do you know how to use one?"

"Sherlock here took me shooting on our honeymoon."

"You sure you want to get involved?"

"You said there may be a connection between all the things that have happened. And in the course of one of those things, my new car and house got shot up. Hell yes I want to get involved."

"Congratulations, Mrs. Britton," Castillo said formally. "You are now a member of the Office of Organizational Analysis. Just as soon as we have a moment, I'll get you on the horn with Agnes Forbison and we'll get you on the payroll."

"You're serious," Jack Britton, surprised, declared out loud.

"In the words of your bride, 'Hell yes.'"

Castillo had just decided that Sandra Britton being here was a fortunate happenstance.

He had also just realized that neither Darby nor Santini had opened their mouths, not even to ask questions.

That could be because my briefing was brilliant, covering absolutely everything that needed to be said.

No questions necessary.

More likely, however, it's because they don't like what they heard and are deciding how and when they can tactfully suggest to the boss that he's about to fuck up by the numbers.

When Castillo walked over to the quincho with the Brittons, Alex Darby, and Tony Santini, sitting on its verandah were Alfredo Munz, Edgar Delchamps, and Jack Davidson. Munz was holding a bottle of Coca-Cola; Delchamps and Davidson, liter bottles of Quilmes beer.

"Kensington?" Castillo asked.

"With our guests," Delchamps said, jerking his thumb toward the interior of the quincho.

"Everybody up to speed?" Castillo asked.

"Ace, is this where you ask, 'Any questions or comments?' " Delchamps said.

Castillo shrugged. "Okay. Any questions or comments?"

"Charley," Darby said, "you're aware that there is a U.S. government agency that's charged not only with trying to get the bad guys—and girls, come to think of it—to change sides but has all the facilities in place to deal effectively with them. Yes? They call it the CIA."

"I've heard that."

"With that in mind," Darby went on, "now that you've gotten Berezovsky and family safely out of Europe—where, I suspect, they were about to be grabbed by the Sluzhba Vnezhney Razvedki and/or the Federal'naya Sluzhba Bezopasnosti, which, I also presume you know is charged with keeping defectors from defecting—"

"Why don't I just get on the horn," Castillo interrupted reasonably, "and call Langley and have them send a plane down here to take our guests off our hands?"

"Yeah," Darby said. "Why don't you?"

"I'm glad you brought that up, Alex. It reminds me of something else I've forgotten to do. Alex, if you happen to have a friendly conversation with your pal Miss Eleanor Dillworth in Vienna, you have no idea where I am, and you never heard of Berezovsky and company."

"What?" Darby said.

"I didn't get into that," Delchamps said.

"Into what?" Darby asked.

"Miss Dillworth is not a big fan of our leader," Delchamps offered.

"*Your* leader. I work for Langley."

"No, Alex," Castillo said, "you don't. Ambassador Montvale has informed the DCI that—at the direction of the President—the CIA is to furnish the OOA—me—with whatever assets I think I need. You are such an asset. I don't mean to get starchy, but it's necessary. You will not tell the CIA or anyone else that you have been requisitioned. That's an order, Top Secret Presidential, as was what I said before about the woman in Vienna. Clear, Alex?"

Darby's face whitened.

"He does have the authority, Alex," Delchamps said. "You'd better say, 'Yes, sir.'"

"Jesus Christ!" Darby blurted.

"That's close enough," Castillo said.

"Are you now going to tell us what's going on, Ace?"

"Two things," Castillo said. "One is that I'm following my original orders, which remain in force until the man who issued them—and no one else—changes them. Those orders are to 'find and render harmless' whoever is responsible for the murder of Jack The Stack Masterson. I think that may be a General Sirinov; Berezovsky mentioned his name. He said Sirinov ordered the elimination of the Kuhls, Friedler, and Billy, Otto, and me. I think he probably had something to do with what happened to Jack and Sandra and to Liam Duffy.

"Second, Berezovsky said—for the two million bucks I promised him—that he would give me the details about a chemical factory in Congo-Kinshasa making some kind of weapon of mass destruction. I thought he was telling the truth, and so did Davidson."

Davidson nodded.

"So," Castillo finished, "I'm going to deal with these people myself until I am convinced that they are fucking with me or that I can't—*we can't*—handle them ourselves."

"Ace, you realize you just bit off a hunk that's going to be hard to chew, never mind swallow?"

Castillo took a long, thoughtful look at Delchamps, then said, "Meaning you think I'm wrong? On some kind of ego trip?"

"Meaning, Ace, I think you're doing the right thing—I can think of fifty ways that Langley could, *would*, fuck this up—and that means what I said, I just hope you realized what size chaw you just bit off."

Castillo nodded.

"Any other questions or comments?" he asked.

When there were none, he gestured toward the sliding door of the quincho. "Let's see to our guests."

Bob Kensington, in a chair against one wall of the quincho, was still in his bathing trunks. He had the Uzi on his lap, the weapon's sling, with a two-magazine pouch hanging from it, slung around his neck.

Sof'ya was sitting on the floor with the pups and Max. The puppies were trying to climb high enough on Max, who was sitting beside the girl, to gnaw on his ears. He didn't seem to mind.

The adult Russians were sitting in a row on wicker chairs. Berezovsky had removed his jacket, revealing a sweat-soaked shirt and what Castillo decided was a really cheap pair of suspenders. His wife and Svetlana had removed their jackets. Their blouses were the opposite of crisp and fresh.

"Did you all get something to drink?" Castillo asked.

Berezovsky and his wife nodded.

Sof'ya said, "Thank you."

Svetlana didn't respond at all.

"The first thing we're going to do is get you some summer clothing," Castillo said. "And the way we're going to do that is that Mrs. Berezovsky will go with Agent Britton"—he pointed to Sandra, not Jack, surprising more than a few—"to the local shopping center. Make sure you know the sizes of everyone, Mrs. Berezovsky.

"While they are gone, I will show the others your accommodations, and you can move your luggage into them. Mr. Darby and Mr. Delchamps will have to take a look through the luggage—"

"Is that necessary?" Svetlana interrupted.

Does that mean you have something you don't want me to find?

Or that you have nothing I might consider contraband, and are going to be amused at our fruitless search?

"Obviously, Colonel, I have decided that it is," Castillo said. "And right now I would like your purses, wallets, money, passports, and all identification. Put them on the Ping-Pong table, please, now. The purses will be returned after Agent Davidson has had a chance to examine them."

"Less the contents, of course?" Svetlana asked sarcastically.

"Colonel, why don't we try to start our relationship as amicably as possible? We are going to be spending a good deal of time together, and I don't see much point in making it any more unpleasant than necessary."

Colonel Alekseeva responded to the proffered olive branch by standing, then walking over to the Ping-Pong table and dumping the contents of her purse on it.

"Okay?" She held up the purse—he thought it looked like something that could be used to hold horse feed—so that he could see it was empty.

"Fine. But leave the purse, will you, please?"

She glowered at him.

What's this, a new tactic?

Now she's going to be a martyr, and I'm going to have to be nice to her, so she'll look deeply into my eyes again?

"One never knows, does one, Colonel, what might be hidden in the lining of a purse? For all I know you might have another .32 in there."

She tried to stare him down and failed.

"Are you about ready to go shopping, Mrs. Berezovsky?" Castillo said.

"May I take my daughter with me?"

"You may. But don't you think she'd rather play with the dogs?"

She looked at her daughter and then smiled.

"Yes, I do," she said.

"Just get enough clothing for three days," Castillo said. "Plus a bathing suit or two."

"Bathing suits?" Svetlana asked incredulously.

"This is a five-star prison, Colonel. With a swimming pool. I also think you will like the food, which will be ready by the time Mrs. Berezovsky and Agent Britton have returned."

She didn't say anything.

"Your choice, Colonel," Castillo said. "Use the pool or don't use it. For that matter, wear a bathing suit or don't wear one. That's up to you."

"There are three bedrooms—actually suites—on the second floor, Tom," Castillo said to Berezovsky, then pointed at a closed door. "The center one here is mine; it has an office in which I will conduct my part of the interrogations. The other two suites don't have the office. Arrange yourselves in them any way you want.

"At night, the doors will be locked and there will be someone in the corridor to make sure we have no 'sleepwalkers.' And there will be someone in the drive to make sure no one opens—or goes through—the windows. That should prove no problem, as only a fool sleeps with an open window in an Argentine summer.

"The point I'm trying to make, Colonel," Castillo went on, making it clear that he was talking to Berezovsky, not to Svetlana, "is that I will make every reasonable effort to make our relationship as business-like as possible, as comfortable as possible, so long as you're here."

"And how long will that be?" Svetlana asked.

Castillo ignored her.

"Every reasonable effort for comfort is dependent, of course, on good behavior. The alternatives range from moving you onto cots in the garage, which is not air-conditioned, to leaving one or both of you trussed up like Christmas turkeys on the driveway of the Russian embassy on Rodríguez Pena."

"I asked, 'How long are we going to be here?' " Svetlana said.

Castillo turned to her after a moment. "Until you earn back the cost of what it cost me to get you here, plus of course the two million dollars we've talked about."

"And how long do you think that will take?" she pursued.

"And now, if you'll excuse me, I'm going to leave you with Mr. Darby and Mr. Delchamps. While they are having a look at your luggage, Mr. Davidson, Max, and I are going to take a dip until supper."

On his way to the quincho five minutes later, Castillo—now wearing bathing trunks—was intercepted by the housekeeper. She was holding up a bathing suit.

"For the poor little *chica*, if that's all right. It belongs to Juanita. I already gave one to the other lady."

Castillo presumed that "Juanita" was either a diminutive maid or one of the housekeeper's children. Or grandchildren.

"That's very kind," Castillo said. "How about going out there with me and helping her get into it?"

When Castillo, trailed by the maid, walked into the quincho, Bob Kensington was standing by the AFC communications device and a stand-alone all-in-one device that could print, scan, and send and receive facsimile transmissions. Kensington was feeding the machine from the stack of passports, identification cards, driver's licenses, and the like that they had taken from the Russians.

Kensington stated the obvious. "This goddamn thing is the slow-link—takes forever to scan this stuff."

"Miller can't run that stuff through NSA at Fort Meade until he has it. Nose to the grindstone, Sergeant Kensington!"

"Yes, sir," Kensington said, then loudly shouted, "Hoooo-rah!"

Castillo laughed. The shouting of "Hoooo-rah!" to indicate their enthusiasm to carry out a difficult task was getting to be almost a hallmark of U.S. Army Rangers, and even some lesser ordinary soldiers.

Most Special Forces people—and almost everybody in Delta Force—thought doing so was ludicrous.

Castillo said: "Your oh-so-commendable enthusiasm, Sergeant, has earned you a promotion. You are now the detachment's classified documents officer."

"I guess I should have seen that coming. Where's the Pride of the Marine Corps when I need him?"

"Lester will be here tomorrow morning. But you will not delegate that responsibility to him. A lot of that stuff's likely to be very important later on, not just now. I don't want any of it lost."

Kensington nodded his understanding. He scanned two pages of Svetlana's passport, then using a flash memory thumb-sized chip, put the chip into a slot and transferred the file to the AFC device. It beeped. Before he could open the scanner to rearrange the passport and repeat the process, the AFC beeped again—and a sultry female voice announced, "All done, baby. Slip it to me again! I never get enough!"

Castillo raised an eyebrow. "I presume that means the file has been received and verified, and the AFC is ready to accept another file?"

"That's about it, sir," Kensington said, a little—but only a little—embarrassed.

"Where'd you get the voice?"

"I played around with the voice-recognition circuits." Kensington now smiled. "I can make anybody say almost anything."

Castillo turned to see what, if anything, Sof'ya thought of the sultry female voice. He saw that she was shyly and politely trying to tell the maid, in English, that she would please like to wait until Mama came back before accepting the bathing suit.

The maid spoke very little English.

Castillo wondered what the child had been told about what was happening, and what rules Mama had told her that now governed her behavior.

He came to her rescue.

"Sof'ya, you can wait for your mother, but why don't you come out and watch Max and the pups?"

"He goes in the pool?" she asked.

"Watch."

Castillo retrieved a soccer ball from the top of a refrigerator. It was the only place where the ball could be kept out of the dog's reach.

Max jumped to his feet, having instantly decided that playing with the ball would be more fun than having his offspring gnaw on his ears.

Castillo went to the quincho door and drop-kicked the ball into the pool. Max raced after it, not even pausing before jumping into the water. He swam to the ball and took it in his mouth.

Then Max saw that the pups had not only followed him to the pool but jumped in it after him.

Sof'ya screamed. "They'll drown!"

Castillo didn't think so, but Max was suddenly overcome by paternal emotions. He dropped the soccer ball, swam to one of the pups, and picked it up gently in his mouth.

The pup howled.

Sof'ya screamed again as she ran to the side of the pool.

Max looked confused. There were two pups, but he could get only one in his mouth at a time. He began to paddle in a circle. The pup that had not been rescued paddled desperately after him.

Castillo slipped out of his sandals and ran, laughing, to the pool and dove in.

He swam to the circling dogs and caught in his hand the one that was free. The pup struggled to regain its freedom, but Castillo managed to get it to the decking of the pool, where he set it at Sof'ya's feet.

"The other one, the other one!" she screamed. "He's going to eat it!"

"Max!" Castillo called. "Come!"

But Max kept circling.

With some difficulty—he was now almost helpless with laughter—Castillo went after Max. Max saw him coming and swam away from him to the wrong—the deep—end of the pool.

There he tried to climb out and failed. All he could do was get his paws on the edge of the pool—and slide back in.

Before Castillo could reach him, Sof'ya ran to the pool's edge there and tried to convince Max to give up the puppy. When that failed, she reached over and grabbed a handful of Max's fur, trying to pull him out.

Max's paws again slipped on the poolside tiles. This time he slid backward into the water with two results: He took Sof'ya with him and, when his head went underwater, he let go of the puppy.

Castillo was by then at the scene. He grabbed the now-yapping puppy and put it on the pool deck. Max reached the surface, saw the puppy, and tried again to climb out of the pool.

The puppy ran to pool edge and started yapping indignantly at its father.

Castillo knew Max would not hurt the pup. Sof'ya did not know Max as well as Castillo did.

"He's going to eat him! Oh, God! He's going to eat him!"

Castillo grabbed Sof'ya so that he could hoist her out of the pool. He didn't know how well she could swim—if at all—and she was still wearing her heavy European winter clothing.

She struggled.

At that point, reinforcements arrived. Or, more accurately, erupted from the water next to Castillo.

"What are you doing to her, you sonofabitch?" Lieutenant Colonel Svetlana Alekseeva of the Sluzhba Vnezhney Razvedki demanded, furiously indignant.

Lieutenant Colonel C. G. Castillo of the Office of Organizational Analysis instantly took his hands off Miss Sof'ya Berezovsky, which caused her to go under the water again, which frightened her, and caused her to struggle rather violently when she felt her aunt's hands on her.

Castillo climbed agilely out of the pool, then got to his feet and surveyed the pool.

Max, apparently having finally realized that he was not going to be able to get out of the pool at the deep end, now was swimming furiously to the shallow end of the pool, where he could walk out using the wide steps there.

Svetlana, without much success, was trying to calm Sof'ya, who was still concerned about Max eating one or both of the pups, which now yapped a chorus. Finally, Svetlana succeeded to the point where she could move Sof'ya close enough to poolside so that Castillo could bend over, or kneel, and give Sof'ya his hand and haul her out and safely onto the deck.

But when Castillo bent over to offer his hand, he became distracted—and nearly fell back into the pool.

There was, of course, a very good reason for his losing his balance. And it was a sight he would not soon forget:

Although Colonel Alekseeva at the moment was wholly unaware of her problem, the fact was that when she had been struggling with Sof'ya, the strap of the top to her two-piece swimsuit had snapped, and said strap had slipped from her neck, and the top itself had fallen from her breasts.

This caused the exposure to Castillo's instantly bedazzled eyes of the most perfect naked bosom—in every respect, including erect nipples—he had ever seen, and the number of those he had seen at one time or another over the course of his life was legion.

He was frozen for a moment, but somehow—miraculously—then reached down and coolly hauled Sof'ya from the pool. He turned her over to the housekeeper, who was hovering with concern nearby.

Then he returned his attention to the pool.

With a little bit of luck, she'll want me to give her a hand out of the pool.

Luck, alas, was no longer to be with him.

Colonel Alekseeva saw Colonel Castillo standing above her, saw where he was looking, looked herself, and in one swift motion, modestly clapped her hands over her bosom and slipped under the water, there to attempt reaffixing her garment.

Castillo heard footsteps approaching.

"You're going to have to teach me how to do that, Ace," Edgar Delchamps said behind him, a laugh in his tone. "Talk about absolutely destroying the self-confidence of the prisoner about to be interrogated!"

Castillo turned to glare at him but found Delchamps walking quickly to Sof'ya, who was sitting on the grass crying and clutching both of the soaking-wet pups to her.

"You know what that means, don't you, Sof'ya?" Delchamps asked her in a kind and gentle voice that Castillo had never heard from him.

She shook her head, not understanding the question.

"In the United States, we have a rule. When a puppy is in danger and some-one rescues him, that person then owns him."

"Really?"

"Which of the pups did you rescue?" Delchamps asked.

With no hesitation at all, Sof'ya hoisted one.

"This little girl," she said. "I call her 'Marina.' "

"Well, Marina now belongs to you," Delchamps said. "That means, you un-derstand, that you now will be responsible for seeing that she has enough to eat, things like that. You think you can do that?"

Sof'ya happily nodded.

On one hand, Castillo thought, *Delchamps may have finally found the out he was looking for after running off at the mouth and announcing he wanted one of Mädchen's pups. How the hell was he going to care for a puppy?*

On the other hand, truth being stranger than fiction, a human heart may ac-tually be beating under the old dinosaur's hide.

Delchamps gently took the other pup, the last one, from Sof'ya and walked to Castillo.

As if he had been reading Castillo's mind, he said, "In the trade, that's known as establishing the good-guy/bad-guy relationship. Guess who's the good guy, Ace? The guy who gave the kid a puppy, or the bastard who tore Auntie's bathing suit from her shoulders and then stared shamelessly at her boobs?"

He handed the pup to Castillo. Castillo took it, shook his head but didn't reply, and returned his attention to the pool.

Lieutenant Colonel Alekseeva had reached the shallow end and was now wading through the last several feet, trying without success to repair the bro-ken strap with one hand as she held the suit top with the other.

Max, who had been lying on the tiles recuperating from his ordeal, stood up and eyed her curiously.

As Svetlana marched past him, he shook to free himself of the water in his fur. The fur of a Bouvier des Flandres holds an astonishing amount of water.

As Svetlana jumped out of the way, the right side of her bathing suit bottom slipped off her right buttock and bunched up in the valley between the opposing buttocks, exposing to view a pink, fleshy orb that put into the shadows all other orbs Castillo had seen here and there in his lifetime.

She pushed and pulled the cloth back into place while marching with what dignity she could muster toward the house.

Castillo felt a stirring in his groin.

Down, boy, down!

If there was ever a really off-limits female, there it is, walking on those lovely long legs into the house!

VII

[ONE]
Nuestra Pequeña Casa
Mayerling Country Club
Pilar, Buenos Aires Province, Argentina
1905 29 December 2005

Colonel Dmitri Berezovsky was the first of the Russians to appear. He was wearing baggy swimming trunks, a knit shirt embroidered with a Ralph Lauren polo player insignia, and rubber sandals, and he had a towel draped around his neck.

Castillo, who was standing at the parrilla turning bifes de chorizo, saw Sof'ya holding the puppy and running happily toward her father, obviously intending to tell him that the dog was now hers.

Berezovsky, without breaking stride, held out his hand to her in a *stop* signal. Shedding the shirt and the towel en route, he took the steps into the shallow end of the pool, waded toward the deep end until he judged it deep enough for swimming, then flopped onto his belly and swam using a breaststroke with his head out of the water to the far end of the pool. There, he stopped, hung on to the side of the pool for several seconds, then flopped back into the water and breaststroked—with his head held high again—back to the shallow end. And, there, he stood, waded until he reached the end of the pool, and got out.

Castillo saw that Berezovsky had managed his swim without getting his hair wet.

The Russian walked to where he had dropped the towel and Sof'ya was now standing. He picked up the towel and dried himself methodically as Sof'ya explained what had happened and tried to hand him the dog.

When he had finally dried himself to his satisfaction, he rolled up the towel, held it between his knees, put the polo shirt back on, draped the towel around his neck, and took the dog.

Berezovsky looked thoughtfully across the pool at Castillo.

He's wondering what we're up to, Castillo thought.

In his circumstances, I'd do the same damn thing.

And by now, of course, in addition to wondering what's going to happen to him and his family, he's almost certainly wondering if defecting was really such a good idea in the first place.

Castillo turned to the parrilla, stuck an enormous fork into a two-pound bife de chorizo—New York strip steak—then held it over his head, signaling Berezovsky to come over.

Still carrying the pup, Berezovsky did so, with Sof'ya at his side.

"My Sof'ya tells me she has been given this animal," he said, making it a question.

"And now she wants me to cook it for her on here?" Castillo asked.

"No!" Sof'ya said, but laughed.

Berezovsky handed her the puppy.

"Why?" he asked simply.

"I guess Mr. Delchamps thought she should have it," Castillo said. "This has to be tough on her, Colonel."

Berezovsky nodded. Castillo couldn't read it.

"Are the women about ready?" Castillo said. "The food is."

He picked up another bife de chorizo to illustrate his point.

"Sof'ya, go tell your mother that supper is ready. And Auntie Svetlana, too."

The girl ran off with her puppy.

"The beef here is the best in the world," Castillo said.

"So I have been told," Berezovsky said.

"It goes down very well with wine," Castillo said, pointing to an uncorked bottle of Saint Felicien Cabernet Sauvignon and some long-stemmed wineglasses sitting beside an open cardboard case of the wine. "You're welcome to help yourself, but you might want to keep in mind that right after we have our supper, we're going to have the first of our conversations."

Berezovsky met his eyes, considered what he had said, then said, "Thank you," and headed for the wine.

I wonder if the "thank you" was for the warning or the wine?

Berezovsky poured wine—a lot of it—into two of the large wineglasses, half filling them and half emptying the bottle, then walked to Castillo at the parrilla and offered him one.

"I started early," Castillo said. He pointed to his now nearly empty glass at the end of the grill.

Berezovsky thrust the glass he held at Castillo again and smiled.

Okay. I get it. You think I have grape juice in my glass.

Then you will drink the real stuff, get plastered and loose-lipped, and I will be absolutely sober and able to take advantage of your naïve trust.

Castillo took the glass Berezovsky held out to him.

"Chug-a-lug?" Castillo asked.

" 'Chug-a-lug'?" Berezovsky parroted.

I don't think, Tom Barlow, ol' buddy, that you have a clue what that means.

Castillo raised the glass to his lips and drained it.

Berezovsky's eyes showed his surprise, but he rose to the challenge and also drained his glass.

Castillo immediately refilled the glasses, but set his down and began to flip the steaks on the grill.

If I chug-a-lug again, I'll probably fall down and begin to sing bawdy songs, or in some other manner manifest behavior unbecoming an officer and a gentleman, such as myself.

Why the hell did I do that?

One of the maids appeared with several large serving platters.

"The bife de chorizo is done," Castillo announced. "Please put it on the table." He turned to Berezovsky. "It's hot, grilling the steaks. I'm going to cool off until the women get here."

He walked to the deep end of the pool, dove in, swam underwater to the shallow end, turned, and swam back. Then he turned to repeat the process. When he came up for air at the shallow end of the pool, he saw the women—Sandra Britton, Lora and Sof'ya Berezovsky, and Svetlana Alekseeva—walking together from the house toward the quincho.

They were all dressed very much alike, in brightly colored cotton skirts and white blouses, and chatting and laughing among themselves.

If it wasn't for Jack Britton walking behind them with that Uzi held at his side, they'd look like members of the Midland Junior League headed for lunch at the Petroleum Club pool.

Jesus, she's really good-looking!

He turned and swam to the deep end of the pool, considered his situation for a moment, and turned again.

By the time Castillo climbed out of the pool, he had completed three more laps, and by the time he took his seat at the big table in the quincho, everybody had already been served and had started to eat.

[TWO]

The housekeeper, Svetlana Alekseeva, and Jack Davidson all came into Castillo's office together. The housekeeper carried a tray with three mugs and a large thermos of coffee. There was no cream or sugar, and Castillo idly wondered whether that was an oversight or because the housekeeper had heard Svetlana refuse both after supper.

Probably the latter, Castillo decided. The housekeeper was more than she seemed to be. She had worked—at exactly what, Castillo didn't know—for Alfredo Munz when El Coronel Munz had been head of SIDE, Argentina's version of the CIA and FBI rolled into one. Munz had vouched for them when Darby and the Sienos had been staffing Nuestra Pequeña Casa, and that was good enough for Castillo.

Davidson carried two small recording devices; a large ashtray; a box of wooden matches; a portable leather cigar humidor (he was as addicted to the filthy weed as was Castillo); what looked like a laptop computer but was actually much more, as was its twin—Castillo's—already on the table; a legal pad; a box of fine-point felt-tip pens; and a small notebook.

Lieutenant Colonel Alekseeva brought only her purse with her. When Castillo had waved her into one of the upholstered captain's chairs at the table, she instead went to his desk and began to unload the purse. Out came a package of Marlboro cigarettes, a disposable lighter, two ballpoint pens, a notebook, a small package of Kleenex, a small bottle of perfume, and a plastic bottle filled with blue gunk. The last item so interested Castillo that he picked it up and read the label. It was Argentine sunscreen lotion with aloe.

"The last time we did this, Charley," Davidson said in Pashtu as he arranged his toys on the table, "neither the prisoner nor the surroundings were nearly as nice, were they?"

Castillo chuckled, as the image of that last time—a really bad guy in a crude stone building that was more of a hut than a building—popped into his mind.

"What was that, Pashtu?" Svetlana asked, but it was more of a statement.

If you know what it was, Castillo thought, *you probably understand it, so there goes our private code.*

And we won't be able to fall back on alternatives A and B, either. We know you speak Russian and Hungarian.

But why did you ask? Why give that up?

Castillo ignored her question. Instead, he said: "Before we get into the fingernail-pulling and waterboarding aspects of this, Svetlana, let me tell you what's going to happen tonight."

She nodded, just once, and did not smile.

"As we speak, your identification and other information we took are being processed in Washington. When we get that back, we can clear up any inconsistencies there may be."

She nodded again.

"For now, to get started, let's clear up a few minor things. First, why don't you identify these account numbers for us?"

He gestured with his index finger, took a sheet of paper that had been stuck into the legal pad, and slid it across the table to Svetlana.

She glanced at it quickly, then looked into Castillo's eyes, not quite able to conceal her surprise and discomfort.

Gotcha, sweetheart!

"That's a printout from the chip Mr. Darby found in the lining of your purse," Castillo said. "Probably the guts of one of those things . . ."

He looked at Davidson, who furnished, "Flash drives, Charley."

". . . those *flash drives* you stick in a computer's USB slot," Castillo finished.

There was no expression on her face, but her eyes showed that she had just been kicked in the stomach.

"Sergeant Kensington," Castillo continued, "who's really good at that sort of thing, had a hell of a time reading it, but finally managed it. Darby thinks they're bank account numbers. Maybe encoded somehow. Anyway, we sent them to Two-Gun Yung in Vienna. . . . Oh, that's right. You never met Two-Gun, did you? Two-Gun is our money guy. He's just about as good at finding hidden money as Kensington is at fooling around with computers."

Svetlana continued to meet his eyes, as if hoping to read something in them, but didn't say anything.

Castillo went on: "In the belief that (a) the list may be encrypted and (b) if encrypted then done so more or less simply, I've sent it to our in-house cryptography lady. If I'm right about (a) and (b), she should be able to quickly crack it. If she can't—and/or if Two-Gun can't immediately determine what they are, I've told our cryptologist to take the numbers to Fort Meade—the National Security Agency's at Fort Meade, Maryland; she worked there for years—where they have, honest to God, acres and acres of computers that can eventually crack anything.

"I'd really rather not have to do that. So if you will identify those numbers for us, it will save us some time and might do a lot to convince me you meant it when you said you'd tell me anything I want to know. Right now, your hiding that chip from me brings that promise into question."

She reached for the pack of Marlboros and put a cigarette in her mouth. Davidson struck a wooden match and held it out to her.

She lit the cigarette. She took a deep puff, held it, looked at the burning tip of the cigarette, and exhaled through both nostrils as she sighed and shrugged her shoulders.

Castillo found this to be erotic.

She turned and met his eyes, which had the same effect.

"The money is, so to speak, our retirement money," she said.

"Is that list encrypted?"

She nodded.

"And are you going to decrypt it for me?"

"It's simple substitution," she said.

She picked up one of the ballpoint pens and demonstrated with underlines on the numbers as she spoke.

"The first block on the second line, the second block on the fourth, the third block on the sixth . . ."

She raised her eyes to Castillo. "You understand?"

He nodded.

"Is the key," she said. "The alphabet is reversed."

"Cyrillic?" Castillo asked.

She nodded again and pushed the sheet away from her.

Davidson took it, lifted the lid of his laptop computer, pushed several keys, waited a moment while watching the screen, then began typing.

"You have the Cyrillic alphabet in there?" Svetlana asked, surprised.

"No, but we're trying to fool you into thinking we do," Castillo said. "And while Jack's doing that, we will turn to Subjects Two and Three on our agenda for this evening."

She took another drag on her cigarette, then crushed it out as she simultaneously exhaled through her nostrils and looked into Castillo's eyes.

He felt it in the pit of his stomach.

"Something else you promised and didn't deliver," Castillo said, "is the reason why you have defected. You said I wouldn't believe you when you told me. Has it got something to do with these bank accounts? Or is there something else?"

"The money is not the reason we defected," she said calmly. "The money permitted us to defect. Is it your intention to take the money?"

"Would you believe me if I said no?"

"I don't know," she said matter-of-factly.

"Before you start telling me the things I'm not going to believe, let's talk about Alekseeva. Starting with his full name."

"Evgeny Alekseeva, Colonel, SVR. I think that would be 'Eugene' in English. It's from the old Greek word for 'noble.' Evgeny's parents were always proud of their bloodline."

What the hell does that mean?

"And he is—or was—your husband?"

"Is."

No shit!

Well, that may—or may not—affect my interest.

"Any children?"

"If I had children, I would be with them here or back there."

"Why didn't Evgeny come with you?"

"He is perfectly happy where he is."

What the hell does that mean?

"And, apparently, you were not?"

"I was not."

"You had trouble with your husband? Is that what you're suggesting?"

"I was not happy. He was. That often causes problems. Are you always happy with your wife?"

She looked deeply into his eyes.

She's probing. . . . How am I supposed to respond?

When in doubt, try the truth. . . .

"I'm supposed to be asking the questions, Colonel," Castillo said. "But since you're curious, no wife. Not ever."

She shrugged.

"Where is your husband now?"

"He may be dead, or under interrogation, or perhaps he's packing his bag to come looking for me."

"He didn't know what you were planning?"

"If he *suspected* what Dmitri and I were planning, he would have denounced us."

"Nice guy."

"He would be doing what he thought he had to do."

"And if he comes looking for you and finds you, what do you think he would think he had to do?"

"The SVR would, of course, prefer to have us back home, but getting us there might be—probably would be—dangerous. So he would kill me. And, of course, Dmitri and his family."

"As I said, a nice guy."

"So obviously, the thing Dmitri and I have to do is not get found."

Castillo picked up the phone and punched one button.

"Bob, get on the horn to Major Miller, tell him I need yesterday (1) the agency's file on Evgeny Alekseeva, Colonel, SVR. I spell." He did so, and looked at Svetlana to see if he had it right, which of course caused him to look into her eyes.

She nodded.

"And (2) tell him to get quietly onto NSA and get me all Russian traffic on the same guy. All of his aliases, too. If he's moving, I want to know all about it.

"And I just thought of (3): Call Two-Gun and our cryptologist and tell them to hold off sending the data on that chip to NSA; I think we can decrypt it here. Got it?"

There was a pause as he heard it read back.

"If you got it, how come I didn't get no *'Hooooo-rah!'*?" Castillo asked, and hung up the phone.

Davidson raised his eyes from his laptop and, shaking his head, smiled at him.

Svetlana looked at Castillo as if wondering why he wasn't in a straitjacket.

"Which brings us back to Question One, Colonel: the reasons I won't believe why you've defected. If it wasn't to make off with the money, then what?"

"Dmitri and I realized that things weren't really changed, that they were going back to the way they were, and that we didn't want to be part of it anymore."

"I have no idea what you're talking about," Castillo confessed.

"How much do you know about the SVR, about Russia?"

"Not much."

That's not true.

I know a good deal about both Russia and the SVR. And she knows I do.

Which means she knows I'm lying to her.

Which she expected me to do.

So why does that bother me?

"I think you think you know a good deal about Russia and the SVR," Svetlana said.

She's reading my mind again!

"Is your ego such, Colonel," she went on, "that you could accept that there's a good deal you think you see that isn't at all what you think it is, and that there is a good deal you don't see at all?"

That's a paraphrase of what General McNab has been cramming down my throat since the First Desert War: "Any intelligence officer who thinks he's looking at the real skinny is a damn *fool, and any intelligence officer who thinks he has all the facts is a* goddamned *fool."*

Castillo glanced at Davidson, who apparently not only could walk and chew gum at the same time but also had been often exposed to the wisdom of General Bruce J. McNab and just now had heard the same thoughts paraphrased by a good-looking Russian spook.

They smiled at each other.

"Did I say something amusing?" Svetlana snapped.

"Not at all," Castillo said. "We just found it interesting that you are familiar with the theories of B. J. McNab, the great Scottish philosopher."

"I never heard of him," Svetlana said.

"I'm surprised," Castillo said. "You'll have to expand on what you said."

"It'll sound like a history lesson," she said. "And I don't like the idea of playing the fool for you."

"I'm always willing to listen. Believing what I hear is something else."

She looked at him intently, rather obviously trying to decide if he was indeed trying to make a fool of her.

"Do you have any idea, Colonel," she asked, more than a little sarcastically, "how long what you would call the secret police have been around Russia?"

"No, but I think you're going to tell me," Castillo said, matching her sarcasm.

"What do you know of the boyars?" she asked.

"Not much."

"Ivan the Terrible?"

"Him, I've heard of. He's the guy who used to throw dogs off the Kremlin's walls, right? Because he liked to watch them crawl around on broken legs?"

"That was one of the ways he took his pleasure. He threw people off, too, for the same reason."

"Nice guy."

She shook her head in tolerant disgust.

"Ivan the Terrible—Ivan the Fourth—was born in 1530," she went on. She switched to English. "In other words, thirty-eight years after Christopher Columbus sailed the ocean blue in 1492."

He smiled, and she smiled back.

Castillo heard Davidson, who was bent over his laptop, chuckle.

Svetlana went back to Russian: "Ivan's father, Vasily the Third, Grand Duke of Muscovy, died three years later, which made Ivan the Grand Duke.

"There was then no Tsar. The country was run by the boyars, who were the nobility, and each of whom had a private army, which they placed at the service of the Grand Duke of Muscovy. Everybody wanted to be the Tsar, but none was able to get everybody else to step aside to give him the job.

"The Grand Duchy of Muscovy—the most important one—was thus governed by *ad hoc* committees, so to speak, of boyars, who 'advised' the Grand Duke what to do, whereupon he issued the Grand Ducal Order.

"This was fine, so long as he was a little boy. But he was growing up, and he might be difficult to deal with as an adult. So they began to impress upon him how powerful they were. One of the ways they did this would now be called 'child molestation.' They wanted to terrorize him, and when they thought they had succeeded, the boyars let him assume power in his own right in 1544, when he was age fourteen.

"They had frightened Ivan but not cowed him. He came to the conclusion that unless he wanted other people to run his life, he was going to have to become more ruthless than the boyars who were running his life and abusing him in many ways, including sexual.

"There is a lovely American expression which fits," Svetlana said. "Ivan had gone through"—she switched to English—" 'the College of Hard Knocks' "—then back to Russian—"and had learned from his teachers."

Again Castillo smiled at Svetlana, and she smiled back and Davidson chuckled over his laptop.

"Ivan selected from among the boyars," Svetlana went on, "a small number he felt were hard enough to deal with the others, and at the same time he could control, both by passing out the largesse at his control and by terrorizing them.

"He also knew that if he had the church on his side, he would also have the support of the peasants and serfs, who were very religious—"

"Wasn't it some other Russian," Davidson asked innocently, "who said, 'Religion is the opiate of the masses'?"

"No, Mr. Davidson," Svetlana corrected him. "It was Karl Marx who said that. He was a German, a Jew with a strong rabbinical background, and what he actually wrote was *'Opium des Volkes,'* which usually is mistranslated."

"I stand corrected," Davidson said, and then wonderingly asked, "I wonder if my Uncle Louie knows that?"

The question so surprised her that she blurted: "Your *Uncle Louie?*"

"He's a rabbi," Davidson explained.

Castillo chuckled.

Svetlana shook her head again in disbelief.

She went on: "So Ivan made a deal with the church. If they would"—she switched to English—" 'scratch his back, he would scratch theirs.' "

When she got the now-expected chuckle from Davidson and exchanged the expected smile with Castillo, she went back to Russian: "The Metropolitan of Moscow found scripture which said that Ivan had a divine right to rule. Ivan developed an overnight religious fervor, and in January 1547, the Metropolitan presided over the coronation of Tsar Ivan the Fourth. He was then seventeen years old.

"As soon as he was Tsar, *his* boyars began throwing into pits the boyars who he suspected weren't so sure he had a divine right to rule. There, they were eaten by starving dogs."

"A *really* nice guy," Castillo said.

"The property—lands and serfs who belonged to the land—were split between the Tsar and the boyars who believed that it pleased God to have Ivan the Fourth as Tsar.

"Over the next eighteen years, while Ivan did a really remarkable job of turning Russia into a superpower, he consolidated his power. He took care of the church, and the church responded by telling the faithful that Ivan was standing at the right hand of God, making the point that challenging Ivan was tantamount to challenging God.

"Then he started separating the best of the good boyars from the bad ones. A good boyar was defined, primarily, as one who didn't harbor any ideas about assassinating him and then taking over. Those he suspected had such ideas were removed from the scene in various imaginative ways—for example, by being skinned alive—which served, of course, to remind those that remained that even thinking of displeasing the Tsar was not smart.

"The more clever boyars came to understand that the key to success was in getting close to the Tsar, most often by denouncing those who could be safely accused of having possibly treasonous thoughts. The most clever of the clever boyars further understood that getting *too* close to the Tsar tended to increase their risk of being tossed to the starving dogs or thrown from the Kremlin walls. The Tsar was naturally suspicious of anyone whose power seemed possible of threatening his own.

"The point here is that as he passed out the serfs taken from the bad boyars to the good boyars, this increased the size of the good boyars' armies. Soldiers, so to speak, were serfs equipped with a sword or a pike, who went into battle because they might live through the battle, and refusing to go into battle would certainly see them killed.

"So he began to recruit a corps of officers from the merchant class, and even from the peasant class. They were treated almost as well as the good boyars, and realized that their good fortune depended on ensuring that the Tsar, who had appointed them to command the serfs he had taken away from the bad boyars, remained in power."

She paused to take another cigarette out of the pack, light it with what Castillo thought was great style, then exhaled.

"By 1565," Svetlana continued, "he thought he had arranged things as well as he could. First, he moved his family out of Moscow to one of his country estates. When he was sure that he and they were safe in the hands of his officer corps, he wrote an open letter—copies of it were posted on walls and, importantly, in every church—to Philip, the Metropolitan of the church in Moscow. The Tsar said he was going to abdicate and, to that end, had already moved out of Moscow.

"The people, the letter suggested, could now run Russia to suit themselves, starting by picking a new Tsar, to whom they could look for protection. This caused chaos at all levels. The people didn't want a new Tsar who was not chosen by God. The boyars knew that picking one of their own to be the new Tsar was going to result in a bloodbath. The officer corps knew that the privileges they had been granted would almost certainly not be continued under a new Tsar, and that the boyars would want their serfs back.

"The Tsar was begged not to abdicate, to come home to Moscow. After letting them worry for a while, during which time they had a preview of what life without Tsar Ivan would be like, he announced his terms for not abdicating.

"There would be something new in Russian, the *Oprichina*—'Separate Estate'—which would consist of one thousand households, some of the highest nobility of the boyars, some of lower-ranking boyars, some of senior military officers, a few members of the merchant class, and even a few families of extraordinarily successful peasants.

"They all had demonstrated a commendable degree of loyalty to the Tsar. The Oprichina would physically include certain districts of Russia and certain cities, and the revenue from these places would be used to support the *oprich-niki* and of course the Tsar, who would live among them.

"The old establishment would remain in place. The boyars not included in the Oprichina would retain their titles and privileges; the council—the *Duma*—would continue to operate, its decisions subject of course to the Tsar's approval. But the communication would be one way. Except in extraordinary circumstances, no one not an oprichniki would be permitted to communicate with the Oprichina.

"The Tsar's offer was accepted. God's man was back in charge. The boyars had their titles. The church was now supported by the state, so most of the priests and bishops were happy. Just about everybody was happy but Philip, the Metropolitan of Moscow, who let it be known that he thought the idea of the Oprichina was un-Christian.

"The Tsar understood that he could not tolerate doubt or criticism. And so Ivan set out for Tver, where the Metropolitan lived. On the way, he heard a rumor that the people and the administration in Russia's second-largest city, Great Novgorod, were unhappy with having to support Oprichina.

"Just as soon as he had watched Metropolitan Philip being choked to death, the Tsar went to Great Novgorod, where, over the course of five weeks, the army of the Oprichina, often helped personally by Ivan himself, raped every female they could find, massacred every man they could find, and destroyed every farmhouse, warehouse, barn, monastery, church, every crop in the fields, every horse, cow, chicken—"

"At the risk of repeating myself," Castillo interrupted, "nice guy."

The look she gave him was one of genuine annoyance.

What's that all about?

How long is this history lecture going to last?

Where the hell is she going with this?

She went there immediately.

"And so, Colonel Castillo, what we now call the SVR was born."

"Excuse me?"

"Over the years, it has been known by different names, of course. And it actually didn't have a name of its own, other than the Oprichina, a state within a state, until Tsar Nicholas the First. After Nicholas put down the Decembrist Revolution in 1825, he reorganized the trusted elements of the Oprichina into what he called the Third Section."

Castillo looked at her but said nothing. He saw that Davidson was also now looking at her in what could be either confusion or curiosity.

"That reincarnation of the Oprichina lasted until 1917, when the Soviets renamed it the All-Russian Extraordinary Commission for the Suppression of Counterrevolution and Sabotage—acronym CHEKA."

"That sounds as if you're saying that the Tsar's secret police just changed sides, became Communists," Castillo said.

It was his first real comment during the long history lesson.

"You're saying two things, you realize," Svetlana said. "That the Oprichina changed sides is one, that the Oprichina became Communist is another. They never change sides. They may work for a different master, but they never become anything other than what they were, members of the Oprichina."

With a hint of annoyance in his voice, Castillo said, "Svetlana, the first head of the CHEKA—Dzerzhinsky—was a lifelong revolutionary, a Communist. He spent most of his life in one Tsarist jail or another before the Communist revolution."

"Challenge your sure and certain knowledge of this with these facts, Colonel," Svetlana said. "Felix Edmundovich Dzerzhinsky was born on the family's estate in western Belarus. The Dziarzhynava family was of the original one thousand families in Ivan's Oprichina. The estate was never confiscated by the Bolsheviks or the Mensheviks or the Communists after they took power. The family owns it to this day.

"The Tsar's Imperial Prisons were controlled by the Third Section. How well one fared in them—or whether one was actually in a prison, or was just on the roster—depended on how well one was regarded by the Oprichina. The fact that the history books paint the tale of this heroic revolutionary languishing, starved and beaten, for years in a Tsarist prison cell doesn't make it true."

She lit another cigarette, considered her thoughts, then went on:

"And don't you think it a little odd that Lenin appointed Dzerzhinsky to head the CHEKA and kept him there when there were so many deserving and reasonably talented Communists close to him?"

Castillo said what he was thinking: "I'm going to have to think about this."

She nodded as if she expected that would be his reply.

"The CHEKA was reorganized after the counterrevolution of 1922 as the GPU, which was renamed later the OGPU. A man named Yaakov Peters was named to head it. By Felix Edmundovich Dzerzhinsky, who was minister of the interior, which controlled the OGPU.

"Dzerzhinsky died of a heart attack in 1926. And there were constant reorganizations and renaming after that. In '34, the OGPU became the NKVD. In '43, the NKGB—People's Commissariat for State Security—was split off from the NKVD. And in '46, after the Great War, it became the MGB, Ministry of State Security."

"And you are suggesting, are you, that this state within a state . . ."

"The Oprichina," she furnished.

". . . the *Oprichina* was in charge of everything? Only the names changed and the Oprichina walked through the raindrops of the purges they had over there at least once a year?"

"You're putting together things that don't belong together," she said. "Yes, the Oprichina remained—*remains*—in charge. No, not all the oprichniki managed to live through all the purges. Enough did, of course, in order to maintain the Oprichina and learn from the mistakes made."

"You're saying the Oprichina exists today?" Castillo said.

"Of course it does. Russia is under an *oprichnik*."

"Putin?"

"Who else?"

"And you and your brother were—are—oprichniki?"

"And my husband is."

"I'm a little confused, Svetlana. From what I understand, the intelligence services live very well in Russia. And from what you've just told me, you and your brother and your husband are members of this state within a state that lives very, very well."

She nodded.

"So then why did you defect?"

She replied by asking a question.

"What do you really know about Vladimir Putin?"

Plenty—far more than you think I do.

"That, for example," he replied somewhat defensively, "while Putin's grandfather might really have been Stalin's cook during the Second World War, he was also a political commissar in the Red Army. Including, among other places, Stalingrad."

I said that because her attitude pisses me off.

What I should've said was, "Very little." And the look in Jack's eyes confirms that I should have.

She smiled. "So you have read a little about my country?"

She's trying to make me mad. And succeeding.

"Colonel, you had best stop thinking about Russia as your country," Castillo said. And then his mouth ran away with him. "But since you seem so curious about Mr. Putin, I know that his father was not foreman in a locomotive factory, or whatever the official bio has him doing, but was at least a colonel in the KGB."

"Actually, a general. I'm impressed."

"Charley, why don't we call this off for tonight?" Davidson asked. "I don't know about you, but I'm beat."

Meaning, of course, that you think I'm about to lose it.

And my behavior suggests that I am.

What the hell is the matter with me?

"Yeah, me, too. It's been a very long day. Couple of days," Castillo said, then stood.

Svetlana said: "You said your question is, 'Why did we defect?' I am about to tell you."

"Okay, tell me," Castillo said more than a little sharply, and sat down.

"Because we came to the conclusion that sooner or later, Mr. Putin was going to get around to purifying us. We know too much. We have one family member who has, if not defected, done the next thing to it."

"Really?" Castillo asked sarcastically.

"Really," she said. "I don't think Putin would throw us to starving dogs or off the Kremlin wall, but keeping us on drugs in a mental hospital for the rest of our lives seemed a distinct possibility."

Castillo looked into her eyes.

I'll be damned if I don't believe her.

Svetlana smiled wanly and shrugged. "I told you that you weren't going to believe me."

"And why did you want to come here?" Castillo asked.

"We have a relative here, who saw what was going to happen long before we did. And got out in the chaos, when the Soviet Union was falling apart."

"And he's here?"

"Somewhere here. I don't know exactly where. I was hoping, frankly, that you'd help me find him. His name is Aleksandr Pevsner. His mother and my mother were sisters."

Castillo was quiet a long moment, hoping that he appeared to be in thought, not caught off guard.

"I've heard the name, of course," he finally said as he stood up. "The last I heard, there were thirteen Interpol warrants out for him."

He motioned for her to go to the door.

"Agent Britton will take you to your room, Colonel. If you need anything, ask her. Breakfast will be served at seven-thirty. I expect you and your brother to be there."

She ground out her cigarette, stood, and walked through the door to the bedroom without saying anything.

Davidson followed her, and Castillo heard murmured conversation between Davidson and Sandra Britton, and then the sound of the door closing.

Davidson came back into the office.

"Thanks, Jack," Castillo said.

"For what?"

"You know damned well for what."

"Okay. Then you're welcome," Davidson said, then added, "Pevsner!"

"Jesus Christ!"

"That would explain why they came to you in Germany," Davidson said. "They know you know him."

"I don't think so. If they were in touch with Pevsner, and he wanted to get them out, he would have sent planes and people. Alex is very good at that sort of thing."

"What did you think of that state-within-a-state business she fed us?"

"It may be proof that I was in no shape to interrogate anybody, much less a pro like that one. I think it's probably true."

"Me, too. You never heard anything like that before?"

"That the SVR is a separate class within Russian society, sure. Not that it goes back to Ivan the Terrible with the same people."

"I always forget not to look in the mirror when I'm thinking about the Russians," Davidson confessed. "Maybe because I'm a half, two-thirds, a bunch of Russian myself. Those Russians are not like our Russians. I should write that on the palm of my hand."

"How'd you do with those account numbers?"

"It worked the way she said it would. But no names." He paused. "Christ, her face when you told her we had the chip. If looks could kill, in other words. I almost felt sorry for her."

"Feeling sorry for Little Red Under Britches would be very dangerous."

Davidson started to speak, stopped, and then went on: "I'm glad you said that, Charley. Otherwise, Colonel, sir, I would have had to say it to you, and sometimes you are not as grateful of my wise counsel as you should be."

Castillo gave him the finger.

"Come on, let's go out to the quincho and see how the professionals did with the colonel. And get those account numbers to Two-Gun and Mrs. Sanders, to see what they make of them."

"I don't suppose we could stop in the living room and have a little taste on the way, could we? Trying to read that dame wore me out."

"Every once in a great while, Sergeant Major, you have a great idea."

[THREE]

"First impressions," Edgar Delchamps said. "Berezovsky is what he says he is, and you don't get to be the Berlin rezident unless you are very, very good. It's almost as important as a posting to Washington or the UN.

"Second, I have the feeling he's not used to being on the receiving end of being scared, which both supports the previous impression and may explain why, I think, operative word *think*, he has been telling us the truth, and will continue to do so. We didn't get into many specifics. I want to do that tomorrow, after I have a chance to ask some questions to verify the unimportant stuff he gave us." He paused thoughtfully, then waved at Alex Darby. "Alex?"

"I agree. I wanted to get more into why they defected, but there wasn't the chance."

"According to Little Red Under Britches," Castillo said, "they were afraid of getting thrown out with the bathwater when Putin inevitably cleans house."

Castillo raised his eyebrows, asking for Delchamps's and Darby's reaction to that.

"Credible," Darby said, and Delchamps nodded his agreement.

"Did Aleksandr Pevsner's name come up?"

Darby and Delchamps shook their heads.

"All we know about him," Castillo said to ensure everyone had the same story, "is that there are fourteen Interpol warrants out for him."

Everybody nodded their understanding.

"What did she have to say about Pevsner?" Delchamps asked.

"They're cousins. His mother and theirs are sisters. He was an oprichniki who got out—"

"A what?" Delchamps said.

"An oprichniki is a member of the Oprichina, the secret police state-within-the-state that goes back to Ivan the Terrible. She gave us quite a history lesson. And Jack and I think it's probably true."

"Wow!" Darby said.

"Anyway, she says Pevsner got out when everything was *upgefukt* when the Soviet Union was coming apart—"

"A lot of them got out when that happened," Delchamps offered. "It explains why the Russian mafia suddenly became so successful: Three-quarters of them are ex-KGB."

Castillo nodded. "—and that he's here. She doesn't know where."

"At noon he was in Bariloche," Alfredo Munz offered. "And there was no indication that he planned to go anywhere."

Alfredo, my friend, Castillo thought, *you have just earned your OOA salary for the rest of this year—and for six months of next year.*

And wasn't I smart to put you on the payroll?

"Alfredo, I'm thinking I may have to go there. Do you think Duffy can arrange for me to borrow his friend's Aero Commander again?"

"Probably," Munz said. "You can ask him in the morning when he comes here?"

" 'When he comes here'?" Castillo parroted incredulously.

"I thought it better to tell him you were here than for him to find out himself then think you were trying to keep something from him. Which would have destroyed his current—if fragile—belief that you are a wonderful human being."

And wasn't I stupid not to realize that the former head of SIDE was not going to ask anybody's advice—or permission—before doing what he thought was obviously the appropriate thing to do?

"What time's he coming?"

"I invited him for breakfast," Munz said.

"You tell him who's here?"

Munz shook his head. "I didn't know how you'd feel about that."

"Well, see if you can get in touch with him and convince him that we don't need any help in dealing with our guests."

Munz nodded.

"Prefacing this by saying I don't think any of them are going to try to escape—operative words *don't think*—how do we keep our chickens in the coop overnight?" Castillo asked. He looked at Sergeant Kensington. "Bob?"

"I just checked the motion sensors, Colonel. A-OK. I also took a look at the house from the driveway. Maybe the colonel and the lady could get into the drive—where they would set off the sensors—by making a rope from sheets. But I don't think Sof'ya or her mother could climb down a rope.

"So we leave the floodlights on in the backyard. The guy on the radio—and, by the way, I checked out Mr. and Mrs. Britton on the AFC—would see anyone out there, and then they'd have to get over the fence.

"What I would suggest, Colonel, is that we station one guy in the foyer of the house, have another guy wandering around, and someone on the radio. And then change the team around, so the guy on the radio could get a little sleep. So I see it as me, the Brittons, and somebody else."

Castillo had used the military technique of soliciting opinions starting with the junior member. As he was trying to decide who would be the least pissed off by being selected as the next-to-junior member, Tony Santini jumped in and answered the question for him.

"Let Sandra get some sleep," Santini said, "so she can deal with the women tomorrow. I'll take her place."

Castillo looked around and saw that the suggestion met everyone's approval. "Anybody else?" he asked.

There were no takers.

"Okay. That's it. I'm off to bed. Breakfast at half past seven."

[FOUR]

Stripped to his T-shirt and shorts, Castillo walked into the bathroom of the master suite—everything but the doors and ceiling was either marble or mirrors—carrying his toilet kit and a clean set of underwear.

He laid the toilet kit on the marble, twin-basin sink, then pulled his T-shirt off, balled it up, and took a basketball shot at the wicker laundry basket against the wall.

"Three-pointer!" he said, then pulled off his shorts. They dropped to the floor. He put one hand on the sink to steady himself, then kicked the shorts into the air and grabbed them. He balled them up and took another shot at the laundry basket.

"Shit," he said, and walked to the basket to pick them up.

As he dropped the shorts into the laundry basket, he noticed a door. He had seen it before, of course. The architect who had designed the house had taken into consideration the possibility that the occupants of the master suite would reproduce. Thus, the room next door, the smallest of the three on the floor, could serve as the nursery. It certainly wasn't being put to that use now, but the fact remained that there was a door leading to it from the master-suite bathroom so that Momma could rush to soothe a squealing baby.

Without really thinking about it, he tried the handle. The door was locked, and there was no key. But his curiosity having gone this far, he bent over and looked through the keyhole. He could see nothing.

He walked to the glass-walled shower and turned on the water. He sniffed his armpit. It didn't exactly exude the fragrance of a flower shop, but he decided it didn't smell as foul as it could—probably should—have considering that the last shower he'd had was at das Haus im Wald, some twelve thousand kilometers away and God Only Knows how many hours before.

When the water had reached a satisfactory temperature, he stepped under it and just stood there.

A forbidden question crept into his mind: *I wonder what Svetlana looks like in the shower starker? I've already been blessed with the sight of those marvelous nipples erect on those marvelous breasts—*

He forced the image from his mind and started with the soap.

What the hell is wrong with me? I'm too old to be behaving like a seventeen-year-old suffering from raging hormones.

And I should be smart enough to realize this is one situation where I cannot, absolutely cannot, let a stiff dick take control of the brain.

When he decided his rigorous shower had cleansed him as well as he could be cleansed, he sucked in his breath and turned off just the hot-water faucet.

When he was actually shivering, he turned off the cold water, opened the shower door, and reached for a towel.

And then he quickly tried to modestly cover his groin with his hand.

Lieutenant Colonel Svetlana Alekseeva was in his bathroom. She was fully covered by a thick white terry-cloth bathrobe, but for all practical purposes it was transparent above the waist—Castillo's memory bank had automatically kicked in and he again was looking at her bare bosom and erect nipples in the pool.

A number of thoughts zipped at a dizzying speed through his brain as he tried to think of something to say, how to say it, and then actually say it.

"I checked that door just now. It was locked." That was what finally came out of his mouth.

She held up something red, about the size of a pencil, and smiled.

What the hell is that?

He looked at the object again.

Oh, shit!

Tradecraft 101: How a Cigarette Lighter Flame Can Turn Ordinary Objects into Other Useful Tools.

In this case, remolding a toothbrush handle into a key for a simple lock.

She opened that door!

"I don't wish to be alone tonight," Svetlana said softly if a bit awkwardly. "Do you?"

"Jesus H. Christ!"

She looked into his eyes and then, as if suddenly embarrassed, averted them.

Then, still looking down, she chuckled softly and said: "I'll take that as 'No, I don't wish to be alone either,' yes?"

"What?"

She nodded toward his groin. He looked.

The father of all erections was standing out from the hands with which he had hoped to conceal the symbol of his gender.

"Jesus H. Christ!" Castillo said when he had regained enough breath to speak.

"I hope that's an expression of satisfaction," Svetlana said.

He turned his head to look at her.

She was also sprawled on her back, with her head turned to him.

"What do you think?" he asked.

"I don't have much to compare it with," she said.

Oh, for Christ's sake, don't try to paint yourself as Little Miss Goody Two-Shoes. You couldn't do what you just did without a lot of practice.

I don't know how you feel, but that was the best piece of ass I've had in a long, long time.

Ever.

"Really?" Castillo asked.

"You're the second man I've been with."

"That's a little hard to believe."

"And you don't believe me?"

"Let it go, Svetlana."

"I can't." She sighed. "Will you listen?"

He shrugged. "Why not?"

"Sexual relations can cause a lot of trouble . . ."

No fooling?

Like this one's going to cause more fucking trouble than I want to think about?

". . . and in the Oprichina there are rules," she went on.

"You don't say?"

What comes next? That the Oprichina is a place where females are virgins until marriage, and faithful ever after?

But he saw the hurt in her eyes and was sorry for his sarcasm.

"A man is, of course, permitted to do what he pleases with women, so long as they are not oprichniki. For women, it is different. If it becomes known that an unmarried woman has taken a lover, that will bar her from a career of her own. She cannot handle her emotions and therefore cannot be trusted.

"Should it come out that the wife of an officer has been unfaithful—"

"She will be shot at dawn?"

"You said you would listen, Charley."

"Sorry."

That's the first time she's called me that.

And I like the way it sounds.

"If it becomes known that an officer's wife has been unfaithful to him, it is the end of his career. If he can't control his own wife, how can he be expected to control other men?"

Christ, I'm starting to believe this!

"He can, one time, and one time only, prove his dependability by killing her."

"And he gets away with that?"

"One time only," she said matter-of-factly. "If he marries again, and the second wife is unfaithful, that's proof that he cannot judge character."

Castillo suddenly realized he had turned on his side.

And then his hand, as if with a mind of its own, reached out and his fingertips brushed her cheek.

"I have never been with another man, Charley. Only Evgeny. Is true."

"Well, what did you think?"

"I didn't know it could be like that," she said, smiling warmly.

"Either did I."

Castillo leaned to her and kissed her gently on the lips.

The gentleness didn't last long.

VIII

[ONE]
Nuestra Pequeña Casa
Mayerling Country Club
Pilar, Buenos Aires Province, Argentina
0705 30 December 2005

Max was having trouble waking Castillo, who was sleeping soundly and who had not responded to either a gentle nudge with Max's muzzle or a paw laid gently on his chest. Finally, Max delicately took the pillow edge in his mouth and, without apparent effort, jerked it out from under Castillo's head.

That did it.

Castillo opened his eyes, saw the dog, and reached out and scratched his ears.

Then he was suddenly wide awake.

He looked quickly to the other side of the bed. It was empty.

"Where the hell were you last night, Max? Getting an eyeful?"

Castillo sat up and swung his legs out of the bed.

Max gave him his paw.

"Okay, okay," Castillo said, and walked somewhat awkwardly to the door to the corridor, unlocked it, and stepped into the hall.

"Who's down there?" he called.

"It is I, the warden," Sandra Britton cheerfully called back. "Seven bells and all is well in the cell block!"

"Let Max out, will you, please?"

"Your wish is my command," she called. This was followed by a shrill and surprisingly loud whistle. "Come on, Max, baby!"

Max happily trotted down the corridor toward the stairway.

Castillo went back into his room, closed the door, and walked to the bed. Then he went back to the door and locked it, cleverly deciding that if someone walked in on him while he was concealing the traces of his nocturnal visitor, there would be a certain curiosity aroused.

He remembered that at some time during the night, she had gone and gotten her cigarettes and an ashtray. And when he had seen her coming back into the bedroom from the bath, starkers, he had decided on the spot that she had to be the most beautiful woman he had ever seen.

Yet there was absolutely no trace of Svetlana.

Nothing in the bed, nothing around the bed, nothing—surprisingly, remarkably—in the bathroom.

That may be, of course, because Lieutenant Colonel Alekseeva of the SVR, as a highly trained intelligence officer, knows how to remove all traces of a clandestine visit to someone's room.

He tried the interior door of the bathroom. It was locked.

Or it may be that it never happened at all, that it was an incredibly realistic wet dream—courtesy of my active imagination and that wine I chug-a-lugged.

That could very well be it: I haven't had one of those since West Point. The sight of those erect nipples really got to me, and I haven't had my ashes hauled in a long time.

You are pissing in the wind, Charley.

It happened.

The proof of that came immediately when he looked in the mirrored wall over the sink. There was an angry, curved, bluish bruise on the soft skin between his right shoulder and armpit.

He remembered when she had bit him.

"Why the hell did you bite me?" he had asked some minutes later.

"I didn't want everybody rushing in here to see who was screaming. I knew I couldn't scream if I had my mouth full of you."

He gently rubbed the teeth marks with his index finger.

I have absolutely no idea what I'm going to do about that, except maybe swim wearing a T-shirt.

And I have absolutely no idea what I'm going to do about Lieutenant Colonel Svetlana Alekseeva.

With whom, I think, as incredible as it sounds, and as fucking insane as I know it is, I think I'm in love.

No, lust.

No, love.

"I couldn't scream if I had my mouth full of you."

Wow!

He stripped off his underwear as he had the last time he had taken a shower, and this time got both the shorts and the T-shirt into the wicker laundry basket, the latter with a rim shot.

And then he stepped under the showerhead. This time he didn't even turn on the hot water. He just closed his eyes and let the cold water stream on him until he heard his teeth chatter.

Edgar Delchamps, Alex Darby, Jack Britton, and Tony Santini were waiting for Castillo, when he came down the stairs dressed in a polo shirt and swimming trunks, five minutes later.

"We need to talk, Ace," Delchamps said seriously. "Okay?"

Oh, shit! They know!

Castillo nodded, gestured toward the door of the library, and raised a questioning eyebrow.

"Fine," Delchamps said.

What the hell am I going to say?

"Sorry, guys, it won't happen again"?

"Excuse the stupidity"?

Or maybe "Well, you guys know how it is. When was the last time you turned down a piece of tail?"

No, that one I won't use.

That wasn't a piece of tail. I don't know what it was, but it was a hell of a lot more than a wham, bam, thank you, ma'am quickie.

The words "a meeting of souls" just popped into my feverish brain.

Castillo was somewhat surprised—*But not really; the help here is incredibly efficient, and thank God for that . . . I need a jolt of caffeine*—to find an insulated carafe of coffee and a half-dozen china mugs on a tray in the center of the library table. There was a red leather-upholstered captain's chair at the head of a library table. Castillo poured a cup, sat in the captain's chair, and made a two-handed gesture signifying *Let's have it.*

"Charley, we've been talking," Delchamps began.

I'll bet you have. And have decided the appropriate course of action for me to take is resign my commission and check into one of the better mental health facilities.

"We think there's something to the chemical factory in the Congo," Delchamps said.

What did he say?

"Something really heavy, Charley," Darby added.

"You ever wonder, Charley, why the ragheads didn't hit us again after 9/11?" Santini asked.

"Other than us good guys are doing a helluva job shutting them down? Last I looked, the Liberty Bell was still intact."

"There is that," Delchamps said. "But there's something more."

"What 'more'?" Castillo said.

They don't know about me and Svetlana?

"You think maybe they're sorry, have gone to confession, received absolution, and ain't gonna do nothing like that never no more?" Santini pursued.

"Where're you headed, Tony?" Castillo asked.

"Hold that thought, Ace," Delchamps said, and gestured to Britton.

"Colonel," Britton asked, "did you ever wonder who was really behind the stolen 727 headed for your beloved Liberty Bell, and why whoever it was had involved the African-American Lunatics in Philadelphia, only a very few of whom can walk and chew gum at the same time?"

Castillo held up both hands in a helpless gesture.

"Same question," Castillo said. "Where're—"

"Same response," Delchamps said. "Hold that thought."

"Okay." Castillo leaned back and slowly sipped his coffee.

"Have you considered the possibility that our Russian friends were already en route to Vienna to defect when you were dumped in their lap?" Delchamps asked.

"Yeah, I have," Castillo said. "What's been bothering me is how they knew that I'm Gossinger—"

"They know who you are, Ace, because Berezovsky is very good and because he runs their show in Germany."

"—and how they knew I was going to be at the Friedler funeral."

"That one's even easier to explain, Ace. It was in the *Tages Zeitung* newspapers, on the front page. 'Tages Zeitung Publisher to Attend Final Rites' or something to that effect."

"Are you going to give me a scenario, or keep me guessing?"

"Berezovsky is in Marburg to supervise the taking out of Otto Görner, following which he will go to Vienna to meet the people with the wax statue of Whatsisname?"

"Peter the First," Castillo furnished.

"Following which, he and Little Red Riding Hood will defect. Hold that thought, too."

"Get on with the scenario, Edgar," Castillo ordered.

"The day before, maybe still in Berlin, maybe in Marburg, he hears that the Kuhls got eliminated. That scares the hell out of him. He didn't know about that.

"Conjecture: Kuhl didn't go to him to try to turn him. Berezovsky went to Kuhl; they knew who he was. Who *they* were.

"Are they onto them? What to do?"

"Keep doing what he was supposed to do, take out Otto Görner. And then he hears that you and Kocian are going to be at Friedler's funeral. . . .

"Now, going off at a tangent: Why was Friedler terminated? Because he was getting too close to what? German involvement in this African chemical factory maybe?

"Then, after Berezovsky orders that you and Billy get taken out, he has a second thought. Or maybe—even probably—Little Red Riding Hood does. She's as smart—"

"Little Red Under Britches," Castillo corrected him without thinking, then had a mental flash of her coming out of the bath sans any britches.

"What the hell is your fascination with her underwear all about?"

"Not now," Castillo said. "Keep going."

"*Little Miss Red Underpants* is as smart as Big Bad Wolf is. She says, 'If they're onto us, maybe Gossinger/Castillo can be useful. If he's alive, of course.

He has an airplane. If SVR is onto us, they're onto Kuhl and the CIA station chief in Vienna, but not onto him.'

"So Berezovsky warns you that you're going to be hit. That makes him a good guy in your eyes. And then he'll find you in Vienna. . . ."

"Instead, we get on the same train," Castillo said.

"Right," Delchamps said. "By that time, he's really scared. When he called off the hit on you, he called it off on Görner, too. Which he was supposed to ensure. And he doesn't know what the hell he's going to find in Vienna. With no other options, short of swallowing his own bullet, now he really has to use you. So he offers you the most important thing he has to barter, the chemical factory in Congo-Kinshasa."

And, very probably, since sex is what makes the world go 'round, he offers up his baby sister, too.

It took you a long time to figure that out, didn't it, Romeo?

"You think that's important?" Castillo said.

"Charley, do you know what's there, what *was* there?" Darby asked.

Castillo shook his head.

"In the bad old days, the West Germans had a nuclear laboratory there," Delchamps said matter-of-factly. "That area was German East Africa before Versailles. We pretended not to know, but when the wall came down, we made them shut it down. It's another of the reasons the Krauts don't like us much anymore; the Israelis have nukes and they don't."

"You're saying there's a nuclear laboratory there?"

"I'm saying there's a *chemical* laboratory there, Ace, and a factory."

"Making what?"

"Maybe something as simple as *Francisella tularensis*," Darby said. "Or . . . you know what I'm talking about, Charley?"

"I think I probably read the same bio-warfare stuff that you did," Castillo said. "It causes rabbit fever, right?"

Darby nodded. "Or something else: anthrax, botulinum toxin, plague . . ."

"I'm not trying to be argumentative, Alex, but what I've read says that, as scary as all that stuff sounds, it's not all that dangerous. Only anthrax and the rabbit fever virus can survive in water, and the ordinary chlorination of water in a water system kills both."

"And both can be filtered out by a zero-point-one-micron or smaller filter, right?" Delchamps asked, paused, and then said, "You want to take a chance that these bastards haven't developed a chlorine-proof bacterium, or something that'll get around or through that point-one filter?"

"You think this is the real thing, don't you?"

Delchamps did not answer directly. Instead, he held up his index finger in a gesture of *Hold that thought*, then said, "Now, throw this into your reasoning."

He nodded at Jack Britton.

"This is conjecture again, Colonel," Britton said. "But it fits. I've been wondering why they tried to whack Sandra and me in Philly. First, they had to go to a lot of trouble to find out who Ali Abid ar-Raziq was—I just disappeared from the mosque, you'll remember; no busts, no questioning by me, nothing that would tell them I was a cop—and then for them to set up the hit. They're just not smart enough to do that, period. Somebody smart found me."

"And why was that so important?" Castillo asked.

"I knew which of the mullahs had gone to Africa, including the Congo, on somebody else's dime," Britton said, "and one of the things I did for Allah was take pictures of the water supply so it could be poisoned. When I turned that in, both to the Department and to Homeland Security, the response was not to worry, chlorine and filters, etcetera."

"Moments ago, Jack, you asked me if I ever wondered why the people responsible for—"

"Stealing the 727 bothered with a bunch of morons?"

"Essentially."

"I have my own theory, which nobody agrees with, except sometimes Sandra."

"And, since last night, me," Santini offered.

"And me and Darby," Delchamps added. "This is what really pushed us over the edge, Charley. Listen to him. Go on, Jack."

"The people behind this, Charley, don't really expect to wipe out half the population of Philadelphia by poisoning the water any more than they expected the morons to be able to find the Liberty Bell, much less fly into it with an airliner."

"Then what?"

"To cause trouble in several ways. First, exactly as the greatest damage done by the lunatics who flew into the Twin Towers was not the towers themselves, but the cost, the disrupted economy.

"There would be mass hysteria, panic, chaos—call it what you will—if it came out that any of those things had been dumped into the water supply. And if they caught one of the AALs pouring stuff into the water supply, it would do the same thing for we colored folks as 9/11 did for the Arabs. You'll recall that every time we saw a guy who looked like he might be an Arab, we wondered if he was about to blow something up. So if a black guy got caught—and those AAL morons are expendable; they might arrange for the whole mosque to get bagged with anthrax spores and the photos I took of the water supply—every time someone who wasn't black looked at someone who was, it'd be, 'Watch out for the nigger; he's going to try to poison you.' "

"Ouch," Castillo said.

"Jack's right, Ace. Nobody will talk about it, but that's the way it is."

"Okay," Castillo said. "I'm convinced that this thing should be looked into, and we're not equipped to do it. So, what you're suggesting is that I get on the horn and call Langley and say I have two defectors?"

"No. That's exactly what we're going to try to talk you out of doing, at least until we have looked into it and have something Langley—and Homeland Security and the FBI—can't look at, then laugh in our face and condescendingly say, 'Oh, we know all about that, and there's nothing to it.' "

"I don't think I follow you," Castillo said.

"Okay. Let's suppose that I'm right, and Berezovsky and the redhead were headed for Vienna, having arranged to defect. Who was going to help them do that?"

"My friend Miss Moneypenny," Castillo said.

"Right, Ace. And they never showed; they have disappeared. So Miss Moneypenny—that's not her name; why do I let you get away with that?— *Miss Eleanor Dillworth,* the station chief, who is about to become famous at Langley for being the one who turned in the Berlin rezident and the Copenhagen rezident in one fell swoop of spook genius, is more than a little worried.

"She would have kept Langley posted on what's going on. So they probably sent somebody over there to help her carry this off. For sure, they have assets in place—an airplane standing by, and someone turning the mattresses and polishing the silver in one of those houses on Chesapeake Bay. Wouldn't surprise me if the DCI already is practicing his modest little speech in which he lets slip, 'Oh, by the way, Mister President, my station chief in Vienna just brought in the SVR Berlin rezident,' etcetera, etcetera. . . .

"But suddenly no Berezovsky. Anywhere. He's vanished. So the DCI asks Station Chief Dillworth, 'What has happened? Has anything unusual happened around here lately?' And Dillworth replies, 'Not that I can think of,' but does think to herself, *Except that good ol' Charley Castillo was in town, very briefly.*"

"Okay, so she suspects we have them. So what?"

"It is not nice to steal the agency's defectors, Colonel. They might let you off with a warning if you promptly hand them over and say you'll never do it again. But don't hold your breath. And if you did hand them over, we're back to: 'We know all about that Congo facility, and there's nothing to it.' "

"So what am I supposed to do?" Castillo said.

"If Alex and I have another forty-eight hours, minimum, I think we can get a hell of a lot more out of Berezovsky than we have so far. One of the problems—and this is where you will get your feathers up, Ace, but that can't be helped—is your method of interrogation. He thinks you're a fool with this 'Let's have a swim and some steak and wine and be friends'—and that makes all of us fools."

Castillo was silent a moment, then put down his coffee mug with a *clunk* that seemed to resonate in the table.

"You're right, Edgar. My feathers are up. But you damn sure aren't going to put him—either one of them—naked into a chair, pour ice water on them, and start shining bright lights into their eyes."

Delchamps shook his head.

"You underestimate me, Ace. Me and Alex and Santini. That doesn't work on people like Berezovsky and Sister, and we know it. What we're going to do is give him a little opportunity to worry while we question him just about around the clock in two-man relays."

Shit. This is really where my new relationship gets rocky.

"What's he going to worry about?" Castillo said.

"Where his sister is and what she is telling us."

What the hell is he thinking?

"And where is the sister going to be?"

"Same place as you, Ace."

What did he say?

"What?"

"Anywhere but here, Ace, when Ambassador Montvale calls to ask if you happen to know anything about Berezovsky. Bariloche would make sense. You're going there to see Pevsner, right?"

"And I should take her with me? Is that what you're saying?"

For a romantic interlude in Bariloche?

Jesus, maybe they do know!

Is that what this is?

They want me out of the way because I just proved my gross goddamn stupidity by screwing a SVR agent?

And since they can't order me out of the way, they're offering me three sex-filled days in beautiful Bariloche.

Well, sanity has returned.

Svetlana, my love, I now understand what happened. I'm not even angry with you. You did what you thought you had to do, and you did it with great skill. I will remember that piece—those pieces—of absolutely superb ass to my dying day.

But . . . Yea, I have seen the light, Praise Jesus, and ol' Charley ain't gonna sin no more.

"Okay, Edgar," Castillo said. "Let's cut the crap. Why do you want me out of here?"

The question surprised—maybe shocked—not only Delchamps but the others as well. It showed on their faces.

"Ace, I just told you. We want to interrogate that bastard for forty-eight hours."

"You could do that if I was here. You know I usually defer to you in matters like this. What else is there? I either get a good answer or I stay and wait for the agency to send people to take these people off my hands."

"Jesus Christ!" Darby said.

"I told you something like this would probably happen," Delchamps said.

"Let's have it," Castillo ordered.

Darby threw up his hands in resignation. "Tell him."

"You're not going to like this, Ace."

"Come on, come on."

"Our egos are involved," Delchamps said.

"What?"

"Nobody in the agency is supposed to know what anybody else has done, right? If you get blown away, they put a star with no name on it on the wall. But that's bullshit. Anybody with enough brains to find his ass with both hands knows what's going on."

"Where the hell are you going with this?" Castillo demanded.

"We weren't going to tell you this until this little escapade . . . scratch 'little escapade' . . . until *this situation* is over, one way or the other.

"What happened after we had our discussion last night, leading to everything I said before, is that Darby and I had a couple of belts and, write this down, Ace, *in vino veritas,* I told him that I had had enough of the agency, even my dealings with it while working for you."

"I keep saying this, but I don't know what the hell you're talking about."

"Okay. If I was a good agency man, when you told me in Vienna that you had these two in the bag I would have insisted that we follow the rules and hand them over to Miss Moneypenny, she being the CIA officer responsible for defectors, according to paragraph nine, subparagraph thirteen. If you had not done that, I was obligated to inform her or a suitably senior agency bureaucrat of your defiance of the United States Code and the rules governing the clandestine service of the CIA."

"You didn't say anything."

"Because you were doing the right thing, Ace. You had the ball and you ran with it."

"Charley," Darby said, "when you told me you were drafting me to work for you again, and not to tell anybody, I didn't."

Castillo looked at him and waited for him to go on.

He didn't. Delchamps answered for him: "Even though he had a direct order from Frank Lammelle, the DDCI, to call him—or the DCI—immediately and personally if he ever had any contact with you about anything ever again. And, of course, not to tell you about the order."

"I'll be a son of a bitch," Castillo said.

"And you thought good ol' Frank just came to see you in the hospital and wish you a speedy recovery from taking that hit in the tail, right? I think his primary purpose in coming down here was to fumigate his people who had been contaminated by you."

"He gave the same speech to the Sienos and Bob Howell," Darby said, mentioning the CIA station chief in Montevideo.

Delchamps said: "No witnesses. Nothing in writing. The sonofabitch even told the Sienos one at a time, so that it would be he-said/she-said." He paused, then went on: "And if you went to Montvale with this—I suspect that thought is running through your head—what would happen, Ace? Not a goddamn thing, and you know it. You could go to the President, and he would have the choice of firing the DCI, the DDCI, the ambassador, or Lieutenant Colonel Charley Castillo—and you know who would win that one."

Delchamps paused and waited until he saw that Castillo couldn't argue with what he had just said, then went on: "Okay, so getting back to why do we want you out of here: I told Alex I was going to stick around until this esc—*situation*—is resolved one way or the other, and then I'm really going to put in my papers."

"You ever hear 'great minds travel similar paths,' Charley?" Darby said. "I told Edgar that I've been thinking about hanging it up since I got the speech about you from Lammelle, and that, when I hadn't called the SOB when you drafted me again, it looked like I'd made up my mind."

"And that started the mutiny," Santini put in. "I said, 'Count me in. If they don't trust me to protect the President because I slipped on an icy step, then fuck 'em.' "

"And," Jack Britton said, "for much the same reasons as my distinguished comrade has offered, Colonel, I, too, have decided that my Secret Service career has been nipped in the bud. Somebody tried to whack me, and getting shot at is just not allowed."

Castillo shook his head. "And why did you think you couldn't, or shouldn't, tell me this?"

"I'm not through, Ace. Now, several things are going to happen when this situation is resolved. I think this factory is heavy. So does Alex. If we're right and something can be done about it, that's a very good way for Alex and me and Santini to be remembered.

"Worst-case scenario: We're wrong. It's bullshit. But it comes out—and it will—that you did indeed snatch Berezovsky and Sister from the CIA, aided and abetted in this criminal enterprise by renegade Clandestine Services and Secret Service agents. They would ordinarily try to make an example of us, but I don't think so. That might get in the papers, and make the agency and the Secret Service look foolish. We'll all just retire—quietly fold our tents and steal away into the night."

"All of you? Two-Gun, for example?"

"Two-Gun can never go back to the FBI, no more than . . ."

He stopped.

"Finish what you were going to say," Castillo said.

"No more than you can go back to the Army, Ace, if the worst scenario is what happens. You know that you've been a pain in the ass to Montvale since this whole OOA business started. Now, when the DCI goes to him—or directly to the President—he has all the reasons he needs—you gave them to him when you snatched Berezovsky—to say, 'I knew all along, Mister President, that something like this was going to happen. Castillo is a loose cannon,' etcetera, etcetera."

"Yeah," Castillo agreed.

"Maybe you could walk on this, Ace, if you truthfully said that you never interrogated Colonel Berezovsky and that as soon as you could, you turned over him and his family to the CIA. You didn't even know that the sister was a spook."

"What makes you think I'd want a walk?"

"Because you're very good at what you do, Ace. You are far too young to retire, and can probably be very useful to the President in the future."

"You know goddamn well that's not going to happen," Castillo said. "Snatching the Russians was my idea. If everything goes sour, I'll take the lumps."

Delchamps nodded. "And lumps there will be, Ace. Whether or not it goes sour. I told you that in Vienna. Let's say we"—he gestured at the others—"are right. And we get Berezovsky to tell all. That would really put egg on the agency's face, and Montvale's. They would really come after you."

"You're all determined to quit, right?"

They all nodded.

"Charley, there's no other option," Darby said, and chuckled. " 'No good deed ever goes unpunished.' You never heard that?"

"Is Duffy here?" Castillo asked.

Delchamps shook his head.

"If I'm going to go to Bariloche, I'm going to need his friend's Aero Commander."

"Duffy's at Jorge Newbery arranging that," Delchamps said. "Where shortly he will be joined by Sergeant Major Davidson and Corporal Bradley, whom he picked up at Ezeiza. Davidson said the Cherub could sit on Red Underpants while you're visiting Pevsner."

"You must have been pretty sure I was going to go along with this," Castillo said.

"Davidson was. He's also a mutineer, Ace."

"He said he's got his twenty years in," Santini said. "And he's sick of being pushed around by a chickenshit, just-promoted light colonel who's younger than he is."

"Don't take it to heart, Charley," Britton said. "He probably didn't mean it."

"And what do we do with Lester?" Castillo asked.

"The Cherub, I am ashamed to say, did not come up in the course of this conversation," Delchamps said. "I don't think the Marine Corps will let him retire at nineteen. But we'll think of something."

"And now I suggest we go in and have breakfast with our guests," Darby said. "And while we're doing that, the housekeeper will throw a few things in a bag for Colonel Alekseeva, just enough for a day or two of fun and romance in the beautiful Llao Llao Resort and Casino."

Castillo looked at him and after a long moment decided that the word "romance" had gone innocently into what Darby had said.

[TWO]
KM 28.5, Panamericana, Southbound
Buenos Aires Province, Argentina
0820 30 December 2005

"Colonel Castillo," Lieutenant Colonel Svetlana Alekseeva said, "we are being followed by three men in a Peugeot sedan."

They were in Darby's embassy car, an armored BMW with diplomatic license plates and equipped with a shortwave radio. Darby was driving. Castillo was in the front passenger seat holding the puppy, his lap protected by a copy of that day's *Buenos Aires Herald,* which had been a sanitary/sartorial suggestion of Sandra Britton.

Max and Svetlana Alekseeva were in the backseat. Darby had confided in Castillo that he had switched on the baby locks, a statement that he had to explain to a baffled Castillo, who was grossly ignorant of most things having to do with any aspect of child rearing, and had no idea there was a device available to keep youngsters—and adult female ex–SVR agents—from opening the rear doors of a car once they had been closed on them.

"Not to worry, Colonel," Darby replied. "They're Gendarmería Nacional. Comandante Duffy doesn't want anything to happen to you before you tell us who ordered the hit on him and his family."

"I have no idea what you're talking about," Svetlana said, somewhat plaintively.

"Right," Darby said. "What about that promise you made to Colonel Castillo to tell him everything he wanted to know?"

She did not reply for a moment, but then said, again, somewhat plaintively, "I know nothing about a Comandante Duffy."

"Your call, Colonel Alekseeva," Darby said.

Aside from a general "good morning" addressed to everyone at the breakfast table, Castillo had not said a word to Svetlana—nor she to him until just now—since he'd gotten up.

But this, Castillo realized, was not because he had inadvertently signaled her—or she had somehow figured out—that he now understood the greatest love story since *Anna Karenina*—or maybe *Doctor Zhivago?*—was really her putting into practice what she had been taught in How to Be a Successful Spy 101: Fucking Your Way Successfully Through a Difficult Interrogation.

She thinks she still has me in the bag, and that I am just trying to make sure our great romance is kept in the closet.

Which of course means that she thinks she has had enough postcoital experience to be able to judge the morning-after reaction of the interrogator.

She's wrong.

Stupid here finally woke up.

[THREE]
Jet-Stream Aviation
Aeropuerto Internacional Jorge Newbery
Buenos Aires, Argentina
0845 30 December 2005

Castillo could see Comandante Liam Duffy, Sergeant Major Jack Davidson, and Corporal Lester Bradley—whom he expected to see—and Alfredo Munz and Captain Dick Sparkman, USAF—whom he did not expect to see—at the airport, standing around the nose of the trim, high-wing, twin-engine Aero Commander 560 when Darby's embassy BMW drove up to the tarmac fence.

"Keep her in the car until I see what's going on," Castillo ordered, and, holding the pup with one hand and the sanitary/sartorial newspaper in the other, got out of the car.

Max nimbly jumped from the backseat, went out Castillo's door, and raced toward Corporal Bradley, clearing the waist-high fence as if it wasn't there.

By the time Castillo reached the gate in the fence, and the airport policeman guarding it, two of the men in the Peugeot sedan that had been following them were out of the car and at the gate. One held it open for him, and the other one said, "I will take that newspaper from you, Colonel, and get rid of it."

Castillo handed it to him, marveling at both how soaked the newspaper had become on the way from Pilar—*You little sonofabitch,* he thought, scratching the pup's ears, *you must be mostly bladder*—and at the unaccustomed courtesy of the gendarmería officers.

They usually stand around practicing how to look dour.

The reason became immediately apparent. Their commanding officer walked toward Castillo, then broke into a trot and, when he reached Castillo, wrapped him in a bear hug, pounded his back, and kissed him wetly on both cheeks.

"Oh, my friend Charley," he said. "It is so good to see you!"

What the hell is this all about?

"El Coronel Munz told me that you understand," El Comandante Liam Duffy said. "But that doesn't make it any better."

"There's nothing to be concerned about, Liam."

"I had three men killed and six wounded—in addition, of course, to the two men those bastards massacred as soon as we were"—he paused, smiled, and switched to English—"boots on the ground"—then back to Spanish—"and there were funerals and I had to deal with the families."

"I understand, Liam."

"I just could not get to Uruguay right away, and when I did, you had already gone to the U.S. of A."

He grabbed Castillo's arms with both hands.

"I should have somehow arranged to go to Montevideo," he said. "You shed blood with us! You are one of us, Carlos!"

He got control of himself.

"You remember Segundo Comandante Martínez and Sargento Primero Pérez, of course?" Duffy said, indicating the two gendarmes who'd opened the gate for Castillo and taken care of the sodden newspaper.

Why do I think the last time I saw these guys they were in camos and had black-and-brown grease all over their face and hands?

"How could I forget?" Castillo said, smiling broadly, offering his hand, and then—*Oh, hell, when in Rome or Buenos Aires!*—hugging them and kissing their coarse cheeks.

"You have luggage, *mi coronel?*" the younger one—*Probably the sergeant,* Castillo thought—asked.

"There's a couple of bags in the trunk," Castillo said.

"And is the Russian woman in the car?" Duffy asked.

Castillo nodded.

"I would like to introduce her to my wife and children," Duffy said, "and then kill her slowly and painfully."

And that, Castillo decided, *is not what they call hyperbole.*

"Liam, she was in Europe when that happened," Castillo said.

"She's one of them," Duffy said simply.

"She and her brother have information I need."

"So Alfredo says. What I want are the names of the people who tried to kill my wife and children."

"I will first have to find out who *ordered* the attack on you," Castillo said. "And then, if you can get him, you can find out from him who actually attacked you and your family."

"You find out who he is—or she is—and I'll get him," Duffy said.

"I'll do my best, Liam."

Munz, Sparkman, Davidson, and Bradley walked up to them.

"Nice flight, Lester?"

"I was never in first class before, sir," Bradley said.

"Well, that was certainly a mistake. We'll take the difference out of your pay."

Bradley recoiled at that, but it didn't take him long to realize he was having his chain pulled.

"Do you have a pistol, Lester?"

"No, sir."

"Get him one, Jack," Castillo ordered. "Make sure Little Red Under Britches sees you give it to him—and that she sees you chambering a round, Lester."

"Yes, sir," Bradley said. "Little Red—what did you say, sir?"

"The lady in the car is a SVR officer, Les. A lieutenant colonel. I don't think she'll try to run away—she'll have no idea where we will be, and I have all of her identification in my briefcase—but she may. I don't want her dead."

"Yes, sir."

"I just happen to have one with me," Davidson said, and took a Colt Model 1911A1 from the small of his back. He handed it to Bradley. "There's already one in the chamber."

"Yes, Sergeant Major," Bradley said politely, then with speed and precision that visibly astonished the gendarmes, he ejected the magazine, worked the action to eject the round in the chamber, caught it on the fly, examined the pistol to make sure the chamber was indeed empty, fed the just-ejected round to the magazine, fed the magazine to the pistol, let the slide slam home, carefully lowered the hammer to de-cock it, and finally slipped the pistol under his belt on the small of his back.

"He's usually much faster than that," Davidson said with a straight face.

"Bradley—" Castillo began.

"May I see you a moment, please, Colonel?" Alfredo Munz interrupted.

Castillo followed him toward the Aero Commander.

Duffy's face showed that he didn't like Munz and Castillo having a private conversation.

But there doesn't seem to be anything that can be done about it.

Munz, his back to Duffy, immediately proved him wrong.

"Take out some money, and count out a lot of it, and hand it to me," Munz said. "I'm making it seem like I don't want Liam to see."

Castillo didn't hesitate.

"Charley, I think I had better go with you to Bariloche," Munz said.

"I can handle her, Alfredo."

"And I can handle Liam's gendarmes in Bariloche," Munz said, "who I suspect are going to try to be far more helpful than you want them to be."

Munz put the money in his pocket, laid a hand on Castillo's shoulder in thanks for the cash, and led him back to the others.

"Colonel," Sparkman said, and handed him a flight plan. "Perfect weather all the way."

"Thank you," Castillo said.

And what happens to you, Dick, if—when—the worst scenario happens?

That would effectively end your Air Force career. Getting shot down in flames for your association with the disgraced OOA will be even worse for you than your association with the Air Commandos.

"Colonel," Davidson said, "I put an AFC device aboard."

"Thank you."

Munz handed Davidson the wad of hundred-dollar bills Castillo had given him.

Duffy's face showed he wondered what the hell that was all about.

"Lester," Castillo ordered, "go with Colonel Munz and put the lady in a backseat in the airplane."

"Yes, sir."

As she walked past him, Lieutenant Colonel Alekseeva asked Castillo if she could ask where they were going.

He didn't reply.

[FOUR]
The Llao Llao Resort Hotel
San Carlos de Bariloche
Río Negro Province, Argentina
1625 30 December 2005

The manager of the luxury resort—who was attired in a tailcoat and striped trousers—met them at the front door, shook Munz's hand, ignored everybody else, and led them through the lobby—where a dozen employees were engaged in changing the holiday decorations from Christmas to New Year's—then to the elevator bank, and on to a top-floor suite.

"This will do nicely, thank you," Munz said after examining the four rooms. "I will need keys for all the doors, of course."

The manager handed him a dozen keys on a ring.

"The boat is available at the dock, Colonel," he said, bowed his head, and left.

"May I use the restroom?" Svetlana asked.

Munz pointed to a door.

"Wait outside for her, Bradley," Castillo ordered. "If she tries to get away, try not to shoot her, but . . ."

"Yes, sir."

Svetlana did not look at Castillo as she walked past him. Max walked after both of them. Castillo set the puppy on the floor, where he immediately followed his father to the bathroom door, then raised his leg against the leg of a small table and puddled the carpet.

"I wonder where he gets it all," Castillo said, almost admiringly.

"You're taking him with you?" Munz asked.

Castillo nodded.

"He's for Elena. For her and Sergei and Aleksandr, but primarily for her."

Munz nodded.

"I'd like to think I'm doing that simply to be a nice guy," Castillo said. "But I'm not sure if it's not because it will get to Pevsner."

"I like the kids, too," Munz said. "And I know you're a nice guy, whether or not you like to admit it."

Castillo looked at him but remained silent.

And what happens to you, Alfredo, when the worst scenario comes down?

A nice settlement payment, of course, but what about after that?

Munz pulled back his jacket, revealing a revolver in a high-mount hip holster.

Castillo recognized the offer and shook his head. "I go in peace. And I would be heavily outgunned, anyway."

"Well, don't worry about Mata Hari. I can deal with her," Munz said, then smiled and added, "Or if I can't, Lester can."

Castillo chuckled.

She's figured that out. She may be curious about Lester, but she saw that very professional display of pistol handling, and as a pistoleer herself, she knows that there is a very strong chance she will be wounded seriously with a heavy-caliber bullet if she tries to run.

And by now she also knows that despite some spectacular initial success in turning me into a chump, that's over. She's given up on the soulful looks into my eyes.

"You know how to get to the boat?" Munz asked.

"Get on the elevator and push the Minus-2 button, and then down the corridor."

"You sure you don't want me to go with you?"

"Yeah, I'm sure."

Castillo walked to the bathroom door, scooped up the puppy, said, "Come on, Max," then nodded at Munz and walked out of the suite.

Castillo heard the boat's engine quietly burbling when he walked out onto the long pier jutting into the lake, but he couldn't see it until he was almost to where it was tied by the stern to the pier.

He was a little surprised by the boat. He expected a cabin cruiser. This was—he searched for the word and after a moment found it—a *speedboat.* There had been one like it when he was a kid, at the beach house on the Gulf of Mexico. That had been a Chris-Craft, and he and Fernando were never allowed to take it out themselves—but of course had—as their grandfather thought it was dangerous in ocean water.

The speedboat waiting for him now was made of mahogany and had two passenger compartments, one fore and one aft, with the engine mounted between them. The forward compartment had the controls and an automobile-like steering wheel. The aft compartment had a leather-upholstered seat for three behind a small windshield that was supposed to protect the passengers from spray—but never did.

The man standing on the pier directed him: "In the rear seat, please, *mi coronel.* For the balance."

"Thank you," Castillo said, and, holding the puppy against him, carefully stepped into the boat and then down into the seat. Max leapt effortlessly aboard, inspected the front compartment, then came back and sat beside Castillo.

Castillo then set the pup on the footboards. He had not thought to bring newspaper or one of the Llao Llao's monogrammed towels with him.

The man untied the stern, then jumped onto the boat, causing it to rock somewhat. He squatted beside Castillo and handed him a cellular phone.

"I know the colonel has probably told you, *mi coronel,* but button seven is my phone and button four is the colonel."

Munz had not said a word.

"Thank you," Castillo said.

"I will take you to the pier. You can get out without help?"

"Yes."

"And then I will go beyond the floodlights, which, if they don't come on as we approach the pier, will do so as soon as you step on the pier. There are motion sensors."

"Okay."

"There is a guard shack, usually only one man, at the shore end of the pier."

Castillo said, "Thank you," instead of what started to come to his lips: "I know. This is not my first visit to 'Karinhall.'"

The man moved on hands and knees to the forward compartment and dropped into it. Castillo both heard and felt the *chunk* as the man engaged the transmission and the propeller began to spin.

Thirty seconds later, the engine revved and Castillo sensed the speedboat going up on the step. Ten seconds after that, he got a face full of spray. Max went down on the floorboards next to the puppy. Castillo sought what refuge he could behind the windshield.

The speedboat slowed and almost stopped as suddenly as it had accelerated twenty minutes before.

Castillo raised his head above the windshield and saw in the faint light that they were very close to a pier. He grabbed the puppy from the floorboard by the loose skin above its neck and stood up on the leather seat.

The man driving the boat skillfully put the stern against the pier and held it there long enough for Castillo to jump out of the boat. The moment Max leapt onto the pier, the engine revved and the boat headed back out on the lake.

Castillo had just enough time to change his grip on the squealing puppy when floodlights came on, blinding him.

It took perhaps twenty seconds for his eyes to adjust enough for him to see down the pier.

Twenty yards away a man came warily, in a half-crouch, down the pier toward him. He held an Uzi. Max was halfway between them; his hair bristled, and he was growling deeply.

The man cocked the Uzi.

"If you shoot the dog," Castillo called in Spanish, "you will die!"

He repeated the same threat in Russian and then a third time in Hungarian.

"Lower the gun!" a voice from farther away called, loudly and authoritatively, in Hungarian.

Castillo could now see the second man, who also had an Uzi.

"Hey, János," Castillo called in Hungarian to Aleksandr Pevsner's bodyguard. "What are you doing out here in the middle of nowhere?"

And then, as János kept advancing toward them, Castillo ordered in Hungarian, "No, Max! Sit!"

Max sat, but Castillo could hear him growling still.

János looked around the pier.

"You are alone?" János asked, then without waiting for a reply: "You didn't bring the redheaded woman?"

"Do you see her, János?"

"He does not expect you," János said, then corrected himself: "He did not expect to see you."

"Well, he knows as well as I do that life is full of surprises," Castillo said.

János gestured for him to walk down the pier. Halfway to the shore, the floodlights died and were replaced with small lights illuminating the pier and a path beyond.

"You are well now, Colonel?" János asked softly.

"It hurts me a little to sit down," Castillo said honestly. "The leg's okay."

"My woman says I now have a zipper," János said, and drew a line from his waist up his side to his armpit." He was quiet a moment, then added, "I never say, 'Thank you, Colonel'—so, thank you."

"You're welcome, János."

A Jeep Wrangler, so new it looked right off a showroom floor, was at the end of the pier. It had a driver waiting behind the wheel.

Max jumped in the front seat and sat there.

"In the back, Max," Castillo ordered.

Max reluctantly complied after the order had been repeated three times.

"He bite me if I get in back?" János asked.

"Probably," Castillo said, and somewhat awkwardly got in the back.

[FIVE]

Aleksandr Pevsner, a tall, dark-haired man, wearing linen trousers and jacket and a yellow polo shirt, was waiting for them under a huge chandelier in the foyer of the enormous house.

"You've lost a lot of weight, Hermann," Castillo greeted him in German. "And some hair, too. Been on a diet here in 'Karinhall,' have you? Nothing but *knockwurst und sauerkraut?*"

Pevsner smiled as if he really didn't want to.

"Frankly, there are times when one wishes never to see dear friends again," Pevsner replied in Russian. "This is one of them."

"I love you too, Aleksandr," Castillo said. "But I hope you aren't going to kiss me."

"Never fear. Where's the redhead?"

"What redhead?"

"The one you flew here in that little airplane."

"A gentleman never discusses his love life. Didn't your mother teach you that?" He held up the puppy and gestured at Max. "Besides, I've come to trust only canines."

Pevsner ignored that. "How is your . . . wound?"

"My leg is coming along just fine. My ass, not so good. Thank you for asking."

"You are absolutely impossible!"

"Does that mean you're not going to offer me a drink?"

"Now that I see you don't have some floozy with you, I would be honored if you would have a glass of champagne with Anna and me." Pevsner gestured toward the open door of the library.

"Where's the statue?" Castillo said, looking around the foyer. "I would have thought it would be at the foot of the stairs."

"What statue?" Pevsner asked automatically, and then his face showed that he understood he was about to have his chain pulled.

"Of Lenin," Castillo said. "To prove you didn't buy this place because of your admiration for the late *Reichsforst-und-Jägermeister*."

He threw Pevsner a stiff-armed Nazi salute.

"Charley, you're not teasing him already?" a tall, svelte blonde asked in Russian as they walked into the library.

"Teasing him?" Castillo replied as he walked to her and kissed her cheek. "If it walks like a duck, talks like a duck, and has a house made from the same plans as Hermann Goering's hunting lodge . . ."

"We didn't realize that until we bought the place, and you know it," she said, laughing. Her attention went to Castillo's arms. "What are you doing with that puppy?"

"Trying to get rid of it," Castillo said. "You don't happen to know of some kind and gentle young lady of thirteen or so who would take it off my hands, do you?"

"You're serious? You brought that for Elena? What is it?"

Castillo gestured at Max.

"A little version of him. By way of Marburg, Germany, and Vienna," Castillo said, looking at Pevsner as he spoke, and not being surprised when he saw that Pevsner's eyes had turned to ice.

"Let me see it," Anna said, taking the puppy from Castillo, then holding it up and rubbing noses with it. "Charley, he's precious! Elena will be crazy with him. Thank you so much!"

"The small horse is the father?" Pevsner asked, indicating Max. "It will grow to be the same?"

"Yes, indeed."

Anna picked up a telephone, waited a moment, and then said, "Will you ask the children to join us in the library, please?" She hung up and turned to Castillo. "Alek said you might be bringing someone with you and . . ."

"I know," Castillo said. "Your husband always thinks the worst of me."

"If it walks like a duck, talks like a duck . . ." Pevsner said.

Castillo laughed.

A maid rolled a bar service into the room.

"What can we offer you, Charley?"

"I'm feeling Russian. Is that vodka I see?"

"How do you want it?" Pevsner asked.

"In a glass would be nice," Castillo said straight-faced.

Anna laughed.

"I meant, from the freezer, or with ice, or room temperature," Pevsner said, shaking his head.

"From the freezer, please," Castillo said.

Pevsner wagged a rather imperious finger at the maid and told her in Spanish to bring a bottle from the freezer.

"Your Spanish is getting better," Castillo said.

"Better than what?" Pevsner asked suspiciously.

"Better than it was," Castillo replied.

"What does he eat?" Anna asked.

"Puppy chow," Castillo said, and took a plastic zip-top bag from his jacket pocket and laid it on a small table. "I have more in the hotel. And I am assured it can be found in any supermarket in the country. This is Royal Canine Puppy Chow For Very Large Dogs. Max loves it."

"I'll have to write that down," Anna said, and went to an escritoire that looked as if it belonged in the Louvre and did so.

"I have a little trouble picturing you, Friend Charley, traveling the globe and caring for a puppy," Pevsner said.

"He brings out the paternal instinct in me," Castillo said piously.

"What were you doing in Germany. Visiting home?"

"Actually, I had to go to a funeral."

"How sad," Anna said. "Family?"

"Employee," Castillo said. He met Pevsner's eyes. "He died suddenly."

Three adolescents entered the room and politely, shyly, made their manners to Castillo. The girl kissed his cheek and the older boy shook his hand.

"Oh, where did that puppy come from?" Elena Pevsner said. She took him from her mother, matter-of-factly held him up to examine his belly, and finished. "He's adorable. What's his name?"

"That's up to you, sweetheart," Castillo said.

It took her a moment to take his meaning. "Really?"

Castillo nodded.

"Oh, Charley, thank you ever so much!"

"Honey," Castillo said, picking up the bag of puppy chow. "Why don't you take him someplace, get two bowls, put the bowls on newspaper, put water in one, and this in the other?"

"How much do I give him?"

"Honey, you're lucky. Dogs are like people. Some are pigs and eat whatever is put in front of them—then get sick and throw it up. The others, like Max and Nameless here, are gentlemen. They take only what they need, when they need it."

My God, her eyes are shining!

Like Randy's eyes.

I just did a good thing,

But if no good deed goes unpunished . . . ?

The maid appeared with a bottle of vodka encased in ice.

"Can Max come?" Aleksandr, the oldest boy, asked.

"If I can have him back," Castillo said.

The children left the room. Max trotted after them.

"That was a very nice thing for you to do, Charley," Pevsner said as he handed Castillo a small glass of the vodka. "Thank you."

"My son has his brother," Castillo said. "I thought Elena would like one."

"You saw your son?" Anna asked.

"His grandfather brought him to our ranch for quail hunting. I hunted with him, and then I started to teach him how to fly."

"And he doesn't know?" Anna asked softly.

Castillo shook his head.

"Oh, Charley!" Anna said, and went to him and laid her hand on his cheek and kissed him. "I am so sorry."

Castillo shrugged.

"Me, too, but that's how it is."

"Would you think me terribly cynical if I suspected there's more to your visit than bringing the children a puppy?" Pevsner asked.

"Alek!" Anna said warningly.

"I don't know about cynical. I guess it's to be expected of an oprichniki. I know you guys have to be careful, even of your friends. Or maybe especially of your friends."

If looks could freeze, I would now be colder than that ice-encased bottle.

He raised his vodka glass to Pevsner and drained it.

"Mud in your eye, Alek!"

Anna's face had gone almost white.

"What did you say?" Pevsner asked coldly.

"About what?"

"Goddamn you to hell, Charley!"

"You're not supposed to have secrets from your friends," Castillo said. "I remember you telling me that. Several times."

"You are on very thin ice, Friend Charley."

"Speaking of ice," Castillo said, raising his glass. "That was just what I needed. May I have another?"

He went to the ice-encased bottle of vodka and refilled his glass.

"Can I pour you one? You look like you could use it," Castillo said, and then asked, "How come you never told me you are a card-carrying member of the Oprichina?"

"*Was* a member," Anna said very softly.

Pevsner glared at her, then moved the glare back to Castillo, who went on: "Okay. *Was* an oprichniki. Did you formally resign? Or just not show up for work one day as the Kremlin walls were falling down?"

"What do you want, Charley?" Pevsner asked very softly.

"I want you to tell me everything you know about Colonel Dmitri Berezovsky."

Anna sucked in her breath. Her lips looked bloodless.

God, I hope she's not about to pass out!

"Berezovsky, Dmitri, Colonel. The Berlin rezident," Castillo pursued. "A high muckety-muck of the Oprichina. Tell me about him, Alek, please."

"Why are you interested in Berezovsky?"

"Fair question. He had a man who worked for me at the *Tages Zeitung* killed. And he tried to take out two people very close to me. Oh, and me. I'm always curious about people who want to kill me."

"If Berezovsky wanted you . . . eliminated . . . you wouldn't be standing here," Pevsner said.

"Well, you're wrong. He did, and here I am. You should not believe your own press releases, Alek. The SVR isn't really that good."

"Why did he try to kill you, Charley?" Anna asked.

He saw that some of the color had returned to her face.

And there was something about her carriage that told him that she had abandoned her just-a-wife-who-doesn't-have-any-idea-what's-going-on role.

And Pevsner has seen that, too. He's not trying to shut her up.

"I don't really know. I think he was trying to send a message for the SVR. Maybe make a statement. 'We're back, and we're going to kill everybody who gets in our way.'"

He gave that a moment to register and then went on. "I know why he took out the reporter for the *Tages Zeitung*. He was getting too close to the connection between the Marburg Group who made all that money sending medicine and food to Iraq, and what's going on in the African chemical factory. I want you to tell me everything you know about that, too."

That was a shot in the dark.

But his eyes—and especially the tongue quickly wetting his lips—show I hit him hard with it.

The proof came immediately.

"In exchange for what?" Pevsner asked.

"Well, for one thing, it will keep our professional relationship where it is. The agency and the FBI will leave you alone . . . presuming you don't break any U.S. laws."

That's bullshit.

The agency and the FBI will no more obey the President's order to leave him alone than they obeyed Montvale's order to leave me alone. They will do whatever they can to silence him. The agency's skirts are the opposite of clean.

"How cynical are you, Friend Charley?"

"Well, probably not as much as I should be. But I can learn, I guess."

"I have personal reasons for not telling you all I know about Dmitri Berezovsky. I won't tell you what they are, and that's not negotiable. I will tell you what I know—which isn't much—about the chemical laboratory in the ex–Belgian Congo, and my price there is very cheap. You don't tell anyone—anyone including the agency—where you got it."

So Berezovsky wasn't lying. There is a chemical laboratory. His big chip to deal with me. Or was Svetlana the big chip?

"Why are you being so good to me, Alek?"

"That's why I asked how cynical you are. Are you capable of believing it's because I think what they're doing there is despicable?"

"Define despicable."

"Biological warfare that would kill millions of innocent people is despicable. Wouldn't you agree?"

"Why would you say that none of this has come out?"

"It has come out. The Muslims boast there will be a caliphate from Madrid to Baghdad and that they will kill how many millions of Christians—and, of course, Jews—as necessary to accomplish that. Nobody wants to believe that, so they pretend they didn't hear it.

"Exactly as they didn't want to hear that Hitler was murdering undesirables by the millions, and Stalin's starving Russians to death by the millions in the gulags, and Saddam Hussein's use of chemical weapons to kill several hundred thousand of his own people."

"So you're suggesting that there's nothing that can be done, that we should lie down and let these people roll over us?"

"I'm suggesting that the best that people like you and me can do is stop a little here, and a little there, and meanwhile try very hard to keep yourself and the people you love alive."

"Is that the voice of experience I hear?" Castillo asked without thinking, and hearing himself, immediately regretted the sarcasm.

Pevsner's icy glare showed he didn't like it either.

For a very long twenty seconds, he said nothing. Then: "As a matter of fact, it is. It is the experience of my heritage speaking."

He paused again, almost as long.

"Friend Charley, you're very good at what you do. God gave you an ability few have."

Where the hell did God come from?

There was no sarcasm in the way he said that.

Alex believes in God?

I'll be damned!

"You didn't come here and throw the Oprichina in my face without knowing something—probably a good deal, but not as much as you think you do—about it."

He paused, obviously thinking, before going on: "You know how far back it goes?"

Castillo nodded. "Ivan the Awesome."

"A terrible, tormented, cruel, godless man, who by comparison makes Stalin and Hitler and Saddam Hussein look like Saint Francis of Assisi," Pevsner said. "But not all of the people he took off into the state within the state were like him. There were good, God-fearing people among them, who went with him because the alternative to being of unquestioned loyalty to Ivan was watching your family being skinned alive and fed to starving dogs."

"Your ancestors?"

"Don't mock me, Charley."

"I wasn't. I was asking a question."

"Our ancestors, Charley," Anna said softly.

"Some of those who went with Ivan were minor nobility, and some were soldiers, like you and me."

"You were a soldier?" Castillo asked.

"Former Polkovnik Pevsner of the Soviet Air Force at your service, Podpolkovnik Castillo. I was simultaneously, of course, a colonel in the KGB. My father and Anna's father were generals. Anna's mother was a podpolkovnik. My mother never served. Her father, of course, did. Are you getting the picture, or should I go on?"

"What did you do?" Castillo asked.

"Is that important?"

"If you feel uncomfortable telling me, don't."

"I was in charge of ensuring the loyalty of Aeroflot aircrew, service personnel working outside the Soviet Union for Aeroflot, and the transmission—the protection—of diplomatic pouches sent by whatever means."

"For all of Aeroflot?"

"I was considered one of the very reliables," Pevsner said. "And I was. But let me get back to what I was saying: In the beginning, it was the women who kept their faith—their faith, not the Church per se; after Ivan had Saint Philip, the Metropolitan of Moscow, strangled"—he paused to see if Castillo was following him, then went on—"the women understood that being too good a Christian was about as dangerous as harboring disloyal thoughts about Ivan, so while paying lip service to the Church, as was expected of them, aided by some clergy, they kept their faith private, within the family. You understand?"

"I think so," Castillo said.

"It was impossible to really be a Christian—standing up to Ivan and the others we served over the years would have been suicide—but it was possible, here and there, from time to time, to act with great caution and, for example, warn the Jews of an upcoming pogrom so that some of them would survive, or arrange for someone about to be executed or sent to the gulag to make it out of Russia to China or Finland. . . . You understand?"

Castillo nodded.

"That's what I meant, Friend Charley, when I said that the best that people like you and me can do is stop a little here and a little there."

"Why did you leave?"

"Because the opportunity was there. Half of what would become the FSB left as Soviet Russia started coming apart."

"Half of the Oprichina left?"

"Not everybody. Probably less than one-quarter, one-fifth of the FSB—or the Cheka, or the NKVD, whatever, by whatever name—was Oprichina."

"In other words, a state within a state within a state?"

"Precisely."

"Okay," Castillo said. "So why, if you were a card-carrying oprichniki, and doing pretty well, did you leave?"

"I told you, there was the opportunity."

"To swap the good life to make a few bucks as an arms smuggler, which would have not only most of the world's police departments trying to put you in jail, not to mention your former pals in Moscow and in Saint Petersburg trying to whack you and your family, as an example *pour les autres*? Come on, Alek!"

This time it was more than twenty very long seconds before Pevsner replied.

"It is only recently—since I have met you, as a matter of fact, Friend Charley—that I have been—my family has been—in any danger from the FSB."

" 'He's pals with Castillo. Kill the bastard!'?" Castillo said sarcastically.

Pevsner looked at his wife.

"Tell him, Aleksandr," she said. "Or I will. You are alive because of Charley. He is now our family."

Pevsner considered that a long moment, then waved his hands, signaling, *Okay. If that's what you want, you tell him.*

"The Communist Party, Charley, was very wealthy," Anna began. "Another state within a state, if you like. There was more than one hundred billion—no one really knows how much, and I'm speaking of dollars; no one cared then or now for rubles—some in cash and some of it in gold and platinum. Tons of gold and platinum. The Communists had no intention of turning this over to a democratically elected government. They planned to take power again, and they would need the money to do this.

"The first thing they did was authorize what was then the KGB to go into business in Moscow—regular businesses, car dealerships, real estate, everything. The idea wasn't to make money—although that happened—but to find places to hide the money.

"But what to do with the gold and platinum? It had to be taken out of the country and hidden somewhere.

"So how to do that?" Anna asked rhetorically, then gestured at her husband. " 'Ask Comrade Polkovnik Pevsner of the KGB and Aeroflot. He has spent more time out of the Soviet Union and been more places than just about anybody else.' "

"And I was a respected oprichnik," Pevsner interjected, "one who was trusted by them. So when they came to me, I suggested that I knew where to hide it. Saudi Arabia, the U.S., places like that. And I even had a cover story. I would leave the KGB, it would be arranged for me to buy several Ilyushin transports, and I would grow rich transporting small arms around the world and bringing luxury cars and French champagne into Russia. No one would notice—and no one did—that when my Ilyushins left Moscow or Saint Petersburg, several of the wooden crates ostensibly holding Kalashnikov rifles or ammunition for them actually held gold bars. Or platinum."

"Jesus Christ!" Castillo said.

"And, to make sure everybody believed that I had really left the Oprichina, it was arranged for Anna and the children to escape."

"What did you do with the gold and platinum?"

"After taking my agreed-upon fee of five percent—"

"You took five percent of a billion dollars' worth of gold?"

"I took five percent of a lot more than *a* billion dollars' worth of gold, Charley. And about twice that much of platinum."

He saw the look on Castillo's face.

"Is true," he said, chuckling. "And when that was over, I began to spend a very great deal of money ensuring that no one I formerly knew would ever see me or hear of me ever again. So you'll understand my annoyance, Friend Charley, when I heard that a young American colonel—no, a young American *major*—was looking for me because he thought I'd stolen a worn-out, old 727 from an airfield in Angola. At the time, I was buying four new 777s—through other people, of course—more or less direct from Boeing."

He smiled and reached out and touched Castillo's arm.

"Who would have thought the night we met in Vienna that one night we would be sitting together halfway across the world, as Anna put it, as family?"

"Jesus Christ, Alek!" Castillo said.

"If I tell you what I know about—and what I can learn about—the chemical factory outside Kisangani, you will not tell anyone where you got the information?"

"You have my word."

"And maybe you will be able to convince your superiors to do something about it?"

"It'll go, if I have to take it out myself."

Pevsner nodded his approval.

"You heard about the factory from your journalist? Is that what started you on this? 'If it's rotten, Aleksandr Pevsner will certainly know something about it'?"

"Actually, Colonel Dmitri Berezovsky told me about it."

Pevsner clearly bristled at that. "All you had to say was 'None of your business.' I don't find that funny. In the old days, I knew Berezovsky. Despite what he tried to do to you, he's a good man."

"Colonel Dmitri Berezovsky told me about the factory," Castillo said. "I don't lie to friends. If you don't believe me, you can ask your cousin Svetlana."

"I told you, I don't think this is funny. Sometimes, when you think you're being funny, I could kill you."

"Did your cousin Svetlana have red hair the last time you saw her?"

It took a moment for Pevsner to take his meaning.

"Svetlana is here with you?" he asked finally.

"I thought, if it's all right with Anna, you might want to ask her to have dinner with us. I am invited, right?"

"And Alfredo is with her?" Pevsner asked.

"And my bodyguard," Castillo said. "You remember him?"

"The boy with the gun," Pevsner said.

Castillo nodded. "Who killed your pal Lieutenant Colonel Yevgeny Komogorov in the garage of the Sheraton Pilar when Komogorov was trying to kill you."

"And they nearly killed János," Pevsner said. "Yes, Charley. I remember."

Castillo took out his cell phone. "Should I call Munz and tell him to put her on his boat?"

"Where is his boat?"

"Bobbing around in the lake, just outside the reach of your floodlights."

"I always keep a boat at the hotel," Pevsner said. "Get him on the line for me, please, Charley."

Thirty-five minutes later, Pevsner and his wife were standing together under the enormous chandelier in the foyer. Castillo had taken a seat at the side of the room.

János came into the house first, then Munz, then Svetlana, and finally Lester Bradley. Two men followed them, carrying everybody's luggage, including, Castillo saw, the AFC radio.

Svetlana, somewhat confused, looked quickly around the foyer, settled her eyes on Castillo, and asked, somewhat plaintively, "Charley?"

And then Anna sobbed, and Svetlana looked at her and for the first time recognized her. Anna held her arms open and Svetlana ran to her.

Without realizing he had gotten out of the chair, Castillo was now standing.

Anna let go of Svetlana, who moved to Pevsner's open arms. Castillo saw tears running down his cheeks.

Pevsner finally let Svetlana go, took a handkerchief from his pocket, and mopped his eyes.

Svetlana looked at Castillo for a moment, then ran to him.

Castillo decided it would be ungentlemanly of him to refuse her gratitude, even if he was aware that her previous manifestations of affection for him had been solely professionally motivated.

She threw herself into his arms and pressed herself against him.

"Oh, Charley, my Charley, thank you, thank you. I love you so much!"

And then her mouth was on his.

Some time later, Castillo heard Anna say, "If you two are about finished, the children are waiting to see Svetlana."

IX

[ONE]
La Casa en Bosque
San Carlos de Bariloche
Río Negro Province, Argentina
0845 31 December 2005

"I love you, my Charley," Lieutenant Colonel Alekseeva announced, and kissed him very quickly, if incredibly intimately, and then went on: "And I love this room! I'm going to have one just like it!"

She jumped out of the bed and trotted naked to the window on her toes. She pulled the translucent curtain aside and further clarified her desire. "With a view of a lake, like this, and the mountains!"

They were in "The Blue Room," so identified by a little sign on the bed-side telephone, the walls of which were covered with pale blue silk brocade—Castillo thought it was the same shade of blue as that on the Argentine flag and had, when he had been shown—alone—to the room, wondered if that was intentional or coincidental.

He had had perhaps three minutes to consider this and a number of other things when the door to the adjacent room had opened and Lieutenant Colonel Alekseeva, attired as she was now—and carrying a bottle of champagne and two glasses—had joined him.

It was some time later that he noticed through the open door that the walls of the adjacent room were covered with dark green silk brocade and wondered if it was called "The Green Room."

By then, he had come to several philosophical conclusions:

Live today, for tomorrow you may die was one of them.

Anything this good can't be bad was another.

So I'm out of mind, so what? was yet another.

Svetlana let the curtain fall back into place and looked at Castillo.

"I see your face," she said. "Anything worth having is expensive."

Then she trotted back to the bed and dove into it.

"You don't like this room?" she asked.

"I like it fine."

"Then I will buy one just like it for you," she said, and then corrected herself. "For us, my Charley!"

He put his arms around her shoulders and she crawled up on his chest and bit his nipple.

He had time for just one more philosophical conclusion, *There's no such thing as too much of a good thing*, when there was a knock at the corridor door.

"Oh, no!" Svetlana said, raising her head to look at it.

"May I come in?" Anna Pevsner called.

"One moment," Svetlana called, rolled onto her back, pulled the sheet—which was also, Castillo noticed for the first time, Argentina blue—modestly over them, and then called, "Okay. Come!"

Anna came into the room and stood at the foot of the bed with her hands folded in front of her.

"This is difficult for me," she said. "But the children . . ."

"What, Anna?" Svetlana said.

"I believe, as I know you do, what Holy John Chrysostom said about 'the sacrament of the brother.' "

"Good," Svetlana said. "Then don't do it."

What the hell is this?

Who the hell is Holy John whatever she said?

"Would you like me to . . . uh?" Castillo asked, pointing to the bathroom door.

"This concerns you, too, Charley," Anna said.

Svetlana nodded to confirm this.

"Then somebody please tell me about Holy John," Castillo said.

"You are a Christian, Charley?" Anna asked.

"I don't think I'm in particularly good standing."

"I'm sorry," Anna said.

"I will fix that," Svetlana said.

"What about Holy John Whatever?"

"Holy John Chrysostom said one must avoid . . ." Anna began.

"What he said was one must *certainly* avoid judging or condemning one's brother or sister," Svetlana corrected her. "*Certainly* avoid."

"And that's what I'm trying to do. If you want to . . . be intimate . . . with a man not your husband, that's between you, God, and Evgeny."

"Between me and God, certainly. It's none of Evgeny's business."

"Evgeny's your husband."

"*Was* my husband. If he's still alive, he's trying to find me so he can kill me."

"He is still your husband," Anna insisted.

You didn't challenge that "he's trying to find me so he can kill me," though, did you, Anna?

"No, he's not. I left his bed four years ago."

Four years ago?

"You can't break the covenant."

"I did. And you know that the Holy John Chrysostom wrote that it's 'better to break the covenant than to lose one's soul.' "

"That's between you and the Lord."

"Yes, it is. And as far as my Charley is concerned, I'll go with what Saint Paul said in First Corinthians."

"That's up to you."

"I'm a little rusty about First Corinthians," Castillo said. "What exactly did Saint Paul say?"

Anna looked uncomfortable. Svetlana blushed.

"Well?" Castillo pursued.

"Why not? You know anyway. 'If they cannot control themselves, they should marry.' The moment I saw you on the train, I knew I was through controlling myself."

"Saint Paul said that about the unmarried and widows," Anna said.

"I told you, I broke the covenant; I'm not married," Svetlana said. "And when I first saw my Charley, I had been controlling myself for four long, long years. You try that sometime, Anna."

"This is getting us nowhere," Anna said.

"Well, at least it's out in the open," Svetlana said.

"All I'm asking is that you try to . . . behave appropriately in front of the children. Especially Elena. She remembers Evgeny."

"The last time she saw Evgeny she was practically in diapers. She wouldn't know him if he walked in the door right now."

But that would certainly be interesting, wouldn't it?

"Breakfast will be in half an hour," Anna said. "And after that, we're going to decorate the Novogodnaya Yolka." She looked at Castillo, said, "Thank you for understanding, Friend Charley," and walked out the door.

Svetlana waited until it was closed, then got quickly out of bed, went to the door, made sure it was locked, and then got back in bed.

She put her hand on the bodily appendage peculiar to his gender and gave it an affectionate squeeze to which it immediately responded.

"Are you happy, my Charley, that I cannot control myself?"

Before his mind moved almost immediately afterward to other thoughts of a more erotic nature, Castillo had time to think, *Both of them are genuinely devout. How the hell can that be?*

[TWO]

"Forgive me for starting my breakfast without waiting for you," Aleksandr Pevsner said absolutely insincerely. "I hope you slept well?"

"Better than I have in years," Svetlana said as she took one of the chairs. Then she asked, "What in the world is that you're eating?"

"American pancakes," Pevsner said. "I thought it would be nice for Charley and Corporal Bradley. They get the sauce by bleeding a tree."

"What?"

"Tell her, you Americans."

"It's maple syrup, Colonel," Bradley explained. "A tap is driven into maple trees, which are common in the northern United States. And, of course, in Canada. Possibly in other similar climates, but I just don't know. When there are below-freezing nighttime temperatures followed by daytime temperatures above freezing, the sap of the tree drips from the tap into a container. It is col-lected, then boiled until the desired consistency is reached."

"And now you know," Castillo said. "Thank you, Bradley."

"You're quite welcome, sir. Was the explanation sufficient, Colonel?"

"Yes, it was," Svetlana said. She turned to a maid and said, in Spanish, "Please bring me black coffee and a pastry of some kind. A croissant would be nice."

"Oh, try a pancake with tree sauce," Castillo said. "Live dangerously."

"I thought I was," she said. "But all right. Bring me one, please, a small one."

Castillo smiled at Elena, who was cuddling the puppy.

"And how did it go with Nameless, sweetheart?"

"Well, he wouldn't stop crying until I took him into bed with me," she said. "Then he was all right. When I woke up this morning, Max was in there with us and he wouldn't let the maid in the room."

"That animal was in bed with you?" her father asked incredulously.

"And he wouldn't let Delores come into the room until I screamed at him," she said. "And the puppy's not nameless anymore. He's Ivan."

"Why Ivan?" her mother asked.

"Well, the first thing he did when I took him to my room was wee-wee on the floor. So I took him outside so he could do his business, and brought him back, and the first thing he did when I put him on my lap was . . . you know. So I told him 'you're terrible' and there it was: 'Ivan the Terrible.' "

"That seems to fit," Castillo said.

"Right after our breakfast, we're going to decorate the Novogodnaya Yolka," Anna said quickly. "Do you know what that is, Charley?"

"No, but I'll bet Lester does," Castillo said, and gestured to Bradley.

"My understanding, Colonel," Bradley began, "is that the Novogodnaya Yolka is sort of the Russian version of our Christmas tree but is symbolic of the New Year rather than of Christmas. It is topped by a star, and decorated with candy and small pastries. Father Frost, sort of a Russian Santa Claus, and his daughter—"

"Granddaughter," Pevsner interrupted. "Ded Moroz's *granddaughter*, Sne-gurochka, the Snow Girl."

"Thank you for the amplification, sir," Bradley said. "I didn't know that. Please feel free to correct me at any time."

"You are doing very well, Corporal," Anna said. "Please go on. My husband will not rudely interrupt you again."

Bradley acknowledged that with a nod and went on: "Father Frost and the Snow Girl bring in presents for the good children and leave them under the

Novogodnaya Yolka. More or less a variation of presents left under the Christmas tree. That is about the sum of my knowledge, sir."

"Thank you, Lester," Castillo said.

"You're very welcome, sir."

"And since I have been a very good girl for years and years," Svetlana said, looking directly at Anna, "and Ded Moroz and Snegurochka knew how very, very hard that was for me, they brought me my present early. Last night."

Castillo realized he was being groped under the table.

"What was it, Aunty Svet?" Elena asked.

"I promised not to tell; if other girls knew what it is, they'd be jealous. Something I really needed. I'll have to take very good care of it."

Anna's face was frozen.

"And while Anna and the children are decorating the Novogodnaya Yolka," Pevsner said quickly, as if trying to shut off that line of conversation, "I need to have a word with Colonel Munz and Charley. And you, too, Svetlana, unless you'd rather help decorate the tree."

"I told you I've already gotten my present," Svetlana said, giving the present a farewell squeeze. "So I'll go with you."

The maid placed a plate with one solitary pancake on it before Svetlana and a plate with a stack of half a dozen pancakes and four strips of bacon before Castillo.

Svetlana watched as Castillo buttered his pancakes and poured maple syrup over them. She buttered her pancake, put maple syrup on it, and then sawed off a small piece and forked it into her mouth.

Then she reached over to Castillo's plate and transferred two pancakes and two strips of bacon to her plate.

She caught the maid's attention and said, "We're going to need some more of this, if you'd be so kind."

[THREE]

János was in the library when Pevsner, Castillo, Munz, and Svetlana walked in, followed by a maid pushing a cart with a silver samovar, a silver coffee thermos, and the necessary accoutrements on it.

Pevsner waited somewhat impatiently for the maid to leave, then gestured to János to arrange chairs in a circle around a small low table. When he had, everybody sat down.

János then served. He poured coffee for Castillo and Munz without asking, asked Svetlana with a gesture whether she wanted tea or coffee, then poured tea for her and Pevsner.

"Since the circumstances have changed somewhat—" Pevsner began. "God, what an understatement that was!" he interrupted himself, and then went on: "*Under the new circumstances,* certain things have to be discussed and dealt with.

"I will start with János. Svet, János has been protecting me and the family for years. We have almost died together. Most recently, I was betrayed and lured to the basement garage of the Sheraton Pilar—near Charley's safe house— where Podpolkovnik Yevgeny Komogorov, whom you know, and several of his friends tried very hard to kill us both. János was severely wounded. Only Charley's people kept us alive. The boy who just now delivered the lectures on tree syrup and the Novogodnaya Yolka took care of Komogorov."

He laid his index finger just below his eyeball.

"From at least fifteen meters with his pistol. Bradley is a very interesting young man."

"Why did Komogorov want you removed?" Svetlana asked. She didn't seem surprised to learn of Bradley's skill as a pistoleer.

"We'll get into that later. Let me continue," Pevsner said. "So, Svet, you may trust János completely."

Svetlana nodded.

"Now we turn to Alfredo, which shames me," Pevsner said. "He was advising me. Not about any of my business enterprises, but how best I could disappear in Argentina, how best I could protect Anna and the children, things of that nature. I repaid his faithful service, when others were betraying me, by suspecting Alfredo was among them. Charley was a far better judge of character than I; he knew Alfredo was incapable of what I suspected. Charley also knew what I was capable of when someone threatened my family, that I believed what the Old Testament tells us in Exodus, 'An eye for an eye, a tooth for a tooth,' rather than in turning the other cheek.

"Charley sent Alfredo's wife and children to his grandmother in the United States to protect them from me. And Alfredo went to work with Charley. And when the time came, when Alfredo had every right in God's world to apply what it says in Exodus to me, he instead turned to Saint Matthew and turned the other cheek."

Castillo was having irreverent thoughts: *While this theological lecture by the Reverend Pevsner is certainly interesting—and Svetlana is swallowing it whole as if he just carried it down from Mount Sinai carved in stone—the truth is if Alfredo could have got a shot at you when your thugs were following him around, he damn sure would have taken it. And then, when you found out he was really a good guy after all and called off your bad guys, he didn't whack you because (a) he doesn't like killing people unless he has to, and (b) it would have caused more trouble than the satisfaction would have been worth.*

Or am I the only near heathen around here? Is Alfredo a Christian in the closet? "As a good Christian, Aleksandr, I forgive you. Go and sin no more"?

Or am I committing the sin of looking in the mirror? Just because I have trouble believing a lot of the things I've heard in church doesn't mean that Alfredo does. And Svetlana and Aleksandr sound like they're perfectly serious.

Jesus, what did she say when I wisecracked that I wasn't a Christian in good standing?

"I'll fix that" is what she said.

Jesus Christ!

"Have you been able to find forgiveness for me in your heart, Alfredo?" Pevsner asked.

"Of course," Munz said. "You thought you were protecting your family, and I knew how you felt about that."

"And will you come back to work for me?"

"No."

"You can name your salary."

"This isn't about money, and you know it. Or should. And anyway, it's moot. I work for Colonel Castillo."

"And there is some reason you can't work for both of us?"

Munz chuckled.

"Yes, there is, and you probably know it as well as I do," Munz said, and then went on to quote effortlessly: "Saint Matthew, Chapter Six, Verse Twenty-four, 'No man can serve two masters: for either he will hate the one, and love the other; or else he will hold to the one, and despise the other. Ye cannot serve God and mammon.' That's from the King James Bible. But there's not much difference between that and other versions of Holy Scripture."

I will be damned.

You have been looking in the mirror, stupid!

"You're right of course," Pevsner said after a moment. "But that's going to cause a problem."

"How so?" Munz asked.

"I was about to tell János to contact everybody and tell them that you are back, and that you speak with my voice."

Munz considered that quickly and replied. "If it's all right with Colonel Castillo, that's probably a good idea."

"How so, Alfredo?" Castillo asked.

Pevsner answered for him: "Before the Buenos Aires rezident learns that you have brought Dmitri and Svetlana here, we're going to have to move Dmitri out of your safe house. The Cubans do most of the work for him, for the obvious reasons—and we've seen the proof—and while they might not know specific details, the Cubans know the Americans have something, most likely a safe house, in Mayerling Country Club, and if the Cubans know, the rezident knows."

Munz nodded his agreement.

And the Central Intelligence Agency, which will also shortly be looking for Bere-zovsky and family, also knows about Nuestra Pequeña Casa.

"Move them where?" Castillo asked. "Here?"

"No," Munz said. "I think the thing to do is for Alek and his family to stay here. So far as I know, the rezident doesn't know anything more than that Alek has a place in Bariloche, but they don't know which one."

"There's more than one?" Castillo asked.

Pevsner nodded. "Plus two more that might be suitable in San Martín de los Andres, which is several hours by car and forty minutes in the helicopter," he said. "One of them, come to think of it, is a fly-fishing estancia. When the fish are not in season, we have paying guests, who find it a beautiful, roman-tic, out-of-the-way place just to get away."

Munz nodded his agreement.

There's that word "romantic" again. Is there an implication that the Reverend Pevsner approves of our sinful relationship? Munz's nod, I think, means simply it would be a good place to hide.

"And there is the second place in the Buena Vista Country Club in Pilar, and then of course the place at the Polo & Golf," Munz said. "I'm sure the Cubans will have an eye on the big house."

"I miss that house," Pevsner said, then turned to Castillo. "Well, Charley, you can see why I need Alfredo's advice and why his speaking with my authority is more than useful, absolutely necessary. Are you willing to take the chance that there are exceptions to what Saint Matthew said, and this is one of them?"

"Why is there any question at all?" Svetlana began. "We're all—"

"He was asking me," Castillo interrupted.

She flashed him a look that was more anger than hurt.

"Far be it from me to challenge Saint Matthew," Castillo said. "Would this be satisfactory? Alfredo will advise you, and speak with your voice, with the clear understanding that he has only one master, me?"

"I thought that was understood," Svetlana said.

Castillo gave her a look he hoped she would interpret as saying, *You are pissing me off.*

"Well?" Castillo said. "Alek?"

"Understood and agreed to," Pevsner said.

"Okay, Alfredo, let's hear your advice."

"As soon as we can, move Colonel Berezovsky to the small house in Buena Vista. Preferably in something that won't attract much attention. Alek, where is the Coto supermarket delivery truck?"

"In the garage," Pevsner said. "János?"

"It's there. But the battery may be dead."

"When you get on the phone, make sure it is not dead."

János nodded.

"If that doesn't work," Munz went on, "Darby can arrange a black embassy car."

"Delchamps and Darby will go with him?" Castillo asked.

"Of course."

"And what about the radio?"

"Leave the radio with Davidson," Munz said. "If they're watching Nuestra Pequeña Casa, a sudden mass exit of people and lack of activity—"

"What radio?" Svetlana asked.

"If I wanted you to know, I would have told you," Castillo said.

Pevsner chuckled.

"This man may be good for you, Svetlana," he said. "You do not cow him."

"I think it would be a very good idea to let Colonel Berezovsky talk to both Alek and Svetlana," Castillo said.

"Yes," Pevsner said. "For both personal reasons and so that he can stop dancing with Darby and Delchamps."

"If they are watching Charley's house and this one, there will be telephone taps," Svetlana said disgustedly.

"Thank you for sharing that with us, Colonel," Castillo said. Then he put his index finger over his lips and said, "Sssshhh."

János and Munz tried not to smile. Pevsner laughed out loud.

"János, what has Bradley done with the radio?" Castillo asked.

János pointed to the window.

"It's up?" Castillo asked, surprised.

"He had it up last night, right after you went to bed."

"Go get him and it, please," Castillo said.

János left the room.

"I would like to know about the radio," Svetlana said.

"So you said," Castillo said.

"I am a podpolkovnik of the SVR!" Svetlana announced angrily. "I will not be treated as a foolish woman!"

"You *were* a podpolkovnik of the SVR," Pevsner said, rather unpleasantly. "And from your behavior, I'd say you just proved you *are* a foolish woman."

"That is between Charley and me. None of your business."

"I don't know what you're talking about, Svet," Pevsner said. "What *I* meant is that only a foolish woman loses her temper when there is nothing whatever she can do about what has angered her. And I know very well that when Friend Charley decides to tease you, there is nothing you can do but smile."

Corporal Lester Bradley entered the room carrying the handset of the AFC radio.

"I can run the secure cable if you would like, sir," he said. "But I rather doubt if there are intercept devices within the hundred-meter possible intercept range. And, of course, Class One encryption is active. In my opinion, sir, the secure cable is unnecessary."

"Your opinion is good enough for me, Lester," Castillo said. "But before I get Delchamps on the radio . . . You may have noticed a certain change in the relationship between myself and Colonel Alekseeva?"

"No, sir. I have not. Is there something I should know?"

"May I speak?" Munz said.

"You don't have to ask, Alfredo."

"I was thinking just then about what Davidson said when you sent Bradley to the Delta camp at Fort Bragg to hide him. Do you recall what he said?"

"He said trying to hide Lester at Camp Mackall was like trying to hide a giraffe on the White House lawn."

Pevsner smiled broadly.

"Am I being called a giraffe?" Svetlana asked suspiciously.

Pevsner put his index finger in front of his lips and made a shushing sound.

"I take your point," Castillo said. "So let's get it out in the open. I can't explain what happened between us. Bottom line, it did. I can't even work up much guilt for doing what everybody in this room, everybody I know in our line of work, will regard at least as goddamn foolish, and—with absolute justification—as gross dereliction of duty, not to mention conduct unbecoming an officer and a gentleman. Bottom line here: I will try to carry out my duties to the best of my ability, and believe I can. And I realize I really don't give a good goddamn what anybody thinks about it; all I care about is what Svetlana thinks about me."

"Oh, my Charley," Svetlana said, and got out of her chair and went to kiss him.

"Obviously, the others are going to find out," Castillo said a moment later. "The later they do, the better. I'll cross those bridges when I get to them."

"If I may say so, sir," Bradley said, "I have seen nothing in your behavior toward Colonel Alekseeva, or in hers toward you, that in any way suggests any impropriety of any kind on the part of either party."

"That sums it up pretty well for me, too, Charley," Munz said. "Anything else?"

Castillo shook his head. He didn't trust his voice to speak.

"Lester, call the safe house, and get Mr. Darby on there, please," Munz ordered.

"I was wondering when you were going to check in, Ace," Edgar Delchamps's voice came over the AFC handset loudspeaker perhaps thirty seconds later. "Your pal the ambassador has been looking for you."

"Ambassador Silvio? Oh, shit. What did he want?"

Juan Manuel Silvio was the American ambassador to Argentina. He had courageously risked his career to help Castillo in the past, doing things an ambassador just should not do. Castillo did not want to involve him in the current *situation*.

"No. The one who doesn't like you. Montvale. *That* ambassador."

"What did *that* ambassador want?"

"Aside from talking to you, do you mean?" Delchamps asked, then went on: "Well, he wanted to know where you were."

"And?"

"And I told him you were off in the Andes with a redhead studying geological formations, and would return after the New Year's holiday. I may have given him the impression I suspected you were going to try to hide the salami in the redhead."

Svetlana's face showed that it had taken her five seconds to take Delchamps's meaning. Then it showed indignation, perhaps even outrage. Then it colored.

"And his response?"

"Something to the effect that if you had been able to keep your salami in your pants in the past you wouldn't be in the trouble you're in now. No. Actually, what he said was '*We* wouldn't be in the trouble *we're* in now.' "

"Did he say what trouble that was?"

"He alluded to a preposterous notion apparently held by the agency's Vienna station chief—which she has apparently relayed officially to the DCI—and unofficially to a former co-worker at the CIA, one Mrs. Patricia Davies

Wilson, who in turn just happened to mention it in passing to C. Harry Whelan, Jr., of *The Washington Post*."

"Did he say what this preposterous notion was?"

"As a matter of fact, he did. He said that a Miss Dillworth—she's the Vienna station chief—has somehow gotten the preposterous idea that you swooped into Vienna and snatched away two very important Russians she had labored hard and long upon to change sides and who were about to do so.

"The ambassador said he found this impossible to believe—even of you—especially inasmuch as you had an arrangement with him to tell him whenever you were going to do something out of the ordinary, but he would like to have a little chat with you as soon as possible to straighten the matter out."

"Well, I guess I'd better call him in the next day or two. How are you and Alex doing with Polkovnik Berezovsky?"

"In Russian, huh? Can I infer from that your relations with Podpolkovnik Alekseeva have been going well?"

"Answer the question, Edgar."

"Not well. He's one tough sonofabitch, Charley. And we're running out of time."

"Well, don't break out the ice water and the bright lights just yet. Get him on the radio."

"Really? You got something out of Red Underpants we can use on him?"

"Get him on the horn, and make sure everybody else can hear."

"The way you said that sounds like maybe I didn't have to put an edge on my hari-kiri sword after all; maybe I won't have to commit *seppuku*."

Castillo happened to glance at Svetlana. She was glaring at him.

"Sit there, Colonel, and just talk in a normal voice. Okay, Ace, we're all gathered here to witness the miracle."

"Colonel Berezovsky, can you hear me?" Castillo asked.

"I can hear you."

Castillo gestured to Aleksandr Pevsner.

"God has mercifully answered our prayers, Dmitri," Pevsner said. "Our mothers are smiling down on us from heaven. Thanks be to God, you are safely out of hell on earth."

And we will now sing Hymn Number One One Four, "Onward, Christian Soldiers."

Castillo was immediately sorry when he heard Berezovsky finally manage to ask, in a choked voice, "Aleksandr?"

And even worse when he saw that Pevsner couldn't find his voice, either.

I hate to tell you, Edgar, but right now neither of them looks like a tough son-ofabitch to me.

"Pity you're not here, Tom Barlow, ol' buddy. You could help us decorate the Novogodnaya Yolka."

That earned him another icy glare from Svetlana.

Pevsner found his voice.

"Dmitri, the situation has changed greatly. Listen to me carefully. Do whatever Mr. Darby—or any of Charley Castillo's people—tells you to do. Tell them anything they want to know. Do what they say."

"You know this man Castillo?"

"He is the next thing to family," Pevsner said. "He *is* family, if you ask Anna."

"Or me, Dmitri," Svetlana said. "So far as I am concerned, before God and the world, he is family."

"Has he met Alfredo?" Pevsner asked Castillo, who nodded.

"Dmitri, Colonel Munz is not only my friend, but he speaks with my voice," Pevsner said. "We're going to move you from where you are to a safer place. Alfredo will explain."

Munz then addressed Darby. "Alex?"

"Here, Alfredo."

"There is a second safe house at the Buena Vista Country Club. Colonel Castillo wants you to go there—you and Delchamps; everybody else stays at Nuestra Pequeña Casa—with Colonel Berezovsky and his family. Within the hour, a Coto supermarket delivery truck will come there and back up to the front door. Load everybody in it."

"Whose truck?"

"Pevsner's, and the men in it will be his. We've got another place at the Golf and Polo Country Club as a backup."

"This is Charley's idea?" Darby asked dubiously.

"Until something better can be worked out, yeah," Castillo said. "By the time I get back to Buenos Aires—"

"When will that be, Ace?" Delchamps asked.

"I'm going to leave here at first light on the second. I'll be at Jorge Newbery—and somebody will have to meet me—four hours and something after that. I'll have Alfredo and Lester with me."

"And me," Svetlana said.

"I'm going to leave Colonel Alekseeva here. And probably move Mrs. Berezovsky and Sof'ya here."

"Is leaving her there smart, Charley?"

"It's out of the question," Svetlana said. "'For wither thou goest, I will go' . . . Read the Bible, my Charley, that's in the first chapter of Ruth."

"I don't want all our eggs in one basket," Castillo said.

"That's right. You trust Pevsner, don't you?" Delchamps asked sarcastically.

"I'm with Charley, Alex," Munz said. "Leaving her here makes sense."

"Well, I guess that makes two of you," Delchamps said.

"I'm going to find out as much as I can about the money from her. Alek is going to tell me what he knows about the Congo operation, but he says he doesn't know much, so get what you can out of the colonel."

"Dmitri, tell them everything you know about that," Pevsner ordered.

It took Berezovsky a long moment to reply.

"You are sure, Aleksandr?"

"Of course I'm sure. We can do something about that, Dmitri, through Charley."

"If you're worried about the two million, Colonel," Castillo said, "Alek will tell you I'm a man of my word. I promised it to you, and I'll pay it."

Castillo saw that Svetlana shook her head as if wondering how stupid just one human male could be.

What the hell is that all about?

"One quick question, Colonel, now that we're no longer dancing," Castillo said. "And we're no longer dancing, right?"

"I trust Aleksandr's judgment, Colonel," Berezovsky said. "We are no longer, as you put it so quaintly, dancing."

"Did you go to the Kuhls when you decided to leave, or did he try to turn you?"

"I went to him. We have known about them for years."

"And he put you in contact with our station chief in Vienna?"

"Finally."

"What about her?"

"I presume you wish an honest, rather than a courteous, opinion?"

"Yes, I do."

"She was the problem. She would do nothing without permission."

"Is that what you meant by she 'finally' made contact with you?"

"She *finally* allowed *us* to make contact with *her*. And it was Svetlana and I who were taking the risk, not she."

"Is that why you suddenly decided to approach me?"

"There was a *possibility* they were onto us. That was a *possibility*. In Svetlana's and my judgment, it was a *certainty* that should it appear to Miss Dillworth that there was any possibility of anything going wrong, we would be left to fend for ourselves."

"Thank you for your honesty," Castillo said.

"And speaking of Vienna, Charley," Delchamps said, "Miller said that guy you wanted an eye on . . . what the hell was his name?"

"Alekseeva?"

"Some kind of a relative of Little Red Under Britches?"

"Yeah. What about him?"

"Miller said NSA said they were already running an eye on him for somebody else. They wouldn't tell him who, but it sounds like the agency. Anyway, he's on an Air France—not Aeroflot—flight to Rome from Moscow sometime this afternoon. And then has a train reservation to Vienna."

"That means they have allowed him the opportunity to redeem himself by eliminating Svetlana," Colonel Berezovsky said. "Be careful, Svet!"

"And you don't think he's coming after you, too?" Svetlana said.

"I can deal with Evgeny. It's you I'm worried about."

"Pride goeth before a fall," she said.

"And I'll bet that's in the Bible, too," Castillo said sarcastically.

"Proverbs 16:18," she replied matter-of-factly.

"I think it might be useful if we knew what everybody's talking about," Delchamps said.

"This guy's out to whack our new friends. Tell Miller to get NSA to keep an eye on him. I want to know if he's in Vienna, and if and when he leaves Vienna. And where he's headed when he leaves."

"And don't bother the agency with this, right?"

"Absolutely don't bother the agency with this."

"Anything else?"

"I can't think of anything."

"You want a call to report we've made the move?"

"Not unless something goes wrong."

"Okay. See you the day after tomorrow at Jorge Newbery."

[FOUR]

"The possibility exists, Aleksandr," Svetlana said, "that even if they weren't onto us, they are now, and consequently may have already learned about the money, and we must presume that if they haven't, they soon will. I have the numbers memorized . . ."

She stopped when a maid came into the library. It was just the three of them. Munz was off somewhere, presumably on the telephone, and Lester had been summoned by Anna to see if he could do something about Max, who was apparently snatching the small pastries off the Novogodnaya Yolka as soon as they could be hung, then growling at any adult who tried to stop him.

It was the fourth time their conversation had been interrupted by one of the help.

"Enough," Pevsner declared in Russian, which caused the middle-aged maid to look at him almost in alarm.

"When you finish whatever it is you have to do in here, please tell Madam Pevsner that we will be in the Green Room, where we do not wish to be disturbed unless it's the Second Coming of our Lord and Savior."

The maid nodded her understanding.

*She almost prostrated herself before Tsar Aleksandr. It was—*Castillo stopped the thought until he came up with the word he was searching for—*serflike. Not almost. Serflike. And she's Russian. So how did a Russian serf wind up in Bariloche?*

"There is a study in the Green Room," Pevsner announced. "Large enough. We will continue this there. With the door locked."

"I want one of those," Svetlana said as Castillo opened the lid of his laptop. "Will you get me one, Charley?"

"No," he said simply.

Pevsner chuckled.

"Then I will buy one myself."

"I don't think that's very likely," Castillo replied. "But speaking of money, as we were when we were interrupted—"

"What about it?"

"Those bank account numbers you told Alek you have memorized—"

"What about them?"

"I've got them in here," he said, tapping the laptop. "Why don't I just put them on a CD if Alek needs them?" He was looking into her eyes and hoping he was at least somewhere close to matching the icy looks Pevsner was so good at.

And I hit home. Her eyes show it.

"Or are we talking about bank account numbers you somehow forgot to mention when you were telling me everything, Girl Scout's Honor?"

"Oh, God, Charley, I was going to tell you about them!"

That look of genuine remorse is either genuine, or she should be on the stage.

Svetlana looked at Pevsner for support and, Castillo saw, got none.

"Before we get into what else may have slipped your mind and you didn't tell me," Castillo said, "what are the memorized account numbers?"

"That's where most of the money is," she said. "Most of it in Lichtenstein, but some in Switzerland and the Cayman Islands. There are five accounts in all."

"And the numbers you gave me?"

"What we did, Charley, is put a little bit of money in those accounts, so in case we were found out, they would think they had found the money and stop looking. You understand?"

"Define 'a little bit of money.' "

"Usually never more than a quarter of a million dollars."

"Looks can be deceiving, Svetlana. I'm not really stupid enough to believe that."

"Before God, it is the truth."

He did the math in his head before going on. "You expect me to believe that whoever chases after dirty money in Russia is going to come across your lousy eight thousand dollars and say, 'Eureka, we found it. Call off the search'?"

"Eight thousand dollars?" she asked in what seemed to be genuine confusion.

Pevsner laughed.

"This is not funny, goddamn it, Alek. First she lies to me, and then she insults my intelligence. What happened to the 'we're all family and have no secrets' bullshit?"

"A moment ago, Friend Charley, you owed her an apology. Now you owe us both one."

"How?"

"First that I consider you family is not bullshit. You have wounded me by thinking that."

"And?"

"What did you do, Charley, divide a quarter of a million dollars by the number of small accounts to come up with eight thousand dollars in each?"

"That's exactly what I did."

"I think what Svetlana was trying to tell you is that there's about a quarter of a million in each of those accounts."

As one part of his brain began to suspect that he had just made an ass of himself, another part did the math.

"Christ, that's almost eight million dollars," he said. "You were prepared to spend *eight million dollars* to throw the SVR off the scent?"

Svetlana nodded. He saw tears in her eyes.

Oh, Jesus, don't do that!

"Before God, it is the truth," she sobbed. "I can't stand it when you look at me with hate and suspicion in your eyes!"

"Oh, baby," Castillo heard himself say.

And then she was in his arms, sobbing.

"I think I will go see how they're doing with the tree," Pevsner said. "It might be wise to lock the door after I go."

"We have just had our first fight," Svetlana said. "And our first makeup, and our first you-know-what in my bed. Up to now, all the you-know-whats have been in your beds."

"Baby, I'm really sorry."

"I know. I can tell," she said. "Can I say something?"

"You can say anything you want."

"I know what it was, why you disbelieved me."

"Because I'm stupid?"

"Because you are a man," she said. "Like other men, insecure. When a woman throws herself at you, you are incapable of just accepting your good fortune. You don't think you are worthy of what you are being given, so the woman has to have some ulterior motive."

"What is that, Psychology 101?"

"It is the truth," Svetlana said. "And I have something else to say. I am not a foolish woman. I am probably less foolish than any woman you have ever known.

"And like you, I have been trained to look for the worst scenarios. I thought about the worst scenarios before I put the toothbrush in the lock of your bathroom."

"And what are the worst scenarios?"

"Actually, there were three," she said, propping herself on her elbow to look down at him, which caused her breast to rest on his chest. "The first was that I was wrong about what I thought I saw in your eyes, and that you felt nothing for me.

"The second was your professionalism would be so strong that you would reject me no matter how you felt. That really worried me."

"And the third?"

"That's still viable, my Charley. You know what the chances are of our spending our lives together? You've never thought about that?"

"I've thought about it," Castillo said softly.

"I don't think there's a chance in a thousand that we will be able to do that."

"Okay. So what do we do?"

"I will pray. I have been praying. Do you pray, Charley?"

"Not in a long time."

"That's between you and God. My father never prayed either. He said that God knew his mind, so it was pointless. God was going to do with his life whatever God wanted to do."

"I'm something like that," Castillo said. "And if God is reading my mind, He knows how I feel about you."

"So there is a tentative scenario we can run. We just put all the reasons we shall most likely not grow old together from our minds and pretend that we will be together forever."

She raised her eyebrows questioningly.

"Deal," he said.

"You mean that?"

"I mean that."

"Good. Then I will go with you to Buenos Aires and you will give me a computer just like yours."

"I've just been taken," Castillo said.

She nodded happily in agreement.

"Can I ask a question?"

"Anything, just so long as it's not about money."

"Actually, it is. How much money is in the accounts, the ones you memorized?"

"So that's it. You're a gigolo? After my money?"

"A lot more, I would guess, than the eight million you were willing to spend to throw the dogs a bad scent."

"If I told you forty, fifty times that, would that make you happy? You want me to give you money, my Charley? Just ask."

"I'm not in that league, but I'm not going to have to sell Max anytime soon to pay the rent. What I've been wondering about is that two million you asked for on the train."

"Two reasons. You needed to hear a reason—right then—why we were willing to defect, a reason you would believe. And if you thought we needed money, you probably wouldn't start looking for any that we might have."

"One more question?"

"*One.*"

"Do you have any idea what it does to me when you rub your breast on my chest that way?"

She blushed, but then confessed: "Oh, I was hoping that would work!"

[FIVE]
The Great Room
La Casa en Bosque
San Carlos de Bariloche
Río Negro Province, Argentina
0915 1 January 2006

Charley had learned the night before that there were two celebrations marking the New Year. First was the family celebration, an enormous meal—there had been two roast geese on the enormous table, plus a suckling pig—starting at half past ten.

The meal itself had been preceded by Pevsner giving a lengthy prayer/speech—not unlike Grace—in which he offered thanks to not only the Divinity but also to a long list of saints, only a few of whom Charley had ever heard of, for God's munificence to the family—including the reuniting "now, of Svetlana, and soon, very soon, of Dmitri and Lora and Sof'ya to the bosom of those who love them" and for the "presence at our table and in our lives of Charley and Lester and Alfredo and János, who have lived the words of our Lord and Savior that there is no greater love than being willing to lay down one's life for another."

At that point, Svetlana had grasped his hand—not groped him—under the table, and he had looked at her and seen tears running down her cheeks.

Then they had moved into the Great Room where the Novogodnaya Yolka had been set up. Servants dressed as Father Frost and his granddaughter, Snegurochka the Snow Girl, danced to the music of a balalaika quartet. The balalaikas were of different sizes, the largest as big as a cello.

Charley was a little ashamed that his first reaction to this was to decide that Father Frost's costume was designed for Santa Claus, the Snow Girl's for Mrs. Santa Claus, and both had probably been made in China by Buddhists.

He was touched, and finally admitted it.

The children—Elena clutching Ivan the Terrible to her—sang several Christmas songs, following which Father Frost and Snegurochka danced out of the room, to dance back in a few moments later heading a column of servants, who deposited gaily wrapped boxes under the tree.

The children, Svetlana told him, would get their presents in the morning.

Charley at this point, possibly assisted by the champagne that had been flowing since they sat down for dinner, came to the philosophical conclusion that maybe the Russians had the better idea, passing out the presents at New Year's rather than at Christmas, which was, after all, supposed to be a Christian holiday—meaning Holy Day—not one of gluttony under Santa Claus's benevolent eye.

He shared this observation with Svetlana, who laid her hand on his cheek and kissed him.

At five minutes to midnight, everybody was out on the pier, trailed by servants carrying an enormous grandfather clock and pushing a cart holding half a dozen bottles of champagne.

The clock was set up, the hands adjusted, and at midnight began to bong its chimes.

Pevsner counted loudly downward from twelve.

As the last bong was fading, there was a dull explosion, which startled Castillo, followed by another and another and another.

He had been enormously relieved when the first of what turned out to be a fifteen-minute display of fireworks went off.

And enormously pleased when Svetlana had kissed him, as Anna was kissing her husband.

The celebration today was for what Pevsner described as "the people."

It was held in the Great Room, which Castillo, perhaps because too much champagne always gave him debilitating hangovers, decided had been converted into a throne room for Tsar Aleksandr I, Empress Anna, Grand Duchess Svetlana, the Imperial Children, and visiting nobility, such as himself, Corporal Bradley, and Colonel Munz.

There were no actual thrones, but the chair in which Pevsner sat had a higher back than that of his wife, which in turn was higher than those of everybody else. János was not around, and Castillo wondered where he was.

Father Frost and Snegurochka were back, as was the balalaika quartet. This time Father Frost and Snegurochka were standing by an enormous stack of packages. The quartet began to play. János appeared, ushered into the room perhaps eighty people, ranging from bearded elders to children, and then walked up to Father Frost.

Father Frost took a small package from the stack and gave it to Pevsner, who unwrapped it, opened a small box, and took from it a wristwatch, which he then held up for everybody to see. There was a murmur of approval from "the people."

Next, Father Frost gave Anna a package, and a moment later, she held up a string of pearls for everyone to see. Next came Svetlana, who also got a string of pearls.

Castillo had just decided that the kids had gotten their presents earlier. He looked at Elena and saw there was a string of pearls around her neck he hadn't noticed before.

Now what?

Father Frost handed him a small box.

Jesus Christ, a Rolex.

"Hold it up, hold it up!" Svetlana hissed.

He held it up.

Corporal Bradley got a small package and moments later held up his Rolex for the approval of the people.

Colonel Alfredo Munz got his Rolex.

Well, Pevsner probably gets a discount if he buys them by the dozen.

What did he say? "I took five percent of a lot more than a billion dollars' worth of gold, Charley. And about twice that much of platinum."

And finally, János got his Rolex, and then began reading from a list of names.

An old man left the group, approached the throne, literally tugged at his hair in front of Pevsner. Pevsner nodded. Father Frost handed the old man a package. He opened it. It contained a small, flat-screen television. The people murmured their approval.

János called out another name, and a young woman approached the throne, and tugged at her hair, then took her package from Father Frost.

It was more than an hour before the last of the people filed out of the throne room carrying their New Year's presents.

Tsar Aleksandr rose from his throne.

"This will displease Anna," he said. "But despite the hour, I am going to have a drink. That always wears me out. But the people expect it of me. You'll join me, of course?"

This is where I am supposed to say, "Alek, neither Lester nor I can accept a gift like those Rolexes."

Castillo saw that Lester was examining the new watch on his wrist.

What the hell. He saved Pevsner's life.

"Just one," Castillo said. "And then I'm going to take a nap. I have to fly in the morning."

———

"Happy New Year, Charley!" Pevsner said, touching his glass of vodka from an ice-encrusted bottle to Castillo's glass.

"Happy New Year," Castillo said. "Alek, those people. They were Russian, right? Or at least most of them?"

Pevsner nodded.

"Where did they come from?"

"Russia," Pevsner said, obviously delighted with himself. When he saw the look on Castillo's face, he said, "I learned that from you. If I do that to Anna, she usually throws something at me."

"How'd they get here?"

"They're Jews, most of them. They have worked for people in the Oprichina for many years. When the Communists decided to let some of the Jews leave to go to Israel, we first warned them they probably wouldn't like it, and then we arranged for them to go first.

"They didn't like it. The culture shock, the climate—what is it you Americans say? 'One more goddamned sunny day in L.A.'?; Tel Aviv is worse—what they saw of the future, the suicide bombers. They wanted to leave, but they didn't want to go back to Russia. So I arranged for them to come here. One day the children will join all the Russian Jews in Argentina. There are forty thousand Jewish gauchos here, originally from Eastern Europe. Did you know that?"

Castillo nodded. "I'd heard that."

"For now the parents work for me."

"Alek, I don't know what to say about that Rolex."

"How about 'thank you'?"

"You have learned, haven't you?"

"The people, the Jews, would say, 'Wear it in good health.'"

"Thank you."

[SIX]
Aeropuerto Internacional Jorge Newbery
Buenos Aires, Argentina
1240 2 January 2006

As Castillo taxied the Aero Commander to the private aircraft tarmac, he saw that there were two Gulfstreams parked side by side.

One was his. The other bore USAF markings and was painted in the paint scheme of the Presidential Flight Detachment.

"Oh, shit," he said.

He parked the Aero Commander by the USAF Gulfstream.

"I see Davidson," Munz said. "And there are several of Pevsner's people, too. And several of Duffy's."

"And I see that Gulfstream. Alfredo, can you take Svetlana to that second safe house you mentioned? Golf and Polo, Polo and Golf, whatever?"

"I am going with you," Svetlana announced.

"You'll do what I say. Fun-and-games time is over. Got it?"

She nodded.

"What I'm going to do is get out and have a word with the pilot," Castillo said. "You stay—everybody but Max—in the airplane. If I walk toward Davidson, stay in the plane until we're gone, then take Svetlana and Lester to the Polo whatever. Got it?"

"What is it, Charley?"

"I suspect it's very bad news. The only thing that could make it worse is if they see me with Svetlana."

"You don't think that's Montvale?"

"I think it's either him or his flunky," Castillo said. "We'll soon find out. Open the door, please."

Svetlana didn't kiss him as he walked, bent nearly double, past her seat. But she stopped him, laid her hand on his cheek, and looked for a long moment into his eyes.

That was at least as intimate as a kiss.

There were two Air Force types in flying suits standing near the nose of the Gulfstream. One drew the attention of the other to Max performing his ritual at the nose gear, and then to the man in khaki trousers and a polo shirt walking toward them.

The taller of them, Castillo saw, was a light colonel wearing command pilot wings, the other a captain wearing ordinary wings.

"You speak English, sir?" the lieutenant colonel asked.

"I try," Castillo said.

"Nice dog," the lieutenant colonel said.

"Thank you."

Max trotted over, sat down, and offered his paw.

The lieutenant colonel squatted and scratched Max's ears.

"Nice airplane," Castillo said. "Presidential Flight Detachment, right?"

The lieutenant colonel looked up at him, then stood up, but did not reply.

"I'm the SVR rezident in Buenos Aires, Colonel. We like to keep up on what our American friends are doing."

He then handed the lieutenant colonel the identification card of Lieutenant Colonel C. G. Castillo, Special Forces, U.S. Army.

The lieutenant colonel, recognizing the card immediately, smiled, then did a double take and examined it carefully.

"I was about to tell you, Colonel," he said, "as tactfully as I could, that I just can't talk about the mission of this aircraft. But since you are the mission . . ."

"Excuse me?"

". . . I will tell you, out of school, that you're probably in the deep shit."

"How's that?"

"Ambassador Montvale just blew his top at the ambassador. You didn't miss them by five minutes. Ambassador Montvale said, and this is almost verbatim, 'I just flew five thousand goddamned miles down here to see Lieutenant Colonel Goddamn Charley Castillo, and you're telling me you not only don't know where the sonofabitch is, but that you didn't even know the crazy bastard is in Argentina?'"

He turned to the captain and asked, "Is that about what the ambassador said, Sam?"

"Almost verbatim, sir," the captain said. "I somehow got the idea, sir, that Ambassador Montvale doesn't like Colonel Castillo very much."

"I always knew that Ambassador Montvale doesn't like anybody very much, but I don't ever remember him being as pissed as he was just a couple of minutes ago," the lieutenant colonel said. "What the hell did you do, Colonel?"

"I guess I have been a very bad boy," Castillo said. "And we never had this conversation, Colonel."

Fully aware that rendering the hand salute while not in uniform is proscribed by Army regulations, Castillo saluted.

The lieutenant colonel and the captain returned the salute.

Castillo turned to the Aero Commander, intending to wave.

He changed his mind and blew a kiss.

Then he said, "Come on, Max," and walked to where Jack Davidson was waiting for him.

"You just missed Ambassador Montvale," Davidson said as they shook hands.

"Did he see you?" Castillo asked.

"No. The gendarmería had a heads-up that an Air Force Gulfstream was coming in, so I erred on the side of caution and waited in Darby's car." He pointed to a BMW with darkened windows and Argentine license plates. "The Mercedes SUV next to it used to be Duffy's. Unless you look close, you can't see where all the bullet holes were."

"You're sure Montvale didn't see you?"

Davidson nodded. "Moot point, though. He doesn't know who I am, much less what I look like."

"Never underestimate Montvale. Was he alone?"

"Three guys with him. Two of them probably his Secret Service . . ."

"Who just might have recognized you."

"If they had seen me, which they didn't, since I had erred on the side of caution, Colonel, sir."

"Sorry, Jack. I'm tired. And the third guy?"

"Six-two, maybe six-three, one eighty, forty-odd, GI haircut, Sears, Roebuck suit. I'd guess he was military. Probably Army."

"Why?"

"Officers of our brother services in civvies tend to look like civilians. Our officers in civvies tend to look like Army officers in civvies."

Castillo chuckled.

"I wonder who he is," Castillo said rhetorically. "What happened?"

"Right after I erred on the side of caution and got in the BMW, Ambassador Silvio showed up. With an embassy Suburban. And no, Colonel, sir, he didn't see me, as I had erred on the side of caution. . . ."

"Okay, Jack," Castillo said.

"But I think it's possible he recognized Darby's car, as he is a clever guy. He did not come over to say 'Howdy.' Then the Gulfstream landed and Montvale and the others got out and had a conversation in which Montvale got red-faced and waved his arms around. I think maybe they were talking about you."

"And then?"

"They loaded into the Suburban and drove off."

"You have any idea where they went?"

"Yes, sir, Colonel, sir, I do. In the BMW to which I retired, erring as I said—"

"Enough, goddamn it, Jack," Castillo said.

"There is an embassy radio, to which I listened, and am thus able to tell you they reported they were going to the embassy."

"Not to the safe house?"

"I'm guessing, Charley, I can't read lips, but I think maybe one of the reasons Montvale was so pissed was that he asked the ambassador about the safe house and the ambassador said, 'What safe house?' "

Castillo turned and looked at the Aero Commander.

Everybody had gotten out of it.

And why didn't I think that at one o'clock in the afternoon of a sunny summer day in Argentina, the sun quickly turns the interior of an Aero Commander into an oven?

He signaled to Alfredo Munz to come over. Munz alone.

And why am I not surprised that everybody's coming over?

When Pevsner's men saw Munz, Svetlana, and Bradley walking to Castillo and Davidson, they got out of their cars and walked to them. When the gendarmería officers saw Pevsner's men walking to Castillo and Davidson, they got out of their cars and walked to them.

Davidson read Castillo's mind.

"Well, maybe they'll think Little Red Under Britches is a movie star and we are her groupies."

"The Air Force Gulfstream brought Ambassador Montvale here," Castillo announced when the little group had gathered around him. "They went to the embassy, which is where Jack and I are going. Alfredo is going to take Svetlana to Pilar. Lester, you take the AFC and go with them."

"Yes, sir."

Castillo turned to the gendarmería officer.

"What are your orders?"

"To place ourselves at your orders, *mi coronel*."

"You have two cars?"

"*Si, mi coronel.* The Mercedes and the Ford."

"Send one of the cars with me, and the other with El Coronel Munz. Follow him and these gentlemen, but go no farther than the gate of the country club; we don't want to attract any more attention than we have to."

"*Si, mi coronel.*"

He turned to the people Munz had called "Pevsner's people" and took a chance and spoke Russian.

"The Panamericana is so busy this time of day that following someone is very difficult."

One of "Pevsner's people" nodded his head in understanding. He was to lose the gendarmería car if possible.

Podpolkovnik Svetlana Alekseeva, presumably reasoning that if it was safe for Lieutenant Colonel Castillo to speak Russian it would be safe for her, too, had a question of her own, which she expressed in Russian:

"When will you join me, Charley, my darling?"

Castillo saw the look on Jack Davidson's face.

Well, fuck it. The cow's out of the barn. I'd have to have told him anyway.

"Just as soon as I can, my love," he said in Russian, then met Davidson's eyes. "Are you all right to drive, Jack? You look like you're in shock."

X

[ONE]
The Embassy of the United States of America
Avenida Colombia 4300
Palermo, Buenos Aires, Argentina
1325 2 January 2006

It was a fifteen-minute drive from Aeropuerto Jorge Newbery, on the west bank of the River Plate, to the American embassy, and their route through heavy noontime traffic took them past six traffic lights, all of which were red when they reached them, and all of which seemed to be timed on a five-minute sequence.

Jack Davidson didn't say a word during the entire trip, even when waiting for the lights to change. But his face showed that he was thinking of what he needed to say—and how to say it.

Castillo spent the trip dreading this inevitable dropping of Davidson's shoe.

Not shoe, Charley thought.

Boot—damned lead-soled, thirty-pound diver's boot.

Castillo, of course, had all that time to think, too. He had known Davidson just about as long as Castillo had been in the Army. Technical Sergeant Davidson had been covering Colonel Bruce J. McNab's back—with a twelve-gauge sawed-off Remington Model 870 shotgun—when Second Lieutenant Castillo had reported to McNab for duty in the First Desert War.

And then Sergeant Major Davidson had manned the Gatling gun in the Black Hawk helicopter that Major Castillo had "borrowed" in Afghanistan to go see if he could get back Major Dick Miller and the crew of his shot-down Black Hawk before the bad guys overran their position, a task that had been solemnly considered by some very senior officers and pronounced absolutely impossible.

Between their first meeting and this latest trip around the block, Charley and Jack had gone around many blocks together.

Castillo also thought about when Lieutenant General Bruce J. McNab had released Davidson from his duties at Camp Mackall to join Castillo at the Office of Organizational Analysis. McNab had called Castillo to tell him: "Just in case you might be thinking I have mellowed in old age, Colonel, and was being a nice guy, know that the sole reason I'm *loaning* you Sergeant Major Davidson is because he's the only guy I know who can pour cold water on you when you're about to fuck up big-time. So, Colonel, one more time I'm telling you something that you should have learned as a second lieutenant: 'When Jack Davidson tells you not to do something, for God's sake take his counsel and don't do it!' "

Castillo knew that that counsel also worked in other ways.

In Afghanistan, when Castillo had told Davidson that he was going to "borrow" the Black Hawk and go after Miller despite just having been ordered not to—"Frankly, Major," the brigadier general had barked, "I'm starting to question your mental health for even suggesting you *try* something so suicidal. What part of 'Absolutely no!' don't you understand?"—all Davidson had said was, "You sure you want to do this, Charley?"

And then Davidson had gone to get them flak vests to wear over their Afghan robes and to make sure he had enough ammo for the door-mounted Gatling gun.

Castillo now thought:

Viewed objectively, as an indication of poor judgment and mental instability, "borrowing" a Black Hawk to fly through a snowstorm to go after Dick and his crew pales when compared to considering oneself in love with a lieutenant colonel of the SVR and deciding that she is telling me the truth, the whole truth, and nothing but the truth.

I knew I was safe to fly that day. I wouldn't have taken Jack along if I didn't really believe I could do it.

And the cold truth here is that whenever I look into Svet's eyes—or in other more intimate situations—and hear the celestial chorus singing "I Love You Truly"—the small, still voice of reason keeps popping up and whispering, "This is wrong, you dumb fuck, and you know it. That violin music you hear is her playing you."

Davidson pulled the BMW nose-in to the curb in front of the embassy. The gendarmería's Mercedes-Benz SUV pulled in beside them.

Davidson put both hands on the top of the steering wheel and turned to Castillo. Their eyes met.

Here comes Jack's lead boot. . . .

After a moment, Davidson said, "Please tell me, Charley, that you are (a) fucking Little Miss Red Underpants as an interrogative technique to gain the confidence of the interrogatee, or at least (b) you had a couple of belts and things got temporarily out of control."

"None of the above, Jack."

"Oh, shit."

Castillo shrugged. "I'm in love."

"Well, then I guess it's a good thing that I'm going to retire. When McNab hears about this, the most I could hope for would be to spend the rest of my days in the Army counting tent pegs in a quartermaster warehouse in Alaska."

"I'll make sure he knows that you did everything possible short of shooting me in the knees with a hollow-point .22 to dissuade me from my insanity."

Davidson shook his head in resignation. "If I thought that would do any good, that's just what I would do."

"I would resign today, Jack, if it wasn't for this chemical operation in the Congo."

Davidson met his eyes again.

"When Berezovsky started talking," Davidson said, "it looked like Delchamps was on the money when he said that was heavy."

"It is. Very heavy."

"Okay. You and Delchamps believe him. I'll grant you that; I'm not going to say both of you are wrong. So I'll give you that. But what the hell do you think you can do about it? Delchamps says the CIA knows about the plant and doesn't think it's a threat. And I don't think they'll listen to you or Delchamps that it is. They probably wouldn't believe Berezovsky and/or your lady friend if they had them. Which they don't. Which opens that can of worms."

"Can I wave duty in your face, Jack?"

Davidson shook his head. After a moment, he softly said: "Yeah. For Christ's sake, you know you can, Charley."

"I think it's my duty to take out that chemical factory, even if the CIA doesn't think it's a threat."

Davidson nodded his understanding. "And how are you going to do that?"

"I haven't quite figured that out yet."

After a moment, Davidson said, "Are you willing to listen to some unpleasant facts?"

"I'll be surprised if you can think of any I haven't thought of myself—that's not a crack at you, Jack; I've really given this a lot of thought—but go ahead."

"The CIA is already pissed that you have the Russians."

Castillo nodded his acceptance of that statement.

"And I don't think you're going to turn either of them over to the agency."

"I'm not, Jack."

Davidson shook his head again. "Which is really going to piss them off. And Montvale, too."

Castillo nodded again.

"Your authority, Charley, comes from the Presidential Finding, which is to 'locate and render harmless' the people who whacked Jack 'The Stack' Masterson. Period. Nothing else. It says nothing about turning Russian spooks and nothing about going into the Congo and taking out a chemical factory—one the agency knows about and doesn't think is a threat."

He paused for a long time, a period that Charley took to mean that Jack was letting that counsel sink in.

Then Davidson shook his head again and went on: "So where do you think we're going to get what we need to take out the factory? That's got to be a helluva long laundry list—"

He said, "What we need."

He's in.

And he doesn't care what that may cost him.

Castillo felt his throat tighten.

When he trusted himself to speak, Castillo admitted: "I haven't figured that out yet either."

"So what happens now, Chief?"

Castillo intoned solemnly: " 'The longest journey begins with the smallest step.' You may wish to write that down."

Davidson chuckled.

"What happens now is that I go in there"—Castillo nodded toward the embassy building?—"and, while trying very hard to keep Ambassador Silvio out of the line of fire, deal with Ambassador Montvale. And while I'm doing that, you go to Rio Alba, taking the gendarmería with you, and wait for me."

"For how long?"

"I don't know. Get some lunch. If I don't call you in thirty minutes, call me. If I answer in Pashtu, hang up and head for the safe house."

"And?"

Castillo was silent a moment, then shrugged and shook his head again, and said, "I just don't know, Jack."

"Okay. We'll wing it."

Castillo glanced at the Mercedes-Benz parked beside them. Then he looked over his shoulder and said, "Max, you stay."

Castillo opened his door. When he did so, one of the gendarmes got out of the Mercedes and stood by the open door.

When Castillo headed for what he thought of as the embassy employee's gate in the fence, the gendarme closed the vehicle's door and walked after him.

Davidson backed out of the parking spot and drove toward the restaurant Rio Alba, which was a block from the embassy in the shadow of—at fifty stories—Argentina's tallest building. The gendarmería Mercedes followed him.

The fence surrounding the embassy had three gates, a large one to pass vehicular traffic and two smaller ones for people. The employees' gate was a simple affair, a turnstile guarded by two uniformed, armed guards of an Argentine security firm.

Castillo was absolutely certain that a couple of Argentine rent-a-cops wouldn't deny entrance to the embassy grounds to a United States federal law-enforcement officer who presented the proper identification.

He was wrong.

The rent-a-cops were not at all impressed with the credentials identifying C. G. Castillo as a supervisory special agent of the United States Secret Service.

The rent-a-cops advised him that if he wished to enter the embassy grounds, he would have to use the Main Visitors' Gate, which was some three hundred yards distant, down a sunbaked sidewalk.

Castillo bit his tongue and started for the other gate, with the gendarme on his heels.

The last hundred yards of the sidewalk was lined with people—clearly not many of them, if any, U.S. citizens—patiently baking in the sun as they awaited their turn to pass through the Main Visitors' Gate to apply for visas and other services.

There has to be a gate for U.S. citizens.

For Christ's sake, this is the American embassy!

He did not see anything that looked helpful until he was almost at the single-story Main Visitors' Gate building. Then he came across a ridiculously small sign that had an arrow and the legend: U.S CITIZENS.

He pushed open the door and was promptly stopped by another Argentine rent-a-cop who—not very charmingly—asked to see Castillo's passport.

After examining it carefully, the rent-a-cop motioned that Castillo was now

permitted to join one of two lines of people waiting their turn to deal with embassy staff seated comfortably behind thick plateglass windows. The scene reminded Castillo of the cashier windows in Las Vegas casinos.

He got in line and awaited his turn. Ten minutes later, it came.

"I'd like to see the ambassador, please."

"Passport, please."

The not-unattractive female behind the thick plate glass examined it, then
carefully examined Castillo, and then said, "What time is your appointment?"

"I don't have an appointment. But if you will get the ambassador on the
phone, I'm sure he'll see me."

The lady scribbled a number on a small pad and slid it through a tray at
the bottom of the plate glass.

"You can call this number and ask for an appointment."

"Is there an American officer around here somewhere?"

Three minutes later, a pleasant-looking young man appeared behind the
woman, looked at Castillo, and said, "Yes?"

Castillo remembered Edgar Delchamps telling him that new graduates of
the CIA's Clandestine Services How-to-Be-a-Spy School were often given as
their first assignment duties as an assistant consul at an embassy where their in-
experience would not get them in trouble.

If I were into profiling, I'd bet my last dime I'm facing one now.

"Good afternoon," Castillo said politely, and slid his Army identification
through the slot under the plate glass. "I'd like to see the ambassador. Would
you be good enough to call his office and tell him I'm here?"

The fledgling spook examined the ID card and slid it back through the slot.

"Let me give you a number you can call, Colonel," the pleasant-looking
young man said.

Castillo slid his Secret Service credentials through the slot.

"Listen to me carefully, please," Castillo began, keeping his voice low but
his tone that of one not to be questioned. "If you don't get on the phone right
now, I will personally tell the DCI that you wouldn't call the ambassador for
me. And the result of that will be that you'll be sitting in one of the parking lot
guard shacks at Langley this time next week."

They locked eyes.

The assistant consul picked up the telephone handset, then spoke into it.

A moment later, he slid the handset through the slot.

"I don't know where he is, Colonel," Ambassador Silvio's secretary said.
"He went to Jorge Newbery to meet a VIP and hasn't checked in. Would you
like to wait for him here?"

Sonofabitch, they're on the way to Nuestra Pequeña Casa!

"No, thank you," Castillo replied. "When you're in touch, tell him I'll call him later."

Castillo slid the handset back through the slot, then without a word turned from the window and took out his cellular telephone.

A rent-a-cop laid his hand on Castillo's arm and pointed to a sign on the wall. It forbade the use of cellular telephones.

Castillo left the building and went back into the one-hundred-degree, one-hundred-percent-humidity Buenos Aires summer afternoon. He saw that the gendarme was waiting for him.

Castillo punched one of the cell phone's autodial buttons. Davidson answered on the second ring.

"He's here with Montvale," Davidson said by way of answering.

"Keep them there if you have to break Montvale's legs," Castillo said, and then began to walk on the sunbaked sidewalk toward the fine steak house called Río Alba, the gendarme on his heels.

[TWO]

Jack Davidson and his gendarme were sitting at a table just inside the restaurant door. Both looked to be halfway through with eating their luncheon of steaks.

Davidson caught Castillo's eye and indicated with a nod toward the rear of the restaurant.

"You wait here with them," Castillo said to his gendarme, motioning to the table with Davidson and the other gendarme. Their table had a clear view of a round table at the rear of the establishment.

Castillo walked toward the round table, seated at which were the Honorable Charles W. Montvale, the United States Director of National Intelligence who liked to be called "Ambassador"—in his long career of public service he had been deputy secretary of State, secretary of the Treasury, and ambassador to the European Union—the United States Ambassador to Argentina Juan Manuel Silvio, and a man in his late fifties, tall and trim with closely cropped hair.

Castillo decided unkindly that the tall, trim man's suit indeed looked, as Davidson had said, as if it had come off a chromed rack at Sears, Roebuck & Co.

At a table against the wall were two neatly dressed, muscular men who Castillo decided were almost certainly from the agency or were Montvale's Secret Service bodyguards. Montvale spotted Castillo, paused momentarily in the act of forking a piece of steak to his mouth, then completed the motion.

"Well, what a pleasant surprise!" Castillo announced as he approached. "I was just at the embassy to make my manners, Ambassador Silvio, but they didn't seem to know where you were. And Mr. Montvale! What brings you down this way?"

"I think you've got a very good idea, Colonel," Montvale said sharply, chewing as he spoke.

Castillo glanced around the room, then looked back at Montvale. "Aside from thinking you've heard the reputation of the Río Alba as the world's best steak house, I haven't a clue."

Montvale swallowed, then sipped at his glass of red wine. "Why don't you sit down, Colonel."

"Thank you very much."

Castillo took his seat, looked around for a waiter, and motioned for him to come over.

"I'm starved. I had breakfast very early," he said in English to Montvale, and then switched to Spanish to address the waiter: "Would you bring me a Roquefort empanada, please, and then a bife de chorizo punto, papas fritas, and a tomato and onion salad?"

He picked up the bottle of wine on the table, read the label, made a face, returned the bottle to the table, and added, "And a bottle of Saint Felicien Cabernet Sauvignon, please."

"Something wrong with that wine, Colonel?" Montvale said, an edge of sarcasm rising in his tone.

"Well, according to the label, it's Malbec."

"Yes. And?"

"And, Mr. Montvale, I thought you knew. 'Malbec' is French for 'bad taste.' I don't know about you, sir, but that's enough to warn me off."

Ambassador Silvio chuckled.

The man in the Sears, Roebuck suit stared icily at Castillo.

Castillo reached across the table and offered him his hand.

"My name is Castillo, sir. Any friend of Mr. Montvale—"

"*Lieutenant* Colonel Castillo," Montvale interrupted, "this is Colonel Remley."

"How do you do, sir?" Castillo said politely.

"Of Special Operations Command," Montvale added.

"Oh, really? Well, if we can find the time, sir, maybe we can play 'Do You Know?' I know some people there."

Colonel Remley neither smiled nor replied.

"Speaking of time, Castillo," Montvale said. "I'd like to get back to Washington as soon as possible. How long is it going to take for you to get your 'guests' to the airport?"

"I have no idea who you're talking about."

Montvale, looking over the top of his wineglass, stared down Castillo. "You know goddamn well who I'm talking about."

The waiter arrived with Castillo's wine. Castillo took his time going through the ritual of approving the bottle, finally taking a long sip, swirling it in his mouth, then shrugging to the waiter as if signifying that it'd have to do.

After the waiter poured the large glass half full and left, Castillo picked up the glass, looked at Montvale, and said, "Even if I did know about whatever it is you suggest that I do, a public restaurant wouldn't be the place to talk about it, would it?"

Montvale glowered.

"Or in front of these gentlemen?" Castillo pursued.

"Then let's go to the embassy!" Montvale said angrily under his breath.

"After I've had my lunch, that would probably be a good idea."

"Castillo," Colonel Remley snapped, "you know who the ambassador is. How dare you speak to him in that manner?"

"Colonel, no disrespect to either ambassador was intended, sir. It's just that I suspect Mr. Montvale was alluding to something that is highly classified, and I know that neither you nor Ambassador Silvio is authorized access to that material."

"Ambassador Montvale briefed me fully on this situation on the way down here, Colonel!"

"With respect, sir, I doubt that."

"You arrogant little sonofabitch!" Remley said sharply, almost knocking over his water glass. "Just who the hell do you think you are?"

"Sir," Castillo replied evenly, "the reason I doubt that Ambassador Montvale would make you or anyone else privy to what I think he's referring to is that only two people have been authorized to decide who has the Need to Know. And as I haven't done so and I have not been informed by the other person so authorized that you have been briefed, I'm reasonably certain that you have not been made privy and thus do not have the Need to Know, sir."

"Goddamn you, Charley!" Montvale said.

Castillo raised his eyebrows in mock shock. "If everybody is going to swear at me, I'm just going to have to be rude and change tables. I'm very sensitive, and I don't want to have indigestion when I'm eating my lunch."

"One of my options, Castillo," Montvale said, ignoring him, "is to ask Colonel Remley to place you under arrest, then have those gentlemen escort you to my airplane."

He nodded toward the two neatly dressed men.

Castillo looked at them, then at Ambassador Silvio, who now looked more than a little uncomfortable, then back at Montvale. "What are they, Secret Service?"

"Yes, they are," Montvale said.

"And I'll bet they're armed, right?"

"Yes, they are."

"Do you see those three men at the table in the other room looking this way, Mr. Ambassador?"

Montvale looked. "What about them?"

"Two of them are officers—commissioned officers—of the Gendarmería Nacional. If either of your Secret Service agents even looks like he's going to do anything to me, the gendarmes will come over, ask them for their identification, and then pat them down. If they are armed—the Secret Service has no authority in Argentina—they will be arrested, their weapons confiscated, and then Ambassador Silvio will be forced to see what he can do about getting them out of the slam. With a little quiet encouragement from your table guest here, they might even detain you and the colonel for questioning."

"I'll see you before a general court-martial, Colonel!" Colonel Remley exploded.

Castillo met Remley's eyes.

"With respect, sir, on what charge?" he said calmly. "I have always been taught that an officer is required to obey his last lawful order unless that order is changed by an officer senior to the officer who issued the initial order. You are not, sir, senior to the officer whose orders I am obeying. And both Ambassador Silvio and Mr. Montvale know that."

"Gentlemen," Ambassador Silvio said with some awkwardness, "this is getting out of hand."

"Mr. Ambassador, with respect, I suggest that I'm trying to keep it from really getting out of hand. And with that in mind, vis-à-vis my going to the embassy to have a private chat with Mr. Montvale, I'm going to have to ask for your word that I will be allowed to leave the embassy whenever I choose to do so."

Castillo saw the waiter approaching with what he guessed was his meal, and he remained quiet as the waiter placed it before him, then picked up the bottle of Saint Felicien and refilled Castillo's large glass before leaving.

"You really should try some of this, Mr. Montvale," Castillo said, raising the glass in his direction. "It's very nice and can get that 'bad taste' out of your mouth."

Montvale just stared back.

"And if I don't give you my word that you will be free to leave the embassy?" Ambassador Silvio asked.

"Then I will have my lunch and leave."

"Colonel Castillo," Colonel Remley said, his tone hard-edged, "I am about to give you a direct order—"

Montvale held up his hand, interrupting him.

"Drink your wine, Castillo," Montvale said. "And have your lunch. Then we will go to the embassy."

Castillo looked at Montvale, then back at Silvio. "And have I your word, Mr. Ambassador, that I'll be allowed to leave?"

"You have my word," Ambassador Silvio said.

[THREE]

Ambassador Silvio's armored BMW was waiting at the curb when everyone in their party walked out of Río Alba fifteen minutes later.

"I suggest that it would be easier to walk," Silvio said.

"Fine with me," Castillo said. "If Mr. Montvale feels up to it."

Montvale glared at him, nodded at Colonel Remley to follow, and set off down the sidewalk.

"The embassy's this way, Mr. Montvale," Castillo said, pointing his thumb in the opposite direction.

Montvale stopped in his tracks, then turned. He walked past Castillo without looking at him and with Remley following suit.

They all walked single file the one block to the employees' gate in the embassy fence with the Secret Service following them, and the gendarmería SUV following everyone.

The rent-a-cops passed everybody through the turnstile. Then one of the rent-a-cops went to the sidewalk to more than a little arrogantly wave the Mercedes away from what was a no-parking zone. One of the gendarmes got out of the vehicle and took up a position near the turnstile. The driver held up his credentials. The rent-a-cop immediately lost his arrogance and slinked back to his station.

Castillo saw that this had not gone unnoticed and said, "Did you ever wonder, Mr. Montvale, what diplomats, members of the gendarmería, and six-hundred-pound gorillas have in common?"

Montvale looked at Castillo in disgust mingled with a little confusion.

"What did you say?" the director of National Intelligence asked.

"They can park wherever they want to," Castillo explained.

"Good God!" Montvale said in disgust.

Montvale followed the ambassador into the building. When Castillo followed him, the ambassador turned to them both.

"May I suggest you use my office for your conversation?" he asked.

"That's very kind of you, Mr. Ambassador," Castillo said. "And, sir, would you clear it with the switchboard in case we have to have a secure telephone?"

"Of course."

They passed through a metal detector guarded by a Marine. Its alarm went off, but a nod of Ambassador Silvio saw them passed through anyway.

They rode an elevator to the second floor and entered the ambassador's outer office.

"Unplug that, please," Castillo said, pointing to the intercom box on the desk of the ambassador's secretary. "And the telephone, too, if it's capable of eavesdropping on the ambassador's office."

Ambassador Silvio's secretary looked at her boss in genuine surprise. And again Silvio signaled with a nod of his head to do what Castillo had requested.

"Mr. Ambassador," Castillo said, "with the caveat that what will be discussed in your office will be classified Top Secret Presidential and is not to be disclosed to anyone, including the secretary of State, you're quite welcome to come with us."

Montvale answered for him: "Please do, Mr. Ambassador. I really would like a witness."

"Very well," Ambassador Silvio agreed, with obvious reluctance.

Castillo turned to Colonel Remley.

"With respect, sir, I don't believe you have the Need to Know."

"And what if I insist that Colonel Remley participate, Castillo?" Montvale said coldly.

"Then we will not have our chat," Castillo said evenly. "And, Colonel, with Ambassador Silvio as witness, I now inform Mr. Montvale that he is not to tell you what is said or what may transpire in the ambassador's office."

"I find it hard to believe that you have the authority to order Ambassador Montvale to do anything," Remley said.

"With respect, sir, in this instance I do."

"Wait here, Remley," Montvale ordered. "I have the feeling that shortly I will be able to point out to Colonel Castillo how far out of line he is."

Ambassador Silvio waved them into his office, followed them in, and closed the door.

"Is there anything I can get for anyone?" Silvio asked.

"I'd like a minute or two in there, Mr. Ambassador," Castillo said, pointing to the ambassador's private restroom. "The waiter in Río Alba kept pouring the soda water, and I kept drinking it, and my back teeth are awash."

"Jesus Christ, Castillo!" Montvale said in disgust.

"Help yourself," Ambassador Silvio said, not quite able to restrain a smile.

When Castillo came out of the restroom, Silvio was sitting behind his desk and Montvale was on a couch. Castillo sat in an armchair upholstered in what appeared to be some type of silk fabric, took a leather cigar case from his trousers pocket, and went through the ritual of trimming and lighting a long thin black cigar.

"If you're quite through with doing that, may we begin?" Montvale asked.

"I'm waiting for you, Mr. Montvale," Castillo said.

"All right, where are they?"

"Where are who?"

"Colonel Dmitri Berezovsky and Lieutenant Colonel Svetlana Alekseeva of the SVR."

Castillo saw interest jump into Ambassador Silvio's eyes.

"Next question?" Castillo said.

"You're not going to deny that you have them, for God's sake?"

"That would depend on what you mean by 'have,' Mr. Montvale."

"I'll be goddamned! Now he thinks he's Bill Clinton!"

Again, Ambassador Silvio could not completely restrain a smile.

"What this is about, Ambassador Silvio—and since *Lieutenant Colonel* Castillo . . ."

Castillo thought his pronunciation of "lieutenant colonel" turned the rank into an obscenity.

". . . has elected to make you privy to this, I can tell you—is that *Lieutenant Colonel* Castillo, without any authority whatsoever, took it upon himself to completely ignore the carefully laid plans of the CIA station chief in Vienna to cause these Russians—important Russians; Berezovsky was the rezident in Berlin and the woman the rezident in Copenhagen—to defect and flew them here."

"Speaking hypothetically, of course," Castillo put in, "what makes you so sure that the station agent in Vienna shared anything with me? I never laid eyes on her. How could I ignore something I didn't know?"

"Then what were you doing in Vienna, for Christ's sake?"

"Carrying out my orders to locate and render harmless those responsible for the assassination of Mr. Masterson."

"And Berezovsky and Alekseeva just popped into your life?"

"Actually, that's just about what happened. Hypothetically speaking, of course."

"You're going to explain that, of course?"

"If you think you can get your temper and indignation under control—and keep them that way—I'll give it a shot."

Montvale made a grand *Go to it* gesture.

"In a twenty-four-hour period starting the day before Christmas Eve, there were three assassinations. Two of them you called to ask me about: the garroting of the Kuhls in the Stadtpark in Vienna and—"

"You told me you had never heard of the Kuhls," Montvale interrupted.

"And I hadn't."

"Am I permitted to ask questions?" Ambassador Silvio said, then went on without waiting for a reply. "Who are the Kuhls?"

"Were," Montvale corrected him. "For a very long time, they were deep-cover CIA assets in Vienna. Primarily, they were involved in identifying Russians—and others—who could be influenced by others to defect. They had a number of successes over the years."

"And they were identified and killed?"

"That's what it looks like," Montvale said.

Montvale and Silvio watched while Castillo relit his cigar.

Then, after exhaling a blue cloud of smoke, Castillo went on: "At just about the time the Kuhls were assassinated, a correspondent of the *Tages Zeitung,* Günther Friedler, was murdered in Marburg an der Lahn. That's a small city sixty miles or so north of Frankfurt am Main, best known for Philipp's University. The body was mutilated in an attempt to paint the murder as the result of a homosexual lover's quarrel. Friedler was investigating the Marburg Group, a collection of German businessmen known to have profited from the Iraqi oil-for-food scam. Specifically, Friedler was looking into the connection between these people and a chemical factory operating on what had been the West German nuclear facility in the former Belgian Congo."

"May I ask how you know this?" Silvio asked.

"I have an interest in the *Tages Zeitung* publishing firm," Castillo said.

Montvale smiled, then while looking at Castillo said: "Actually, Mr. Ambassador, in his alter ego role as Karl Wilhelm von und zu Gossinger, Castillo *owns* the *Tages Zeitung* publishing empire."

Silvio's eyebrows rose in surprise.

Castillo calmly went on: "I was, when we heard about this, in Washington with a man named Eric Kocian, who is publisher of the Budapest *Tages Zeitung.* An attempt to murder him in Budapest was made some time ago. Kocian was our man who reopened the Vienna *Tages Zeitung* after World War Two. And he was an old friend of the Kuhls. And he considered Friedler a close friend. He announced he was going to (a) go to their funerals and (b) find out who had murdered them. There was no way I could stop him, so we got on the Gulfstream and flew to Germany.

"Going off at a tangent, there were, within the twenty-four-hour period I mentioned, two more assassination attempts, both of which failed. One was here—actually in Pilar; that's about forty-five klicks from here, Mr. Montvale—when Comandante Liam Duffy of the Gendarmería Nacional and his family were leaving a restaurant. . . ."

"I heard about that," Ambassador Silvio said softly.

"Duffy was in on the operation when we got the DEA agent back from the drug people in Paraguay. The second attempt, in Philadelphia, was on Special Agent Jack Britton of the Secret Service and his wife. They took fire from fully-auto AKs as they drove up to their home. For years, Britton had been a deep-cover Philly cop keeping an eye on an aptly named bunch of African-American Lunatics involved in, among other things, the lunatic idea of crashing that stolen 727 into the Liberty Bell and making mysterious trips to Africa—including the Congo—financed, we found out, with oil-for-food money.

"Britton was on the Vice President's security detail. When he was informed 'of course, you're off that assignment' and otherwise made to feel he was being punished for having been the target of an assassination attempt, he said some very rude things to various senior Secret Service people, then told them what they could do with the Secret Service and came to see me before we flew to Germany. I sent him and his wife down here—"

"And why did you think you had the authority to do that?" Montvale demanded.

Castillo ignored the interruption and, looking at Silvio, continued: "I was initially thinking Jack would be just the guy to help protect Ambassador Masterson in Uruguay. And since Jack had, so to speak, burned his Secret Service bridge, I didn't think—and still don't think—that I had to ask anyone's permission."

He met Montvale's eyes.

"So what happened in Germany?" Montvale said after a moment.

"I was at the Haus im Wald, near Bad Hersfeld—it used to belong to my mother, but now Otto Görner, who runs Gossinger Beteiligungsgesellschaft, the holding company, lives there—when there was a call for me—as Castillo—from quote the U.S. embassy in Berlin unquote.

"When I answered it, a guy asked in Berliner German if he had Gossinger—not Castillo—and when I said 'yes,' he switched to English—faultless American accent—and said, 'Sorry to bother you, *Colonel Castillo,* but I thought you would like to know an attempt will be made on your life and Görner's and Kocian's during the Friedler funeral.' Sometime during the conversation, he said his name was 'Tom Barlow' and that I should be careful as the workers were ex-Stasi.

"And then he hung up.

"Friedler's funeral, the next day, was in Saint Elisabeth's church in Marburg. We had reserved seats. Two of my guys checked them before the ceremony. They found an envelope addressed to me—Gossinger—in one of the prayer books. It contained a photocopy of Berezovsky's passport and four cards with the name 'Tom Barlow' on one, and 'Vienna,' 'Budapest,' and 'Berlin' on the others. 'Berlin' had been crossed out.

"What it looked like was that Berezovsky wanted to meet me in either Vienna or Budapest and would be using the name 'Tom Barlow.' "

"You mean he wanted to defect?" Montvale asked, his tone now somewhat civil.

"It didn't say that, but we thought that was likely."

"And it never occurred to you to contact the station agent in either Berlin or Vienna or Budapest?"

"I considered that and decided against it."

Montvale shook his head in obvious disgust. "So you went to Vienna to see what would happen?"

"Let me tell this through, please," Castillo said, and after a visibly annoyed Montvale nodded his assent, went on: "Nothing happened at the church, possibly because my people and the local cops were all over it. Afterward, Kocian said he wanted to go to the Kuhl funeral in Vienna and wanted to go there on the train. I sent the airplane ahead to Vienna, and Kocian and I—plus Kocian's bodyguard and one of my guys—caught the train in Kassel."

"Which one of your guys?" Montvale said.

"That's not germane."

"The one General McNab sent to make sure you didn't do anything stupid, as you're so wont to do? The one sitting in there with the gendarmes? Sergeant Major Davidson?"

"We went to lunch on the train," Castillo said, ignoring the question. "Berezovsky, his wife and daughter, and Alekseeva were having their lunch. I recognized him from the photocopy of his passport picture and spoke to him. He said he would like to talk a little business, so I invited them to my compartment.

"Thirty minutes later, they showed up—just Berezovsky and Alekseeva—told me who they were, and said they were willing to defect for two million dollars. I asked him what he had that was worth two million dollars, and he promised to tell me all about the chemical factory in the Congo once he was where he wanted me to take them in the Gulfstream."

"Where did he want you to take them?"

"Next question?"

"Okay. And at no time during all this did it occur to you that you were in way over your head with something like this, and what you should do was take these people to the U.S. embassy in Vienna and turn them over to the CIA station chief? Or call me, for Christ's sake, and ask me what you should do? I thought we had an agreement."

"That implies that you have some authority over me, and we both know you don't," Castillo said. "We do have an agreement, but I came to understand that this did not fit its guidelines. Berezovsky and Alekseeva were antsy, and it came out they knew that the Kuhls had been whacked, and I decided that's why they had come to me. They were afraid of what they were going to find in Vienna—from anyone who ultimately reports to you. Thus, the loophole in our agreement."

Montvale didn't say anything for a moment as he looked across the room in thought. It was clear he was not happy with what he was hearing. He then said: "How did they come to contact you in Germany?"

"My theory at the time was that Berezovsky went to Marburg to see that the ex-Stasi guys did a good job on Kocian and Göerner. Then—in what sequence, I don't know—they saw my picture—Gossinger's picture—in the *Tages Zeitung*—"

"What was that all about?"

"There was a front-page story that announced that the publisher—Gossinger—had returned to Germany from the States for Friedler's funeral and was offering a reward—a large reward—for information leading to the people who had taken him out.

"I decided that Berezovsky knew who Gossinger is—who I am—and saw in the newspaper photograph that I was traveling in the Gulfstream, and decided I was his safe ticket out of Europe.

"What I guessed then turned out to be pretty much on the money. They told me that they had heard about the Kuhls, which suggested the SVR would be waiting for them in Vienna. And they had very little faith in the CIA station chief in Vienna, fearing that she would leave them hanging in the breeze if the SVR was onto them.

"So I slipped them out of the West Bahnhof in Vienna, onto the Gulfstream, and got them the hell out of Dodge."

"And brought them here," Montvale finished for him. "Where are they, Charley? To salvage anything from this mess, we have to get them to Washington and turned over to the agency just as soon as possible."

"No. That's out of the question, I'm afraid. They are not going to turn themselves over to the agency."

Montvale exhaled audibly.

He said: "You're telling me that you offered to give them two million dollars to tell you all about the chemical factory in the *Democratic Republic of the Congo*? God, you don't even know its name!"

I'm not even going to respond to that ridiculous remark.

He's trying to get a rise out of me.

"I know all about that chemical factory," Montvale went on. "There's nothing of interest there." He grinned. "You have been conned out of two million dollars, my young friend."

Castillo caught his pulse rising at the condescension.

Let it go. . . .

He counted to ten, then said in a reasonable tone: "Tell you what. Why don't we call the agency and ask them? If they say there's nothing of interest to our national security there, then once again you've put blind faith in who feeds you your intel. Because they and you are wrong. More egg on their face and more, I'm afraid, on yours. There is a very active chemical laboratory and factory there, funded with oil-for-food money. It has the mission of poisoning the water supplies of our major cities and, they hope, poisoning as many millions of Americans as possible as collateral damage."

"Berezovsky told you this?"

Castillo nodded.

"And you believe him?"

Castillo nodded again.

"I don't have to call the agency to verify what I already know."

"If I were you, I would call," Castillo said. "If you do, and they tell you they're on top of the situation, and there's nothing to worry about, then you'll be covered, with Ambassador Silvio and I as witnesses, when this comes down. You asked and they assured you everything was hunky-dory."

For a moment, Castillo thought Montvale would not reach for the thick-corded secure telephone on Ambassador Silvio's desk, but in the end he did.

"How does this thing work?"

Silvio held out his hand and took the handset from Montvale.

"What we're going to have to do is get a secure line to the State Department switchboard. They can connect you with the CIA," Silvio said, then switched on the secure telephone.

"This is Ambassador Silvio. Get a secure line to State, then get a secure line to the director of Central Intelligence. Ambassador Montvale is calling."

Toward the end of saying "Ambassador Montvale is calling" Silvio had raised his voice questioningly while looking at Montvale, in effect asking, *Did Montvale want the DCI or someone else?*

Montvale had nodded, signaling that DCI was fine.

"Put it on the speakerphone," Castillo said. "That way Ambassador Silvio and I can both testify that you asked the DCI personally."

Montvale gave him a dirty look, then looked at the phone base and pushed the speakerphone button in time for everyone to hear, "Office of the DCI."

"This is Ambassador Montvale. Get me the DCI, please."

Moments later, the voice of John Powell, the director of the Central Intelligence Agency, inquired cheerfully: "How are you, Mr. Ambassador?"

"I'm well, thank you, Jack."

"What can I do for you?"

"I'm sitting in Ambassador Silvio's office in Buenos Aires."

"Little warm down there, isn't it?"

"Brutal. Jack, Lieutenant Colonel Castillo is with us."

"Oh, really?"

"The question has come up—actually, Castillo raised it—about activity in the Democratic Republic of the Congo; specifically, on that experimental farm the West Germans used to operate down there. You know what I mean?"

"Yes, of course."

"Do you know of anything going on down there?"

"Is that what Castillo suggested?"

"Yes, it is."

"Where did he get that?"

Castillo clapped his hands, then drew his right hand in a cutting motion across his throat.

"He'd rather not say," Montvale said.

"I see. Well, as I said, I haven't heard anything. But if you'll give me a minute, I'll check to see if anything has happened that I missed. Hang on a minute, please."

There came the murmur of unintelligible voices in the background, and then Powell came back on: "It'll take a couple of minutes. Are you on a speakerphone?"

"Yes, Jack, we are."

"How are you, Colonel?"

Castillo said: "I'm very well, Mr. Powell. Thank you. And yourself?"

"I understand you've been in Vienna."

"There is a rumor circulating to that effect, sir."

"Apropos of nothing whatever, Colonel, to kill the time while we're waiting to hear about Africa, so to speak, a couple of interesting Interpol warrants crossed my desk this morning."

"Yes, sir?"

"The Russians say that several of their diplomats—Dmitri Berezovsky and Svetlana Alekseeva, known to be SVR officers, one in Copenhagen and the other in Berlin—have absconded with large amounts of money. More than a million dollars from Copenhagen, and twice that from Berlin."

"Well, I suppose that goes to show we're not the only ones with crooked diplomats," Castillo said, and winked at Ambassador Silvio, who smiled and shook his head.

"The Russians seem really upset about these two," Powell went on. "They've offered a large reward for information leading to their arrest. And no one seems to know where they are or how they got there."

"Well, I'll keep my eyes peeled for dishonest-looking Russians, Mr. Powell. And you'll be the first to know if I find any."

"I don't like to think what will happen to these people—Lieutenant Colonel Alekseeva is Colonel Berezovsky's sister, and his wife and little girl are apparently with them—if the SVR catches up with them. As they will eventually."

"Well, just off the top of my head, Mr. Powell, I'd say if anyone knew how to dodge the SVR it would be a couple of senior SVR officers. Especially if they had a lot of cash. What did you say they're supposed to have stolen? Three million dollars?"

"And off the top of my head, Colonel Castillo," Powell said with more than a little impatience in his voice, "if the situation presented itself, I'd think obviously would be in their self-interest to place themselves under the protection of the CIA."

"And you'd really like to talk to them, right?"

"Yes, we would really like to talk to them."

"Well, I'd say that might be possible somewhere down the pike, but not any-time soon."

"Why do you say that?"

"Well, if I have heard that the Vienna station chief has a big mouth—I understand she's been telling wild stories to her old pal, Mrs. Patricia Davies Wilson, who in turn has been running her mouth to C. Harry Whelan, Jr."—Castillo glanced at Montvale to gauge his reaction to the mention of the journalist who'd tried to crucify Castillo but was outsmarted by Montvale—"I think we have to presume these people have heard it, too. Under those circumstances, I don't think if I were them I would place a hell of a lot of faith in the agency to protect them. Would you?"

There was a long silence, then Powell asked, "Did you ever hear of Lieutenant Colonel Oliver North, Colonel Castillo?"

"Isn't he one of those talking heads we see on Fox News?"

"Before that, he was a serving Marine officer who was given more authority than he could handle."

"The story I get, Mr. Powell, is that Colonel North saw what he was doing as his duty as an officer sworn to protect the United States from all enemies, foreign and domestic, and to do what he was doing despite a lot of opposition from what he called the 'LAs.' "

"The what?"

"I think it stands for 'Langley Assholes,' but I'm not sure."

Silvio suddenly had the urge to clear his throat. Castillo looked at him, but the ambassador apparently was finding the tips of his shoes fascinating.

Powell shot back: "Can I infer from that that you share North's opinion of the agency?"

"I don't know what Ollie thinks of the CIA. But if you're asking for my opinion?"

"Yes, I am."

"Some really wonderful people struggling to stay afloat in a sea of politically correct left-wing bureaucrats."

"Interesting," Powell said icily.

"This is getting us nowhere," Montvale said. "How long is it going to take to get the information on the alleged chemical factory in the Congo?"

"I think Mr. Montvale means the *Democratic Republic of the Congo*," Castillo offered.

"It was just handed to me," Powell said. "The latest analysis is dated five days ago. It states that there is no discernible activity there of interest to the United States. They are apparently experimenting with fish farms."

" 'Fish farms'?" Castillo parroted.

"Yes, Colonel. I spell: Foxtrot-India-Sierra-Hotel farms."

Castillo shook his head. "Are you open to a suggestion, Mr. Powell?"

"I'll listen to one, Colonel Castillo."

"You might consider the possibility that whoever filed that, and whoever analyzed and approved the raw data, are cut from the same cloth as Mrs. Davies."

"Thank you for sharing that with me, Colonel," Powell replied again with more than a hint of sarcasm. "I will indeed take it under consideration."

"Nice to talk to you, Mr. Powell," Castillo said.

"Did you ever hear the old Russian proverb, Colonel, that people who dig their own graves usually are buried in them?"

"I think you just made that up," Castillo said.

"I'll get back to you later, Jack," Montvale said.

"I think that would be a good idea, Mr. Ambassador."

Montvale's face showed he didn't know what to do with the telephone. Ambassador Silvio took it from him and said into the handset, "Break it down, please."

"Satisfied, Castillo?" Montvale asked.

"Not really. With all the money we spend on the CIA, it seems to me they ought to be able to find their ass with only one hand, let alone both."

"As a matter of curiosity, why did you go out of your way to insult the DCI?"

"What's chiseled there in stone on the wall of the lobby at Langley? 'You shall know the truth and the truth shall make you free'? If hearing the truth insults the DCI, maybe he should look for other work."

"Okay. I've had enough. I am now going to tell you what's happened, and what's going to happen."

"Correction: What you would like to think is going to happen," Castillo said. "Unless I hear from the President to the contrary, I'm not subject to your orders."

"Do me the courtesy of hearing me out," Montvale said.

Castillo met his eyes, then shrugged, then leaned back in his armchair and relit his cigar. "I'm listening."

"A board of medical officers convened at the Walter Reed Army Medical Center has examined your case and determined that the stress of your duties has rendered you psychologically unfit for active service, and therefore decided that you will be medically retired as of 1 February—"

"What the hell!" Castillo said, sitting upright.

Montvale held out his hand, palm out, as a *Wait* sign.

"Hear me out," he repeated, then went on: "The degree of psychological damage you have suffered in the line of duty has been determined to be twenty-five percent. You will thus receive a disability pension of twenty-five percent of your base pay. There has been some talk that at your retirement ceremony you will be awarded the Distinguished Service Medal.

"Turning to the retirement ceremony—at which Major Miller will also be medically retired and may be decorated with the Legion of Merit—it will be the regular monthly retirement ceremony at the Army Aviation Center, Fort Rucker, Alabama. At this time, it is currently planned that General Allan Naylor will preside.

"Major Miller has been placed on terminal leave. You are also on terminal leave—or will be, as soon as you sign the papers Colonel Remley has brought with him.

"I will be present at your retirement ceremony, as will Mr. C. Harry Whelan of *The Washington Post,* and DCI Powell. On the flight down, Mr. Powell will tell Mr. Whelan, in the strictest confidence, that there is absolutely nothing to the story Mrs. Davies has told him that you interfered with the CIA operation to turn Colonel Berezovsky and Lieutenant Colonel Alekseeva. And that the Russian defectors are—and always have been—in CIA hands.

"If it seems to DCI Powell to be the appropriate thing to do—and as a proof of the high regard the CIA holds for Mr. Whelan, as a patriotic American—he will ask my permission to take Mr. Whelan, immediately on our return to Washington, to the CIA safe house in Maryland where Berezovsky and Alekseeva are being interrogated. I will, as proof of my own regard for Mr. Whelan's patriotism and high standing in journalism, grant my permission.

"Mr. Whelan will thus have proof of what I told him the first time you got us in a mess like this, that Mrs. Davies is a disgruntled former CIA employee who doesn't know what she's talking about. You, rather than running some super-secret operation of the President, are in fact a distinguished warrior who has been pushed beyond his limits and were assigned to an innocuous little agency in the Department of Homeland Security while the psychiatrists and psychologists at Walter Reed tried to help you regain your mental stability. Lamentably, they failed, and Mr. Whelan will see you retired with flags flying, bands playing, and a new medal to add to your already impressive display."

He paused and met Castillo's eyes as all that sank in.

"Getting the picture, Castillo?"

Castillo leaned back in his chair and puffed his cigar. "I've got it."

"All you have to do now is sign the papers Colonel Remley has for you and get the Russians to the airport, and we can put this all behind us."

Castillo pointed with his cigar to the secure telephone. "There's the phone. Call the President."

"Why should I do that?"

"Because he doesn't know about this. Does he?"

Montvale shrugged, then confessed: "No. I want to protect him as much as possible from the mess you have caused."

"You're going to present him with a *fait accompli*?"

"That's the idea."

"Bad idea," Castillo said. "Now, is it my turn to tell you what's not going to happen and what is—"

"You don't have any choice here, Castillo, for Christ's sake!"

"Wrong again."

Montvale glowered at him but said nothing. He started to stand.

"You want to hear me out?" Castillo asked.

Montvale looked at him, then took his seat. "If you insist."

Castillo puffed his cigar as he gathered his thoughts.

He exhaled, then said: "First of all, the Russians are not going to get on your airplane to be flown to a CIA safe house in Maryland. I don't think I could talk them into that if I wanted to, and I don't. Second, I have no intention of signing anything Colonel Remley may have in his briefcase. That's the 'what's not going to happen' part of my scenario.

"The second part, 'what is going to happen,' is that—with or without your help—I'm going to the *Democratic Republic of the Congo* to verify what I've been told is going on there."

"You're out of your mind!"

"And when I have proof of that, I'm going to take that factory out myself, and if I can't do that, lay the proof on the President's desk and tell him I did what I did because the CIA refused—again—to believe what I told them."

"You know I can't permit you to do anything like that," Montvale said.

"And you know you can't stop me," Castillo said. "So here is a possible compromise that should cover most of the bases:

"First, we get Dick Miller on the first plane down here. I need somebody to help me fly the Gulfstream, as Colonel Torine and Captain Sparkman are going to return to Washington with you. Another proof for you to show your pal the journalist that I was not running OOA—Torine is a full-bird colonel; I'm a lowly lieutenant colonel.

"Jack Doherty of the FBI is now in Vienna with Dave Yung. They are no longer needed there, as I have turned up another very reliable source of information vis-à-vis who assassinated the Kuhls and Friedler . . ."

"Your new Russian friends, obviously," Montvale said sarcastically.

". . . and tried to kill Duffy and the Brittons. When all the *t*'s are crossed and all the *i*'s dotted, I will turn that information over to you.

"I spoke with Doherty and Yung last night. Yung's resignation from the FBI will be in the mail this morning. So he will not be available to anyone, like Whelan, to be questioned.

"Doherty, on the other hand, wants to return to the J. Edgar Hoover Building. So he's on his way to Washington, where, if Whelan finds him, he can tell Whelan that he was on temporary duty with the OOA, analyzing the operations of Homeland Security, had always worked for Torine, and knows almost nothing about me except that he heard I wasn't playing with a full deck.

"Alex Darby and Edgar Delchamps are going to retire from the agency and won't be available. Jack Britton will resign from the Secret Service, as will Tony Santini; Whelan won't be able to find them, I don't think, and even if he does, will learn nothing from them."

"Ambassador Silvio," Montvale said, "I put it to you that you've heard enough of this to fairly conclude that Lieutenant Colonel Castillo is not only as unstable as the doctors in Walter Reed have concluded but that he is threatening to do a number of things—which he is entirely capable of undertaking in his delusional state—that are not only illegal but which will almost certainly cause great embarrassment not only to the President personally but to the country, and that under these circumstances, it is your clear duty to help me get him on my airplane and to the United States, despite any promises you made to him not knowing the seriousness of his mental condition."

"You sonofabitch!" Castillo said. "If I am held here against my will, much less forced to—"

Ambassador Silvio made a gentle gesture with his hand, silencing Castillo.

"Ambassador Montvale," Silvio began in a measured tone, "first let me say that I don't need you to point out my 'clear duty' to me. As ambassador, by law I am the senior American officer in Argentina. And let me be frank: As I've listened to the exchange between you and Colonel Castillo, and between Colonel Castillo and Mr. Powell, I wondered about my responsibilities in that regard in this matter.

"When Colonel Castillo first came to Argentina, the President told me personally that Colonel Castillo was acting on his behalf and with his authority, and directed me to provide him with any assistance he required. Given that—"

"You've heard this insanity!"

"Pray let me continue," Silvio said. "Given that, Mr. Ambassador, I don't think you have the authority to force Colonel Castillo to go anywhere or do anything he doesn't want to do, absent a specific order from the President placing him under your authority. Quite the opposite, actually, I see it as my 'clear duty' to do whatever I can to assist him in carrying out his orders from the President and to prevent anyone from interfering with him."

"His orders say nothing about abducting Russian defectors from the CIA," Montvale argued, "and certainly nothing about conducting any kind of an operation in the Congo."

"Since what exactly his orders actually entail seems to be in question, it seems obvious that the only person who can clarify them is the President himself. Absent that clarification, I am not going to challenge Colonel Castillo."

Montvale met his eyes for a long moment.

He then said: "May I use your secure telephone again, Mr. Ambassador?"

"To call the President?"

"To call the President."

"Certainly. But if that is your intention, I think I should tell you that when I speak with the President—and I will do so—I will tell him that Colonel Castillo is, in my judgment, in full possession of his extraordinary mental faculties, and that it seems to me that, motivated by your desire to spare the CIA and yourself embarrassment for losing the Russian defectors, what you and the DCI are trying to do—please forgive the colorful speech—is to throw Colonel Castillo under the bus."

Montvale looked at him in angry disbelief.

"I shall also tell him," Silvio went on, "that it is my judgment that if he goes along with you and orders Castillo to Washington, it will be some time—probably years—before the CIA will be able to locate the Russian defectors, much less get them to the United States. I will point out to the President that it took decades for Mossad, the Israeli intelligence service, as you know, to find Adolf Eichmann, who they knew was in Argentina, and wasn't until a couple of years ago that Erich Priebke, who gained infamy for his role in the Ardeatine Caves massacre outside Rome, could be brought to justice, even though he had been in Argentina since 1948 and owned a hotel in Bariloche."

Montvale's face was white. Castillo wondered if the director of National Intelligence was going to lose control.

He didn't.

"Well, it seems our little chat is over, doesn't it, Castillo?" Montvale said.

"Not quite, Mr. Montvale. I would like to know whether you are going to obstruct my operation in Africa, or provide what assistance I'll need to carry it out under my existing authority."

Montvale contorted his face. "Why in hell would I do that?"

"Because, if you give me the help I need, I give you my word that I will go along with your charade about my medical retirement, and even show up for my retirement parade."

Montvale looked as if he didn't believe his ears.

"You'll go along with that?" Montvale asked after he'd taken a moment to consider the ramifications. "Why?"

"I'm as interested in protecting the President as you are. And after this the President would have to choose between us—and, self-evidently, you're far more valuable an asset than I am. I know when it's time to fold my tent."

Montvale considered that, then nodded once. "I'll give you what you think you need."

"I don't want the CIA, or anybody else, to know what I'm going to do. Understood?"

"You have my word."

"Before a witness," Ambassador Silvio put in.

"It will take me a couple of hours to explain the situation to Colonel Torine and get him and Captain Sparkman to Jorge Newbery."

"To where? Oh, the airport." He looked at his watch. "Okay. We'll be there."

Without thinking about it, when Montvale looked at his watch, Castillo looked at his. Montvale saw it.

"That looks like a brand-new stainless steel Rolex," the director of National Intelligence said.

"Actually, it's white gold. A gift from a friend."

Castillo, using his eyes, then asked for permission to use the secure telephone from Ambassador Silvio, who responded by handing him the handset.

"Get State on here, please," Castillo said into it, "and get them to give me a secure line to Major Richard Miller at OOA in the Nebraska Avenue Complex."

In the silence of the room, with Montvale's and Silvio's eyes on him, Castillo took a puff on his cigar while the telephone operator put the call through.

"Dick? I'll call you back in an hour or so. But right now make plans to get yourself on a plane down here tonight. If there's any trouble with that, call the Presidential Flight and have them fly you down in one of their Gulfstreams. If there's any trouble about that, tell them Ambassador Montvale authorized it."

Montvale rose from the couch and, without saying a word or looking at either Ambassador Silvio or Castillo, walked out of the ambassador's office.

Castillo heard Montvale say, "Okay, Remley, we're through here."

After Castillo broke off his call with Miller, he looked at Silvio.

"Mr. Ambassador, I didn't realize that you'd wind up in the middle of that. I am indeed sorry. And of course very grateful, sir."

"No reason for you to be sorry, Charley. Or grateful. I did what I thought it was my duty to do."

XI

[ONE]
Nuestra Pequeña Casa
Mayerling Country Club
Pilar, Buenos Aires Province, Argentina
1605 2 January 2006

When Jack Davidson turned the embassy's BMW into Mayerling, the gendarmería Mercedes-Benz SUV following them made a U-turn, then stopped and backed off the road into a position from which it could easily follow the BMW when it left the country club, no matter which way it turned when it came out.

Seeing what the gendarmería vehicle had done, Castillo realized that he was going to have to somehow dump his protective tail. As soon as he could, he wanted to join Svetlana at the Pilar Golf & Polo Country Club, and he didn't want the gendarmes to follow him there. They would attract unwanted attention.

When they got to the safe house, Jack Britton, holding an Uzi along his leg, opened Castillo's car door and told them that "everybody" was out back by the quincho.

"Everybody" turned out to be more than Castillo expected.

When he walked up to the shaded verandah of the quincho, "everybody" was comfortably sprawled like passengers on a cruise ship in lines of teak deck chairs on the verandah and in teak chaise lounge chairs along one side of the pool.

Susanna and Paul Sieno, Sandra Britton, Bob Kensington, and Dick Sparkman, all in bathing suits, were at the pool. Castillo knew that Paul Sieno had come from Asunción while he had been in Bariloche. Jake Torine, Tony Santini, and Jack Britton, wearing slacks and polo shirts, were in deck chairs in the shade of the verandah. A garbage can full of iced-down beer was helping them deal with the heat, and a mound of jumbo-sized packages of pretzels and potato chips on a table was giving them sustenance.

Castillo had not expected to see either Edgar Delchamps or Alex Darby, who were also on the verandah. They were wearing somewhat sweat-soaked dress shirts, and their suit jackets and the shoulder holsters they had worn under them were lying on the tiled floor beside their deck chairs.

They're supposed to be with Berezovsky and his family at Pevsner's second safe house way the hell the other side of Pilar!

Castillo's mouth went on automatic: "What the hell are you two doing here? Who's sitting on the Berezovskys?"

Delchamps didn't like Castillo's tone, and his voice showed it when he replied.

"In reply to the first question, Ace, we're sucking on a cerveza while waiting for you to tell us all about your chat with Montvale." He took a long pull on his Quilmes beer bottle to illustrate. "As for the second question, Polkovnik Berezovsky and his family are being sat upon by half a dozen heavily armed men working for our own Alfredo Munz, four of them Argentines and the other two former associates of the colonel."

He paused, and when he saw by Castillo's expression that that information had registered, then went on: "And when you have finished telling us what the ambassador had to say, Ace, we need to have a little chat ourselves."

Max interrupted the exchange by making a quick run to a table between two of the deck chairs, delicately snatching a jumbo-sized package of potato chips in his mouth, then effortlessly jumping the fence around the swimming pool and trotting to the far side of the pool, away from the deck chairs, where he lay down with the bag between his paws. He tore the bag fully open, took a mouthful of chips, then more or less casually looked up at the humans to see if there was any objection to his action.

"Max, you sonofabitch!" Castillo called.

Max took this as permission to proceed—with haste—and dug his nose back into the bag.

Castillo shook his head but couldn't help but smile.

"To err on the side of caution, I think I had better deliver the bad news inside," Castillo said as he signaled the swimmers to join him.

Everybody hoisted themselves out of the deck chairs and filed inside the quincho.

"Gather 'round me, children," Castillo said after "everybody" had entered and he had hoisted himself to sit on the pool table. Everybody shifted chairs so that they formed a half circle facing him.

"How did you know I was with Montvale?" Castillo asked, looking at Delchamps.

"I called here right after Davidson had called saying you were on the way here, had just left Montvale, and wanted everybody here. Alex and I decided we could consider ourselves 'everybody.' "

"And that it would be all right to leave the Berezovskys with those people?"

"The only question in my mind, Ace, was whether the sitters would let us go. There were six of them and two of us. It finally took a call to Alfredo before they would."

"You think they're still going to be there when you go back?"

"You're not listening, Ace. There were six of them. Alex and I were outnumbered and outgunned. If Berezovsky wanted to leave, he would have left."

"Interesting."

"He told me what he wants to do is to have a little chat, *mano a mano*, with you."

"About what?"

"Why don't we get into that when you've finished telling us about the ambassador? Starting at the beginning and leaving nothing out."

"Fair enough," Castillo said, and began: "When I parked at Jorge Newbery, there was a Presidential Flight Gulfstream on the tarmac. The pilot told me not only that it had carried Montvale down here, but that Montvale had blown his stack when Ambassador Silvio told him he had no idea where I was.

"So I went looking for him. I found him in the Río Alba and then we went to the embassy for a little chat. . . ."

It took Castillo about five minutes to bring everybody up to speed.

"Okay. That's about it. Anybody?"

Colonel Jake Torine shook his head in wonder. He—and everyone else—

had just heard that he was being sent to the Nebraska Avenue Complex, where—aided and abetted by Mrs. Agnes Forbison, their very own expert on all things bureaucratic—he was to be prepared to convince Mr. C. Harry Whelan of *The Washington Post* that the Office of Organizational Analysis was in fact what its name suggested, just one more small governmental agency charged with analyzing government organization, in this case that of the Department of Homeland Security.

Castillo looked at Torine. "Jake?"

"Why do I think you have a hidden agenda here, Charley?"

"Because by nature you are simply unable to trust your fellow man?"

"How about because I have been around the block with you too many times, ol' buddy."

"Did I forget to mention that I hope you and Sparkman will be able to tear yourself away from your analytic duties for a few hours so that you might consider the problems of getting whatever matériel and men into the Democratic Republic of the Congo in complete secrecy so they can take out a chemical laboratory/factory?"

"No, I guess that slipped your mind," Torine said.

"And of course once they have accomplished that little task, to get them *out* of the Democratic Republic of the Congo as unobtrusively as they entered?"

"That presumes that you will be allowed to use the Delta Force 727."

Castillo nodded. "And some people from Delta Force. Uncle Remus comes to mind."

Chief Warrant Officer Five Colin Leverette, a legendary Delta Force special operator, was an enormous, very black man who was called "Uncle Remus" by his close friends—and only by his close friends—in the special operations community.

"From what you have told us of your little chat with Ambassador Montvale, are you sure that's going to happen?"

"No," Castillo said simply.

"Then what, Charley?"

"I haven't quite figured that out."

"Wonderful!"

"If you're uncomfortable with this, Jake, don't do it. Just con C. Harry Whelan and leave it at that."

"Every time you lead me around the block, I'm uncomfortable," Torine said. "But I always go, and you know that."

"That was before," Castillo said, "when you were able to con yourself into thinking I wasn't really crazy."

"Not without difficulty," Torine said, chuckling.

"I've got something to tell you that will probably make you conclude I have finally really gone over the edge."

"Frankly, Charley, that wouldn't be hard."

"I'm emotionally involved with Svetlana Alekseeva," Castillo said.

Torine looked at him intensely, his eyes wary, but otherwise there was no expression on his face at all.

"To prevent any possible misinterpretation of that, Jake, let me rephrase: I am in love with her, and that emotion, I believe, is reciprocated."

"I'm really glad to hear you say that, Ace," Delchamps said.

Castillo instantly decided he had not correctly heard what Delchamps had said.

"Excuse me?"

"If you had said anything but almost exactly that, we would have had, added to our other burdens, the problem of protecting you from the lady's big brother. In my brief association with him, I have learned he is one smart, tough sonofabitch, and protecting you from him might not have been possible."

Castillo thought he saw a look of disbelief in Susanna Sieno's eyes, then wondered if it was disbelief or contempt.

Paul Sieno and Sparkman had their eyes fixed on the floor.

"Charley," Torine said finally, "I hope you weren't crazy enough to tell Montvale about this."

Castillo shook his head.

There was another long pause before Torine went on: "Insofar as reciprocity is concerned, would this explain Colonel Berezovsky's otherwise baffling sudden change of attitude?"

Castillo first noticed the near-stilted formality of Torine's question, then realized: *He's thinking out loud. Not as good ol' Jake, but as Colonel Jacob D. Torine, USAF, a senior officer subconsciously doing a staff study of a serious problem and, specifically, right now, doing the Factors Bearing on the Problem part of the study.*

"Pevsner told him that I was almost family. . . ."

"Supported," Torine went on, "by Lieutenant Colonel Alekseeva's statement, which I thought was odd: 'So far as I am concerned, before God and the world, he is family.' "

"That's what she said," Castillo agreed.

Delchamps put in: "If I'm to believe Polkovnik Berezovsky—and truth being stranger than fiction, I do—the whole family, including the infamous

Aleksandr Pevsner, is deeply religious folk with quote family values unquote that would satisfy the most pious Southern Baptist. Make that Presbyterian; they do like their booze."

He looked at Alex Darby.

"That's my take," Darby said, nodding gently.

Susanna Sieno looked like she was going to say something but changed her mind.

"Following which," Torine went on almost as if he was in a daze and hadn't heard Delchamps, "Colonel Berezovsky began not only to answer questions he had previously answered evasively and ambiguously—if at all—and began not only to answer such questions fully, but also to volunteer intelligence bearing on the questions."

"One explanation for the change in attitude," Susanna Sieno said more than a little sarcastically, "might be Charley repeating his offer of two million dollars for the information."

Delchamps looked at her coldly but didn't challenge her.

He respects her, Castillo thought.

Susanna may look like a sweet young housewife in a laundry detergent advertisement, but she's a good spook who has more than paid her dues in the agency's Clandestine Services.

"No, Susanna, that wasn't his motivation," Castillo said. "They asked me for two million on the train to establish a credible motive for their defection. But they don't need money. They brought out with them—it's in various banks around the world—far more than two million. So much money I have trouble believing how much."

Torine, deep in thought, looked out the quincho's doors.

"That is the belief of their interrogator," he went on in the military bureaucrat cant of the staff study, which sounded even more stilted when spoken. "Inevitably raising the question of the soundness of the interrogator's judgment, inasmuch as the interrogator in his admission of romantic involvement has also admitted he has abandoned the professional code he has followed throughout his adult life."

Torine stopped and tapped his fingertips together for a good thirty seconds.

Then he raised his eyes to Castillo's. "So, you see, Colonel, the dilemma into which you have thrust me?"

"Jake, you say the word and I'll get on Montvale's airplane. If you tell me you think I can't . . ."

He stopped when Torine held up his hand.

"—said dilemma makes me seriously consider that you may have in fact lost your fucking mind."

Jack Davidson chuckled.

"So you think I should get on Montvale's airplane?"

"No, that's not what I said. Or mean. I just think you should keep in mind that you're not acting rationally."

"That's . . ." Susanna Sieno started and then stopped.

"Go on, Susanna," Castillo said, gesturing. "Let's hear it."

She met his eyes for a moment, shrugged, then went on: "What I was about to say, Charley, was that that's something of an understatement."

"Guilty," Castillo said. "That thought has occurred to me."

"And you still think you're in love?"

He nodded.

"In that case, maybe I should just shut up."

"I wish you wouldn't," Castillo said. "Let's get it all out."

She considered that a moment, shrugged again, then said: "Here're a couple of things to consider. Charley. . . . Oh, hell, I was about to say that Svetlana is at least as good a spook as I am, maybe even as good as you are. But you've considered that, I'm sure. Anyway, given that, if I were in her shoes, snaring somebody like you by whatever means—certainly including spreading my legs—would be a no-brainer."

"Jesus Christ, honey!" Paul Sieno exclaimed.

"Stop thinking like a husband, Paul," Susanna said.

"And," Jack Britton said, "since we're all running at the mouth, Charley, you were on the rebound after Betty Schneider dumped you, ripe to get plucked by any female, and certainly by a really good-looking, smart one with every reason to have a 'protect my ass' agenda."

"Betty dumped him?" Sandra Britton asked, surprised. "You never told me about that!"

"I didn't think it was any of our business," Britton said.

"How'd you hear about that?" Castillo asked.

"I heard Agnes and Joel Isaacson talking," Britton said.

Castillo shrugged. "She did dump me. What she said was that she didn't want to be married to a guy who instead of coming home for supper would leave a voice mail that he was off to Timbuktu. But what I really think it was is that being with me would interfere with her new Secret Service career; that what she really wanted to do was be more of a hotshot cop than her brother. And I really don't think I was on the rebound."

Britton's face showed he didn't believe that at all.

"The flaw in your argument, Susie," Alex Darby said, "is that none of the Russians need Charley now. If she had, to use your apt if indelicate phraseology, spread her legs before he brought them here . . ."

"We don't know when or where that happened," Susanna said, and looked at Castillo.

He was on the verge of telling her that it was none of her goddamn business when he had first been intimate with Svetlana, but then realized that, in fact, it was.

Castillo made a grand gesture with his right index finger, poking the felt of the table. "Here, the first night."

There was a resounding silence.

"On the pool table?" Sandra Britton blurted. "Charley!"

"No, I mean in Argentina, not before."

"Right after her swimsuit top 'accidentally' came off, right?" Susanna said, undeterred.

Castillo nodded.

"That was an accident," Sandra said. "I saw what happened."

"Well, she really covered herself up just as fast as she could, I'll say that for her. Top and bottom," Susanna said.

Castillo's memory bank kicked in, and he had a clear image of Svetlana adjusting her bathing suit back over her exposed buttock.

"If I didn't know better, Susie," Darby said, "I'd suspect you don't like Podpolkovnik Alekseeva very much."

"That's the point, you asshole," Susanna snapped. "She *is* a podpolkovnik of the FSB—"

"*Was* a podpolkovnik of the *SVR*," Delchamps corrected her without thinking.

"*Et tu*, Edgar?" Susanna said, thickly sarcastic. "You're into this true-love-at-first-sight bullshit?"

"Well, what the hell's wrong with that?" Sandra challenged. "It happens."

"Bullshit!" Susanna said.

"I don't know about you people," Sandra snapped back. "But it does happen to certain cops and schoolteachers. Tell her, Jack."

"Guilty," Britton said.

"Oh, for Christ's sake!" Susanna said disgustedly.

Darby said: "What I started to say, Susie, what seems an hour or so ago, before we got into the romantic aspects of all this, is the flaw in your argument is that the Russians don't need Charley anymore."

"Meaning what?" Susanna challenged.

"Well, for example, we weren't at the second safe house thirty minutes when the Russians came in, bearing gifts."

"Like what?"

"Passports and national identity cards for everybody—Argentine, Uruguayan, Paraguayan, South African, Mexican."

"All good forgeries, I'm sure," Susanna said, her tone making clear her contempt for counterfeit passports, which everybody knew were good only until immigration authorities could run them through a computer database.

Darby took two passports and two national identity cards from a zip-top plastic bag and handed one set to Susanna and the other to Castillo. "These are genuine. I have an asset in Argentine immigration and he checked them for me."

Castillo found himself looking at photographs of Svetlana looking at him through the sealed thick plastic of a Uruguayan national identity card and passport identifying her as Susanna Barlow, born in Warsaw, Poland, and now a naturalized citizen living in Maldonado, Uruguay. He remembered from somewhere that Maldonado was just north of the seaside resort town of Punta del Este.

"What's the name on yours, Susanna?" Castillo asked as he extended the documents to her.

She didn't reply. She simply handed him the set of documents Darby had given to her. When Castillo examined them, Svetlana's photo—the same one as on the Uruguayan documents—was on both an Argentine passport and a national identity card identifying her as Susanna Barlow, born in Warsaw, Poland, and now a naturalized citizen living in Rosario.

Delchamps said: "The Paraguayan, South African, and Mexican documents may be fake, but I don't think so. As soon as I can, I'll check them."

Susanna looked at him but didn't say anything.

"What's interesting here, Susanna," Delchamps went on, "aside from Svetlana's new first name, I mean, is that when I told Berezovsky I was going to meet Charley here and I thought Svetlana would be with him—" He stopped and turned to Castillo. "Where is she, by the way?"

"At yet another of Pevsner's safe houses, in the Pilar Golf and Polo Club. Munz and Lester are with her," Castillo furnished.

Delchamps nodded, then turned his attention back to Susanna: "Berezovsky just handed me this stuff and asked me to give it to her. I don't think he would have done that if he planned to take off."

"Who is Berezovsky now?" Castillo asked.

" 'Thomas Barlow,' who else? Born in Manchester, England," Delchamps answered.

"The Russians also showed up with a little walking around money," Darby said. "One hundred thousand dollars of it, fresh from the Federal Reserve. Still in the plastic wrapping. It makes up a package about this big." He demonstrated with his left hand, fingers and thumb extended in what could have been the mimicking of a bear claw. "And it was the real thing, too, Susie. Nice, crisp, spendable hundred-dollar bills."

He waited until she reacted. All he got was a sort of *so what* shrug, but it was enough for him to go on.

"All of which leads Edgar and me to believe that if all they—especially she—wanted out of Charley was getting them here from Vienna and a little help until they got settled—or disappeared—that that time has passed. Berezovsky is still singing like a canary and—"

"And Charley is still alive," Delchamps said. "Taking Charley out when he was in Bariloche would have been the smart thing for them to do, covering their tracks, and it is a given that both Pevsner and Berezovsky are very good at doing that sort of thing and lose no sleep whatever when they do it."

"So what are you saying?" Tony Santini asked.

"I can't wait to see the look on Susanna's face when I say this," Delchamps said. "I believe, and so does Brother Darby, that (a) Polkovnik Berezovsky and Podpolkovnik Alekseeva risked all to get out of Russia because—subpara lowercase *i*—they came to believe that Vladimir Putin was about to resurrect the bad old days of the Soviet Union and they wanted nothing to do with that . . ."

"I don't believe I'm hearing this," Susanna Sieno said.

". . . and—(a) subpara lowercase *ii*—they suspected that because Brother Putin, himself a member in good standing of the Oprichina—you'll recall his father was Stalin's cook—knows all about what a threat heavy-duty oprichniki would pose to his regime, they stood a very good chance of spending the rest of their lives in a mental hospital with their veins full of happy juice, said mental hospitals having replaced the gulag in the new and wonderful Russian Federation as depositories for potential troublemakers."

"You're telling me that you and Alex"—she looked between them—"believe those ludicrous yarns about a state within a state?"

"With all my innocent trusting heart, Susie," Darby said, putting his right hand to his chest. "But then again, you have to remember that throughout my long career in the Clandestine Services I earned the reputation of always being the guy who believed everything he was told."

"If I may go on?" Delchamps said. "Darby and I also believe that (b) the Berezovskys, the Pevsners, and at least Charley's new friend Svetlana are Christians who take it seriously—we're not so sure of the lady's husband, he's one mean sonofabitch who may well be a godless Communist. . . ."

"She's married?" Susanna asked, shaking her head.

"To Polkovnik Evgeny Alekseeva of the SVR," Delchamps confirmed, "who at last report was scouring the streets of Vienna in high hopes of finding his wife, who he no doubt then hopes to kill in the most painful way he can think of."

"Oh, Charley!" Sandra Britton said.

"Once again, if I may go on?" Delchamps said. "Now, where was I? Oh, yes! (b): *are Christians who take it seriously*, and for that reason—subpara lowercase *i*—regard the poisoning of a couple of million innocent women and children as un-Christian and are therefore willing to help Charley take out whatever the hell those bastards have in the Congo, about which Berezovsky apparently knows a hell of a lot.

"Subpara lowercase *ii*, would be deeply offended if Our Leader—known to the Secret Service as 'Don Juan'—as I really expected to hear just now when he returned to our little nest—had been pleasuring Podpolkovnik Alekseeva simply to get her to talk—or simply for fun—rather than as a manifestation of his intention to marry the lady when that is possible, and thereafter to walk hand in hand and in the fear of God in the bonds of holy matrimony until death do them part. Amen." He paused. "Getting the picture, Susanna?"

"If I heard all that from anybody but you two . . ."

"That wasn't the question."

She nodded. "I got it, Edgar."

"Now tell our leader you're sorry, baby," Paul Sieno said.

Susanna looked at Castillo.

"Is the wedding going to be simple, Don Juan, or are you both going to wear your uniforms?"

"Uniforms, I think. But only if you're going to precede us down the aisle scattering rose petals while singing 'I Love You Truly.'"

[TWO]
Pilar Golf & Polo Country Club
Pilar, Buenos Aires Province, Argentina
1740 2 January 2006

After thinking about it, Castillo decided there was more to be lost than gained by eluding the gendarmería SUV that was waiting for them outside the gate of the Mayerling Country Club.

Comandante Liam Duffy would be annoyed, Castillo understood, and now was not the time to annoy the Latin-tempered (his mother was Argentine) gendarmería officer. That was, annoy him any more than he already was annoyed.

Castillo knew that Duffy remained furious about the assassination attempt on Christmas Eve on Duffy and his family, and while Castillo had almost identified the SVR officer who had organized and probably participated in that, he would have to check with Berezovsky before he was sure. And as soon as Duffy learned that name, he was going to do his very best to find him and then kill him and his close associates in the most imaginatively painful ways he could think of.

While Castillo fully sympathized with Duffy, he didn't want that to happen until the Congo operation was over. Taking out the SVR officer who had replaced Lieutenant Colonel Viktor Zhdankov in South America would tell the SVR more than Castillo wanted them to know about the extent of his knowledge of SVR operations.

Replacing Zhdankov had become necessary after Corporal Lester Bradley, USMC, using his Colt Model 1911 .45-caliber semiautomatic, had taken Zhdankov out with a well-placed head shot in the basement garage of the Pilar Sheraton Hotel and Convention Center when Zhdankov had been engaged in trying to take out Aleksandr Pevsner.

The initial order, according to both Aleksandr Pevsner and Svetlana, had come from Lieutenant General Yakov Sirinov, who was the man in charge of that sort of thing for the Sluzhba Vnezhney Razvedki. He ran either Directorate S, the oddly brazenly named Illegal Intelligence arm of the SVR, or Service A, which was the arm of the SVR charged with planning and implementing "active measures," which meant such things as assassinations.

Or General Sirinov ran both Directorate S and Service A.

Or Directorate S and Service A were really one and the same entity.

Svetlana and Pevsner had told Castillo the order from General Sirinov had probably been rather vague in nature, stating only that the individuals on a list had been determined to be posing a threat to the Russian Federation and were to be eliminated as soon as the local rezidents could arrange to have it done, preferably within the same twenty-four-hour period.

That, Svetlana had matter-of-factly told Castillo, would serve both to keep the others on the list from suspecting they were in danger because one of their number had been eliminated, and would also make a statement, when the assassinations had been successfully carried out, that the SVR was back and dealing with its enemies as the KGB, the NKVD, and the Cheka had done in the past.

The names certainly listed were Frau und Herr Kuhl in Vienna, Herr Friedler in Marburg, Mr. Britton in Philadelphia, and Comandante Duffy in Buenos Aires. Both Svetlana and Pevsner felt that some people on General Sirinov's list who would be eliminated, if possible, as a second priority included Otto Görner, Eric Kocian, and Karl Wilhelm von und zu Gossinger, aka C. G. Castillo.

Neither Svetlana nor Pevsner had mentioned that the Berlin rezident ordered to implement the successful termination of Herr Friedler and, if possible, as a second priority, Otto Görner, Eric Kocian, and Karl Wilhelm von und zu Gossinger aka C. G. Castillo, was one Dmitri Berezovsky—and, although this thought had run through Castillo's mind more than once, neither had he.

When Jack Davidson had driven the BMW out of the Mayerling gate, Castillo had signaled cheerfully for the gendarmes in their Mercedes SUV to follow them.

When finally he had to deal with Liam Duffy's impatience—angry impatience—to learn the name of the man who had tried to kill Duffy and his family, at least the Argentine cop wouldn't have his Irish temper already inflamed by Castillo having eluded his protectors. Read: tail.

Several miles past the end of the Autopista del Sol, where the six-lane toll road had turned into a two-lane macadam highway, Castillo saw a sign reading PILAR GOLF & POLO COUNTRY CLUB, and moments later saw the gatehouse of the place itself.

Unlike either the Mayerling or Buena Vista country clubs, where a combination of high fences, closely packed trees, and thick shrubbery hid everything inside from anyone on the roadway, the Pilar Golf & Polo Country Club presented an unobstructed view of immaculate fairways and greens as far as the eye could see. A dozen electric golf carts were on narrow, concrete paths that picturesquely wound near the fairways and the greens.

At least a mile from the gatehouse, sitting on a gentle hill, were a dozen houses—maybe more—all of which seemed to Castillo to be larger than Nuestra Pequeña Casa.

There might have been a fence around them, but Castillo didn't get a good enough look at them before Davidson had to stop at the gatehouse, which itself was a substantial two-story building. Castillo saw that there were two barrier gates in series, each a substantial affair that opened by rolling to the side; the interior gate was two car lengths distant from the exterior one.

From behind thick glass windows in the gatehouse, three uniformed, armed guards examined the BMW and its occupants. Castillo could see on an interior wall a row of video monitors mounted over a rack of shotguns. The monitors gave the guards a clear view of what the surveillance cameras were recording—at the moment, six views of the BMW, including its undercarriage.

At this point, Castillo had a somewhat unnerving and embarrassing thought: He knew Svetlana, Munz, and Lester were inside the Pilar Golf & Polo Country Club, but not exactly where.

Nothing beyond "in another of Pevsner's safe houses."

You should have asked how to get in here, stupid!

It didn't turn out to be a problem.

First, a black KIA sport utility vehicle with darkened windows appeared from the side of the gatehouse in the area between the barriers and stopped its nose against the interior barrier. A large and sturdy man in a business suit got out of the KIA, in the process unintentionally revealing that he carried a large semiautomatic pistol in a shoulder holster.

Next, the red light in a traffic signal mounted on the side of the gatehouse went off and the signal's green light came on. The exterior barrier then rolled slowly to one side. When there was room, Davidson drove up to the KIA as the barrier now behind him closed.

The man who had gotten out of the KIA walked to the BMW, smiled, and bent down beside it.

When Davidson rolled down his window, Max erupted from the backseat, where he had been sitting beside Edgar Delchamps, put his head between Davidson and the lowered window, then growled deep in his chest and showed the man his teeth.

The man jumped three feet backward—moving so quickly that Castillo thought he was going to lose his balance.

The man quickly regained his composure.

"El Coronel Munz has been expecting you, gentlemen," he announced. "If you'll be so kind as to follow me?"

The interior barrier rolled away, and they followed the KIA down a serpentine macadam road that skirted the golf course—as they did, Castillo concluded that the club had two eighteen-hole courses—then past four polo fields, two of which were in use, and then an enormous building with half a dozen tennis courts that suggested it was the Club House.

Finally, they approached the sort of compound of houses he had seen from the road.

There was no road in front of the houses, just a line of six-foot-high fencing, nearly invisible from even a short distance away. A second look showed that inside the fencing there was an even less visible line of wire suspended between insulators two or three feet above the grass.

That's motion sensing, Castillo decided. *The outer fence is designed to keep the golfers, and their golf balls, off that last expanse of grass. The motion-sensing wire inside goes off if something larger than a golf ball gets close to the houses.*

Whoever designed this knew what he was doing, and was not constrained by financial considerations.

Proof came as they approached the houses from the rear. He now saw that the houses were lined up in a gentle curve, their front doors facing away from the road and toward yet another guard shack and barrier. Two other KIAs, identical to the one they were following, sat facing out just inside the barrier.

The barrier here was different. It consisted of four five-foot-tall painted steel cylinders about eighteen inches in diameter in the center of the road. They could be raised and lowered hydraulically. They sank into the road as the lead KIA approached.

Inside the compound, the KIA stopped before the third house, and the man got out and nodded toward the house.

The house, of timbered brick, looked as if it belonged in the Scottish Highlands as the ancestral hunting lodge of at least a duke.

Offering his unsolicited observation that "these fucking Krautmobiles weren't designed for full-size people," Edgar Delchamps opened the rear door of the BMW and started to haul himself out.

He had one leg out the car's door when Max saw not only that the door of the house had opened but who had come through it.

He exited the car in a leap, using Delchamps's crotch as the springing point for both rear legs, which served to push Delchamps back in his seat. Delchamps said unkind things about Max and his mother.

Max bounded to Svetlana, yapping happily and dancing around her. She bent and scratched his ears.

Then she saw Castillo and waved to him.

Max lapped her face and then ran to Castillo, who was by then out of the front seat. Max yapped at him as if saying, "Hey, boss! Guess who I found here?" before returning to Svetlana, where he stood on his rear legs and draped his paws over her shoulders.

A very large man rushed out the front door, looking as if he was in the act of drawing a lethal weapon from a shoulder holster.

"Nyet!" Svetlana ordered in a voice befitting a podpolkovnik of the Sluzhba Vnezhney Razvedki on a Moscow parade ground. The man stopped as if frozen.

Svetlana's voice softened as she pushed Max off her shoulders, then dropped to wrap her arms around his neck. "It's okay, Stepan. Max is our dog, isn't he, my Charley?"

Castillo nodded.

He walked up to her. She kissed him chastely and not very possessively on the cheek.

"You remember Edgar, of course, honey?"

"Certainly," she said. "He's the one who took the stitches out of my good purse."

She looked at Delchamps and then at Castillo. Then she pulled Castillo's face to hers and kissed him on the mouth—passionately, possessively, and at length.

"Please come in the house, Mr. Delchamps," she said a moment later. "We'll have a cocktail, and then I will show you and Mr. Davidson around our house."

She tucked her hand under Castillo's arm, leaned her head against his shoulder, and led him into the house.

"What's this 'our house' business?" Castillo asked.

"I love it," she said. "And so will you when you see it. I'm going to buy it. And this is Mr. Lee-Watson, who's going to sell it to me."

Three people were standing in the high-ceilinged foyer: El Coronel Alfredo Munz, Corporal Lester Bradley, USMC, and a very tall, elegantly tailored man in his forties.

"Delighted to make your acquaintance, sir. Cedric Lee-Watson."

His accent suggested he was the duke who owned this Scottish Highlands castle.

Castillo took the proffered hand and looked at Munz, asking with his eyes, *Who the hell is this guy, and what's he doing in Pevsner's safe house?*

"Mr. Lee-Watson handles real estate for our mutual friend in Bariloche," Munz explained.

"Indeed, for he whose name is only rarely, and then very carefully, spoken," Lee-Watson said.

"Cedric built this place—the club—for our friend," Munz said.

Lester Bradley caught Castillo's attention. "Colonel, can I see you for a minute, please?"

"What's up, Lester?"

"Privately, sir?"

"Won't that wait until after I show him the house?" Svetlana protested.

Castillo took Bradley's arm and led him farther into the house, to one side of a wide stairway at the end of a foyer.

"Okay, what, Lester?"

"As soon as I got the AFC set up, there was a call for you from Mr. D'Allessando."

"What did he want?" Castillo asked, surprised.

On his retirement from twenty-four years of service—twenty-two of it in Special Forces—Chief Warrant Officer Five Victor D'Allessando had gone to work for the Special Operations Command as a Department of the Army civilian. Theoretically, he was a technical advisor to the commanding general of the John F. Kennedy Special Warfare Center at Fort Bragg. What he actually did for the Special Operations Command was not talked about.

"He said a friend wants to talk to you, sir."

"Well, get on the horn and get him back, Les."

"Yes, sir."

Bradley walked to the foot of the stairs, then ran up them, taking them two at a time.

Svetlana, trailed by Delchamps, Davidson, and Lee-Watson, crossed the foyer to Castillo.

"Vic D'Allessando was on the horn," Castillo reported. "He said a friend wants to talk to me."

Delchamps and Davidson both shrugged, indicating they had no idea what D'Allessando might have on his mind.

Everybody started up the stairs to the second floor.

[THREE]

Ten minutes later, as Svetlana and Lee-Watson had just about finished showing all the comforts the master suite offered, Bradley walked in and announced, "I've got Mr. D'Allessando for you, sir. The AFC is just down the hall."

Delchamps read Castillo's mind.

"You want us to wait here, Ace?"

Castillo exhaled audibly.

"The wheezing, I suspect, reveals a certain indecision," Delchamps said.

"I was thinking that Svetlana probably should hear this," Castillo said.

"Or wondering how you could keep her from hearing it?" Delchamps said.

Svetlana flashed him an icy look.

"I was about to say, 'What the hell, the barn door's open; there's no way to get the cow back in,'" Delchamps went on, which earned him an ever more frigid glare, "but I was afraid she might take it the wrong way."

Davidson chuckled.

"Mr. Lee-Watson, will you excuse us for a few minutes? There's an important call I—we—have to take."

"Of course."

The AFC radio was set up on a small escritoire in a small room off the corridor. There was an interior door. Castillo opened it and saw that it opened on the bedroom of the master suite.

He closed the door, and noticed that Bradley was about to leave the room.

"Stay, Lester," Castillo said, and sat down carefully on an elegantly styled and obviously fragile chair.

"Thank you so much, my ever thoughtful Charley," Svetlana said sarcastically.

He started to get up to give her the chair, then changed his mind.

"You're welcome," he said, and checked the LEDs on the AFC. They were all green. One of them indicated the conversation would be conducted with the protection of AFC Class One encryption, which Aloysius Francis Casey had personally informed him that even the master National Security Agency eavesdroppers at Fort Meade, Maryland, could not penetrate.

Castillo pushed the SPEAKERPHONE button.

"How they hanging, Vic? What's up?"

There was no immediate reply, and when a reply did come, it was not in D'Allessando's familiar Brooklynese but rather in the crisp diction that immediately and unequivocally identified the other party to Castillo as Lieutenant General Bruce J. McNab, Commanding General of the United States Special Operations Command: "Colonel Castillo."

"Good evening, sir."

"I wasn't sure Vic could get through to you, Colonel. I didn't think they would permit you to take one of Aloysius's radios on your terminal leave."

"General, I'm not on terminal leave."

There was a pause.

"But now that I have you, Colonel: Although you have caused me a lot of grief during our long relationship, on balance you were far more useful than I ever thought you would be. Given that, I wanted to tell you personally that I did my best to dissuade General Naylor from going along with Ambassador Montvale. I failed. I'm sorry, and I wanted to tell you that myself."

"Sir, I am not on terminal leave."

"Well, if you're not, you soon will be. Colonel Remley, my G-1, is on his way down there with the appropriate papers for you to sign." He paused. "That presumes, of course, that he can find you. He's not one of us, so that's quite possible. Where are you?"

"Sir, I met briefly with Colonel Remley. And Ambassador Montvale. Several hours ago. They are both by now on their way back to the States. I declined to sign whatever it was he wanted me to sign."

"Did Colonel Remley inform you that I had sent him down there at General Naylor's direction to have you sign your acceptance of the medical board's conclusions?"

"No, sir. Neither your name nor General Naylor's was mentioned. Ambassador Montvale made it quite clear he wanted me to sign whatever Colonel Remley had for me to sign. I declined to do so."

"Charley, if the President has decided it's time for you to go, it's your duty to go. You should know that."

"Sir, the President is unaware of what Ambassador Montvale had planned for me."

This time the pause was longer before McNab spoke again.

"Forgive me, Charley. I am ashamed to say I was sitting here trying to decide who would be more likely to lie to me, you or that lying sonofabitch Montvale."

"No apology required, sir."

"How much truth is there to the tale Montvale tells that you—for reasons he can't imagine—snatched two Russian defectors from the CIA station chief in Vienna and flew them to Argentina?"

"They were never in the hands of the CIA, sir."

"But you did fly them from Vienna to Argentina?"

"Yes, sir."

"Off the top of my head, Charley, that sounds as stupid as . . . well, for example, as borrowing a Black Hawk. Why the hell did you do that?"

"You mean borrowing the Black Hawk? Or flying the Russians here?" Castillo asked innocently.

"You know goddamn well what I mean, Charley," McNab said. But he chuckled.

"Sir, at the time I thought it—both things—was the thing to do."

"And now that you've had time to reflect?"

"Now I know, sir, that I did the right thing. Both times."

"Why?" McNab asked simply. "Skip the part about Dick Miller and his people still being among the living."

"Sir, I had good reason to believe the SVR was onto them, and unless I got them off the train and out of the Westbahnhof in Vienna, they'd be grabbed."

There was another long pause before McNab went on: "That raises the questions 'What train?' 'What were you doing on the train?' and 'How did you get together with the Russians in the first place, since getting the bastards to turn is none of your goddamn business?' But I will not ask them, because that is what is known as water under the dam. Pick it up where you got them out of the Westbahnhof and to Gaucho Land instead of turning them over to the agency in Vienna."

"Sir, the Russians suspected that the CIA station chief also knew the SVR was onto them and was going to let them hang in the breeze. I think they were right."

"Montvale's version is that you rode into town like Jesse James and blew up the carefully laid plans of the CIA to arrange their defection."

"Yes, sir. I'm aware of his story."

"You don't sound very repentant about all this, Charley. Even though it's going to end your colorful military career on something of a sour note."

"Sir, what I got from the Russians is worth more than my career."

"Their heartfelt gratitude for helping them dodge the SVR?"

"Sir, they've put me onto an operation in the ex–Belgian Congo—run by Iranians with other raghead cooperation and funded by oil-for-food money—that's going after our water supplies."

"And you don't think the agency, as incompetent as we both know it sometimes can be, doesn't know the bad guys would love to poison our water supply? And if they're seriously working on an operation would know just a little bit about it?"

"As of a couple of hours ago, the agency believes—sir, this is just about verbatim—that, quote, there is no discernible activity there of interest to the United States. They are apparently experimenting with fish farms, unquote."

"How the hell could you possibly know that?"

"I heard the DCI tell Montvale that. We were in the embassy in Buenos Aires, and Montvale called him."

"And you think the agency is wrong?"

"Yes, sir. I believe they are."

"One of the defectors told you that?"

"Both of them did, sir."

"And you believe them?" McNab asked incredulously. "Two whys, Charley: Why would they tell you, and why do you believe them?"

"I can give you a long answer, sir, or—"

"Short one first."

"They happen to be Christians who take it seriously and don't want several million innocent people poisoned."

"Jesus Christ! And you believe *that*?"

"I do, and so does Edgar Delchamps."

"The guy who stuck a needle in the traitor's neck in the Langley parking lot?"

"That has been alleged, sir. He and Alex Darby, the station chief here, both believe what the Russians have told us."

"Correct me if I'm wrong, but what I'm hearing here is that a brand-new lieutenant colonel with a well-deserved reputation for being a world-class loose cannon, an agency dinosaur who takes out people he doesn't like in the CIA's parking lot, and another agency type who got himself banished to Gaucho Land because he still thinks the Russians are a threat all have decided, based upon what a couple of Russian defectors—who the Russians say took off because they stole three million dollars, not because they're born-again Christians—told them that there is a bona fide terrorist threat that the agency, having looked into it, says is nonsense. Does that sum it up fairly accurately, Colonel Castillo?"

"Yes, sir. That's about it."

"And what do these three lunatics plan to do about it?"

"This lunatic, sir, is going to go over there and find out for himself what's going on."

"And then?"

"Either take it out myself or lay proof on the President's desk of what's going on."

"All by yourself, John Wayne?" McNab asked, bitterly sarcastic.

There was a moment's pause before Castillo responded.

"Well, sir, now that you've brought it up, I was hoping I could borrow Uncle Remus for a couple of weeks. He has the right complexion and he speaks Swahili."

"If you are referring, Colonel Castillo, to Chief Warrant Officer Five Colin Leverette of this command, he not only speaks Swahili, but Lingala and Tshiluba as well. And not only is Mr. Leverette far too valuable to be put at risk in a dangerous—not to mention unsanctioned—operation such as you propose, but he is far too wise and experienced to even momentarily consider volunteering for anything like it."

"Yes, sir."

There was a very long pause.

"Lieutenant generals, as you should know, Lieutenant Colonel Castillo, do not bargain with lieutenant colonels."

"Yes, sir."

"But if I should suddenly lose my mind and discuss this situation with Mr. Leverette and he similarly suffers a temporary loss of his good judgment and agrees to talk with you about it, it will be with the understanding that if I do not approve—personally, here in the States—every detail of your proposed operation to snoop around this chemical factory in the Congolese jungle, you will not undertake it. Agreed?"

"Yes, sir. Thank you, sir."

"When and where do you want Uncle Remus, Charley?"

"Here, as soon as possible, sir."

"I can't get him on a plane today."

"Sir, Major Miller will probably be coming down here in a Presidential Gulfstream. It could stop at Bragg . . ."

"And you don't think Montvale will hear about that?"

"Montvale knows about it, sir. I made a deal with him, too."

There was a pause.

"What kind of a deal, Charley?"

"No matter what happens in Africa, sir, I will retire at the end of this month."

"Even if you're right and everybody else is wrong?"

"Yes, sir. That was the deal I made."

There was another long pause.

"I'll get back to you—or Vic D'Allessando will—with the details of Mr. Leverette's travel," McNab said finally. "And now I'm going to have a word with General Naylor."

"I wish you wouldn't do that, sir."

"Why not?"

"General Naylor decided that he was doing the right thing when Montvale went to him with this. I'm sure it wasn't easy for him. He saw it as his duty."

Another long pause.

"That's the problem a good officer has to face every once in a while, isn't it, Charley? Knowing just what doing your duty really calls for?"

Castillo didn't reply, and a moment later one of the green LEDs went dark, signaling the call had been broken.

Castillo shook his head, then looked around at the others.

"Who was that, my Charley?" Svetlana asked.

"The man who heads our version of Spetsnaz," Castillo said softly. "Lieutenant General Bruce J. McNab. Who just decided to help me deal with the chemical factory, even though he's fully aware that may very likely see him standing beside me in the Thank You for Your Service and Don't Let the Doorknob Hit You in the Ass on Your Way Out retirement parade."

"I do not understand," she said.

"I'm getting kicked out of the Army," Castillo said, and stopped. "Correction: For what I like to think is 'for the good of the service,' I will go along with being medically retired as psychologically unfit for active service."

She looked at him thoughtfully but didn't say anything.

"Not to worry, Svetlana. I will receive a pension of twenty-five percent of my base pay. You may have to flip burgers in McDonald's to help out with our bills, but we can probably get by."

She ignored the comment.

"You work for this man? You are American Spetsnaz?"

"Not anymore. I used to be. I used to work for General McNab."

"And now who do you work for? This Ambassador Montvale?"

"You and your brother were right to be worried about the CIA station chief in Vienna," Castillo said, ignoring the question. "She probably would have left you swinging in the breeze, since she probably knew the SVR was onto you. What happened is that when she figured out that I had gotten you out of Vienna safely, instead of saying 'thank you' or keeping her mouth shut, which also would have been nice, she told the director of Central Intelligence—and also told a friend of hers who she knew would promptly tell an important journalist—that I had swooped in out of nowhere and snatched you and the colonel and family away just as she was about to put you in the bag and send you to Washington."

"So you are in trouble because of what you did for us? I will kill this woman!"

"Hold that thought, Svetlana," Delchamps said.

Castillo looked between them and thought: *The truth is both of them are more than likely dead serious.*

"Both of you drop that thought," Castillo said.

"And this Ambassador Montvale, who you do work for, believed this woman?" Svetlana asked.

"I don't work for Montvale. But yeah, sure, he believed her. Right now his priority, which is one I agree with, is to protect the man I work for."

"Who is? And this man you work for will believe this bitch in Vienna?"

"Two profound thoughts, Ace," Delchamps said. " 'Hell hath no fury like a woman protecting her man.' "

Davidson and Castillo chuckled.

"You said two," Castillo said.

" 'The cow is already out of the barn,' " Delchamps said. "If you won't tell her, Ace, I will. Svetlana, Charley works for the President."

If she was surprised by this announcement, it didn't show on her face.

"And your President will take the word of the bitch in Vienna over yours?"

"That's not the point," Castillo explained. "But no, I think he'd accept whatever I told him as the truth. The point is that he'd be deeply hurt politically if it came out that—"

"That he has been running his own private CIA–FBI–American Spetsnaz rolled into one," Delchamps interrupted, "in contravention of American law and—maybe even worse—without taking the Congress into his confidence. He would be crucified, unless they could think of something more painful."

Svetlana looked at Castillo, who nodded to confirm what Delchamps had said.

Castillo said: "So far, the President doesn't know anything about this?"

"Wrong, I think," Delchamps interrupted again. "I think the DCI probably got carried away and told the President that—to use Svetlana's delightful terminology—the bitch in Vienna was about to put—after long, brilliant, and expensive CIA labor—Svetlana and her brother into the bag. He probably thinks they're in a safe house in Maryland right now."

Castillo didn't reply.

"He came down here to get them, Ace. I rest my case."

"Could very well be," Castillo admitted.

"This man, the ambassador, came down here to get us and take us to the United States?" Svetlana asked.

Castillo nodded. "That was one of the things on his agenda. Understandable."

"What did you say to him?"

"I told him that two hundred dollars, a bottle of scotch, and a mule wasn't even in the ballpark pricewise, but if he wanted to reconsider and up his offer, I'd listen."

It was obvious on Svetlana's face that Castillo's remark made no sense to her.

Davidson took pity on her.

"Svet," he said in Russian, "I don't know how to translate this into Russian, but the essence of Charley's reply to Montvale's suggestion that he turn you over to the agency was that the ambassador"—he switched to English—"should try a flying fuck at a rolling doughnut."

After a long moment, Svetlana said seriously: "I think I understand. But what is a 'doughnut'?"

"Think of a Berliner," Delchamps said, "but round. And with a thumb-sized hole in the middle." He held up his thumb, then mimed rolling the pastry across the floor.

She smiled as the mental picture formed.

"My Charley, you are *very naughty*. But I love you anyway!"

She demonstrated this by leaning over and kissing him.

"Edgar," Davidson asked, "do you think there's any chance that when Romeo and Juliet are finished we can get that drink we were promised when we got here?"

[FOUR]

"Oh, Charley, look! Isn't that sweet?" Svetlana exclaimed as they walked into a basement room of the house.

Marina was across the room, tugging as hard as she could on a woven twine rope, the other end of which was in her father's mouth.

Castillo took a quick double-take around the room. It held a rack of golf club bags. Next to that was a rack of cues for the billiards table that was in the center of the room. One side of the room was given over to a bar, at which stood Cedric Lee-Watson and ex-Polkovnik Dmitri Berezovsky of the SVR. They had drinks in their hands. Lora and Sof'ya Berezovsky were sitting on bar stools, drinking what looked like Coca-Cola.

Castillo snapped his head to look at Svetlana.

"Oh, I didn't tell you, did I, my Charley? We're going to have dinner with my brother Tom and his family at the Club House," Svetlana said as she crossed to the bar to kiss first Sof'ya and then her sister-in-law.

Castillo looked at her and then at Munz.

Munz smiled knowingly, which pushed Castillo even closer to losing his temper.

"Is this smart, for Christ's sake?" Castillo snapped.

"Sooner or later, Karl," Munz said in German, "Mr. Barlow and his family, including of course Susanna, are going to have to start living their new identities. Why wait? For what?"

Castillo didn't reply.

"And you did notice, didn't you, the security measures around here?" Munz went on.

"I did," Edgar Delchamps said. "This place is tighter than a drum."

He saw the look on Castillo's face and went on: "Smile, Ace, you've been had," and then he walked to the bar, with Davidson on his heels.

"I thought I'd find you near the liquor, Tom, old buddy," he said in Russian.

"My Russian is not so good," Berezovsky/Barlow said in English. "Would you mind if we speak English?"

"Not at all."

Castillo walked to the bar.

Tom Barlow set his drink on it and took two steps toward Castillo. He grabbed Castillo's upper arms.

"I can call you Charley, right?" he asked in accentless American English.

"Why not?"

"One of the reasons I accepted my sister's kind invitation to break bread with you tonight was that I'd hoped to have a private word with you about her."

"Really?"

"She's my little sister, Charley. You understand. I wanted to make sure I understood your intentions."

The Russian words for *Go fuck yourself, Dmitri* leapt to Castillo's lips.

At the last possible split instant, he bit them off.

"But when I saw how you looked at each other when you walked in, I realized that wouldn't be necessary."

"Good," Castillo said in English.

Barlow looked intently into Castillo's eyes, reminding Castillo of the first time Aleksandr Pevsner had done that to him.

"So I think we should both be very grateful to God that things in Marburg turned out the way they have, don't you?" Barlow said. "They could—so easily—have gone differently."

Castillo neither replied nor blinked.

But finally Barlow let go of his arms, and Castillo looked away.

Svetlana was squatting beside Max and Marina.

"Hey, Susie," he called. "Do want something to drink?"

She looked at him and smiled uncertainly. "Susie" hadn't registered.

"That's you, baby. 'Susie.' You'd better get used to it."

She got up and walked to him. He put his arm around her shoulder.

XII

"Then it is agreed, is it not," Tom Barlow said, "that tonight what we have is friends having dinner together, and we do not talk—or even think about—the business we will deal with tomorrow?"

I didn't hear any proposal to agree to, Castillo thought, *but what the hell, why not?*

"Fine with me," he said.

"You know a little about our family, Charley, but Susanna tells me she knows nothing of yours," Barlow said.

"There are nine of us," Castillo said. "There were ten, but my brother Fritz was hung a couple of years ago for cattle rustling in the Texas Panhandle."

Barlow shook his head.

"Aleksandr told me you have an . . . interesting sense of humor," Barlow said.

"If it's all right with you, Charley," Alfredo Munz said, "I'll pass on dinner. My wife has the odd notion that I should have dinner with her and the girls once in a while."

The translation of that is: Will I feel safe to be left here alone?

"Go ahead, Alfredo. The Marine is here and the situation is well in hand."

Davidson and Lester understood and both smiled. Lester looked pleased at what he took as at least some small recognition of his self-appointed role as Castillo's bodyguard.

Davidson also saw the look on Svetlana/Susanna's face.

"Susie . . ." he said.

"Susanna," she corrected him.

"We already have a Susanna. How about simply Susan?"

She looked at Castillo.

"Hello, there, Simply Susan," Castillo said, smiling.

"I was about to say there's something you don't know about Charley," Davidson said.

"Is there?"

"You know the Bible verse *'Whither thou goest . . .'*?"

"Yes, of course." She looked at Charley again. "It's in Ruth. *'For whither thou goest, I will go; and where thou lodgest, I will lodge: thy people shall be my people . . .'*"

"That's it," Davidson said.

Castillo, who knew what was coming next, looked uncomfortable.

"Well, Simply Susan, so far as Charley goes, our version says, 'For whither Charley goest, Lester and I goest, and where Charley lodgest, Lester and I lodge, etcetera.' "

"You are mocking Holy Scripture!" she snapped, and looked to Castillo for help.

Castillo held up his hands in a gesture of helplessness.

"What is this all about?" Susan demanded angrily.

"Simply Susan, you're a formidable female," Davidson said. "Maybe the most formidable female I've ever met. But you're not in the same league as General Scotty McNab. And my orders from him are not to let Charley out of my sight. Amen."

"There's an exception in there for closed bedroom doors," Castillo said.

"Right," Davidson agreed. "I guess McNab would go along with that."

"And how long is that going to last?" Susan asked.

"Until, Simply Susan," Castillo began, then looked at Barlow—"Forgive me, Tom, I know I promised not to talk business"—he turned back to Susan—"until we come back from Africa. Then Jack can go back to his usual duties of pulling the wings off flies and teasing beautiful women."

"Susan," she said. "Not Simply Susan."

"Whatever you prefer," Castillo said magnanimously.

Susan mentally gathered her arguments, then earnestly began: "There is absolutely no reason for them to be here. You have seen the security. . . ."

"I think," Barlow said, smiling, "that we are about to see the irresistible force meet the unmovable object."

"I'm not going to get in the middle of this," Munz said. "Tom, slide that phone to me, please? I'll call my wife and tell her I'm coming home."

Barlow did, and Munz reached for the telephone. His hand was almost on it when it rang. He was so startled that he pulled back his hand for a moment before picking up the handset.

"Yes?" Munz said into it. He nodded at the reply, as if he expected it. He met Castillo's curious eyes and said, "Please escort Comandante Duffy here," and hung up.

Castillo was reminded once again that Munz was not in the habit of asking for his permission—or even advice—before taking what he thought was the appropriate action.

"Jesus Christ, Alfredo. Couldn't you have stalled him until we figure out how to deal with him?"

"Karl, I've given how to deal with him some thought. And we might as well find out here and now if what I intend to do is going to work."

"That's the policeman who was at the airfield?" Susan asked.

"The gendarmería comandante," Munz corrected her. He smiled at Davidson and added, "A formidable man. If he's so inclined, he can cause us a great deal of trouble. He is smart, honest, and a patriot. For people in our business, that combination often spells trouble."

"Before you just do it," Castillo said more than a little sarcastically, "you're going to tell us how we're to deal with him, right?"

Munz nodded, the sarcasm apparently lost on him. "As best I can, Karl. Basically, what I'm going to do is follow your advice: 'When all else fails, tell the truth.' "

Castillo bit off the reply that came to his lips. Now was not the time to get in a scrap with Munz.

The cold truth is I don't have any better idea how to deal with the problem of Comandante Liam Duffy than telling him the truth and seeing what happens.

"Okay, Alfredo," he said. "Tell us how we should handle Duffy. And make it quick; in a couple of minutes, he'll be coming through the door."

"Should we be here?" Susan asked.

Munz answered: "I think it would be best if it were only Charley, Colonel Berezovsky, Señor Lee-Watson, and me. In the study upstairs?"

Berezovsky and Lee-Watson nodded their agreement. Charley was surprised that neither Delchamps nor Svetlana—especially Svetlana—objected.

[TWO]

The study—which actually was more of a library, the room lined with bookshelves—had not been on Svetlana's tour of the house. Four red leather armchairs were arranged around a large, low table on which sat a telephone and an ashtray designed for cigars. Next to the ashtray was a large, silver-plated lighter.

Castillo sat in one of the chairs, then took out and trimmed a cigar. The silver-plated lighter didn't work. He then produced what he called his "terrorist tool"—a butane cigar lighter, a replacement for one that had been seized by the ever-vigilant Transportation Safety Administration inspectors at Washington National Airport as enthusiastically as if it had been an Uzi—and lit the cigar.

He looked at the door to see if Duffy had arrived. His eyes fell on one wall of books. There was something wrong, something odd about them. He got up and went to the shelf. He tugged at one book spine—and suddenly a flimsy shelf-long sheet of something designed to look like book spines fell from the shelf.

"What this is, old boy," Lee-Watson said, laughing, "is what I think you Americans call a model house. Designed, don't you know, to show potential customers how nice-looking these very expensive houses can be when furnished."

"No wonder the toilet wouldn't flush," Castillo said.

Lee-Watson looked horrified.

"Gotcha!" Castillo said.

Lee-Watson sighed. "Quite."

Liam Duffy walked confidently into the study a minute later. He was in civilian clothing. His unbuttoned double-breasted suit jacket revealed a large semiautomatic pistol carried in a high-rise cross-draw holster.

He looked quickly around the room until his eyes fell on Berezovsky.

"Well, I see that everybody's here," he said, mockingly jovial. He looked at Tom Barlow. "Including Colonel Dmitri Berezovsky."

Castillo said: "This is Señor Barlow, Liam. Señor Thomas Barlow, may I introduce Comandante Liam Duffy?"

"*Mucho gusto*, Señor *Barlow*," Duffy said. "But I have to tell you that you look just like the man in the photograph on an Interpol warrant that just crossed my desk—for one Colonel Dmitri Berezovsky."

"You're mistaken, Comandante," Lee-Watson said.

"Like hell I am!" Duffy snapped, then looked at Lee-Watson.

"Do you have the pleasure of Señor Cedric Lee-Watson's acquaintance, Liam?" Munz asked.

The question got to Duffy.

"I know who you are, señor," he said. "I must say I'm surprised to see you in this company."

"How are you, Comandante?" Lee-Watson said.

"Liam, listen to me carefully," Munz said. "Are you going to take his word that this is Señor Barlow, or will it be necessary for Señor Lee-Watson to call the foreign minister and have him tell you that you're wrong?"

Duffy didn't immediately reply. After a moment, he said, "Alfredo, we seem to have a problem here."

"One that can be worked around, I'm sure," Munz said.

"One way to do that, Alfredo, is for you to give me the name of the bastard who tried to kill my wife and children. If I had that, I would just leave and forget I had even seen . . . Señor Barlow."

"Unfortunately, it's not quite that simple."

"I will have that name, Alfredo. That's not negotiable."

"Liam, I know a good deal about you. You're not only a good policeman but an honest one, and we both know that's not always the case in Argentina. I sincerely admire you."

Duffy looked at him a long moment. "But?"

"But there are forces in play here that you don't understand."

"Such as?"

"I had two reactions when I heard of the attack on you and your family," Munz explained. "The first was personal—that it was a despicable act, beneath contempt."

"And the second?" Duffy asked softly.

"That your quite natural reaction to it was going to cause Carlos and me trouble."

"I don't need any help from you or Carlos to kill the bastards—"

"We know that, Liam," Castillo interrupted. "But why don't you let us tell you why we don't want you to go out and eliminate the bastards right now?"

Duffy looked at him angrily.

"Pay close attention to me, Liam," Castillo said, his tone of voice now suddenly the opposite of mockingly amused. "We can do this nice, between friends, or we can do it the other way."

"You're not actually threatening me, Carlos?"

"That was a statement of fact, not a threat," Castillo said. "You ready to listen?"

They locked eyes for twenty seconds, then Duffy nodded.

"The same day that you and your family were attacked, Liam," Castillo then said, "a German journalist was assassinated in Germany, an Austrian couple was murdered—garroted—in Vienna, and an attempt was made to murder an American policeman and his wife in Philadelphia."

Duffy considered that for a moment, then asked softly, "There was a connection?"

"And General Sirinov also ordered the elimination," Berezovsky added, "when they were to attend the journalist's funeral several days later, of two other journalists, and, if possible, of Colonel Castillo."

"How could you know this?" Duffy said, and without waiting for an answer went on: "General who? They tried to kill you, too, Carlos?"

Castillo nodded.

Berezovsky went on: "Lieutenant General Yakov Sirinov runs Directorate S of the Sluzhba Vnezhney Razvedki, SVR. He ordered the appropriate SVR rezidents—those in Berlin, Vienna, New York, and Buenos Aires—to carry out the eliminations."

"How is it that you know this?" Duffy demanded.

"Because, Comandante, I was at the time the Berlin rezident. Something that I doubt one might find noted on anything from Interpol."

Duffy took a moment to consider that.

"You're telling me this man," he then said, "this General *Sirinov* . . . is that right?"

"Lieutenant General Yakov Sirinov," he furnished.

". . . ordered the murder of my wife and children?"

"Of you, certainly," Berezovsky said. "I don't think your family was on the order. But, on the other hand, I don't think his order said, 'Make sure this man's family is not hurt while you are eliminating the comandante.' " He paused while that sank in, then went on: "On the other hand, considering what we believe to be his second purpose, he very well may have ordered the elimination of your family."

"What do you mean, 'second purpose'?" Duffy asked.

Castillo answered: "The primary connection between all these assassinations, Liam, both successful and failed, with the possible exception of yours, is that everybody either knew or soon would uncover more details about an Islamic terrorist operation than the SVR wanted them to know."

"What kind of a terrorist operation?" Duffy asked.

Castillo ignored the question, and instead replied: "The assassination of the German journalist—his name was Friedler—was because he was getting too close to the Germans who were involved in the oil-for-food cesspool."

"Did you ever hear, Comandante," Berezovsky said, "that 'it is impossible to cheat an honest man'?"

"What?" Duffy asked.

"The corollary of that is that you *can* cheat—or otherwise steal from—a *dis*honest man."

"I have no idea what you're talking about," Duffy said, as much indignantly as in confusion.

"When the Iraq oil-for-food program was in operation," Berezovsky went on, "there were many people who grew rich from it. One of the ways to turn a nice profit was to raise the price of the food and medicine and medical supplies being sold to Iraq. Hands were washed . . ."

"Greased, Tom," Castillo corrected him.

". . . *greased,*" Berezovsky went on, his face and tone making it clear he was unaccustomed to being corrected and certainly not grateful for the clarification now, "and the appropriate authorities found nothing wrong with, for example, a microscope of the type used in elementary schools to examine the wings of a fly and available in a store for, say, fifty dollars being shipped to Iraq as the latest item in medical microscopy and valued at a thousand times the fifty dollars it had actually cost.

"The man—the example here is a member of what we're calling the Marburg Group—took the fifty-thousand-dollar check, cashed it, made a small gift—say, five thousand dollars—to the invoice examiner, and pocketed the difference, not mentioning it to the tax people, of course, and went away patting himself on the back for being a very clever businessman.

"It wasn't all medical equipment, of course. A great deal of food was in fact shipped to Iraq and fed to the hungry. Possibly as much as ten percent of that was purchased at shamelessly inflated prices. One hundred cases of canned chicken became a thousand cases by the 'mistaken' adding of a zero to the invoice. The invoice examiner, of course, missed the mistake. You getting the picture, Comandante?"

Duffy nodded.

Castillo said: "All of this stopped, Liam, when we deposed Saddam Hussein. What these thieves then found to be necessary was to clean things up to make sure none of the very important people who profited—the name of UN Secretary General Kofi Annan's son has been mentioned—would be caught. One man who we know not only profited—to the extent of sixteen million dollars—but also knew who had been paid off and for what was a UN official. His name was Dr. Jean-Paul Lorimer and he had then been living in Paris. But Lorimer saw what was coming and fled to Uruguay, where he had bought an estancia, changed his name, and set himself up in business as an antiquities dealer.

"Lorimer's sister was married to the number-two man at the American embassy in Buenos Aires, J. Winslow Masterson. When what we have come to call 'the cleaners' couldn't find Lorimer, they decided his sister probably knew where he was. So they kidnapped her from the parking lot of the Kansas Restaurant in San Isidro. That's when I became involved, Liam."

"How? Why?"

Well, if nothing else, I have his attention.

Let's see how he reacts to this:

"I work for the President of the United States, Liam, dealing with matters like these. Surely, you must have suspected?"

"When you had those helicopters flown off your aircraft carrier . . ."

"The USS *Ronald Reagan*," Castillo furnished.

". . . I suspected you were more than a simple lieutenant colonel."

"Well, until now, Liam, I was not in a position to explain more."

"I understand, Carlos," Duffy said.

"Just about as soon as I got down here," Castillo went on, " 'the cleaners' tricked Jack Masterson into going to the riverside in downtown Buenos Aires, where they killed him in cold blood before his wife to make the point that unless she told them where her brother was they were perfectly capable of killing her children, too.

"The problem was that Mrs. Masterson had no idea where her brother was. Fortunately, I had a pretty good suspicion. My people and I got to the estancia in Uruguay—"

"How did you find him, Carlos?"

Castillo looked at Duffy without speaking.

The cold truth is, Liam, it was dumb luck.

God takes care of fools and drunks—and I qualify on both counts.

But I can't tell you that, because we are trying to dazzle you into believing I am a combination of 007 and Bruce Willis with a shave.

"If I could tell you, Liam, I would," he said finally. "You understand?"

Duffy held up both hands.

"Carlos!" he said emotionally. "I understand your position. Forgive me for asking."

Castillo went on: "We got to Lorimer's estancia about ten minutes before 'the cleaners' did. There were six of them, probably ex-Stasi—East German Secret Police—commanded by Major Alejandro Vincenzo of the Cuban Dirección General de Inteligencia."

"I know that name," Duffy said, and then really remembered, adding excitedly: "He was Fidel Castro's chief of security when Castro was here. You remember, Alfredo?"

Munz nodded.

"We of course were prepared for them," Castillo continued, "and it was unfortunately necessary to terminate Major Vincenzo and his people. In the firefight, Dr. Lorimer lost his life."

What actually happened, Liam, is that we didn't have a clue that anyone else was around, much less pros working for the fucking Russians.

The first we knew anything was when the bastards put their first round into Lorimer's head. Their second round would have gone into my head if not for Lester taking the bastard out with a head shot.

And because of my incompetence and stupidity, Seymour Krantz is now pushing up daisies in Arlington National Cemetery.

We didn't have a clue as to who the guys who had damned near killed us were. Or even, then, why they had whacked Lorimer.

But that's not the picture of Charley Castillo that Munz said we have to paint for you.

And you seem to be swallowing everything whole.

So let's see how this goes down:

"The trail has led us many places since then, Liam," Castillo said. "And frankly, it took us a long time to put it all together. We couldn't have done that without Colonel Ber—*Mr. Barlow* and his sister. They confirmed what we had only suspected."

"What?"

"That there's a monstrous plan to bring down—if not outright kill, then to terrorize—millions of Americans by poisoning the water supplies of major U.S. cities."

Now, why did that sound phony?

It's the only thing I've told him that's the truth, the whole truth, and nothing but the truth.

Because it's so monstrous—and that's the only word that fits—that the mind simply does not accept it.

Cannot accept it any more than we can accept a bearded character in a bathrobe telling us he wants to kill every last infidel—Christian, Jew, Buddhist, whatever— and is perfectly willing to blow himself up if that's what it takes to do it.

"In a remote area of the Democratic Republic of the Congo . . ." Berezovsky began, then stopped when he saw by Duffy's expression that he had little or no knowledge of what that was.

"They keeping changing the name," Berezovsky explained. "It was once the Belgian Congo, and then Zaire—"

"I understand," Duffy interrupted.

Berezovsky nodded. "Between Stanleyville—now called Kisangani—and the borders of Sudan and Uganda, there is a chemical laboratory—a very good one—dedicated to developing water-poisoning materials that will either get through any known filtering systems or overwhelm them, then remain chemically active for a very long time and, to the extent possible, resist any chemical attempt to neutralize them. Once this has been accomplished, the factory will produce these materials in whatever quantities are required to attack the water systems of all major American cities."

Duffy considered that, then said: "Colonel, forgive me, but that"—the door opened and Svetlana walked in—"is incredible."

As she walked toward Castillo, all eyes on her, he thought: *I should have known that she was not going to be a good little girl and stay in the bar.*

"Don't let me interrupt," she said, sitting on the arm of Castillo's chair. "What's incredible?"

Duffy was visibly surprised but quickly recovered.

"You must be *Lieutenant Colonel* Alekseeva," he said, then asked in heavy macho-laden sarcasm, "Are there many female officers of your rank in the Russian secret police?"

"My name is Susan Barlow, Comandante. I'm Tom's sister. I really don't know what you're talking about."

Screw it, Castillo thought. *I can play, too.*

"Now I'm curious, Liam," Castillo said. "How many senior female officers are there in the gendarmería? I didn't know you had any."

"Carlos," Duffy said. "You're not going to deny that this woman is the Russian defector?"

"Carlos?" Svetlana asked. "Why did you call Colonel Castillo 'Carlos,' Comandante?"

He looked at her incredulously, then sarcastically snapped: "Because that's his name, Colonel."

"I didn't know that," she said in what was almost a purr. "Carlos is *much* nicer than Charley. Hello, there, *Carlos!*"

Castillo could not resist smiling at Svet. This visibly confused Duffy and visibly annoyed Munz.

"Please go on, Alfredo," Svetlana said. "I didn't mean to interrupt. You were saying something was incredible. No. The comandante was saying that."

Yes, you did mean to interrupt, baby.

You decided to confuse Duffy.

Knock him off balance, knock some of that self-righteous confidence out of him, make the point that he's not as important as he would like to think he is.

"If everyone is through being clever," Munz said, quietly furious, "may I get on with this?"

"Susan," Castillo said, "Comandante Duffy finds incredible the notion of a chemical laboratory in the Congo and the whole idea of poisoning the water supplies of major American cities."

"Yes, I do," Duffy said firmly.

Svetlana smiled. "So did I, Comandante, when I first heard about it. You do have to expand your mind even to begin accepting it."

" 'Expand your mind'?" Duffy parroted.

"Consider this, Comandante," Svetlana said. "The day before Hiroshima, how many people could have accepted that the Americans had developed an *incredible* bomb with the explosive power of thousands of tons of dynamite? Or, on the tenth of September, how *incredible* would it have been to hear that the next day two one-hundred-story buildings would be taken down by religious zealots flying passenger airliners into them?"

Duffy thought about that a moment. "I take your point, Colonel. Which is not to say that I suddenly believe this Congo thing."

Castillo met Munz's eyes, then Berezovsky's.

They heard it, too.

Duffy called her "Colonel"—and without a hint of sarcasm or condescension. What comes next is the truth. . . .

"Then," Svetlana went on, "you have to ask yourself why we would make up something such as this."

Duffy began to argue: "If there was anything to this at all, certainly the CIA must have some idea—"

"As of a few hours ago, Liam," Castillo interrupted, "the CIA sees no threat in the Congo operation. Specifically, the CIA believes that what's there is nothing more than a fish farm."

"How do we know they're wrong?" Duffy asked reasonably.

Operative words, "How do we know?"

We've got him.

Except, of course, when he asks, "What has this to do with Argentina? It's none of Argentina's business."

"We know, Comandante," Berezovsky offered, "because of the Marburg Group. Those businessmen—ones who can be cheated and manipulated because of their dishonesty—were my responsibility when I was the Berlin rezident."

Duffy looked at him, waiting for him to go on.

"The laboratory in the Congo," Berezovsky explained, "requires not only chemicals unavailable in Iran—or anywhere else in the Arab world—but, of course, the laboratory equipment, centrifuges, that sort of thing, with which to manipulate these chemicals. Also unavailable anywhere else in the Arab world. It has been credibly suggested that one of the reasons why the Muslims hate the West is that they are scientifically four hundred years behind the West.

"What the laboratory in the Congo needs is available only in three places—

six if you include Russia, China, and India and refer in the latter countries only to the raw chemicals.

"Conversely, everything is available in the United States, Great Britain, and Germany. The United States and Great Britain, especially after both rejected chemical and biological warfare, pay very close attention to their stocks of chemicals and to the allied processing equipment.

"They don't want anyone else developing stocks of chemical and biological weapons now that they have destroyed their own stocks.

"Germany's chemical and biological warfare capability died when they lost the Great War, but the chemicals and processing equipment are available in Germany and used for medical purposes."

He paused, then asked, "Can you see where I'm going with this, Comandante?"

Duffy nodded. "I think so."

"Enter the SVR," Berezovsky went on. "The Foreign Intelligence Service knew which German businessmen had profited handsomely from the sale of medicine, medical chemicals, and medical equipment at grossly inflated prices when the oil-for-food program was in full swing—"

"You knew?" Duffy interrupted. "How?"

"It was our business to know. We had assets at every step." Berezovsky paused, then went on: "It became in our interest to see that the Congo operation had what it needed. So we went—in the case of the Marburg Group, I went—to see these dishonest businessmen. I told them there was more money to be made by acquiring certain chemicals and laboratory equipment—in some cases, manufacturing the equipment themselves—and shipping it quietly to a transfer point, often in Egypt, Syria, and Lebanon, but in other places as well."

"And they were willing to do this?"

"Of course they were. They saw another golden opportunity to make a great deal of money without a tax liability. But then, when they were not paid, they of course came to realize, in that charming American phrase, that 'there is no such thing as a free lunch.' "

"You didn't pay them?" Duffy asked.

"Of course not," Berezovsky said. "All we had to do was tell them that if they made any trouble, the German government would learn not only of their involvement in the oil-for-food business but also of their involvement in shipping chemicals and equipment without the proper licenses. And, of course, evading taxes. The SVR decided it needed the money the Iranians paid for all this matériel more than these already-rich-by-dishonest-means German businessmen."

"And none of them went to their government?"

"Of course, we considered that scenario," Berezovsky said. "We fed a jour-nalist from the *Tages Zeitung* newspaper chain enough information to attract his interest toward one of the smaller players. We knew they would learn of his interest."

"'We' being defined here as General Sirinov," Susan said. "He prides him-self in taking a personal hand in the more interesting operations. Feeding that information to Herr Freidler was the general's idea. We didn't think it was nec-essary and told him so. He didn't pay any attention to our recommendation, and ordered that it be done. And it turned out badly. Friedler was getting too close to the heart of the operation—not just to the man we'd pointed him to."

"And he had to be eliminated?" Castillo asked, but it was a statement.

Susan met his eyes. "Yes, and that, too, was General Sirinov's decision."

"Now that I've had time to think about it," Berezovsky said, "what I think happened was that Sirinov—possibly, probably, we have to consider this, Susan—at the recommendation of Evgeny, who has always been prone to think of termination as the best solution to any problem—"

Castillo's mouth ran away with him. He blurted in Russian: "You're talking about her Evgeny?"

Berezovsky nodded.

"He hasn't been my anything for years, Carlos," Svetlana replied, also in Russian. "I thought I had made that quite clear."

"I was talking about Colonel Evgeny Alekseeva," Berezovsky continued in Russian, smiling, "who belongs to Directorate S. What I was suggesting was that General Sirinov concluded—possibly on the advice of Colonel Alekseeva—that Herr Friedler had become a threat and had to be terminated. Then, with that decision made—and here is where it sounds like Evgeny—it was decided that it would also make sense to eliminate the policeman in Philadelphia."

"Why?" Castillo asked.

Out of the corner of his eye he saw that Duffy was uncomfortable not un-derstanding the conversation.

"Because Sirinov knows—"

"I don't want to leave Comandante Duffy out of this," Castillo interrupted Berezovsky. "Can we speak English?"

"You're the one, Carlos, who started speaking Russian," Susan said in English.

"Sorry," Castillo said.

"I didn't understand a word, of course," Lee-Watson said. "But it's a melodic language, isn't it? I thought it would be more guttural, like German."

"What we were talking about, Comandante," Berezovsky said in his American English, "was the possibility that when he prepared the list of people who were ultimately attacked, General Sirinov was very likely getting advice from an SVR colonel attached to Directorate S, which General Sirinov runs. A man named Evgeny Alekseeva, whom both my sister and I know well.

"What I was suggesting was that once the decision to eliminate Herr Friedler had been made, Alekseeva encouraged him to also eliminate the policeman in Philadelphia."

"I heard that much," Duffy said.

"Why?" Castillo asked again.

"Because he knows that those black people in Philadelphia are being funded by oil-for-food money. And Sirinov probably heard that the policeman now works for you. That could also explain your presence on his list."

"I dunno, Tom," Castillo said dubiously. "That seems stretching. And when they tried to whack Britton, he wasn't working for me; he was on the Vice President's Protection Detail."

"I could be wrong, of course, but let me run the scenario out. We're working pretty much in the dark. I'm trying to put things together. My theory is that the decision to eliminate two people opened the door to eliminating the others. We don't *know* that Sirinov knew that we—Svetlana and I—had been in touch with the Kuhls. There were only two meetings with them, and I'd be surprised if we were detected.

"But the SVR has known about them for a long time. I can see Evgeny reasoning that this would be a good time to terminate them on general principles."

"Nice guy, Susan," Castillo said.

Berezovsky said: "Colonel—or may I also call you 'Carlos'?—he is ambitious and quite ruthless, something I strongly suggest you keep in mind. And he has an agenda."

"An agenda?"

"Do we have to get into this?" Susan asked.

"I think we should," Berezovsky said simply. He met her eyes for a moment, waited until, just perceptibly, she nodded, and then went on: "Evgeny was shamed by the breakup of the Soviet Union. By the near dissolution of the KGB. By what he regarded as the shameful behavior of Aleksandr—and there were others like Aleksandr—who not only left their successful careers in the KGB but left Russia to become very rich.

"He was determined to stay; to be faithful to the Motherland; to do what he could to restore the Soviet Union—he never really accepted the words 'Russian Federation'—to what he thought of as its former greatness. And, of course, the KGB to its former, now greatly diminished, power.

"He was not alone. There were thousands like him, ranging from privates in the border patrol to highly placed KGB officers. Colonel Vladimir Putin, for example. They flocked to the 'new' SVR. It wasn't what it once was—many of the brightest officers had left—but it could form the nucleus of what Putin and the others were determined would be an even better, stronger organization than the KGB had ever been.

"And they immediately set out to do so.

"Just about everyone who had remained loyal and was not a certified moron was promoted. I was reminded of Hitler after France fell, when he made field marshals of all those generals. Among those promoted before his time was Evgeny Alekseeva, first to lieutenant colonel and then, after his wife was promoted to lieutenant colonel, to colonel.

"I was not promoted, and as I was not certifiably stupid, I suspected that this was because Putin didn't like me very much. I had once been his commanding officer, and my reports on him were not flattering. But I had too many friends for Vladimir to ship me off for psychological evaluation, as happened to others. I think he was hinting that I might do well to join Aleksandr wherever he might be.

"I therefore resisted as well as I could any foreign assignments when they were proposed to me. The result of that, of course, was I was *given* the assignment—one I think I would have killed for, literally—as rezident in Berlin.

"Meanwhile, Evgeny was having domestic problems. His wife wanted a divorce. In the new SVR as well as in the old KGB, an officer is supposed to control his wife. Divorce was and is frowned upon. If she left him—much less divorced him—his career would have been severely hurt."

"And he didn't have any proof that she had ever been unfaithful to him," Svetlana said. "Because she had never been unfaithful. If he had been able to even credibly allege that she had been in someone else's bed, that would have solved the problem. He just would have killed her, and that would have been the end of the problem."

Castillo looked up at her on the arm of his chair and thought: *If you think that speaking in the third person, Simply Susan, my love, is going to disabuse Duffy of his suspicion that Dmitri is talking about you, have another think.*

That cow was out of the barn a long time ago.

"So," Berezovsky went on, "they acted as if nothing was wrong, continued to live together. Then Evgeny, who has always disliked me, had one of his inspirations. Who better to watch the Berlin rezident than the rezident's sister—who happened to be Evgeny's own wife?"

Did I mention the cow being out of the barn?

"It was no secret that I could not stand him, and that I had told my sister that she would be a fool to marry him. So far as they knew, she was Evgeny's loyal, faithful wife, who hadn't spoken to me or my family since we failed to show up for their wedding."

"Causing her great embarrassment," Svetlana chimed in. "Women don't forget insults like that."

"So Evgeny's wife was appointed the rezident in Copenhagen," Berezovsky said. "Which of course gave us the opportunity to defect that we took. I detect the hand of God in that."

"Excuse me?" Duffy blurted.

Castillo saw the look on Duffy's face.

Write this down, Liam, because there will be a quiz:

All Communists are godless, but not all Russians—not even all senior SVR officers—are Communists. Some of the latter are almost as devout as the Pope.

"There had to be divine intervention," Berezovsky said. "It was all too much for coincidence, a series of coincidences. There was my assignment to Berlin, which placed me in contact with the Marburg Group. Then Svetlana being sent to watch me, and her seeing Charley's photograph in the *Tages Zeitung* and"— he stopped and looked at Castillo—"her convincing me that eliminating you would be counterproductive. And, finally, you being on the 'Bartok Bela.'"

"The what?" Duffy asked.

"The train to Vienna from Marburg," Berezovsky explained. "My sister and I were on our way to Vienna to defect. Charley . . ."

"Carlos," Svetlana corrected.

" . . . was on the train. He had his airplane; he could have flown to Vienna— he *should* have flown to Vienna. But he was on the train. If he hadn't been on the train, to save us from that incompetent CIA station chief in Vienna, Svetlana and I would have been arrested in Vienna. Our Lord and Savior put Carlos on that train."

Castillo looked between Duffy and Berezovsky, and thought:

Actually, Billy Kocian put me on that train—"The dogs have suffered enough from the miracle of travel by air," he said.

If you want to chalk it up to divine intervention, Dmitri . . .

But why the hell not?

He's right. There were a lot of odd coincidences.

I expected to meet him in either Vienna or Budapest. If we had flown to Schwechat, the SVR would've bagged both of them in the West Bahnhof.

And I never would have seen him or Svetlana again.

She wouldn't be sitting here on the arm of my chair, her fingers playing with the hair on my neck.

Was there more to Jack and me being on the train than Billy's concern for the puppies? To this entire sequence of events?

Jesus Christ! Am I starting to believe him?

"Are you a Christian, Comandante?" Berezovsky asked.

"I'm Roman Catholic," Duffy replied.

"My father's brother was a priest," Berezovsky said. "He taught me there were only two kinds of sins. One commits a sin. Or one fails to do what he knows he is called upon to do—the sin of omission. In this case, I know what the Lord is calling upon me to do: help Carlos deal with the chemical factory. I am going to resist the temptation of sin, as I had planned to do."

"Excuse me?" Duffy asked.

Uh-oh!

Has the Reverend Berezovsky gone too far?

Duffy sounds like he smells a rat.

"On the long flight here, I decided that what I was going to do was tell Carlos what I knew of the chemical factory. That would be payment enough for getting us safely out of Vienna. Then I would simply disappear to begin a new life with my family. But then, and I see the Lord's hand in this, too—"

Now what has the Lord been up to?

"—I didn't have to look for our cousin Aleksandr. Carlos took Svetlana to him. And Aleksandr told her that he owed Carlos his life. Like you, Comandante, I am a man of both strength and experience. I would not have believed a word Carlos told me had not Aleksandr told Svetlana he thought of him as family, as a brother."

Oh, shit! I think our little morality play is over.

Duffy's not going to swallow that whole. Not even a little piece of it.

"As it says in Scripture," Duffy said, and interrupted himself. "I don't want to call you 'Colonel.' May I call you by your Christian name?"

"Of course. Dmitri."

"I know," Duffy said.

Of course you know, Liam.

It's on the fucking Interpol warrant—probably next to a picture of a cow having left a barn.

"But for your safety," Duffy said, and glanced at Svetlana, "and for your family's, I will honor you as 'Thomas.' "

Out of the barn and the door locked tight.

Duffy is no fool. . . .

"So, Thomas, in Scripture it says, 'Greater love hath no man than to lay down his life for another,' " Duffy said.

Berezovsky nodded.

"My friend, my brother, Carlos," Duffy went on, his voice quivering with emotion, "has already shown that he is willing to do that for me. I could not deny him anything he asked of me."

I'll be damned!

"His name is Lavrenti Tarasov," Svetlana said matter-of-factly, if not coldly.

"What?" Duffy said.

"Lavrenti Tarasov," Svetlana repeated, then looked at her brother. "I trust this man. I can see in his eyes that he is a good, Christian man."

"Thank you," Duffy said.

"Tarasov is a lieutenant colonel of the SVR," Berezovsky furnished, "and rezident for Paraguay and Argentina. His cover is commercial attaché in the Russian embassy in Asunción."

"For Paraguay *and* Argentina?" Munz asked.

"Alfredo," Berezovsky said, smiling, "as I understand it, your SIDE spends a good deal of time and effort keeping an eye on the man you have been allowed to *think* is the rezident in Buenos Aires."

"Who never does anything out of line?" Munz said.

Berezovsky nodded.

Munz shook his head.

"Liam," Castillo said, "just so that we're still clear on this: I don't want a damn thing to happen to this Lavrenti Tarasov until I get back from Africa."

Duffy met his eyes.

"Clear?" Castillo pursued.

"I hope you're not going to be in Africa long, Carlos."

"Not ten seconds longer than absolutely necessary."

"I can wait that long," Duffy said.

[THREE]
Pilar Golf & Polo Country Club
Pilar, Buenos Aires Province, Argentina
0725 3 January 2006

Very carefully—so as not to wake Svetlana—Castillo got out of bed, walked across the tile floor to the bathroom, and closed its door behind him. The door was substantial; he didn't think Svetlana would hear the sound of the shower through it.

He had seen the bathroom during Svetlana's quick tour of the house, and again just before they had gone to bed, but he hadn't paid much attention to it. Now, taking a good look, he decided that this bathroom made the all-marble bath in the Presidente de la Rua Suite of the Four Seasons Hotel, which at the time he had thought was pushing opulence to new heights, look like the plywood-holed-planking honey bucket sanitary facilities he had known so well in Iraq, Afghanistan, and other exotic locales.

The Club House—where everyone, including Max and Marina, had gone for dinner in a convoy of electric golf carts—had been similarly mind-boggling. It looked more like one of Saddam Hussein's palaces in Baghdad than, for example, the Southern Hills Country Club in Tulsa. And the furnishings and service made the Petroleum Club in Dallas look like a Motel 6.

He remembered Abuela telling him that before World War II, when people wanted to describe someone as stinking rich and needed a more elegant phrase, they said, "Rich as an Argentine." Abuela had also told him that Juan Domingo Peron had managed to squander, during his tenure as dictator, what in 1938 had been the largest gold reserves in the world.

But some of that enormous wealth, to judge by the miles of high-rise luxury apartments in Buenos Aires and those lining the beaches of Punta del Este, had somehow managed to elude Peron's grasp.

Then another part of his brain kicked in. He remembered documents he'd read—ones still classified sixty years after the war's end—about the movement to Argentina of vast sums of money by senior members of the about-to-crumple Nazi structure. That, in turn, triggered memories of Aleksandr Pevsner's Bariloche copy of Göring's hunting estate mansion, Karinhall. The odds that that had been built by a successful cattle breeder were pretty damn slim.

That was his final profound philosophical thought before he stepped away from a sanitary facility mounted on the marble wall of its own softly lit cubicle. A red light flickered in a gold-plated box and the urinal flushed.

"Oh, God, how did I ever get through life having to flush my own pissoir?" he asked aloud, then left the cubicle and headed for the shower.

He looked at his new wristwatch. He would have just about an hour until Delchamps and Davidson—who had gone to Nuestra Pequeña Casa after dinner—would bring just about everybody—which, it was to be hoped, would include Uncle Remus and Dick Miller, who should have arrived sometime during the night and been taken to the safe house—for the first meeting on what would happen in Africa and—more important—how in hell they would make it happen.

"Oh, God," he again asked aloud, "how did I tell time all those years without a Rolex?"

He pulled open one of the two doors to the shower, stripped, and stepped inside. He picked up a bar of soap and started to bathe. Then he smelled himself, decided the bar of soap was the causative factor, and sniffed it.

"Oh, God," he once more asked aloud, "how did I ever get through life without soap like this?"

He soaped his body and then closed his eyes and soaped his hair and face.

"Jesus Christ!" he exclaimed as he suddenly felt hands on his body that weren't his.

"If you let me wash yours, I'll let you wash mine," Svetlana said, and stuck her tongue in his ear.

[FOUR]
0840 3 January 2006

The bar had been turned into a meeting room.

Everyone—including Dick Miller and Uncle Remus—was there when Castillo and Svetlana walked in.

"Overslept, did you, Ace?" Delchamps greeted them.

"Sorry," Castillo said. "Everybody met?"

There were nods and a chorus of "Uh-huhs."

"This is Svetlana, aka Susan," Castillo said. "Honey, these two are really old friends, Colin Leverette and Dick Miller."

Miller and Leverette stood up and took her extended hand. Both mumbled, "How are you?"

Then they sat down.

Svetlana took her hand back, looked at both of them, and shrugged. "Okay, to clear the air: Yes, I'm the diabolic Russian who has taken your innocent friend to my boudoir and done all sorts of wicked things with him. But since that has nothing to do with taking out the chemical factory in the Congo, may I suggest we turn our attention to that?"

"You tell 'em, Susie!" Delchamps said, laughing.

Leverette stood up. "Colonel, my friends call me Uncle Remus. And any friend of Charley's . . ."

"Thank you," Svetlana said. "It used to be Colonel, Uncle Remus. Now it is Susan."

"Susan it is," Leverette said, and sat down again. He shoved his elbow into Miller's midsection. "Gimpy, that's your cue to stand up and make nice to the lady. Otherwise, I'll break your good knee."

"And just off the top of my head," Delchamps said, "I'd say Uncle Remus is big enough to do that without a hell of a lot of effort."

Miller stood.

"If an apology is in order, herewith offered."

"Accepted," Svetlana said.

"When I met him," Miller then blurted, nodding at Castillo, "we were both kids, about to become plebes at the Academy. I've been trying to keep him out of trouble ever since. He's done some wild things, and I didn't think he could surprise me anymore. But I didn't know about . . . about *this situation* until twenty minutes ago."

"You were surprised? Nobody is more surprised than Carlos . . . except perhaps me. Okay? Dramatic confrontation concluded?"

Miller nodded and sat down.

Delchamps slid a sheet of paper across the table to Castillo.

"I think it would save some time if you took a look at these before we get started," he said. "Everybody else has seen them."

"Okay," Castillo said, and started to read:

TRAVEL PERMITS: US NATIONALS REQUIRE A VALID PASSPORT AND A VISA TO ENTER THE DEMOCRATIC REPUBLIC OF THE CONGO.

AIRPORTS: KINSHASA (N'DJILI) (FIH) IS 25KM (15 MILES) EAST OF THE CITY. BUSES RUN TO AND FROM THE CITY. TAXIS ARE AVAILABLE.

FACILITIES: 24-HOUR BANK/BUREAU DE CHANGE, POST OFFICE, RESTAURANT AND CAR HIRE, BUT ALL SERVICES ARE ERRATIC AND UNRELIABLE.

HEALTH: YELLOW FEVER VACCINATION IS A REQUIREMENT. VACCINATIONS AGAINST CHOLERA, TYPHOID, AND POLIO ARE

HIGHLY RECOMMENDED. THERE IS A SIGNIFICANT MALARIA RISK
THROUGHOUT THE COUNTRY, AND ADVICE SHOULD BE SOUGHT IN
ADVANCE ABOUT PREVENTIVE MEASURES. HIV/AIDS IS
PREVALENT. RABIES IS ENDEMIC TO THE DRC. REGULAR
OUTBREAKS OF PNEUMONIC PLAGUE ALSO OCCUR, PARTICULARLY
IN THE DISTRICT OF ITURI, AND IS FATAL IF UNTREATED. AN
OUTBREAK OF THE DEADLY EBOLA VIRUS OCCURRED IN
SEPTEMBER 2007. THE CENTER PRIVÉ D'URGENCE (CPU) CLINIC
IN KINSHASA IS ABLE TO COPE WITH BASIC HEALTH PROBLEMS
AND TO STABILIZE A PATIENT AFTER MOST SERIOUS
ACCIDENTS. HOWEVER, MEDICAL EVACUATION TO SOUTH AFRICA
(OR ELSEWHERE) WOULD BE ADVISED AS SOON AS POSSIBLE.
OUTSIDE KINSHASA, WESTERN STANDARD MEDICAL FACILITIES
ARE PRACTICALLY NON-EXISTENT. VISITORS ARE ADVISED TO
TAKE THEIR OWN BASIC MEDICAL SUPPLIES WITH THEM, AS
MEDICINES ARE IN SHORT SUPPLY. MEDICAL INSURANCE WITH
PROVISION FOR EMERGENCY AIR EVACUATION IS ESSENTIAL FOR
VISITORS. ALL WATER SHOULD BE REGARDED AS CONTAMINATED,
AND MILK IS UNPASTEURIZED; THEREFORE CONSUME ONLY
IMPORTED BOTTLED WATER AND AVOID DAIRY PRODUCTS.

SECURITY: THE EAST AND NORTHEAST OF THE COUNTRY ARE
INSECURE AND TRAVELERS SHOULD BE CAUTIOUS IF TRAVEL TO
THE REGION IS NECESSARY, PARTICULARLY NEAR THE BORDERS
WITH UGANDA AND RWANDA. THERE ARE FREQUENT ARMED CLASHES
IN THE DISTRICT OF ITURI NEAR THE UGANDAN BORDER, AS
WELL AS KIVU PROVINCE AND NORTHERN KATANGA. THERE IS A
HIGH LEVEL OF STREET CRIME AND ARMED ROBBERY,
PARTICULARLY IN KINSHASA, WHERE ARMED GANGS OR CRIMINALS
POSING AS PLAIN-CLOTHES POLICEMEN REGULARLY ATTACK
FOREIGNERS. SECURITY OFFICIALS HAVE ALSO BEEN KNOWN TO
ARREST FOREIGNERS AND DEMAND PAYMENT FOR THEIR RELEASE.
DO NOT DISPLAY VALUABLES ON YOUR PERSON, WALK THE
STREETS ALONE, OR CARRY LARGE AMOUNTS OF MONEY. KEEP CAR
DOORS AND WINDOWS LOCKED. DEMONSTRATIONS AND POLITICAL
GATHERINGS SHOULD BE AVOIDED. BOATS AND FERRIES ARE
POORLY MAINTAINED AND HAVE LOW SAFETY STANDARDS; ON 16

JANUARY 2004 AN OVERCROWDED FERRY ON THE KASAI RIVER
SANK, KILLING 35 PEOPLE. DUE TO VIOLENT ATTACKS, THE
BORDER BETWEEN ANGOLA AND THE DRC IS NOW CLOSED.

When he had finished, he slid the printout to Svetlana.

"Where'd you get that?" he asked.

"Courtesy of our friends in the CIA," Delchamps said.

"Jesus, you asked them?"

" 'Hi, there! We're about to blow up a chemical factory in the Congo that you say doesn't exist, and need a little help.' "

"Then what the hell are you talking about?"

"Gotcha, Ace." Delchamps smirked. "I did a quick Internet search. The CIA has data like that on the Web for anyplace you can think of. So does your State Department page boy pal's Web site—maps, data, even the address of your favorite home away from home, the U.S. embassy."

"And the odd thing, Charley," Uncle Remus said, "is that what Edgar got off the Web is just about the same thing as this."

Leverette slid a manila envelope to Castillo. He opened it. The document, on official CIA stationery, was classified SECRET and its heading read: "CONGO, DR of, Basic Conditions as of 1 Jan 2005."

"See? Says just about the same thing," Leverette said. "D'Allessando gave me that. I don't know where he got it, but there's no tie to you."

Castillo took a quick look, then slid it to Svetlana.

"Only one airport? That's hard to believe," Castillo said.

"The whole Democratic Republic of the Congo is hard to believe," Leverette said.

Castillo's cellular vibrated in his shirt pocket.

"Hola?" he said, and then listened.

"Jesus. Thanks, Liam. I'll get back to you."

He put the cellular back in his shirt pocket and looked at Svetlana.

"That was interesting," he said. "Comandante Duffy just told me that the Lufthansa flight from Frankfurt this morning had aboard a Russian diplomat by the name of Evgeny Alekseeva, who was met by a Russian diplomat from Paraguay by the name of Lavrenti Tarasov."

"He will have to be terminated, Carlos," Berezovsky said evenly.

"No," Castillo said firmly. "What we're going to have to do is get out of here, out of Argentina."

XIII

"Colonel," Dick Miller said, "may I have a word with you in private?"

Castillo looked around the room.

They're a motley bunch, but they're my motley crew—my team.

"No, Dick. Unless you want to confide in me that you contracted a social disease on the way down here."

Delchamps and Davidson chuckled.

"I think it's important," Miller pursued.

"No. You know Rule One: Everybody on the team knows everything."

"Go ahead, Carlos," Svetlana said. "Talk with him. I don't mind."

"Whether or not you mind is beside the point, Susan. And Rule Two is that when I speak *ex cathedra* it's not open for debate."

"You are now the Pope?" she snapped.

Castillo raised an eyebrow toward her. "Actually, that means 'from the chair,' not 'from the cathedral,' if that's what you were thinking. And Rule Three is never be sarcastic unless you're sure you know what you're talking about."

Berezovsky laughed and applauded. Delchamps joined in.

Svetlana with obvious effort kept her mouth shut.

Castillo looked at Miller. "Okay, Dick, let's have it."

Miller hesitated.

"The colonel just used the term 'terminated,' " Leverette then said. "Presuming it means what I think it does, who and why?"

"Is that what you were going to ask, Dick?" Castillo said.

"Among other things," Miller said.

"Okay," Castillo said. "What Tom Barlow—not Colonel Berezovsky; no one ever heard of him—wants to do is take out two SVR people. One of them, Lieutenant Colonel Lavrenti Tarasov, is the rezident for Paraguay and Argentina. The

other, Colonel Evgeny Alekseeva, works for Directorate S and came here looking for Tom and Susan."

"What's the connection?" Leverette asked, and when Castillo didn't immediately answer, said, "Alekseev, Alekseeva, whoever you said?"

Castillo looked at Svetlana.

"What did you say Rule One was, Carlos?" she said, giving him her okay.

Castillo looked back at Leverette. "*Alekseeva* was once married to Susan."

"Davidson, you didn't happen to mention that," Leverette said.

Miller rolled his eyes and shook his head.

"Because of that connection . . ." Berezovsky began and stopped. "I don't
know what to call you. 'Mister Leverette'?"

Leverette looked at Castillo, then back to Berezovsky. "Tell you what, Tom.
Against my better judgment, and until I decide you really are the nice guy
Charley seems to think you are, you can call me 'Uncle Remus' . . ."

"Thank you."

"Everybody else seems to be crazy, so why not me?" Leverette finished.

Berezovsky said: "As I was saying, Uncle Remus, because of that connection,
Colonel Alekseeva has, in addition to a coldly professional interest, a personal
interest in our defection. Unless he either can return us to Russia—which is just
about an impossible ambition—or terminate us, his career will be finished. An
officer who could not prevent the defection of his wife and her brother obviously is unreliable." He met Castillo's eyes. "I am suggesting, Carlos, that because Evgeny Alekseeva is highly skilled in this sort of thing, and we know
highly motivated, eliminating him is the thing to do."

"No," Castillo said.

"Was that also *ex cathedra*, Carlos?" Berezovsky asked softly, but with a tone
that was challenging.

Castillo nodded. "Yes, it was, Tom."

"Dmitri!" Svetlana said warningly.

"I think I should tell you, Carlos," Berezovsky said, "that I have several options. One is to smile at you and agree, then pretend to be surprised when we
learn that Evgeny is no longer with us. Stepan—the larger of the two men
Aleksandr assigned to watch over our Susan—he used to work for me. He
would eliminate Evgeny Alekseeva with at least as much enthusiasm as Comandante Duffy would take out Lavrenti Tarasov."

"Please don't try that, Tom," Castillo said.

Berezovsky ignored the comment.

"My second option," he went on, "is to try to reason with you, one professional to another, to try to show you why eliminating Evgeny now makes

more sense than anything else. And if that failed, to go to you as Svetlana's brother and point out that this very dangerous man is determined to kill the woman we both love and my wife and child."

"Don't you think I've thought of that?" Castillo said.

"Dmitri," Svetlana said evenly, "the woman you both love is perfectly capable of taking care of herself. And stop treating Carlos as if he started in this business last week. If he has his reasons—"

"May I continue?" Berezovsky said.

She made a face but motioned for him to go on.

"But, I am sure that Carlos would agree with me that there can be only one man in charge, so I will consider myself at his orders and defer to his judgment."

Castillo looked him in the eyes a long moment as he considered that, then nodded once. "Thank you."

Berezovsky looked at Leverette.

"As you so colorfully put it, Uncle Remus, 'Everybody else seems to be crazy, so why not me?' "

"That's very kind, Tom," Leverette said. "But let the record show that Uncle Remus would vote, if asked, to whack this guy while we have the opportunity."

"I second the motion," Delchamps said. "Ace, if we don't deal with this guy now, then sooner or later it's going to come around and viciously bite us on the ass."

"I didn't say I wasn't going to deal with him; I said I didn't want him whacked," Castillo said. "Speaking of everybody being crazy, hasn't it occurred to anyone but me that the enemy you know is less dangerous than the one you don't?"

"Meaning?"

"That if we take out Evgeny—"

Jesus, I'm talking about the husband of my lover!

That's one helluva strange feeling—not to mention dangerous ground!

"—they'll just send someone else, who may be more dangerous than Evgeny."

"So how are you going to deal with the one we have?" Delchamps said.

"Sic Liam on him for now," Castillo said, "while hoping I can keep him from whacking him on general purposes." He turned to Alfredo Munz. "How safe is Aleksandr's house in Bariloche from somebody like this guy?"

"There's only one road leading to the house," Munz said. "It's patrolled and secure. The only other way to get there is by air, which is impossible to do quietly, and by boat, which you've seen yourself."

Castillo nodded. "Worst-case scenario: How would the Pevsners and the Berezovskys get out if Evgeny showed up with a platoon of Ninjas?"

"Platoon of what?" Berezovsky asked.

"The ex-Stasi or ex-ÁVH—Államvédelmi Hatóság—or whatever the hell they were—the only one we ever identified was the Cuban who eliminated Dr. Jean-Paul Lorimer at his estancia. They were dressed up in black and wearing balaclava masks like characters in a bad movie—or a comic book. We called them 'the Ninjas.' "

"I doubt if anything like that is likely," Berezovsky argued. "They were sent—they *were* Hungarian, by the way—to deal with that particular problem. You dealt with them. Sending in another team to replace them just in case they might be needed would be difficult and dangerous. Just keeping a half-dozen people like that around and out of sight . . ."

"With respect, Dmitri, it would appear that Evgeny's been sent, as you say, 'to deal with this particular problem,' " Castillo said. "So indulge me." He turned to Munz. "Alfredo?"

"There is Alek's Bell helicopter. If anything like you suggest did happen, they could quickly leave on it and go anywhere, including Chile, on short notice."

Castillo looked at Berezovsky.

"Then you would say, Alfredo, that Mrs. Berezovsky and Sof'ya would be safe in Bariloche? Maybe even safer than where they are now? While we're off to I-don't-know-where or for how long?"

"Yes, I would."

"You're talking about Africa?" Berezovsky said.

"No. Or at least not yet. I have the gut feeling we should get out of the Buenos Aires area. I just haven't figured out where to go."

"That's a no-brainer, Ace," Delchamps said. "Shangri-La."

Uncle Remus made a thumbs-up gesture.

Svetlana asked, "Where?"

"All any of us really know about the Congo is to keep your hand on your wallet and don't drink the water," Delchamps said. "But Ambassador Lorimer was stationed there. He was running through the bush around Stanleyville with a couple of ASA guys when the cannibals were eating missionaries in the town square."

"They didn't eat all of them, Edgar," Leverette said. "I mean, they ate only their livers. That kept them from being hurt by bullets."

"I stand corrected," Delchamps said.

"When we jumped the Belgian paratroops on Stanleyville to save the missionaries," Castillo said, "it was called Operation Rouge; I read the after-actions. They jumped them onto the airfield. So there's an airport there."

"Maybe was," Jack Davidson said. "According to GoogleMaps and the CIA, there's no airport now."

"Supplies to the laboratory would have to be flown in," Svetlana offered. "So there has to be an airport. What is this 'Shangri-La'?"

"Charley, McNab wasn't kidding about wanting to know everything," Dick Miller said. "If you don't have your oral Ph.D. thesis in African studies ready to recite when we go to see him, he'll pull the plug on you. And we're going to need that 727."

"Carlos, my darling," Svetlana said. "What about Rule One?"

He looked at her until he took her meaning.

"Shangri-La is a mythical city of splendor somewhere in Asia," he said solemnly, then added: "It's also the name of the estancia Lorimer bought in Uruguay. His father—a retired ambassador—and mother inherited it and moved there when they lost their home in New Orleans to Hurricane Katrina."

"And," Davidson added, "where they have a half-dozen guys from China Post keeping them company. Odds are one or more of them will know more about the Congo than any of us do."

" 'China Post'?" Berezovsky asked, smiling.

"Shanghai China Post Number One of the American Legion in Exile, Tom," Leverette said. "Surely you've heard of it?"

"Of course," Berezovsky said.

"Okay," Castillo said, chuckling. "Shangri-La it is. Chief of Staff, let's hear your plan."

Miller looked at him in disbelief.

"Charley, I wouldn't know where to begin . . ." he protested before he realized his chain was being pulled.

"He got you, Gimpy, didn't he?" Delchamps said.

Miller shook his head in mock disgust. "My experience with him, over long years, is that he's most dangerous when he thinks he's being funny."

"And that evens the score, doesn't it, Ace?"

Castillo said: "Okay, let me have a shot at it, then, since our crippled friend here has owned up to his inadequacy. First question: Are you all right to fly, Dick?"

Miller nodded.

"I don't think Paul or Susanna needs to go to Shangri-La, because they're not going to Africa. We can bring them up to speed after we find out what we can find out at the estancia. That will leave Paul free to deal with Duffy."

He looked at the others. With the exception of Berezovsky and Svetlana, who showed no reaction, everyone either nodded or gave a thumbs-up.

"You all right, Tom, with sending your wife and Sof'ya to Bariloche?" Castillo asked.

Berezovsky nodded.

"Two ways to do that," Castillo went on, "three, if they fly there commercial, and commercial means that Sof'ya would have to leave Marina here with Susanna. The other two options are to drive them there—which would attract the least attention, but it's a hell of a long ride—or for Dick and me to fly them there in the Gulfstream. Comments?"

"No-brainer, Charley," Leverette said. "The Gulfstream."

The others showed their agreement, except Berezovsky, whose face was inscrutable.

Castillo went on. "All right, then. Alfredo, get on the horn to Aleksandr and let's hear what he thinks. When we know that, Paul, you call Duffy and see what he has to say about how to get the women to Jorge Newbery without attracting any attention."

"I'm sure you are considering that the comandante will then know where my wife and daughter will be," Berezovsky said.

"He's a smart cop, Tom," Castillo said. "He already knows where they are now, and I think he'll suspect they're going to Aleksandr's place; he knows that I took Susan there. And with that in mind, Paul, tell Duffy we're moving the women to Bariloche."

Munz stood, walked to a corner of the room, and took out his cell phone.

"And while he's doing that," Castillo said, "we can begin to contemplate the interesting problem of getting everybody else from here to Shangri-La. Alex, you're confident about Tom's and Susan's new documents?"

"They're good," Darby said.

"Which should they use? Uruguayan or Argentine?"

"Argentines can travel back and forth to Uruguay on their national identity cards. I say use the Argentine."

"Done," Castillo said.

"Charley, it might be a good idea to get them U.S. visas," Darby said.

"I see a couple of problems with that," Castillo said after a moment.

"Such as? All I have to do is hand them to a consular officer I know and tell him to stamp them." He paused, then explained himself: "He's a spook-in-training, and knows what I really do for a living."

"I think I met him yesterday," Castillo said. "My problem is Ambassador

Silvio. I don't like going around him, and he was there when I had my little chat with Montvale."

"Your call," Darby said. "But visas may come in handy somewhere down the pike."

Castillo considered that a moment.

"Alex, when this can be worked in, go see the ambassador. When all else fails, tell the truth. Hand him the passports. Say, 'Mr. Ambassador, Castillo would like to see these fine Argentines get multiple entry visas, but only if it doesn't put your ass in a crack.' Or diplomatic words to that effect. If he seems to be thinking hard about it, tell him I said, 'It's okay. Thanks anyway.' "

"Done," Darby said. "Another thing, Charley. Maybe me driving to Uruguay—I mean, taking a vehicle on the Buquebus to Montevideo—would be a good idea. I'm accredited in both places, so no luggage searches. In case you want to take weapons. . . ."

"There're weapons in the Gulfstream," Castillo said.

"Getting them out of the airplane in Uruguay might be a problem, and I have all we'll need at the embassy." He stopped and smiled. "Last week, I *permitted* the consular officer I mentioned to come in at night and clean and inspect them for me. He was thrilled."

There were chuckles.

"And one more thought, Charley: I take either Tom or Susan with me. There would be less chance that some zealous immigration guy who may have seen the Interpol warrants would have his attention heightened by seeing just one or the other. They'll be presumed to be traveling together."

"And if you drove, we'd have at least one set of wheels in Uruguay, wouldn't we? Okay, you drive. Next question: Where do you drive? Where do Dick and I take the plane?"

Alfredo Munz walked back to the table. "Aleksandr suggests flying into San Martín de los Andes . . ." he began.

Castillo's face and shrug showed he didn't understand.

". . . a small town several hours' drive from Bariloche."

"Can we get the Gulfstream in there?"

"Aerolíneas Argentinas flies a 737 in there once a day, weather permitting. When they're not expecting that flight, the control tower shuts down. What Aleksandr suggests—this is what he often does in the Lear—is file a flight plan to Bariloche, then land at San Martín, unload most of the passengers there, then go on to Bariloche. If any questions are asked, the pilot made a precautionary landing. Aleksandr will have people waiting in both places. Then they will drive to the house, instead of going to Llao-Llao and taking a boat from the hotel dock."

"Okay, done. Still-open question: How do we get from where we're going—where *are* we going?"

"Alek suggests Punta del Este," Munz said.

"Why?" Castillo asked. "That has to be a couple of hundred miles from the estancia."

Munz smiled.

"Maybe he thinks you'd have some trouble landing the Gulfstream at Tacuarembó International," he said.

"Stupid question," Castillo said, chagrined.

"And it's the busy season in Punta," Munz said. "One more private jet won't attract much attention—certainly less than at Carrasco in Montevideo."

"After deep and profound consideration, I have decided that we'll go to Punta del Este," Castillo said.

He took his cellular telephone from his pocket and slid it across the table to Miller.

"Autodial five will get you the weather at Ezeiza, Dick. Get us the weather to Bariloche and Punta del Este."

Miller opened his laptop, waited until it awoke from its sleep mode, then picked up the cell phone.

"Alek also suggests we take Lee-Watson with us," Munz said.

"If I ask why, would my stupidity show again?"

"He has a connection with the Conrad," Munz said. "Alek thinks you should stay there. Keep the apartments in case we need them."

"What apartments?"

"He owns half a dozen, maybe more, luxury apartments in those high-rises along the beach. Lee-Watson manages them for him; people rent them for a week, two weeks. They're not safe houses but could be used for that purpose. No questions would be asked if strangers show up, rent cars, etcetera."

Castillo nodded his understanding, then asked, "So, stay at the Conrad and then drive to Shangri-La in the morning?"

Munz nodded.

"Where is Lee-Watson?"

"Having a cup of tea in the breakfast room. I didn't think you'd want him here for this."

"Ask him to join us, please."

[TWO]
Aeropuerto Internacional Capitán de Corbeta Carlos A.
  Curbelo
Maldonado Province
República Oriental del Uruguay
1705 3 January 2006

The wheels hardly chirped when the Lorimer Charitable & Benevolent Fund Gulfstream III touched down on the runway.

"You must have been practicing, Charley," First Officer Miller said to Captain Castillo over the intercom. "That wasn't your usual let's-bounce-three-times-down-the-runway-and-see-if-we-can-blow-a-tire landing."

"With all the time you've spent flying right seat with me, First Officer, I would've thought by now you'd have learned that landings come to me naturally, as a by-product of my superb reflexes and, of course, genius."

A grunt came through Castillo's headset.

"You ain't no genius when you're thinking with your dick, Captain. In fact, you ain't never been too smart in that department."

Castillo turned to look at Miller. "If you have something to say, Gimpy, say it," he said unpleasantly.

Miller held up both hands, suggesting it had been only an idle, general comment.

Bullshit, Dick!

You're just waiting to offer your heartfelt, well-meaning philosophical wisdom vis-à-vis my outrageous relationship with Svet.

Well, I should've expected it.

Everything so far today has gone well, almost perfectly, far better than one could reasonably expect.

Berezovsky's wife and little girl and Marina, their Bouvier des Flandres pup had arrived quietly at Jorge Newbery at exactly the right time. The Gulfstream had gone wheels-up five minutes later. The odds were strong that no one had seen them.

Forty minutes into the flight, Sergeant Kensington had called over the secure AFC radio and reported: "Mr. Darby said to tell you that Ambassador Silvio says ambassadors can't do visas—but that he asked the consul, who does, and who was delighted to authorize multiple-entry visas for any friends of Colonsel Castillo."

Thirty-five minutes after that, they landed at the San Martín de los Andes airport. Max had barely begun his nose gear ritual when three Mercedes-Benz SUVs pulled up beside the Gulfstream.

There had been a brief but intensely emotional moment as everybody, tears running shamelessly down their cheeks, embraced everyone else. Castillo had been a little wet-eyed himself.

Then everyone—including Ivan the Terrible and Marina—loaded into the SUVs and took off.

Max looked at Castillo with his head cocked, as if asking, *Where the hell are those people going with my children?* But when he heard the whine as Miller began to restart the engines, he trotted quickly up the stairs into the fuselage without waiting to be told.

Five minutes later, they broke ground.

The fuel stop at Bariloche posed no problems whatever, and when Miller checked the weather he learned it would be perfect all the way to Punta del Este.

And they found that the immigration authorities had the same immigration setup at Bariloche as the Buquebus had in Buenos Aires. Which was: An Argentine immigration officer put the DEPARTED ARGENTINA stamp in their passports, officially stating that they had left Argentina. Then he slid the passports to a Uruguayan immigration officer sitting next to him, who put the ENTERED URUGUAY stamp in the passport. There would be no immigration formalities when they got to Punta del Este.

An hour into what would be the final leg, Sergeant Kensington called again to report that Alfredo, Darby, and "their friend" were aboard the Buquebus about to leave for Montevideo. That meant there had been no questions asked about Berezovsky's new national identity card.

And the flight to Aeropuerto Internacional Capitán de Corbeta Carlos A. Curbelo had been smooth, uneventful, and had ended in what Castillo with all modesty considered to be one of his better landings.

And what that means, as stated clearly in Castillo Rule Seven, is:

"That inasmuch as everything has gone perfectly so far, something will surely fuck up big-time in the next couple of minutes."

"The last time I landed here, we were the only airplane on the field," Castillo said as they turned off the runway to trail a FOLLOW ME pickup truck to where they would be parked. "Now look at it!"

There were too many airplanes on the field to count, but the bigger aircraft among them were four glistening Boeing 737s. Two bore the logotypes of LAN-

Chile and Aerolíneas Argentinas. The other two—GOL and OceanAir—Castillo had never heard of, but to judge by the flag on their vertical stabilizers, both were Brazilian.

The FOLLOW ME pickup truck led them between lines of private aircraft—mostly Beechcraft turboprops, but there were two Gulfstreams, one with Brazilian tail numbers and the other with American.

"What is this place, anyhow?" Miller asked.

"Where the rich of South America come in the summer to rest up from counting their money. In the winter, it's just about deserted. The last time I was here, it was winter and it looked like a science fiction movie. Lots of plush apartment houses, multimillion-dollar beachfront houses—and just about no people."

"What were you doing here?"

"Trying to grab Howard Kennedy." He paused and made a question of the statement: "The renegade FBI agent who went to work for Pevsner?"

Miller nodded his understanding.

"Well, Kennedy sold Pevsner out. He tried to have him whacked, and in the process damned near got me. *Would have gotten* me if Lester hadn't been there. My payback plan was to take Mr. Kennedy home so the FBI could arrange for him to be sent to the Federal ADMAX prison in Florence, Colorado, thereby earning me the profound gratitude of the FBI. For some reason, the FBI doesn't seem to like me very much."

"I've heard that," Miller said. "Jesus, look at all these airplanes!"

"The last time I was here, it was just little ol' me."

"Somebody had already whacked Kennedy when you got here, right?"

"Yeah, unfortunately. Pevsner decided that being raped on a regularly scheduled basis was not sufficient punishment for Howard having taken Pevsner's money and then betrayed him. When we got to the Conrad, which essentially is the Caesars Palace of Punta del Este, it looked like every cop in Uruguay was there.

"There's a Uruguayan cop—the chief inspector of the Uruguayan Policía Nacional, one José Ordóñez—who also doesn't like me, by the way. I hope not to see him—"

"Charley, I've never been able to understand why so few people actually do like you."

Miller then pointed out the cockpit window.

The FOLLOW ME truck had stopped, and the driver and another man were getting out.

"Finally," Castillo said. "I thought he was taxiing us back to Montevideo."

They were wanded into a parking space, and they shut down the aircraft. Miller unfastened his harness.

"Hold it a second. Let me finish," Castillo said.

"Okay."

"Ordóñez was in the lobby of the Conrad when we walked in. He took us to one of the better suites, where taped to two chairs were the bodies of Howard Kennedy and a guy who Delchamps recognized as Lieutenant Colonel Viktor Zhdankov of Putin's Service for the Protection of the Constitutional System and the Fight Against Terrorism. Taped because they had been beaten to death. Slowly, with what in Chief Inspector Ordóñez's professional opinion was an angle iron. They started by smashing fingers and toes, then worked up to the larger parts. It was pretty gruesome."

"I wonder what your good buddy Pevsner would do to some guy who didn't do right by his cousin?" Miller asked lightly.

Castillo shook his head. "Not a problem, my friend, because that's not going to happen."

"I remember you telling me something in those exact words before. Actually, on several occasions. The first was years ago in that motel in Daleville, when you were contemplating nailing the deputy post commander's daughter. . . ."

Where the hell did that come from? Castillo thought.

He said: "That's a long time ago. This is now."

Miller shrugged.

"Cutting this short," Castillo went on, "Ordóñez has twice told me I'm not welcome in Uruguay. The day we found Kennedy and Zhdankov, he told me to get out and stay out. And he told me again the time I used Shangri-La as a refueling point when we flew those black choppers off the *Gipper*. He sees me causing trouble for Uruguay."

"But he took the helicopters, right, when you were through with them?"

"Not the way you make it sound, Dick. He's a good guy, ethical, but not bribable."

"Really?" Miller replied sarcastically.

"Yeah, really," Castillo said angrily. "The point of this little lecture is that I want to pass through Punta del Este as quietly as possible. I do not want to have Ordóñez adding to our problems."

"As quietly and *inconspicuously* as possible, right?"

"Right."

"That may be just a little difficult, the inconspicuous part."

He pointed out the cockpit window again.

A glistening white Lincoln stretch limousine had driven up beside the Gulf-stream.

"That's a mistake; that can't be for us," Castillo said. "What that looks like is the Conrad Resort & Casino meeting a Brazilian high-roller."

Miller chuckled.

The liveried chauffeur got from behind the limousine wheel and opened the passenger door. An elegantly dressed man got out and with a welcoming smile waved at the airplane.

There was the electrical whine as the stair door unfolded.

"I hope Edgar has got Max on the leash," Castillo said.

Edgar did not.

Max came down the stairs, trotted to the limousine—causing the smiling man to lose his smile—stuck his big furry head into the open rear door of the limousine, and then, curiosity satisfied, headed for the nose gear.

Castillo unstrapped himself and went into the passenger compartment.

"Terribly sorry, my fault, old chap," Cedric Lee-Watson greeted him. "I should have known something like this would happen."

"What the hell is going on?" Castillo demanded angrily.

"The thing is, you see, is that I have something of a vice."

"No!" Miller said in mock horror.

Castillo could not restrain a smile.

Lee-Watson mimed throwing dice.

"You're a crapshooter?" Miller asked. "Shame on you!"

"The car is from the Conrad," Lee-Watson said. "When I called to ask about accommodations for all of us, they must have assumed I was bringing friends."

"High-rolling friends?" Miller asked.

Lee-Watson nodded.

"And so you have," Miller went on. "Sometimes, when I've known that Lady Luck was smiling at me, I have been known to wager as much as two dollars on the turn of a card."

Castillo chuckled. Then he said, "Well, what the hell do we do?"

"One option, Ace," Edgar Delchamps called, "would be to get in the limousine and go to the hotel. It's getting hot as hell in here."

Castillo saw a Chrysler Town & Country van pull up behind the limousine, then a Chrysler Stratus behind the van. Two large men wearing wide-brimmed straw hats, sunglasses, and flowered Hawaiian-style shirts—which failed to conceal the outline of holstered pistols under them—got out of the front passenger seat of each and stood looking at the airplane.

"Let me deal with this," Lee-Watson said, and went down the stair door.

Max appeared at the foot of the steps and started barking.

Castillo turned to look at Svetlana.

"Didn't you hear Max, Cinderella? Your pumpkin is here."

[THREE]
Restaurant Lo de Tere
Rambla Artigas and Calle 8
Punta del Este, Maldonado Province
República Oriental del Uruguay
2025 3 January 2006

Charley held Svetlana's hand as they waited for her to judge if the Uruguayan caviar—as the waiter had promised them with a straight face—was really as good as that from the Caspian Sea.

Castillo sensed eyes on them and saw that an elderly, nice-looking couple a few tables away was smiling at them.

Romeo and Juliet are holding hands, sipping a very nice Chardonnay, waiting for their caviar, while an elderly couple, probably remembering their youth, smile kindly at them.

And Romeo and Juliet are also under the watchful eyes of two Russian gorillas and Corporal Lester Bradley, USMC—all of whom are prepared to deal with however many bad guys, having miraculously located us, might at any moment crash through the door with Uzis blazing.

"What are you thinking?" Svetlana asked.

He lied.

"I was wondering if you're going to be honest enough to admit that the Uruguayan fish eggs are as good as Russian."

"I will be polite and say 'very nice' if they are at all edible, which I rather doubt."

Everything else was still going so smoothly that he could not get Castillo Rule Seven out of his mind.

They had attracted much less attention than he expected when the limousine rolled up to the door of the Conrad. He thought there would be at least some people gaping at the limo to see the bride of the rock star or the rock star himself or a combination thereof emerge.

There were no gapers.

Their accommodations were first class, suggesting that Cedric Lee-Watson was not only a heavy roller, indeed, but a very unlucky one as well. They were all on an upper floor of the hotel, in suites with balconies that had provided Lester with an easy place to set up the AFC radio and Svetlana with a view of the swimming pool.

"I've got my bathing suit," Svetlana had announced, instantly triggering memories in Castillo's mind of the last time he had seen her in—actually mostly out of—it.

He had restrained his carnal urges until they returned from their swim, but had been on the verge of unleashing them when she entered the shower.

The telephone had dashed that hope. It was Alex Darby calling from Montevideo to announce that he and the others were in Montevideo and what he suggested was that they stay there overnight and drive to Shangri-La in the morning, rather than meet in Punta del Este and drive to the estancia together.

Castillo immediately decided that that was a sound proposition, based on a careful analysis of the tactical situation, which would also provide the opportunity for him to have a romantic dinner with Svetlana in some restaurant overlooking the blue South Atlantic.

With Svetlana and no one else.

"That's fine with me, Alex," he had pronounced solemnly. "We'll see you at the estancia, say, about eleven, maybe a little later."

Why jump out of bed in the morning?

All sorts of interesting things could likely happen if we don't rise with the roosters.

Those plans hadn't gone off perfectly. No sooner had he hung up the telephone and gone into the bedroom than Svetlana had come out of the shower and stood in her unmentionables while aiming a roaring hair-dryer at her hair.

When she saw him looking at her, she flicked off the dryer. "What do we do now?"

He gallantly put aside the first thought that occurred to him and suggested instead that when she had finished dressing—"No hurry, sweetheart"—that they walk along the beach until they came to a nice restaurant.

She'd smiled and flicked the dryer back on.

But that hadn't gone off exactly as planned, either. They were perhaps a quarter-mile down the beach when he noticed that walking along the roadside, with a car trailing, were Corporal Lester Bradley and two of the Russian gorillas who had met the plane. The former wore a black fanny pack, which hung heavily, as if it possibly held, for example, a Model 1911A1 Colt .45 ACP semiautomatic and three or four full magazines, while the latter wore coats and ties and who knew what weaponry concealed.

The headwaiter of the Restaurant Lo de Tere discovered a last-minute reservation cancellation a remarkable thirty seconds after Castillo had slipped him the equivalent of twenty-five U.S. dollars.

"I'm in a generous mood," Castillo then had told the headwaiter, holding up another twenty-five dollars' worth of Uruguayan currency. "There's a hungry-looking young man, looks like a college student, hovering near the door, probably wondering if he can afford your excellent restaurant. You tell him you have special prices for students and put the difference on mine."

The extended Uruguayan currency had been snatched from his hand.

Let the gorillas bribe the maître d' themselves.

Five minutes later, as Bradley was shown to a table near the door, he saw the gorillas in conversation with the maître d', and a minute or so later another canceled reservation was apparently discovered, for they were shown to a table near Lester.

The Uruguayan caviar was delivered in an iced silver tub, with toast triangles and a suggestion that it really would go nicely with champagne, and they just happened to have several bottles of Taittinger Comtes de Champagne Blanc de Blancs 1992 on ice.

"Bring us a bottle of your finest Uruguayan sparkling wine," Castillo said. "I'm told that, like your caviar, your sparkling wine is much better than what's available in Europe."

The wine steward was visibly torn between national pride and selling expensive French champagne, but smiled.

He returned shortly—as Svetlana dubiously eyed the caviar—with a bottle of Bodegas y Viñedos Santa Ana Chef de Cave '94.

Finally, as Castillo sipped at the wine, she steeled herself and used a tiny spoon to extract from the tub enough Uruguayan caviar that would partially cover a fingernail, then put it—with what Castillo thought was exquisite grace—into her mouth.

Her face contorted.

"Bad, huh?"

"It has to be Russian! It is marvelous!"

Using the tiny spoon, she thickly covered a toast triangle with caviar and put it into his mouth. And immediately began to do the same thing for herself.

This is not the time to confess I'm not too fond of fish eggs.

"Well?" Svetlana asked.

"Marvelous," Castillo said, forcing a smile and a swallow.

They found themselves looking into each other's eyes.

Svetlana put her hand to his face and slowly ran her fingers down his cheek.

"Oh, Carlos, my Carlos, I am so happy!"

"Me, too, Svet."

And I mean it.

And the evening is still young.

And I am not going to remind myself of Rule Seven.

[FOUR]
Estancia Shangri-La
Tacuarembó Province
República Oriental del Uruguay
1215 4 January 2006

When Castillo stopped the Hertz rental Volkswagen in front of the main house, there were already five vehicles parked there. All were nosed-in at the hitching rail, to which were tied three magnificent horses.

One of the vehicles was a Chevy Suburban with Argentine diplomatic license plates. That told Castillo that Alex Darby and Dmitri Berezovsky had arrived. There were two identical Ford pickup trucks, which Castillo guessed belonged to the hired hands from China Post Number One. And there were a smaller, older Ford pickup and a Chrysler Town & Country minivan. The older truck, he reasoned, was being driven by Ambassador Lorimer; the minivan by his wife.

As Castillo opened his car door, Colin Leverette, at the wheel of an identical rental Volkswagen, pulled in beside him.

Castillo looked around, wondering where the hell the guys from China Post were—then saw one, a portly, graying black man in his fifties or sixties, come around the corner of the building, a CAR-4 at his side.

When he saw Castillo looking at him, he smiled faintly and gave him a very casual salute. Castillo waved back.

Another black man, this one very small, very black, and with closely cropped white hair, came out the front door of the main house. He was wearing what Castillo thought of as the "Gaucho Costume"—the lower legs of the Bombachas trousers stuffed inside soft black leather boots, a white, open-collared billowing shirt, and a flaming red kerchief tied around the neck.

He also held an enormous *parrilla* fork in one hand.

"You seem to have gone native, Mr. Ambassador," Castillo greeted him.

"If you insist on calling me 'Mr. Ambassador,' Castillo, not only will I have no choice but to call you 'Colonel' but I will see that you get nothing to drink but Coca-Cola," Ambassador (Retired) Philippe Lorimer said.

"It's hard for me to call you 'Philippe,' sir."

"Suit yourself, Colonel. Drink Coke."

"I will call you 'Mr. Ambassador,' sir," Colin Leverette said, "because I am bigger and meaner than you are."

"Larger, perhaps," Lorimer said, waving the parrilla fork.

"And I come bearing gifts, sir," Leverette said.

"Good God, I hope you didn't bring flowers!"

"No, sir. Bitters. Peychaud's Bitters."

He handed him a small bag.

Lorimer opened it and took out three small bottles; the bag obviously held more.

"You will be rewarded in heaven, Colin," the ambassador said. "I'm out. And they're not available here."

"May I respectfully suggest, Mr. Ambassador, sir, that we put the essence of the Crescent City to the ultimate test to see if it has endured the rigors of travel?"

"Making Sazeracs is the best idea I've heard this week," the ambassador said. "But not until I welcome this lovely lady to Shangri-La. How do you do, my dear? Welcome to Shangri-La."

"Thank you," Svetlana said.

"I now understand," Lorimer said.

"Understand?"

"How you captured the heart of the colonel. You're stunning."

"You heard about that, did you?" Castillo asked.

"I hear everything, Colonel. I thought you knew that."

"Okay, Philippe, I surrender."

"It was inevitable," Lorimer said. "Corporal Bradley, you are always welcome here." He gave Bradley his hand and looked at Dick Miller. "And you, sir, are?"

"My name is Miller, Mr. Ambassador."

"Oh. Charley's Hudson High classmate. I'm Norwich, but I will not hold West Point against you. You probably didn't know any better."

Leverette laughed.

"Why don't we go into the house—actually, *through* the house; the parrilla is in the interior garden—while Colin makes us one of his famous Sazeracs?"

He looked at Svetlana. "We can watch as your brother, my dear, and my wife ruin some wonderful Uruguayan beef on the parrilla."

He got the expected chuckles.

Lorimer turned to Castillo. "And then you can tell me what this is all about. I am old but not brain-dead, and therefore suspect that you didn't just drop in because you were in the neighborhood."

He switched the parrilla fork to his left hand, offered his right arm to Svetlana, and marched with her through the door. She towered at least a foot over him.

The portly black man who had come around the corner of the house holding the CAR-4 when they had arrived now walked into the interior patio as the ambassador was slicing an entire tenderloin of beef. He laid the weapon on the table, sat down, and reached for a silver cocktail shaker.

"Colin," he said, "this better be what I think it is."

"Have I ever failed you, DeWitt?" Leverette replied.

"Yes," the man said. "I shudder recalling how many times, where, and how." He picked up the cocktail shaker, poured himself a Sazerac, sipped it appreciatively, then announced, "This will do."

Castillo chuckled.

The black man looked at Castillo and smiled. "You don't remember me, do you, Colonel?"

"No," Castillo confessed.

"All we black folk look alike, DeWitt," Leverette said. "You know that."

"Fuck you, Uncle Remus!" Castillo flared.

Leverette knows that was uncalled for.

And bullshit besides.

There are five "black" people here. The ambassador and his wife, Big Mouth Uncle Remus, Dick Miller, and this old guy, who I never saw before, and now that I think about it is older than I first thought. He's at least sixty.

And the one thing they have in common is that they don't look alike.

One's uncommonly small (the ambassador), another's uncommonly large (Uncle Fucking Remus), one's trim (Miller), and one's more than pleasingly plump (the China Post guy).

And the color of their skin ranges from as light as mine (Mrs. Lorimer) to the you-can't-see-him-when-the-lights-are-out pigmentation of Leverette, who until just now I thought was one of my best friends.

"Easy, Charley," Dick Miller said. "He didn't mean that the way it sounded."

"Yeah, I did," Leverette said.

"Well, then fuck you, too!" Miller said angrily. "You know better than that, Colin. Goddammit!"

Castillo glanced at the ambassador and saw concern on his face; his wife's face looked even worse.

"Goddamn you, Colin!" Castillo flared. "How many of those Sazeracs have you had?"

"Just this one, Boss Man," Leverette said in a thick accent, then raised the glass to Castillo.

Castillo, literally speechless, looked at him in shock. His eye caught the fat old man, who was holding his hands in the form of a T, signaling *Time-out*.

"We got him, Colin," the black man said. "Enough's enough."

"DeWitt, we got *both* of them," Leverette said, laughing. "As ye sow, Carlos, so shall ye reap! You might want to write that down."

Castillo glanced at Dewitt.

DeWitt . . . DeWitt, he thought, then a faint bell tinkled in his memory banks.

"When I saw Colin," the fat man was saying, "I said, 'I just saw Hotshot Charley and he looked right through me.'"

"To which I replied," Leverette picked up, " 'DeWitt, I hate to tell you this, but you are no longer the Green Beanie poster boy you were in The Desert.' "

"Master Sergeant DeWitt!" Castillo said, suddenly remembering.

"And then," DeWitt said, "we said—simultaneously—'Let's pull his chain.' Which we then proceeded to do, with what you'll have to admit was conspicuous success."

"I will now say something I didn't have the courage to say in The Desert," Castillo said. "Go fuck yourself, DeWitt!"

"It's really good to see you, Charley," DeWitt said. He spread his arms wide and a moment later they were embracing, pounding each other's backs.

"Now that the show is over," Delchamps said drily, "may I infer from that obscene display of affection that you have crossed paths on the road of life?"

"You know General McNab?" DeWitt asked.

Delchamps nodded.

"He was then a colonel," DeWitt went on, "running special ops in The Desert. I was his intel sergeant. Right after it started, the colonel came to me and said he had a new chopper driver, a twenty-one-year-old, five-months-out-of-Hudson-High who he wanted to keep alive because he already had the DFC and a Purple Heart and somebody like that would probably be useful somewhere down the pike.

"He was bad enough when he got there, but after he grabbed the Russians—"

" 'Grabbed the Russians'?" Berezovsky parroted.

DeWitt looked at him for a moment before replying. "This is probably still classified Top Secret, Kill Anybody Who Knows, but what the hell. The Scotchman?"

"This Colonel—General—McNab?" Svetlana asked.

"Yes, ma'am. That's what we call him—behind his back, of course. Anyway, the Scotchman mounted an operation to grab a Scud. You know what a Scud is?"

"A Russian missile based on the German V-2," Svetlana said matter-of-factly. "The Iraqis had a number of the R-11/SS-1B Scud-A's, which had a range of about three hundred kilometers."

This earned her a very strange look from Master Sergeant P. B. DeWitt, Special Forces, U.S. Army, Retired, but all he said was, "Yes, ma'am. What we wanted to do was grab one, first to see if it was capable of either being nuclear or to put chemicals or biologicals in the head, and then to send it to the States.

"So we mounted an op to go get one. Two UH-60s—"

He looked at Svetlana, who nodded.

"The Black Hawk," she said.

"—with a reinforced A-Team—"

Svetlana nodded again.

"—with Charley flying the colonel in a Huey."

Svetlana nodded her understanding one more time. Castillo saw that Leverette and Delchamps were having a hard time keeping a straight face.

"So over the berm we go," DeWitt went on. "We reach the Scud site. Everything goes as planned, until somebody notices that among the people lying on the ground with their hands tied behind them there's a lot of heavy brass. First thought, Iraqi brass. Then Hotshot Charley here hears a couple of them whispering to each other in Russian. So he says—in Russian, the first time any of us knew he spoke it—'All Russians please stand up and start singing "The Internationale.' "

Berezovsky laughed.

"So that was you, Carlos!" Berezovsky said. "When I debriefed them after you sent them home, they said that the Americans had a Russian who sounded as if he was from Saint Petersburg."

"Why do I think I'm not fully briefed on this situation?" DeWitt asked.

"Sergeant DeWitt," Delchamps said. "Permit me to introduce Colonel Dmitri Berezovsky and Lieutenant Colonel Alekseeva, formerly of the SVR."

"No shit?"

"And you thought she was just Charley's latest redheaded lady friend, right, DeWitt?" Leverette asked.

"They didn't tell me about you making them sing 'The Internationale,'" Berezovsky said. "You really made them do that?"

"People tend to do what heavily armed men with black grease all over their faces tell them to do. We even took pictures of the chorus and gave everybody a copy before we put them on the Aeroflot plane to Moscow."

"I guess the pictures somehow got lost," Berezovsky said, chuckling.

"Is somebody going to tell me what's going on around here?" DeWitt asked.

"I want to hear the rest of the story," Svetlana said. "Including all about Carlos's previous redheaded girlfriend."

"The Green-Eyed Monster just raised its ugly head. Actually, it's 'rather attractive redheads,' plural," Delchamps said.

Svetlana, in Russian, raised questions about the marital and social disease status of Delchamps's ancestors.

He laughed delightedly.

"There were no women in the desert," DeWitt said. "Colin was just talking. Anyway, we brought two Scuds back, sling-loaded under the Black Hawks, and the Russians. We took their identification and mug-shotted them, and then the agency sent a plane in and flew them to Vienna. Charley went along with them and saw them take off for home."

"You know," Delchamps said conversationally, "I've noticed that Vienna has a lot of women, many of them Hungarian, with red hair. Did you go right back to the desert, *Carlos*, or take a little vacation first?"

"Carlos taught me how to do this, Mr. Edgar Delchamps," Svetlana said, and gave him the finger. Then she turned to DeWitt. "Why do you call him 'Hotshot Charley'?"

"There was a character in the comics, a fighter pilot, they called 'Hotshot Charley,'" DeWitt said. "And it fit him like a glove. Here he was, a twenty-one-year-old second lieutenant, and he already had the DFC, and now there was a DP TWX from the President—"

"A what?" Berezovsky asked.

"A message from the President. DP means Direction of the President. It has the highest priority. Former DCI Bush was the President then, and he was so excited that he forgot he wasn't a sailor anymore. The message read: 'Pass to all hands Operation SNATCH'—that's what we called the op—'Well done. George H. W. Bush, Commander in Chief.' That's pretty heady stuff, especially for a second lieutenant. And it went right to his head."

"Untrue. I have always been the epitome of modesty and self-effacement," Castillo said.

Leverette laughed out loud.

"I can see him now," he said, "strutting around in his desert suit, a CAR-4 in one hand, a .45 in a shoulder holster, frag grenades in his shirt pockets, a KA-BAR knife stuck in his boot top, and peering through his aviator sunglasses as master of all he surveyed."

DeWitt chuckled.

"The cold, honest-to-God truth, ma'am," DeWitt said, "was that Hotshot Charley here thought he was God's gift to the Army and that it was necessary for me to sit on him pretty hard from time to time. As a general rule of thumb, second lieutenants don't like sergeants telling them what to do. And then making them do it."

He looked at Castillo.

"But it worked, didn't it? Here you are, two wars later—three if you count the one we're in with the Muslims—a light colonel doing interesting things for the President himself."

"Raining on your parade, DeWitt, what I am is a light colonel who is not only in the deep stuff up to my ears, but is getting booted out of the Army at the end of this month."

DeWitt looked at him for a long moment, then at Leverette, who nodded.

"Are you going to tell me what happened?" DeWitt asked. "Not to mention what the hell is going on around here?"

"It's liable to cast a pall on our lunch," Castillo said. "Let's let fate decide. You ever been to Sub-Saharan Africa, DeWitt?"

"Yeah, and I didn't like it much."

"The Congo?"

"Both of 'em. There's two, you know. And Sudan, Uganda, Rwanda, Burundi, places like that. I was bodyguarding a candy-ass from the agency who was 'observing' the UN. He didn't speak any of the languages—"

"And you do?"

DeWitt nodded.

"Uncle Remus and I spent a wonderful year at the Language School in the Presidio. Just before we went to The Desert."

"Why don't we talk about this situation over lunch?" Lorimer said.

"Mr. Ambassador," Castillo said when he had finished what in effect was a briefing about the chemical factory, "we were hoping you could tell us something of the Congo. We're really in the dark, and only you and DeWitt have ever been there."

Ambassador Lorimer looked at him coldly.

Oh, shit, I called him "Mr. Ambassador."

What he's doing now is considering how to point out to me how unforgivable that blunder is.

"It's been some time, of course, since I have been there," Lorimer finally said. "But on the other hand, I spent a long time in that part of the world, and I have since—akin to someone not being able to stop looking at a run-over dog—kept myself as up to date on it as possible."

"Please, whatever you could tell us, Philippe," Castillo said.

"Better," the ambassador said. "The best way to do what you ask, I think, is to begin at the beginning. But where is the beginning?"

He paused as he considered his own question.

"In 1885," he began, "the Association Internationale Africaine, chairman and sole stockholder Leopold the Second, King of the Belgians, announced they now owned what today we call the Democratic Republic of Congo. Nobody challenged him. The Germans were doing the same thing—I can't recall the name of their company—in what is now Burundi, Rwanda, and Tanzania, and the French right next door in what later became known as Congo-Brazzaville.

"They were going to bring Christianity and culture to the savages, and also see about making a little profit from the copper, rubber, other minerals, and from whatever else they could exploit.

"They established the capital in a town they called Leopoldville, now called Kinshasa, and others at the interior navigational end of the Congo River. They called this one, now called Kisangani, the one in which you are interested, Stanleyville, after the famous explorer Henry Morton Stanley, who went looking for a missionary who was bringing Christ to the savages in the bush and had gone missing.

"Stanley found him on the rapids of the river and with great élan said, 'Doctor Livingstone, I presume,' as we all heard about in the eighth grade."

There were the expected chuckles.

"This went on for about twenty years," the ambassador continued. "Then, somewhere around 1906 or 1907, the King got some bad press, a lot of it American. An English diplomat named Roger Casement toured the Congo and learned that the Belgians had been unkind to the natives; Casement said they had starved to death or murdered large numbers—thousands upon thousands—of them.

"We Americans tend to be a little self-righteous, and there was a predictable hue and cry in the press.

"To which King Leopold replied that he had no idea that anything of the sort was going on and he would put an end to it. The Belgian Government, in the name of His Majesty, Leopold Two, annexed the Congo in 1908, with un-specified compensation to the Association Internationale Africaine.

"The bad press stopped, and now the Belgian parliament was in charge of improving the lot of the natives, who now found honest employment harvest-ing rubber, extracting copper, etcetera for Belgian firms, many of which had close ties to the Association Internationale Africaine.

"This situation lasted until 1960, and to be honest, what was termed 'pa-ternalistic colonialism' wasn't all bad. They brought schools, religion, and med-icine to the Congo. Their hearts were in the right place, but very little of it stuck on the natives. It's politically incorrect to say this, but the natives of Sub-Saharan Africa weren't ready to govern themselves.

"I guess the best way to make that point is to quote Doctor Albert Schweitzer, organist, philosopher, and physician, who was awarded the Nobel Prize for his lifelong humanitarian services to Africa. He built a hospital in French Equatorial Africa and did a great deal else for Africans, to whom he re-ferred to his dying day as 'Les Sauvages.'

"I was in Leopoldville as a junior consular officer in June 1960 when the Belgians gave in to UN pressure—a lot of that generated by the United States—and granted the Congo its independence. It became the Republic of the Congo. So did the former French colony Middle Congo, next door. So we had two new independent countries with the same name. They became Congo-Brazzaville and Congo-Kinshasa, when the new government renamed Leopoldville.

"At that time, there were two—yes, two—university graduates in Congo-Kinshasa. There were some other very bright people, however. Some were friends of mine. I had one particular friend, a fellow named Joseph Désiré Mobutu, who had been a corporal in the Belgian gendarmerie. He loved to hear about the formation of the United States. I used to loan him books. He was re-ally impressed with George Washington and Thomas Jefferson.

"As soon as parliamentary elections could be held, they were. Mobutu was at the inauguration. In his new uniform. He was now a colonel in the Congolese Army.

"Things promptly started to come apart. Katanga, where the copper mines are, could see no reason to share its wealth with the rest of the country and an-nounced its secession under a lunatic named Moise Tshombe. The Congo's second-richest province, Kasai, also announced its independence a couple of weeks later. A military coup broke out in the capital and there was rampant looting.

"The prime minister of the Congo, Patrice Lumumba, turned to the Soviet Union for help. Khrushchev promptly started to send technicians and some really fancy weaponry to the Congo. They denied anything but honorable intentions.

"And we denied, of course, that we were sending weapons and CIA people to 'advise' President Joseph Kasavubu, even though that was about as much of a secret as the fact that it will grow dark when the sun goes down tonight.

"In my long government service," Lorimer said, looking at Castillo, "I never saw a sitting U.S. President or heard from one. But the word going around then was that President Eisenhower was not going to tolerate the Russians in Sub-Saharan Africa and that he had decided that Nikita Khrushchev's pal Lumumba was a bump on the road to international peace, harmony, and goodwill, and therefore had to be—to use the euphemistic terms I have heard so often since becoming friendly with Charley—whacked, terminated, eliminated.

"What happened was that in December 1960—this is six months after independence, mind you—Kasavubu overthrew the government. To make sure he wouldn't come back, Lumumba was removed from the scene, it was rumored, by Colonel Joseph Désiré Mobutu.

"When I asked my old friend, the great admirer of Washington and Jefferson, that he tell me the rumors were not true, his response was that it would well behoove me to keep my nose out of Congolese internal affairs, and further that it might be a good idea for me to request a transfer home before something happened that would force President Kasavubu to declare me persona non grata.

"I received the same advice from a co-worker at the embassy who I had reason to believe was getting his orders from Langley, Virginia. Consequently, I remained in the Congo as long as I could, another six months.

"Then, after an assignment to the Philippines, I returned in time for the tragedy at Stanleyville. That was August to November 1964. I left the day we jumped the Belgian Paras on Stanleyville; a large Belgian Army medical officer took one look at me and ordered me onto an airplane. Actually, he carried me onto it.

"I haven't been back to the Congo since. But in 1965, shortly after by then-Lieutenant General Mobutu had become commander in chief of the Army and had appointed himself president for five years"—he looked at Svetlana a moment—"I was then political counselor in our embassy in Copenhagen; we must exchange opinions of what makes a really good smorgasbord when we can find the time"—he looked back at Castillo—"someone, who I suspect was the agency man who advised me to seek a transfer, apparently remembered that I had once been friendly with the general, and of course that I had been in the bush outside Stanleyville during the tragedy and I was proposed as ambassador to what was by then Zaire. The word quickly came that I was considered not acceptable. I later learned that my report on what had happened there was considered insulting to Congolese national dignity."

He stopped, looked thoughtful, exhaled audibly, and finished: "Further deponent sayeth not."

"Sir," Castillo said after a moment, "please don't misunderstand this. That background was fascinating, but what I hope you'll tell us is what we can expect when we get there."

" 'We get there'?" Lorimer parroted.

"Yes, sir," Castillo replied, not taking his point. "Me and my team."

The ambassador remained silent and glanced at the others as he considered his reply.

Then he looked at Castillo and said: "First of all, my dear friend, if *you* were found anywhere near Stanleyville—and found you would be, with that rosy complexion—you would be killed and possibly cannibalized. The liver of a white man is considered good juju against bullets.

"As to what anyone else might find, if they were foolish enough to go to that area, it would be the sad remnants of a European attempt to superimpose their culture on the Congo. The Europeans, if I have to say this, are long gone. The airport—which used to have daily flights of Boeing 707 aircraft to and from Brussels—has been closed for years. There is rampant disease. And little or no electricity because little or no oil makes it up the Congo to power generators small or large. They would find stacks of decomposing bodies in the bush not unlike what the Khmer Rouge scattered around Cambodia. Need I go on?"

Castillo didn't reply.

"The only way you could destroy that factory would be by air," Lorimer said.

"We don't even know where it is, within a hundred miles," Castillo said.

"Oh, we can find it," DeWitt said.

" 'We,' DeWitt?" Castillo asked sarcastically.

"I thought this was an employment interview," DeWitt said straight-faced. "You mean it wasn't?"

"Charley," Leverette said, "we could HALO a team, maybe just four, five shooters. Find the sonofabitch, paint it, and call in the Air Force."

"You'd have to—" Castillo began. He stopped when a bell rang loudly, and then a telephone buzzed.

Lorimer picked up the telephone, listened, said, "Thank you," and hung up.

"Someone else just happened to be in the neighborhood and is dropping in. Chief Inspector Ordóñez."

"Oh, shit!" Castillo said.

"May I suggest that Dmitri and Svetlana might be more comfortable if De-Witt took them for a ride around the estancia?"

"How about just putting them in another room?" Castillo asked. "This could just be a coincidence."

Or . . . he could be waving that Interpol warrant.

"If you'd like to come with me, Svetlana, Dmitri?" Ambassador Lorimer asked politely.

"No rush. It'll take him five, six minutes to get here from the highway," De-Witt said professionally.

XIV

[ONE]
Estancia Shangri-La
Tacuarembó Province
República Oriental del Uruguay
1505 4 January 2006

Chief Inspector José Ordóñez of the Interior Police Division of the Uruguayan Policía Nacional—an olive-skinned, dark-eyed man in his late thirties who was well-tailored—walked into the interior patio five minutes later.

"The door was open, Mr. Ambassador," he greeted Lorimer politely. "I just came in."

"You're always welcome here, José. I'd hoped that I had made that clear when you last visited." He gestured toward the table. "We're just finishing lunch, but there's more than enough—"

"That's very kind, Mr. Ambassador. My day has been extraordinary, and I haven't had my lunch." He looked around the table, nodding.

"Good to see you, José," Munz said. "Extraordinary, you say?"

Ordóñez took an open seat at the table. "Quite. I began the day very early."

"Is that so?" Castillo said.

"Someone rang my doorbell at an unholy hour," Ordóñez said. "But when I got out of bed, no one was there. This, however, had been slipped under my door."

He handed Castillo a plain white letter-size envelope. It was unsealed. Ordóñez nodded at it. "Please. Have a look."

Castillo opened the envelope, took out a single sheet of paper, and read it.

Castillo handed it to Alfredo Munz, who read it, then handed it to Edgar Delchamps, who read it, than passed it to Alex Darby, who read it:

```
REFERENCE INTERPOL WARRANTS EUR/RU 2005-6777 FOR
BEREZOVSKY, DMITRI AND EUR/RU 2005-6778 FOR ALEKSEEVA,
SVETLANA

RELIABLE SOURCES SUGGEST BEREZOVSKY AND ALEKSEEVA MAY
BE IN THE COMPANY OF C.G. CASTILLO. LTCOL CASTILLO IS A
US ARMY INTELLIGENCE OFFICER WHO ALSO POSSESSES OTHER
IDENTIFICATION, INCLUDING THAT OF A SUPERVISORY SPECIAL
AGENT OF THE US SECRET SERVICE. HE WAS SEEN IN BUENOS
AIRES 2 JANUARY 2006

IT ALSO HAS BEEN LEARNED THAT THE RUSSIAN OFFICER IN
CHARGE OF THE BEREZOVSKY/ALEKSEEVA CASE, COLONEL EVGENY
ALEKSEEVA, OF THE SVR, IS EITHER IN BUENOS AIRES OR EN
ROUTE. HE IS TRAVELING ON A DIPLOMATIC PASSPORT.
```

Darby folded it and handed it back to Ordóñez, then said: "If I didn't know better—no member of the FBI would ever do something like this, as we all know—I'd say that *somebody* has slipped a confidential FBI backgrounder to a member of the local law-enforcement community."

Ordóñez did not respond to that. Instead, he said: "So, Colonel, before I had my breakfast, I made a couple of calls—these reports would have been on my desk anyway when I went to work, you understand—and learned both that your beautiful airplane had landed at Punta the previous afternoon and that Mr. Darby had taken the Buquebus to Montevideo.

"I then called the Conrad, thinking maybe you might be there playing a little Vingt et Un or something like that. And, sure enough, they told me you were there, in the company of what the manager told me was a truly striking red-haired lady.

"I asked myself, 'Since I made it so clear that I personally and the government of Uruguay semi-officially have stated that we would prefer that you take your tourist business elsewhere, why are you unable to resist the temptation to return to Punta?' "

Ambassador Lorimer placed a plate heaped with slices of beef tenderloin on the table before him.

Castillo avoided the question. He gestured at Ordóñez's lomo. "There are some lovely grilled peppers to go with that, José. Won't you try some? And some really nice Cabernet Sauvignon. I'll get you a glass. Unless, of course, you're on duty and not drinking?"

Castillo got up from the table, and returned with a bottle and held it up.

"It's called Bodegones del Sur, and it's from the Bodega Juanicó. The label says it has a complex aroma, whatever that means, with notes of mature fruits—which calls to my mind a mental image of a cologne-soaked elderly gentleman of exquisite grace. . . ."

Ordóñez shook his head. "Pour the wine, please, Colonel. But, for the record, I'm always on duty."

Castillo half-filled the large glass before Ordóñez, then helped himself to one.

"I'll join you, so there will be two of us always on duty giving in to Demon Rum. Or Demon Cabernet."

They touched glasses.

Ordóñez put some beef in his mouth and chewed.

When he had finished, he said, "Very nice, Mr. Ambassador," and then turned to Castillo.

"So I hopped into my car and drove to Punta. I thought I might be able to have breakfast with you, Colonel, to chat about this.

"When I got there, I heard that you had rented a car and gone for an early-morning drive. But, as you can certainly understand, Colonel, my professional curiosity was piqued."

Ordóñez took a sip of his wine, then went on: "So I showed the picture on the warrant of Miss—or is it Mrs.?—Alekseeva to the manager. He said that it sure looked like the lady who was sharing 1730 with you.

"And then I showed it to the maître d' of the Restaurant Lo de Tere—which is the sort of place I would take a lovely redhead if I was having a romantic interlude in Punta—and he said a woman who looked very much like the woman in the photo had been in his restaurant last night eating caviar and drinking champagne with a big tipper who looked just like the picture I showed him of you.

"But you weren't in the Conrad. Or on the beach. Or having coffee in one of our quaint seaside coffeehouses. So I asked myself, 'If I were in Uruguay and knew that I was not exactly welcome, where would I go?'

"And here I am."

"And here we are," Castillo said.

"So it would seem," Ordóñez said. "On the way here, I wondered if maybe it had occurred to you that Shangri-La might be an ideal place to hide these fugitives from Russian justice."

"That thought never entered my head," Castillo said.

"There have been too many foreigners' bodies here as it is," Ordóñez said, and when he had, his eye caught Lorimer's. "Forgive me, Mr. Ambassador, but that had to be said."

Lorimer made a deprecating gesture.

Ordóñez looked again at Castillo. "And, for that matter, more than enough bodies in the Conrad. Everywhere you go, Colonel, there seem to be bodies."

Castillo could think of no reply to make.

"That's not going to happen anymore," Ordóñez said simply.

"There's more going on here, José, than you understand," Munz said.

"Alfredo, whatever it is, I don't want to know about it." There was a moment's silence, then Ordóñez went on: "Something else occurred to me on the drive here. How much easier it would be if you weren't one of my oldest friends, Alfredo, or if I didn't like—and admire—Colonel Castillo despite all the trouble he's caused me. I even thought it would be very nice if I was one of those people who have a picture of Che Guevara on their office wall."

Ordóñez smiled as he saw that the Che Guevara reference was lost on his audience.

"Why? Because if I were in the Che camp of followers, I would first find the people on the Interpol warrants, arrest them, then turn them over to the Russian embassy and see if the Russians really would pay the two hundred fifty thousand euros they're offering as a reward.

"I would then escort Colonel Castillo and the rest of his entourage to their airplane, see that their passports were stamped 'Not Valid for Reentry into Uruguay,' and watch until the aircraft was in the air.

"That would allow me to go to my superior and report that the situation had been dealt with."

He took a moment to have some more beef and wine.

"But I can't do that," Ordóñez finally said. "So I'll tell you what's going to happen. About ten o'clock tomorrow morning, I am going to tell my superior that although I rushed to Punta immediately on learning that Colonel Castillo and possibly the Russian embezzlers might be there, I got there an hour after Colonel Castillo and entourage flew away from Aeropuerto Internacional Capitán de Corbeta Carlos A. Curbelo, having filed a flight plan to Porto Alegre, Brazil."

There was quiet while the pronouncement was considered.

Ordóñez met Castillo's eyes, then Munz's.

"Thank you, José," Munz said.

There you go, Alfredo, Castillo thought, *once again acting before asking. But once again you're right.*

"Me, too, José," Castillo said.

Ordóñez made a gesture that said, *Of course. It is nothing.*

He said, "And so, having of course never been here, I'm going to have another glass of the perfumed fairy Cabernet and leave."

[TWO]

Berezovsky and Svetlana came out of the room where they had been waiting.

Castillo handed the FBI backgrounder to Berezovsky, who read it and then gave it to Svetlana.

"I do not know what this is," Berezovsky said.

"It's a backgrounder," Castillo said. "The FBI sends this sort of thing to people they think would be—or should be—interested. It's unofficial, but of course in effect it is official."

"The question," Darby said, "is: Where did it come from? My primary suspect is Montvale."

"Ye olde knife in Ace's back?" Delchamps said. "Despite his promise to lay off?"

"Could be Montvale," Castillo said. "But it could be the FBI itself, never mind the President's standing order of hands off the OOA. The FBI's under the Department of Justice, not Montvale. They don't like him any more than they like me. And by now the story of me having snatched Dmitri and Svet from the agency station chief in Vienna has had plenty of time to get around Washington. They have the capability of locating the Gulfstream; they know it was in Buenos Aires. That'd explain the 'was seen in Buenos Aires' line.

"So, thinking that it would be very nice indeed if they could embarrass Montvale *and* stick it to me *and* get credit for bagging the Russian defectors, they sent that backgrounder to both Buenos Aires and Montevideo. Shines a different light on their motto, 'Fidelity, Bravery, and Integrity,' eh?"

Darby, DeWitt, and Davidson chuckled. Delchamps grunted.

"In Buenos Aires," Castillo went on, "a couple of things might've happened. Maybe Artigas got the backgrounder and 'lost' it—"

"Who, Charley?" Dick Miller said.

"Julio Artigas. Used to be an FBI agent in Montevideo. He looks like Ordóñez's brother. Smart. Good guy. He learned—intuited—more about us than was comfortable, so we had him transferred to OOA and moved him to the embassy in Buenos Aires. Inspector Doherty has made it clear to him that if he behaves, Doherty will take care of him in the FBI."

Miller nodded his understanding.

"So he got the backgrounder and tore it up. Or he didn't get it. Some other FBI agent did and took it to Ambassador Silvio for permission to tell SIDE or whatever, and Silvio said 'Not yet' or even 'Hell, no.'

"The backgrounder also went to Montevideo, where (a) the FBI guys are still pissed at Two-Gun Yung, who they now know works for us, and (b) the ambassador is still pissed at us generally because of Two-Gun, and me personally. I can see McGrory—"

"Who?" Miller said again.

"The ambassador," Castillo furnished. "I can see him smiling broadly, saying that he thought the local authorities should be made aware of the contents of the message. But then McGrory also says to slip it under Ordóñez's door in the middle of the night, thus covering his ass by producing what is called 'credible deniability.' I thought it interesting that 'FBI' was nowhere to be found on this."

He tapped the backgrounder with his fingertips.

"Yeah," Darby said.

"Ol' Ace really isn't as dumb as he looks, is he?" Delchamps said, earning him a cold look from Svetlana.

"So, what does it mean?" Berezovsky said.

"Since we don't know where else that backgrounder may have gone, I just don't know what it means. But I don't think it's a very good idea for you and Svet—for that matter, any of us—to go back to Argentina right now."

Delchamps said, "One thought that pops into my mind is that you face facts and abandon this wild idea of yours to take out the chemical factory."

"Is that what you really think I should do?" Castillo said evenly. "That is, not do?"

"It's an option, Ace."

"That's not what I asked."

"It's obviously the most sensible thing to do," Delchamps said. "But on the other hand, I still have this romantic, second-childhood notion that I'd like to go out in a blaze of glory."

Miller grunted. "You're saying your idea of going out in glory is being boiled in a pot for somebody's juju supper? You heard what the ambassador said about the chances of a white guy in the Congo."

"And the ambassador is right, Mr. Delchamps," DeWitt said.

"If you call me 'Mr. Delchamps' one more time, I'm going to start calling you Bee Fu Om—that's short for Bald Fat Ugly Old Man."

"Let me think a minute," Castillo said.

When it seemed to Delchamps the minute had expired, he said, "Well, Ace, since we can't go to Argentina, and Ordóñez made it pretty clear Porto Alegre is not a viable destination option, *wherever* shall we go?"

"Washington," Castillo said.

"That I think is what is known as an off-the-wall thought," Delchamps said.

"Hear me out," Castillo said. "We send Alfredo back to Argentina. He can catch a civilian flight, Aerolíneas or something else. Maybe even catch a flight today. The minute he gets there, he calls Pevsner and tells him we're headed for Cancún, and to set that up for Dmitri and Svet."

"You've lost me," Delchamps said. "Cancún?"

"Actually, an island just off Cancún. With an airport that will take the Gulfstream. Cozumel. On which is the Grand Cozumel Beach & Golf Resort, featuring sandy beaches, a golf course, deep-sea fishing, and some really nice cuisine. You'll like it, Svet—"

"I am not going to . . . wherever you said."

"—and not only because it is owned by your cousin Aleksandr. It also has, for reasons I don't wish to think about, a security system that is at least as mind-boggling as the ones in Bariloche and Pilar Polo & Golf. Or Golf & Polo. Whatever the hell it is."

"Where, my Carlos, do you think you would be going without me?"

"To Washington, Svet. You heard what the ambassador said, what DeWitt said. Thinking that we can find the chemical factory, much less take it out, is pissing in the wind. What I can do is go directly to the President.

"According to Montvale, as of the day before yesterday, the President has been shielded from my 'outrageous behavior' in Vienna. I can see no reason for him to have told him since then, because that would mean the CIA would have to fess up that they don't have either of the top SVR agent defectors wanted on an Interpol warrant that they claim they do.

"That means I can get to the President. Just as soon as we drop Svetlana and Dmitri into the arms of luxury on Cozumel and go wheels-up, I get on the AFC and call him. Unless he's in Nome, Alaska, we can go direct to wherever he is. And with a little luck, get there before Montvale hears what's going on.

"Even if Montvale's sitting there with the President when we get there, and has told him his version of the story, the President will hear me out." He paused and looked at the men seated around Delchamps. "That is, hear *us* out. You're going with me, Edgar. And you, too, Alex. And Davidson, Leverette, and De-Witt. Everybody who has heard what Dmitri and Svetlana have told us and believe there's more in the Congo than a fish farm."

There was a moment's silence.

"Either the President will hear us out, or we go directly to jail without passing Go. Going with me will be on a voluntary basis, and I would be neither surprised nor disappointed if everybody elected instead to go trolling for sailfish with Svet and Dmitri off sun-drenched Cozumel."

There was another long moment of silence.

"May I speak?" Ambassador Lorimer asked.

"Yes, sir, of course," Castillo said.

"I was thinking, Colonel, that if you thought it would be useful, I could prepare a short paper on the history of activity in that area of the Congo. For example, its initial use by the then–West Germans as a nuclear facility. That isn't well-known, and I think it's possible that he's unaware of it."

"Your President wouldn't know about that?" Berezovsky asked incredulously.

"Washington is a strange place, Dmitri," Ambassador Lorimer said. "President Truman was informed of the nuclear weapons that the United States was developing only the day after President Roosevelt died. While Truman was Vice President, he was not told one word—he had been kept completely in the dark."

"So, you are agreeing that my going to the President makes sense?" Castillo said.

"From my vantage point, which I am aware is one of near-total ignorance, it looks to me as if it is your only viable option."

Castillo nodded thoughtfully. "Then yes, sir, Mr. Ambassador, I would be very grateful if you would prepare a paper like that."

"Then I shall, even though I am about out of patience with your refusal, my friend, to address me by my Christian name."

"I'm in, Ace," Delchamps said.

"Me, too," Darby said.

Castillo looked at Davidson.

"Jesus Christ, Charley! Do you have to ask? Yes, sir, Colonel, sir, I will go with you to see the President, sir. Not only that, I will bring Uncle Remus and this bald, fat, ugly old man with me, and do my best to keep them sober."

[THREE]
Cozumel International Airport
Cozumel, Mexico
2005 5 January 2006

Castillo saw that Miller had a hard time getting out of the co-pilot seat—that it was painful for him—but pretended not to notice.

It was understandable. Castillo was a little stiff, too, and during the long flight often had been reminded of his wounded buttocks and leg.

And it had been a long one indeed: Six hours fifteen minutes from Punta del Este across the South American continent to Quito, Ecuador, and then after an hour for fuel and a really bad chicken supper, another three hours and something from Quito to Cozumel.

On both legs he had sent Miller back to the passenger compartment so that he could stretch out on one of the couches with his knee unbent for an hour or so. And on both occasions, Svetlana had come forward and sat in the co-pilot seat. They had tried to hold hands, but the Gulfstream flight deck had not been designed for romance, so they just sat there and watched the fuel gauges drop and the GPS image of the Gulfstream inch its way across the map.

There had been plenty of time to think, and a lot to think about, and a number of decisions to be made, one of which he thought of as Step One of Biting the Bullet.

Castillo started to implement Step One of Biting the Bullet now, after Miller left the cockpit and he heard the whine of the stair-door motor.

As he reached for the AFC handset in its rack beside the co-pilot seat, Svetlana again came into the cockpit. She asked with her eyebrows what he was doing.

To hell with it; she'll learn what's going to happen soon enough anyway.

He pointed to the handset. She handed it to him, then slid into the seat and listened to his side of the conversation.

"C. G. Castillo," he said to the handset.

"Yes, Colonel Castillo?"

The voice-recognition circuit reacted more quickly, he thought, than a human operator would have answered.

And it doesn't sound at all like a computer-generated voice.

"General Bruce J. McNab. Encrypted Level One."

"One moment, please."

Then McNab's voice: "Thank you ever so much for checking in, Colonel. I was beginning to wonder if you had decided to retire earlier than scheduled."

"Good evening, sir."

"Or if you were in the arms of the Argentine cops in Gaucho Land. I presume you're aware of the FBI backgrounder?"

"Yes, sir. You've seen it?"

"Oh, yes. And the 'locate but do not detain' message."

"I didn't hear about that one, sir."

"Well, if you ever try to come to the United States, you'll know why the Border Patrol is so fascinated with your passport."

"Yes, sir."

"Where the hell are you?"

"Sitting in the airplane—we just landed—in Cozumel."

"A fuel stop? Or are you planning to rest from your trip overnight?"

"Both, sir."

"I've given some thought on how to get together—"

"Sir . . ."

"—since your coming to Fort Bragg would be ill-advised. What I've been thinking—"

"Sir . . ."

"—is that I would fly to Rucker, which wouldn't attract any attention, then chopper down to Hurlburt. No one would even know I'd done that. And—I presume you have your German passport—if you went through immigration at Lauderdale—"

"Sir . . ."

"Goddamn it, Charley, stop interrupting me! If you went through immigration at Fort Lauderdale, which makes even more sense now that you'll be coming from Cozumel, since they're both vacation spots, you could fly on to Pensacola—"

"Sir, I'm not coming to see you."

There was a short pause before McNab replied, "Say again?"

"I'm not going to come see you, sir, at least—"

"Your coming to me was not in the nature of a suggestion, Colonel. More like an order. You remember, from your time in the Army, what an order is, right?"

"I'm going to see the President, sir."

There was a long pause.

"He sent for you?"

"No, sir. I'm going to call him and ask to see him just as soon as I get off the horn with you, sir."

There was another long pause before McNab said, "Charley, I don't think the President is going to buy 'I'm sorry, and it won't happen again, sir.' "

"What I'm hoping he will buy, sir, is that there is a chemical laboratory and factory in the Congo."

"You're aware, of course, that the CIA thinks what that is is a fish farm."

"I'm taking Mr. Delchamps with me, sir."

"Ol' Lethal Injection in the Neck Delchamps? You know what the agency thinks about him."

"And Mr. Darby."

"He who sees a Mad Russian bent on world domination behind every tree?"

"And Jack Davidson and Uncle Remus and P. B. DeWitt. They all have—"

"*P. B. DeWitt? My* P. B. DeWitt? Master Sergeant Phineas Bartholomew De-Witt, Retired?"

"Yes, sir. He's one of the China Post guys I hired to sit on Ambassador Lorimer."

"I haven't seen him since his wife's funeral," McNab thought aloud.

"They all have talked to the Russian defectors and believe them, sir. And so does Ambassador Lorimer. And the ambassador has prepared a background paper for the President, sir, outlining the history of the factory site, when the Germans—"

"And it is your intention to march all these people into the Oval Office—he's not there, by the way, he's in Saint Louis, giving a speech—and then what?"

"Try to convince him there is a chemical lab and factory, sir. And get his permission to take it out. There's no way I can do that myself."

"I recall suggesting something like that to you, Colonel," McNab said sarcastically. "Now listen to me carefully, Colonel. This is what they call a direct order. You are not to get on the horn to the President. You are not going to see the President."

Castillo did not reply.

"What you are going to do, Colonel, and again this is a direct order, you are tomorrow morning going to enter the United States as Karl Wilhelm von und zu Gossinger at Fort Lauderdale. You then are going to fly to Pensacola, Florida. When you have procured suitable accommodations in some luxury beachside hotel, you will then contact me on the AFC—I will most likely already be in Fort Rucker—and I will give you my ETA at Hurlburt, to which you will send Jack Davidson to pick me up. No. Make that P. B. I want to have a word with him."

Castillo didn't reply.

"I hope that silence I hear," McNab said a long moment later, "is not one of the finest officers I have ever known contemplating willful disobedience of a lawful order."

Yes, sir.

That's exactly what it was, General.

Key word "was," as I consider you one of the finest officers I have ever known. And without question you're thinking a helluva lot smarter than I am right now. Case in point: Me even considering disobeying your order. . . .

"Sir, I'll get on the horn just as soon as we're in the hotel in Pensacola."

After another long moment, McNab said, "Get some rest, Charley. It's a long flight from Gaucho Land and tomorrow's probably going to be pretty busy. Out."

"Break it down," Castillo said, and turned to Svetlana.

She met his eyes for a long moment and then turned away to put the handset back in its holder. And then she got out of the co-pilot seat and went into the passenger compartment.

Castillo had the feeling she had wanted to say something but had changed her mind.

He looked out the cockpit window and saw that Mexican customs and immigration officials were examining passports and aircraft documents. Behind their truck were two white GMC Yukon XLs with the Grand Cozumel Beach & Golf Resort logotype on their doors.

Four gorillas—these looked Mexican—stood by the GMCs, waiting to make themselves useful.

[FOUR]
The Tahitian Suite
Grand Cozumel Beach & Golf Resort
Cozumel, Mexico
2125 5 January 2006

"So that's it," Castillo said. "For a number of reasons, instead of going to see the President tomorrow, we're all going—except, of course, Svet and Dmitri, who will stay here and watch the waves go up and down—to see General McNab tomorrow. Maybe, after he hears what all of us have to say, he'll say, 'Okay, go see the President.' And maybe not."

"Well, I know McNab well enough to know he's not doing this to cover his ass," Leverette said. "So what's he thinking?"

Castillo shrugged. "We'll just have to wait and find out. Without him, we're dead in the water. And I have had, since I had our little chat, another unpleasant thought. Even if I went to the President and he believed me, he would want a second opinion about staging an op to blow the place up, and the man he'd go to for that second opinion would be Lieutenant General Bruce J. McNab."

"May I speak, Colonel?" Berezovsky said.

"Colonel"? That sounds pretty serious.

"Of course," Castillo said.

"And does that 'what anyone knows, everyone knows' rule of yours apply to me and Svetlana, or would you rather hear what I have to say in private?"

"Let's hear it, Dmitri."

"Does the name Colonel Pietr Sunev mean anything to you?"

"Ol' Suitcase Nukes himself," Delchamps said. "Talk about egg on the agency's face!"

Castillo chuckled. "Yes, we have heard of him, Dmitri. Friend of yours?"

"As a matter of fact, yes. Or he was."

"I'm in the dark," DeWitt said.

"Dmitri's former associates," Delchamps furnished, "let the agency find out that about a hundred briefcase-size nuclear weapons had been cleverly smuggled into the States, and were scattered all over the States waiting to be detonated at the appropriate moment—"

"And," Darby picked up, "this was confirmed by a Russian KGB defector named Pietr Sunev—"

"Who then led the boys in Langley on a merry chase all over the country," Delchamps resumed, "during which they found no bombs, because there were none."

"But," Darby interjected, smiling, "Colonel Sunev was such a nice guy and a convincing liar—and knew how to work a polygraph—that the agency believed him so much that—"

"They never used more efficient—if less pleasant—truth detectors on him," Delchamps said.

"—believed him so much," Darby went on, "that they gave him not only a very substantial tax-free payment for his services but also put him in the CIA's version of the Witness Protection Program, which gave him a new identity—"

"As a professor of political science!" Delchamps interjected. "I always loved that little nuance."

"At a prestigious left-wing college—"

"Grinnell. In Iowa," Delchamps furnished.

"—from which one day the professor disappeared—with, of course, the money he had been paid. To turn up a week or so later in Moscow."

"That's the man," Berezovsky said.

"You guys done good with that operation, Dmitri," Delchamps said.

"That operation did go well," Berezovsky said. "And I would rather suspect that General McNab is aware of it."

"What you're suggesting now is that he thinks you're Sunev Two?" Castillo asked, now quite serious.

"The United States would be excoriated in world opinion," Svetlana said, "if a team of your Spetsnaz was killed or captured trying to destroy a fish farm in a country whose population is starving. It would be worse if your aircraft was successful in destroying it."

"Where are you going with this?" Castillo asked.

"I think it would be much smarter, my Carlos, for Dmitri and me to go with you tomorrow than for us to stay here and watch the waves go up and down."

"To do what?"

"To convince General McNab of the truth," Berezovsky said. "And to make ourselves available, if that should become necessary, to the appropriate authorities."

Delchamps grunted. "Let me give you a scenario, Dmitri. You go through agency debriefing, which means this time the use of the less pleasant methods of truth detecting, and they believe what you have to say. Which isn't much. What you have told us is hearsay. We believe you, but that won't count with the agency. What they are going to think is that here is the guy—"

"And his sister," Darby interjected.

"—who humiliated the station chief in Vienna, and thus the agency. They conveniently will conclude that you are the embezzlers the Russians say you are, and have concocted this fantastic story, à la Sunev, to cover your ass, and the thing for them to do is turn you over to Interpol for return to Russia."

"Neither of you is going to turn yourselves in to the agency," Castillo said.

"If you think that through, Colonel," Berezovsky said, "that is not your decision to make. How would you stop us?"

Castillo met his eyes. "How about reminding you of your wife and daughter in Argentina?"

"Did you notice how well my wife and Susanna Sieno got along? Even better than you and I, Carlos. Both women know of the roles their husbands play in the world in which people like you and I live. From time to time, when God wills it, unpleasant things happen.

"We are back, Carlos, to what we have talked about before. The sin of omission. If I went back to Argentina without seeing this through, that would be a sin. What happens now is in the hands of God."

No, it fucking well isn't.

It's in the hands of C. G. Castillo—but I don't have a fucking clue how to handle it.

When you don't know what the hell you're doing, stall.

"Dmitri, if I allowed you and Svetlana to come with us to Florida, would you give me your word, swear to God on the lives of your family, you wouldn't turn yourself in to the agency without talking to me first?"

Berezovsky considered that a moment.

"I so swear," he said, and crossed himself.

And I swear that you're going back to your wife and little girl if I have to drug you, roll you in a carpet, and ship you as FedEx freight.

Or carry you on my back.

And I'll die before I see Svetlana in the hands of the agency, who would— Delchamps is right on the money about that—send her back to Russia and then congratulate themselves for "dealing with the situation in a way that reflected credit upon the agency."

[FIVE]

Svetlana was wrapped in a white terry-cloth robe—under which Castillo happened to notice she wore the lacey red underpants he had first happened to see in Vienna's Westbahnhof—and leaning on the jamb of the bathroom door as she watched him conduct business on the telephone.

She asked with her eyes what was going on. He signaled for her to wait.

"I appreciate your understanding," he said into the phone. "The animal is a symbol of the strength and devotion of the Lorimer Fund, and I can't imagine Max not being at a board of directors meeting."

Svetlana raised her eyebrows even higher in question, as whoever Castillo was talking to said something else.

"Thank you very much," Castillo said politely, "but I think we can make do with the space in the larger suite for our meeting."

The door chime sounded and Svetlana, in bare feet, ran quickly to answer it.

Castillo saw that it was a room-service waiter pushing a cart on which sat a champagne cooler and something else he couldn't see.

"I'm afraid we won't have time for offshore fishing," Castillo went on, "but I must admit it certainly sounds like fun."

The room-service waiter opened the champagne and Svetlana attacked whatever else was on the table by jabbing at it with a fork.

"A cocktail party at the pool is something we'll have to consider when we get there," Castillo said. "But that, too, is certainly an interesting option."

Svetlana signed the room-service check and showed the waiter out the door, carefully fastening the lock after he'd gone.

She returned to the room-service cart, picked up two champagne stems with the thumb and two fingers of her right hand, then picked up something with her left hand and walked to Castillo.

"We look forward to seeing you, too, and will do so tomorrow," Castillo said, his tone suggesting he was past ready to finish the business conversation. "Thank you so much for your courtesy."

He hung up the telephone and said to it, "Sonofabitch wouldn't stop selling!"

Then he looked up at Svetlana.

He started to say something else but could not, because she had thrust something into his mouth.

"Beluga," she said, and showed him the label on the small jar.

Great . . . more goddamn fish eggs.

"Wonderful," he said a moment later.

"And Pommery *extra brut*," she said, offering him one of the glasses. "That Uruguayan champagne was not bad, but it was not French, and we're celebrating."

What the hell are we celebrating?

Dmitri volunteering that the both of you commit suicide?

She saw something in his eyes.

"Not to worry, my Carlos, I am rich. I will pay for it."

He touched his glass to hers.

"Exactly what is it that we're celebrating?"

"Us. You and me. Being in love."

"Sweetheart, what would I have to do to get you to stay here?"

She ignored him. "And after you finish the caviar and the champagne, I have a small present for you."

"Did you hear what I asked?"

"It is something I know you like. . . ."

"Jesus Christ, honey. Listen to me, please."

"No," she said flatly. "There is nothing you can say, my Carlos."

He looked at her for a long moment.

She flipped the robe open and then closed it. "What sort of a present, my darling, do you think Little Miss Red Under Britches has in mind for you?"

He smiled—*So, she's heard her codename*, he thought—then reached for her and wrapped his arms around her. Even through the thick terry cloth, he could feel the softness and warmth of her belly against his cheek.

He felt a tightness in his throat, and then his chest heaved.

Jesus Christ, I'm crying!

[SIX]
Portofino Island Resort & Spa
Pensacola Beach, Florida
1530 6 January 2006

"Welcome to the Portofino, Mr. Castillo," the manager on duty said.

Castillo recognized his voice.

This is the sonofabitch from the phone call yesterday.

The same sonofabitch who tried selling me everything in the place as a "surprisingly inexpensive option to enhance your visit."

"Before we get going here," Castillo said pointing to a signboard standing beside the reception desk, "can you please get rid of that? Our donors might not understand."

The signboard had movable white letters on a black background that announced:

```
        THE PORTOFINO ISLAND RESORT & SPA
                     WELCOMES
    THE BOARD OF DIRECTORS OF THE LORIMER CHARITABLE &
                  BENEVOLENT FUND
        C.G. CASTILLO, EXECUTIVE DIRECTOR
```

"I understand completely, Mr. Castillo," the man announced with an unctuous tone. "Consider it gone!"

He snapped his fingers to attract the attention of a bellman, and when a languid youth appeared, the two of them carried the sign somewhere out of sight.

"Until just now," Delchamps offered, "I had no idea you were our executive director. Just what does that entail?"

Castillo gave him the finger.

"I just had a very discomfiting thought," Delchamps said seriously. "If there's a 'locate but do not detain' out on you, our friends in the FBI are going to know where you are as soon as your sales manager buddy runs your credit card."

"Jesus! I didn't think of that."

"Well, you're in love. That tends to make people forgetful."

The manager returned.

Delchamps handed him an LC&BF platinum American Express card. "Put everything on this, please."

"Mr. Castillo won't be using his card?"

"Oh, no. Our executive director never pays for anything. That's my job. I'm director for corporate gifts. And while we're here, perhaps you'll be able to give me a few minutes of your valuable time?"

[SEVEN]

They were in a large suite on what looked like the top floor of the high-rise resort on the beach.

Lester Bradley checked the AFC, which he had installed on a wide balcony overlooking the beach and the Gulf of Mexico, then gave Castillo a thumbs-up signal.

Castillo picked up the handset and told the computer to connect him with General McNab with Level One encryption.

When he heard McNab's voice, Castillo said, "Advance party reporting, sir. We hold the high ground. No unfriendlies have been sighted."

"As strange as this may sound, I'm really glad to hear from you."

"Yes, sir."

"What was the meaning of what you just said?"

"I'm in a very nice room on the top floor of the Portofino Island Resort & Spa, which is on Pensacola Beach about half an hour from the Pensacola Airport and about thirty miles from Hurlburt."

"It must be nice not to have to worry about living on per diem."

"Yes, sir. It is."

"You have wheels?"

"A small fleet, sir."

"I'm in the Hurlburt O Club. On the beach?"

"Yes, sir. I know where it is."

"The question would then be: Does Phineas know where it is?"

"I'm sure he can find it, sir."

"What kind of wheels?"

"Two Suburbans and a Mustang convertible, sir. A red one."

"The Mustang sounds nice, but I have with me my aide, an old friend of yours and Miller's, and the co-pilot. And, of course, the AFC. I don't think we'd all fit in a Mustang. Send Phineas in one of the Suburbans."

"Old friend"?

Probably Vic D'Allessando.

But more likely somebody from the Aviation School, maybe somebody from the 160th.

"Is putting everybody up going to cause any problems?"

"No, sir. I'm sure they'll be happy to accommodate everybody."

Especially since this place doesn't seem to be turning away people rushing to pay them two hundred and fifty bucks a night minimum.

"Well, make sure."

"Yes, sir. I will. Sir, if DeWitt leaves now, he can be there in, say, thirty-five, forty minutes."

"Does this Porto Whatever Resort & Spa have a restaurant? One I can afford?"

"Sir, you will be an honored guest of the Lorimer Fund."

"We didn't have any lunch, and until seventeen hundred, all the O Club has to offer is stale peanuts and even more stale popcorn."

A wild hair popped into Castillo's mind. He considered it briefly.

Well, why the hell not?

He's a general officer and a gentleman.

He's not going to throw one of his celebrated tantrums in McGuire's.

"General, there's a great steak house in Pensacola called McGuire's. We need to eat, too. May I suggest you have DeWitt take you there directly? And then we can come to the hotel."

"I know McGuire's," General McNab said. "Every once in a great while, Colonel, you have a decent idea. This one, however, is an excellent one. We'll see you at McGuire's when we get there. McNab out."

[EIGHT]
Ruprecht O'Tolf Wine Cellar
McGuire's Irish Pub
Pensacola, Florida
1750 6 January 2006

The only thing the obliging management and staff of McGuire's would not do to accommodate the Lorimer Charitable & Benevolent Fund's board of directors dinner was permit its executive director to smoke a cigar. They had even sneaked Max in through a fire exit door.

The management had made available to them the Wine Cellar, which was both a bona fide wine cellar—with, so the menu said, more than seven thousand bottles of wine—and a private dining room with a long banquet table in a sunken room within sight of the wine.

By the time DeWitt opened the door for Lieutenant General Bruce J. McNab's spectacular appearance on the passageway between the door and the wine cellar—McNab was in uniform, which was adorned not only with an impressive display of multicolored ribbons representing the wars he had been in and the decorations he had been awarded but seven sets of parachutist's wings and two aiguillettes—Lieutenant Colonel C. G. Castillo had had ample time to consider that coming to a festive Irish pub (with, for example, some two hundred thousand dollars in one-dollar bills stapled by "honorary Irishmen and lasses" to its ceiling and walls) might not be, after all, one of his brightest ideas.

To say that the general was going to be surprised when he found everyone—Castillo, Dick Miller, Colin Leverette, Jack Davidson, Alex Darby, Edgar Delchamps, Lester Bradley, Jack and Sandra Britton, plus, of course, Dmitri Berezovsky and Svetlana Alekseeva—gathered around a table covered with an impressive display of hors d'oeuvres and numerous bottles of wine from the cellar was something of an understatement.

But what proved to be the real surprise, which caused Castillo's mouth literally to momentarily gape, was that one of the three officers—also in full uniform, trailing the general, "the old friend" who McNab had mentioned—was not Chief Warrant Officer Five (Retired) Victor D'Allessando. Nor was it some old crony from the 160th Special Operations Aviation Regiment with whom Charley and Dick could swap war stories.

It was, instead, Lieutenant Colonel Randolph Richardson III, of the Army Aviation School.

Corporal Bradley broke the silence as he shot to his feet, sending his heavy chair loudly screeching five feet backward across the hardwood flooring.

"Attention on deck!" he bellowed as loud as he could. "Flag officer on deck!"

"As you were," McNab said. "Good evening, gentlemen." He then saw Svetlana and Sandra. He looked at Castillo. "And ladies."

McNab came regally down the stairs and headed for Svetlana and Sandra, who were standing at the table, washing oysters down with Chardonnay.

"Bruce McNab, ladies. May I ask what two beautiful women are doing with all these ugly men?"

"I'm Sandra Britton, and I'm waiting for the good time that ugly man promised if we came along with him," Sandra said, pointing at her husband. "All he's produced so far is a couple of lousy oysters."

Svetlana laughed, and McNab turned to her.

"And you, my dear. What did the ugly man promise you?"

"I thought it would probably be more than oysters. But I have to admit these are very good."

"And you are?"

"Susan Barlow, General, and this man is my brother, Tom."

McNab's eyes said, *Like hell. I know who you and Brother Tom are.*

"An honor, General," Berezovsky said. "I've heard a lot about you from Carlos."

"I'll bet you have," McNab said.

"I'm Edgar Delchamps, General. Ditto."

"Ditto?"

"I've heard a lot about you, General."

"Ditto. From some mutual acquaintances in Virginia."

"Alex Darby, General." Darby offered his hand, chuckled, and added, "Ditto, ditto, ditto."

"Meaning?" McNab said.

"I've heard a lot about you, and I'll bet you've heard a lot about me. From the same mutual acquaintances in Virginia."

"True," McNab said, and turned to Lester Bradley.

"Why do I suspect you're the Marine Corps representative?"

"Sir, Corporal Bradley, Lester, sir."

"And I have heard a lot about you, son," McNab said. "All of it from people I respect, and all of it good."

Corporal Bradley's face turned red.

McNab looked at Miller. "How's your knee, Dick?"

"Coming along just fine, sir."

McNab wordlessly shook hands with Davidson and Leverette, then turned to the others in his party. They still stood on the passageway. He pointed them out, left to right, and said: "Lieutenant Colonel Peter Woods, the second-worst aide-de-camp I've ever had; the worst by far was Colonel Castillo. Next is Major Homer Foster, who kept Colonel Richardson from making fatal flying errors on the way down here. On the end is Colonel Richardson, who was a classmate of Castillo and Miller at West Point. Make your own introductions, please, gentlemen."

Max padded up to McNab, sat before him, and offered his paw.

"General McNab, Max," Castillo said. "Max, General McNab."

McNab squatted and shook Max's paw.

"I met one of your progeny today, Max. He was soiling General Crenshaw's office carpet at Fort Rucker at the time."

"And my son Randy has his brother," Colonel Richardson said.

Svetlana caught that and looked at Castillo. He nodded.

"Are we about finished making nice?" McNab asked. "Those appetizers look like a great starter, but I really could eat a horse."

"Oh, I would say you'll fare better than that in here, General," Berezovsky said. "May we offer you a glass of wine?"

"A man after my own heart," McNab said. "Is there some Malbec?"

"Sir?" Colonel Richardson said.

McNab looked at him.

"Sir, while I hate to pass up what looks to be a wonderful—"

"You have the name of the place we're staying?" McNab cut him off.

"The Portofino Island Resort & Spa on Pensacola Beach, sir."

"Check in with Woods at 0700," McNab said.

"Yes, sir. Thank you, sir."

Richardson made his apologies around the room and quickly left.

McNab looked at Castillo. "Mrs. Richardson is chaperoning a bunch of kids from Rucker. Including their boy. They're at a motel near the Naval Air Station; the kids are visiting the Naval Aviation Museum."

"That's one hell of a museum."

"General Crenshaw told me you taught the boy to fly."

"Yes, sir."

"Well, perhaps you'll have a chance to say 'hello' tomorrow."

"Yes, sir."

"If there's time. Since we are not going to talk business at dinner and our time later tonight will be short, I suspect we'll really be busy tomorrow."

"Yes, sir."

"And maybe by then you'll have come up with some suitable explanation, Colonel."

Explanation? Castillo thought. *For what exactly?*

That damn list is long—and complicated.

"I'm not sure I follow, sir. An explanation for what?"

McNab helped himself to some of the seared-rare ahi tuna appetizer. He chewed slowly, clearly enjoying the delicacy, then swallowed. "I told you on the phone that I was starving."

And here we are. Eating.

"Yes, sir?"

"Then why the hell did you send the Suburban all the way to Hurlburt to then haul us back here to Pensacola?"

"But, sir—"

"We right now could be finished with our meals at the McGuire's in Destin."

Damn!

There's a McGuire's in Destin?

"There's a McGuire's in Destin, sir?"

"Not ten miles east of the O Club," McNab said, shaking his head, "I was so informed by the lovely hostesses here. And you have the nerve to call yourself a seasoned world traveler."

He looked past Castillo and suddenly grinned.

"Ah, there we are," McNab said as Berezovsky handed him a glass of wine. "Now, where the hell's the big menu I remember so fondly?"

[NINE]
The Malaga Suite
Portofino Island Resort & Spa
Pensacola Beach, Florida
2125 6 January 2006

"Get on the horn, Peter, and have room service bring us coffee," General McNab ordered as he slumped onto a rattan couch. "Lots of coffee. I ate so much I'm half asleep, and this may go on for some time."

"Yes, sir," Lieutenant Colonel Peter Woods said.

"And then, if you'd like, you can hit the sack," McNab said.

"Sir?"

"If you leave now, Peter, you will thereafter be able to swear under oath that you have no idea what was said in this room, or even who was in here."

"I'm in, sir," Colonel Woods said.

"Say 'Hoo-rah,' Peter."

Woods laughed, said, "Hoo-rah," and reached for the telephone.

"Lady and alleged gentlemen," McNab said, making a grand gesture around the room. "If I may have your attention?"

He waited until he had it.

"If this didn't come up before," McNab then said, "Major Homer Foster is from the 160th. He's one of us, and he's in on this."

The insignia on Major Foster's uniform indicated he was a senior Army Aviator assigned to the Army Aviation School and Center; there had been nothing to identify him as a special operator.

Castillo couldn't remember Foster having said a word during dinner, but he had caught Foster examining everybody very carefully.

"Reverend Castillo will now give the invocation, which begins: 'You are hereby advised that anything and everything'—"

He gestured for Castillo to pick it up, and Castillo did so: "—discussed in this meeting is classified Top Secret Presidential and is not to be disclosed in any manner to anyone without the express permission of the President or myself."

"And since we're not going to bother the President with any of the details at this time, that means only Colonel Castillo. I would like to add my own little caveat, and that is that every serving officer here, me included, is putting his career at risk by participation in the very discussion we're going to have. By that I mean that if we get caught doing what we are going to do, we will all be standing beside Colonel Castillo at his retirement ceremony the end of the month. This is your last chance to get out of here, Pete and Homer. My advice is go."

"I'm in, sir," Colonel Woods said.

"I'm in, General," Major Foster said.

"Okay. Next item: opening remarks. When you get to be as old as I am, and have been around the block as many times as I have, you flatter yourself to think that you wouldn't have all these stars, or, for that matter, have come back so often from around the block, unless you are a pretty good judge of character.

"And you have learned to trust the judgment of those who have been around the block with you, or those individuals you know have been around the block many times by themselves. So if there is anybody here who thinks that Colonel Bere . . . *Mister Barlow* and his charming sister have not told us the truth, the whole truth, and nothing but the truth with no mental reservations whatsoever, raise your right hand and speak now, or else forever after keep your mouth shut."

He ran his eyes around the room, looking intently for a moment at everybody. No one said a word.

"Okay. That's it. It is now established that there is a chemical laboratory slash factory in the Congo established by the Iranians, the Russians, or both, with the intent of waging chemical slash biological warfare against the United States, despite the fish farm opinion of the intelligence community, specifically the CIA, and that we see it as our duty to take it out before they can bring the aforementioned chemical slash biological weapon into play."

He looked around the room again.

"Hearing no objections, the motion carries.

"Facts bearing on the problem: Colonel Castillo has concluded that the way to deal with the problem is to go to the President, lay what he believes—and I believe—are the facts before him, whereupon the President will take the necessary action.

"Colonel Castillo is wrong. The President would not take—with an exception I will get into in a minute—the necessary action without running it past the secretary of State, the secretary of Defense, and the DCI. They would all object. The DCI would insist all it is is a fish farm and the whole idea is nothing more than from the fevered imagination of a loose cannon who has, among other outrages, snatched two high-level defectors from the CIA and now refuses to turn them over for interrogation by those who know how to do that sort of thing.

"The DCI, if I have to say this, would be wrong. The secretary of State and the secretary of Defense, when the President asked them for their opinion of his intended dispatch of the military might of the United States into a poor African country, would both say, 'Mr. President, there simply is no proof.'

"And they would be right. All we have is the word of these two, plus some circumstantial stuff, and nobody believes circumstantial.

"And then there is the problem of the Russians making fools of us with Colonel Sunev, which no one wants to see happen again."

"General—" Berezovsky began.

"Let me guess, Colonel. You're here because you are willing to go to the CIA and let them interrogate you using any means they think will work, including chemical. I admire that. I truly do. But it wouldn't work. You want to know why? Because as people believe what they want to believe, they disbelieve what they don't want to believe. If the agency had you in one of their Maryland rest homes and they couldn't prove you were lying, they would blame the sodium pentothal, or whatever else they had been sticking in your veins, and keep trying something else until you were dead, dead, dead. Getting the picture, Colonel?"

"What you're leading up to," Svetlana said, "is that Carlos has to lay proof— not just what we offer as 'facts'—on the President's desk. Am I correct?"

"Precisely," McNab said. "Without proof, we're pis . . ."

"Pissing in the wind?" Svetlana asked innocently.

McNab couldn't repress a smile. "If you're so smart, why is it you keep looking at Charley like he's the man of your dreams?"

"I suppose that's because he is. Now, how do we get the proof?"

"First, we have to define proof," McNab said.

"How do we do that?" Svetlana asked.

"We get us an expert," McNab said.

"Fort Dietrich," Delchamps said.

"Fort Dietrich," McNab confirmed. "Corporal Bradley, I presume you have the AFC up and running?"

"Yes, sir," Bradley said. He walked to General McNab and gave him the handset.

"Pay attention, please," McNab said. "We are about to take the irreversible step. Cross the Rubicon, so to speak. This is everybody's absolutely final last chance to bail out. And I have to say that I really wish I wasn't running this circus, because I would be the first one out the door."

He looked around the room one final time, then picked up the handset.

"Bruce J. McNab. Encryption Level One. Get me the White House switchboard."

"White House. Good evening, General McNab. How can we help you?"

"Get me the commanding general of the U.S. Army Medical Research Institute at Fort Dietrich, Maryland, on a secure line, please."

"The what?" Berezovsky asked, confused.

McNab put his hand over the mouthpiece. "They used to call it the Chemical Warfare Lab. That was before political correctness took over."

XV

[ONE]
The Malaga Suite
Portofino Island Resort & Spa
Pensacola Beach, Florida
2359:30 6 January 2006

One of the many things then—Second Lieutenant Castillo had learned during his tenure as aide-de-camp to then–Brigadier General McNab was that McNab believed that no matter how noble one's intentions, working when fatigued usually produced little that was useful and too often what was produced was sloppy or in error—or both.

He began a meeting like this one by judging the participants and himself and deciding how long it could profitably last.

Castillo, therefore, was not surprised when Lieutenant Colonel Peter Woods interrupted McNab in the middle of a sentence to announce, "Midnight in thirty seconds, General."

When they had walked into the suite after their dinner at McGuire's, McNab had caught Woods's eye and said, "Midnight." Colonel Woods had nodded his understanding.

One thing all the participants had learned tonight was that General McNab did not like to be interrupted. Everybody but Woods and Castillo therefore waited for the explosion when Woods announced the time.

Instead, McNab turned to Svetlana and smiled. "As your boyfriend—I would say 'gentleman friend,' Susan, but that would not be accurate—may have told you, at the stroke of midnight I change from being a kindly friend of man and mentor to the world into an ogre."

"Oh, I can't believe that," Svetlana said.

This earned her another smile.

She had become one of the four people in the room who could talk back to McNab—even interrupt him—without triggering a scathing response, the others being her brother and Phineas DeWitt.

"We'll resume at oh-nine-hundred," McNab then announced. "Brief recapitulation: As is often the case, our major problem is ignorance. We don't know *exactly* what the evil Iranians and their Russian mentors are cooking up for us in the Congo—only that they're doing it.

"We won't even know precisely what to look for until Colonel . . ." He stopped and looked at Woods.

"Hamilton, sir. Colonel J. Porter Hamilton," Woods furnished.

". . . *J. Porter Hamilton* of the U.S. Army Medical Research Institute at Fort Dietrich arrives . . ." He looked at Woods again.

"At oh-eight-fifteen. Delta flight 616 from Atlanta," Woods furnished.

". . . and having been met by . . ."

"Colonel Richardson, sir."

". . . comes here to share with us what the CG of Fort Dietrich says is Colonel Hamilton's encyclopedic knowledge of the subject.

"Meanwhile, rushing ahead blindly in our overwhelming ignorance, it is tentatively planned for our people to enter the Democratic Republic of the Congo on the ground via Rwanda, as Phineas tells us that's our only option except by HALO insertion, and that's not much of an option, because we wouldn't know where to drop them, which would leave us with between twelve and twenty-four of our people in the middle of we-know-not-where and without wheels.

"Our people being defined as 'as black as possible' Delta Force operators to be selected by Mr. Leverette, who will go to Bragg as quickly and as quietly as possible to do so.

"And, speaking of black people, inasmuch as Brother Britton feels that (a) those he insists on calling the Afro-American Lunatics may be in possession of useful information and (b) that he may able to obtain it from them, we have to get him—"

"And his lovely wife," Sandra interjected.

McNab looked irritated at the interruption but did not flare up.

"—*and his lovely wife* to Philadelphia as soon as possible, and quietly, which may be difficult, as he is what is known as a 'person of interest' to the Secret Service.

"Presuming all this can somehow be accomplished, our people will be transported to . . ." He looked to Castillo.

"Gregoire Kayibanda International in Rwanda, or Bujumbura International in Burundi," Castillo furnished.

"Depending on which looks like the better place to Phineas, who will reconnoiter both on the ground, having entered both countries surreptitiously from Uganda, presuming he can persuade the Ugandan embassy in Washington to give him a visa. A little cash may help in this regard.

"Phineas, equipped with large amounts of currency, will also purchase a fleet of vehicles that will be waiting for our people at either . . ."

"Bujumbura International or Gregoire Kayibanda," Castillo furnished again.

". . . when they arrive aboard our 727 . . ."

"Or are HALO'd in," Leverette said.

"Thank you, Uncle Remus. May I continue?"

"Sorry, sir."

"The vehicles will be waiting for our people when we somehow get them in, either in our 727—dressed in the color scheme of some ragtag African freight hauler, to be determined by Colonel Jake Torine—or, as Uncle Remus was so kind to point out, are HALO'd in.

"Once they have the vehicles, Phineas will bribe their way across the bridge at the southern end of Lake Kivu, from which they will proceed up Congo National Route Three.

"How far they proceed up Route Three depends on our finding out just where the laboratory is. It is to be hoped that Brother Britton, after eluding his former associates in the Secret Service, will be able to get from the AALs at least a hint about the location of the lab.

"Once that little detail is out of the way and we can tell them where to go, they will infiltrate the plant area in search of whatever . . ." He looked at Colonel Woods.

"Colonel J. Porter Hamilton."

". . . Colonel *J. Porter Hamilton*—why does someone ashamed of his first name worry me?—tells them to look for. Once they have done that, they will bring whatever it is they have found—and themselves—out of the Congo to a yet-to-be-determined location by means yet to be determined.

"Once the matériel and our people are safely aboard our Tanzanian Air Freight and Gorilla Transport 727 and en route to the U.S. of A., Colonel Castillo will have to abandon his search for interesting seashells on the sandy beaches of Cozumel, Mexico, or whatever else he's doing with Tom and Susan down there, and return to the United States to lay evidence before the President of what the evil Iranians and the Russians are really doing on what CIA intel heretofore labeled a fish farm."

"Sir," Castillo said, "there is really no reason I couldn't go as far as Uganda with DeWitt, and run the op from there."

"I don't recall asking for your opinion, Colonel, but since you insist on muddying the waters: Yes, there is. The primary reason, of course, is that I say you can't."

"Ex cathedra?" Svetlana said.

"I'll just bet among the many other secrets our *Carlos* has shared with you, my dear young woman, is that I don't like to be interrupted."

"No, he never said a word."

McNab looked at Delchamps. "Tell me, Edgar, why do I think those two deserve each other?"

"Because at the stroke of midnight, you change from being a kindly friend of man and mentor of the world into an ogre, and it's already five past the witching hour?"

"True," McNab said. "Charley, if that 'locate but do not detain' that the FBI has out on you changes, as I suspect it might, to 'put him in the bag,' this whole op goes out the window. I'm surprised you can't figure that out all by yourself.

"Second, or thirdly, or whatever, you are going to have to keep in touch with Edgar and Darby so that the guy who runs your newspapers and that Hungarian character really give them—us—everything they've got on the Germans sending matériel down there. The more of that you can lay before the President, the better."

"Yes, sir."

"The more astute of you may have noticed we have a few little problems as yet to be resolved. One of these is how do we get Charley and Susan—and, of course, her brother as chaperone—down to sunny Cozumel, since I am offering ten-to-one that some FBI agent is at this minute at the Pensacola airport watching the Gulfstream to see if he shows up. And I don't think we can count on them not knowing who Karl Gossinger is, either."

He exhaled audibly.

"But . . . this is enough for tonight. Try to have some useful suggestions in the morning."

He banged his fist on the table.

"Meeting adjourned. Go in peace."

[TWO]
The Malaga Suite
Portofino Island Resort & Spa
Pensacola Beach, Florida
0620 7 January 2006

Castillo, carrying fresh linen and his toilet kit, quietly closed the door of the second, unused bedroom of the suite, then turned to head for its bathroom. He immediately saw that the bedroom in fact was in use.

Max was stretched out—not curled up—on the bed.

"Don't let me disturb you, buddy. I am in my kindly don't-wake-the-weary-sleepers mood."

Charley had not disturbed Svetlana, who was soundly asleep in the master bedroom. He had thought—but of course did not tell her—that the way she slept was like Max slept: completely limp, sort of melting into the sheets and mattress.

Max took him at his word, closed his eyes—the only part of him that had moved when Castillo came into the room—and went back to sleep.

Castillo moved to the bathroom, where on the sink he found a coffeemaker beside a hair dryer. He got the coffeemaker going, then performed his morning ablutions, which included shaving under the running water of the shower.

The coffee was ready when he was finished, and tasted as bad as he had been afraid it would.

The options were calling room service, or drinking it. Calling room service would mean a waiter would eventually appear and make enough noise to wake Svet. Perhaps worse, there was no guarantee the room-service coffee would taste any better than what he had.

He left the bathroom, carrying both the coffeepot and a plastic mug, and headed for the balcony that overlooked the beach.

Max followed.

It was a beautiful day. A little chilly, but going back in their bedroom for one of the terry-cloth robes probably would wake Svet. And there were no robes in the second bathroom; he had looked.

He took another sip of the coffee, grimaced as he swallowed, set down the cup, and then, resting his hands on the balcony railing, looked down at the beach.

A group of sturdy souls in T-shirts and shorts were double-timing down the beach, headed by Lieutenant General Bruce J. McNab.

Immediately, memories came to him of Second Lieutenant Castillo jogging after Brigadier General McNab all over picturesque Fort Bragg. General McNab was a devotee of physical conditioning in general and early-morning jogging in particular.

"I wonder how I got excused from this morning's jaunt?" he asked Max, who didn't reply.

He had just acquired the answer—*If the general thinks the FBI is watching the airplane, to locate if not detain me, the general thinks there is a strong possibility they might be watching the Portofino Island Resort & Spa for the same purpose*—when a bonging announced that someone was at the door.

"That, Max, is either the FBI or, more than likely, someone McNab sent to summon me for the morning run."

Castillo worried more than a little about the former possibility—particularly as it might apply to Svetlana—while he rushed to open the door before the chimes bonged again and awoke her.

He pulled it open.

"Good morning, sir," a trim, dark-haired young man of fourteen said. He wore khaki pants and an obviously brand-new T-shirt bearing Naval Aviator wings and the legend U.S. NAVAL AVIATION MUSEUM.

"Did I wake you, sir?" Randolph J. Richardson IV said politely.

"No, Randy. I had to get up to answer the doorbell. Come on in."

They somewhat formally shook hands.

"Thank you, sir."

Max put his front paws on Randy's shoulders and enthusiastically lapped his face.

"You're with your dad?" Castillo asked.

"He had to come here to get wheels to meet some guy at the airport."

"Yes, that's right. I'd forgotten."

Colonel J. Porter Hamilton of the U.S. Army Medical Research Institute is due in at 0815.

McNab sent Righteous Randolph to meet him.

"I told him that you had called and said you wanted to introduce me to General McNab."

What the hell?

"Why did you do that, Randy?"

"Otherwise, he wouldn't have brought me over here."

"Why did you want to come over here?"

"I have a couple of questions, sir."

Castillo waved the boy onto a couch.

"Have you had your breakfast?"

"No, sir."

"Neither have I. There's a room-service menu on the table there." Castillo gestured to it. "Order up."

"Thank you, sir."

He took the menu from the coffee table and began to study its possibilities.

"See anything you like?" Castillo asked after a moment.

"Yes, sir. They have buckwheat pancakes with genuine Vermont maple syrup, not that usual molasses crap they call pancake syrup."

"Well, that sounds good. Then that's what we'll have." He paused. "What kind of questions, Randy?"

"Like, what's going on here, sir?"

"I don't understand."

Randy shrugged. "The last thing I heard was that you were getting kicked out of the Army."

Jesus H. Christ!

"Where did you hear that?"

"Last week my father came home . . ."

He's not your father.

I am.

". . . and told Mom that you were getting kicked out of the Army. Some guy he used to work for in the Pentagon . . . Colonel Remley? . . ."

"I know Colonel Remley," Castillo said evenly.

". . . told him General McNab was sending him to Argentina to get you to sign the papers."

Castillo didn't answer.

"And here you are," Randy finished, "with General McNab."

"Randy, what you got, what your father got, is called 'a garbled message.' I'm *retiring* from the service."

"And when he came to the motel last night, I was in the bathroom. I heard him tell Mom that she wouldn't believe it, but you were having a party with General McNab in McGuire's restaurant."

"And so we were. Your father was invited, of course, but he wanted to be with you and your mother."

"How are you going to retire? You don't have enough service to retire; you're a classmate of my father's."

I will be goddamned if I'll lie to my son and tell him I'm "psychologically unfit to remain on active service."

Damn that paper-pushing, straight-leg-chair-warming sonofabitch Remley!

"Medically," Castillo said. "I'm being medically retired."

"What's wrong with you?"

Sonofabitch!

There was the sound of a door opening, and both automatically looked toward it.

"Good morning," Svetlana said from the doorway to the master bedroom.

She was wrapped in a terry-cloth robe, running a heavy wooden-handled brush through her lustrous hair.

Randy politely got to his feet.

"Randy, this is Miss Barlow," Castillo said. "Svet, this is—"

"I *know* who he is," she said, smiling warmly and looking between them. "One look at those eyes and I'd know him anywhere!"

Oh, shit!

Svetlana saw something on both their faces but didn't know what it was. Her smile disappeared.

"Oh? You are not Carlos's son, his son who lives with his mother and her husband?"

Where the hell did she get that?

From me, of course—that's where the hell she got that, stupid.

I told her—and Pevsner and damn near everybody else—that I had a son who lived with his mother.

"Well, I guess that answers most of my other questions," Randy said.

"What?" Castillo asked.

Randy looked him in the eyes. "Like why I look just like the pictures of your father, Colonel Castillo, sir. And why Abuela wanted me to call her Abuela. And—"

"He didn't know?" Svetlana suddenly exclaimed. "Oh, Carlos!"

"No, ma'am. I didn't know. I think everybody else knew. My Grandfather Wilson has known all the time. And, of course, I think it's safe to assume Mom knows—"

"Randy!" Castillo said.

"Why the hell didn't anybody tell me?" Randy asked.

Castillo saw that the boy was on the edge of tears.

"I don't think your father knows," Castillo said gently.

Which is true.

I don't think Righteous Randolph would be able to believe his wife ever had been to bed with me.

Much less believe that their honeymoon child was mine.

"Is that an admission, Colonel Castillo, sir, that I am in fact your bastard son?"

"Oh, Randy!" Svetlana said.

"Why the hell didn't you tell me?" Randy demanded, his voice cracking. "What kind of a man would—"

"Shut up!" Castillo ordered.

Both Svetlana and Randy looked at him in shock.

"I have a habit of saying—and, of course, thinking I'm clever when I say it—that when you don't know what to say, try telling the truth. Are you able to handle the truth, Randy?"

The boy nodded.

"Okay, let's start with being a bastard."

"Carlos!" Svetlana said warningly.

"My parents were not married. That makes me a bastard. You learn to live with it. My mother loved me deeply and I deeply loved her. I am sure that my father would have—but he never knew about me. He was killed before I was born."

Charley looked at Svetlana.

"He was a helicopter pilot in Vietnam, Svet. And Randy's grandfather was his co-pilot."

"At Fort Rucker," Randy said, "there's a picture of them in a building they named for Colonel Castillo's father—or should I say 'my other grandfather'? He won the Medal of Honor. I look just like him. Did you really think nobody would ever know?"

"Well, *I* didn't know until we flew down to see the Mastersons and the Lorimers—yeah, Svet, our Ambassador Lorimer—right after Hurricane Katrina."

He met Randy's eyes.

"I honest to God didn't know about you, Randy. Worse, in Mississippi, after Ambassador Lorimer told me, 'Your son has eyes just like yours,' I told him I didn't have a son."

"My God!" Svetlana said. "You really didn't know!"

"So he says," Randy said more than a little sarcastically.

"I'm getting off the track here," Castillo said. "One point I was trying to make, Randy, is that I can't work up a hell of a lot of sympathy for you. You have a loving mother, and she's still around. Mine died when I was twelve. I never knew my father, and you've had a good man all of your life who thinks he's your father and who loves you."

"You sonofabitch!"

"No," Castillo replied more calmly than he expected. "I am *not* a sonofabitch, and neither are you. My mother was the antithesis of a bitch, and so is yours. Think what you like of me, but never *ever* apply that term to me. And never allow anyone to apply it to you."

The boy glared at him but didn't reply.

"Clear, Randy? Say, 'Yes, sir.'"

After a long moment, the boy nodded. "Yes, sir."

"This is not to suggest that I am a man of principle and sterling character," Castillo went on. "The opposite is true, as a great many people, including your mother, have learned from painful experience.

"And that's the reason that your mother, when she found out that you were on the way . . ."

Castillo paused. He made a face as he visibly gathered his thoughts.

"Did I lie to your mother? Yes, I did. Did I feed her martinis knowing full well how they would affect her? You bet your ass I did. Did I take advantage of her naïve notion that because I was a West Pointer I had the same moral attributes as her father and Lieutenant Randolph Richardson III—and that I would not lie, cheat, or steal to get what I wanted from her? You can bet your naïve little ass I did.

"Getting the picture?"

Randy stood stone-faced.

"Your mother had a tough call to make. She had to decide between who would be the better father to the child she was carrying—a thoroughly decent man who loved her or . . ."

"You," Randy said.

". . . or a man who would lie, cheat, and steal to get whatever he wanted, and never lose a moment's sleep over it. And it is now self-evident that she made the right decision."

The boy just looked at him.

"So now you have a decision to make, Randy. You can wallow in self-pity—'poor little me'—and tell everybody how everyone—your mother, your grandfather, me, Abuela, the man you call Uncle Fernando—has abused you. And if you do, the result of that will be that you will hurt, deeply hurt, not only all of them but also the only man who's absolutely innocent in all of this— the man who has been *de facto* your father all of your life. You owe him better than that."

Castillo let that sink in a moment.

"Or . . . you can keep this secret a secret."

After looking at Castillo for a full ten seconds, Randolph J. Richardson IV's face contorted. He blurted, "I have to piss."

Castillo pointed toward the bathroom door, and the boy ran to it.

They heard the door close, then the unmistakable sound of him being nauseated.

Castillo looked at Svet.

"Jesus H. Christ," he said softly.

"How much of what you said to him was true?" she replied as softly.

"I don't know, baby. I don't even know what I said, or where it came from; my mouth was on autopilot."

She ran the balls of her fingers down his cheek.

They heard the sound of water running for a long time, and when Randy came out, his new T-shirt was almost soaking wet.

He didn't make it to the john before he threw up; he fouled himself.

Then washed the shirt.

What have I done?

"Want to borrow a shirt?" Castillo asked.

"If I did that, my father would ask what happened to this one," the boy replied logically. "If I keep it on, it will dry pretty quick."

"Makes sense. Your call."

The boy met his eyes.

"If you're really such an all-around sonof—*bastard,* as you say you are, why should I believe anything you said?"

"I guess that's your call, too, Randy," Castillo said evenly.

Randy considered that, then nodded once.

"I guess, even after everything, I don't think you're a liar."

"Well, counting Abuela, Max, and Svetlana, that's three of you against the rest of the world."

"Is that your real name? Svetlana?"

"Yes, it is."

He looked back at Castillo. "You going to tell me what's going on around here?"

"No."

"I should have known that the story of you getting kicked out of the Army was bullshit."

"Why?"

"Grandfather Wilson, when you started showing up at Abuela's house when I was there, said I should never ask you what you do in the Army. He said you couldn't talk about it, that you were an intelligence officer. He said that General McNab told him you were the best one he'd ever known."

It took Castillo a good fifteen seconds to find his voice.

Finally, he said, "Well, Randy, your grandfather and General McNab, between you and me, are a little too fond of the bottle. When they've been at it, you just can't believe anything they say."

The boy smiled at him.

Castillo turned to Svetlana.

"Randy and I are about to have our breakfast. Following which, I will locate the ogre in his den and introduce Randy to him. Would you care to join us for either or both?"

"Ogre? Is that what you call General McNab?" Randy asked.

"Only behind his back," Castillo said.

"Do they have those flat little round cakes with that sauce they bleed from the tree?" Svetlana asked.

Randy looked at her in confusion a moment, then understood. "If you're talking about buckwheat pancakes with genuine Vermont maple syrup, yes, ma'am, they do."

"Can you handle calling room service, Randy?" Castillo asked.

"Yes, sir."

"And while he's doing that, my Carlos, you can put on your pants."

[THREE]

It was not necessary to locate the ogre in his den.

As they were finishing their breakfast, there came a knock at the door. Castillo opened it, and through it marched Lieutenant General Bruce J. McNab, now in camouflage BDUs, trailed by Lieutenant Colonel Peter Woods and Major Homer Foster, similarly attired.

"I see I'm wrong," McNab greeted them. "That does happen from time to time, despite what you've probably heard."

"Sir?"

"You're out of bed. I gave Foster ten-to-one we'd have to throw you out of bed and then watch you eat."

McNab walked into the living room.

"You look like you're about to attack Baghdad," Svetlana said.

"Good morning," McNab said to her. "And I've already done that twice." He turned to Woods. "Get the others up here."

"Yes, sir," Woods said, and headed for the telephone.

McNab spotted Randy.

"I thought it was the young females of the species who wore wet T-shirts," he said.

"General," Castillo said, "this is Randolph Richardson the Fourth."

"Really?" McNab said. He looked at Castillo. "I know your father."

Jesus H. Christ!

Did everybody know but me?

McNab redirected his attention to the boy. "And, of course, your grandfather. If you will give me your word to give General Wilson my best regards, I will give you my word that I will keep that cross-dresser's wet T-shirt between us."

Randy grinned as McNab shook his hand.

"Yes, sir. Will do."

"And while we are waiting for the others, yes, I will, thank you, have a cup of coffee, if that meets with your approval, Colonel Castillo."

"Yes, sir, it does. And I will even order up some fresh for you, sir."

"Why don't we let Woods do that?" He turned to his aide. "Coffee and pastry, Peter, please. Lots of sugar on the doughnuts."

"Yes, sir."

"Sugar does all sorts of terrible things to your body, Randolph—they don't really call you Randolph, do they?"

"Randy, sir."

"So, *Randy,* you should avoid it if at all possible. However, sugar does provide a sudden burst of energy. And a sudden burst of energy is just what the motley crew that's soon to drift in here is going to need."

He looked at Castillo.

"As Colonel Castillo knows, a morning jog feeds blood to the brain. Feeding it greater amounts of blood causes the brain to function with more efficiency. And while some people, Randy—nothing personal—have been sitting around a hotel room, stuffing their faces, some others of us have been out on the beach jogging."

By 0850, everybody who had been at the last meeting had shown up, and all were drinking coffee and eating pastries.

At 0855, the door chimes sounded once again. Major Foster opened the door. Two officers wearing Class A uniforms—heavily starched shirt, trousers, tunic, and tie—marched in.

One of them was Lieutenant Colonel Randolph J. Richardson III. The other was a very slim, very tall, ascetic-looking officer who was even blacker than Uncle Remus. His stiffly pressed, immaculate, perfectly tailored uniform bore the silver eagles of a full colonel, the caduceus of the U.S. Army Medical Corps, a shoulder insignia Castillo could not remember ever having seen, two—but only two—rows of I Was There ribbons, and, somewhat incongruously, a set of parachutist wings. Basic wings, which meant he had jumped fewer than thirty times.

The colonel, who appeared to be in search of a suitably senior officer to whom to report, looked around at the coffee drinkers and doughnut munchers slumped in chairs—or sitting on the floor—and only then finally found the senior officer present. This luminary was on his hands and knees, holding one end of a web strap between his teeth, and exchanging growls with Max, who had the other end in his mouth.

"Sir!" the colonel barked as he raised his hand to his brow in a crisp salute, "Colonel J. Porter Hamilton reporting to the commanding general, Special Operations Command, as ordered, sir!"

McNab let loose the web strap, leapt rather nimbly to his feet, and returned the salute with something less than parade-ground precision. Max went to inspect the newcomer.

"At ease, Colonel," McNab said, then turned to Charley. "Invocation time, Colonel."

"Yes, sir." Castillo looked at Hamilton. "You are hereby advised—"

"Pay attention, please, Colonel Richardson," McNab interrupted. "This now applies to you."

He signaled for Castillo to continue. Randy watched raptly.

Castillo noticed that Righteous Randolph seemed delighted that he was about to be included in whatever was going on around here.

Castillo recited: "You are hereby advised that anything and everything discussed in this meeting is classified Top Secret Presidential and is not to be disclosed in any manner to anyone without the express permission of myself or the President."

"Got that, the both of you?" McNab asked.

"Yes, sir," they chorused.

Colonel Hamilton looked askance at Castillo, who had added khaki trousers to his clothing but still was barefoot.

"Richardson," General McNab ordered, "this is what you're going to do. Go see the commanding general at Hurlburt. Him only. Tell him I sent you to get the maps."

"Yes, sir."

"See that they are securely packaged, then go to Base Ops and wait for us; we'll be along shortly."

"Yes, sir. Transportation, sir?"

McNab considered that for a full two seconds.

"Any reason they can't take the Mustang, Charley? Randy would like a ride in a ragtop."

"No, sir," Castillo said, and tossed Richardson the keys to the convertible.

"See you at Hurlburt, Richardson," McNab said. He turned to Randy. "It was a pleasure meeting you, son. Give my best to your grandfather."

They shook hands.

"It was nice to see you, Colonel Castillo," Randy said as he walked to Castillo with his hand extended.

I have never wanted to put my arms around anyone, Svetlana included, more than I want to put them around Randy.

But that's obviously out of the question.

He swallowed hard and said, "Good to see you, too, Randy. Give my regards to your mother. And see if you can get your granddad to bring you out to the ranch. Between Fernando and me, we'll get you some more PT-22 stick time."

"I'd like that, sir," Randy replied a little roughly as they shook hands.

Svetlana felt no restrictions on her conduct. "You get a kiss and a hug from me, Randy." And she proceeded to give him a long one of each.

Thirty seconds later, Richardson and Randy were gone.

"Make sure that door's locked, Peter," McNab ordered.

He turned to Colonel Hamilton.

"Colonel, you have been represented to me as the Army's—maybe the country's—preeminent expert on toxins, that sort of thing. True?"

"Sir, that is my area of knowledge and some expertise."

"I don't suppose you know much about Africa, do you, Colonel? Specifically, what used to be called the Belgian Congo?"

"Sir, I don't know much about the Democratic Republic of the Congo, but I do know something—far more than I would prefer to know, frankly—about Rwanda and Burundi, which, as I'm sure you know, both abut the Congo."

"Colonel, please run that past me—past all of us—again, if you don't mind."

"Sir, what I said was that I know something about Rwanda and Burundi. I was there—"

"You were there?"

"Yes, sir. I was there in '94 during the worst of the Rwandan genocide of the Tutsis—hundreds of thousands massacred."

"What were you doing there?"

"Observing, sir."

"Observing for whom?"

"Sir, with respect, I am not at liberty to say."

McNab raised one of his bushy red eyebrows. "Colonel, do you know who I am?"

"Yes, sir."

"And you can't tell me?"

"No, sir. With respect, I cannot."

"Who would it take to get you released from that?"

"Sir, what I could do is contact certain people and ask for permission to tell you what I know about the genocide. I'm sure they would take into consideration who you are, General McNab."

"We're not talking about the CIA, are we, Colonel?"

"No, sir. We are not. Or any of the alphabet agencies, so called."

"I will be damned," McNab said.

Castillo was surprised McNab had not lost his temper.

"Sir, the way it works: I call a certain number in New York City and tell them I need to talk. They call back, often immediately, always within an hour or so, and direct me to a secure telephone. Would you like me to commence that process, sir?"

McNab gave the subject twenty seconds of thought.

"You are a serving officer, correct?"

"Yes, sir, I am. Actually, I'm Class of '83 at the Academy, General."

"Well, then as soon as we can find the time, you and me and Barefoot Boy there can get together and sing 'Army Blue.' But right now what you're going to do, Colonel, is listen to what I have to say to these people.

"Understand, this is simply to bring you up to speed on what's going on here. You are specifically forbidden to relay any of this to these mysterious people you seem to be associated with. I want you to have what you hear in your mind when you get them on the horn. Clear?"

"Yes, sir."

"Then please sit down, have a doughnut and a cup of coffee, and pay close attention."

"Yes, sir."

"Surprising me not at all, ladies and gentlemen," McNab then announced, "as the increased flood of blood to my brain derived from my morning jog caused that organ to shift out of low gear, I realized that there were certain solutions to our problems that had not occurred to me last night.

"The problem of getting Colonel Castillo and the Barlows to the sandy beaches of Cozumel past the vigilant eyes of the FBI and the Border Patrol no longer exists, as there is no good reason, thanks to the blessed Aloysius Francis Casey's generosity, for them to go there. Colonel Castillo, if I'm wrong thinking that you can control this operation from anywhere—say, your farm in Midland—please be good enough to explain why I err."

"I could control it from there, sir. I'd prefer, though—"

"I didn't ask what you would prefer," McNab cut him off. "Now, since Major Porter has confirmed that your Gulfstream is in fact being surveilled by what we strongly suspect are minions of the FBI, the question then becomes:

'How do we get Barefoot and his Friends to the farm in Texas without the FBI knowing?' as they would if we used the Gulfstream or commercial aircraft.

"And again, as I jogged happily down the beach while others unnamed enjoyed a leisurely morning repast, the answer came to me. Then, the moment I came out of the shower, I communicated—using the AFC, of course—with Colonel Jacob Torine."

McNab looked at Colonel Hamilton. "We consider Colonel Torine, although he is USAF, as one of us."

Hamilton nodded.

McNab went on: "Colonel Torine, as he frequently does, agreed with both my analysis of a problem and the solution thereof. As we speak, Colonel Torine is either at, or will soon be at, Baltimore/Washington International Airport, where he will sign the dry lease for a month of a Learjet aircraft from Signature Flight Support, Inc., to the Lorimer Charitable and Benevolent Fund, of which he is a director.

"As soon as that is done, the Lear will be flown here to the Pensacola Regional Airport by Captain Richard M. Sparkman, USAF—and parked. While, technically, two pilots are required to fly the Lear, it can be flown by one good pilot.

"Captain Sparkman, if I had to say this, will be in civilian clothing and flying as a civilian pilot. He will go to the passenger lounge, where he will be met by Major Dick Miller, who will also be in civilian clothing, and Mr. and Mrs. Jack Britton. Sparkman will file a flight plan to the Northeast Airport in the City of Brotherly Love for the Gulfstream. The Gulfstream requires two pilots, hence Miller.

"It is possible that this may elude the attention of the FBI. But in the event it does not, their investigation will cleverly learn that shortly after a pilot appeared with an authorization from the Lorimer Charitable and Benevolent Fund to take possession of their G-III aircraft, three black people, one of them a pilot, having earlier arrived by taxicab from the Hilton Garden Inn—which is right down the beach from here—then got in the G-III and took off on a flight plan to Philadelphia.

"Having cleverly deduced that the object of their 'locate but do not detain' order was not among the trio who boarded the G-III—Colonel Castillo would've had to acquire one helluva dark tan during his short visit to the beach—they then will theorize that he either sneaked aboard the airplane while they weren't looking, or that he left the area by other means, such as an automobile.

"They will probably cover all their bases by having co-workers waiting at the airport in Philly. What those people will see will be Mr. and Mrs. Britton getting off the airplane and being met by Philadelphia police officers. Mr. and

Mrs. Britton then will be taken to the Four Seasons Hotel—their home is *hors de combat,* Colonel Harrison; and so their accommodations will be benevolently covered as long as necessary by the Lorimer Fund—but the FBI won't notice this, as Mr. Britton will have told his former law-enforcement buddies 'lose the Feds,' or words to the effect, a suggestion with which, there being little love lost between the Philadelphia police and the FBI, they will happily comply.

"The Gulfstream will then fly to BWI, where it will be turned over to Signature Flight Support, Inc., for necessary maintenance.

"The more astute among you will have noticed that this series of events leaves Mr. Britton in Philadelphia, where he will see what he can learn from the African-American Lunatics about the chemical laboratory in the Congo. And it leaves Captain Sparkman and Major Miller in Washington, where Miller can take over for Colonel Torine, who will be traveling."

McNab stopped and looked at Miller.

"Surely, Major, after you went and got yourself shot up in The Desert, you didn't think you were going to be running around the Congo bush with Phineas and Uncle Remus, did you?"

He turned to Colonel Hamilton.

"The big one is Uncle Remus, Colonel, and the ugly one Phineas DeWitt." He pointed. "Counting them, that's two of us who know anything about that part of Africa or have ever been there. Now you make it three."

"As a matter of fact, sir," Hamilton said, "I remember seeing Mr. DeWitt. At the Hotel du Lac in Bujumbura, Mr. DeWitt?"

"Yes, sir," DeWitt said. "I stayed there a lot. But I don't remember you."

"I was trying very hard to pass myself off as a Tutsi," Hamilton said.

"That made two of us, sir. I didn't speak Kinyarwanda, so I tried to keep my mouth shut."

"General," Hamilton said, "I'm sure that Mr. DeWitt knows as much about that area as I do, and I am therefore . . ."

"Wondering why I need you? Indulge me a little longer, please, Colonel."

"Yes, sir. You said something about a chemical—"

"What I politely asked you to do, Colonel, was to indulge me a little longer."

"Yes, sir. Sorry, General."

"So we have Britton in Philadelphia, Miller in Washington, and Colonel Castillo—and the Lear—here in Pensacola. By nightfall, I suspect the FBI will have more important things to do than hang around the Pensacola airport hoping for a glance at you. The Gulfstream, they will probably have learned, is in Baltimore. But, as I have been wont to say, people in our business can never have too much in the way of dark nights. So, Charley, wait until dark before you and go out to the airport with the Barlows, Corporal Bradley, and Jack Davidson."

"Yes, sir."

"Two questions. Are you going to have enough security? And can you land at your farm in the dark?"

Castillo glanced at Davidson. "As you know, sir, I've always had to worry a little about Jack, but as long as I have Corporal Bradley, we'll be all right."

Castillo got chuckles from a few. Davidson gave him the finger.

"I'll call somebody—my cousin Fernando, most likely—and have him have somebody light the strip. Worst scenario, I'd have to go into Midland. Lears in Midland go as unnoticed as Hatteras and Bertrams in Lauderdale. Not a problem."

"That brings us to these two," McNab said, nodding at Edgar Delchamps and Alex Darby. "Your call, Charley; who goes where?"

"I think that's Edgar's call," Castillo said.

"Alex to Fulda-slash-Marburg to deal with your guy there," Delchamps said immediately. "Me to Vienna or Budapest or wherever the hell Uncle Billy is. Okay, Alex?"

Darby nodded.

It occurred to Castillo that it was the first time Delchamps had opened his mouth since the session began.

It's not that he's shy—nor is Darby.

For that matter, nobody's shy; more the opposite.

It means they've agreed with everything McNab has said.

God, what a man!

"Communications?" McNab said.

"There's an AFC in Görner's office," Castillo replied, "and I gave one to Sándor Tor."

"We're going to have to do something for Aloysius." He looked at Woods. "Peter, send Mr. Casey a new green hat."

Lieutenant Colonel Peter Woods smiled. "Yes, sir."

"The one he has is a little ratty," Castillo said.

"All communications to me go through D'Allessando," McNab said. "From the moment I walk out that door, I don't know where you are, or what you're doing, or anything about you except that I agree you're not playing with a full deck."

"Yes, sir," Castillo said.

"I presume you two are not going to need any help to get to Germany and wherever Kocian is."

Delchamps and Darby nodded.

"And, Ace, I presume that the Benevolent Fund is going to benevolently provide these two dinosaurs with first-class tickets over there."

"Absolutely, Edgar. How are you fixed for money?"

"Your credit's good," Delchamps said.

McNab looked at Castillo. "If you will be so good as to indulge me a moment longer, Colonel, a few loose ends to tie up. DeWitt and Uncle Remus and you will go back to Bragg with me. At Bragg—" He paused and turned to Hamilton. "How long since you've given a pecker-check, Colonel?"

"It's, uh, been some time, General."

Castillo couldn't tell if Hamilton was pissed, amused, or had thought it was a straight question.

"Well, while we're waiting for the pieces to come together, we'll see if we can't give you some practice. The pieces that have to come together are—this is yours, Uncle Remus—picking the Delta Force shooters."

"Yes, sir."

"And making sure Air Tanzania gets painted."

"Yes, sir."

"All that military crap, Uncle Remus. Shots, last wills and testaments, insurance, all of it. Phineas and Colonel Hamilton will be tied up teaching everybody all about Africa."

"Yes, sir."

"You'd better work out of the Stockade."

"Yes, sir."

"I can't think of anything else. Can anybody?"

No one said a word.

"Now, Colonel Hamilton, thank you for your patience. Do you have any questions?"

"Oh, yes. Do I correctly infer you are planning an operation of some sort in the Democratic Republic of the Congo?"

"Yes, we are."

"May I ask what type of operation?"

"We have reason to believe the Iranians, assisted by the Russians, have a chemical-slash-biological-warfare laboratory-slash-factory there, and we wish to get proof of that to show to the President before the bastards can do us any harm."

"Frankly, sir, I'm delighted to hear that someone agrees with me."

"Excuse me?"

"I passed that—the distinct likelihood of a bio-chem facility in the Congo—to the CIA some time ago. They looked into it and concluded that I was wrong; I thought they were."

"Would you be good enough to amplify that, Colonel?" McNab asked.

"Well—" he began, then stopped. "How much do you know of the subject?"

"Virtually nothing," McNab said.

"Well, as I said before, that's my area of knowledge, in which I have some expertise. I try to keep an eye on it, so to speak. Some time ago, I noticed an anomaly in the production of certain chemicals, especially in Germany, suggesting to me that they were being either consumed in testing or stockpiled, or both."

"What chemicals?" McNab asked softly.

"Would the names be of any use to you, sir?"

"What kind of chemicals?"

"In layman's terms, those used in chemical and/or biological warfare. Forbidden under international treaties. Such as sarin. What really caught my attention was the increased production of DIC—diisopropylcarbodiimide."

"Which is what?"

"In layman's terms, it permits, to varying degrees, the storage of sarin in aluminum."

"Such as a missile head?"

"Or a coffeepot. The point is: If the possession of sarin is against the law, why does one need anything aluminum in which to store it?"

"I take your point."

"There were other areas which attracted my attention: unusual production, again in Germany and India, of the chemical precursors of the polypeptide family, the doxycyclines, trichothecenes, mycotoxins, and so on."

"All poisonous substances?"

"Oh, yes."

"And you informed the CIA?"

"I even suggested to them that if there was activity we should look into, it was taking place at the former German nuclear facilities on the Nava and Aruwimi rivers in the Congo, which is not far from Kisangani, which was formerly Stanleyville. You know, Henry Morton Stanley? 'Doctor Livingstone, I presume?' Stanleyville is where Stanley found Livingstone."

"So I had heard," McNab said. "Why did you think this?"

"Because both types of laboratory operations, nuclear and chemical, require large amounts of water, for cooling and other purposes. I think this is perhaps where the CIA got the idea the old German facilities are now a fish farm; the cooling tanks, etcetera, I suppose could be used for that purpose."

"Who did you deal with at the CIA, Colonel? Do you remember his—or her—name?"

"I didn't deal with anyone at the CIA. I just wrote it up, paper-clipped to it an inter-office memorandum saying it should be sent to the CIA, and put it in my out-box. I'm a scientist, not someone in the intelligence community."

"So you don't know if your reports ever got to the CIA?"

"I simply assume they did. I heard back—I forget how—of the CIA fish-farm theory."

"Colonel," McNab said, "just now you said you were a scientist. You're wearing the caduceus of the Medical Corps . . ."

"I'm a physician."

"And you're wearing the eagles of a colonel, and you said you were West Point '84, which would suggest you're a soldier. Which is it, Colonel?"

"I am a serving officer, a West Pointer, a colonel, who also is a physician. And a bio-chemist, Ph.D. Oxford '86. And a physicist, Ph.D., MIT '93."

McNab nodded. "I'm awed, and there is nothing that should be interpreted as sarcasm in that statement."

"General, with respect, I think I had better call those people now," Hamilton said.

"I was about to suggest that very thing. But on my terms, Colonel, not yours. Unless you want to tell me who they are and have me call them myself?"

"Sir, again, with res—"

"Yeah. I know. But before I have Phineas and Uncle Remus throw you on the floor and hold you down while Barefoot Boy pulls out your fingernails to get you to tell me who 'those people' are, why don't we try this: You get on the telephone to 'those people' and you say you're with me and I have the idea that the Iranians and the Russians are up to something nasty in the Congo. Then ask 'those people' how much you are allowed to cooperate with me, up to and including telling me just who 'those people' are. How about that?"

"Yes, sir," Hamilton said. "But what about the secure telephone, sir?"

"Tell them you don't have time to go to a secure telephone. Tell them if they have a number at which you can call them, we'll put it through the White House switchboard, which is about as secure as it gets."

"That sounds logical, sir."

"There's the telephone," McNab said, pointing.

"With your permission, sir, I'd prefer to use this," Colonel Hamilton said.

He took a cellular telephone from his trousers pocket and walked out onto the balcony, closing the sliding door after him. They saw him punch a long number into the phone.

"Memorized," Dmitri Berezovsky said. "Not autodial."

"I noticed," McNab said.

"You were joking about the fingernails, right?" Sandra Britton asked.

McNab looked at her. "If I thought that would work, he would now look as if he was wearing Red Passion nail polish."

"That is a very interesting man," Svetlana said.

"That has just earned you the award for Understatement of the Week, Sweaty."

" 'Sweaty'?" she repeated with some obvious displeasure.

"Isn't that what our Carlos calls you?"

"He calls me 'Svet.' That is short for—"

"He got you, Sweaty!" Delchamps said.

"I'm good at that," McNab said, smiling. "Didn't our Carlos tell you?"

"He's spending longer on that telephone than setting up a callback," Berezovsky said.

"Yeah," Darby said.

Colonel Hamilton put his cellular telephone back in his pants, slid the door open, and came back into the room.

"They will call me back," he announced. "But I'm afraid they are going to insist on a secure telephone."

"While we're waiting," McNab said, "why don't you tell us how you got all those degrees, Colonel?"

Hamilton nodded. "Yes, sir. Well, right after I graduated from the Point, I was a Rhodes Scholar. I went to Oxford—Mansfield College—with the idea of taking the equivalent of an American master's degree in biochemistry. It was supposed to be for a year.

"It all came surprisingly easy to me, and when they told me I could probably earn a doctorate if I spent another year, I asked the Army for another year.

"And when that was over, I went through the Officer Basic Course at Benning, then applied for and was accepted for jump training. I went through that and was given command of a chemical platoon in the 82nd Airborne at Bragg."

Castillo met Uncle Remus's eyes. Both had the same mental image of the faces of the platoon when they learned their new commander was a tall, skinny, black guy with a Ph.D. who spoke with an English accent and who had graduated from jump school just last week.

"While I was at Bragg," Hamilton went on, "I took some correspondence courses from MIT—"

He stopped when his telephone buzzed.

"Yes?" he said into it, and then, a little surprised, "Very well."

He handed the telephone to McNab, who—causing a momentary look of shock to appear on Hamilton's face—pushed the SPEAKERPHONE button.

"General McNab?" a voice said.

"Yes. Who is this?"

"Under the circumstances, General, I think we can dispense with a secure line."

"Your call."

"I have just instructed Colonel Hamilton to cooperate in every way but one in your current project."

"Thank you."

"He is not authorized to tell you anything about us."

"Okay."

"We really wish you well in this project, General."

McNab held the telephone at arm's length and looked at it.

"Sonofabitch hung up on me!" He then looked around the room and asked, "Anybody recognize that voice? I've heard it before. Goddamn it!"

He slowly walked back and forth in front of the sliding glass doors for thirty seconds or so, obviously searching his audio memory.

Then he turned, put his hands on his hips, and said, "Okay, children. Fun-and-games time is over. Let's get this show on the road! Hubba hubba!"

"Hoo-rah!" Castillo called.

Lieutenant Colonel Woods laughed.

"You'll pay for that, Peter!" McNab said, and without another word marched out of the room.

XVI

[ONE]
Double-Bar-C Ranch
Near Midland, Texas
2305 7 January 2006

The runway lights at the Double-Bar-C were lit as the result of a somewhat less-than-loving, not to mention less-than-civil, conversation between cousins—one Lieutenant Colonel Charley Castillo and one Mr. Fernando Manuel Lopez—some thirty minutes previously:

"Hello?"

"Mr. Fernando Lopez, please. The White House is calling."

"Yeah, sure it is."

"Are you Mr. Lopez?"

"Guilty."

"I have Mr. Lopez for you, Colonel."

"Fernando?"

"Damn it, Gringo. I just this moment fell asleep."

"Thank you for sharing that with me."

"What won't wait until the morning? Or is it already morning?"

"I need the runway lights turned on at the Double-Bar-C."

"Then what you should do is call the ranch and say, 'Turn on the runway lights.'"

"I don't have the number handy."

"You're on your way to the ranch?"

"No. But I thought it would be fun to wake you up and have you turn on the lights to scare hell out of the rattlesnakes keeping warm on it."

"You're not only a wiseass, Gringo, you're a pain in the ass, you know that?"

"I'm thirty minutes out, Fat Boy. Now call the fucking ranch and have the fucking lights lit. And don't let anybody know I'm there."

"Why am I not surprised?"

"If the lights aren't on when I get there, I will tell María you have been chasing blond cocktail waitresses again."

"And you would, you miserable prick. So hang up so I can call."

"It's never a pleasure to talk to you, Lard Ass. Break it down."

When the conversation had been concluded, Svetlana Alekseeva, who was sitting in the co-pilot seat of the Learjet, inquired, "Carlos! Who were you talking to?"

"My cousin, Fernando. He's actually more like my brother. He's a really good guy."

And then he had activated his microphone and politely requested permission from the air traffic controller to close out his flight plan to Midland and instead land at a private field in the vicinity.

Two GMC Yukons were waiting at the hangar for them.

Castillo was the last person off the airplane. When he had closed the stair door, put chocks under the wheels, and slid the heavy hangar doors shut, a short, massive, swarthy woman got out from behind the wheel of one of the Yukons and rushed up to him. She called him "Carlos," took his face in her hands, and kissed him affectionately.

"Svet," Castillo said, "this is Estella. She has been running this place since . . . forever. Estella, these are my friends Susan Barlow and her brother, Tom." He motioned at Davidson and Bradley. "You know Jack and Lester. They'll all be staying with us for a couple of weeks, and we don't want anyone to know."

She didn't seem surprised at the announcement. She wordlessly and formally shook everybody's hands.

"Well," she then said, "come on up to the house, and I'll get you something to eat. Ernesto will get your luggage."

"I'm sorry there wasn't more," Estella, hands on her hips and surveying the table, said after the group had gorged themselves on ham steaks, eggs, and Caesar salad. "But Fernando only called a little while ago."

"It was wonderful," Svetlana said.

"I put Lester and Sergeant Davidson in their usual rooms," Estella announced, "and the gentleman in the last room on the right, and the lady in the room next to him."

To hell with it, Castillo thought. *Bite the bullet.*

I am not going to sneak around my own house.

Besides, Abuela's not here.

He said, "Estella, the lady will be staying with me."

Estella looked at him in disbelief, then crossed herself.

"Estella," Dmitri Berezovsky offered, "I am her brother and, like you, a Christian. I know what that might look like. But I have found some comfort in the Scripture that enjoins us to judge not, lest we be judged."

Estella looked between them.

"We will make sure Doña Alicia does not find out," she said somewhat anxiously. "Or Fernando. Or, God forbid, María!"

"Okay," Castillo said twenty minutes later. "The AFC is up and running. Starting first thing in the morning, it gets monitored twenty-four/seven. And that means we will have to teach Dmitri and Svet how to use it."

"Just Dmitri, my Carlos. Sweaty already knows how to operate it."

"Dmitri, then, will require instruction," Castillo said. "And we'll have to come up, Sergeant Major, with a duty roster."

Davidson nodded.

"And after breakfast tomorrow, having come up with a necessary equipment list—printers, scanners, tape recorders, etcetera—and having submitted same to Corporal Bradley for his approval, either Davidson or Bradley or both will drive into Midland and find an office supply or something similar to acquire what's needed.

"We'll then set up a CP in the library. That being accomplished, we can then all sit around with our thumbs in our . . . ears, waiting for the AFC to go off reporting how others are doing what I'd really prefer to be doing myself."

"Come on, Charley," Davidson said. "You heard what Phineas said. If we went over there we'd wind up in some cannibal's pot."

"You can really be stupid sometimes, my Carlos," Svetlana said.

Castillo raised an eyebrow at her. After a moment, he said, "And on that romantic note, I'm going to bed."

"Is this the place where I am not supposed to sleep?" Svetlana asked five minutes later.

Castillo didn't reply. He went into the bathroom. When he came out ten minutes later, Svetlana walked wordlessly past him into the bathroom.

When she hadn't returned ten minutes later, Castillo considered the pros and cons of going in after her.

He had just about decided that that would not be a very good idea when she suddenly appeared nude—then rushed across the room and jumped in beside him in the bed.

"This place is like Siberia. I am freezing. If you were a gentleman, you would make me warm."

That, Romeo, is as close to a peace offering as I'm going to get. . . .

He hugged her.

"Don't let this go to your head," she said a moment later, "but you were an adorable little boy."

"I know."

"That's not what you were supposed to say." She momentarily laid an icy hand on his crotch.

He squirmed. "Jesus!"

"You're going to have to learn not to blaspheme," she said.

"What was I supposed to say?"

" 'How do you know?' And then I would say, 'I was looking at your pictures on the wall.' "

"What is this leading up to?"

"Does it always shrink when it is cold?"

"Why don't you try putting a *warm* hand on it and see what happens?"

Svetlana vigorously rubbed her hands together, then did so.

After a moment, she declared, "Ah. Is much better."

"Yeah."

"When you were a little boy, did you ever think you would lie here one day with a beautiful woman putting her warmed hand on your you-know-what?"

"Every night from the time I was thirteen."

She squeezed. "When I was thirteen, I wanted to be a nun. I wanted to marry Christ."

"And then you turned fourteen, and that didn't seem like such a good idea?"

She made a soft grunt and after a long moment said, "Why is your farm in the middle of an oil field?"

"It's a ranch, not a farm. You raise cattle on ranch. And things like corn on a farm. Unless you have milk cows; then it's a dairy farm."

"And then they found oil on it?"

"Actually, my great-grandfather found the oil. It was there all the time, but he didn't know about it until he put down the first hole. They call it the Permian Basin. You really want to talk about this?"

"You have some income from this oil?"

"Sure."

"Then it is *your* oil? Not the government's?"

"They call that the concept of private property. It goes hand in hand with capitalism. And speaking of hand in hand . . ."

"Stop that! What do you think you're doing?"

"At least I warmed my hands first."

"And what I heard about those newspapers in Europe—somebody said you own them?"

"Did they?"

"Oh, God, don't do that! They'll hear us all over the house."

"Let jealousy eat their hearts out."

"You're rich, my Carlos?"

"We say 'comfortable.' "

"Oh, I am glad!"

"And I'm pleased you're glad."

"Now I'll never have to worry that you say you love me only because of my money."

"Actually, you have certain other attributes that attract me."

"Oh, God, when you do that, I go crazy!"

"I've noticed."

[TWO]
Double-Bar-C Ranch
Near Midland, Texas
0715 8 January 2006

Svetlana decided to let her Carlos sleep. She knew that he was exhausted both emotionally and physically, maybe especially physically. And not only because he'd done all that flying all over in such a short period of time.

My God, I love that man!

After their last romp—whenever that had been; three, three-thirty, four in the morning—he had rolled onto his back, closed his eyes, and not moved since.

He hadn't even stirred when the airplane landed, making enough noise to wake her from her sound sleep.

Svetlana did not know what time it was. She had been confused by the one-hour time difference between Fort Lauderdale and Pensacola, which were both in the same state. And then, when they had flown west in the Lear—which Carlos had said was even faster than his bigger Gulfstream—she had been confused again, because they had covered far more distance than inside Florida—and logically that would indicate several time zones—yet Midland and Pensacola shared the same time.

The only thing she knew for sure was that she desperately needed a cup of tea and maybe a piece of toast or something. Then she would come back to bed and go to sleep again, curled up against her Carlos.

Carefully curled up, so as not to wake him.

In this situation, not only would taking a shower be unnecessary, but the noise it would make would almost certainly wake him. When the water closet flushed, it sounded like a fire hydrant exploding.

That then raised the question of dress. It simply made no sense to get dressed to sneak quietly into the kitchen and make a cup of tea and maybe some toast, then come back to the bedroom only to get undressed again.

She went snooping, and the solution she found pleased her.

In the first closet she came to, she found a bathrobe hanging from a hook. It was old, well-worn and frayed, but it was wonderfully soft to the touch, and when she held it up and examined it she saw that it was clean, too. And then she was even more pleased to finally recognize it for what it was—from Carlos's military college. It read "USMA" in large letters on the back, and there was an insignia, sort of a coat of arms, on the breast.

She put it on, and smiled warmly at the thought of wearing Carlos's military college bathrobe.

Is nice.

Intimate. . . .

She did not put on any underwear. She disliked putting on underwear once she'd taken it off, and it really didn't make much sense to put on fresh linen without showering first, only to have to take it off ten minutes later.

She opened the bedroom door and looked and listened before finally going into the corridor. Then, barefoot, she ran down it until she reached the kitchen.

She listened at the door to make sure no one was inside, then quickly stepped inside, quietly clicking the door closed behind her.

Then she turned—and came face-to-face with three unfamiliar people who were sitting at the kitchen table.

One was a very large, swarthy man. The other two were women—a dark, attractive Latina a little younger than the man and an erect, silver-haired lady who appeared to be in her late sixties, maybe a little older.

Svetlana smiled awkwardly and nodded.

The older lady stood and smiled back. "Well, my dear. I see that Randy was right on the money. He said you were 'a real looker.' "

Svetlana said nothing.

"I'm Alicia Castillo, my dear. Carlos's grandmother."

Svetlana said nothing.

Doña Alicia gestured. "And this is my other grandson, Fernando, and his wife, María."

"You talked to Randy?" Svetlana suddenly said.

"As soon as he got back to Fort Rucker, he called me. He was quite excited to report that Carlos 'has a girlfriend. A real looker.' "

Svetlana said nothing.

"He said your name was Svetlana—what a pretty name!—and he told me that my grandson was no longer alone, and wasn't that great?"

"Randy is a nice boy, a very nice boy," Svetlana said. "And you're his great-grandmother?"

"He calls me Abuela."

Svetlana sighed. "The bull is out of the pen, or whatever Carlos is always saying. I stupidly let it out when I met Randy. But now that I think about it, I am glad that I did."

"The cow is out of the barn?" Fernando said.

"Yes," Svetlana said.

"Randy knows?" Fernando pursued.

Svetlana nodded.

"Oh, my," Doña Alicia said. "How did that go?"

"Very well. They had a long talk, and agreed to keep the secret."

Fernando grunted. "It was bound to come out. It's hardly going to be a 'secret' long."

"Goddamn you, Fernando," María said furiously. "I knew it all along, and you kept saying I had a dirty, suspicious mind."

"Where is the Gringo?" Fernando asked.

"Fernando!" Doña Alicia said warningly.

"Who?" Svetlana asked.

"Carlos Guillermo Castillo, or Karl Wilhelm von und zu Gossinger, or whatever name he's using today."

"I let him sleep; he was exhausted."

"I can imagine," María said with a knowing look, then sipped her coffee.

Svetlana shrugged. "I guess that bull is out of the barn, too."

"Is Estella aware of the sleeping arrangements?" Fernando asked.

Svetlana nodded.

He looked at Doña Alicia and grinned. "Well, that explains the missing housekeeper, doesn't it, Abuela? She heard us land, saw you get off the plane, and decided that anywhere else would be the safest place to be."

The kitchen door opened again. Corporal Lester Bradley, USMC, walked in.

"Well, the Marines have landed," Fernando said, "but I don't think the situation is well in hand."

"Be quiet, Fernando," Doña Alicia said. "Hello, Lester."

"Ma'am," Bradley said politely.

"*Semper Fi,* Les," Fernando said.

"I told you to be quiet," Doña Alicia said. "What can we do for you, Lester?"

Bradley turned to Svetlana.

"Colonel, do you know where the colonel is?"

"What did he call her? 'Colonel'?" María said.

"The colonel is looking for his goddamn bathrobe, that's where he is," Castillo called from the corridor, and then came into the kitchen, buttoning the shirt he'd worn the previous day. Its tail covered—mostly—his undershorts.

Svetland pulled the robe tighter around her as she crossed her arms. "Oops!"

"Surprise, surprise, Casanova," Fernando said.

Bradley said, "Sir, Mr. D'Allessando's on the AFC. He says it's important."

"Stall him for a couple of minutes, Les."

"Yes, sir."

Lester quickly disappeared from the room.

"I didn't know you were here, Abuela," Castillo said.

"We sort of guessed that," María said.

"Or you," Castillo added.

"We were just having a nice chat with Svetlana, Carlos dear," Doña Alicia said. "Fernando and María were nice enough to fly me up here, and now they're about to leave."

"And you're not?" Fernando asked.

"I need to talk to Carlos," Doña Alicia said. "Privately."

Fernando, to no one in particular, said, "That's what she used to say in the old days when the Gringo was caught, so to speak, with his hand in the cookie jar. It means she's about to drag him to the stable and have at him with a quirt."

"I'll have someone drive me home," Doña Alicia said. "You and María want to get back to the children, I'm sure."

"I wouldn't think of leaving until I hear how the two colonels met," María said. "You're old Army buddies, is that it?"

"Something like that," Castillo said. "I've got a plane here; I'll take Abuela home."

"I saw the Lear in the hangar," Fernando said. "What happened to your G-III?"

"I've got to take that call," Castillo said, avoiding the question. "You're going to have to excuse me."

"May I stay, Carlos?" Doña Alicia asked.

He looked at her for a moment.

"You know you don't have to ask, Abuela," he said finally.

[THREE]
0735 8 January 2006

"Sorry to keep you waiting, Vic," Castillo said. "I was in bed."

"I heard about that," D'Allessando said. "When do I get to meet her?"

"Soon enough. Look, Lester's rounding up the others; it'll take a minute."

"Everybody knows everything, right?"

"Right."

"You were just a wee slip of a lad when I taught you that," D'Allessando said. "And you still had hair, Vic. It was a long time ago."

"Actually, I thought about those days this morning, while jogging around Smoke Bomb Hill with Colonel Hamilton."

"And the general?"

"I have no idea who you're talking about, Colonel," D'Allessando said.

Castillo waved for Bradley to bring the crowd into the room.

"Everybody's here, Vic," Castillo said.

Including my grandmother, whom I'm not going to run off; she's not a Russian spy. I'm sleeping with the Russian spy. Who is here with her brother, also a Russian spy, who just shook hands with my grandmother.

"Hello, one and all," D'Allessando said. "Our problem is Colonel Hamilton, with whom, as I just told Charley, I took a jog down memory lane around Smoke Bomb Hill. He was crushed to learn that the barrack in which he once commanded a platoon was long ago torn down.

"He also told me, 'Of course I'm going into the Congo.' "

Castillo said, "Absolutely out of the question. He can go as far as Bujumbura, and even that makes me uncomfortable."

"Well, you're going to have to tell him that, Charley."

"I'm a lowly lieutenant colonel. He's a more than a little starchy full bird. Get McNab to tell him."

"Get who?"

"General McNab."

"I thought he told you . . ."

"Told me what?"

"The general doesn't know you anymore," D'Allessando said. "He hasn't seen you since you went off to Washington a long time ago, where he hears you went off the deep end. He knows you snatched two Russian spies away from the CIA and won't give them back. He thinks you're a disgrace to the uniform and has already taken steps to see that you're booted out of the Army. He wouldn't talk to you even if, by some wild stretch of the imagination, you had the effrontery to try calling him."

Castillo saw the look on Svetlana's face and then on Abuela's.

"I'd forgotten," Castillo said.

I remember him telling me, "From the moment I walk out that door, I don't know where you are, or what you're doing, or anything about you except that I agree you're not playing with a full deck."

But, until just now, what it meant just didn't sink in.

"Keep it in mind, Charley," D'Allessando said.

"Where is Colonel Hamilton?"

"I choppered him out to Camp Mackall. I thought maybe seeing what the guys in the last stages of training have to go through might discourage him. I'm not holding my breath, Charley."

"Get him back. Get him on the horn. How long will that take?"

"An hour, give or take."

"Do it. Anything else?"

"Air Tanzania is all painted and ready to go. Uncle Remus is in the process of picking shooters; he's almost finished, he said. The maps we got from the Air Force at Hurlburt have been digitalized and sent to you. Lester didn't tell you?"

"Not yet. I'm going to have to go buy printers—"

"And/or some external drives. Those things do eat up the bytes."

"I remember. That it?"

"I'll call you when I get Hamilton back to civilization. D'Allessando off."

"Russian spies?" Doña Alicia asked. "General Naylor said something about that."

"*General Naylor* said something?"

"He came to see me. Very upset."

"Well, Abuela, I'm as anxious to hear about that as you are to hear about the Russian spies. But for right now, as I go to take my morning shower, you'll have to be satisfied with me pointing them out to you."

He pointed.

"Oh, my!" Doña Alicia said.

"One of them is not only a Russian spy, but steals people's personal robes."

"I'll go find Estella and get some breakfast started," Doña Alicia said.

[FOUR]
0840 8 January 2006

"Actually, Carlos," Doña Alicia said as she poured tea into Svetlana's cup, "General Naylor got quite emotional toward the end. He said he felt responsible for so much that's happened to you in the Army."

"I would love to have seen that," Castillo said. " 'Old Stone Face' emotional?"

"He said that he should have known the Army would do something—because of your father and the Medal of Honor—like send you to the Desert War before you were prepared, and done something to stop it."

Castillo shook his head. "Fernando was over there, and he was even less prepared for that war than I was. I knew more about flying helicopters than he did about commanding a platoon of tanks."

"And then he said—and this surprised me, because I always thought they were great friends—that his greatest regret was in sending you to General McNab after you were shot down and they gave you the medal. He said that once you were 'corrupted' by General McNab, everything followed. I thought 'corrupted' was a very strong term."

"Just to keep the record straight, Abuela, they gave me the medal for *not* getting shot down. And Naylor sent me to McNab to keep them from putting me in another Apache, which he correctly suspected they would do. I really wasn't qualified to fly Apaches, and if I had kept it up, which I would have been stupid enough to do, I probably would have killed myself. General Naylor's conscience should be clear on that score."

She looked at him but didn't say anything.

Castillo went on: "And General McNab didn't corrupt me, Jack Davidson corrupted me—"

"Go to hell, Charley," Davidson said, laughing.

"—because every second lieutenant is taught to find a good senior NCO, then do what he says and follow his example. And what this corrupter of young officers did was teach me how to blow safes and steal whiskey."

Davidson laughed again.

Doña Alicia shook her head. "Carlos, I'm being serious here."

"So am I, Abuela. Go on, Jack, fess up. Tell Doña Alicia that you talked me into sling-loading a dune buggy under McNab's Huey so we could 'reconnoiter the American embassy in Kuwait by air and land before the Marines could get there.' And that when we got to the embassy, you blew the safe and stole all the diplomats' whiskey."

"Really?" Svetlana said. She did not seem disapproving.

"He's an evil man, Sweaty," Castillo said. "Rotten to the core."

"Sweaty?" Doña Alicia repeated.

"Was that before or after you made the Russian colonels sing 'The Internationale'?" Dmitri Berezovsky asked.

"What?" Doña Alicia asked.

"A couple of days after, Colonel," Davidson said. "We needed a little something to drink to celebrate the Well Done message we got from Bush One."

"What Russian colonels singing?" Doña Alicia asked.

Berezovsky and Davidson related the Russian and American versions of the story.

"I should be ashamed of myself," Doña Alicia then said. "My curiosity always seems to get out of control. We were talking about how bad General Naylor feels about your . . . *retirement*."

"He shouldn't," Castillo said seriously. "He went along with Montvale because that's what he thought his duty called for him to do. I did the same thing; I did what I thought was my duty. I'm not angry with Naylor, Abuela. Really. He's always been one of the good guys."

"What are you going to do when this is over and . . ."

"When I am 'Lieutenant Colonel Castillo (Retired)'? Right now what I'm thinking is that I'll move into Sweaty's new house in the Pilar Golf and Polo Country Club and maybe even learn how to play golf. Or polo. Or both."

My post-retirement plans are a little vague, probably because I don't want to even think about them.

What the hell am I going to do?

I can't imagine playing golf or polo. . . .

"What about coming back here?" Doña Alicia asked.

Lester came into the kitchen, saving him from having to answer the question.

"Mr. D'Allessando's got Colonel Hamilton on the AFC for you, Colonel."

And what happens to you, Lester, when this merry little band folds its tent and steals off into the night?

"Thanks, Lester."

He motioned for everybody to follow him into the library, where Bradley had the AFC set up.

[FIVE]
0855 8 January 2006

When Castillo walked into the library, he saw that the first steps to convert it into the Command Post for what he was now thinking of as Operation Fish Farm had been taken by Corporal Bradley. The AFC had been set up on a table near a window. A bed for the 24/7 posting had been dragged in from somewhere and there was a coffeemaker on another table against the wall.

Chairs had been arranged around the table, and there were lined pads and several ballpoint pens on each pad. Aside from that, there was nothing on the table but Castillo's and Davidson's notebook computers and the AFC handset. The rest of what they were going to need was going to have to wait until Lester or Jack went shopping.

Castillo took the seat at the head of the table, with his back to the fireplace, which held a crackling fire. Dmitri Berezovsky took the seat on the left side of the table. Davidson slipped into the seat across from him. Svetlana and Doña Alicia sat together on the left at the other end of the table, and Bradley sat across from them.

A Winchester lever-action .44-40 rifle was mounted on pegs above the fireplace. Large, accurate-scale models of a U.S. Army AH-64 Apache attack helicopter and an M1A1 Abrams tank sat on the mantelpiece under it. Castillo had bought the Apache model in the bookstore at Fort Rucker shortly after having been rated in that aircraft and had it shipped home. Fernando had done about the same thing with the Abrams model: bought it at the Fort Knox bookstore and sent it home just before shipping out for the Desert War.

The Winchester was a family treasure, having been used on many dozen occasions to protect the Double-Bar-C and its cattle from marauding Apache Indians.

The M1A1 Abrams was named for one of the Army's most distinguished Armor generals, Creighton W. Abrams. Among his great achievements, Abrams, as a lieutenant colonel, had broken through the German ring surrounding Bastogne to rescue the 101st Airborne.

The AH-64, an instructor at Rucker had told Castillo before he'd even been allowed to get close to one of them, was named after the Apache Indians in tribute to their characteristics as warriors. Castillo had had trouble believing his ears—and even more keeping his mouth shut.

He had thought of that instructor every time he had climbed into an AH-64 Apache thereafter, wondering again and again if the Pentagon chairwarmer—or chair-warmers, plural—who had given it that name because of the warrior characteristics of the Apache Indians had done enough research. For example, to learn, as Castillo well knew, that the Apaches had expressed their contempt for settlers against whom they waged war by capturing settlers and hanging them alive upside-down over a small fire and slowly roasting their brains. Or, for example, leaving their captors spread-eagle in the desert sun with eyelids hacked off and enough small bloodletting incisions made in the genital area to attract ants and other desert fauna.

And now Castillo thought of chair-warmer types again as he reached for the SPEAKERPHONE button on the AFC.

"Good morning, sir. Castillo here."

"So it says on this amazing device," Colonel Hamilton replied. "I am taking Mr. D'Allessando's word for it that we are now in Class One encryption."

"Yes, sir, we are."

"I have been hoping you would get in contact, Colonel Castillo, inasmuch as General McNab has informed me the press of his other duties forces him to leave this operation in your hands, so to speak."

"Yes, sir. That is my understanding."

"Are you alone, Colonel? Mr. D'Allessando suggested you might wish him to be privy to this, and he's with me."

"I have my people with me, sir, and we're on speakerphone."

"Specifically, our new Russian friends?"

"Yes, sir."

"Colonel Berezovsky, I regret I didn't have more time to talk with you and your charming sister when we were in Florida," Hamilton said. "But if you will continue to be available while we're doing this, no real harm done."

"Good morning, Colonel," Berezovsky said. "We will be here."

"There are some things that have to be done in the immediate future, Castillo, before Mr. DeWitt and I go into the Congo."

"Sir, I wanted to talk to you about that," Castillo said.

"About what?"

"Sir, what I'm thinking is that it would better if you didn't actually go into the Congo."

"That's absurd. Wherever did you come up with that?"

"What I was thinking would make more sense, sir, would be if you remained outside the Congo—say, in Tanzania or Chad. . . ."

"I repeat, that's absurd."

"Colonel, you're too valuable an asset to be put at risk."

"I will make that judgment, Colonel. I have made that judgment. Now, as I was saying—"

"Sir, with respect, I must insist."

"Colonel, you are in no position to *insist* on anything."

"Sir, as you told me, General McNab has been forced to place this operation in my hands."

"What General McNab said to me, Colonel, was that in the inevitable event we should find ourselves in disagreement, we could not look to him for resolution; we would have to do that ourselves."

"Yes, sir, I understand that. Sir, may I say that I regard myself as the operation commander and you, sir, as very likely our most important asset, and that it is therefore my responsibility to protect you to the best of my ability."

"What did you say your class was? At the Academy?"

" 'Ninety, sir."

"Then I can't believe you said what you just said. You're a West Pointer."

"Yes, sir. I am."

"Well, Colonel, unless the course of instruction at our alma mater has dramatically changed since you and I last marched across our beloved plain above the Hudson, they are still teaching that he who is senior is in command."

No shit, Hamilton!

And no one is more senior than the commander in chief.

And the President is my senior—but I damn well can't say that.

I've got to somehow beat this sonofabitch at his own game . . . but how?

"Sir, with respect, I don't think that applies when one of the officers is of the combat arms and the other in the medical corps. In that situation, the senior combat arms officer is in command."

"Good God, Castillo! You didn't think I was going to go into the Congo wearing a Red Cross and caduceus—caduci? Is that the plural? I never seem to remember—and claiming the protection of the Geneva and other applicable conventions, did you? I'm not out of my mind. I'm going in armed as heavily as I can arrange. Mr. D'Allessando is taking me out and teaching me to fire the Mini Uzi as soon as we finish this conversation."

Berezovsky saw the look on Castillo's face.

He first laid a gentle hand on Castillo's wrist, and when Castillo looked at him, Berezovsky signaled *Slow down, calm down, take it easy* all with one motion of his hand and a gentle, understanding smile.

"That's very good of Mr. D'Allessando, sir."

D'Allessando's voice, his tone very serious, came over the speaker: "I always try to be helpful, Colonel Castillo. You know that."

Hamilton went on: "So let's clear the air between us, Castillo. My view of our relationship is this: When my people . . ."

You can stick "your people" up your ass, Hamilton!

I've had enough of your secret "protectors"!

". . . authorized my participation in this operation, it was understood between us that General McNab was in command. Now that the other calls upon his time have taken him out of the picture, command thus falls to the next senior officer, which happens to be me. I will, of course, defer to your judgment in those areas of your expertise and seek your counsel. Now, Colonel, do you have any trouble with that?"

Berezovsky touched Castillo's wrist again and shook his head.

"No, sir, I do not."

Berezovsky gave Charley a thumbs-up.

Charley looked at Svetlana. He couldn't tell if she felt sorry for him or thought what was going on was just short of hilarious.

"Fine, Colonel Castillo. On reflection, I'm glad this came up when it did, rather than later. Now, as to what has to be done."

"Yes, sir."

"Mr. DeWitt and I have to go to Washington. My people have arranged for visas for us—it usually takes weeks, I was told—for not only Tanzania but for Rwanda and Burundi, and—this should please you, Castillo—for the Democratic Republic of the Congo as well. But they cannot get around the requirement that the passport must be presented by the holder—or is that the holdee?—personally."

"Then I have to go to Fort Dietrich to pick up my equipment."

"Your equipment, sir?"

"Yes. It will be taken, Mr. D'Allessando assures me, to Africa aboard your airplane with the 'shooters.' I had never heard that term before, but, especially after what I saw at Camp Mackall just now, I'm rather assured by what it connotes."

"Sir, what sort of equipment are we talking about?"

"My testing equipment. There are three rather large soft-sided suitcases. Getting them through customs would have posed a major problem, but your shooter's airplane has solved that. Getting them from Fort Dietrich here is the instant problem."

"Sir, I can—"

"Mr. D'Allessando suggests that Mr. DeWitt and I leave Bragg and fly to Washington today. There is a Delta flight at 1620 to Washington, via Atlanta."

Castillo thought quickly, then said, "As usual, Colonel, Mr. D'Allessando knows what should be done. And I'll have Major Miller—you remember him, sir?"

"Yes. The officer with the injured knee."

"I'll have Major Miller meet your plane, sir."

"That's very kind of you, Colonel, but I can make it from Reagan to my home without assistance, and I'll be happy to have Mr. DeWitt's company. It'll give us a chance to get to know one another, so to speak, before our trip."

"Sir, with respect, this is my area of expertise."

Hamilton was silent a moment, and apparently remembered his offer to listen to suggestions. "Go on, Colonel."

"I will have Major Miller meet you, sir. We have a house in Alexandria—for that matter, we keep a suite at the Mayflower Hotel—where I'm sure you would be comfortable. It's central—"

"I know where it is, Colonel," Hamilton interrupted. "In some circles, it's known as the Motel Monica Lewinsky."

"Yes, sir, I'd heard that. Major Miller can take you to the various embassies, and then out to Fort Dietrich for your equipment."

"How are we going to get that back here to Fort Bragg, Castillo? Have you given that any thought?"

"If you'll bear with me a moment, sir?"

"Go ahead."

"Major Miller will then take the equipment to Baltimore, where a plane will be waiting to bring you and Mr. DeWitt—and, of course, your equipment—back to Bragg."

"Is there some reason that I don't know why Mr. DeWitt and I should come back to Fort Bragg?"

Shit.

"No, sir. I didn't think that through."

"Obviously." He paused dramatically. "Now, once we have our visas, we can be on our way."

"Yes, sir. Major Miller will also arrange your transportation to Africa."

"That would be helpful."

"Mr. D'Allessando will inform Miller of your ETA at Reagan," Castillo said.

There was a long pause as both men thought. Finally, Colonel Hamilton broke it: "That would seem to be it, wouldn't you say, Castillo?"

"I can't think of anything else, sir."

"We'll be in touch, of course."

"Yes, sir."

"How does one hang this thing up, Mr. D'Allessando?"

[SIX]
0940 8 January 2006

"I know what you're thinking, Carlos," Dmitri Berezovsky said after Castillo had set things up with Miller. "But that could have gone wrong and it didn't."

"I thought you done good, Charley," Davidson said, then added admiringly: "He *is* one starchy sonofabitch, ain't he?"

"Starch melts in hot water. Like in a cannibal's pot?"

Berezovsky chuckled but said: "I have the feeling the colonel knows how to handle the cannibals."

Castillo looked at him and shook his head. "Well, now that your boundless optimism has removed that weight from my shoulders, we can turn to Bradley's shopping list." He looked at him. "What did you come up with, Les?"

"Sir, while I know what we should have in terms of equipment capability, I'm afraid I haven't been able to convert that into what we need in terms of specific equipment that might—or might not—be available in an Office Depot or Radio Shack store."

"Which, off the top of my head, Les, means that you don't get to go to bed until after you've gone shopping. Sorry about that. Let me see what you have."

Bradley handed him a sheet of paper. Castillo looked at it a moment, then tossed it onto the table.

"I don't know what I'm looking at, and it just occurred to me—some of you may have noticed that I am not functioning too well in the I'm-on-top-of-everything department—that when you don't know something it usually helps to ask somebody who does."

He leaned forward and touched a button on the AFC handset.

"C. G. Castillo. Dr. Casey. Encryption Level One."

"One moment, please, Colonel," a sultry, electronically generated voice replied. "I will attempt to connect you."

The voice of Aloysius Francis Casey, Ph.D.—in an interesting mixture of the accents of a Boston Irish "Southie" and a Southwesterner—came over the speaker ten seconds later.

"Hey, Charley. What the hell are you doing twenty-two-point-five miles outside of Midland, Texas?"

How the hell does he know that?

"Good morning, Dr. Casey."

"You call me that one more time, and I'll not only hang up but will make the handset blow up in your ear."

"Sorry."

"You're forgiven. I know you can't handle the booze. I can't detonate the handset—but that's a thought; I may work on that—but that GPS function works all right, doesn't it? Providing you are twenty-two-point-five miles from Midland, Texas."

"That's where I am."

"I can whittle down that tenth-of-a-mile indicator some—probably to within a couple of meters—when I have more time to fiddle with it. What can I do for you, Charley?"

"I'm about to send Lester shopping in Radio Shack or someplace—"

"The Boy Jarhead is there? *Semper Fi,* Les!"

"Good morning, Dr. Casey," Bradley said.

"You can call me that. You Gyrenes should always show a little respect for people like me."

Bradley grinned at the term Marines normally took some offense at. "Yes, sir."

"Charley, you're sending Les shopping for what?"

"We need storage devices to receive a lot of data from a long way away from one AFC to another—maybe multiple more AFCs. So they'll have to be high speed."

"And portable? Self-powered and/or uninterruptible battery powered for at least a couple of hours?"

"All of the above."

"And what else?"

"High-speed printers with lots of resolution for photos and maps. And a similar scanner or three, ditto. I need to keep in contact with one—or two—teams of shooters and a couple of people maybe running around by themselves."

"Charley, the limiting factor is the speed of the relay in the satellites. I have to run them a lot slower than their capacity because of the equipment on the ground—equipment I didn't make. I'm getting the idea you're about to run an op?"

"Yes, we are. Operation Fish Farm."

"I think I know what you need, Charley. No problem."

There was a long silence. Then Castillo said, "You are going to tell me what it is, right, *Aloysius*?"

"You'll see what it is when I get there. If it doesn't work, we'll work on it until we get it right."

"I called to ask you to tell me what we need, not with my hand out."

"Is there an airport any closer to where you are than Midland? Where do I tell the pilot to go?"

"Home. You go home after you tell me what we need. Then Les will go buy it."

"Like hell he will. Now, where do I tell the pilot to go?"

Castillo shook his head, but he was smiling. "You have my coordinates?"

"Yeah. Like I told you, within a tenth of a mile and maybe five hundred feet altitude."

"There's a strip three-tenths of a mile to the south."

"Will it take a Gulfstream V, or should I bring something smaller?"

"It'll take a G-Five, but I can't get something that big in my hangar, and if you park it here, people might get curious."

"That kind of an op, huh? No problem. I'll just have them drop me off—not to worry, they won't remember where—and worry about getting back to Vegas later. It's seven hundred nautical miles. Figure an hour to get to the airport and off the ground and an hour and three-quarters in the air. Add all that up, Charley, and I'll see you then. Casey out."

Castillo pushed a button, turning off the AFC speakerphone function.

"You really have such interesting friends, Carlos," Svetlana said. "That *was* the Casey of the AFC Corporation?"

"You know about him, huh, Svet? What that was was a very lonely man—his wife just died—who I think I just made very happy. He's sitting all alone in a house about twice the size of the one in Golf and Polo, or vice versa, that you like so much, on several hundred hectares of very expensive real estate overlooking Las Vegas and of course the AFC labs and plants."

"I don't understand," Berezovsky said.

"When Aloysius was a kid, Colonel," Davidson offered, "he was in the Vietnam War, the commo—communications—sergeant on a Special Forces A-Team operating black in Cambodia and other places. When he gets here, you will learn how he almost won that war all by himself. He never really took off the suit."

"What does that mean?" Svetlana asked.

"He still thinks of himself as a special operator," Castillo said.

"And Charley just told him he could come out and play. No, not play. This is for real, and that makes it better; he can tell us young guys how to do an operation the right way. For Aloysius, that's better than Christmas, his birthday, and Saint Patrick's Day all rolled into one."

"He's stopped talking to Billy Waugh," Castillo said. "Did you hear that?"

Davidson nodded. "Uh-huh."

"Isn't that the fellow who caught Carlos the Jackal?" Berezovsky asked.

"One and the same," Davidson said. "Aloysius and Billy were young green beanies together, and Billy's still out there—the last I heard he was in Afghanistan again—going after the bad guys. Meanwhile, Aloysius is behind a desk—and can't stand that Billy isn't pushing a walker rather than making HALO jumps."

"How old are they?" Castillo mused. "Seventy-five, anyway. Pushing eighty."

"Then they ought to have enough sense to stand down," Svetlana said. "If they're that old."

"And do what?" Berezovsky said. "The American general Patton said it, Svet. The only good death for a soldier is to die from the last bullet fired in the last battle."

Castillo said, "How about me having a heart attack on the ninth green, or whatever they call it, of Golf and Polo, and then you having one trying to load me into the golf cart? That way, we could go out together and wouldn't have to look for a job. Or play golf."

"I think I'd rather take that last bullet," Berezovsky said. "Even though it no longer seems we have that option."

"Or we could go fishing in that lake with Aleksandr, fall out of the boat and drown," Castillo said.

"Your William Colby went out that way," Berezovsky said.

"Who?" Svetlana said.

"He was a director of Central Intelligence," Berezovsky said.

"And he fell out of his canoe," Castillo said. "And drowned."

"I think I'd prefer the bullet," Berezovsky said.

"Me, too," Castillo said. "All things considered. God knows I can't see myself on a golf course."

"The both of you make me sick!" Svetlana said furiously. "May God forgive you both!"

She stormed out of the library.

"What the hell's the matter with her?" Castillo asked.

"She's a woman," Berezovsky said. "I suspect your learning about women is going to be an interesting experience for you. Painful, but interesting."

[SEVEN]
1250 8 January 2006

Casey's Gulfstream V—which Castillo thought was both beautiful and probably carried the most advanced avionics in the world—touched smoothly down, turned at the end of the strip, and taxied back to the hangar.

The stair door opened and Aloysius Francis Casey, Ph.D., came down the steps carrying an open laptop computer. He was wearing clothing not often seen in South Boston: a Stetson hat, Western World ostrich-skin boots, a sheepskin-lined denim jacket, and matching trousers.

He saluted. Castillo returned it.

"We cheated death again," Casey announced triumphantly, then nodded at the computer. "This little sonofabitch was right on the money."

He handed the laptop to Lester Bradley.

"You can carry this. I wouldn't want a Marine to rupture himself trying to carry anything heavier."

"Yes, sir," Bradley said. He looked at the screen. "Dr. Casey, why does this show we're in Dallas?"

Casey took a quick, shocked look at the screen.

"You little sonofabitch, you got me!" Casey said approvingly.

A man wearing the shoulder boards of a first officer came down the stairs carrying a large cardboard box, followed by a man wearing the four-stripe shoulder boards of a captain and also carrying a large cardboard box.

"That's the delicate stuff," Casey barked. "Be careful with it."

"Yes, sir," they said in unison as they headed for one of the Yukons. Bradley went to the nearest and opened the rear door.

"Where'd you get the cowboy suit?" Castillo asked.

"Weren't you paying attention in the Q course when they said you should always try to blend into the native population? And this is Texas, right? At least Dallas, if one were to believe the Boy Marine."

Castillo chuckled.

"Well, hello," Casey said, having spotted Svetlana.

"I like your cowboy suit," Svetlana said. "Carlos, I want one just like that."

"*Aloysius*, this is Susan Barlow," Castillo said. "And her brother, Tom."

"You don't sound like a Texan," Casey said. "But as pretty as you are, you can sound like anything you want."

"My grandmother's in the house, setting up lunch," Castillo said.

"Your *grandmother*?"

"We need all the help we can get," Castillo said.

"And here I am," Casey said. "Let's get this crap off the airplane."

The "crap off the airplane" nearly filled both Yukons.

Less than an hour after it touched down, Casey's Gulfstream went wheels-up.

"What we're going to need before too long are a couple of large, very large, monitors," Casey announced. "Better, three. Better yet, four. That's presuming the Marine Corps doesn't smash everything taking it out of the boxes."

He nodded toward Bradley, who was half inside one of Casey's large cardboard boxes that crowded the library.

"Not to worry, sir. I know how delicate vacuum tubes are."

"*Vacuum tubes?*" Casey asked incredulously, then said, "The Boy Marine got me again!"

"So it would appear," Berezovsky said.

"I may decide not to like you, Tom. And I don't even know who you are."

"You tell me what kind of monitors you want, and I'll go into town and get them," Castillo said. "And while I'm doing that, Davidson can tell you who Tom is and otherwise bring you up to speed."

Casey said, "Go to Radio Shack and get a bunch of precision soldering irons and hand tools, that kind of thing. Mine are in my kitchen. As far as the monitors go, get the best they have. I don't want to have to fix monitors in addition to everything else I have to do around here."

He reached for his wallet. "Let me give you a credit card."

"I have a credit card, thank you. The Lorimer Charitable and Benevolent Fund will pick up the tab."

Castillo was almost out the front door when he remembered that if he used the Lorimer AmEx, or anything with his name on it, the FBI would quickly learn his whereabouts.

Abuela, Estella, and Svetlana were cleaning up the kitchen after breakfast when he walked in.

"Abuela, I need you to go into town with me to buy some things. And bring your credit card, please. I'll pay you back later."

"Carlos, you don't have a credit card?" she said incredulously, if disapprovingly.

"I do. But if I use it, the FBI will know I'm in Midland, and I don't want them to know that."

That announcement didn't faze her.

"I was just about to ask, Carlos, if it would be safe for Svetlana to go into Midland."

Castillo looked at her. "Why do you want to, Svet?"

Doña Alicia answered for her. "I promised her I'd show her St. Agnes's, where you sang in the choir . . ."

"*Before* you grew up and became a heathen," Svetlana said.

". . . and she wants to buy some denims," Doña Alicia picked up.

"I became neither a heathen nor a Roman Catholic," Castillo said.

"He doesn't mean that the way it sounds, dear. He's a Protestant—"

"He's not a very good anything now," Svetlana said. "That I will change."

"And I was thinking if you could get what you need in Sam's . . ."

"Sam's and Radio Shack, probably."

". . . Svetlana could get the denims there. And if you're going to have to go to Radio Shack, that's right down the street from Western World. They have some very nice ready-to-wear boots, and blouses and things. That's if it's safe for her to go into town."

The odds are pretty slim that the local FBI people would spot this Interpol fugitive in Sam's or Western World, or riding around in a Yukon with a Double-Bar-C sign on the door.

"Whenever you're ready, ladies," Castillo said.

"Svetlana can ride with me. That would attract less attention," Doña Alicia said.

[EIGHT]
1745 8 January 2006

The Yukons returned to the Double-Bar-C each transporting two fifty-six-inch flat-screen liquid-crystal monitors, one strapped to each roof and one extending four feet out the rear door of each with a little flag flying from the boxes—Lester Bradley had said there was no reason not to avoid a conflict with the cops for having something hanging out the back of the truck.

Doña Alicia and Svetlana, carrying boxes of denim clothing and whatever the big box labeled WESTERN WORLD contained, disappeared into the house.

Ernesto—Estella's son—and Bradley and Castillo started off-loading the monitors. After they had carried the first one into the library—which was now a sea of electronic devices and parts there for—Davidson came out to help with the others.

"Miller called, Charley."

"And?"

"Colonel Hamilton and Phineas will arrive at Reagan at oh-nine-something. He'll take them to the Motel Monica. Tom McGuire has some Secret Service guys who'll sit on them tonight and tomorrow without asking any questions. He said there's nothing to connect them with us anyway.

"And Delchamps is on the 2130 Lufthansa flight to Munich, and Darby on the 2150 American flight to Frankfurt, both out of Dulles. Miller gave them $9,900 apiece—a hundred under the law requiring anything over ten grand taken out of the country to be declared."

Castillo nodded. "What else?"

"He's got a Beechcraft King Air laid on from noon tomorrow to take Hamilton's stuff to Bragg. Actually to Fayetteville, where Vic will have somebody meet it. No jet was available, and he said it won't make any difference anyhow, as Torine can't leave without that stuff or the shooters, and Uncle Remus is not finished with the paperwork for the shooters."

"But he has them, right?"

"Uncle Remus said he's got eighteen coal-blacks, five a little lighter, and one he says they may have to leave in Tanzania he's so light."

"Okay. I guess that leaves us with nothing to do now but set up Casey's toys and wait."

"I have the feeling we'll be doing a lot of that, Charley. Waiting."

"Do they have sophisticated tools like this in Marine Corps communications, Bradley?" Casey asked, holding up a very-fine-pointed soldering iron from Radio Shack.

"I don't know what they have in Marine Corps communications, sir," Bradley replied. "I was a designated marksman, not in that. I think they mostly use semaphore flags."

He mimed waving semaphore flags.

Casey shook his head. "What's a designated marksman? That anything like a shooter?"

"I really don't know how well your shooters shoot, Dr. Casey, so I don't know if they would qualify to be a Marine Corps designated shooter. But if you were asking can I use that soldering iron, then yes, sir, I can. Before I joined the Corps, I was in the AARRL. I made most of my stuff."

"I was also in the American Amateur Radio Relay League," Casey said. "That's how I got suckered into Special Forces; they needed people who knew the difference between an ohm and a watt."

He pointed to a rat's nest of twisted-together wires on the table.

"Why don't you see what you can do with that?" Then he turned to Castillo, Ernesto, and Davidson, who were resting from their monitor-carrying labors. "Why don't you guys get out of here and leave those of us who know what we're doing to do it?"

Castillo and Davidson went to the kitchen, carrying an AFC handset with them. Estella offered them coffee. Castillo had just picked up his mug when Svetlana came into the room, almost causing him to drop the mug.

She was wearing her cowboy suit, which included a light gray Stetson hat, a denim jacket worn open over a translucent blouse of Western cut—through which he could see her upper undergarment—a pair of lizard-skin boots, and of course denim trousers.

She spun around.

"No comment?" she asked.

"How the hell did you get those pants on? With a paintbrush?"

"You're not supposed to ask questions like that of a lady, my heathen," she said.

"Jesus, Charley!" Davidson said in mock disapproval of his query. "Even I know that."

Svetlana smiled at Davidson, then went to Castillo, put her arms around him, and whispered in his ear, "If you will be a good boy, later I will show you how I get them off."

[NINE]
0700 9 January 2006

When Castillo walked into the library he saw that while it was not going to win any prizes for order and cleanliness, it was a great deal cleaner and more in order than it was the last time he had seen it the night before.

He also saw Lester Bradley sound asleep in an armchair, and that Casey, heavy-eyed, was sitting in another.

"He wouldn't go to bed when we finished about oh-five-hundred," Casey greeted him. "Said he 'had the duty.' He's been like that since about ten after five."

Castillo gently shook Bradley's shoulder and, when he opened his eyes, said, "Wake up and go to bed, Lester."

Bradley was on his feet a second later.

"Sir, I guess I dropped off for a second."

"Go to bed, Lester. Say, 'Yes, sir.' "

"Aye-aye, sir."

Castillo waited until Bradley had walked sleepily out of the room, then asked, "What would you say, Dr. Casey, sir, if I gave you the same order?"

"I would say, 'Yes, sir, whatever the colonel desires, sir.' Right after I tell you what Miller had to say and I show you what we've done."

"What did Miller have to say?"

"Delchamps's and Darby's planes got off the ground, and so far there has been no report that they dropped into the Atlantic. And he said Doherty and Two-Gun Yung arrived. He said he's going to install Doherty in the office to keep an eye on the FBI trying to put an eye on you, and that Yung will arrive at the Midland Airport at twelve twenty-five. He said he thought he might be useful here."

"He will be. Thanks. And now why don't you get some sleep?"

"You'll notice that all four monitors are glowing dully," Casey continued. He pointed at the monitors, one of which was on a table too small for it, and the others sitting on the floor. "But when the proper buttons are pushed, they begin to show us things. For example, the physical location of the AFCs in which I have activated the transponder."

One of the monitors showed a map of the world. Lightning-bolt symbols showed the locations of the radios in Germany, Argentina, Uruguay, Hungary, and the United States.

"At various scales," Casey went on, "for example, here in the States."

A second screen lit up, with a map of the United States, showing lightning bolts in Nevada, Texas, North Carolina, and the District of Columbia.

"Or closer."

The first screen went blank, then lit up with a map of the Washington area, with lightning bolts at the Nebraska Avenue Complex, the Baltimore airport, and the safe house in Alexandria.

"Or closer."

The second screen now showed a map of the Baltimore airport, with a lightning bolt coming out of a hangar.

"That's the one in your Gulfstream. And thanks to the friendly folks at Google, we have this view of that, as well."

A third screen lit up showing a three-dimensional image of the Signature Flight Support, Inc., hangar.

"God knows that picture wasn't taken yesterday, or even last month, but it's better than no picture. And I sure as hell didn't want to hack into Fort Meade."

"Could you do that?"

"Who do you think set up their imagery? Whenever we need that, we can. Just didn't think it wise in the middle of an op."

Castillo was awed. He smiled. "Go to bed, Aloysius."

"And so far as people are concerned"—Casey punched more buttons on a keyboard. The world map reappeared with symbols of humans—"this shows the last known location of everybody of interest."

Casey then repeated the process of demonstration, which this time ended with a three-dimensional view of the ranch house, above which was a line of numbered symbols. A chart to the right identified the numbers. Castillo was represented by the number 1, Casey by the number 2, and so on.

"I'm awed."

"This is pretty rough, Charley, but it's up and running."

"Now, go to bed. We're going to have to wait for what comes next."

"I think I will."

"Thanks, Aloysius."

Casey yawned, then made a deprecating gesture and walked out of the library.

Castillo sat down in the armchair Lester had vacated, reached for the coffee thermos, poured himself a cup, and began to wait for what would come next.

XVII

The first thing Castillo had to wait for was the arrival of former FBI Special Agent David W. Yung, Jr. Jack Davidson, who had gone into Midland to meet Yung at the airport, called at half past twelve to report that Yung hadn't been on the plane, had probably missed his connection at Dallas/Fort Worth International Airport and might be on the next plane, or planes, one of which was due at two something and the other at four something.

Castillo told him to wait. He didn't want a record, should the FBI have a "locate but do not detain" out on their former co-worker, that Two-Gun had rented a vehicle and driven himself from the airport to the Double-Bar-C.

That hadn't happened. Yung walked off the next regional jet that landed at Midland International.

Minutes before Two-Gun and Davidson walked into the ranch's library, Corporal Bradley had updated the data bank with new information. Colonel Hamilton's suitcases were now in Fort Bragg. But the 727 had not yet left for Africa. It had been discovered that an Air Tanzania already existed, which made it necessary to remove most of that color scheme and replace it with a scheme identifying the aircraft as part of the fleet of Sub-Saharan Airways, Ltd.

Corporal Bradley was thus able to demonstrate the command post's new installed technical capabilities to Yung.

While he was doing that, one of the AFCs went off, the caller identified as Alex Darby. He was in Fulda, in Otto Görner's office. A conversation followed, during which it was learned that Edgar Delchamps's going to Vienna had been something of a mistake, as Eric Kocian was in Budapest. God only knew when he'd get to Budapest now. It was also learned that the transmission of the late Herr Friedler's notes would be begun as soon as they could be scanned.

As Lester was demonstrating how the changed data—Last Known Location of 7-Darby, A—could be entered into the data bank so that it could be shown on one of the monitors, Svetlana came into the library. She wore another new cowgirl suit, one much like the other—just as form-fitting—but the denim was red in color.

She kissed Castillo somewhat less than chastely on the mouth, then whispered something in his ear, and then finally said, "Lester, if you'll show me how to do that, I can do it."

"It's not hard, Colonel," Bradley replied, at which point Castillo deduced from the look on Two-Gun's face that he now understood the cowgirl was one of the Russians Castillo had gotten out of Vienna, and also that Miller had not advised him that the relationship between the Russian defector and Colonel Castillo was not one that one would normally expect.

"Close your mouth, Two-Gun," Davidson advised, "and pay attention to what Lester's teaching Sweaty. You're here; you're going to be on the duty roster."

[TWO]
0700 10 January 2006

The world map now showed that the Sub-Saharan Airways 727, having refueled in Morocco, was somewhere over the Sahara Desert, en route to Kilimanjaro International Airport, Tanzania.

It also showed Colonel Hamilton and DeWitt in Brussels, Belgium, where they would board an Air France flight to Dar Es Salaam International Airport, Tanzania, at 2300.

They learned from Sándor Tor, via the AFC installed in Eric Kocian's Hotel Gellert apartment overlooking the Danube in Budapest, that Edgar Delchamps had gotten as far as Vienna. He had telephoned to say he would be along in a day or two, just as soon as he took care of something he had to do in Vienna.

Because Delchamps was not answering his cellular telephone and had not provided an alternate number at which he could be reached, Colonel Castillo could not ask him what the hell that was all about. And Castillo needed Edgar in Budapest to go through Billy Kocian's files to choose what would be scanned and sent to Midland.

At supper—Doña Alicia and Estella prepared a rack of pork, Svetlana made garlic mashed potatoes, and an enormous salad, and there were several bottles of a very nice Chilean Cabernet Sauvignon—Dmitri Berezovsky confessed to

Castillo that he was a little worried about Delchamps. The Russian said that while he really liked Edgar—he thought they had become friends—he struck him as the kind of man who had to be kept on a short leash.

"I think he was kidding when he said he'd like to whack the CIA station chief lady," Castillo replied.

Svetlana said, "Of course he was, my Carlos. I was the one who wanted to kill her."

Judging by Doña Alicia's face, Castillo could not tell whether or not she thought that Svetlana was only making a little joke.

After supper, Dmitri beat Two-Gun at chess six games in a row, one lasting an exhausting two minutes and twenty seconds by the clock.

And they watched television and the monitors and waited.

[THREE]
0700 11 January 2006

The monitor showed the updated data that Colonel Torine had called in: that the Sub-Saharan Airways 727 and its cargo and crew were on the ground at Kilimanjaro International and that Uncle Remus was looking around to see what pickup trucks or similar vehicles were available for purchase in the nearby towns of Arusha and Mosi.

Sándor Tor reported that Edgar Delchamps had called again and said that he would arrive by train from Vienna at 1415.

"I guess he did whatever he had to do in Vienna," Dmitri observed.

"He spent a lot of time in Vienna," Castillo said. "So far as we know, he has a Fräulein—more likely a Fräu, I suppose—with whom he passed a little time. He knew there was no rush."

"Isn't he a little long in the tooth for that sort of thing?"

"I don't think so. Sándor Tor told me that Billy Kocian has two very good friends in Vienna. And you know how old he is."

"An inspiration to all of us," Berezovsky said.

An Internet inquiry of Air France revealed that flight 434, nonstop Airbus service from Brussels to Dar Es Salaam, had arrived on time.

And they watched the monitors and talked a little about what exactly would be the best format for the data Castillo would lay before the President, and Two-Gun said he'd start making up a dummy to be filled in as the data arrived and was digested.

And they waited.

[FOUR]
1310 11 January 2006

"Colonel Hamilton for Colonel Castillo, Encryption Level One," the sultry voice of the AFC announced. Castillo looked at the monitors. The one showing Sub-Saharan Africa showed a now-flashing lightning bolt in Bujumbura, Burundi. It also indicated the local date and time beside the flashing lightning bolt: It was now 0110 12 January 2006 in Bujumbura.

Castillo pushed the SPEAKERPHONE button.

"C. G. Castillo."

"I have Colonel Castillo for you, Colonel Hamilton. Encryption Level One confirmed."

"Thank you very much," Hamilton said.

"You don't have to thank her, sir," Castillo said. "She's a computer."

"I'm aware of that, of course. Force of habit."

"Yes, sir."

"It's ten past one in the morning here, Castillo. I'm in the Hotel du Lac in Bujumbura."

Castillo looked at another of the monitors. It showed a three-dimensional picture of the Hotel du Lac.

"Yes, sir, I know."

"In Washington and on our way here, I discussed a number of things with Mr. DeWitt and I must say I was very impressed with him."

"He's a very impressive man, sir."

"Among the things we discussed was our mode of operations. I also discussed this with Colonel Torine when DeWitt and I got to the Kilimanjaro airfield. And a third time, with Mr. Leverette, when we finally arrived here in Bujumbura."

"Yes, sir?"

"I thought we had resolved, once and for all, the command structure of this operation. I am of course in overall command. Colonel Torine will handle the transportation and logistics outside the Congo. Inside the Congo, Mr. Leverette and Mr. DeWitt will be responsible for transportation and security, and I will be responsible for the investigation."

"That seems to be a practical solution for your situation, sir."

"So I would have thought. When I went to bed tonight, I thought it had been agreed between us that we would get some rest tonight. Not only was it a long flight, but we have passed through—I don't know *precisely* how many but a number of time zones. . . ."

"Six, sir," Castillo furnished.

"And the natural clock of the body has been disturbed. Rest obviously was called for. Tomorrow morning, I thought it was agreed, when fresh from our rest, we would plan our incursion of the Congo."

"I awoke about fifteen minutes ago, Castillo. I had trouble sleeping, and with the thought that perhaps Mr. Leverette and/or Mr. DeWitt were having the same problem, I decided I would see if they did, and if so, we could perhaps get a jump on our morning planning session."

"Uh-oh," Jack Davidson said.

"What was that, Castillo?"

"Nothing, sir. One of my men came in the room."

"So I started out of my room. I was startled by a man dressed in the local clothing—or lack of it—sitting directly in a chair across from my door. He had in his lap an Uzi—the full-size one, not the Mini Uzi Mr. D'Allessando was kind enough to loan me.

"He addressed me in English, by rank. He said, in effect, 'Is there something I can do for you, Colonel?' to which I replied, 'What are you doing outside my door?' to which he replied, 'Uncle Remus said we should sit on you, sir.'

"By then I realized the man was one of our shooters, so I asked him to direct me to Mr. Leverette's room. He replied, 'I can, Colonel, but *Uncle Remus* is not in his room.'" Colonel Hamilton paused. "And what is *that* all about, Castillo? Everyone calls him 'Uncle Remus.' Why do they do that?"

"Only his friends, sir, are permitted to call him that."

"I asked you why they do that. You are aware of the inference, the implication, I presume?"

"Yes, sir. Well, sir, the best answer I've ever been able to come up with is that the Uncle Remus character in the books was a kindly old gentleman who was always telling stories, and Mr. Leverette seems to fit that description."

"Be that as it may, Castillo, permitting your subordinates, particularly your subordinate *enlisted* men, to call you by the name of a fictional character in a series of children's books that some think—and here you may take my point—are racist in tone is pretty odd behavior for a chief warrant officer of the highest grade, wouldn't you agree, Colonel Castillo—"

Castillo caught himself smiling. "I honestly never gave it much thought, sir. I will look into it—"

"It comes perilously close to conduct unbefitting an officer and a gentleman, Castillo, and you know it."

"I must respectfully disagree, sir. Mr. Leverette is one of the finest officers with whom I have ever served."

"Well, let me tell you what he's done."

Castillo glanced at Davidson, who was grimacing.

"Yes, sir."

"I asked the shooter with the Uzi," Hamilton went on, " 'If Mr. Leverette isn't in his room, where is he?'

"To which he replied, 'He and Phineas went over the fence, Colonel.' Then he handed me a letter and said, 'Uncle Remus instructed me to give you this in the morning, Colonel. But I guess it's okay to give it to you now.' "

"A letter, sir? What did it say?"

"I will read it to you," Colonel Hamilton said. "Quote. Dear Colonel Hamilton. Phineas and I decided it would be a good idea if we conducted a preliminary reconnaissance of the border area prior to the planning of the incursion. Since you were so tired, and we felt sure you would agree this was a wise step, we didn't wake you. We will return in forty-eight hours. Respectfully, Colin Leverette CWO5 USA. End quote. Well, what about that, Castillo?"

"What about what, sir?"

"If that isn't direct and willful disobedience of orders, what is it?"

"Sir, did you order Mr. Leverette and Mr. DeWitt not to conduct a reconnaissance of the border area?"

"I thought it was understood. I told you that."

"Well, to judge from Mr. Leverette's letter, sir, I'd have to say the understanding wasn't unequivocally clear. He would never disobey an order, sir"—*Unless, at the time, Colin thought it was the right thing to do*—"Sir, why don't you have a word with Mr. Leverette when he and Mr. DeWitt return?"

"You can take that to the bank, Castillo," Colonel Hamilton said. "I'll give the both of them a dressing-down they'll remember the rest of their lives."

Probably more like two seconds.

Uncle Remus and Phineas DeWitt have been dressed down by Bruce J. McNab, and with all possible respect, Colonel Hamilton, sir, you just ain't in the same ball club.

"Sir, I realize I shouldn't say this, but I respectfully suggest you not be too hard on either of them. They mean well."

"I will contact you on their return, Castillo."

"Yes, sir. Thank you, sir."

"Colonel J. Porter Hamilton. Please terminate the communication link."

"Anything else I can do for you, Colonel?" the sultry voice asked suggestively.

"Uh, no," Hamilton replied somewhat uneasily, then in a stuffy tone added, "That will be all, thank you."

Castillo looked at Davidson, who said: "Well, Colonel Castillo, sir, I guess we'll just have to wait and see, but I would not be surprised if Colonel Hamilton ignores you vis-à-vis not being too hard on Uncle Remus and Phineas. He will lecture them both severely and probably reduce them both to tears. But nice try."

[FIVE]
0200 12 January 2006

"Otto Görner for Colonel Castillo, Data Transmission Not Encrypted," the sultry voice of the AFC announced.

Davidson pushed the VOICE TRANSMIT button.

"John Davidson. Colonel Castillo available in five minutes."

"Hold one, Sergeant Davidson," the voice said, then twenty seconds later added: "Not Encrypted Data Transmission begins. Pass to Colonel Castillo when available."

Davidson hadn't even reached the printer when it started to whir and the voice—which, or *who,* Davidson very privately had begun to think of as "Sexy Susan"—announced: "Not Encrypted Data Transmission complete."

Three seconds later a hard copy of the data came out of the printer.

Davidson read it, then began to push keys on the printer keyboard.

The printer monitor showed what he'd typed: TRANSLATE GERMAN TO ENGLISH DRAFT.

The translation began to appear on the printer monitor.

Davidson studied it, made a few minor corrections—the AFC translator was good but not perfect—then typed, FILE AS GÖRNER 0203 12 JAN PRINT 3 COPIES."

The printer began to spit out the three copies.

Davidson stapled the German original and the translation together, then said, "Sorry, Casanova, duty calls," and walked out of the library.

Svetlana answered his knock in a few seconds.

"He's asleep," she said.

Davidson held out the papers.

"Sweaty, I think he'd want to see this."

She took them from him, stepped into the corridor where there was enough light to read, then scanned both versions, and sighed. "Dmitri was afraid of something like this would happen. I will wake Carlos."

Davidson went back to the library.

Castillo, wearing his West Point bathrobe, came in almost immediately behind him.

"Goddamn that Edgar Delchamps!"

"You're not really surprised, are you, Charley?"

"*Pissed* is the word that comes to mind. At Delchamps, and at me for not seeing this coming."

Dmitri and Svetlana came into the library. Berezovsky was wrapped in a terry-cloth bathrobe.

"Have a look at social notes from all over," Castillo said, gesturing to the papers.

"Svetlana told me," Berezovsky said.

"Read it," Castillo said, "then give me the benefit of your thinking, please."

Berezovsky took one of the copies of the translation, and his eyes fell to it.

TAGES ZEITUNG VIENNA

0900 12 Jan

Immediate

For All Tages Zeitung Newspapers

TAG: RUSSIAN DIPLOMAT FOUND MURDERED OUTSIDE U.S. EMBASSY

By Wilhelm Dusse

Staff Writer/Tages Zeitung Vienna

The body of Kirill Demidov, cultural attaché of the Russian embassy, was found early this morning in the passenger seat of a taxicab near the United States of America embassy at Boltzmanngasse 16. He apparently had been strangled to death.

Mr. Demidov's body was found by a U.S. Marine guard as he walked to the embassy to begin his duty day.

"I thought it was funny for somebody to be sitting in the back of a cab with no driver, so I took a look, and when I'd seen what it was

I went inside the embassy and called the cops," Staff Sergeant James L. Hanrahan told this reporter before the interview was interrupted by an officer of the embassy, who took Sergeant Hanrahan away and announced the U.S. embassy would have no comment.

Mr. Demidov's body was still sitting erect in the taxicab when this reporter arrived at the scene shortly before officials of the Russian embassy then arrived and, claiming diplomatic privilege, had the body removed to an undisclosed location by ambulance.

Vienna police officials said that the taxicab had been stolen from its garage earlier last evening, and that the police had been looking for it. They also reported that there had been a "metal noose" around Mr. Demidov's body, with which he had apparently been strangled.

It is known that Mr. Demidov

had earlier been at the Kunsthistorisches Museum at ceremonies marking the closing of the exhibit of the Bartolomeo Rastrelli's wax statue of Russian Tsar Peter the First, which had been on loan from the Hermitage Museum in Saint Petersburg.

STORY OPEN
MORE TO FOLLOW

"Let me make a wild guess, Dmitri," Castillo said. "Demidov was the Vienna rezident?"

Berezovsky nodded.

"Who sent us this? Darby?" Castillo asked.

"Otto Görner," Davidson said.

"Well, then let's see what else Otto knows. For all we *know*, Edgar may be as pure as the driven snow in this. Demidov may have been done in by his homosexual lover; there's been a lot of that going on."

Davidson laughed.

Castillo went to the radio. "C .G. Castillo. Otto Görner. Encryption Level One."

"Hold one, Colonel. I will attempt to make the connection."

"Sweaty, she sounds a lot like you. Ever notice?" Davidson asked. "I've started to think of her as 'Sexy Susan.'"

Svetlana gave him the finger.

"Well, Karl," Otto Görner's voice came over the speakerphone, "what are you doing up in the middle of the night?"

"Reading the newspaper. What else have you got?"

"I just got off the phone with Willi Dusse. Two little tidbits that probably don't mean anything"

"What, Otto?"

"An unnamed source in the Vienna police, whose name Willi always spells correctly, with two *s*'s, said that while they were waiting for the police heavyweights and the Russians to show up, he happened to notice that the victim's face was not contorted and blue, as is common in strangulations, and that what he described as the 'metal noose' was not embedded in the victim's neck, but just sort of hanging there. He did notice, however, that there was a mark on the neck, below the ear, that could perhaps have been made with a needle."

"Willi thinks it's possible the victim did not die of strangulation, but of some other cause. But we'll never know, as any autopsy will be conducted in Moscow."

"That's interesting. They have any idea who did this to Mr. Demidov?"

"Not according to Willi. Willi was told, however, that the taxi was wiped clean; no fingerprints. Suggesting, possibly, that this terrible act was done by someone who knew what he was doing."

"That's all? What's the second little tidbit?"

"Well, one little thing, which probably means absolutely nothing. As the police wrecker was hauling the taxicab away, Willi's friend noticed a calling card at the curbside. It could have simply been dropped there prior to all this, but it also could have been in the taxi and dislodged when the police initially examined the cadaver."

"What was the name on the calling card?"

"It was an American diplomat's, a woman named Eleanor Dillworth. She's the consul."

"Oh, I do love a man who can *really* hold a grudge," Davidson said.

"Goddamn it," Castillo said.

"That mean something to you, Karl?" Görner asked.

Castillo avoided the question. "Otto, please send me whatever else your man Dusse comes up with, will you?"

"Of course, Karl."

"Does Darby know about this?"

"I showed it to him when it came in. He's just about finished here, he said, and is moving to Budapest."

"Is he there now?"

"No. Alex said he was going to his hotel to pack."

"If you see him, have him call me, please."

"I suppose if you knew anything about those two Russian defectors, you'd tell me, right?"

"Absolutely."

"You don't suppose somebody stuck needles in their necks, do you? Or hung a garrote around their necks and they just haven't found the bodies yet? That's a story I'd love to write myself. And give to Friedler's widow."

"I'm going back to bed, Otto," Castillo said. "End transmission."

Berezovsky then said, "Carlos, you seem to be genuinely surprised by this."

"'And you're not?"

Berezovsky didn't immediately reply.

"You knew about this?" Castillo asked, then thought: *Of course you did!* "You knew Edgar was going to whack this guy and you didn't tell me?"

"Why do you think he did this?" Berezovsky asked.

Castillo said: "He wants to go out in style, be remembered when the other dinosaurs gather as the dinosaur who whacked the Vienna rezident the week before he retired."

Berezovsky shook his head.

"No?" Castillo snapped. "Then, damn you, why?"

"We talked—" Berezovsky began.

Castillo saw Svetlana nodding in agreement.

"*We* being who?" Castillo interrupted. "You, Delchamps, and who else? You, Svet?"

"Yes, my Carlos. Me, too," she said.

"Anybody else?" Castillo flared. "Lester, maybe? Aloysius?"

Davidson raised his hand.

"Oh, Jesus H. Christ!" Castillo exclaimed.

"Don't blaspheme," Svetlana said.

"You're pissed because I am 'taking the Lord's name in vain,' but it's all right for you and everybody else to sit around planning to whack people? *Jesus H. Christ in spades!*"

Berezovsky calmly went on: "What we talked about—Darby, too—Carlos, was how to stop the killing."

Castillo could not believe what he was hearing. "You mean, by whacking this guy in Vienna, then leaving the CIA station chief's calling card? I'll bet when that Marine opened the cab door, that calling card was pinned to Demidov's lapel with a rose."

"We didn't get into how anything was to be done, Charley," Davidson said. "Just agreed that it had to be done."

"*Et tu,* Brutus? Jesus Christ, Jack. Nobody was interested in what I might have to say?"

"I told them what you would say, Charley. 'No.' Was I right?"

"You know fucking well that's what I would have said."

"But Dmitri and Edgar and Sweaty were right, too," Davidson said.

"How the hell do you figure that?"

"My Carlos, hear out Dmitri," Svetlana said, then added, "Please, my darling."

"I'm all ears," Castillo said after a moment, and gestured impatiently for him to explain.

Berezovsky nodded. "Carlos, it is said that the Germans and the Russians are very much alike; that's why the wars between us kill so many millions—"

"What I draw from that philosophical observation is: 'So what?' " Castillo interrupted.

"—That we are either on our knees before our enemies when we believe we cannot win a conflict, or tearing at their throats when we think we can triumph. The only time there is peace between us is when both sides realize that the price of hurting the other is being yourself hurt."

"There is a point to this, right? And you're going to get to it soon?"

"When it was the U.S. versus the U.S.S.R., this concept was called 'Mutual Assured Destruction,' " Berezovsky went on. "And thus there was no exchange of nuclear weapons."

"Where are you going with this?"

You know where he's going with it, stupid!

Berezovsky started to say something. Castillo silenced him with an upraised hand, and said, "We have to take out some of their people, preferably the ones who whacked some of ours, to teach them there's a price to pay?"

"Otherwise, this won't stop," Davidson said.

"Knowing something of how Putin's mind works," Berezovsky picked up, "I can tell you he is going to evaluate the five assassinations we know about—and I'm sure there were more—and decide, depending on the speed and ferocity of the reaction to them, whether he should pull in his horns or see how much more he can get away with before the enemy charges a price he doesn't wish to pay."

"Some of this is personal for me, Charley," Davidson said. "I really don't want to spend the rest of my life—on whatever sunny beach I find myself in retirement—looking over my shoulder."

"Nor I," Berezovsky said.

Svetlana didn't say anything out loud, but her eyes also said, *Nor I.*

And neither do I, goddamn it.

Sexy Susan said, "CWO Leverette for Corporal Bradley, Class One Encryption."

"C. G. Castillo."

"It's okay, sweetheart," Leverette's voice said, "I'll talk to him."

"Go ahead, gentlemen," Sexy Susan said.

"You're watching the radio in the middle of the night, are you, Colonel? What did she do, kick you out of bed?"

"I understand you've already displeased Colonel Hamilton. You sure you want to do that with me, too, Mr. Leverette?"

"Negative."

"I didn't expect to hear from you for another twenty-four hours or so."

"As I just explained to Colonel Hamilton, sir, I meant that forty-eight-hour period to mean the longest time we might be gone."

"He's there with you?"

"Good morning, Colonel Castillo," Hamilton said.

"Good morning, sir."

"Mr. Leverette has assured me that our little problem was a communications breakdown."

"I felt sure it was something like that, sir."

"Some good news and some bad, Colonel," Leverette said.

"Good first. I've just had some bad."

"As we speak, Phineas is taking the vehicles and a dozen shooters across the bridge. I found several Congolese officials who became very sympathetic to our desire to collect small fauna for the Fayetteville Zoo after I gave them a great deal of money."

"Only a dozen shooters?"

"I'll explain that when I get to the bad news. These same officials were also kind enough to rent me four outboard motorboats—not bad ones, with 150-horsepower Yamahas; they told me they stole them from the UN—at a price I would say is only four or five times what they're worth, even in this neck of the woods. And further, to show us the place where the boats will be hidden from sight until—and I hope this never happens—it is necessary to launch them as an alternative method of leaving the Congo.

"It is my intention to use four of the shooters as guards on the fleet while the rest of us try to catch parrots—"

"Parrots?"

"—and whatever else we might happen across. Yeah, parrots. Our new friends are in the wild livestock business. They offered us everything up to and including gorillas. We settled on parrots."

"The Congo African Grey Parrot," Hamilton furnished, "*Psittacus erithacus erithacus,* is regarded as the most intelligent of the species. They bring anywhere from a thousand dollars to several times that much in Washington."

"As I said," Leverette went on, "our new friends somehow got the idea we're trying to catch and illegally export African Grey Parrots. They said the birds may be found in large numbers along the Ngayu River, on both sides of National Route 25.

"They also said—I'm not sure if this is bad news or good news—that we should be very careful not to go past kilometer marker 125 on Route 25, because beyond that is where the Arabs and the bad water are.

"I asked them what the Arabs are doing in that area, and they said they didn't know, possibly poaching elephants for their ivory, or maybe engaged in the slave trade, but the bottom line being that very few people who go deep into that area are ever seen alive again.

"The bodies of those who do venture too far, my new friends told me, are often found on the shoulders of Route 25, as far west as Kilometer 120. And I mean *bodies*—none are buried. Seems that some missionaries—I didn't know until they told me that there were Congolese missionaries, black guys, who didn't take off when the Belgians and Germans and French were mostly run out of this paradise—did try burying the dead, then suddenly came down sick and died very unpleasantly. As did large numbers of various carnivores that thought they'd found free lunch on the roadside."

"Jesus!" Castillo said.

"Amen, brother. And, to round off this *National Geographic* lecture on the fascinating Congo, there are no fish in the crystal-clear waters of that stretch of the scenic Ngayu River. Sometimes, in the past, there were fish kills, but no longer. Suggesting, perhaps, one fish kill too many—"

"All of this, as you can well imagine, Castillo," Colonel Hamilton said, "has rather whetted my curiosity."

"—So, as soon as I hear from DeWitt that the shooters and the pickups are across the border, Colonel Hamilton and I are going to join them. We will drop four shooters at the boats, with one truck, to ensure our new friends don't rent them to other parrot hunters.

"The rest of the scientific expedition will then drive up Route 25, which we pick up in Kisangani, to Kilometer 120. There, we'll split into three groups. Colonel Hamilton said he can learn a lot from the bodies and—presuming, of course, that our new friends have been telling the truth—the water in the Ngayu. The other two will reconnoiter the area beyond Kilometer 125.

"This time, Charley, when I say we'll be back in seventy-two hours, that's conservative."

Castillo said, "Same question: Why are you not taking the other team?"

"I'm going with my gut, Charley. The fewer of us the better. Less chance of detection."

"Your call, Uncle Remus," Castillo said.

Hamilton cleared his throat. "I thought you and I had discussed that unfortunate appellation, Colonel Castillo."

Go fuck yourself, Hamilton.

"Yes, sir, we have. It won't happen again, sir."

"Charley, don't call us. We'll call you. I don't want some raghead with an RPG and a Kalashnikov wondering who the broad with the sexy voice is."

"Isn't there a way to disable the audio function of the radio?" Colonel Hamilton asked.

"It doesn't always work, sir. Watch your back, Colin."

Of course the voice can be shut off.

Uncle Remus is telling me (a) he doesn't want to have one of the shooters wasting time sitting around the bush with an earpiece waiting for a call, and (b) more important, that he doesn't want soon-to-be-retired Lieutenant Colonel Castillo looking over his shoulder and offering unsolicited advice.

What Uncle Remus is saying loud and clear: "Butt out, Charley, and let us do our thing."

"See you when I see you, Charley. Leverette out."

Castillo turned to Davidson. "Jack, is there a countdown function?"

"Seventy-two hours?"

Castillo nodded. "Put it on all of them."

Davidson tapped keys.

In the upper left-hand corner of all the monitors, a line of numbers appeared: 72:00:00. Which a second later turned to: 71:59:59.

[SIX]
0615 12 January 2006

When Castillo, in his bathrobe, walked into the library and sat down at the table, the countdown on the monitors read 68:20:25 and continued declining.

"Les, if you can find my—and Jack's—laptops in all this crap, how about putting the countdown on them?"

"Yes, sir."

Bradley had come to his room and said Susanna Sieno wanted to talk to him.

"C. G. Castillo."

"Mrs. Sieno," Sexy Susan said, "I have Colonel Castillo for you. Encryption Level One."

"Hey, Susanna. How's the temperature down there? It's ten above zero here."

"Is Svetlana with you?"

"No. You want her?"

"No, I don't," Susanna said.

While Castillo was trying to interpret the meaning of that, three seconds later Sexy Susan said, "Not Encrypted Data Transmission complete."

Castillo went to the printer as it spit out a sheet of paper.

"The morning newspaper was just delivered," Susanna Sieno said. "Read that. There's more. Alfredo heard about this around midnight, and has been working on it since. He just came here."

Castillo glanced at one of the monitors and saw that "here," according to a flashing lightning bolt and a three-dimensional image, was Nuestra Pequeña Casa in the Mayerling Country Club in Pilar.

The printout he held in his hand was a scan of part of the front page of *The Buenos Aires Herald*:

RUSSIAN DIPLOMATS MURDERED NEAR EZEIZA AIR TERMINAL

From Staff Reports

Officers of the Gendarmería Nacional discovered shortly before midnight the bodies of two Russian diplomats, later identified as Lavrenti Tarasov and Evgeny Alekseeva, in an automobile of the Russian embassy parked just off the Autopista Ricchieri approximately two kilometers from the airport entrance.

According to a spokesman for the Russian embassy, Tarasov—the commercial attaché in the Russian embassy in Asunción, Paraguay—was apparently taking Alekseeva to the airport, where Alekseeva had reservations on the 10:35 p.m. Lufthansa flight to Frankfurt, Germany. Both had been in Argentina participating in a diplomatic conference.

Comandante Liam Duffy of the gendarmería, the first senior police official on the scene, told *The Herald* that "at first glance, pending full investigation" it appeared to be a case of mistaken identity, that the diplomats were mistaken for drug dealers.

"From the condition of the cadavers," Duffy said, "it would appear that they were fatally shot with shotguns, this after both had been wounded several times with a small-caliber weapon, probably a .22, in the knees and groin areas. Inflicting this type of excruciatingly painful, but not immediately lethal, wound is almost a trademark of the [drug criminals] to get their fellow scum to talk."

The murders recalled the still-unsolved murder of the U.S. diplomat J. Winslow Masterson, who was found shot to death on Avenida Tomas Edison in late July of last year.

Comandante Duffy said that while the most thorough investigation would be conducted, he had "to say in candor" that he doubted very much that it would be any more successful than the investigation into the Masterson murder had been.

"When these faceless, cowardly rats of drug dealers go back into the sewers, only good luck ever sees them get what they so richly deserve," Duffy said.

Alfredo Munz, despite what Susanna had said, didn't have much to add to what was in the *Herald* story, except to put in words what had been pretty obvious as soon as Castillo had read the story: that Duffy had learned that Alekseeva was going back to Europe, which meant that Tarasov was going back to Paraguay, and Duffy just wasn't going to let that happen.

Castillo told him thanks and broke the connection.

How the hell am I going to handle this?

"Les, print some copies of that story and pass them around, please," he said, then he pushed himself out of his chair and headed for his bedroom.

"Svetlana, sweetheart."

She opened her eyes and stretched.

"I've got some bad news, baby."

She sat up.

"Duffy went off the deep—"

"Is that it?" She snatched the story out of his hand before he had a chance to reply.

After a moment, she said softly but matter-of-factly: "And so I am now the Widow Alekseeva."

Castillo didn't say anything.

She swung her legs out of bed.

"Pray with me, my darling," she said as she knelt next to the bed. She saw the look on his face. "Please, my Carlos."

She bent her head and put her hands together.

Shit!

Castillo, more than a little awkwardly, knelt beside her and put his palms together.

He glanced at Svetlana. Her lips were moving, but no sound was coming out of her mouth. Twice she crossed herself.

So what am I supposed to pray for?

"Thank you, God, for letting Duffy take out my lover's husband"?

Or, "God, I hope you didn't make him suffer too long between Duffy shooting .22-rounds in his balls and finishing him off with the shotgun"?

Damn, I am indeed a prick.

Oh, Jesus, why didn't I think of this before? *"Dear God, please make this as easy as possible on Svetlana. She's really a good woman, a good Christian, and she's going to blame herself for this. If you want to punish anybody, punish me for not being able to get that cold-blooded Irish bastard to back off.*

"Let her really be pissed at me, just so long as she doesn't blame herself. She's sure as hell going to get into the sin thing, because we've been sharing a bed while she was still married, and will decide that this is her punishment.

"Well, lay that on me, too. She didn't rape me. It just happened. I take full responsibility. Let her be really pissed at me. I probably deserve it, and after a while, maybe she'll come around. Just make this easy on her.

"I'll even take the blame for the other Russian Delchamps whacked in Vienna. I should have seen that coming and stopped it.

"Just be good to Svetlana, Lord. Amen."

Svetlana stopped praying and got to her feet. More than a little awkwardly, Castillo stood, too. She touched his face and kissed him.

He held her.

"Thank you," she said.

"Don't be silly."

"What did you pray for?"

"Evgeny's soul," he lied.

Where the fuck did that come from?

On top of everything else, I'm lying through my teeth.

Add that to my demerits list, God.

"Me, too," she said. "But mostly I prayed for us."

"For us?"

"Evgeny knew the rules."

"Excuse me?"

"He knew them, and I know them, and you know them. I prayed to God to excuse us from them, my Carlos."

What the hell is she talking about?

"Saint Matthew," she went on as if reading his mind. "When the Romans came to arrest Jesus Christ, Simon Peter drew his sword to protect him. Our Lord told him to put it away. 'For all those who take up the sword perish by the sword.' You never heard that?"

"Now that you mention it . . ."

"I prayed to God that he will excuse you and me from that, my darling. It might not hurt if you did the same thing."

She kissed him quickly on the lips, then gently pushed away from him. She announced, "I'm going to have a shower. You want to go first, or after? Or . . . ?"

"Or," he said, and followed her into the bathroom, shedding his West Point bathrobe en route.

[SEVEN]
2130 12 January 2006

"Major Miller for Colonel Castillo," Sexy Susan announced.

Castillo looked up at the monitors from the playing cards he held. The countdown timer read 53:05:50, and there was a flashing lightning bolt above a picture of the house in Alexandria.

He looked across the table at Dmitri Berezovsky and Aloysius Casey, then back at his hand: two aces, two sevens, and a nine.

"I think you're bluffing, Aloysius," he said, picking up chips and tossing them in the pile at the center of the table. "Your two dollars and two more." Then a little more loudly and officially he said, "C. G. Castillo."

Sexy Susan said, "I have Colonel Castillo for you, Major Miller."

"How they hanging, Gimpy?"

"Montvale's looking for you, Charley."

"So, what else is new?"

"He just called here on the White House secure phone. He asked me if I knew where you were."

"To which you responded?"

"That you were at the moment out of touch. And then he said, 'Where is he, and don't tell me you don't know,' to which I cleverly responded, 'I'm afraid I'm going to have to say exactly that, Mr. Ambassador, sir.' "

"Why do I think that didn't end your little chat?"

"He said it was urgent that he speak to you, and please have you call him; he has to talk to you about Vienna."

"If I call him, since the sonofabitch owns the wiretappers in Fort Meade, he will know where I am. Let me think about it, Dick. I'll call you back."

"Figure something out, Charley. Or he will change that 'locate but do not detain' on you to 'put the bastard in chains.' "

"How do we know he already hasn't?"

"As of three minutes ago—according to Inspector Doherty; I called him before I called you—they haven't. Doherty said this was probably because they need something called a warrant before they can throw you on the ground and slap on the handcuffs."

"At the risk of repeating myself, let me think about it. I'll call you back. Castillo out."

Aloysius Casey put down his cards, faceup. "All I have is three jacks and a pair of fours," he said, mock innocently. "What do they call that, a full house?"

As he pulled the money in the center of the table to him, he said, "You want to talk to this Montvale guy, Charley?"

"I don't want to, but I would if I could figure out how to do it without having him find out where I am."

"Ask and you shall receive." He turned toward the AFC radio. "White House, via the Venetian."

"Right away, Dr. Casey," Sexy Susan said.

"What this does is activate a cellular in a suite we keep at the Venetian," Casey said. "Not encrypted—I'm working on that—but what it does is tell the phone company—and Meade, Langley, anyone who's curious—that the call is being made on a cellular in Vegas. That's all. I don't know how many rooms there are in the Venetian, a couple of thousand, anyway . . ."

"You are a genius, sir."

"White House."

"Colonel Castillo for Ambassador Montvale."

"On a regular line?"

"Yes, ma'am."

"Ambassador Montvale's line."

"Lieutenant Colonel Castillo for Ambassador Montvale," Sexy Susan announced. "The line is not secure."

"It's Castillo," they heard Truman C. Ellsworth, Montvale's deputy, say.

"On the White House line?" Montvale then said, and then the director of National Intelligence came on the line. "Good evening, Colonel Castillo."

"Burning the late-night oil, are you, Mr. Ambassador?"

"Where are you, Charley? We've been looking all over for you."

"So I have been led to believe by Major Miller."

"He told me he didn't know where you are."

"Did he? Well, I don't always tell him where I am."

"Are you aware of what happened in Vienna this morning?"

"What?"

"The Austrian foreign minister called the American ambassador and asked him if, in the spirit of international mutual cooperation, he would be willing to have Miss Eleanor Dillworth, his consul, answer a few questions the police had for her."

"That's the same lady who accused me of stealing some Russians from her? What did she do, go further off the deep end? What did the Viennese cops think she did?"

"You're not going to make me lose my temper, Castillo, so you can knock it off."

"Yes, sir. I'm deeply sorry, sir."

Castillo saw Casey shaking his head, but he was smiling.

"What the police wanted to know was if she could shed some light on why her business card was found on the chest of a man by the name of Kirill Demidov. He was found sitting with a garrote around his neck in a taxi just down the street from the American embassy."

"I just can't believe that Miss Dillworth could have anything to do with anything like that, even if the bastard was the Russian rezident who ordered the garroting of the Kuhls."

"Who told you that?" Montvale snapped.

"I have some Russian friends, you know. They tell me all kinds of interesting things."

They heard Ellsworth trying to mask his voice in the background, then Montvale said into the phone, "What the hell are you doing in Las Vegas?"

Casey smiled again and gave Castillo a thumbs-up.

"Who told you I was in Las Vegas?"

"I'm beginning to think Miss Dillworth and a growing number of other people, including General McNab, are right."

"About what?"

"That you really have lost it."

"No. That's just a story you cooked up to convince C. Harry Whelan, Jr., of *The Washington Post* that a fruitcake like me could not possibly have stolen two Russian defectors from her, as Miss Dillworth alleges. Remember?"

"I think I should tell you that Miss Dillworth has told the Vienna police, the State Department, and of course Mr. Whelan, that if they are looking for the persons responsible for the Demidov murder, they should start with you and your crony Mr. Edgar Delchamps."

"Is that what they call loyalty to your co-workers? I thought agency types never ratted on one another."

"I don't suppose you know where that dinosaur is, do you?"

"He could be in Budapest, I suppose—"

"Budapest?"

"—Or Buenos Aires. Or just about any place in between."

"He's not with you in Las Vegas?"

"I never said I was in Vegas. You did."

"Wherever you are, the FBI will inevitably find you."

"I'll bet there'll be a lot of volunteers to look for me in Las Vegas. Who did you say told you I was here—I mean, there?"

Casey and Berezovsky grinned widely.

"All right, Castillo, enough. I have told the DCI I want a separate investigation of the allegations your Russian friends have made about a secret factory in the Congo. You have accomplished that much, if they are not making a fool of you. And now, it seems to me, it's time for you to put up or shut up."

"Meaning what?"

"Berezovsky and Alekseeva should step forward and tell the agency what they know."

"That's unlikely. They trust the agency a little less than even I do."

"Charley, I don't care where in the world you have them hidden. You tell me where, and I'll have a plane there in a matter of hours."

"Which will transport them to one of those nice houses the agency has in Maryland? I don't think so, Mr. Ambassador. But I'll tell you what I will do: In a couple of days, when I get it all together, I will send you everything they have told me about what the agency thinks is a harmless fish farm. Plus what I've managed to dig up myself."

Montvale didn't reply for a long moment.

"I'm surprised. I thought there was nothing you could do that would surprise me. But I should have thought that you would be doing something like this."

"Something like what?"

"You still want to go over there yourself, don't you, John Wayne? Jump on your goddamn horse and gallop off to fight the fucking Indians. You think if you can put before the President enough of your bullshit, mixed with the bullshit your fucking Russian friends are feeding you, the President will say, 'Sure, hotshot. Go over there and show up the agency. Have Montvale set it up.' All the while ignoring whatever damage you can do to the President if you fuck it up—when you fuck it up."

"I thought you weren't going to lose your temper."

"Mark my fucking words, Castillo, you will go to Africa and embarrass the President and the country and me over my dead body. You will not have access to any assets over which I have control—"

"Well, it's always a pleasure to talk to you, Mr. Ambassador," Castillo said. "Break it down, White House." When he heard the click, he said, "Castillo out."

"In about a minute," Casey said, "I suspect a cell phone will start to ring in the Venetian. No one will hear it, because the ringer's been muted. And I wouldn't be a bit surprised if, shortly thereafter, lots of gun-toting guys in bad suits with emission detectors in their ears will start prowling the miles of Venetian corridors. That won't work, as I thought of that and came up with a fix. But was that smart, Charley?"

Castillo looked at him but said nothing.

"Thank you, Carlos," Berezovsky said.

"For what? I told you I'd never turn you over to the agency, and that was before—"

"Before Cupid's arrow struck? No. Thank you for not backing down from that assault. You reminded me of David and Goliath."

Castillo pointed his finger at him. "You shut up." Then he pointed at Casey. "And you deal."

Doña Alicia and Svetlana came into the library fifteen minutes later. They had been watching an old Paul Newman movie on television in the ranch house's main living room. They joined the game.

When they quit playing—just before midnight, when Lester Bradley came in for his watch duty with the AFC—Doña Alicia had won almost twenty dollars and Sweaty had shown that she was a lousy loser by twice throwing her cards angrily on the table and uttering thirty-second recitations of Russian expletives that Castillo was glad Doña Alicia didn't understand. As Castillo stood, he noted on the monitors that the countdown read 50:45:15.

[EIGHT]
0900 13 January 2006

Castillo walked into the library carrying a mug of coffee.

Davidson shook his head and said, "Not a fucking peep, Charley."

Castillo sat at the table.

"I think what you were supposed to say was, 'Good morning, sir. I hope the colonel slept well. I beg to report there have been no reports from any of the reconnaissance parties, sir.' "

Davidson gave him the finger. "Uncle Remus said seventy-two hours, Colonel, sir."

He pointed at the countdown. Castillo saw that it read 41:40:40.

"I think we have a surfeit of precision. Why the hell are we counting in seconds?"

"I don't know. Because we can?"

"Let's wake up the Air Force and see what they're doing to earn all the money the taxpayers are throwing at them," Castillo said. "C. G. Castillo for Colonel Torine. Encryption Level One."

Sexy Susan said: "One moment, please, Colonel."

Davidson's fingers attacked his keyboard.

The monitor Castillo was watching changed its data display. It now showed a three-dimensional picture of the terminal building at Kilimanjaro International Airport, Tanzania. A lightning bolt at the top of the screen began to flash, then the screen showed the local date and time at the airport: 1701 13 JAN 06.

"Back that up, Jack," Castillo said. "Let's have a look at the Congo."

Sexy Susan said: "I have Colonel Torine for you, Colonel. Encryption Level One."

"What's up, Charley?" Jake Torine asked.

"Hold one, Jake," Castillo said.

The screen showed the last known positions of 5-Leverette, C and 6-DeWitt, P. They were now inside the Congo, eighty-some kilometers northeast of Kisangani. Their symbols were nearly superimposed on each another, which could have meant that they were together, or in the same area just a klick or two apart.

"Speaking of precision," Castillo said.

"That's it, Charley," Davidson replied. "It won't go any closer. What they did was turn on the AFC just long enough for the computer to get a GPS position."

Castillo's fingers flew over the keyboard of his laptop.

"Jake, I've got a last-known position on Uncle Remus. He's in the Congo."

"He told me that's where he was going. Anything a little closer than that? The Congo is a great big place, Charley."

"You have a pencil or something to write this down?"

"The Lorimer Fund bought me the latest and greatest laptop computer just before I came over here. I thought maybe it would come in handy."

Castillo read from his laptop screen: "One point zero six north latitude; twenty-five point nine east latitude. That's eighty-odd klicks northeast of Kisangani."

"Let me have those coordinates again. Slowly."

Castillo read them again slowly.

"Got it. Where the hell did you get that?"

"We Army special operators try to stay on top of things," Castillo said. "I think this place we're interested in is another fifty or sixty klicks farther northeast of Uncle Remus's LKP."

"That would fit," Torine said thoughtfully.

"It's possible, repeat possible, that we'll get position updates, and I thought that while we're waiting maybe we might consider what we could do if this place turns out to be what it is, and where we think it is."

"The Air Force, as usual, is way ahead of you. There's a number of options,

ranging from nuking it from a B-1 through having Uncle Remus sneak up and
throw a spear at it."

"And you've been thinking about them?"

"If you had to make an educated guess, Charley, would you say the target
would be within a fifty- or sixty-klick radius of Uncle Remus's LKP?"

"I'd be happier with seventy-five klicks, but you could probably narrow it
down some from a radius. I have an educated guesstimate that it's not farther
than ten klicks either side of National Route 25, and no more than that from
the Ngayu River."

"That will narrow it down a lot. I'll work on it. Give me an hour or so,
Charley, and I'll send you my thoughts."

[NINE]
1150 13 January 2006

Two hours and thirty-two minutes passed before Sexy Susan announced that
Colonel Torine wanted to speak with Colonel Castillo, and when Castillo went
on the AFC, she announced, "Commencing data transmission, Encryption
Level One-D."

Moments later, the printer began to spit out sheets of paper—and then
kept spitting them out. After four minutes, it stopped suddenly and Sexy Susan
announced: "Partial failure of data transmission to file and printer. Printer
paper supply, or printer toner supply, possibly exhausted. Transmission to file
will resume momentarily. Check printer paper supply and or printer toner supply, replenish as necessary, and enter RESUME PRINT FILE."

Doing that consumed another seven minutes.

And it was another five minutes before Sexy Susan announced, "Transmission of data, Encryption Level One-D, to file and printer verified complete."

As Svetlana helped Castillo stack the printer's output, he noticed the countdown, no longer reflecting seconds, was down to 37:16.

When he had finished glancing at the information Torine had sent, he was
surprised at how little time Torine had spent detailing the options, not how long.

There were eight separate "Proposed Operational Order: Congo Chemical
Complex" papers. A quick glance showed they called for the use of aerial
weaponry ranging from missiles, through the B-1 Stealth bomber, to the F-15E
fighter bomber, and the aerial tankers needed to refuel them, and two involved
U.S. Navy F/A-18C fighter bombers operating from carriers in the South Atlantic and Indian oceans.

And there was a ninth paper: "Proposed Operational Order: Bomb Damage Assessment, Congo Chemical Complex." It suggested this could be done by satellite overfly; a U-2 high-altitude photoreconnaissance aircraft; Predator Unmanned Aerial Vehicle; return to the bombing site by bomber or low-flying fighter aircraft, or by "clandestine entry into the Congo of U.S. Air Force or U.S. Army Special Operations personnel to make such evaluation on the ground."

The ninth was the only one Lieutenant Colonel Castillo, himself a military aviator with a good deal of experience, felt he more or less understood.

But he was going to have to try to understand the strengths and limitations of the various things Torine was proposing. He was going to have to show them to the President, and he didn't want to look or sound like a goddamn fool when inevitably the President asked him a question and he didn't have the answer.

He collected everything that Torine had sent him, plus the draft of the report Two-Gun Yung had prepared from his own notes and from what had come from Fulda and what he'd gotten from Dmitri and Svetlana. And he went to his old desk in his old bedroom, where he hoped he would have a little privacy.

Yung's draft would have to be modified when Yung had a chance to review what had just started coming in from Budapest—Delchamps had finally shown up there—but Yung had put it to him that now was the time to have "a quick look" to make sure it was what he wanted, rather than have him continue "to break his ass on what might well be a waste of everybody's time."

He had just made himself comfortable at his old desk and poured himself a cup of coffee when Svetlana came into the room. He was convinced he'd pissed her off by telling her that he didn't need help or company right now, thank you very much.

She simply replied, "Joel Isaacson is on the radio."

[TEN]
1150 13 January 2006

The countdown on his laptop read 36:58 when Castillo sat down at the desk and reached for the AFC handset.

"C. G. Castillo."

Sexy Susan said: "I have Colonel Castillo for you, Mr. Isaacson."

I don't have to be Sherlock Holmes to figure out this has something to do with the President, Joel having been in charge of his Security Detail.

Confirmation of that came immediately when Isaacson began the conversation by announcing, "Charley, I had a call five minutes ago from the President."

Castillo waited for him to go on.

"He wanted to know if I knew where you were," Isaacson said. "When I told him I honestly didn't know, he asked if I could find you. I said—I don't lie to the President, Charley—'I think I can, Mr. President.'

"To which he replied, 'Do so, Joel. If you can, tell him to call me. If you can't, call me back within ten minutes.'

"To which I replied, 'Yes, Mr. President.' He hung up. I then called Jack Doherty, who said to get on the AFC. Jack is not capable of lying to the President, either, even secondhand."

"I understand, Joel. I'm sorry you got in the middle of this."

"So am I, Charley. What do I tell him?"

"You won't have to tell him anything. I'll call right now."

"White House."

"C. G. Castillo for the President on a secure line, please."

"Hold one, Colonel, please. I have special instructions . . ."

What "special instructions"?

"The President's private line," an executive secretary to the President answered.

Private line?

The one in what he calls his working office?

"Colonel Castillo for the President, please."

"Colonel, the President is in a do-not-disturb conference in the Oval Office. If you will kindly give me a second—"

"Can you tell me with whom?"

There was a long pause, then:

"The secretary of State, Ambassador Montvale, and the directors of the CIA and the FBI. However, the President's given special instructions should someone call about you, sir."

There was another long pause, then Castillo heard the President's voice snap, "Yes, what is it?"

"Are you free to speak with Colonel Castillo, Mr. President?"

"Oh, am I ever. Are you on here, Castillo?"

"Yes, Mr. President."

"Hang on a minute. I'm going to the little office."

"Yes, Mr. President."

Castillo quickly formed a mental picture of what was happening. The President of the United States was rising from his desk in the Oval Office—or from an armchair or a couch—and marching into the smaller office just off the Oval Office, officially known as "the President's working office," leaving behind him Secretary of State Natalie Cohen, FBI Director Mark Schmidt, Director of Central Intelligence John Powell, and Director of National Intelligence Charles W. Montvale, all of whom had just come to the same conclusion: that the President didn't want any one of them to hear what he was going to say to a lowly lieutenant colonel, and that they were going to be furious to varying degrees, none of them minor.

"Okay, Charley, I'm in here."

"Yes, Mr. President."

"I think you'd agree that Mark Schmidt is not given to colorful speech," the President said.

"Sir?"

"He just came up with something very colorful. He said, 'As far as out-of-control loose-cannons rolling around are concerned, Castillo by comparison makes Oliver North look like the Rock of Gibraltar.' "

The President let that sink in.

"Of course, that may be because he is just a little humiliated that the FBI can't find you or those two Russians you stole from the CIA."

Castillo didn't reply.

"Why did you steal those defectors from the CIA, Charley?"

"Sir, the CIA never had them."

"Then there is another side to this horror story I have just heard?"

"Yes, sir, there is."

"Did you tell the DCI that you refused to turn over the stolen Russians to him?"

"Sir, they were not stolen. I told him that the Russians did not wish to turn themselves over to the CIA."

"And also that the CIA was nothing more than a very few very good people, or words to that effect, trying to stay afloat in a sea of left-wing bureaucrats?"

"Yes, sir. I'm afraid I did."

"What are you doing in Las Vegas?"

"Sir, I'm not in Las Vegas."

"Charles Montvale says you are."

"Ambassador Montvale has been wrong before, too, sir."

"Right now, Charley, you are not in a position where you can afford sarcasm."

"Yes, sir. No offense intended. I actually meant it as a statement of fact. Sorry, sir."

The President sighed. "Charley, I have to ask this: Did you personally assassinate or did you set up the assassination of a Russian in Vienna in circumstances designed to make it appear the CIA station chief was the villain?"

"I learned of that, sir, only after it happened."

"Frankly, I didn't believe that one."

"Yes, sir."

"Okay, Charley, here it is. You've earned the right to tell me your side of the incredible things I have been hearing that you have been doing. The question is how to do that? Where are you?"

"In Texas, sir."

"In about an hour, I'm going to Philadelphia. Two speeches, one tonight and one tomorrow at lunch. If you can give me a more precise location than 'Texas,' I'll send a plane to pick you up. I can give you half an hour tomorrow morning. Say, at nine. The Four Seasons Hotel."

"Sir, I'm in Midland, Texas. On my ranch."

"Is that where you'll go after you retire?"

"Possibly, sir. Sir, you don't have to send a plane. I have one."

"I have to ask this, too: You're not thinking of getting on your plane and flying off to, say, Argentina, are you?"

"No, Mr. President, I'm not. I'll see you in Philadelphia tomorrow morning."

"And once more, probably proving that there is such a thing as too much loyalty downward, I'll give you the benefit of the doubt."

There was a click.

Castillo, in deep thought, stared wordlessly at the handset.

"Colonel?" Sexy Susan said. "Colonel . . . ?"

"Disaster time," Castillo announced five minutes later. "I just promised the President I would report to him at nine tomorrow morning in Philadelphia. I also told him where I am.

"Priority one is keeping Sweaty and Dmitri out of the hands of the CIA."

He looked at Casey. "I need a really big favor, Aloysius."

"I'll take care of them, Charley."

"I'll need you to fly them to Cozumel . . ."

"I'll take care of them, Charley," Casey repeated.

" . . . as soon as possible."

Casey turned to the AFC. "Casey. Ellwood Doudt."

"Good afternoon, sir," Doudt answered almost immediately.

"Pick me up an hour ago."

"Roger that. On our way, sir."

"Casey out." He looked at Castillo. "Soon enough, Charley?"

"Thank you."

"Why don't I go with you, Carlos?" Dmitri Berezovsky asked.

"I *am* going with you," Svetlana announced.

"Thanks, but no thanks," Castillo said. "For one thing, they wouldn't let either of you get near the President. For another, even if I could get you in to see him, you'd be Russian embezzlers facing Montvale and the DCI, and they both are convinced you're liars.

"Jack will go with you," Castillo went on. "Les, I'd like you to go with me, if you're willing. And you, too, Two-Gun. Les to work the radios, Two-Gun to explain the money trail in his report if I can get the President to listen."

"Sure," Yung said.

"Yes, sir," Bradley said.

"Jack, as soon as you can," Castillo went on, "get on the horn to the Pilar safe house. Have someone there get in touch with Aleksandr, give him a heads-up that Dmitri and Svetlana are headed back to his Cozumel resort. He'll have an idea or two on how best to get them from there back to Argentina quietly and safely."

"Done," Davidson said. "When are you going to leave?"

"Just as soon as I can wind it up, I've got to stop at Midland for fuel and to file a flight plan. Keep an eye on my pal Max, okay?"

Dmitri repeated his offer to go with them as they shook hands at the house, and Castillo repeated his reasons why that wouldn't make any sense.

Svetlana and Doña Alicia went as far as the plane. Bradley and Two-Gun boarded the Lear, and Doña Alicia waited in the Yukon while Castillo and Svetlana said their good-byes.

"I have this terrible feeling I will never see you again, my Carlos," Svetlana said.

"Don't be silly. The worst that can happen to me is that they'll have somebody sit on me until I go through that retirement charade. As soon as that's over, I'll get on a plane and fly to Gaucho Land, where you'll have my golf clubs all waiting for me."

"I wish I was with child. At least I would have that."

"I already have one of those, and from what I have seen, one is enough."

"It is all right, my Carlos. We had what we had, and we both know the rules of the game we're in. I will pray for you."

If I thought it'd work, I'd pray myself.

"I have to go, sweetheart."

They kissed.

The kiss was unlike any he could remember. That frightened him.

The last thing he saw as the Lear broke ground was Doña Alicia and Svetlana standing in front of the Yukon. Doña Alicia had a comforting arm around Svetlana, who was weeping.

Castillo caught himself thinking that it looked funny.

Sweaty's so much taller and larger than Abuela.

Jesus Christ, that's tremendously touching, not funny.

I really am a callous bastard!

[ELEVEN]
Atlantic Aviation Services, Inc.
Philadelphia International Airport
Philadelphia, Pennsylvania
0810 14 January 2006

Getting to Philadelphia should have been as simple as Castillo had hoped: fuel the Lear, file the flight plan, get in the bird, and three and a half hours later give or take, land in the City of Brotherly Love.

It wasn't. There was really bad weather all up and down the eastern seaboard—which he learned when he tried to file his flight plan—and it was not much better most of the way between Midland and the eastern seaboard.

Arriving in Philadelphia at 1800 for a long conversation with Jack Britton over a nice lobster dinner somewhere and then getting a good night's rest before facing the President the next morning at 0900 proved impossible.

He hadn't been able to get off the ground at Midland until almost eight at night, and then only because he was going to fly first south-southeast from Midland to Houston, then due east to pass over Louisiana, Mississippi, and

Alabama, then north-northeast over Georgia and on to Norfolk, Virginia, the closest airport to Philadelphia that was not experiencing weather-interrupted operations.

At 0720, he finally received clearance to fly ORF-PHL direct, which was fortunate inasmuch as a good deal of research had revealed there was no ground transportation that could carry them there from Norfolk rapidly—if at all—as the roads were covered with snow and ice.

En route, Corporal Bradley managed to contact Jack Britton, who said he would do his best to meet them on arrival, but the roads were icy and he would be personally surprised if the airport didn't shut down again before they got there.

Britton was waiting for them when they landed.

The Lear had forty-five minutes' remaining fuel.

Waiting with Britton was Chief Inspector F. W. Kramer, who commanded the Counterterrorism Bureau of the Philadelphia Police Department. Perhaps equally important, Kramer had done much of his military service with the Tenth Special Forces Group.

"How they hanging, Charley?" Kramer greeted Castillo. "Getting much? What can we do for you?"

"I need to be at the Four Seasons Hotel at five minutes to nine, and Corporal Bradley and Two-Gun Yung have to be there ten minutes before that."

"I can get you there by then, but maybe not in. The President's in town, and that's where he stays."

"I know," Castillo said.

"Why don't we send them in that?" Kramer said, pointing to a fully equipped patrol car. "And I'll take you in mine."

"Can they use your room to set up the AFC, Jack?"

"Hell, no," Britton said. He tossed Bradley a door-opening plastic key. "Show that to the doorman if you get there before we do. He's a retired cop."

[TWELVE]
The Four Seasons Hotel
130 North 18th Street
Philadelphia, Pennsylvania
0855 14 January 2006

There was no sign of the patrol car or of Bradley or Yung when Chief Inspector Kramer's unmarked car pulled up before the door of the Four Seasons.

"I'll put the arm out for them, Charley," Kramer said. "You go on in. You don't want to keep the President waiting."

"Let him in," the President of the United States said when the Secret Service man announced there was a Lieutenant Colonel Castillo seeking an audience.

"Good morning, Mr. President," Castillo said. His eyes scanned the room, and he added, "Madame Secretary, Gentlemen," to the secretary of State, the DCI, the secretary of Defense, and Ambassador Charles Montvale.

"And you didn't think he would show, did you, Charles?" the President said, then looked at Castillo, and added, "I don't think I've seen you needing a shave before, Charley."

"I apologize for my appearance, Mr. President."

"Don't worry about it. Needing a shave pales to insignificance beside the manifold other sins Mr. Powell and the ambassador are alleging you have committed." He paused, then turned to a steward. "Get the colonel a cup of coffee. He looks as if he desperately needs one."

"Thank you, sir. I do."

"Good morning, Charley," Secretary of State Natalie Cohen said.

None of the others said a word.

"Okay, let's get to it," the President said once the steward had delivered Castillo's coffee and left the room. "In as few words as possible, Charley, take it from the beginning. You have five minutes."

It wasn't hard for Castillo to start. He had expected the question and had spent all of his time in the air mentally rehearsing what he would say.

It took him longer than five minutes, however, and he wasn't quite finished when the door opened and a Secret Service agent put his head in.

"Excuse me, Mr. President. There's a kid being held at the elevator who says he's Colonel Castillo's bodyguard. He also says he's a Marine corporal. He says he has something Colonel Castillo absolutely has to have."

Montvale looked at the agent and blurted: "Jesus Christ! You actually came in here with something like that for me?"

"I think he was talking to me, Charles," the President said, and looked at Castillo.

"Corporal Lester Bradley, sir," Castillo confirmed.

"Get him in here. I can't pass up the opportunity to see the colonel's bodyguard."

"Yes, Mr. President."

Bradley came into the room two minutes later. He carried Castillo's laptop, Yung's report, Torine's Proposed Operational Orders, and the AFC handset.

He popped to attention and saluted the President, who crisply returned it.

"You're Colonel Castillo's bodyguard, are you, son?" the President asked.

"Sir, yes, Mr. President, I am, sir."

"For God's sake, he's not old enough to vote," Montvale said disgustedly.

"Sir, no sir, I'm not old enough to vote, but I am Colonel Castillo's bodyguard, sir."

"Who has twice saved my life, so lay off him, Montvale," Castillo snapped, then heard himself. "I'm sorry, Mr. President."

"If he's your bodyguard, I would presume he already knows what we're talking about here?"

"Yes, Mr. President, he does."

"Stick around, son. I want a word or two with you when this is finished."

"Aye-aye, Mr. President, sir."

"Okay, Charley, wrap it up. We're running out of time."

It took Castillo another three minutes.

"That's about it, sir."

"It's about time," Ambassador Montvale said.

"Shut up, please, Charles. I'm thinking," the President said.

That took a full twenty seconds.

"Bottom line, Charley," the President said. "Even if I believed everything you have told me, there's just not enough there for me to authorize a clandestine mission—or even an overflight, except by satellite—to look into it."

"Mr. President, may I say how relieved I am to hear you say that?" Secretary Cohen said. "The ramifications of a black operation going wrong—"

"Right now," the President interrupted, "the answer is no, Colonel Castillo. But I will give you one more chance to turn your Russians over to the agency. If they are able to convince the DCI there is even a remote chance that what they're selling is true, I will authorize a mission to the Congo."

"Mr. President, I have people in the Congo," Castillo said.

"*What* the hell did you just say?" the DCI barked.

"I find that hard to believe, Charley," the President said. "Why should I?"

Castillo turned on the AFC handset, and his speakerphone.

"C. G. Castillo. Colin Leverette. Encryption Level One."

I know Colin's twenty-four hours are far from up, but, please, Lord, let him answer.

"What is that thing?" the President asked. "Some kind of telephone?"

Sexy Susan's voice said: "Colonel Castillo, I have Mr. Leverette. Encryption Level One."

"Hey, Charley! You bastard—I haven't been here an hour."

"Where are you, Uncle Remus?"

"Kisangani. You want to buy a parrot?"

"What is that, some sort of a code?" the secretary of State muttered.

"What are you doing in Kisangani?" Castillo asked.

"Well, the colonel needed someplace to set up his laboratory, so we rented a house. He's using the kitchen for his lab, and I'm buying parrots in the living room. I have fifty of them and have promised to buy another hundred."

"Uncle Remus, I'm with the President and some very important people—"

"Oh, God! I have a sick feeling that you're not pulling my chain."

"Do you think the colonel has come up with anything the President should hear?"

"Yes, sir. He has."

"Can you get him on here, please?"

"Hold on."

"What colonel is that?" Montvale asked.

"Colonel J. Porter Hamilton of the U.S. Army Medical Research Institute at Fort Dietrich," Castillo said. "Ring a bell?"

"Not with me it doesn't," the President said. "Who is he?"

"The preeminent expert on biological and chemical warfare," the DCI said.

"And you sent him into the Congo?" Montvale said. "You really are crazy, Castillo."

"Charles, go get yourself a cup of coffee," the President said.

"Excuse me, Mr. President?"

"Come back in ten minutes—*if* you have your mouth under control by then."

Montvale didn't know what to do. He hesitated, and then decided he'd wait when he heard the speakerphone come alive with a new voice.

"Colonel Castillo?" Colonel Hamilton asked.

"Yes, sir."

"If this, your being with the President, is one more manifestation of that odd sense of humor of yours . . ."

"This is POTUS speaking, Colonel. I have just been told that you are our preeminent expert regarding biological and chemical warfare." It was a statement but sounded more like a question.

"Good day, Mr. President. Yes, sir. There are some who have said that, sir."

"Colonel, have you come across anything that suggests there is a laboratory or factory—"

"Mr. President," Hamilton interrupted, his officious voice hitting a deadly serious tone, "it indeed is a far more dangerous situation than even Colonel Berezovsky suggested."

"Colonel Berz—you don't mean the Russian?"

"Yes, sir. What I have found here is far worse than Colonel *Berezovsky* suggested, Mr. President. I am not a religious man, but what I have seen here in the most elementary of investigations is an abomination before God."

"You have proof of this, Colonel?" the President asked softly.

"Yes, sir. The first samples will be sent out via Tanzania just as soon as the natives finish construction of the parrot cages."

"Excuse me?"

"We—I should say Mr. Leverette, sir, who is known as Uncle Remus and who is a genius of ingenuity—are covering our incursion by posing as dealers in African grey parrots. He feels sure, and I have every confidence he's right, that when we truck out the first fifty parrots later today no one will look in their cages as they cross the border."

"And what will happen to them in Tanzania?"

"Well, Mr. President, I was going to suggest to Colonel Castillo, who is running the tactical end of Operation Fish Farm for me, to see if he can't have another aircraft sent into Kilimanjaro to pick them up, either an Air Force fighter or perhaps something from an aircraft carrier. That way, the samples could get to Fort Dietrich much more quickly than they could aboard our aircraft, and doing so would leave our aircraft there. I am trying to think of some way to get some of the human bodies to Fort Dietrich so that thorough autopsies can be performed. The first problem there is to get them to Tanzania without them contaminating human and plant life along the way. And, of course, we can't hide them in the parrot cages."

The President flashed a concerned look at everyone in the room, particularly the DCI and DNI. When no one had anything to offer, Castillo thought that the look changed to a simmering anger.

"Colonel, please think your answer over before replying. In your judgment, should the laboratory—this factory, fish farm, whatever you want to call it—should it be destroyed?"

Colonel Hamilton did not think his answer over long.

"Mr. President, what we have here is a fairly large and well-supplied laboratory and an even bigger manufacturing plant. I would recommend the immediate destruction of both—I repeat, both—sir. I am amazed that the processes involved have not already gotten out of control. If that happens, Mr. President, it will be a hundred times, perhaps a thousand times, more of a disaster than Chernobyl. Living organisms are far more dangerous than radiation."

"Colonel, I'll be talking to you soon. Thank you very much."

"Mr. President, it has been an honor to speak with you."

"Uncle Remus," Castillo said, "get the colonel's samples in Jake's hands as quickly as you can."

"Yes, sir."

"Castillo out."

"Colonel Castillo," the President said. "From your . . . I guess 'tone of command,' one would suppose that you consider yourself still in charge of this . . . what did Hamilton call it? 'Operation Fish Farm'?"

"Yes, sir."

"Sadly, that is not to be the case. You're just too dangerous a man to have around. Too many people have their knives out for you, and some of them have involved the press. I can't involve the press in this. You understand me, Colonel?"

"Yes, sir."

"You are relieved as chief, Office of Organizational Analysis. You will go someplace where no one can find you, and you will not surface until your retirement parade. Understood?"

Loud and clear, sir.

And so the other shoe finally fucking drops. . . .

It took Castillo a moment to find his voice. "Yes, sir."

"After your retirement, I hope that you will fall off the face of the earth and no one will ever see you or hear from you again. Understood?"

"Yes, sir. I've been thinking of learning how to play polo. Or golf."

"The same applies to everyone in the Office of Organizational Analysis. Understood?"

"Yes, sir."

"I don't know how much of that sixty million dollars you had is left, but it should be enough to provide reasonably adequate severance pay to everyone. If it isn't, get word to me and we'll work something out."

"Yes, sir."

"Since we understand each other, Colonel, before you disappear, I think you have the right to hear this."

"Hear what, sir?"

"Mr. Secretary of Defense, you are ordered to take whatever steps are necessary to get Colonel Hamilton's samples from where Colonel Castillo will tell you they are to the U.S. Army Medical Research Institute at Fort Dietrich as quickly as possible."

"Mr. President," Cohen interjected, "you can't just fly warplanes—"

"I'll get to you in a moment, Madame Secretary. Right now I'm giving orders, not seeking advice."

She started to say something but didn't.

"I think we are in this mess because I've listened to too much well-meaning advice," the President went on. "In addition, Mr. Secretary of Defense, you will immediately prepare plans to utterly destroy this hellhole in the jungle."

"Sir, Colonel Torine has prepared some proposed op orders," Castillo said.

"Give them to the secretary, please," the President said. "I'm sure he will find them valuable in preparing the plan, or plans, I want presented to me yesterday."

Cohen again tried to reason: "Mr. President, you're not thinking of actually—"

"And what you are going to do, Madame Secretary," the President interrupted her, "is return to Washington, where you will summon the ambassador of the Democratic Republic of the Congo to your office. You will tell him (a) that you are sorry to have to tell him that without the knowledge or permission of his government this—what did Hamilton call it?"

" 'An abomination before God,' sir," Castillo offered, earning him dirty looks from the others.

"That this abomination before God has been erected on his soil, but (b) not to worry, because his friend the United States of America is about to destroy it and no one will be the wiser.

"If he gives you any trouble about our airplanes overflying his country—or anything else—tell him his option is that we will destroy this abomination and *then* take it to the goddamned United Nations.

"Natalie, say, 'Yes, Mr. President,' or I will with great reluctance have to accept your resignation, then have the bastard appear in the Oval Office tomorrow and tell him myself. They knew goddamn well it was there. Palms were greased."

After a long moment, the secretary of State said, "Yes, Mr. President."

The President turned to Castillo.

"I hope this eases the pain of getting the boot a little, Charley."

"It eases it a great deal, sir. Thank you."

"For what? For defending the United States from all enemies, foreign and domestic? That's what I was hired to do."

"Yes, sir."

"Is there anything else I can do for you before you start vanishing from the face of the earth?"

Castillo had seen this question coming, too, and was prepared for it.

"Yes, sir. Three things."

The President made a *Let's have it* gesture with both hands.

"First, sir, I would like to see Corporal Bradley here promoted to gunnery sergeant in the Marine Corps. He loves the Corps, but obviously, tainted with this, and knowing what he knows, he could never go back. He'll have to take a discharge."

The President pointed to the secretary of Defense.

"Do it," he ordered, then turned back to Castillo. "And?"

"I'd like to see Berezovsky and Alekseeva taken off the Interpol warrants. They didn't embezzle any money. And three, I would like myself, and anybody else connected to me, to be taken off the FBI's 'locate but do not detain' list—and any other list we may be on."

The President pointed at the DCI. "You can take care of that. And since the Russians have not defected to the CIA, I want the CIA to take no action to encourage them to do so. Understood?"

The DCI did not appear the epitome of happy. "Yes. Mr. President."

The President looked at Castillo.

"I'm sorry it turned out like this, Charley. But bad things happen to good people."

He put out his hand.

Castillo shook it, then he and Bradley walked out of the room.

[THIRTEEN]
McCarran International Airport
Las Vegas, Nevada
1530 14 January 2006

Castillo had made two calls on the AFC from Jack and Sandra Britton's suite in the Four Seasons.

The first was to Dr. Aloysius Francis Casey. Casey told Castillo that while he'd said no problem to Charley's request to get Dmitri and Svetlana to

Cozumel, he admitted now that he'd instead brought them to Vegas, and what he suggested was that Castillo come, too, until he could straighten things out.

The second call was to Major Dick Miller in the Office of Organizational Analysis. He lied to Miller. He said he would explain the whole thing when he had the chance, but right now the President wanted them both out of sight, and he was going to go out of sight in Vegas, and the way they were going to do that was that Miller was going to meet him at BWI, where they would turn in the Lear, pick up the Gulfstream, and fly out to Nevada.

That had a secondary reaction. Castillo decided that there was no reason Jack and Sandra Britton should not enjoy the cultural advantages of Las Vegas. For that matter, Two-Gun Yung either.

The G-III went wheels-up out of Baltimore and four hours and forty minutes later touched down at McCarran. Somewhere over Pennsylvania, Castillo had called Aloysius again, told him who was now aboard the Gulfstream, and asked that rooms for one and all be arranged.

"Our last excursion, so to speak, on the tab of the Lorimer Charitable and Benevolent Fund."

"I'll send somebody to meet you," Casey said.

What met them at the AFC hangar was a gleaming black Lincoln stretch limousine with THE VENETIAN lettered in gold on the doors.

Sandra was thrilled.

"I've always wanted to be mistaken for a rock star with five lovers," she said.

When they were off-loaded at the Venetian's grand entrance, there was one assistant manager in gray frock coat and striped pants for each of them.

"May we show you to your suites?" each asked.

Castillo, who still had not shaved, felt a little uncomfortable in the elegance of the lobby, but he reasoned he would soon be alone with Svetlana and right now that was all that mattered.

"The center door, sir. You are expected. Just go right in," his assistant manager ordered.

Castillo pushed open the door.

"Sweaty?"

"In here, Charley," Aloysius Francis Casey called.

Shit!

Swapping war stories with Aloysius is not what I had in mind.

He found himself at the head of a set of sweeping glass stairs leading down a floor to a dimly lit sunken living room. Aloysius Francis Casey and half a dozen men he could not remember ever having seen before sat on a circular couch that appeared to be upholstered with gold lamé.

Castillo started down the stairs, then realized he knew two of the men. Tom Barlow and Jack Davidson were sitting with their feet on a piece of furniture in front of the circular couch. And then he heard a familiar whine—Davidson was barely holding back Max.

What the hell is going on? he thought as Max broke loose and ran to him.

Then Castillo realized that he did recognize some of the others. One was a legendary character who owned four—maybe five?—of the more glitzy Las Vegas hotels.

But not this one, a voice from the memory bank told him.

Another was a well-known, perhaps even famous, investment banker.

And another had made an enormous fortune in data processing. Castillo remembered him because he was a Naval Academy graduate.

The others he couldn't place.

"Need a little taste, Charley?" Aloysius asked. "You look like you could use one."

"Yes, thank you. I do." He petted Max. "How are you, buddy?"

A butler in striped pants and a gray jacket took his order, and delivered it in a nearly miraculous short time.

"Gentlemen, now that the colonel has his drink," Casey said, "I propose a toast to Colonel Hamilton, Phineas DeWitt, and the incomparable Uncle Remus. They did the job of getting Operation Fish Farm off the ground better than anyone in this room thought they could."

Glasses were raised and clinked and there was a chorus of overlapping voices.

"Charley, word has come back-channel that a scrambled sortie comprised of F-16A, F-15E, and F-15C attack aircraft—on a black op devised by one Colonel Torine—has turned a so-called 'fish farm' into a flaming crater."

All these people know about Op Fish Farm?

I can't believe Aloysius has been running at the mouth.

Or Dmitri or Jack—and what the hell are they doing here?

"Everybody pay attention," Casey said. "You don't often get a chance to see Charley with a baffled look on his face."

"Okay, Aloysius, you have pulled my chain—more than it's ever probably been pulled. What the hell is going on around here?"

"How many times since you made the acquaintance of Colonel Hamilton have you said dirty words when he told you of 'his people'?"

"Every damn time. So what?"

"Here we are, Charley. We're Hamilton's people. And now that you're soon to be unemployed, we'd like to be yours."

"What the hell does that mean?"

"Colonel," the Naval Academy graduate said with a Texas twang, "what we are is a group of people who realize there are a number of things that the intelligence community doesn't do well, doesn't want to do, or for one reason or another can't do. We try to help. And we're all agreed that you're just the man to administer the program."

"You've got the wrong guy. The intel community hates me, and that's a nice way of describing it."

"Well, telling the DCI that his agency 'is a few very good people trying to stay afloat in a sea of left-wing bureaucrats' may not have been the best way to charm the director, even if I happen to know he agrees with you."

"Colonel," the man who owned the glitzy hotels said, "this is our proposal, in a few words: you keep your people together, keep them doing what they do so well, and on our side we'll decide how to get the information to where it will do the most good, and in a manner that will not rub the nose of the intelligence community in their own incompetence." He paused. "And the pay's pretty good."

"Carlos," Dmitri said, "you don't want to learn to play golf any more than I do. And maybe we can do some good on another occasion."

"Think it over, Charley," Davidson said. "I'm in."

"Fair enough," Castillo said. "I will."

I am being dishonest again.

This sounds almost too good to be true.

"Where's Sweaty?" Castillo asked.

"Freddy put her in the Tsar Nicholas II Suite," Casey said. "He thought she'd like it. It's even got one of those big copper teapots."

"Samovars," Castillo corrected him without thinking. "Where is it?"

"You go up the stairs into the foyer. There's three doors. This is the center. You and Svetlana are in the right one. I'll give you a call in a couple of hours, and maybe we'll have dinner and hoist a couple."

Max was already waiting at the top of the stairs.

Svetlana kissed Charley and held him and told him he needed a shave.

"I usually shave while I'm in the shower, Sweaty."

"Is that so? How interesting. Can I watch?"

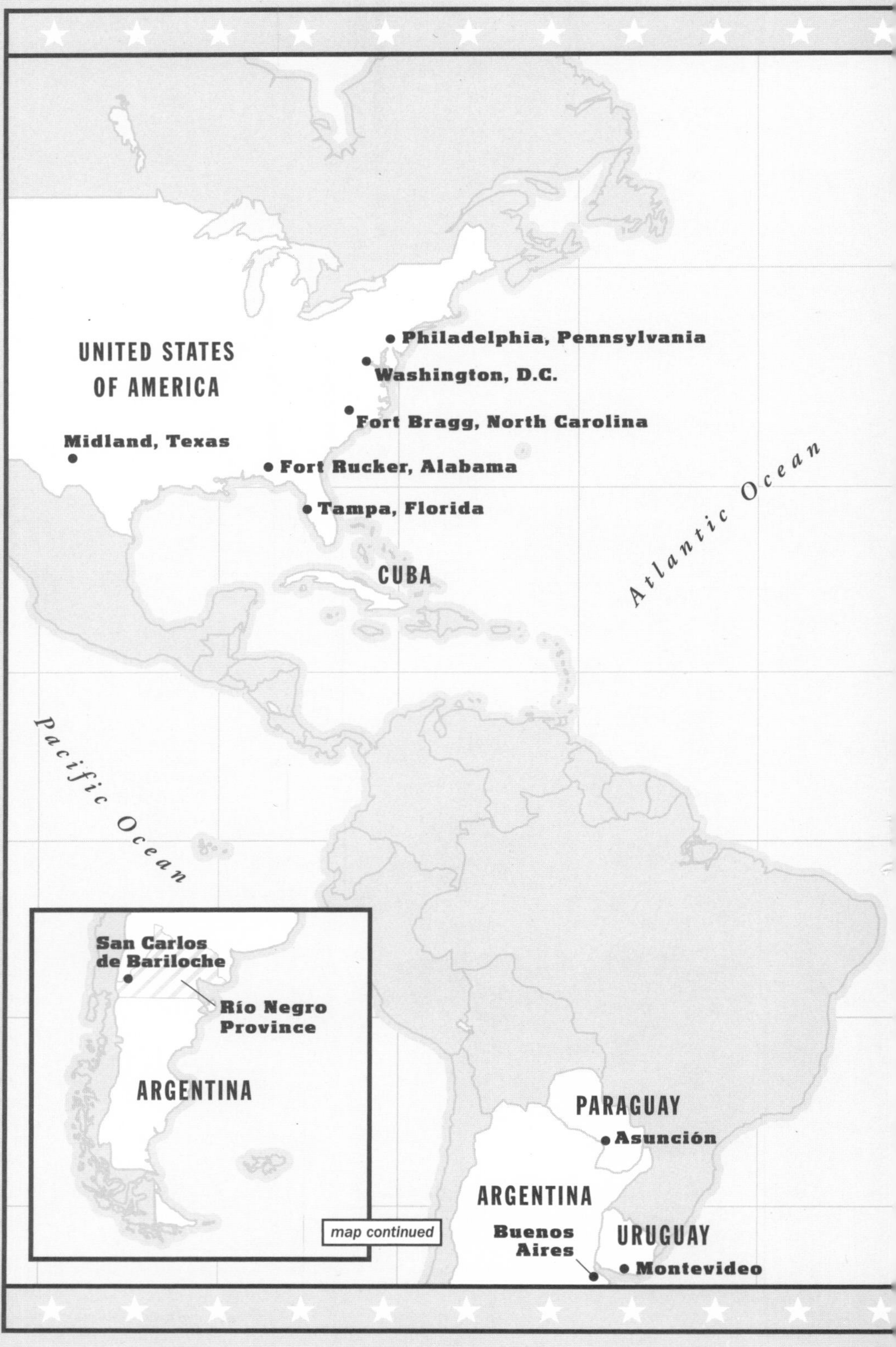
UNITED STATES
OF AMERICA
Philadelphia, Pennsylvania
Washington, D.C.
Fort Bragg, North Carolina
Midland, Texas
Fort Rucker, Alabama
Tampa, Florida
Atlantic Ocean
CUBA
Pacific Ocean
San Carlos
de Bariloche
Río Negro
Province
ARGENTINA
PARAGUAY
Asunción
ARGENTINA
Buenos
Aires
URUGUAY
Montevideo
map continued